TRIFLES AND FOLLY 2

A DEADLY CURIOSITIES COLLECTION

GAIL Z. MARTIN

CONTENTS

Trifles & Folly 2   v
Introduction   ix

Part I
The Final Death   I

Part II
Fatal Invitation   79

Part III
Redcap   127

Part IV
Bloodlines   165

Part V
Predator   197

Part VI
Fair Game   289

Part VII
Unraveled   387

Part VIII
BONUS   469

Afterword   551
About the Author   553
Also by Gail Z. Martin   555

TRIFLES & FOLLY 2

A DEADLY CURIOSITIES COLLECTION

by Gail Z. Martin

ISBN: 978.1.939704.64.1
Copyright © 2017 by Gail Z. Martin
All rights reserved.

The Final Death © 2014, Fatal Invitation © 2015, Redcap © 2015, Bloodlines © 2016, Predator © 2016, Fair Game © 2016, Unraveled © 2017, Steer a Pale Course © 2014, The Low Road © 2015, Among the Shoals Forever © 2015

Cover art by Lou Harper
SOL Publishing is an imprint of DreamSpinner Communications, LLC

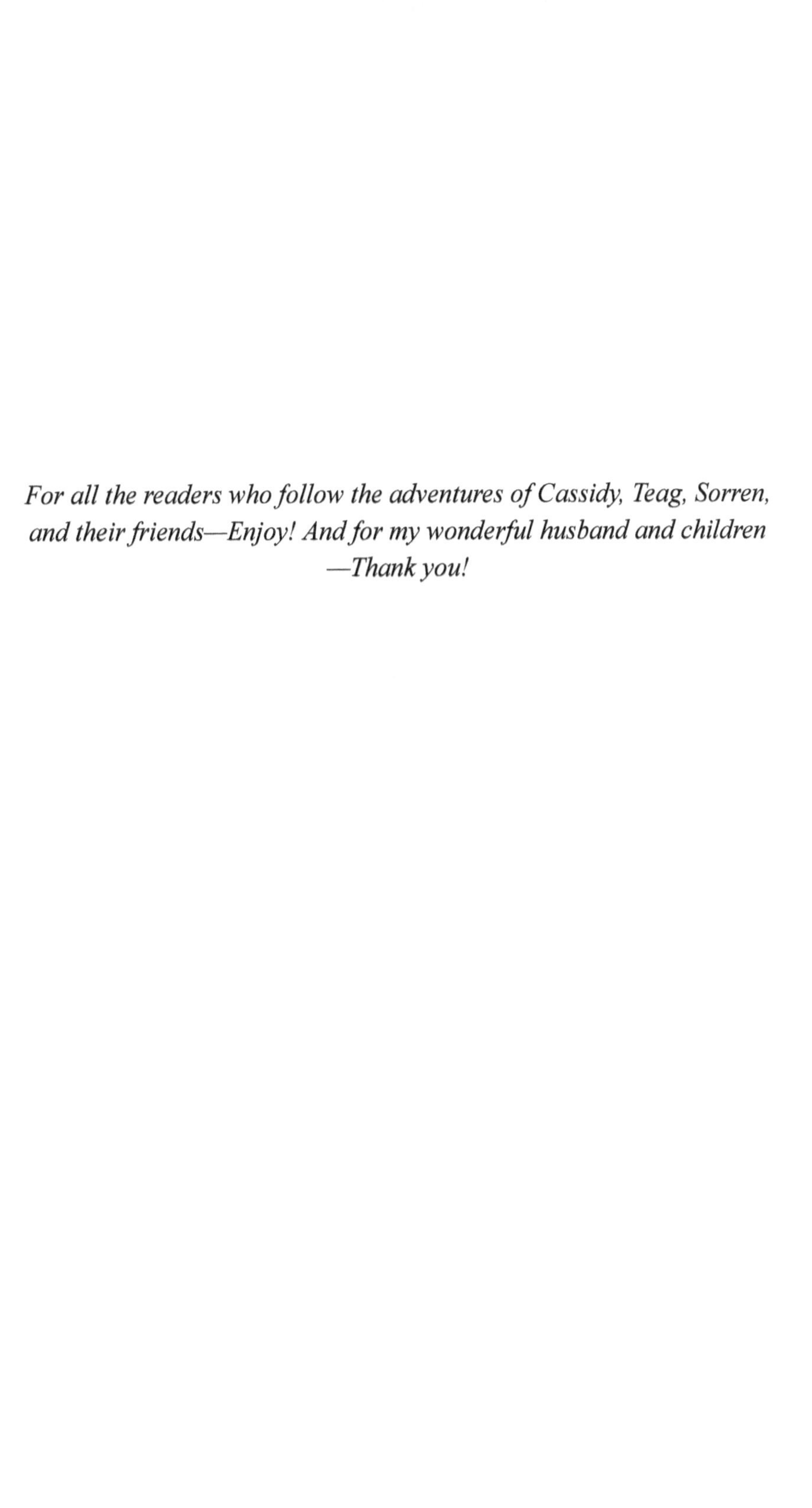

For all the readers who follow the adventures of Cassidy, Teag, Sorren, and their friends—Enjoy! And for my wonderful husband and children —Thank you!

INTRODUCTION

WELCOME TO MY world. This is the second collection of short stories and novellas from the Deadly Curiosities' universe, and as odd as it sounds it began with real life. Authors take inspiration from many places and for me, life events took me down a dark and mysterious road. It all began with *Buttons*, (Included in *Trifles & Folly,* Volume 1) I was asked to participate in the Solaris anthology *Magic: The Esoteric and Arcane* and had to come up with a new story. I'd written several involving Sorren set in earlier times but I wanted a fresh take and a modern setting, and Cassidy was born.

At the time I was dealing with the recent death of my father, and my husband and I were settling his estate, dealing with auctions and appraisers, and sorting through a life-long collection of stuff. Not ordinary stuff, but the kinds of things that provided fodder for ghost stories. Though obviously I took some creative liberties, some everyday items do have unusual providence, and oh, the things they've seen!

Over the course of the short stories and novels, the characters grow and change, as you'd expect if they were real people. When we first meet Cassidy in *Buttons* and in *Deadly Curiosities*, she is very new in using her gift of psychometry, and the visions often throw her for a loop. As time goes on, she gains more skill—both in controlling her magic and in using it defensively. Teag also grows in his magical abilities, and Sorren proves that continued growth and change are part of a successful long existence. By the time the stories in this collection happen, Cassidy and Teag have gained much greater mastery over their abilities.

I hope you enjoy these stories and if so, there are more available and more to come, including the full length novels: *Deadly Curiosities*, *Vendetta*, and *Tangled Web*.

Also included in this collection are three bonus stories set in the 1700s featuring Sorren, Dante, and Coltt. These were the first stories written about Trifles & Folly, and two of them were written for anthologies that required both pirates and magic. Dante is Cassidy's ancestor. They provide a little different perspective, both on the shop and the city. I hope you enjoy them!

PART I
THE FINAL DEATH

SCRIMSHAW

Sometimes, big trouble starts with small things. If I knew then what I know now, I might have put that carved piece of ivory back in its envelope and marked "return to sender" on the outside. But I had no way to know that pretty little disk was going to lead me straight into a tangle of old secrets, restless ghosts, and people who just wouldn't stay dead.

"Hey, Cassidy! What do you make of this?" Teag Logan, my assistant store manager, best friend, and occasional bodyguard held up a yellowed, carved oval disk.

"I'd need to see it up close to tell, but off-hand, I'd say it's scrimshaw, carved ivory," I replied. "And depending on how old it is, that little oval could get us in a heap of trouble."

"I'm pretty sure it was made long enough ago to be legal," Teag replied. "The real question I've got is, is it haunted?"

I'm Cassidy Kincaide, owner of Trifles and Folly, an antiques and curio shop in historic, haunted Charleston, South Carolina. Most people think we're just a place to find the perfect funky knick-knack or an awesome piece of vintage jewelry. Truth is, we protect the people of Charleston—and the world—by making sure dangerous magical objects get taken out of circulation. When we succeed, no one notices.

When we screw up, the damage usually gets blamed on a natural disaster.

I've got a couple of secrets. Few people know that I'm a psychometric—I can "read" the history of objects by touching them. It's a talent that runs in the family. Trifles and Folly has been around for over three hundred and fifty years since Charleston was first founded. My business partner, Sorren, has been around for nearly six hundred years. He's a vampire and was once the best jewel thief in Belgium. That's my second secret. I'm the latest in a long line of family members who use our magical talents to protect the good people of this city and keep the dark things at bay.

When Teag held up the ivory disk, I guessed that it might be a "sparkler"—what we call something that has enough psychic resonance to carry a touch of magic, but nothing dangerous. I was hoping it wasn't a "spooky"—our term for objects that are either haunted or potentially dangerous. No way to tell until I touched it and no telling what the effect would be on me until it was too late to change my mind.

"Let's close up. Then I'll take a look," I said. It was quiet for a summer day, probably because of the heat. Charleston is known for its beautiful gardens, but most people forget that those plants grow so well because of our high temperatures and insanely high humidity. Even with the air conditioning on, the store was warm. I slipped a limp lock of strawberry-blonde hair behind my ear. My Scots-Irish coloring means I burn easily in the sun and get pink in the face when I'm too warm, not ideal for a Charleston summer.

Teag flipped the door sign to "Closed." We turned out the lights in the shop and went into the break room. Just in case, Teag poured me a glass of sweet tea, made the Charleston way with enough sugar to give your fillings a buzz. I sat down at the small table, and Teag pushed the envelope toward me.

"Where did it come from?" I asked.

"I've got a friend who's an urban explorer," Teag replied. "He found it near the ruins of an abandoned plantation house.

"Urban explorer, huh?" I replied, eyeing the envelope, not ready to touch the contents yet. "You mean someone who goes poking around forgotten subway tunnels and spooky deserted amusement parks to take pictures?"

Teag grinned. "Got it in one. The UrbEx folks like to document urban decay and explore man-made places everyone else has forgotten about." He poured himself a glass of sweet tea and sat down in a chair facing me. "Of course, we don't have some of the really amazing old stuff like they've got in New York and Chicago below street level, but they still manage to find some great places to explore."

"Does your friend have a name?"

"He posts his photos as Nikon Ninja," Teag replied. I understood. From what I had read, although some UrbExers try to get permission to access sites, a lot of the exploration also counts as trespassing, maybe even breaking and entering. I could relate. In our work to handle supernatural bad behavior, we had picked more than a few locks ourselves and evaded our share of cops when we were places where we didn't belong.

"Okay, enough stalling," I said, taking a deep breath. "Let's see what I can read from this."

I braced myself and stretched out my hand. I felt a tingle when my fingers brushed the envelope. Then I jostled the ivory disk onto the table and took a good look.

The yellowed disk probably came from a whalebone or an elephant tusk. Back in the 1800s, such things were legal. Sailors have been making elaborate carvings to while away the time almost since the first ships left sight of land. Some of the pieces are in museums. Modern scrimshaw artists work from materials that don't come from endangered animals, and a slew of government agencies take a dim view of people harming protected species to make jewelry.

This particular piece looked very old. I was betting it was ivory from the rich patina. It might have been a button for a cloak or even a pin. The carving was neatly done, and ink had been rubbed into the cuts so that the design stood out in contrast. "It looks like a very embellished 'W,'" I said.

Teag nodded. "That would make sense. My friend said he was over at the Wellright plantation."

I glanced at him. "The Wellright place isn't abandoned."

"You're thinking of the 'new' mansion—the one built in the 1850s, just before the Civil War," Teag said. "Ninja explored the old mansion —not much left now except the foundation and some old cellars. Burned down in the late 1840s. Lots of places did back then, with all the candles and lamps and cooking on open hearths."

I had friends over at the Historical Archive and the Lowcountry Museum. Once I'd handled the disk, I decided to do some digging on the Wellrights' history. "Here goes," I said, and closed my hand over the ivory disk.

I saw the scene through the eyes of the person who had worn the disk. She—I was certain the person was female—was running through the woods, in fear for her life. It was dark, and the branches tore at her clothing. My heart thudded in terror. I didn't know what was chasing me through the darkness, but I was sure that if it caught me, I would die.

Looking through the eyes of the ivory disk's owner, I could see glimpses of moonlight breaking through the thick canopy of trees. The path ahead was shadowed, and I kept stumbling on the uneven ground. I knew that whatever was behind me was getting closer. I was crashing through the underbrush. It moved noiselessly. It was faster than I was, but I knew the forest. I kept running, barefoot now since I had kicked off my shoes long ago. Sweat ran down my face. I gasped for breath. If I could make it to the edge of the forest, I might find help. I ran until I glimpsed a clearing with a well and a half-circle of tall trees. Almost there.

Behind me, I heard a growl: then something ripped the cloak from my shoulders—

The scene disappeared. I was myself again, sitting at the break room table, heaving for breath as if I had been the one running for my life. My hand was shaking too badly for me to trust reaching for my sweet tea.

"Cassidy, are you okay?" Teag was a veteran of these little performances. He knew how to calm me down. There was a reason we had smelling salts in the cupboard. As visions went, this wasn't too bad. I hadn't passed out, thrown up, or fallen out of my chair.

"Yeah. Just give me a minute," I said. My voice sounded shaky, even to my own ears. I managed to drink my sweet tea without spilling it, and Teag waited patiently until I was together enough to tell my story.

"Any idea what the woman was running from?" he asked once I filled him in.

I shook my head. "No, but from how scared she was, I'm betting it wasn't human. She was beyond terrified. And unfortunately, I think that whatever was chasing her got her."

The tea helped calm my nerves. "So your urban explorer friend found this at the old Wellright plantation?"

Teag nodded. "Yeah. He said that it was the first time he had gone exploring there, and he wants to go back. Apparently, not many people have found the place."

"Or maybe, something made sure they didn't want to come back," I replied. "Do you think you could dig up some info on the Wellrights?"

Teag grinned. "Not a problem." Teag's ability to find information, especially online, is more than just awesome computer skills. He's got some magic of his own, Weaver magic. That means he can weave magic into the warp and woof of fabrics, tie ropes into knots that store magical power, and find strands of information and data threads no matter how encrypted or deeply hidden. It's a talent that comes in handy in our line of work.

"The new mansion is open for tours," I added. "And I think Drea's folks have it on their list." Andrea Andrews—Drea for short—owns Andrews Carriage Rides, one of Charleston's busiest tour companies. Tours and tourists are the lifeblood of a city like Charleston, and Drea's team did them better than anyone else. "What say we go pay the new mansion a visit and see if we get any idea what our ivory lady was running from?"

"Sounds great. Mind if Anthony comes along?" Anthony and Teag had been an item for almost a year, and I was hoping it would last.

Teag is good looking, tall and lean with skater boy dark hair. He was working on his doctorate in history before we recruited him to Trifles and Folly and he fell in love with our mission to protect the world, one cursed or haunted magical item at a time.

Anthony looks like he would be Teag's total opposite. He hails from an old Charleston family with a home on The Battery, and now that he's in the family law firm, he's definitely in the "young movers and shakers" category. Anthony is buttoned-down shirts, khakis, and boat shoes. Teag is more of a jeans, t-shirt, and hoodie guy. Personally, I thought they made a great couple.

"Am I ruining a romantic evening? I've gotten used to Anthony working late hours."

Teag shook his head. "We didn't have anything planned. And you know both of us like touring old mansions. Good thing that Charleston has so many to pick from!"

I had Drea on speed dial and got us booked for a candlelight tour of the new Wellright mansion right after dinner. "Drea says we can pick up our tickets when we get there since the others will be arriving by bus," I reported. "Nice to have a friend in the business."

"If you're right about the scrimshaw disk's owner being chased by something nasty, it might have been better to do the tour by daylight," Teag said. "Or did you get a ticket for Sorren, too?"

"Sorren doesn't get back in town until tomorrow," I replied. "Alliance business." The Alliance was a group of mortals and immortals who worked together to hide, bind, or destroy dangerous supernatural objects and keep the bad guys from getting their hands on them. Sorren was one of the group's leaders. He was the long-time silent partner behind Trifles and Folly's business, and I knew he had similar stores elsewhere around the world and other mortal partners. That meant Sorren traveled a lot, and we sometimes didn't see him for weeks at a time.

"The Wellrights have been in Charleston for a long time—and so has Sorren," Teag said. "He might know something about them. Hell, he might have attended a ball at the old plantation before it burned down, for all we know."

"I'll email him," I said. I snapped a picture of the ivory disk with my phone and texted it to Sorren. "Maybe that will jog his memory," I said. Yes, my vampire boss uses email and a smartphone. Sorren says that immortals who can't or won't adapt to changing times don't last very long. Since he's been around nearly six hundred years, it's safe to say he's pretty good at adapting.

I looked at the piece of scrimshaw again and blinked. Out of the corner of my eye, I caught a glimpse of a shadowy woman's form, but when I turned to look, she was gone.

"What?" Teag asked, following my movement.

I frowned. "When I looked at the ivory just now, I could have sworn I saw something—someone—moving just at the edge of my vision."

"Seeing ghosts now, in addition to feeling memories?" Teag's tone was teasing, but the concern in his eyes was real.

"It's been known to happen, especially if whatever imprinted the memory on the object involved a very strong emotion."

"Like running for your life because something wants to eat you?"

I nodded. "Yeah. I think that would do it."

A few hours later, after we closed up the shop for the day, Teag and I met Anthony for pizza, then headed out to the Wellright plantation. "I can't believe that I've never toured this one before," I said. "I thought I had hit all the big antebellum houses, plus quite a bit of The Battery during the Garden Show."

"The Wellright house has only been open to the public for a couple of years," Teag replied. "It's still owned by the family, but you can imagine what the upkeep on a place like this is. Allowing tours helps defray the costs."

"Which is better than letting another grand old mansion fall into ruin," Anthony replied.

"I can't even imagine what their electric bill is like," I said, eying the lit-up old mansion. Wellright plantation was a Greek Revival-style beauty, looking like something straight out of a movie. Tall white columns graced the three-story front, and sweeping stone steps welcomed guests. Each of the mansion's floors had its own wrap-around porch with decorative railings. Twin rows of century-old live oaks lined the carriageway leading up to the house. Every window glowed with light, casting a warm glow. Artfully placed spotlights illuminated the house and lit the entrance path.

"I imagine it's gorgeous in the daylight," Anthony said, and I guessed at what he did not say out loud.

"But right now, with all that Spanish moss in the trees and how dark it is, it's kind of creepy," I finished for him. He nodded.

"Yeah," Teag said. "I was thinking the same thing. The shadows look awfully dark."

Drea was waiting at the foot of the plantation's steps, surrounded by a group of twelve tourists eager for the tour to begin. "Yoo-hoo, Cassidy!" Drea called, waving. Petite and dark-haired, with the same energy as a Level Five hurricane, Drea's enthusiasm is contagious.

Valerie was next to Drea. She was Drea's top tour guide, a real favorite with the customers. Many repeat visitors to Charleston requested Valerie by name when they scheduled tours with Andrews Carriage Rides. Valerie's red hair was tied back in a ponytail, and with her delicate features and retro-ironic eyeglasses, she looked a bit like a bookish pixie.

"Everyone's here, so let's get started," Valerie said. "As we tour the house and some of the gardens, I'll tell you about the Wellright family. They have a long and storied history, with many colorful ancestors including senators and pirates, scalawags and saints, and a few family ghosts as well."

Having been born and raised in Charleston, I was willing to bet there was a skeleton or two in the closet of any family that old, but since the mansion was still owned by the Wellrights, I figured I would have to wait on scandals until Teag was done with his research or Sorren got back to town.

"How do you feel, Cassidy?" To anyone else, Teag's question might have sounded like friendly concern for my health. Anthony and I knew he was really asking if I had picked up any psychic resonance.

"Okay for now," I replied, trying to pin down exactly what I was feeling. I hadn't touched anything yet, but there was a restlessness that seemed to come from the house and grounds that felt off-kilter. Not exactly dangerous, but certainly not neutral.

Anthony knew that I was a psychometric, and it was only recently that he had learned about Teag's Weaver gift. He started out skeptical, but after he saw our abilities in action, he turned into a believer. Teag and I suspect that Anthony has a touch of clairvoyance himself, although he won't admit it. Now, heading into unknown territory, one of them walked on either side of me, which was sweet but not likely to be much protection if any of the objects in the Wellright house served up a particularly strong vision.

We followed Valerie into the home. She chatted on in a tone that managed to be knowledgeable and engaging without sounding like a lecture. Teag and I had decided ahead of time that he would listen to Valerie's spiel for interesting details, while I focused on the objects in the home. Anthony was free to enjoy the tour, but I knew he was going to watch our backs whether we asked him to or not.

I tuned out Valerie and tried to tune in to the beautiful furnishing and decorations. From the website, I knew a little about the Wellrights. They had settled the old plantation farther up the Ashley River in the early seventeen hundreds, raising crops and livestock to feed a growing nation. Fertile soil, good crops, and savvy business dealings soon made the Wellrights a wealthy and prominent family. When a series of disasters struck the family, and the old plantation house burned down, the Wellrights built on a new location and started over, managing to rebuild their fortune.

By the look of it, the Wellrights had lived very comfortably. Chippendale and Queen Anne furnishings, Oriental rugs, and paintings by artists whose work I'd seen in museums decorated the rooms. I shied away from the big, gold-framed mirrors since mirrors were favorite portals for supernatural nasties. And since old objects could pack a psychic wallop, I was being very careful about touching anything. Mostly, I was hoping to make a connection with the girl I had seen in the vision, the one who had owned the ivory disk. But as we moved from one lovely room to the next, I began to think that finding a link was going to be impossible.

"We owe the Wellrights' collection of scrimshaw mostly to Theodora Wellright," Valerie said as we entered the next room, and my ears pricked up. Valerie went to stand next to a glass case on a stately mahogany table.

"Theodora fell in love with Aaron Baskin, a well-to-do ship's captain," Valerie continued. "Baskin traveled around the world, and when he came back to Charleston, he often brought Theodora a scrimshaw trinket as a gift." She glanced up at an oil portrait that hung over the table. "Sadly, Theodora died in a Yellow Fever epidemic before she and Baskin could marry." I startled at the similarity to the ghost I kept glimpsing out of the corner of my eye and wondered if she could be the one from my vision. Unfortunately, I hadn't seen a reflection so had no clue as to her appearance.

"Is she buried on the land near this mansion?" Teag asked.

Valerie shook her head. "We know her grave was near the old house, but some of the records were destroyed in the fire that claimed the mansion, so we aren't exactly sure where she and the other victims were buried."

I maneuvered closer to the table with the glass case. Anthony casually shifted his position so that he blocked Valerie's view. I knew the case would be locked, but I let my fingers brush the lid, hoping that the plantation wasn't fancy enough to have a touch-sensitive security system. No alarms sounded, but the images hit me hard enough that I swayed on my feet.

Love. Loneliness. Images of old-fashioned script on parchment letters that had been smudged from being read over and over again. A glimpse of a proud sailing ship leaving the Charleston Harbor, and the memory of a broad-shouldered, dark-haired man with a full beard and serious brown eyes.

"Cassidy," Teag murmured. "We're moving into the next room."

Teag's comment jolted me out of the vision, and as I turned to follow the group, I caught a glimpse of the young woman's ghost near the case, her image much clearer now. She seemed to be looking straight at me as if she knew I could see her. The look on her face was fierce, but I could not tell whether she was angry or frightened, or merely determined. The image faded almost as soon as I saw it, and I hurried to catch up to the others.

The rest of the house was lovely, but I didn't pick up any more impressions that seemed connected to Theodora. We finished the tour in the large kitchen, and Valerie led us out onto the wide porch and a beautiful summer evening.

"Wellright House has always been known for its elaborate gardens," Valerie continued. "It's a tradition that began with the old house. When that home was destroyed, the family brought cuttings of the garden plants as well as the statues and fountains from the grounds, and created this beautiful landscape," she said, sweeping her arm to indicate the carefully tended banks of flowers, flowering bushes, greenery, and hedges.

"The boxwood maze was built in Theodora's honor since she had loved the maze at the old house," Valerie said. "There's a statue in the center of the maze that was a gift to her from Captain Baskin. The grounds are well lit, and we have some time before we need to head back, so you're welcome to explore the gardens. Just please stay where the lights are, and listen for me when I call you back to the bus."

I wasn't surprised when Teag, Anthony, and I all made a beeline for the maze. The boxwood's sharp scent contrasted with the roses and jasmine. The blue glow of the path lighting made it easy to find our way, although the hedge was taller than either Anthony or Teag. But as we wound our way deeper into the maze, the shadows seemed to grow darker, and the sound of the rest of the tourists faded.

"I hope we can find our way out as easily as we've gotten in," Anthony said.

"I had a package of peanuts in my pocket," Teag said. "I've dropped one every few feet."

We both turned to look at him. "Seriously?" Anthony said, with an expression torn between admiration and friendly mocking.

"Hey, I come prepared," Teag replied. "Unless there are hungry squirrels."

"Let's go get a look at that statue and get back," I said. The maze made me nervous, and the farther we went, the cooler the night became. Sudden cold spots often went with supernatural phenomena. I was torn between hoping we would learn something, and being afraid that we might.

The maze doubled back on itself and presented us with a few dead ends that made us turn back. I took comfort in the crunch of the gravel beneath our feet, the only sound as we wound toward the center.

"There it is," Teag said as we emerged from the narrow boxwood alley into the wide center circle. A bronze statue of a woman stood in the center of a mound of flowers, weathered into a blue-green patina with age. It was a good likeness of the person from the oil painting, a pretty young woman in her early twenties in a flowing cape and long skirts. The woman seemed to be scanning the horizon, and in her hands, she held a model of a sailing ship.

"Watching for her ship's captain to come home," Anthony murmured.

"Take a look at her cloak," Teag said, adjusting his glasses. He pulled out a small pocket flashlight and shone it on where the cloak gathered at the statue's neck. "There." Clasping the cloak shut was an oval disk engraved with an elaborate "W."

Just then, the lights went out.

Something pushed me from behind, and I staggered. I stretched out a hand to catch myself, knowing that I had stumbled into the flowerbed, and I steadied myself against the statue. Longing and loneliness washed over me again, stronger than before, and fear so real that I struggled to breathe.

Theodora Wellright's image bore down on me, fixing me in a piercing glare. She was saying something, but I couldn't hear her. I felt suddenly weak as if something was draining the energy right out of me. My knees buckled, and I was afraid I was going to faint. Theodora came right at me, and I cried out as I felt the spirit's icy touch as she rushed to—and through—me. The awful drain stopped, but I was dizzy with exhaustion, and I collapsed into the petunias.

When I came around, I was lying on the gravel path on my back. Anthony knelt next to me, while Teag shone his flashlight into the air like a beacon, flashing it on and off in a signal even I knew was SOS in Morse Code.

"What happened?" I asked groggily.

"You fainted," Anthony replied. "And when we tried to carry you out, we had trouble finding our way back. The peanuts were gone."

"So I sent up a flare, so to speak," Teag said, nodding toward his upturned flashlight. "Learned this trick in one of the Harry Potter movies."

Sure enough, we heard footsteps coming toward us on the gravel. "Is everyone okay?" It was Valerie, and she sounded worried.

"Cassidy got a little light-headed," Teag fibbed. "Must not have had enough to eat for lunch. Then we got turned around, and couldn't find our way out."

"I'm fine," I said, standing up with a little help from Anthony, who gallantly offered me his arm as if we were going to the prom.

"If you feel up to it, we'd better get going," Valerie said. "It's time to head back." I was just as glad that it was dark and she couldn't see how I'd accidentally trampled the flowers.

"We'll follow you," Teag said, staying close behind us as we wound our way back to the main garden.

"Don't worry, Anthony drove," he assured Valerie as I climbed into the back seat of Anthony's car. Since we had booked the tour late, we had needed to drive ourselves.

"Glad you're okay," Valerie said. "I don't know what could have happened to the lights."

No one said anything until we had followed the bus out of the plantation carriageway and were back on the main highway.

"What happened?" Teag asked. I gave him a quick recap.

"The thing is," I said, "I didn't faint from the vision itself. I felt as if something was draining all my energy and then the ghost came after me." The full impact of what had happened hit me, and I felt shaky. "Something supernatural attacked me."

BURIAL GROUND

THE NEXT DAY WAS QUIET AT THE STORE, AND WHEN MAGGIE, OUR part-time helper, came in I ducked out to do a little research. Alistair McKinnon, Curator of the Lowcountry Museum of Charleston, is a friend of mine. He knows everyone worth knowing in town, and more importantly, he knows the historical dirt on those old families, and he's willing to dish for a good cause.

I had already arranged to meet Alistair for lunch, and I was running late so I hurried, even though in the heat that would mean I'd be sweating when I got there. I swung by Honeysuckle Café to pick up boxed lunches for both of us, and took him his favorite latte, just to sweeten the bribe.

"Good to see you, Cassidy," Alistair greeted me when I reached his office. My guess is that Alistair is in his early sixties given how long he's worked for museums, but he's a sharp dresser and an avid runner, so he wears the years well. "That's not a cinnamon latte, is it?"

I held out the cup and handed him his boxed lunch. "Yep. And the turkey/cranberry/gorgonzola on ciabatta from Honeysuckle Café."

Alistair raised an eyebrow. "Wow. Looks fantastic. You must really want some major information," he added with a grin.

"Absolutely! I'll tell you what I need while you eat, and you can fill me in while I eat. Deal?"

Since Alistair was already unwrapping his sandwich, I figured we had an understanding. I gave Alistair an edited version of events, leaving out the urban explorer and minimizing the drama at the plantation the night before. Alistair may suspect about my psychometry, but he doesn't know for sure, and I'd prefer to keep it that way.

"So," I said as I wrapped up my recount, "what can you tell me about the Wellrights? I'm especially interested in Theodora, and the disaster that destroyed the first mansion."

Alistair sat back in his chair and tented his fingers as he thought. I opened up my sandwich and took a bite, which I washed down with some sweet tea, ready to listen.

"Since you were kind enough to tip me off about your interest in your email, I looked into what we have in the museum holdings before you came," Alistair said. "The Wellrights claimed land in the Charleston area not long after the city was settled. That makes them one of the city's oldest families. The name comes up often over the last three hundred years—Wellrights have played prominent roles in city leadership and philanthropy for a long, long time. The story of the old mansion—and of Theodora's death—are a bleak chapter in an otherwise very successful history."

"I understand that old houses were at risk from fire back in the day," I said, swallowing so I didn't talk with my mouth full. "But why didn't they rebuild on the old site? Why move the mansion so far away from where it was located before?"

"You know that history requires reading between the lines," Alistair said. "People are often less than truthful, even in their diaries, and certainly in public documents. But I'd say that the short answer is: they were afraid."

"Of what?"

"The fire that destroyed the mansion was the last in a series of incidents that went beyond bad luck," Alistair replied. "At the time, there was talk of a curse."

"What kind of curse? Cursed by whom?"

Alistair shrugged. "Well, that's where the record gets spotty. A blight hit the Wellright crops, and then something killed some prize horses worth a small fortune. There was an outbreak of Yellow Fever that claimed Theodora and half a dozen of the servants, and then the house burned." He leaned forward. "There was a rumor that the fire was set by one of the slaves," he said in a conspiratorial tone. "A witness swore that the slave admitted to setting the fire to 'stop the Devil' and break the curse."

"Did anyone believe the account?" I asked, finding that I was sitting on the edge of my chair.

Alistair nodded gravely. "The man was hanged, and it was generally said that he had gone mad. Several of his family members had been among the servants who died of the plague."

"They didn't know how Yellow Fever was transmitted back then, did they?" I mused.

"No. The fact that mosquitoes carried the infection wouldn't be discovered for nearly two hundred years," Alistair replied. "You can imagine how terrifying that was for people. The disease seemed to rise out of nowhere, kill thousands of people in a few weeks, go away for a while, and come back years later. And if people don't know what causes something, they'll make up an answer. So there was talk of everything from curses and black magic, to the Devil or the wrath of God."

I wasn't going to tell Alistair, but at least the part about curses and black magic wasn't as far-fetched as he thought. "What year did all this happen?"

"Seventeen Thirty-Two," Alistair replied. "Charleston got hit by two Yellow Fever epidemics just four years apart, in Seventeen Twenty-Eight and in then again in Thirty-Two. According to the diaries and records, people prayed and fasted and repented of their sins to try to end the plague, and when that didn't work, they drove out anyone they thought might have brought judgment down on the city and hanged some unlucky folks on various charges, but it's widely suspected the victims were said to be witches."

His voice dropped. "Unofficially, more than a few folks tried some magic of their own to protect themselves. Even some of the wives and daughters of the prominent folk went to their slaves from the islands looking for root cures and Voudon protections."

Everyone thinks of New Orleans when Voodoo—or Voudon as its practitioners prefer— gets mentioned. But in reality, slaves from Africa, Haiti, Barbados, and the other Caribbean islands were traded throughout the Deep South, and they brought their beliefs with them. Many wives and daughters of slaveholders adopted some of those practices to tide them over in areas where the Christian teaching was a bit thin, or where desperation called for desperate measures, like childbearing, sick children, and plague. All done secretly but done nonetheless.

"So the Wellrights moved the plantation because of the plague?" I asked.

Alistair nodded. "That was the official reason, and the fact that the new mansion was farther away from marshlands probably did help cut their chance of infection, although they didn't know it at the time. But it's interesting to note that they also located their new property on land that was inside the circle one could draw connecting the city's outlying churches."

"Sanctified ground?" I asked, surprised.

"After a fashion," he said. "During the Yellow Fever epidemics, people didn't want to hold funerals in the same churches where they also held worship services, baptisms, and weddings. Remember, they had no idea how the disease spread. So many cities built 'plague churches' that were only for funerals. St. Roch Church—invoking the patron saint of plague victims—was built as one of these funeral churches. The new Wellright mansion is on land that placed the church between it and the old property."

"St. Roch?" I repeated. "Charleston has an awful lot of churches, but I've never heard of that one." Charleston's over four hundred churches have earned it the nickname of the "Holy City," and some of those churches date from the city's earliest days.

"It doesn't exist anymore," Alistair said. "It had a history as tragic as its purpose. St. Roch survived several fires and hurricanes, and more than one bout of madness among its clergy. The Great Quake of 1886 finally destroyed it."

I made a mental note to ask Sorren some questions about the Wellrights and St. Roch's. Both had runs of enough bad luck that I wasn't quite willing to take at face value.

"What about Theodora?" I pressed.

Alistair smiled. "Ah, that's where we're in luck. We have a number of items from the Wellright family in our holdings, and because Theodora's tragic story is so poignant, we actually have some items that belonged to her."

"Could I see them?" The words were out of my mouth before my better judgment could stop them. Teag wasn't here to pick me up if I got a vision that knocked me on my butt. But I didn't want to miss this opportunity.

"I thought you might ask," Alistair replied. "Come with me."

I followed him out of the office and through the museum. I generally avoid museums for a very good reason: I can pick up strong resonance from items that were involved in highly emotional situations even without touching them. And what kind of things do people put in museums? Just the sort of thing that sends my psychic gift into overdrive. I was willing to bet Alistair still remembered the time I passed out cold in a "Plagues and Pestilence" exhibit.

Fortunately, we cut through exhibits on women's fashions and fine china, so I was spared. We stopped in front of a display case filled with items that once belonged to the doomed young woman whose portrait I had seen at the "new" Wellright mansion. There was a new portrait that I had not seen, one painted of Theodora when she was just in her early teens.

"She was very pretty," I commented, leaving out the fact that I had glimpsed what I believed to be Theodora's ghost up close and personal on more than one occasion.

"Theodora Wellright was just in her early twenties when she died—probably near the age you are now," Alistair said, looking at the portrait. "Everyone loves a tale of star-crossed lovers, and Theodora Wellright and Aaron Baskin certainly fit the bill."

"I heard a little of their story when I toured the mansion," I said. I leaned in for a good look at what was in the display case.

"You never really said what prompted your sudden interest," Alistair said, and I tried to look casual.

"Someone brought us a cloak-fastener that might have belonged to Theodora," I replied, not turning to look at Alistair. "We're trying to authenticate it, and I got caught up in the history."

Alistair nodded as if that explained everything. "Theodora was very well educated for a woman of her time. She had tutors from England and Scotland in classical literature and theology, as well as the classes in music and needlepoint which were required for a woman of her standing."

"She died before her lover returned from the sea," I murmured.

"And lately, some of the museum staff claim that she hasn't stayed completely dead." Alistair's inflection gave nothing away, but the mere fact that he mentioned it made the hair on the back of my neck stand up.

"Oh?"

"You know Charleston—we have nearly as many ghosts per square inch as Savannah or New Orleans," Alistair replied, trying for a light tone and not quite making it convincing. "And here in the museum, we're resigned to having some resident spirits who have tagged along with their belongings. The Wellright exhibit is fairly new. And ever since we added Theodora's things, the staff has reported getting a glimpse of a young woman in period clothing who isn't there when they look again."

I repressed a shiver. Peering into the case, I saw several more pieces of beautiful scrimshaw given to Theodora by her beloved Aaron. There was also a framed, elaborate baptismal certificate, a few yellowed needlepoint samplers and a time-worn Bible. Something drew me to the old leather-bound book. "Was there anything unusual about Theodora's Bible?" I asked.

"Not about the Bible itself, no," Alistair said. "But Theodora kept a journal, and some of her last entries are still being debated by the Charleston historians who have studied it."

"Why?" I asked, sensing that I was getting to something important.

"Theodora was an educated woman for her time," Alistair said. "Quite knowledgeable on science, and above some of the common hysteria of the masses. But her last entries are dark—almost verging on delirium. There's some debate among scholars whether Theodora suffered from madness."

"What makes them think that?" I tried to keep my voice casual.

Alistair met my gaze. "Her last several entries describe visions and dreams that are disquieting. And she seemed to be obsessed with a single verse from the Bible. 'There is a generation whose teeth are as swords and their jaw teeth as knives.'"

"Yikes," I replied. That didn't cover it by half. A nasty suspicion started forming in the back of my mind. If I was right, poor Theodora hadn't been mad, although what she might have discovered would have sorely strained her sanity. I had some pointed questions to ask my vampire boss.

When I got back to the shop, Maggie was taking care of a customer, and I figured that Teag had taken advantage of the lull to do some research of his own. I waved at Maggie and headed to the office, where I found Teag hunched over his laptop.

"Anything?" I asked.

"Plenty," he said, not bothering to look up. "Give me a sec, and I'll fill you in." I waited until he finished what he was doing and looked up. "I think I know why the Wellright lands are seeing so much super-natural activity. Some of the land near the old plantation was sold to a developer for condominiums, and when they began clearing the land, they uncovered about a dozen old graves—probably from the 1700s."

"And?"

Teag shrugged. "And—I don't know more than that. Yet. I'm checking around. The construction company and the new landowners are being extremely quiet about things, which makes me wonder what they're hiding. Especially since the Darke Web has heated up on the topic."

Teag wasn't your average hacker or even your average genius hacker. His Weaver magic meant that firewalls couldn't keep him out and encryption didn't stop him. He had no trouble finding stuff on the Deep Web that wasn't on the search engines, or on the Dark Web—the Internet's back alleys where criminal and unsavory activity flourished. But Teag's magic meant that he could also navigate the Darke Web—currents of information shared by immortal, supernatural, and magical communities, protected by enchantments law enforcement couldn't break, but that didn't slow Teag down a bit.

"Why does the Darke Web care?"

Teag met my gaze. "That's a good question. And I'm still digging for an answer. So far, what's being said out there is like coming into the middle of a conversation—they're talking about something but not defining what it is since it's assumed those in the conversation already know." He grinned. "Don't worry—I'll get to the bottom of things."

"I'm sure you will," I said. "But just the fact that the folks on the Darke Web are talking about the Wellrights means there's something bigger going on here than a haunting."

"Agreed," Teag replied. "And the folks aren't just talking about it—they're definitely scared of something."

I remembered the ghostly attack in the maze. "I'm still trying to figure out whether it was Theodora's ghost who attacked me, or whether something else hit me first and Theodora drove it away. Either way, we've got an aggressive spirit out there that's capable of knocking someone out—and maybe worse. That's different from Charleston's run-of-the-mill spooks."

"We need to go out to the old plantation—what's left of it—before the developers get in there and make a mess of things," Teag said.

I was still a little shivery remembering what happened in the maze, but I knew Teag was right. "When?"

"It's still light after closing time," Teag said. "Let's take an hour to get changed into hiking clothes, and drive out there. If anyone questions us, we can always say we were out for a walk and got lost, golly gee whiz." I was willing to bet that Teag had never said "golly gee whiz" before in his life, and the overdone look of aw-shucks innocence was so unbelievable it made me laugh out loud. At the same time, I had seen Teag talk his way out of tight situations, so I didn't doubt that he could bamboozle our way past a rent-a-cop if the developers had anyone patrolling the grounds.

"Sounds like a plan," I said, resolutely ignoring the tight knot in the pit of my stomach.

A DARK PAST

My Mini Cooper is cute but too recognizable for sneaking around. Teag's old Volvo, on the other hand, is both reliable and nondescript. By the time Teag came to pick me up, I had fed my dog, Baxter, and changed into an old pair of jeans, low hiking boots, and a thin, long-sleeved shirt. Though it was early evening, it was still very warm since Charleston didn't really cool off at night until October. South Carolina's woods were home to all kinds of snakes and bugs, including ticks. Long pants and sleeves weren't cool, but they were practical.

I threw a first-aid kit into the back of Teag's car along with several bottles of water. The pockets of my hoodie were full of other things we might need. I had Theodora's ivory disk in the pocket of my jeans, and I hoped that taking the disk back to the old manor might help me get another vision; something that would help put the pieces together and figure out how she died. There was a packet of salt, good for protection against a lot of supernatural nasties. I wore a necklace of agate, a stone known for its protective qualities, and a bracelet of woven hemp with a wooden amulet made of teak and birch intertwined in a complicated carved knot. Sorren had given the bracelet to me when I first took over the store. He had told me that it wasn't a bullet-proof vest, but that it could protect me from a lot of bad stuff. I wasn't taking any chances.

We picked up burgers at a drive-through. In the short time since we left the store, Teag had managed to download and print out a topographical map of the area that included the old Wellright place, as well as a very old map that showed the boundaries of the first plantation. I finished my burger and studied the maps while Teag drove.

"So the developer is going to take the back third of the old plantation land," I said, squinting at the lines Teag had drawn on the copy of the old survey map.

"Yeah, that's the plan," he replied. "The historic preservation folks fought them to keep them from getting any closer to the old foundation. In theory, all they're going to take is old farmland."

"In theory," I echoed. "You have doubts?" Teag was All But Dissertation (ABD) for his Ph.D. in History before he started working at Trifles and Folly, and he knew his stuff.

He shrugged, keeping his eyes on the road. "There are a lot of things that don't always make it onto official maps," Teag said. "Slave quarters, for example. Outbuildings like summer kitchens and granaries, since they were so much smaller than the main house. Cemeteries, sometimes."

"That's what you think is back there?" I asked. "An unmarked cemetery?"

"When you've got restless ghosts, seems logical to me to go looking for their graves and figure out why they aren't content to stay in them," he replied. It occurred to me that what passed for normal conversation for us was way off the radar for most folks.

"Other than Theodora, there don't seem to be a lot of reports of ghost activity in that area, at least, not that anyone has admitted."

"True," he said. "But the first issue you just touched on. Just because there's no record or report, doesn't mean there aren't any ghosts. There are a lot of reasons—pride being one of them—that people might not want to report or admit to having ghosts wandering around."

And among the Charleston blue-bloods, pride meant a lot. Especially for a family like the Wellrights who had seen their fortunes wax and wane over the years. Sometimes, pride was all a once-notable family had left. Reporting ghost sightings was an invitation to ridicule.

"Okay," I replied. "We know there are ghosts now, but how long has it been a problem? Just since the developers came, or longer?"

"My money is on 'longer,'" Teag answered. "And I'd be willing to bet that regardless of what was said in public, ghosts were at least part of the reason the Wellrights didn't rebuild on the old land and moved the mansion closer to town."

"With a plague church as a bulwark between them and whatever they were running away from," I said.

Teag nodded. "Exactly. That's an expensive proposition. Lots of people in Charleston live in haunted houses. Plenty of them are mighty proud that great-great grandpa or grandma sees fit to wander the family home. But the Wellrights got the hell out of Dodge, so to speak. Why?"

"Ghosts aren't the only supernatural creatures out there," I said. "Most ghosts are pretty tame. A lot of them are just stone tapes, images caught in a perpetual loop, not even really conscious."

"And from what I've read about the founding fathers of the Wellright clan, they weren't afraid of much," Teag added. "That's how they amassed their fortune. They weren't above benefitting from piracy, and they were wheelers and dealers of the first order, so they had a pretty high tolerance for risk. But something scared them so much they tucked tail and ran for town."

"You know what they say about fools who rush in where angels fear to tread," I replied.

"I don't think angels have anything to do with this."

The old Wellright place was down along the Ashley River, home to many of Charleston's historic plantations. We weren't far from downtown, but we might as well have been in another world. Huge old live oaks spread their sprawling, graceful branches while tufts of Spanish moss draped from their boughs. It was summer, so the smell of honeysuckle was almost cloyingly sweet, like a woman wearing too much expensive perfume. Oleander bushes, left over from plantings around the old mansion, were in sumptuous blossom.

Nature had reclaimed the land with such thoroughness that it was difficult to find the ruined foundations. Teag and I battled our way through brush and nettles, slapping off mosquitoes and chiggers. Charleston's heat and humidity send plants into a hothouse frenzy, and some things—like kudzu—grow too well. I was wishing we had machetes to cut through the vegetation, but eventually, we found the weathered cut stones that marked all that remained of the original Wellright mansion.

"Not much to look at, is it?" Teag said, mopping his brow with the back of his sleeve. He guzzled a drink from his water bottle, and I did the same. "Do you think you could read anything from the foundation?" he asked.

I was wondering the same thing myself. Large stone blocks outlined the footprint of the house. They were overgrown in places, covered with debris in others, and along one side, several of the blocks were missing. Holding my breath, I walked over and then placed my hand on a weather-beaten foundation stone and closed my eyes.

I felt as if I was trying to listen to a radio station that was out of range, or watching a TV show that wasn't coming in clearly. My gift picked up faint images and voices, but too distant and diffused to be readable. I sighed and shook my head. "Nothing I can read," I said. "Unless we're in a place where something really emotional happened, I don't usually get a lot of information from buildings."

Thank heavens, or I might be overcome by everyone's life traumas just going to the grocery store or the doctor's office. Not every object or antique resonates either, which is a mercy. The relatively few items that do more than make up for the large number that don't.

"The land goes back that way," Teag said, pointing. Not far behind the foundation, trees had encroached on whatever lawn the mansion might once have had. It looked like much of the rest of the land was forest. Whatever else we found; at least there would be shade.

Theodora Wellright was long dead, but the land that had been her home buzzed and chirped with life. Squirrels chattered in the trees overhead. If it weren't for the mosquitoes, I would have enjoyed the walk. They reminded me that there could be something else lurking in these woods that also fed on blood. I shivered, despite how hard I was sweating.

"Things have grown up so much, it's hard to see anything," I muttered, staggering as my boot caught on a tangle of vines. Wild rose bushes snagged my jeans and scratched my hands.

"Look for periwinkle," Teag said, scanning the ground. "It was a popular plant in old cemeteries. It grows well where the ground has been disturbed."

I tried to imagine what the land might have looked like two hundred years ago. Many of the trees around us were far too young to have been here back then. Big old trees cast more shade, meaning the ground would have been clear of all the weeds and brambles that held us back.

"Looks like there might be an old well over that way," I said, spotting a mound of stones that looked like they had once been stacked in a square. We walked over, but what remained of the well had been capped long ago with a rusty metal plate that didn't look like anyone had bothered it.

I closed my eyes, trying to remember what I had seen through Theodora's eyes the first time I touched her ivory disk. My fingers brushed the disk in my pocket, and I knew we were in the right place. Then I spotted the clue I was looking for: eight trees all nearly the same height planted in a neat semicircle.

"I'm certain this is the area I saw in the vision," I said. "I remember those trees. Theodora was attacked near here." *Did she die here?* I wondered. I folded the disk into my fist, hoping for a hint, but Theodora was silent.

"Head that way," I said pointing. As we walked toward the trees, I saw a depression that might once have been a wagon road. I was sure that if there had been a cemetery on the Wellright land, we were heading right for it.

"The development deal takes the back third of the old property," Teag said, stepping carefully around downed branches. "You can see where they stopped digging."

Sure enough, large construction equipment sat idled along a raw tear in the ground. A hastily built barricade of orange plastic netting cordoned off the area where the unmarked graves were found. We kept well away from that section, as we were hoping to avoid guards although no one appeared to be on duty at the moment.

Teag and I tramped back and forth beneath the half-circle of old trees. "There's periwinkle everywhere, but no markers," he said, kicking at the dirt.

"I don't even see broken headstones."

"During epidemics, they often buried people in mass graves," Teag said somberly. "The survivors often had more urgent things to do than make tombstones."

Bad enough if Theodora died of Yellow Fever, I thought. But the vision suggested a worse fate. *Why was she running for her life out here, so far from the manor house? And what was behind her diary entries about fangs and sharp teeth?* My fear that Theodora's killer was a vampire rather than a virus grew stronger, and I was impatient for Sorren to return.

"There's a lot I want to ask Sorren," I said. "I wish he'd get back."

"No luck with email?"

I shook my head. "I've left a voice mail and sent an email, but he hasn't responded. So we'll have to muddle on by ourselves."

While we had been exploring, the sun had gotten lower on the horizon, and shadows were lengthening. "We'd better get back," I said, eyeing the forest that had been sun-dappled and alive with nature when we left the plantation ruins.

"It's gotten cooler," Teag said, glancing around us. "And the birds aren't singing."

We both knew what that meant. Spirits were beginning to stir. We were far off the main road, and close to recently disturbed graves. It was definitely time to go home.

The trip had already gotten us what we wanted. I had validated the vision I'd gotten from Theodora's disk, and we had a good guess as to where the epidemic victims had been buried. Plus, we now knew the lay of the land around the old mansion, and that might be valuable. We had nothing to gain by sticking around.

Teag and I headed back at a brisk pace. The land around the semi-circle of trees had been relatively open and still lit with the fading sun. Under the trees, it was much darker. Shadows seemed to close around us, and the temperature seemed much cooler than normal for a South Carolina summer night.

"Did you see that?" I pointed to where the gray shape of a woman in a long, old-fashioned dress slipped behind some trees and disappeared. I thought it might have been Theodora, and then I realized that the profile was wrong. Another ghostly outline caught my eye to the left, and I thought I saw something stir off to the right as well.

"I've seen enough to know that we've got company," Teag replied, breaking into a jog. I tried to keep up, but the tangle of bushes, vines, and fallen branches made it difficult to move very fast without falling.

"They're not trying to stop us," I said, hoping the spirits didn't suddenly change their mind.

"It's almost like they're leading us back."

The sun was low in the sky, setting the horizon afire in an orange glow. Overhead, the bright blue sky was rapidly darkening to indigo. I fished my phone out of my pocket and turned on the light. Teag did the same, and together we cast a jerky beam over the uneven landscape, hoping we remembered the path back to the mansion. Once again, I closed my hand over Theodora's disk and concentrated. A sense of certainty filled me.

"Veer right," I called to Teag. "We're on the right path."

I had a sudden vision of Theodora standing in front of me, looking in terror at something over my shoulder. She screamed wordlessly and turned to run, hiking her long skirts and stumbling across the bumpy ground. *Am I seeing a different view of the night Theodora lost her life,* I wondered, *or is this a fresh vision, a warning for here and now?*

Behind me, I heard a rush of air and a hiss. Ghostly hands grabbed for me, unable to clutch my clothing, but capable of sinking through flesh and bone, momentarily robbing me of breath. I cried out as the strike made me stagger, and I nearly lost my footing.

"Cassidy!" Teag had been a few steps ahead of me. He turned, looking past me with an expression of horror.

I knew whatever struck me was going to try again. I held tightly to my phone with my left hand, and with my right I pulled the bag of salt out of the pocket of my hoodie and let the contents fly as my arm made a wide arc, spraying the crystals as far as I could.

The hiss was louder this time, and angry. Whatever it was, I bet it didn't like the salt, but I couldn't pull that trick again. The salt might make a barrier between me and my pursuer, but I hadn't cast a full circle, and I couldn't stay here all night. And the salt wasn't going to do anything for Teag.

The hiss came again, moving now, circling around to the side. I scrambled to my feet, clasping my agate necklace in my right hand and shining the phone light with my left, where the wooden amulet dangled from its cord.

Cautiously, I backed toward Teag, keeping my light shining in the direction where I had last heard the creature hiss. I listened for footsteps, crackling twigs, anything that would reassure me that our pursuer was something normal and physical. I wanted to convince myself that I'd let my imagination get the best of me and that we had spooked a coyote or a fox from cover, maybe a frightened possum. Hell, I would have gladly faced down a rabid raccoon rather than what I feared we were up against.

Teag and I could handle the raccoon. At worst, we'd end up with rabies shots. There's no vaccine against vampires.

Teag and I were back to back, slowly moving in the direction of the plantation. I could glimpse a band of twilight at the edge of the forest. If we could get out into the open, we might make it to the car. Who was I kidding? We'd never outrun him.

The hiss came from the shadows, closer now. Teag had grabbed a fallen branch and broken it to make a staff. Against a mortal enemy, with his martial arts training, it would have been a formidable weapon. But what was sizing us up from the shadows wasn't mortal.

The hiss became a roar, and I felt a rush of icy air as something barreled toward us at full speed. I shone my light straight at the noise, and for an instant I glimpsed the translucent figure of a man, his face twisted with rage, long eye teeth leaving no doubt as to what he was.

Before I could even scream, the ghost attacked, slamming into me with enough force to nearly take me off my feet, and going through my body like a frozen knife. I dropped my phone and fell to my knees. My right hand broke my fall, and as I felt the ghost circle again, I thrust my left hand out, holding the wooden amulet in the palm of my outstretched fist.

The icy blast washed over me again and then recoiled as it brushed my fist. An awful, ear-splitting keen filled the darkness. A vision sprang from the wooden amulet, obliterating everything around me.

I saw the same figure whose ghost had been chasing us, but now he was solid, and if not exactly mortal, then at least corporeal. His dark hair was shoulder-length, tangled from the wind. The clothing he wore was stained and torn, but from the loose shirt and knee-length breeches, I guessed it to be early seventeen hundreds. A large iron key hung on a chain around his neck.

"Leave this alone," the man snarled. "It's none of your concern."

"You stole the Key, and used it to cast a plague curse." I knew that voice with its hint of a Dutch accent, even though I couldn't see the speaker. Sorren had faced this enemy, and the memory of that encounter sprang from the amulet in my fist. "That makes it my concern."

A woman joined the man from the darkness of the forest. Both she and the man had dark skin turned corpse ashen, with long black hair braided in the fashion on the sugar islands of the Caribbean.

"Plague makes for good feeding," the woman vampire said with a leer. Her voice was languid with a deep drawl, thick as chilled blood. "They're going to die anyhow. Where's the harm in feeding from them? Puts them out of their misery."

"You brought a plague down on a city full of people," Sorren snapped. "That ends now."

"You can try," the man replied, standing in a confident slouch that suggested he felt no fear.

Everything in the visions seemed to happen at once. I glimpsed Sorren moving toward the stranger in a blur of motion, and his enemy meeting the attack with the same speed. Another voice I did not recog-

nize, a different woman's voice that also had an Islands' lilt started chanting.

A streak of white fire like lightning crackled through the air, striking the stranger in the chest on the key itself. The dark-haired vampire screamed and began to jerk and buck as if struck by seizure, his skin charring and peeling back to reveal bone.

Sorren barreled into to the woman, hitting with enough force to take her off her feet though she struggled and fought his grip. She was shrieking curses in a language I did not understand, clawing at Sorren with immortal strength, but unable to break his hold. Sorren held the woman's arms pinned and pivoted to face another person, one I still could not see clearly.

"Now!" Sorren ordered through gritted teeth as if it took all his strength to hold the screaming woman. I saw another figure, a large woman dressed in white, chanting in the same heavy islands drawl. A man wearing a priest's shirt ran into my view. A glowing blade glinted in his hand, and I saw the blade sink deep into the female vampire's chest, between the ribs and into the heart.

One last piercing scream of pain and fury filled the night, and the vision ended.

"Come on!" Teag's voice brought me back to the present. I was trembling all over, and I thought I was going to be sick. Teag jerked me to my feet. I grabbed my phone from where it had fallen as he dragged me with him. We staggered and ran toward where the mansion used to be.

"That thing—" I started, barely able to talk.

"Whatever you did, you got rid of it," he replied, his breath ragged as he pulled me along with him.

"It's not gone," I said, not sure how I knew that to be true, but certain nonetheless. "It'll be back."

I dared to glance behind us. Dozens of ghostly figures glowed dimly in the darkness. Theodora Wellright was one of them, but there were many more. Men and women, children, and old people. These were likely the victims of the vampires I'd seen Sorren destroy. They had formed a line behind us, a bulwark in case the vampire's spirit came back, doing their best to buy us the time that had run out for them. We ran.

We almost slammed into the car in the darkness. Teag and I threw ourselves into the car, and he roared away, sending up a spray of dirt and gravel behind us. My heart was thudding so hard I thought I might pass out, and Teag looked just as shaky. Neither of us spoke, and I saw that Teag's hands trembled on the steering wheel.

We wanted answers, I thought. *And we got them. The epidemic that killed thousands of people was caused by a vampire with a cursed object. They fed on the dying. Theodora was right. There were vampires. And they killed her.*

URBAN EXPLORER

I HEARD THE BELL JINGLE ON THE DOOR TO THE SHOP, AND THE exchange of voices told me someone had come in as Maggie's customer went out. Their voices didn't quite carry to the back room.

I was just getting up to go to the front when Maggie stuck her head around the corner. "Cassidy—there's a gentleman here who wants to speak with you."

I followed her out to find a tall, handsome man casually glancing at our display cases. Being five foot nine, I tend to notice height. He was in his late twenties or early thirties with chestnut hair and brown eyes, and he looked more like he was dressed for hiking than for window-shopping on King Street. I got the feeling that being in the shop made him nervous.

"Can I help you?" I asked, trying to place him and deciding I had never seen him before.

"You're Cassidy Kincaide?" When I nodded, he looked relieved. "I really need to talk with you." He glanced around, but Maggie had busied herself with something in a cabinet near the back of the store. "I'm Ryan Alexander. You might know me as Nikon Ninja—and I really need your help."

Teag overheard the conversation and came up to the front. It only took him a few moments to confirm that Ryan Alexander was indeed Teag's urban explorer friend. Things were still quiet in the store, so Teag and I ushered Ryan to the break room table in the back and gave him a glass of sweet tea.

"I'm sorry to show up without calling first," Ryan said. "But I wondered whether you were able to learn anything about that ivory disk I mailed to you."

"I've found out a few things," I said cautiously. "Why the urgency?"

Ryan was silent for a moment as if debating what to say. "Teag's probably told you that I'm an urban explorer in my spare time. I've got a group that's been exploring in a lot of Southern cities—old ruins, abandoned manufacturing plants, forgotten infrastructure like storm drains and old railway tunnels, that sort of thing."

"He mentioned it," I replied, still trying to figure why Ryan seemed so nervous.

"We've seen some odd things poking around in the dark, but we leave the ghost hunting to other folks," Ryan continued. "We actually cooperate with several of the area ghost hunting groups—we scout the location, and they come back with their woo-woo finders."

Sounded to me like Ryan was a skeptic. Which made his connection to the ivory disk all the more curious. "But ever since we started exploring the old Wellright plantation, there have been too many unexplained things happening," he continued. "I've never been completely sold on the idea of ghosts. But I may have to change my mind."

"Why's that?"

Ryan tugged at the collar of his shirt. "Because in the three times my group has gone exploring around the plantation, we've had sightings of a woman's ghost each time—and enough of us have seen her to make it hard to write off as imagination."

"I'm an antique shop owner," I answered. "Why tell me?"

Ryan gave me a no-bullshit look. "I've heard things about you. Folks say you have a talent for handling haunted objects. Before the

Wellright incidents, I wouldn't have put much stock in such things. Now, I'm not so sure."

"I'm not sure I can speak to the rumors you've heard," I replied carefully. "But I'm curious about what you've seen."

Ryan took a deep breath and let it out. "You need to understand how unusual this whole thing is. We have logged hundreds of hours in dark, abandoned places and never saw anything that made us think we'd seen a ghost. Sure, your mind plays tricks on you for a moment when you're in a strange place, but the odd noises or the weird shadows have always turned out to be rats or raccoons or a water leak —something very natural and normal."

He paused, and I waited for him to go on. "We wanted to explore the old Wellright place because we knew developers were going to cut into it and we'd lose the chance forever. The first time, we went in daylight, and we found the foundation of the original mansion. One of my group had turned up a description of the house from the Archive, and so we knew that there should be cellars and tunnels running beneath the mansion. We went looking for them."

"Weren't you afraid that anything down there might have collapsed by now?" Teag asked.

Ryan grinned. "That's part of the fun of being an UrbExer. You never know what you're going to find. Only this time, we found a bit more than we bargained for," he added, and his grin slipped.

"We poked around and found a way into the old cellars. The roof had come down in a few places, but the whole thing was made with brick and stone, and they built stuff to last back then. Most of it was passable." Ryan combed his fingers back through his hair. "But what got our attention was that there were no signs of animals in the cellars or tunnels. None at all. That's very unusual."

"If it was sealed up, maybe they couldn't get in," Teag suggested.

Ryan shook his head. "You'd be amazed. Even in newer buildings, rats and other critters always find ways in. That was the first thing that seemed very odd. Then, several members, each said they felt like they were being watched. That's not usual for our group," he said, leaning forward to rest his forearms on his knees. "We've been doing this long enough that we don't jump at shadows. But I agree with them. I felt it too."

"Could the developers have had security people out there?" I asked.

"No. We're good at what we do," he said, looking up to meet my gaze. "We know how to check for police or security before we explore. None of us fancies spending time in jail."

"I still don't see—"

"Several of us saw a woman in a long dress near the ruins," Ryan cut me off. "We saw her in different places at different times, and no one said anything until after we started back. When we compared notes, we each had the same impression, even though we only glimpsed her before she disappeared."

"What about the ivory disk?" I asked. "What made you send it to me?"

Ryan looked self-conscious. "One of us found it when we disturbed some dirt to find a way into the cellars. We couldn't figure out where the entrance was underneath the ruins, so we used the old drawings and found where one of the tunnels came up near a well in the woods. Right after that, we started to see the ghost girl."

"How much do you know about the Wellrights?" I asked. Part of me wanted to believe Ryan's story. I was certainly convinced that something supernatural—and dangerous—was going on. But Ryan's experiences could be explained away pretty easily as a combination of jitters and suggestion, especially if he had studied the family history or visited the new mansion.

"Before the incidents, not much," Ryan admitted. "We focused on the terrain and the house plans, safety and exploration kinds of things. Until we visited, we weren't even sure we could get into the cellars. Sometimes, there's not much to see."

"The disk belonged to Theodora Wellright," I said, deciding to share a little of what we had learned. "She was in her twenties when she died in a Yellow Fever epidemic right before her fiancé returned from sea. She could be buried somewhere behind the old plantation, along with the others who died of the disease."

"Do you think hers was one of the graves the developers accidentally dug up?"

"Maybe," I replied. "But you still haven't really told us why you're so interested in the disk, interested enough to risk being outed as a trespasser or worse… maybe a grave robber."

"We had nothing to do with the graves," Ryan snapped, and I saw anger in his eyes. I had deliberately provoked him to see what kind of a reaction I would get, and his body language suggested that he was telling the truth. "And the reason I'm so intent on figuring out what's going on is because the last time my group went out, one of my people got attacked. Something's prowling around that forest, and I'll be honest with you. Whatever it is scared the shit out of me."

Now we're getting somewhere, I thought. "Attacked how?" Teag asked.

Ryan leaned back in his chair and shook his head. "I don't really know. That's the hell of it. Tandy is one of our regular explorers. She's tough—had two tours in the Army before she left the service. Not much freaks her out. We went back after dark the last time because we knew the developers had broken ground and we were trying to steer clear of their people. But we all wanted another look at the cellars, just in case the developers destroyed them."

"But you said there was nothing in the cellars," I said.

Ryan shook his head. "Tandy wasn't attacked down there. We were in the forest, not far from where I had found the disk. Tandy was in the rear. She said she had the feeling there was something out there, and she was used to night patrol," he added with a rueful grimace.

"It got real cold all of a sudden, even though the night had been warm. Andy and Jason both saw the ghost girl at the same time, off to the right of us," Ryan recounted. "And then, Tandy screamed." He looked like the memory unnerved him. "Tandy is not the screaming kind. She went down, and either she had a convulsion, or she was trying to fight off something no one else could see. We all went running back toward her, and the cold disappeared as quickly as it came."

"And Tandy?" Teag asked.

Ryan looked from me to Teag as if he were desperate for us to believe him. "Tandy was almost unconscious. When she came around, she said that it felt like something very cold slipped through her, and was trying to drain all of her energy." He met my gaze. "If we hadn't somehow chased it off, I think it could have killed her. What kind of thing can do that? And why is it out there?"

I had a few ideas, and I figured Teag did, too. But I didn't know Ryan well enough to say what was on my mind. "I don't have an answer for you," I replied. "But I'd like to get a look at the place where you found the disk for myself. How soon do you think you could take us out there?"

"I can't go tonight," Ryan said apologetically. "The group has another exploration planned. We're going to look for the crypts beneath St. Roch's church."

"Can we come?" I asked without even thinking to shoot a glance at Teag. St. Roch's, the plague church, the church that the Wellright family was careful to place as a bastion between them and the horrors of the old plantation. St. Roch's had something to do with the hauntings and the supernatural attacks, I was sure of it.

My request startled Ryan, but Teag managed to take it in stride, and I wondered if he had been thinking the same thing. "Sure," Ryan said, regaining his composure. "Have you ever been urban exploring before?"

If you only knew, I thought, thinking of the times Teag and Sorren and I had headed into abandoned and deserted buildings after supernatural threats. "Just a couple times," I said, smiling disingenuously. "But I promise we won't be any bother."

Ryan seemed to make up his mind and nodded. "Okay. We'll meet at seven." He wrote down an address for me. "The church itself is long gone, but we believe some of the old cellars can be accessed through the utility tunnels underneath the buildings in that area. Wear clothing you don't mind throwing out and waterproof shoes. If you mind bugs in your hair, cover it up. And bring good flashlights with fresh batteries."

"See you there," I assured him. "What about the Wellright plantation?"

Ryan's smile slipped a little. *He's afraid,* I thought. "I can take you another time if you don't mind going after dark."

I fully hoped to get Sorren to shadow us and let me know what his sharper vampire senses made of things. "That works," I replied. "Looking forward to it." Funny, but from the look on Ryan's face, I would have said he wasn't.

SLEEP SOUNDLY AND WAKE NOT

AFTER RYAN LEFT, TEAG AND I CLOSED UP THE STORE FOR THE DAY and bid Maggie good night. Then Teag motioned for me to come to the office, where he had been doing some more online digging.

"I didn't want to mention this in front of Ryan," Teag said. "But I found out more about the development project near the old Wellright plantation. The good news is that because of the old graves; they're going to be tied up in paperwork for a bit. So we shouldn't have to worry about activity there."

Something in his tone made me wary. "Why do I have the feeling there's more to it?"

Teag grinned. "Good instincts. I had to do a little hacking to get the official report. Turns out the Charleston coroner's office has its panties in a wad over what they found when they opened the old caskets that the construction folks uncovered."

I felt a shiver down my spine. "This isn't going to be good, is it?"

"All of the bodies had their heads severed and placed upside-down above the bodies, and each one had a wooden stake through the rib cage."

I met his gaze. "Someone thought they had been killed by

vampires," I said quietly. "We've got to find out what Sorren knows about this."

Teag nodded somberly, his grin replaced by a worried expression. "I agree. And the sooner, the better. Because I have a theory about what attacked you the other night."

"I'm not sure I want to know, but go ahead."

"Think about that vision you had... What if there had been a vampire running around Charleston killing people back in 1732?" Teag speculated. "It wouldn't be the first time the Alliance covered up a supernatural killing spree as an epidemic, especially since there really was a Yellow Fever outbreak at the time. And what if disturbing the graves has somehow not only roused Theodora's ghost but others as well?"

He leaned toward me. "You said that Theodora's journal talked about infernal creatures with long teeth. And both you and Ryan said that being attacked by one of the ghosts made you feel drained. What if they weren't completely successful when they killed the vampire back in 1732, and the construction woke up his ghost?"

"A vampire's ghost?" I echoed. "Draining energy instead of blood?"

Teag nodded. "It's not unheard of. People talk about psi-vampires, people or spirits who can drain psychic or life energy."

I made a face. "I think one of those was a college roommate of mine."

Teag laughed. "I know I had one for a dissertation advisor. But seriously, this goes beyond grumpy people who bring everyone down. A real psychic or emotional vampire can get sustenance from the life force of other people. You won't see citations in regular medical litera-ture, but on the Darke Web there are some pretty reputable studies documenting it." He paused. "Of course, in those cases, the psy-vamp was corporeal—not a ghost."

"I want to know Sorren's take on all this," I said. "And I can't shake the feeling that St. Roch's is the key—I just don't know what we're looking for.

"We'll find out soon enough," Teag said drolly.

~

I HAD A lot on my mind as I headed home. I live in an old Greek Revival Charleston "single house," a design style that the Holy City has claimed as its own. The footprint of the house is one room wide, with a single room on each side of a central hall. The front of the house faces into a walled garden, putting the skinny side of the house facing the sidewalk. The door to the street actually opens onto the wide front porch (what Charlestonians call a "piazza"). I bought the house from my parents when they moved to Charlotte, or I never would have been able to afford it. It had been in the family for more than a century. I loved it.

I parked my Mini Cooper at the curb. When I reached the door, I could hear Baxter, my Maltese dog, going nuts on the other side. Baxter is six pounds of pure attitude, a dog with the soul of a mastiff and the body of a Guinea pig.

The door swung open, and Baxter jumped and rolled at my feet. Sometimes I take him with me to the store, but dogs are sensitive to supernatural activity, and I noticed that taking him too often seemed to bother him. I don't know what his extra-sharp senses picked up, and I'm not sure I want to know. I tried living in the apartment above the shop when I first moved back to town and being that close all the time to the objects we had tucked away in the back to get rid of made me jumpy as hell.

I put the mail on the counter, got Baxter's leash, and took him for his evening walk. Despite my resolve to put the Wellright situation out of my mind for a little while, my thoughts kept coming back to it, and my sense of foreboding grew stronger. Something had stirred up the Wellright ghosts. Theodora seemed to be a dead woman with a mission. If she hadn't died of Yellow Fever as accounts reported, and if the real cause of her death had been a vampire, then maybe whatever roused the vampire's ghost from slumber had also brought Theodora back to sound the alarm.

I was well aware of the fact that most normal people don't think these kinds of thoughts when they walk their dogs on a sunny summer afternoon. Then again, I'd never been like most people, even before my great-uncle Evanston decided to leave me a three-hundred and fifty-year-old antique shop and a mission to help save the world, one haunted piece of silverware at a time.

The sun was getting low in the sky by the time Baxter and I got home, and I had already speed-dialed for pizza delivery. I munched my veggie pizza deep in thought, sharing bits of broccoli with Baxter who thinks it's the best treat in the world. Go figure.

I knew it was dangerous to go to St. Roch's, but I didn't see an alternative. Still, I didn't want to go unprotected. I made sure I was wearing my agate necklace since the stone is good for warding away evil. I didn't try to find my silver bracelet. Sorren had told me once that silver doesn't work in real life like it does in the movies. It doesn't kill vampires; it just irritates their very sensitive skin. That means a vampire will avoid silver, but a really determined one will deal with the welts later. Since we might be dealing with a vampire ghost, I didn't think it would be worried about a rash. On a hunch, I took Theodora's ivory disk and put it in my pocket.

As Ryan had suggested, I wore black jeans and a black t-shirt and sneakers with good tread. I had a lightweight black hoodie, more for concealing my face if necessary than because I expected to be cold. My cell phone was charged and in my pocket. I might not get a signal underground, but I could still take pictures. I stuffed a garlic bulb into the pocket of my hoodie, just to be safe, and I filled a small plastic bag with salt and put it in my other pocket. Salt was a kind of all-purpose evil repellent, and I figured it couldn't hurt. I stuck a hand towel in my pocket as well, just in case there was something I wanted to pick up without touching. And I grabbed my heavy-duty flashlight with brand new batteries.

Baxter began to yip at the door, so I knew Teag was there to pick me up. I checked my cell phone again, hoping to have a message from Sorren, but no such luck. Sometimes work with the Alliance takes him off the grid. We would just have to do without him.

"Ready?" Teag asked as I slipped into the passenger seat.

"Yep. What did you tell Anthony? We might be ever-so-slightly trespassing."

Teag chuckled. "He had to work late. No worries."

"Did you bring any lucky charms?" I was feeling a little foolish, but at the same time, the whole idea of having a vampire ghost after us gave me the creeps.

"I brought the hamsa I bought in Greece a few years ago," he said.

"You brought a Greek hamster?"

He rolled his eyes. "Hamsa. It protects against the evil eye." He withdrew a woven cord from inside his t-shirt to reveal a charm in the shape of a hand with an eye in the middle. "I stuck a shaker of salt in my backpack, along with two flashlights, some sage to purify negative energy and a small chunk of amethyst to ward off psychic attack." He paused. "Oh, and a bottle of water."

"Holy water?"

"Mineral. I get thirsty."

Between the two of us, we were about as well-prepared as we could get. I sincerely hoped we didn't need any of the special items, but I felt safer knowing we had them.

Ryan had set the meeting place as a parking garage on the outside edge of Charleston's historic district. Just a few blocks over were a number of important homes including the new Wellright mansion. On the other side of the garage were several blocks badly in need of renovation: some abandoned storefronts, low-rent retail shops and a boarded up house or two. Tourists didn't come out this way, and neither did anyone else, by the looks of things.

Under normal conditions, I wouldn't have set foot in a parking garage that looked like that. It was a 1960s architectural monstrosity, made of brick and steel, left to deteriorate. Graffiti was scrawled across one brick wall, and I almost expected it to read "abandon hope" but it wasn't that poetic.

"Grim little place, isn't it?" Teag said, looking around cautiously. I was starting to wish that I had worried more about encountering the living than the dead. A canister of pepper spray would have made me feel a lot better.

"Thanks for being on time." Ryan's voice made me jump. He was standing next to an old panel van, and three more people, also dressed in dark colors, were climbing out, a man and two women.

"Wouldn't miss it for the world," Teag said, although I knew his real feelings were more ambivalent.

"Let me introduce you to who's here tonight," Ryan said. "Some of our folks couldn't make it. This is Penny," he added with a nod toward a dark-haired, petite woman who carried herself like she had been in the military. "Karen," he said, acknowledging a blonde with a short, pixie cut and freckles that were jarringly at odds with the no-nonsense look in her eyes. She wore a form-fitting lycra jumpsuit that seemed a little overly noir until I saw the rock climber shoes on her feet and the coiled rope she carried over one shoulder.

"And Kurt," Ryan added. The fourth member of their group, a red-headed man with wire-rimmed glasses and nervous blue eyes, gave me a nod.

"Everybody, this is Cassidy and Teag," Ryan finished. I noticed the group wasn't much for last names. I was just as glad to stay relatively anonymous, and since the group's activities skirted the edges of the law, I figured the caution was justified. I noticed that none of Ryan's team who were attacked at the old Wellright place were here tonight.

"The entrance to the service tunnel is over here," Ryan said, gesturing for us to follow him.

To my surprise, our cars weren't the only ones in the garage, but the others could generously be described as "clunkers." No self-respecting car thief would be seen dead in any of them. Some sat on flat tires, suggesting that their owners had abandoned them. Others were covered with enough dust that it was clear no one had driven them in a long time. A few were up on blocks, missing wheels, and other parts. The whole garage felt stagnant and depressing, and I wondered if the fact that it was built on ground once consecrated for a plague church had anything to do with it.

If the garage ever had inside lighting, no one had replaced the bulbs for a long time. The glow of streetlights provided some illumination near the edges of the garage, but farther in was very dark. Ryan led us to a service stairway, then down to a lower level that was pitch black. Our flashlights didn't make much of a dent, and I really hoped he knew where he was going.

"This way," Ryan said. We followed him to a rusted fire door that led down a narrow stairway never intended for the public. The paint peeled on the walls and the cement steps were stained with substances I didn't want to examine. It occurred to me that ghosts might not be the only things to worry about in a place like this. Vagrants, junkies, stray dogs, and rodents wouldn't be pleasant to run into either.

"This takes us down into the sub-basement," Ryan said. "It's where the utilities run. But on the other side of the sub-basement there's a door that opens into an old brick corridor, and from the blueprints I've been able to find, it's a good bet that will open up into what's left of St. Roch's cellar."

It was cool down here, but still heavy with Charleston humidity. I could hear water dripping somewhere in the distance. Like most cellars, the sub-basements smelled of mold and neglect. From the heavy layer of dust, it didn't look like anyone had been down here for a long time. That was probably a good sign. I was worried enough about supernatural threats. I didn't want to have to worry about getting mugged, too.

Ryan's crew had obviously done this kind of thing before. They each carried the heavy, military-style indestructible flashlights that could easily double as a weapon. I noticed that Kurt and Penny had sheaths on their belts for respectable-sized knives. Down here in the dark, I found their equipment reassuring.

"In case you're wondering, the company that built this garage went bankrupt, and it's been tied up in legal wrangling for years," Ryan said. "The bank foreclosed, then even that fell through. The title is so muddied it'll take years to straighten out. So there's no one to care that we're here."

Maybe not among the living, but I couldn't shake the feeling that something was watching us. We moved carefully around the old boxes and crates that had been stored in the sub-basement and were nearly falling apart. Ryan led the way toward the door at the far side of the room, and we followed, brushing away cobwebs as we went.

Karen and Kurt shone their lights on the doorway while Ryan put some muscle into yanking the stubborn door open. I noticed that Penny had a hand on her knife, making me wonder what the group had encountered in the past. Then again, in these parts, anything from feral cats to coyotes to wild pigs were possible, though I didn't think we'd have much problem with the pigs this close to town.

Nothing but cold, musty air rushed out as Ryan hauled the door open. Penny had moved up to the front with Ryan, and she looked like she was used to being on patrol. We slipped through the doorway and found ourselves standing in an old brick corridor. The walls were wet and covered with slime. Underfoot, stepping stones kept us from getting our sneakers wet, but brackish water lay on the bottom of the corridor floor. Cobwebs were thick as cotton candy, and I saw that Ryan and Penny produced telescoping poles from their backpacks to battle with the webs and clear the way.

I fought down claustrophobia. Ryan had assured me that one of their group's safety precautions was that one member always stayed home and knew the details of every outing so that help could be summoned if the team was late to check in. I had left a message for Sorren and a packet for Maggie at the store, which I could retrieve before she got there if everything went well. Still, the knowledge that we were underground in a very old tunnel in the dark made me fight with myself not to run away screaming.

"We're heading in the right direction," Ryan called back to the group. "We should have about ten more feet before this opens into St. Roch's lower levels."

I did my best to make sure my shoulders didn't brush the tunnel walls. The closer we got to the old church cellar, the stronger my sense of being watched grew. Something knew we were down here. Someone was watching, waiting to see what we were going to do.

We came to an abrupt stop. Our flashlights formed a pool of light where we stood, but the tunnel behind us was completely dark.

"There's a door here, but it's nailed shut. This is going to take a little doing," Ryan said.

Ryan and Kurt pulled gloves and crowbars from their packs and handed off their flashlights as they went to work on the boarded up door. We were definitely crossing the line between trespassing and breaking-and-entering. Kurt and Ryan wielded the crowbars as if they had done this kind of thing a lot, leveraging their weight against the old boards and rusted nails that creaked and groaned in protest.

The old wood splintered and gave way. Behind the boards was another door, but its old lock broke easily. The door swung inward, hinges creaking.

"We're in," Ryan murmured, and I could hear the excitement in his voice.

One by one, we filed into the chamber. Our lights shone over the walls, and I understood why whoever had built atop the old church had left the basement. We were in a crypt.

"Wow," Karen said as her flashlight played across the stone slabs. "Do you think all the people down here died from Yellow Fever?"

"Yellow Fever, smallpox, measles—all the epidemics were bad," Kurt said, pushing his glasses up on the bridge of his nose.

"I'm surprised the families didn't protest," Penny said. Even she looked a bit subdued by our discovery.

"Maybe there wasn't anyone left to care," Teag replied. "Back then, epidemics wiped out whole families."

A loud bang made us all jump. "What was that?" Karen asked, her voice a few notes higher than before.

Ryan shone his light in the direction of the noise. "Looks like a piece of stone fell. Not too surprising given the way we had to battle our way in." He studied the ceiling for a moment, but considering the age of the crypt, it looked to be in good shape. "Don't let your nerves get the best of you," he said, but I could hear an edge in his voice.

The tunnel had been cool, but the crypt itself was cold. Even with my hoodie, my arms were cold. I caught a glimpse of motion and turned, but there was nothing behind me.

"Is this it?" Penny asked. She had made a slow circle of the chamber, shining her light across the walls. "There are four small passage-ways that lead off from the main room, but I can see from here that they're dead-ends. Probably more tombs."

Ryan shrugged. "St. Roch's was a burial church. It didn't have a congregation, so it didn't need a lot of space. People only came here to die or attend a funeral."

There wasn't enough space for anyone to get lost, so for a while, we all meandered at our own pace, studying the names on the marble tombs and looking around. Most of the inscriptions looked hastily chis-eled, and I guessed that the stonemasons hadn't wanted to spend any more time here than necessary.

"Look at that," Teag said in a voice pitched for only me to hear. He pointed to an inscription carved into the stained marble. *I pray you remain at rest,* the epitaph said. Not the most common thing for a tombstone.

"Hey, this is weird." Karen had crouched down to have a look at one of the other slabs. "This says 'Rise not, until the final trumpet call.'"

"One over here says, 'Sleep soundly, and wake not,'" Kurt added.

"Are they all like that?" Penny asked. Even she sounded a little concerned.

Karen stood up and glared at Kurt, who was right behind her. "Hey, quit poking me!"

Kurt spread his hands. "I didn't touch you."

I caught motion again in my peripheral vision and turned to follow it. This time, I glimpsed the shadow of a woman who looked a lot like Theodora. I signaled to Teag and began to move toward the nearest of the four small passageways.

Behind me, I heard what sounded like a shower of pebbles. "What the hell!" Penny snapped, batting at the air in front of her. "Where did that come from? I just got hit with a handful of rocks. Quit playing around!"

"Nobody threw anything at you, Penny." Kurt sounded annoyed. "Get a grip."

I had a theory, and I was betting that it was one that Ryan and his team wouldn't like. Falling rocks, mysterious pokes and gravel sprays were all well within what a cheesed off poltergeist could do. The feeling that we weren't welcome here was growing stronger by the minute, but unfortunately, so was the conviction that there was something in the crypt we were supposed to do. I closed my hand around Theodora's ivory disk, and the shadow came into sharper detail. The ghost looked straight at me, and then deliberately turned and walked away, as if she expected me to follow.

Theodora's shadow led me into the right-side corridor, which was only a few feet deep. Both sides of the walls were covered with tombs, and those that had inscriptions were as unnerving as the ones in the outer chamber. *Answer no call to rise but the Almighty's. Surrender to the final sleep. Let no one disturb your rest.* There were more, but I got the idea. Whoever buried these people was not entirely sure they were going to stay dead.

A flicker of movement toward the back of the chamber caught my eye, and I glimpsed Theodora right before something pushed me off balance. I almost cried out, but I didn't want to call the others. Teag was standing guard at the end of the corridor, so I knew no one had gotten past him. Our ghostly friends were getting pushy.

I avoided falling by putting an arm out to steady myself against the tomb wall. Just as I regained my balance, I felt another shove. I was being herded toward the right-hand corner, and the ghost wasn't being subtle.

This time, as I straightened up, I saw a small nook to one side of the top mausoleum drawer. The burial spot was inscribed with the name Theodora Wellright, and the epitaph, *Let the final death take you, my love.* I shone my flashlight into the nook and saw a dark wooden box. There was no way I was sticking my hand in there, so I used my flashlight to ease the box out to where I could reach it.

"We need to get out of here," Teag said. "Everyone's getting jumpy."

"Just a couple of minutes," I said. The wooden box was about as wide across as my hand and about three inches deep, maybe seven inches long. I wasn't about to risk getting a vision down here with

Ryan's explorers around, so I used the towel to grab the box. I was just heading over to put the box into Teag's messenger bag when everyone's flashlights suddenly went dead.

Karen screamed. I heard Kurt cry out in dismay, and Penny cursed. "Stay calm, everyone," Ryan said. I could hear him cranking up an emergency light.

The air grew even colder, and the hair on the back of my neck stood up. Something was coming my way, and it felt dangerous, corrupt. Teag gave an angry shout as a presence bore down on us. I dropped the garlic bulb onto the ground and stomped hard on it, crushing it and releasing its pungent odor. I heard Teag stumble, and instinctively, as the malicious spirit came at me, I held the wooden box up as a barrier.

The cloth slipped, and my hands touched the weathered wood. A vision flooded my senses. *I saw a middle-aged man dressed in black. He wore a white clerical collar, a priest. The priest grappled with a man I had never seen before, and judging from the second man's clothing; the time was again early in the seventeen hundreds. The priest held something in his hand, and he brought his right hand down against the other man's chest. The stranger arched back, shrieking in agony, and reached out to grab the priest by the throat. Blood soaked the stranger's ruffled shirt and spattered the priest's pristine collar. The stranger's teeth were bared, showing his long fangs. He struck with his right hand, slashing the priest on the chest.* The vision went dark.

The presence let out an unholy screech that echoed deafeningly in the stone and brick chamber. Theodora's ghost glided past—or maybe through—me like an arctic wind, standing between me and the presence. With one last angry wail, the presence blinked out. Theodora's ghost turned to me, then dissipated.

The flashlights blinked into life, flooding the crypt with light.

"What the hell was that about?" Ryan demanded, and I could hear fear beneath his anger. In the confusion, I slipped the wooden box into Teag's bag.

"Kurt's down." Karen's voice sounded panicky.

Teag and I came back to the main chamber to find Karen and Ryan kneeling over Kurt. Kurt looked pale, and his breathing was rapid. "I think he's just fainted," Ryan said.

Kurt groaned and began to come around. When he realized where he was, his cheeks colored and he stared up at the others with a sheepish expression. "What happened?"

"Damned lights failed," Penny replied. "You must have lost your balance." She was obviously trying to help him save face, but Kurt's cheeks reddened even more.

"One minute I remember shaking my flashlight to turn it on again, and then I felt really cold, and it was like something pulled my plug," Kurt said, struggling to his feet without accepting the helping hand Ryan offered. "My knees just buckled, and I don't remember anything after that."

"Who knows what kind of bad air could be down here," Teag said, leading the way toward the door back to the tunnel. "After all, the room's been sealed up for a long time. You'll feel better once we get aboveground."

"Yeah, that's a good idea," Ryan said with a glance toward Teag that told me he didn't quite believe the explanation but was willing to let it go, for now. "Let's get out of here."

We moved as fast as we could down the slippery stepping stones of the brick tunnel. I knew that the malicious ghost we had confronted was still down here. We'd made him back off, but we hadn't destroyed him or banished him. And while whatever was in the box I had hidden in Teag's bag had held the ghost away this time, it was no guarantee he wouldn't come looking for a rematch.

I halfway expected an ambush when we came back up the stairs into the abandoned parking garage. None of the cars our group had parked were new or expensive, but by comparison with the heaps left to rot in the old garage, they might as well have been an advertisement for carjacking. To my relief, the garage was still deserted. Given what Teag and I had experienced down below, I wondered if even the local riff-raff felt something dangerously amiss about the garage and stayed away.

Ryan's team looked worse for the wear. Kurt was still pale and shaky, though he tried to cover it. Penny looked angry, and I guessed she didn't handle fear well. Karen seemed to be thinking hard, probably trying to come up with a scientific explanation. Ryan just looked glad to make it out in one piece.

"What happened when the two of you went off?" he demanded. "We heard a god-awful noise."

"Spiders," I said with what I hoped passed for embarrassment. "Had a couple of them go down my back. Sorry."

Ryan gave me a skeptical look as if he suspected there was more to the story. Penny just muttered something under her breath and rolled her eyes. "You'll need to get over that if you do more exploring," he said. "Creepy crawlies go with the territory."

They certainly did, but the kinds of things Teag and I usually ran into were much creepier than anything Ryan had in mind. "Thanks for letting us come along," I said. "I imagine you'll want to go back sometime and get a better look at the crypts we found."

Ryan shook his head. "Probably not, now that we know it's just a burial site. We don't want to disturb the dead. We'll let them rest in peace."

That was the problem. Whatever Teag and I had tangled with wasn't resting, and it sure wasn't peaceful. And until we got to the bottom of it, I was pretty sure that the dead would be the ones disturbing us.

CALL FOR BACKUP

TEAG AND I WERE TOO JUMPY FROM THE ENCOUNTER BENEATH ST. Roch's to consider calling it a night, so we headed back to my house. We had just pulled up to the house when my cell phone rang with a text from Sorren.

Cassidy—important information. Need to discuss. Time to talk tonight?

Come on over; I texted back.

I was not surprised to hear a knock at the door a few minutes later. Baxter ran for the door, growling and barking with as much viciousness as his fluffy six-pound self could muster. I opened the door to let Sorren in, and he immediately knelt down to talk to Baxter.

"You're a very protective, good dog," he said in a very soothing voice as he made eye contact with Baxter, who was nearly beside himself. Immediately, Baxter sat down with a glazed, happy look on his confused little face.

I shut the door and sighed. "If he ends up with brain damage from being glamored, how do I explain it to the vet?"

Sorren rose and gave me a grin. "If he had a better memory, we wouldn't have to go through this every time he sees me."

"You've probably given him doggy Alzheimer's," I said, leading the way into the living room. It was an old, friendly sparring match. I didn't really believe that Sorren's vampire compulsion hurt Baxter. In fact, there were plenty of times when I wouldn't have minded being able to pull the same trick myself.

"I'm sorry to have been out of touch; it took much longer than I expected," Sorren said, with a nod to acknowledge Teag. "I was working on an Alliance situation in the Ural Mountains, and had no way to get or retrieve messages until I got back." He paused. "I'm afraid my silence has put you in danger. Tell me what's going on with the Wellright problem."

Sorren sat down in one armchair while Teag took a seat in the other. I sat on the sofa, and Baxter curled at my feet and fell asleep. Judging from the slight flush to Sorren's complexion, I guessed he had fed recently. The bond between Sorren and my family is nearly four centuries old, and I believe him when he swears he would never and has never harmed any of my relations. Still, I feel better knowing he isn't feeling peckish.

Nothing about Sorren's appearance would make someone wonder whether he was undead, although someone might question whether he was out of graduate school. He looks about my age since he was turned in his twenties, but that was back in 1465. Tonight he was wearing a hoodie over a t-shirt, jeans, and sneakers that when combined with his dark blond hair and boy-next-door looks let him blend in. As with the cell phone and email, Sorren adjusts well to the times.

I filled him in on what had happened and what we knew thus far. He listened with a serious expression, which was never a good sign.

"I remember the Wellright incident," Sorren said. One of the curses of immortality, he had told me once, was that immortals never forgot anything. Forgetfulness, he had told me, was an underrated blessing. "There was an outbreak of Yellow Fever that year, but many people who died didn't die of the fever."

"Let me guess," I said. "Some bad vampires came to town."

Sorren nodded. "They came in with one of the pirate ships from the

Caribbean. By the time the ship made port, a third of the crew had died. The vampires had altered the memories of the others enough that they didn't seem to notice."

He was looking past me, not really at me as if seeing those long-ago days. "When they got to Charleston and realized there was a plague in town, they decided to make the most of it."

"The epidemic hid the killing spree," I said, feeling nauseated. "People were dying left and right, and it was easy to hide the bodies."

"No one wanted to handle the corpses. They didn't know the fever spread from mosquitoes, and they were terrified of contagion," Sorren recalled, a note of sadness in his voice. "If the bites were carefully placed, they could easily be overlooked. Many of the dead were just dumped into mass graves."

I shivered. "What stopped the vampires?"

"I did." Something in his face looked harder, much older. Most people can't meet a vampire's gaze without being glamored, put under a compulsion that makes them do the vampire's will. Maybe it's my magic, or maybe it's the old bond between Sorren and my ancestors, but glamoring doesn't work on me. I met his gaze then, and I saw the centuries filled with losses and compromises and sorrow.

"Then how did one of them come back?"

Sorren grimaced. "We destroyed one of the vampires, body and soul. I thought the other destroyed as well. Apparently, I was wrong."

"Who were they? The vampires you fought." Teag asked.

"Betienne and Renya had been thieves in Haiti back when the French-controlled part of the territory," Sorren replied. "They were turned sometime in the late 1600s. Eventually, they decided to find a larger hunting ground. So they came to Charleston."

"How did you defeat them?" It still blew my mind that Sorren could reminisce about things that had happened three centuries ago. On a few occasions, Teag and I have gotten him talking about the old days, and hearing about history from someone who was actually there is very different from what's in those boring textbooks.

"I didn't do it alone," Sorren said. "Your ancestor—another Evann

—helped me. So did Mama Nadege. She was a powerful Voudon mambo, even then." I had heard him talk about Mama Nadege many times. And it made me think about what Alistair had told me, that even some of the gentry secretly used Voudon amulets to protect against dark forces.

"What do you know about St. Roch's?"

Sorren frowned. "It was built as a plague church, to bury the dead without endangering the living. The rector there was a very good man. Father Conroy. Anglican priest. He was part of the Alliance, and he helped Evann and me on more than one occasion."

A vampire, a Voodoo mambo, and an Anglican priest walk into a bar... I made myself focus on the serious business at hand, and left the matter of unlikely partnerships for another time.

"This is what we found in the crypt," I said, and Teag withdrew the wooden box from his bag. He set it on the coffee table between us, and carefully opened the lid. Inside, something was wrapped in a long piece of old, stained purple cloth.

Teag touched the cloth and let his Weaver magic stretch out to gather its secrets. "Not just cloth," he murmured. "Consecrated. A priest's stole." He paused, then went on to describe the stole's last wearer, someone who resembled the man I had seen in the vision at the crypt. "Is that your Father Conroy?"

"I'm certain that it is," Sorren said. "And that means I'm also sure what you'll find wrapped in that stole. You'll have to be the one to handle it. I can't, and Cassidy shouldn't."

Reverently, Teag unwrapped the layers. The stole was long enough for a priest to drape it around his neck like a scarf, reaching nearly to the hem of his cassock. Though the cloth was faded and stained, I could still make out the careful embroidery that marked both ends, and the fragile silk fringe. "Purple," I murmured. "For funerals." Underneath all the layers lay a knife with a long, steel blade and a bone handle carved with runes. Even without touching it, I could sense its power to destroy.

"Father Conroy hid a powerful weapon in the basement of the

church," Sorren said. "A knife that could destroy a vampire's soul as well as the body. He used that knife to destroy Betienne." He shivered. "For obvious reasons, the knife must be wielded by a mortal."

"I saw Father Conroy in my vision," I said. "And there was another woman. With dark skin dressed in white."

"That was Mama Nadege," Sorren said.

"How did you get a Catholic priest to work with a vampire and a mambo?" Teag asked.

Sorren chuckled. "Father Conroy was Anglican, not Roman Catholic," he said. "And although the hierarchies don't acknowledge it, throughout the centuries people on the front lines are more practical than dogmatic."

"Strange bedfellows," I quoted.

"Indeed," Sorren said. "Father Conroy was a member of the Expeditus Society, a secret group within the Anglican clergy who fight dark supernatural forces. They have long been allies of the Alliance."

"And he was okay working with a mambo?" I mused.

Sorren smiled. "In the islands, the slaves took the names of Christian Saints for their Loas, their Voudon gods, so that they could blend both traditions and escape punishment from their masters. Saint Expeditus corresponds to a powerful Loa, Baron Samedi." I recognized that name. Baron Samedi was the Loa of the dead, the protector against curses.

"So Betienne isn't our problem," Teag mused.

Sorren shook his head. "No. It's Renya we need to worry about. Father Conroy and Mama Nadege had their hands full with Betienne. I took on Renya. In the battle, Father Conroy destroyed Betienne with that knife, but his injuries cost him his life. I badly damaged Renya, but he must have managed to escape."

"The thing that attacked me at the new Wellright mansion and at the crypt was a ghost," I said. "That squares with the attacks on Ryan's people as well." I frowned. "The ghost drains all the energy from whoever it touches. Could we be dealing with a vampire's ghost?"

"Unusual but possible," Sorren replied. "It's possible that the damage I did to Renya was fatal after all," Sorren said. "It destroyed his body, but he was able to tether his soul here. As a Conjure, he may have been able to work a spell to keep himself from passing on. It's not impossible for vampires to become ghosts, but it's very rare."

Sorren looked concerned. "Renya was Betienne's maker, and he was quite loyal to her. His grief at her destruction—and his fury with me—may have been enough to bind his soul to Charleston, waiting for a chance at revenge."

"I felt as if something was draining all of my energy," I recounted. "It took my body heat, my will, my strength. Kurt felt the same thing, and Ryan said it also happened to one of his exploration crew."

Sorren nodded. "Renya would still be a vampire of sorts, even without a body or a thirst for blood. As a spirit, he needs to drain energy in order to keep from passing over. I suspect he has been gaining power, a little at a time, for a while now. Waiting for something to shift the balance in his favor and let him avenge his Betienne."

"Something like having the old graves disturbed?"

"Violating the graves would have weakened the spells we laid on them," he replied. "Mama Nadege placed binding spells on the graves of the victims, and other magic to dampen any remaining power. Both on the grounds and at St. Roch."

As we had been talking, Teag had logged into my laptop. He let out a low whistle. "I think we got very lucky," he said. "There've been killings at the construction site by the old Wellright place. Five workers dead. All of them working a night shift, and not a mark on any of the bodies."

"You've likely aroused his anger. Using my talisman brought the memories to the fore and showed him that you were in league with those who took his Betienne," Sorren replied. "He needed energy to replenish. And he will strike again."

"How is the developer explaining the deaths to the media?" I asked.

Teag shook his head. "It's not public. I hacked into the police files."

"What next?" I asked.

Sorren met my gaze. "We go see Mama Nadege."

~

CHARLESTON IS AN old city. Unless they burned down or fell down in the earthquake, most things built in Charleston are still here, especially from the old days. Tourists love to see the historic homes, the streets and alleys that look just like they did several hundred years ago. But those same old houses and alleyways anchor the past in other ways that aren't always pleasant. Restless spirits and unhappy memories are tied to those buildings and byways.

Some folks call this anchoring a "stone tape"—the idea that the energy, memories, emotions, and even spirits made an indelible impression that never gets erased. Maybe. That might account for the visions I get from objects that I touch. Maybe I'm a better than average psychic DVD player for left-over drama. It might even explain the ghosts that seem to "loop" a particular action over and over again. What it doesn't neatly explain are the ghosts who interact with the living, either for good or bad. I don't have an explanation for those kinds of spirits. I just know they're real.

After dark, only the main streets are still bustling with people in Charleston. After midnight, that traffic has slowed to a trickle except near the most popular nightspots. Side streets and narrow alleys are dark and quiet. People in this town have as much reason to be wary of the dead as they do the living, so they stick to the bright lights. Normally, I do too. But with Teag beside me and Sorren leading the way, I almost felt safe as we headed down a winding, cramped passageway where slave cabins had once stood. Almost—but not quite.

"Sorren," a man's voice said from the shadows. "It's been a long time."

Teag fell into a defensive stance, and I reached for the packet of salt in my pocket, but we both relaxed when a muscular young man who was very much alive stepped into the light. His hair was cut close to his head, and he had dark skin and black eyes. The man's deep voice had an island's lilt to it. And even without touching him, I felt a buzzing sensation that told me he had his own type of powerful magic.

"Good to see you, Caliel." Sorren turned from the newcomer back to Teag and me. "This is Caliel. He's a descendant of Mama Nadege—and a gifted medium." He looked to Caliel. "I'd like you to meet Cassidy and Teag. They run the shop now."

Caliel's laugh was deep and musical. "Always, Sorren has his partners with the shop. A long, long time he's been here. We do business together, Sorren and me." He met my gaze. "Just like Sorren works with your family a long time, mine too. We have history."

"Thank you for coming," Sorren said.

"I see your name on my phone, I pick it up," Caliel replied, chuckling. "I know if you call me, trouble's comin'. I talk to you first; maybe I see it before it sees me."

"I need your help," Sorren said, and Caliel grew serious. "Something evil that Mama Nadege and I fought a long time ago has returned." He gave a terse explanation, and Caliel let out a low whistle.

"When you bring trouble, you don't go halfway," he said, shaking his head. "All right. I'm in."

Sorren looked to Teag and me. "Caliel can not only channel Mama Nadege's spirit, he is also a *houngan asagwe*, a Voudon high priest."

"I know all the right spirits," Caliel said with a chuckle. "Come with me."

We followed Caliel down the narrow street, into the shadows. The air was thick with the smell of gardenia and honeysuckle, heavy with humidity. At the back of the dead-end alley, Caliel stopped and bowed his head. "Mama Nadege," Caliel murmured quietly. "We've come to see you. I need your help."

We were far enough in from the main street that the light behind us seemed dim and shadows from the neighboring buildings loomed over the narrow walkway. I should have felt safe with a martial arts expert and a vampire, but I didn't. I could feel the power in this place. My magic reads objects, and even without touching the old brick walls around me, I could sense the press of memories, sadness, and pain. The impressions carried the weight of bondage and rage, hopelessness, and desire.

"Mama Nadege." Caliel repeated the name, a little louder this time. He placed a smooth black stone on the cobblestones at his feet. I could see the intricate pattern of lines that had been scratched on the stone, and recognized it as a *veve*, a mark of one of the Voudon Loas or guardian spirits. I recognized that *veve*. It belonged to Papa Legba, the Loa who opened and closed the gateway to the spirit world.

The air around us became colder than a walk-in freezer. Nothing outdoors in Charleston is that cold in the middle of summer. I felt powerful magic stirring around me. And while I'm not a medium, and seeing ghosts isn't my special gift, the resonance from the walls around me and the stones under my feet opened my magic to sense the coming of spirits.

I smelled a whiff of pipe smoke and heard the distant barking of a dog, and I knew that both were associated with Papa Legba. I blinked, and then I saw her, Mama Nadege. She was a big woman in a white, loose gown. Her hair was tied up in a kerchief, and her skin was as black as the night and eyes dark as drowning pools. She looked straight at us, and I knew her image was no stone tape.

"It's been a while, Sorren." It was Caliel who spoke, but the voice that issued from his mouth was not the deep, rich baritone of a few moments before. Mama Nadege's image faded, and Caliel's stance shifted, becoming entirely different. Part of Voudon priesthood requires allowing the Loas to speak through the priest or priestess, even possess their body during a ceremony. He would be used to sharing himself with the spirit world, so having his ancestor speak through him wouldn't be that unusual. Caliel stood in front of me, but I knew that Mama Nadege had returned.

"Renya is back," Sorren said. Mama Nadege, speaking through Caliel, spat out a string of curses in a patois I didn't understand. I didn't need to speak the language. I got the gist.

"I thought we killed that bloodsucker good," Mama Nadege replied. Her accent was thick as cane syrup, heavy with the tones and pacing of the islands, tenor to Caliel's normal baritone.

"We did," Sorren said. "It's his ghost this time."

Mama Nadege gave a laugh that made me shiver. "Then you got your work cut out for you, uh huh. But there is a way to do it." She paused. "Who you got with you now, Sorren?"

Sorren introduced Teag and me and told Mama about my touch magic and Teag's Weaver gift.

"Then we got what we need to face down Renya," Mama replied. "But it sure would help if we had that priest with us."

"Father Conroy died a long time ago," Sorren said. "But I have a resource with those skills."

"You bring him with you," Mama said in a tone that was used to being obeyed. "Caliel and I will make preparations. My spirit can travel with him for a while. We'll handle Renya's magic. Your people can help," she said with a nod of Caliel's head. "You attack, and let the priest use that knife."

"Tomorrow night," Sorren said. "We'll meet you behind the old plantation house at sundown, near the well. We'll fight Renya where we fought him before."

"We'll be there," Mama said, chuckling. "And we'll call the spirits to finish this thing." Caliel's lips spread in an unpleasant smile. "This time, we make sure he's dead all the way."

THE NEXT NIGHT, Teag and I were waiting at my house for Sorren to arrive. If we wanted to get to the Wellright place and trek back to the old well before dark, we needed to leave soon.

The bell rang, but it was the door to the sidewalk piazza entrance, not the front door. That meant someone who wasn't authorized to get through Lucinda's wardings. I looked out the window, expecting to see Sorren, so I was surprised when a woman with short auburn hair in a pompadour, dressed all in black. She toggled the intercom.

"Cassidy?" She said. "Sorren told me to meet him here. I'm Father Anne."

It took me a moment before I noticed the clerical collar. "Come in,"

I said, failing miserably to mask my surprise. "I'm sorry," I said. "We were expecting a priest." I opened the wardings for her, and welcomed her into the house.

She laughed. In the light, I guessed her age to be mid-thirties. Her simple hairstyle was stylish and classy, with a bit of an edge, especially for Charleston. Understated makeup gave her a sense of quiet authority, but a colorful tattoo on her left upper arm, just below her short sleeve, suggested independence. The black Doc Martens under her dark jeans gave me the feeling she was ready for tonight's action.

"And a priest is what you got," she replied. "I'm the Reverend Anne Burgett, assistant rector of St. Hildegard's Episcopal Church. But most folks call me Father Anne."

Of course. The Episcopal Church, Anglicanism's American offspring, allowed not only married priests but female ones as well. Teag snickered, and introduced himself, shaking Father Anne's hand.

"St. Hildegard's has been in Charleston for a very long time," he said with a glance in my direction. "It founded St. Roch's as a burial church."

"I'm Father Conroy's many-times great-granddaughter," Anne said. "And I also inherited his role in the Expeditus Society." I took a second glance at her. There was mischief and purpose in her blue eyes. Her tattoo was custom-inked and beautiful, but mysterious. I saw a Roman soldier with his foot on a black crow, a man in a bishop's miter reaching up into a thundercloud, and a fish with a pearl in its mouth.

"Obscure saints—Expeditus, Deodatus, and Petroclus—all of which are good against evil, demons, black magic," she said in response to my unanswered question. She wore a plain iron cross on a chain around her neck. Her small pierced earrings were agate, like my necklace, good for protection against things that went bump in the night, and on her right hand, she wore an onyx ring. Father Anne met my gaze, and we had an understanding.

Teag handed Father Anne the wooden box with the knife and carefully folded stole. "Sorren said you'd know what to do with this," he said.

Father Anne opened the box and looked at the knife with a startle of recognition. "You found the knife," she said quietly. She let her fingertips brush the faded purple stole. "He managed to keep it safe all these years."

She took the knife from the box and then offered the stole to Teag. "Please, take the stole with you. Sorren's told me about your gift. Consecrated items have a power all their own."

Father Anne slipped the knife into a sheath on her belt. I noticed it wasn't her only knife. At least two other blades hung from her belt, one that gleamed like real silver, and another of iron. I also noticed she had a small messenger bag.

"It's good to be prepared," she said with a smile. "Bell, book, candle, and all that. A little holy water, some other things most spooks don't like." Her tone was light, but her eyes were serious.

Sorren wouldn't join us until after sundown because he couldn't, but the rest of us had work to do, preparing for the night's confrontation. Caliel had his own transportation, and when we arrived at the old Wellright mansion, I saw a black motorcycle parked off to one side. Teag, Father Anne, and I tromped through the brush, following the path Teag and I had beaten down on our previous visit.

We found Caliel already in the clearing with the half-circle of trees and the old well. He had paced a large circle in the high weeds, and also stomped down a big "X" a short distance away. Inside the circle, it looked as if he had burned away the tall grass to leave a charred, clear area in which to work. I saw a gourd rattle covered with a loose web of beads and bones with a small bell. Next to it was a cylindrical wooden drum marked with *veves* and covered with a skin drumhead.

Caliel wore a white t-shirt and denim pants, and a white bandana was tied on his head. I saw several amulets hanging from leather straps around his neck. Some I recognized as *veves*. One was a St. Peter's medal—for Papa Legba—and another was a medal with the same Roman soldier with his foot on a crow that I had seen on Father Anne's tattoo. I was certain that all conveyed a level of protection on their wearer.

"St. Expeditus is the stand-in for Baron Samedi," Caliel said, noticing my interest. He looked up and grinned, welcoming the others.

"I thought I'd make ready," Caliel said in greeting, sweeping an arm to indicate the area. Since he could not chalk the *veves* to call the Loa on the uneven ground, Caliel had brought two small smooth boards, on which he had marked the symbols of Papa Legba and Baron Samedi. These he placed near the large X on the ground. Near the X Caliel had left offerings to the Loas of rum and yams, pipe tobacco and cigars along with a freshly killed chicken and candles of yellow and red.

"I have some things to do as well," Father Anne said, taking in Caliel's preparations. He walked widdershins around the circle and lay down a thick line of salt for protection, leaving a quarter of the circle's outline open, to be closed later. That would let us hold something in, or keep something out. Father Anne moved clockwise around the area, stopping at each of the compass points and bowing her head in prayer to the Almighty and the archangels for assistance.

The sun was sinking toward the horizon. I was worried that Renya's spirit would not appear and equally scared that he would show up with a vengeance.

"The developer ordered a total work stoppage after the crew was killed," Teag said. "There haven't been other reports of unusual deaths —public or covered up. So he's hungry." Neither of us had called Renya by name. Names have power, and we weren't ready to confront an angry, hungry vampire ghost just yet.

Teag and I had carried in four camping lanterns, and we set them in the circle and lit them. Supernatural energy could drain batteries, and none of us wanted to be out here in the dark. Just in case, we each had flashlights, but I had seen what Renya could do to those down in the crypt.

I wore my agate necklace, and I had Theodora's disk in my pocket, as well as my own supply of salt. Teag had Father Conroy's stole, and a vest he had made for himself out of bits of cloth that had a strong positive resonance. He had salt, a bag of rice, and a quartz crystal, all things that were supposed to ward off malevolent spirits. Unwilling to be caught in the darkness, we had each gotten the largest, thickest glow sticks we could find and tied a couple with string to the belt loops on our jeans. It seemed like a paltry defense against a vampire ghost.

The sun set. Now it was a race to see which vampire showed up first: Sorren or Renya.

"Thank you for coming." Sorren stepped out of the shadows just a few moments after the sky darkened, giving me to guess that he had found a day crypt nearby, perhaps in the ruined cellars under the old mansion.

Sorren wore a dark t-shirt and jeans. He had nothing to fear from the mosquitoes that buzzed around the rest of us. Sorren scanned the clearing, taking in our preparations and the ominous darkness of the tree line.

"He's out there. Watching."

"Oh yes," Caliel agreed. For the moment, his voice was his own. But as he had moved through his rituals of preparation, it was almost as if I could see his energy and that of Mama Nadege's ghost swapping back and forth. "I can sense him, smell his energy," Caliel replied. "He's waiting. And he's hungry."

For the moment, Teag and I stood inside the half-formed salt circle. I wasn't entirely sure what we could do to help, since the others all had prior training for this kind of thing, while Teag and I were feeling out the limits of our psychic gifts as we went along. But I was ready to do whatever I could, and thinking about Theodora and Father Conroy, and all the victims that Renya and Betienne had claimed made me angry.

My hand closed over Theodora's ivory disk, and I opened my gift. I could sense Theodora's presence. When I opened my eyes, I was certain that I saw misty shapes in the distance, near where the construction had disturbed the graves. *Maybe the spirits want to watch Renya get what's coming to him,* I thought.

The air grew suddenly colder. I felt the temperature change, and a sense of hopelessness washed over me like a riptide, dragging me under. *Failure. Utter failure. Wasting our time.*

Tears rose in my throat, and I wanted to fall to my knees and weep. Movement seemed too difficult; even breathing seemed like a strain. I was cold and growing colder, so suddenly tired and overcome. *Why fight? It's a lost cause.*

I looked around and saw my companions stopped in their tracks, their expressions bereft of hope, eyes heavy and bodies slumping. Only Sorren seemed unaffected. He rushed toward a spot not far from the edge of the glow cast by our lanterns. In that single spot, the darkness seemed absolute, as if no light dared enter. Sorren moved with immortal speed, and I caught a glimpse of a stout metal bar in his hand, which he wielded like a sword, slicing it through the darkness. An agonized shriek filled the air, and the dark space broke apart, scattering on the wind. Immediately, the haze that had gripped my thinking disappeared.

My left hand rose to stroke the agate disks at my throat, and the despair lifted. I saw Teag slump, then rally as he touched the crystal that he wore on a strap around his neck. Caliel clutched a small cloth pouch, a *gris-gris*, and his eyes cleared, then filled with determination. Father Anne had a white-knuckled grip on her iron cross, and she looked at the darkness with defiance.

Fortified, we knew how to drive back that attack if it came again. Caliel took up his gourd and drum, chanting in an island patois, raising his voice to call down the power of his Loas. The darkness reformed, gliding at us like a faceless winged creature, blotting out the stars.

Father Anne muttered, "God help me," as she drew Father Conroy's knife and ran for the rippling darkness. She slashed at the blackness, but it buckled and snapped like a sheet on a laundry line, evading her strikes. Caliel paid them no attention, continuing his drumming, his gourd-rattle making a gravelly rhythm of its own.

Sorren pivoted and came at the void that was Renya's ghost, stabbing at it with his iron pole. I knew that spirits disliked iron, as did many supernatural creatures, but it was one weapon Sorren could wield with impunity since it had no effect on vampires. He moved faster than Father Anne, and several of his strikes pierced the center of the apparition. Another scream echoed from that churning darkness, and once again the blackness vanished.

Father Anne had fallen, but she struggled to her feet looking wan and drained. She still clutched the knife in her right hand and the iron cross in her left. Sorren stood protectively next to her and scanned the horizon watchfully.

"He'll be back," Sorren said.

The knife was our ace in the hole. The plan was that the rest of us would weaken and distract Renya's ghost to give Father Anne a chance to strike with the knife and destroy what remained of his corrupted soul.

"I slashed everywhere in that darkness," Father Anne said. "And it didn't seem to make any difference at all."

"You wounded him," Sorren replied. "His energy level dropped. Consider it a glancing blow."

I gripped Theodora's disk and felt her presence. When I opened my eyes, I saw that the rippling line of spirits had drawn closer, waiting for us to gain their long-overdue vengeance. *If there's any way you can help, we could use it,* I begged silently.

"The Loas have heard us," Caliel said quietly. "I can sense them, out there. They're watching to see what happens." I caught a whiff of pipe smoke and the scent of black coffee.

"Can you keep the connection?" Sorren asked.

"Oh yeah," Caliel said, and I heard Mama Nadege's voice in his laugh. "The Loas, they like a good show. Baron's prob'ly taking bets. We show ourselves worthy, they'll do their part."

Caliel walked toward the burned circle. "I set up a few things in case we needed a Plan B," he said. "Let's get Renya to dance in the circle," he said.

The ring of salt could either trap or protect, depending who was on the inside and who was sealing the circle. "I'll draw him in," I said, stepping forward.

Father Anne looked worse for the wear, but she wore a grim smile. "And I'll get him," she promised, the old knife gripped in her hand. She moved behind me, into the nearly-complete circle of salt. Teag looked nervous, standing just outside of the circle, looking for a way to make the most of his gift.

"He's tried twice to get me," I said when Sorren looked like he might object. "Well, here I am!" I shouted to the darkness with far more confidence than I felt.

Part of the night sky grew blacker than the rest. A rush of cold air dropped the temperature far below the summer swelter. I stood just inside where the salt circle would have been completed. The dark shape came at me fast, and just as quickly Sorren was behind it, ready with his iron bar to drive it into the circle.

Caliel's chanting and the rhythm of the gourd rattle grew faster. The darkness settled just at the entrance to the circle, and I could make out Renya's ghostly shape in the mist. Sorren swung with the iron bar, forcing the spirit into the confines of the nearly-full circle of salt, and I saw the shape waver.

Caliel shouted in a voice of triumph, and a glittering, reflective curtain formed around the dark shape out of nowhere. It was insubstantial and yet blindingly intense as if thousands of mirrored beads had been hung with the sun at their center.

"Mirrors trap evil spirits," Caliel shouted. "Turns them all around, so they lose their way. Get ready. When the lights go out, you strike fast!"

Abruptly, the glittering curtain of power winked out. Father Anne threw herself toward Renya's silhouette as Sorren barred the open space of the circle with his body and the iron bar.

Father Anne brought the old priest's knife down with a powerful overhand blow, a strike that would have dug the blade deep into the chest of a mortal opponent with deadly results. The silhouette writhed and shrieked, tearing away and leaving part of itself behind, as if the knife had shredded an old garment.

Renya's ghost wheeled, and before Sorren could interpose himself, the ghost hit Father Anne full on, passing through her. For an instant, her body hung suspended off the ground, blood starting from her nose and the corners of her mouth, and the knife dropped from her fingers. Sorren ran at the darkness, beating at it with the iron bar wherever he could strike the ghost and not hit Father Anne.

Caliel stopped his drumming. Still chanting, he tore a pouch from his belt, opened it wide and raised it to it mouth. He blew a cloud of dust into the air, right into the space where Renya's silhouette was tearing itself free from Father Anne's body. Again and again, Caliel blew lungfuls of air across the powder in the pouch, sending it to cover Renya's outline.

The ghost vampire screamed in rage, throwing Father Anne clear. She fell just inside the boundary of the salt circle and lay still for a moment catching her breath. Whatever Caliel had done with the dust, Renya had grown nearly solid, no longer a translucent wraith.

I saw a flash of purple as something whipped out to encircle Renya's form. Teag held Father Conroy's stole, the one that had been wrapped around the knife. The sacred energies of consecrated cloth met the power of Teag's Weaver gift, magic that channeled through every thread, into the warp and woof, until the old vestment glowed with intention.

"Cassidy, quickly! Grab the knife. It's blessed and has divine power… you must finish for me." Father Anne rolled out of the way as Renya lunged at her again, fighting against the stole.

I dove for the fallen knife and sprinted toward Renya's newly-solid form. My fingers closed around the knife hilt as I barreled toward where Teag had trapped the revenant. Renya was screaming curses, trying to charge Teag as he had attacked Father Anne, but Teag kept moving, using the stole to keep Renya from coming at him full on. Renya got close enough to land blow after blow with his outstretched hands, raking Teag with his spectral claws, each strike draining Teag's energy.

Sorren worked with Teag, helping to keep Renya at bay and distracting him from what I was doing and moving him away from Father Anne.

It was a race to see who would weaken first. Renya was grounded by salt and Caliel's Hoodoo dust, and by the power of Father Conroy's consecrated stole. But he had been both a powerful vampire and a strong Voudon *houngan*. Even weakened, Renya was a formidable foe.

Memories flooded through me as I ran toward Renya's shade, knife raised. In a blur of images, I saw glimpses from Father Conroy's life: his ordination, his work with the Expeditus Society fighting evil in a direct and hands-on battle, his joy in administering the sacraments, and his final, fatal battle with Renya. Power swelled with those memories, flooding through me. Father Conroy's memories resonated through the knife, lending the moral force of consecrated purpose.

Even with Sorren's help, Teag was pale and bleeding as I threw myself at Renya's form. No longer insubstantial, Renya's nails clawed at Teag's skin, and he snapped at Teag with his fangs. That same substance let my knife find purchase as I struck with all my might and all the borrowed power of Father Conroy's psychic shadow. The blade bit into a solid body, instead of passing through thin, dark air. Renya shrieked again, abandoning his attack on Teag to wheel, trying to grab me with his hands or rip into my flesh with his teeth.

My left hand clutched Theodora's disk. And as I screamed, trying to keep hold of the knife and prevent Renya from jerking it out of his chest, Theodora's presence overwhelmed me. Surrounded by powerful magic, I could see the spirits of the dead surging toward us, flooding into the circle through its opening, hungry for vengeance on the vampire that had sent them to their long-forgotten graves.

Renya thrashed, trying to beat off the wave of angry ghosts, bucking to throw me clear and dislodge the knife, straining to free himself from the tangle of Father Conroy's stole. I gritted my teeth, and twisted the blade, aiming for the heart. Teag still had a grip on the stole. He staggered, but his martial arts training came through. Teag jerked back on the stole, and brought one foot up into a high kick, driving Renya back toward me, forcing the knife deeper into his body, through the heart.

At the same instant, Sorren swung the iron pipe with his full immortal strength, connecting with Renya's skull with a sickening crunch, and ripping the head from the neck.

Renya's spirit gave one final, enraged curse, then the magic that had grounded his spirit and forced it into nearly solid form began to unravel.

"Get back, all of you!" Caliel shouted, then began to chant and drum at a frenzied pace, shaking his gourd rattle as he traced a stagger-step dance from the salt circle toward the X trodden into the weeds.

A wisp of mist, all that remained of Renya's corrupted spirit, was compelled to follow, bound by Caliel's ancient magic.

"Look!" I gasped. Two insubstantial but very clear figures stood one on either side of the X. Not an "X" I realized, but a crossroads, the place mortal spirits met the immortals. The figures were not solid, but they glowed from light within, not of this world. One was an old man leaning on a cane, puffing a pipe. A bony-ribbed dog stood by his side. I recognized him as Papa Legba, one of the most powerful Voudon Loas. The other was a tall man in a dark, formal suit with a high hat and dark glasses. He held a cigar in one hand, and his face was white like a skull. He could be no one else but Baron Samedi, a Voudon *ghede*, master of the dead.

Caliel drummed and chanted, and the *skritch-skritch* of his gourd rattle sounded to me like the scratch of a shovel against cemetery ground. The closer Caliel got to the two men at the crossroads, the more I could see that Renya's withered spirit now knew what it was to be compelled by someone else's will, trapped by powers greater than his own.

Caliel stepped aside as he reached the crossroads, and the Baron reached out a long, bony arm. His skeletal fingers grasped Renya's puff of mist and dragged it to him, into the crossroads, the place between the realms of the living and the dead.

The Baron looked straight toward me as if he knew that I could see him, and he pointed to me, Teag, and the fallen form of Father Anne, then gravely shook his head left to right, three times. Abruptly, the figures vanished.

I sagged to my knees. I could taste blood in my mouth, and I ached in every joint and muscle. Teag collapsed beside me. His face and chest were covered with bloody scratches, and he was far too pale. I tried to crawl toward where Father Anne lay, but Sorren was already there, rolling her onto her back and checking for signs of life.

"She's alive," he said. "Weak, injured—but alive."

Caliel's chanting had slowed. I knew that he was closing down the portal he had opened, dispelling the power he had gathered, and thanking the Loas who had come to his aid. I glanced up at the night sky, never feeling so glad to see an unobstructed view of the bright, distant stars, and said a silent "thank you" to the Powers that Be. Something much greater than my abilities or Teag's magic had imbued both the knife and the stole. And then I looked deep into the darkness, toward where the graves lay, and whispered my thanks to Theodora and her nameless companions, for their warning and their protection.

Finally, Caliel finished his ritual and trekked back toward the circle. His skin was wet with sweat, and his face was gaunt as if he had gone days without eating. He managed a broad grin, a flash of gleaming teeth.

"That was some show, huh?" Somehow, I knew that the triumphant speaker was Mama Nadege, not Caliel.

Sorren stood and gave a shallow bow. "Thank you, Caliel and Mama Nadege."

"You sure know how to have a fine evening," Mama Nadege replied, altering Caliel's voice just enough that I knew she was the one talking. "I'm glad we got that bloodsucker. He did enough harm back when. The Baron'll see that Renya gets what he deserves, true enough."

"Time for you to return to your rest as well," Sorren said, and his half-smile was sad.

"I know I've worn out my welcome," Mama Nadege answered. "I can feel it. I'm proud as I can be of this one," she said, and I knew she meant Caliel, her grandchild many times over. "He fought well."

"Until the next time," Sorren said.

"Oh, I'm sure there'll be a next time," Mama Nadege chortled, but her voice was already growing faint. Caliel closed his eyes, and his whole body gave one long shudder from head to toe. When he opened his eyes, I knew he was himself again.

"Everyone alive? Then it's been a good, good night," he said heartily, though I could hear the exhaustion in his voice.

Sorren lifted Father Anne in his arms as Teag got to his feet and gave me a hand up. I looked past Caliel to the dark clearing, where the crossroads had been.

"Before they left, the Baron pointed to us and shook his head. What did that mean?"

Caliel laughed. "He was telling you, no one dies tonight. The Baron, he's the one who lets the souls into the next world. If he refuses to dig your grave, you won't die."

"That's good to know," I said, utterly exhausted. "But now, it's definitely time to go home."

PART II
FATAL INVITATION

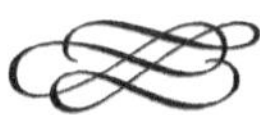

FATAL INVITATION

I reached into the shipping crate. My hand closed around a newspaper-wrapped piece from a china dish set, probably a gravy boat from its contours. The warning tingle from my psychic gift was too little, too late. By the time I realized the danger, I was already immersed in a vision of tragedy and terror.

Images strobed in my mind, searingly clear for an instant and then suddenly dark. A dining room table set with holiday finery for a Thanksgiving feast. Eight people—no, nine—but the one person's face was hidden. Dinner began with high spirits. The person whose memories I was experiencing was a man, the father of the family gathered for the feast, happy that he was surrounded by loved ones—and a guest.

Despite the high spirits, a warning tingled at the edge of my host's senses. It had been a mistake to invite the stranger, *he was thinking.* They say the road to Hell is paved with good intentions.

The stranger didn't say much as the meal began. Everyone else laughed and talked as silverware rattled and food was passed around the table. His son, the youngest at the table, was the first one affected. He complained about his stomach, folded his arms across his midsection, and fell forward onto his plate. I saw the man's hand set the gravy boat down on the table as he stood.

Everyone rose in alarm—everyone except the stranger. I couldn't get a clear look at the guest's face. The others were in sharp focus, but the one I knew was the stranger had blurred features, and the baggy clothing made it impossible to tell gender. The stranger stepped back as everyone rushed to the boy, who fell back, eyes staring blankly, unresponsive, into his mother's arms as she screamed.

The others began to stagger, hands going to their heads or abdomens, faces frightened and worried. The boy's mother collapsed across his body. Others crumpled to the floor or sagged from their chairs.

The person whose memories I shared tried to go to them, but his legs failed him. His heart raced but it was hard to breathe, and his mouth had gone dry. Vision blurred, and despite his panic, he was so utterly tired. Still, he dragged himself toward his family, but halfway across the room, his body no longer responded to his mind's commands. He reached out to the stranger, one hand raised in a plea for help. The stranger only smiled.

He couldn't move, but consciousness remained. He could see and hear the chairs being moved and his family's bodies being dragged across the carpet. Glassware clinked as the stranger reset the table. A few moments later, strong hands lifted him and hauled him back to his chair, dumping him into his seat and arranging his arms and legs just so. The terror in his gut was building, and he wanted to scream, to fight, to stop this madness, but all he could do was watch helplessly as he and those he loved were arranged at the table in a macabre tableau.

He heard footsteps behind him, someone else had come into the room.

"Everything's ready," the stranger said.

I came out of the vision gasping for air as if I were drowning. Teag was already beside me. He's seen me do this enough that he knows how to protect me while I'm having a vision, and Teag's good at helping me come back to myself. He gently took the wrapped piece of dishware out of my hands and put it back in the box.

"That's one hell of a gravy boat," I managed, as he guided me to a chair. A moment later, he had poured me a strong, cold glass of sweet tea and pressed it into my hands. It said something about our normal workday that we had this part of the job down to a routine.

I'm Cassidy Kincaide, and I own Trifles and Folly, an antique and curio shop in historic, haunted Charleston, South Carolina. The shop has been in my family since the city was founded over three hundred years ago. In all that time, we've managed to keep a very important secret. We're not just a great place to buy unique knick-knacks or sell off grandma's silver. Our real job is saving the world from really bad things that go bump in the night.

My magic is psychometry—I can read the magic or imprinted strong emotions of an object by touching it. It's a dangerous gift to have in a business like ours, filled with heirlooms that were witness to history that was good, bad, and downright ugly. Touch magic runs in my family. The person who possesses the gift most strongly ends up inheriting Trifles and Folly, and the secrets that come with it.

Teag Logan is my assistant store manager. Teag's got Weaver magic, which means he can weave spells into cloth and find hidden threads of online data to expose secrets and hack just about any computer system. But our biggest secret is Sorren, my silent partner in the business. Sorren's a vampire, part of a covert Alliance that exists to get dangerous magical objects off the market and out of the wrong hands, and he founded Trifles and Folly back in the 1600s. When we do our jobs right, no one notices. When we make a mistake, the damage usually gets blamed on a natural disaster.

"How bad was it?" Teag asked, watching me carefully as I sipped my tea and tried to stop shaking. Teag settled his tall, thin frame into a chair and brushed a lock of dark hair out of his eyes.

"Bad," I replied, wishing I could un-see the vision. But I couldn't forget it, and I felt a bond to the doomed man whose memories I had shared, memories so strong they had imprinted themselves onto that piece of china. Though I hadn't seen what happened to him and his family, I was certain it hadn't ended well. And I was equally sure that the stranger who had joined them had gotten away with murder.

Teag listened silently as I recounted what I'd seen. "Yikes," he said when I was finished. "So you think whoever owned this dish set was poisoned by someone they invited for Thanksgiving dinner?"

I nodded. "I'm certain of it. There was someone else involved too, but I never saw either person's face." I frowned. "That was very strange. I could see everyone else clearly, but not the stranger."

Teag met my gaze. "Magic?"

"That's my thought," I replied. "But why would someone with magic want to poison a family? Why use poison if you've got magic? And what's up with setting people back in their seats like dummies in a wax museum?"

"Nothing says people with magic can't be psychopaths," Teag observed, rising to pour himself a glass of tea. "But that kind of detail should have made the news, and I swear I would have remembered a story like that."

"Me, too." I finished my tea and set the glass on the table. "Unless the police withheld the information, which wouldn't be uncommon for a mass murder." I shivered, thinking of how cold-blooded the killer had to be to strike down a family on a day that had begun with great joy.

"If it's in a database, I'll find it," Teag said, flashing me a confident smile. "And I'll start by contacting the auction house to see where the dish set and silverware came from. That might help me narrow down the search. Right now, we don't even know whether the murders happened in Charleston or not."

I toyed with the condensation on my tea glass. "You bought the dishes at auction?"

Teag nodded. "Yeah. Remember the unclaimed and abandoned odd lots auction I went to last month? Most of the stuff was junk, but there were a few pieces that caught my eye, and the china set was one of them."

He pulled one of the dishes out of the box and unwrapped it. Teag's magic works differently than mine, so he can touch things like that all he wants, and it won't knock him flat on his ass. On the other hand, he would be just as vulnerable if he happened on a spelled piece of clothing or fabric with malicious magic woven into it. I'm learning that magic can do some amazing things, but it has a price.

"I still think it's beautiful," he said, staring at the gravy boat.

I shuddered. "The vision's spoiled my appreciation. Maybe that's what Charles Dickens meant about a ghost having 'more grave than gravy' about it," I added with a weak smile. I bent forward to have a closer look without touching the china.

It was a very pretty pattern, one of the china company's classics that had been in demand for decades. I wondered if it had been passed down from one generation to another, or purchased new. Someone had high hopes for a lifetime of happy holidays, and I was angry that whoever this stranger was, he or she had destroyed those hopes.

"If it *is* magic, it felt different from the kinds of power we usually run into," I said, leaning back in my chair and staring at the dish. Teag and I have worked with Voudon mambos and Hoodoo root women, kick-ass Episcopalian priests and Native American shamans, along with clairvoyants, spirit mediums, and necromancers. Every type of magic I'd seen so far had its own signature, sort of like a supernatural frequency. The faceless stranger's power didn't match any of the "frequencies" I had encountered.

"Let's ask Sorren what he makes of it," Teag said. "He's been kicking around for almost six hundred years. Maybe it will ring a bell with him. And in the meantime, I'll get digging."

We closed up the shop for the night, and I headed home. Teag promised to call me if he found anything out from his research, and I had a call, email, and text message in to Sorren, asking him to get back to me right away.

Yes, my vampire boss uses modern technology. He says that immortals who can't adapt don't continue to survive, and he plans to be around for a while. But the nature of his work with the Alliance means that Sorren travels a lot, often out of the country, and sometimes he's in situations where he can't get a signal or doesn't dare respond. There was no telling when we'd hear from him, but Teag and I were getting better at making progress on our own, and I figured we'd get Sorren's opinion whenever he surfaced.

My mood was off. The visions I get from handling tainted objects are as real to me as if I were experiencing the situation myself. Since problem objects never have good magic or happy emotions imprinted on them, that means I had my work cut out for me to bounce back after something like I saw today.

Fortunately, there's Baxter. His high-pitched yips greeted me before I'd even managed to open the door. I live in a Charleston single-house, where the side of the home faces the street, and my "front" door actually opens onto the side of my covered porch, what Charlestonians call a "piazza," Which meant I could hear Baxter yipping it up while I was still out on the sidewalk. No person can ever match a dog for being glad to see you.

I opened the door to the house, and Baxter bounced around my feet. He's a Maltese, six pounds of boundless attitude. Heart of a warrior, body of a guinea pig. I scooped Bax up in my arms and let him lick my nose and chin as he squirmed to climb higher. Just holding him eased the tension I felt, and I gave him a big hug, then went to fill his bowl with kibble.

"I think we've got trouble coming," I said to Baxter as I looked in the fridge for something to eat. Leftovers from last night's Chinese take-out caught my eye, and soon they were in the microwave as I poured a glass of water and a glass of wine.

Baxter didn't look up. As long as he's got food in his dish and some popcorn when we snuggle on the couch, he's good. I was still restless, envying him his doggie perspective. My mind cycled back through the images, and I doubted I'd get a good night's sleep tonight, even after the wine.

I could see the faces of the family clearly in my memory—all but the father, through whose eyes I had seen the tragedy. I was certain I would recognize them if I saw them again.

Setting my warmed-up stir-fry to one side, I opened up my laptop as Baxter settled himself at my feet. I don't have Teag's magic, but my Google-fu is strong. The problem was, without more to go on, I had no idea where the deaths occurred. They might have been in Charleston—or in Seattle, for all I knew.

I took a deep breath and closed my eyes, forcing myself to see the setting of the murder as well as the people, looking for any clue to their location. I started searching on "Thanksgiving deaths." That got me a depressingly long list of car accidents and house fires, as well as other unfortunates who met their maker through a variety of causes. I never realized Thanksgiving was so dangerous.

I changed my search to "Thanksgiving murders." The search returned a shorter list this time, though longer than I had expected. I steeled myself and examined my memory, looking for clues in the vision. From how people were dressed, I was willing to bet the scene took place in the last few years. I whittled the list down to the past decade. Very few involved more than one victim. None of the reports I found matched the number of people in my vision.

"I'm striking out, Bax," I muttered. On impulse, I Googled "mysterious holiday deaths." I got a list of items that ranged from missing planes and boats to vanishing tourists, including a YouTube video of *Grandma Got Run Over by a Reindeer*. Nothing useful.

Just then, my phone buzzed. "Are you on your computer?" Teag asked. "I found something I'd like you to take a look at." He gave me a web address, and I typed it in. "You might have to scroll down a bit, but I think some of these stories sound like what you described. I'll call you back in a bit. I've hit on some good information, and I want to get as much as I can."

I looked at the web page Teag had sent me to explore. "Urban Legends: The Deadly Stranger." Intrigued, I clicked through and caught my breath.

"Bingo!" I said. Baxter looked up and cocked his head curiously, then laid back down when he realized no food was involved.

The link took me to a compilation of urban legends, stories everyone has heard, but no one can prove, like the tales of alligators roaming the New York City sewers and the guy with the hook for a hand who preys on horny teenagers parked at Lovers' Lane. I'd always dismissed the legends as being fodder for ghost stories told around the campfire by kids trying to scare each other. Then I remembered how in the movie *Men in Black*, the tall tales in grocery store tabloids were really true, just embellished a little for the press. I poured myself a cup of coffee and read further.

By the time I had worked through about a dozen stories, my heart was racing. Many of the tales sounded like the kinds of dangers Teag and Sorren and I fought as part of the Alliance. I knew that monsters were real. A lot of the urban legends sounded like what I imagined a second-hand account might sound like if someone told about one of our encounters with bad nasty supernatural creatures. I could personally provide an explanation for several of the legends, just from the cursed objects and dark magic we had fought.

What if there's a kernel of truth in all of these stories? I wondered. The thought made me shiver. Most people take comfort in believing that there are no monsters and that the strange noises and shadows in the middle of the night are just their imagination. Teag and I know better. In fact, some of the threats we had fought went way beyond the "imagination" of these urban legends, too fantastic for someone to believe even recast as a tall tale.

"The Deadly Stranger is an urban legend that has been around since the mid-1900s," the website article said. *"The murders are always on a holiday, although the holiday itself may vary. Embellishments abound, but at its core, it is a warning about being too quick to bring a stranger into one's inner circle. Stripped down, the Deadly Stranger legend has several basic elements: a stranger is befriended and invited to come for holiday dinner. Everything goes well to a point, when the host family collapses, likely from being drugged or poisoned. The stranger kills the family and sets their bodies up in a ghastly tableau as if they were seated around the table, enjoying a holiday feast. Whether the legend has a basis in a few unfortunate incidents or whether it has inspired copycats is debated. Law enforcement sources refuse to comment, unwilling to confirm or outright deny the legend's reality."*

"Wow," I said aloud. Baxter pawed my leg for attention, and I picked him up, giving him a hug that was more to reassure myself than for his benefit. This time, I searched on "unsolved murders of families." The results were depressing and more numerous than I expected. My food went cold as I worked my way through the articles, eliminating anything that didn't occur on a holiday. After a couple of hours, I had a list of twenty-five accounts that went back almost fifty years. There were Thanksgiving deaths, but also ones on Christmas, Easter, and Mother's Day. Some were suspicious fires, while others just noted "unusual circumstances" and "remains open for further investigation."

I jumped when my phone rang and nearly dumped Baxter off my lap. It was Teag. "You scared me half to death!" I greeted him.

"Did you get a chance to check out that site? I think I've found some more information about our dinner murderer," Teag said. "Would you mind if I came over?"

Having company sounded great since I was jittery from the stories I'd been reading online. "Come on over," I offered. "I've found some things I want to show you."

"Any word from Sorren?"

"Not yet," I said. "But maybe he can connect the dots if we have enough information together for him."

Twenty minutes later, Teag rang the doorbell at the door from the sidewalk to let me know he was on his way, then knocked at the main door. We've had enough scares and intruders that we developed routines, so there are no unexpected surprises. Baxter went ballistic, as usual, bouncing and barking. A Voudon mambo friend of ours put powerful protective wardings around my house a while back, which have saved my bacon on more than one occasion. She's warded Teag's house and the store, too. Teag and Sorren are two of just a handful of people who can enter the wardings around my house without consequences. At least that's the theory. We try not to take chances. I consider Baxter to be the backup alarm. He could wake the dead—and make their ears bleed.

"Down, Killer," Teag chided Baxter affectionately, then picked him up for the requisite snuggle that was the price of admission. Then he came into the kitchen and pulled his laptop from his messenger bag. "You're never going to believe what I've found," he said.

"I might," I replied, pouring some sweet tea for both of us. "I've got some interesting—and disturbing—things that I bet are related."

Teag got settled in at the table, and I sat down next to him so I could see his screen, pulling my own computer around to make it easier to show him what I had discovered.

"You first," he said, listening intently as I told him my suspicion that the urban legends might be more of a watch list than a compilation of tall tales.

"I'll keep my eye on those sites from now on," Teag promised. "Good catch. And you saw what I meant about the Deadly Stranger 'legend?'"

"Yeah, I think you're onto something," I replied. "What else did you find?"

He pulled up a scattergram on his screen. "I found one hundred unusual holiday deaths involving multiple people that weren't car accidents," he replied. "I bet they include most of the ones you logged. The others weren't from publicly accessible sites." That meant he'd been hacking into law enforcement databases, maybe even the Feds. His Weaver gift made him a scary-good hacker.

"I plotted them by official 'cause,'" he said. "Fires are popular. So are gas leaks, ptomaine poisoning, botulism, even one or two for 'unknown wild animal attack.' But the largest group are 'undetermined.'" He brought up another chart.

"This chart shows the deaths grouped by holiday," he said, sounding like the Ph.D. student he had been before Trifles and Folly opened up a whole new calling for him. "And this one plots the deaths by year and city." He glanced at me. "What do you see?"

I leaned forward to study the charts. "The deaths happen more often at Thanksgiving and Christmas than any other holidays," I mused. "A few in a particular city for a year or two, then it looks like whoever's behind this moves on." I squinted, peering at the screen. "The locations are all big or medium-sized cities. From the dates, it looks like he—she—it—has been moving steadily south."

Teag clicked a key, and a new screen came up with the path of the murders tracked against a map of the Eastern United States. A red line zig-zagged from Portland, Maine down through the New England states, hitting Boston before moving on to New York, Philadelphia, and points south. A circled number told the tale of how many incidents in each location. Only a few in smaller cities like Portland, Rutledge, or New Haven, a dozen in New York, half that many in Boston and Philadelphia, more in Washington, DC, and Baltimore. Richmond, Fredericksburg, Raleigh, and Charlotte were on the map. But what drew my attention and made my heart pound was the red dot on Columbia, South Carolina.

"The killings in Columbia happened last year and the year before," Teag said quietly. "The murderer only stays two years in a city that size. If the killer holds to pattern, Charleston will be next—and the deaths will happen this year." Thanksgiving was less than a week away.

I sat back in my chair. I was frightened, but then I thought about the vision I'd had from the gravy boat, and I got angry. Some kind of monster was preying on innocent people, families that were kind enough to invite a stranger to share a holiday with them, and the reward for their kindness had been death. Whatever it was would strike again, here, unless Teag and Sorren and I stopped them.

"Charleston may not be as big as New York City," I said, "but it's big enough that we can't be everywhere at once. What are we going to do, go on television and tell people not to invite psycho strangers for dinner?" I hated to think about turning away innocent travelers, college students, and others who might be alone on the holiday. "Do we have any description of either the 'stranger' or the accomplice?"

Teag shook his head. "We don't have any information at all on the stranger except for your vision. The cold case files I hacked acknowledged the deaths were unlikely to be suicide." He met my gaze. "They weren't just poisoned, Cassidy. All the bodies were drained of blood."

The knock at my front door startled me, and I jumped, nearly spilling my tea. Ramifications of what Teag discovered were spinning in my mind as I got up to answer the door. Baxter went tearing toward the porch, then stopped when he reached the door and sat down with a goofy grin on his face. That confirmed who my guest had to be.

"Hi, Sorren." I opened the door, and Sorren walked in. Sorren looks like he's in his mid-twenties, but he's almost six hundred years old. His blond hair had a trendy, European cut. I could tell from the warm tone of his skin that he had already fed. Before he was turned, Sorren was the best jewel thief in Belgium. Now he puts those skills to use for the Alliance. "How did you manage to glamor my dog through the door?"

Sorren chuckled and bent down, scratching Baxter behind the ears. "Dogs can sense more things than humans. He could tell it was me by my approach, and I've glamored him enough times that it's become habit. Literally like Pavlov's dog." Since vampires don't make any noise, Baxter being able to sense Sorren's presence was a neat trick. I'd have to remember that, for times when we might meet less friendly vampires.

Teag greeted Sorren with a wave. Sorren joined us at the table and listened as we both caught him up on what we had discovered. He grew more concerned as we spoke. "Have you tried reading any of the other pieces of china or the silver?" he asked me.

I shook my head. "Not yet, although the idea occurred to me." I really didn't want a repeat of the vision I'd had, but the killer was on the loose and likely to strike again unless we did something fast.

Sorren seemed to guess my thoughts. "I can understand why you're reluctant," he said. "And maybe it would just put you through unnecessary anguish. But there's also the chance that one of the other objects might provide a clue."

I took a deep breath, then nodded. "I'll do it. At least this time, I'll have an idea of what I'm getting into."

"Do you think we're dealing with a rogue vampire?" Teag asked. "Or something else?"

Sorren leaned back in his chair. "Did any of your pilfered reports describe wounds on the bodies?"

Teag grimaced. "They all did, in graphic detail. Coroner's reports manage to be gory and boring at the same time. Bottom line—the methods of bloodletting aren't consistent. Sometimes the throats were slit, other times the wrists. A few of the reports make it sound as if the bodies had been chewed on, along with some partial dismemberment. Once or twice, the victims were stabbed."

"I thought serial killers repeated their patterns compulsively," I said. "That's often how the police catch the killer and link the murders together."

"That's one reason the cops haven't said much publicly about the deaths," Teag said. "The notes show they can't agree on whether it's one killer or several, maybe even some 'copycat' murders."

"I'm sure they're not considering supernatural possibilities." Sorren stood and began to pace. "Vampires aren't the only creatures that feed on blood. But few of the other beings could pass for human. No one would be likely to invite them for dinner."

"The stranger I saw in the vision definitely looked human," I said. "Except for the blurry face. But there was someone—or something—else who came later that I never saw.

Sorren nodded, frowning. "That's the part that might be the key to this. The mysterious stranger incapacitates the victims so the killer can feed. If that's correct, then the stranger isn't using a deadly poison. Maybe something that will drug the victims, make them unconscious or at least keep them from fighting back."

"The man whose viewpoint I shared in the vision certainly seemed drugged," I agreed. "He was still conscious and aware, but unable to move or speak." Just thinking about it made me angry again.

"I suspect that whoever—or whatever—does the actual killing prefers the victims conscious enough to register horror and pain," Sorren said with distaste. "Whatever type of supernatural creature this is, it's a monster."

"But who's working for whom?" Teag asked. "Is the stranger feeding his pet? Or setting up the situation for someone more powerful?"

"That's what makes me uncertain whether or not we're dealing with a vampire," Sorren confessed. "The various methods of death might just be a way to throw off the authorities. A vampire could heal the puncture wounds almost immediately, so there wouldn't have to be marks on the bodies at all, if he—or she—stopped shy of death."

A chill went down my spine. I trust Sorren completely, and he's sworn to me that he is oathbound not to harm my family—and by extension, that includes allies like Teag and even Baxter. But occasionally, Sorren knows something that reminds me just how dangerous he can be, and makes me wonder what he's done in all those long-ago centuries.

"Wouldn't a vampire just be able to glamor the family and feed, regardless?" Teag asked.

Sorren nodded. "Nearly always, yes. There are a few exceptions. Glamoring is a part of the Dark Gift, part of how we hunt. But some vampires are better at it than others." He gave a wistful smile. "After all, we began as mortals. Some individuals have tremendous charisma. They can move an audience to its feet and win over strangers with a smile. Their charisma is very close to a vampire's glamor, just a matter of degree." He shrugged. "And for famous con men who put their victims under their sway, I'm not sure there's much difference at all."

"Are there socially awkward vampires?" Teag asked. I chuckled, but he looked serious. "I mean, what if you had someone who was really bad at glamoring because he or she was terrible at social things as a mortal. Maybe a dorky vampire would team up with a smooth henchman who was good at gaining people's trust and they'd work together in exchange for—something."

"Was anything stolen from the homes where the murders occurred?" The thought had just occurred to me. I had been focused on the murders, but it was possible the real goal was theft.

Teag shrugged. "The police weren't certain, because the families were all dead. No one walked out with the television or the silverware if that's what you mean, nothing obvious."

"A careful thief who has the advantage of time can make a house appear untouched," Sorren said. "That's something I know for a fact. I used to be quite good at it." He smiled. "It's a skill that still comes in handy, now and again, on Alliance business." Breaking and entering was often a part of chasing down supernatural bad guys.

"There's another possibility, even more disturbing than theft," Sorren continued. "Some supernatural creatures feed on death and fear, as a vampire feeds on blood. It could be that the pair have complimentary goals, and can achieve them more effectively working together than they could separately."

"We've got a lot of questions, and no answers," I said. "Thanksgiving is coming up soon, and people are going to die unless we figure out how to stop these psychos. What do we do?"

"I think the one clue we have lies in the fact that you can't make out the stranger's face," Sorren said. "That suggests magic to me. And if we're going up against magic, we'll need a good witch."

THE NEXT EVENING, Teag and I waited nervously at Trifles and Folly. The store was closed, the lights in the front were dark, and we were in the break room, awaiting Sorren's arrival. Teag had unwrapped all of the china and silverware from the auction and set it out on the table. It was a lovely set in excellent condition, with tiny little pink flowers and silver accents, something that should have been passed on to make a new generation of users happy. Now, we'd probably have to destroy it, since objects with such strong negative emotional resonance don't make good gifts.

"I heard back from the auction house," Teag said as we paced. "They received the china and silver from a guy who picks things up cheap at sales of abandoned storage unit items and lost suitcases—and police property."

"You think they came from him?"

Teag couldn't help a satisfied little smile. "I'm sure of it. He remembers the items. Got it at a sale up in Columbia. The police take items into evidence and sometimes, there's no one to return them to. When that happens, they sell the stuff to buyers looking for a good deal."

"So the police took the dishes into evidence after the murders," I said, putting the pieces of the puzzle together. "And since the family was all dead, no one wanted them back."

Teag nodded. "Yep. The man at the auction didn't buy anything else that sounded like it was related. I asked, just in case."

Just then, the back door opened. Sorren entered with a woman I didn't recognize. "This is Rowan," Sorren said as they came into the break room. I knew a little about witches, enough that I was certain "Rowan" wasn't the name on her birth certificate. It was a "use-name," an alias to keep others with power from using her real name to gain power over her. Rowan was in her early thirties. Her blond hair was loose around her shoulders, and she wore a loose, light blue dress that fell to her ankles. The dress was embroidered with runes and symbols. I glanced at Teag, and he gave me an almost imperceptible nod, letting me know that he sensed magic in the fabric of her clothing.

Rowan was pretty in a girl-next-door way, and she didn't seem worried about what we thought of her. Rings of silver and onyx glinted on her fingers, and she wore bracelets of agate beads. A silver necklace with the three phases of the moon—a symbol of the goddess—lay against her throat.

"Rowan, I'd like you to meet my business partners, Cassidy and Teag," Sorren said. He turned to us. "It's all right to speak freely—Rowan knows about what we do here, and about the Alliance. We've worked together before."

I felt myself relax, just a little. Our work is dangerous, and knowing we can trust a new person helps a lot. "Nice to meet you," I said. "Would you like some sweet tea?" This is Charleston. We're polite to a fault. Death and destruction might be imminent, but manners were still important.

Rowan shook her head. "Not yet, thank you. Afterwards—definitely." I knew what she meant. Here in South Carolina, we put enough sugar in our tea to raise the dead and give them the jitters. I always found that an ice cold glass of sweet tea puts my nerves back together again, and usually keeps me from passing out after a bad working.

"Just in case, I brought bourbon," Teag said, and waved a small flask that he withdrew from his jacket pocket. "Cassidy might need something a bit stronger than tea, depending on what you have in mind."

I smiled my thanks at him, sure that my grin was a little twitchy. "What did you want to do with the china?" I asked nervously.

Rowan met my gaze. "Sorren says you're a psychometric."

I nodded. "Yep. That's me. But he didn't really say what your magic specialty is."

She chuckled. "I don't have a 'specialty' exactly. I'm more of a general purpose witch, with more practice than I'd like to admit in defensive magic. One thing I think I can do if we join our magic together is not only show everyone what you're seeing, but put ourselves into the scene—in a matter of speaking."

"How?" I pressed. Teag had "hitchhiked" on a vision or two by linking me to him with a piece of spelled cloth. *Would a witch make the connection differently?*

"You hold the objects in your hand, one at a time. I hold your other hand and Sorren's hand, and Teag connects through Sorren," she explained. "I should be able to protect you to a degree from the impact of the visions, while projecting the images into a three dimensional setting all around us." She managed a deprecating smile. "Of course, we won't be able to interact with the figures. It's just a memory. But we might pick up a clue if the objects give us different perspectives."

"All right," I said, taking a deep breath for courage. "Let's get this party started."

I sat at the center of the table. The dishes and silverware were all within my reach. Rowan took my left hand, and then Sorren and Teag moved into position. I reached for one of the other serving dishes, figuring that it was a piece everyone might have touched.

My hand grasped the deep bowl, one that probably served up steaming hot stuffing, or fluffy homemade mashed potatoes, perhaps even sweet potato casserole. I sensed echoes of those foods and others, just like I felt a faint remainder of happy times gone by. Then the vision came rushing to the fore, and all the other images were crowded out.

I was back in the dining room I had seen before. This time, I saw the scene through different eyes. I was certain the person whose memories I sensed was a woman, perhaps the wife of the man through whose perspective I had seen the other vision. As the memories began to unfold, I could pick up the woman's gratitude for the company of family, welcome for the new "friend" who had joined them, contentment for the bounty on the table.

She sat at one end of the formal dining room table, at the far end from the man I'd seen. Her youngest son sat to her right, a boy who looked to be around eight years old. A girl who might have been fourteen was next to him, then an older boy who looked like high school age. On the left were an older couple, probably the parents of the husband or wife. In the last seat on the left was the stranger.

I opened my eyes, and realized that the scene I had envisioned in my mind's eye had unfolded around us like a hologram, filling the break room. Ghostly, translucent figures sat at an equally insubstantial table filled with images of the china we had in the shop. Rowan nodded for me to continue, and I closed my eyes, since that's the way I'm used to "seeing" what my magic shows me.

I focused my magic on the stranger, but every time I almost glimpsed the newcomer's face, the features blurred. The doomed figures at the table were silent, but their images moved as if they were laughing and talking. Unfortunately, my gift doesn't always come with a sound track. It's happened, but it's not a given for my magic, and I couldn't hear any sound now, no matter how closely I listened.

From the body language, the other adults at the table tried to engage the stranger in conversation. She—I was certain once I glimpsed a hand reaching for a spoon that the outsider was female— nodded and murmured, saying as little as possible. The two youngest children ignored the stranger. The older son was keeping an eye on her while trying not to stare. Something about the newcomer bothered him. Even though I knew how the scene turned out, I found myself hoping he would do something, say something, to warn the others.

I felt an odd shift, a subtle tension I hadn't felt in the first vision. It almost felt as if the stranger was somehow deflecting attention from her, making it difficult to think about her. I noticed the effect it had on the others, redirecting them so that they almost seemed to forget the stranger was among them.

I forced my attention back to watch the stranger, reminding myself that I stood outside the scene as an onlooker, not a participant, and that the remembered magic shouldn't be able to affect me. Even so, I had to focus to keep her in my view. I noticed something else strange: the outsider was touching as few items as possible.

More than one heaping serving dish was passed her way, and she shook her head, indicating for the dish to pass by her. She removed a couple of slices of turkey from a tray with her fork and a dollop of mashed potatoes with a serving spoon, but I had the feeling she was either worried about fingerprints or leaving a magical trail—or both. She did not eat anything she put on her plate.

I gritted my teeth and let the remembered scene play out. The boy to my right doubled over, falling forward onto his plate. The woman through whose perspective I viewed the scene rose to help him, and staggered, feeling the effects herself. Everyone else was rising to their feet and then falling to the ground, all except for the stranger.

This time, the vision lasted longer. The woman was slumped across her son, but she had fallen in a way that she could still see. The stranger moved back and forth, dragging the victims back to their chairs and arranging them in their seats. I could glimpse enough of the table to see the bodies placed as if they were a display in a wax museum, or mannequins in a department store window. The stranger rolled the woman from atop her son's body and picked the boy up, sitting him upright. He was still alive, though his breathing was shallow.

Though the eyes of the woman lying on the floor, I saw a new set of feet enter. Small shoes, sneakers, sized for a woman or a child. The stranger came back to lift the woman whose perspective I shared, settling her roughly into her chair as if she were just a rag doll. I willed myself to focus on the stranger as her face was just inches from the doomed woman's, and for an instant, the illusion broke. I saw the stranger clearly—a woman of average build with shoulder-length dark hair and a plain face made remarkable by the intensity of the hatred that glinted in her eyes.

The illusion snapped back into place. Of course there was no reaction from the stranger. I was seeing the imprint of memories, not people acting in real time. But the anger and hatred I had glimpsed in her eyes made me shudder. I tried to get a better look at the newcomer, the one in the sneakers, but the vision from the woman whose perspective I shared was fading quickly. I saw the newcomer from the back, not enough to tell much except the second person was short and had short blond hair.

Abruptly, the vision went dark.

My hand was shaking as I set the bowl down. "Did you all see that?" I asked, hearing the unsteadiness in my voice.

The others nodded. "Are you okay, Cassidy?" Sorren asked, looking at me with concern.

"I wouldn't say I'm having fun," I replied. "But if this helps us stop the killer, I'll keep going until I drop." I looked at Teag. "Did the police find odd fingerprints at the scenes of the murders?"

"Very few," Teag replied. "That makes me think the 'stranger' knows to cover her tracks. But there were two prints that came up clearly—from the first Boston murders and then from the second Baltimore attack. They matched."

"Did the police make anything out of the match or I.D. the prints?" I asked.

Teag shook his head. "The police couldn't identify the prints—not that unusual. Prints aren't in the database unless a person's been arrested for something. I ran the prints through the supernatural terrorist watch list on the Darke Web, but I haven't gotten the results back yet." Teag's hacker abilities mean no database is safe from him, whether it's the firewalls of the FBI or the unindexed content of the Deep Web, the heavily-protected illegal sites on the Dark Web, or the ensorcelled encryption on the Darke Web, where the immortal and supernatural community conducts its online business.

"You don't need to," Rowan said. "I think I recognize your 'stranger.'" We all turned to look at her. "She's a witch who goes by the name Alia Corona. Very powerful, very dangerous—seriously twisted, and not in a good way. The mortal authorities won't have anything on her, but she's been banned in the sorcery community for years. She disregards the Rede and uses her magic as an assassin and swindler. Preys on mundanes," she added, meaning people without magic.

I looked to Sorren. "What about you? I tried my best to get a look at the newcomer, but I didn't get much."

Sorren looked worried. "What you saw might have been enough. It brought someone to mind I haven't thought of in a long time." He glanced toward Teag. "When we're done here, I want you to run the name Brevard LaRive and see what you come up with."

"You think he's our killer?" I asked, puzzled.

"I think there might be a connection," Sorren replied, and I knew he wasn't going to elaborate until Teag was able to see if his hunch panned out.

"Rowan's buffering a lot of the nasty emotional impact," I said, realizing that—unlike what normally happens when I do a stressful reading of an object—I wasn't a total wreck. "I can read a few more objects, if you're up for it."

Rowan nodded her assent. I frowned, trying to remember just which pieces of the table service the mysterious stranger had actually touched. Then I had Teag push the silver-plated pile toward me, and looked for the large serving fork. I closed my hand around the cool, smooth handle, and immediately found myself back in the dead family's dining room, at an earlier point in the meal than my previous vision.

Everyone except the young boy had touched the serving fork. I sifted through the impressions. The older boy resented a stranger at the family's gathering. I suspected that his anger covered a gut-level warning he didn't know how to process. The teenage girl was bored, and the woman whose viewpoint I had shared before felt relief that the meal was on the table. From the grandfather, I picked up hunger and impatience, but the grandmother's impression was wistful, as if she was remembering past holidays shared with people long gone. Little did she suspect how quickly she would join them.

Then I found the dark witch's resonance. I nearly recoiled from the malevolence. She must have used her magic to appear harmless, because the depth and strength of her contempt for mortals took my breath away. I could believe Alia Corona was a magical assassin. She was a stone cold killer, remorseless and vengeful. Just the memory of her tainted power was enough to make me pull away.

For one awful moment, I saw her clearly without the glamor and her gray eyes locked with mine. I told myself it wasn't really her, that she couldn't really see me. Just a memory. Just a vision. But for that instant that our gaze connected, I was certain of something: She was looking forward to seeing the people around her die horribly, with just as much anticipation as the others held for the Thanksgiving feast. The serving fork clattered to the table, released by my fingers as if it had burned me.

I came up gasping from the intensity of the vision, brief as it was. The three-dimensional projection winked out around me as I opened my eyes, just as well since I didn't think I was up to facing down Alia Corona right now, even if it was just her psychic imprint.

Sorren and Rowan packed the dishes and silverware into the box. Teag handed me his flask, then went to look up Brevard LaRive. I knocked back a slug of bourbon and let its warmth stop me from shaking. I could never un-see the awful vision of the family being set up for murder, but a little Knob Creek did the trick and made me numb enough to block it out, for a while. I'd see that family in my dreams for the rest of my life.

Sorren glanced my way, checking on me, and I gave him a nod. I was okay enough for now. He and Rowan withdrew to the other side of the room to talk, giving me a little space to pull myself together, for which I was grateful. I raised my right hand to touch the agate necklace that I always wore. Agate is a gem of protection. Just brushing my fingers across the cold stone sent purifying energy through me, helping me recover.

"You're going to want to hear this," Teag said when he emerged from my office about half an hour later. He carried several sheets of print-outs with him.

"Did you find any information?" Sorren asked, looking more worried than he had in a long while.

Teag nodded. "Yeah. Brevard LaRive's name came up several

times on the Darke Web. Nasty piece of work. Some of the mentions suggested he had a taste for the theatrical when it came to killing, but overall I thought that people sounded scared of him."

Sorren turned away. "Thank you, Teag."

"Why do you think he'll choose Charleston? And how do we stop him?" I asked, feeling the warmth of the bourbon taking the edge off my nerves.

"Serial killers follow patterns that sometimes only make sense to themselves," Teag said. "Charleston is the next city on his way south. So it would make sense for him to come here."

"Yeah, but how do we figure out where he's planning to show up for dinner?" I asked. "Charleston's too big to go door to door."

"I need to contact my coven," Rowan said. "While you were focused on the images in the vision, I concentrated on what remained of Alia's personal magical energy signature." She gave a lopsided smile. "It's a bit like giving a scent to a bloodhound. If my coven and I work together, we might be able to track her. It's something of a long shot, but then again, her energy signature is pretty powerful, even though I'm sure she's trying to mute it."

"Do you think you could confirm whether or not she's in Charleston?" Teag questioned.

Rowan shrugged. "That's the idea. And if we pick up the residue of her energy, we might get lucky and be able to follow her—hopefully head her off before anyone else gets killed."

"We would be very grateful to you—and your coven," Sorren said. "Thank you." Rowan nodded in acknowledgement, said goodbye, and slipped out.

"What can we do, while she and her coven are looking for Alia Corona?" I asked. "We can't just sit and wait."

"Let's start with the obvious—public events and any kind of open listing of people willing to take in strangers for the holiday meal," Teag said. "Since he seems to pick his victims by chance, it's as good a way as any to predict who he might target."

"Charleston's a pretty hospitable city," I replied. "There are going to be a lot of houses of worship and soup kitchens."

"I don't think Brevard would take on such a large gathering," Sorren said shaking his head. "No. I think we're looking for intimate, private gatherings. They would be smaller, easier to control, with less chance he might be interrupted."

"It seems awfully complicated," I said. "If he's hungry, why make such a production out of it?" I asked.

Sorren's expression was bleak. "Brevard was turned as a child. There are reasons such things are forbidden among our kind. Even after decades, Brevard has a child's understanding and an immortal's power."

"Why does he need a witch?" I pressed, deciding that there wasn't enough bourbon in Teag's flask to make me feel better about the direction this conversation was taking.

"He's not powerful enough to control all of them." We turned to look at Teag. "That's it, isn't it? He can't glamor them thoroughly enough to keep them all subdued while he attacks, and he needs someone to invite him inside."

Sorren nodded. "Yes. At least, I believe so. Brevard will always appear to be ten years old. His instruction in the ways of the Dark Gift was interrupted when he lost his maker, so he's damaged and untrained —doubly dangerous. He needs someone to win his victims' trust. Apparently, Brevard and Alia Corona have come to some type of arrangement."

"Why Thanksgiving?" I looked at Sorren.

"I suspect he wants to recreate going home for the holidays."

Two days passed before we heard back from Rowan. The store was busy with people looking for last-minute additions to their formal table settings or purchasing silver service pieces to make a splash with their decorating. Being busy helped a little to keep my mind off the possibility of another impending murder, but Teag and I still spent every moment we could looking for information, anything that might help us narrow things down and save some lives.

"That's interesting," Teag mused. "Brevard LaRive's mother was from Charleston."

My heart sank. "So he's got a personal connection here?" If so, that made it even more likely that Charleston was next on his list.

"Yeah. His mother was a Wilmot, from a prominent family. I started tracing his family tree, just in case I got a lucky hit. It's amazing what shows up in those ancestry web sites."

Just then, the bell on the door jangled. I looked up, and Rowan walked in. "Got something," she said, not bothering with any greeting. She looked gaunt, a change since the last time I had seen her, and I wondered what all had been involved with having the coven try to track Alia Corona.

"Let's go in the back," I suggested. Maggie gave me a thumbs-up, indicating that she could handle customers. Maggie has figured out that we're more than an antique store, and while she doesn't know all the details, she's happy to support us in any way she can.

"You could have just called," I said as I led her into the break room.

Rowan shook her head. "Witches and cell phones don't mix well," she replied. "Ditto computers and other electronics. Something about our energy tends to fry them. Believe me; it's a real pain."

Teag brought us both glasses of iced tea, and we sat down at the break room table. "All right," he said. "What did you find out?"

"We're certain Alia is in Charleston," Rowan said. "Searching for her was a delicate business because she's very powerful, and we didn't want her to know we were looking for her. That made it easier to track where she's been than where she is."

"Did you get any ideas about where they might target?" I asked.

Rowan sighed. Up close, she looked really tired. Whatever she and her coven had done to locate Alia Corona must have taken a lot out of them. "If we get too close to her, she'll know, so we have to keep our distance. She's also good at cloaking her power, so that complicates things too."

"Would Alia have the same kind of difficulties with technology that you do?" I asked suddenly.

"Worse, I'd imagine," Rowan said. "Why?"

"I'm betting Alia doesn't pick her targets at random," I said as an idea formed. "I think she enjoys the hunt too much. Stalking the target is part of the fun for her. So she's going to scope out the possible sites ahead of time, figure out the best location for them to not be bothered when they're playing their little 'game.'"

Rowan nodded. "You're probably right."

"If she can't use computer or cell phone technology to research her possibilities, she's probably got to visit in person," I speculated. "Did your coven get any idea of where she's been, even if you aren't sure where she is?"

"A little but we were focused on confirming that she was near without tipping our hand," Rowan said. "Even that required a great deal of energy."

"Could you tell how long she'd been in Charleston?" Teag asked.

Rowan nodded. "The energy traces we picked up started just a few days ago. The longer she's in town, the more likely someone like me might notice." She gave a knowing smile. "There are more witches around than most people realize."

"So she might not have had a chance to plan too much in advance," I mused. "Maybe that's part of the excitement, making it up as they go." Sorren has mentioned that immortality can get boring after a while. Apparently, that's a hazard, pushing some immortals to increasingly risky behavior in search of new thrills, or sending others into depression and suicide. I never thought too much life could be a good thing, but apparently, everything has its downside.

"They've been doing this kind of thing for a while now," Teag said. "They've probably got a routine."

"I'm sorry to ask for more," I said, truly sympathetic since Rowan looked like she'd been up all night. "But it could save lives if we could narrow things down."

"We know a few details that could shorten the list," Teag said. "I did some more digging. None of the family murders happened in apartments or condos."

I nodded. "Makes sense. Too many people around, plus security cameras and thin walls that carry sound."

"So we're looking at stand-alone homes," Teag continued. "Sorren suspects that Alia can't control a huge crowd, so we can probably rule out big gatherings, like the ones organized by houses of worship, soup kitchens, and restaurants."

"Alia is powerful, but not all-powerful," Rowan said. "That's important to remember. I think Sorren's right. Exerting control takes a lot of energy. That kind of spell would be hard to put in place, and very difficult to sustain. The more people, the more energy it takes, and the shorter the time the witch can hold the spell."

"I think she and Brevard want to do their killing in a home because they're recreating something in a sick sort of way," I thought out loud. "I'm betting she would want to do some reconnaissance. If we could track where she's been, that might tell us more than where she is. We'd know where they were considering staging their murders, and we might be able to get there first."

"Already on it," Rowan said. She produced a print-out from her purse. "We think Alia has raised wardings on where she's staying to keep anyone from finding her. But it's more difficult to hold that kind of spell when you're moving around, especially for any length of time. Here's what we have, a list of some of the streets she's visited. It's still going to be like hunting a needle in a haystack, but it might make for a smaller haystack."

"Thank you," I said, glancing down the locations on the page. "This is a huge help."

Rowan gave a tired smile. "Happy to help. We'll stay on it. Maybe we'll get a break."

Teag and I thanked her again, and Rowan left. I was hoping she had time for a nap. She looked exhausted, and I figured she'd earned it.

I handed the list to Teag. "How about if you see what you can turn up on the computer with these addresses, and I'll go up front and help Maggie." From the sound of it, we'd gotten several customers while we had been in the back, and Maggie could probably use some assistance.

"I'm on it," he said, taking the list and heading for the office.

Normally it helps take my mind off problems when the store is busy. Although Trifles and Folly is technically a cover operation for the Alliance, it's also been my family's business for centuries, and I take pride in it operating profitably. I'm certain Sorren would underwrite us if need be, but I liked running the store like a real business, and that meant viewing customers as a good thing, not a distraction from saving the world.

"Thanks, Cassidy," Maggie said when I came up front. "We've been slammed—which is great."

I headed over to answer questions about some antique books while Maggie went to help a woman who was eyeing our estate jewelry. Fortunately, most old objects don't carry any resonance, or if they do, it's neutral or positive. The objects that have a negative vibe to them, we try to cleanse. The pieces that are magically malicious or have tainted energy, Sorren takes to the Alliance to either be safely stored or destroyed.

We were so busy; I lost track of time. It's the holiday season, and if people aren't looking for a one-of-a-kind centerpiece for Thanksgiving, they're searching for the perfect gift for the person who has everything. Fortunately, we can help with both. Maggie and I finally got a break in the traffic late in the afternoon, and we sagged against the counters and shared a sympathetic glance.

"Damn, that was a lot of people!" Maggie said. She fanned herself. "At this rate, we'll have a banner month for sales." Maggie is a retired teacher who started working for Trifles and Folly part-time when she got bored. She's smart and sassy, with a wardrobe from Woodstock and a mind for business that's all Wall Street.

"Why don't you go take a break, and I'll hold the fort," I suggested. Teag hadn't surfaced yet, but I figured he would have some data soon, and I knew Maggie needed a break.

No one was in the store, so I took out my phone. Teag had mentioned Brevard's mother being a Wilmot, and I that name triggered a memory. I did a search and turned up what I was looking for. The Wilmots had, indeed, been important in Charleston, though the family had now died out. *Hmm, did Brevard and Alia have anything to do with that?* I wondered. A few more clicks got me pictures of an old brick home that had seen better days. The Josiah Wilmot house had a historic plaque on the front and had been named a site for preservation, but right now, it looked sad and dilapidated from years of disuse.

"Damn," I muttered under my breath. I had been hoping to find out the house was occupied. Given the connection, that would have made it the prime suspect for Brevard's murder spree.

A few more customers came in, and I tried to keep my attention from wandering as I answered their questions. People seemed to be in the mood to buy, and I rang up several sales. But I couldn't get my mind off the danger at hand. If we didn't figure out Alia's plan, more people were going to die. I didn't want to live with the knowledge that we failed to protect them. There had to be a way to figure out their next move.

"Teag asked me to send you back to talk to him," Maggie said as she came up front. "Go on. I've had some coffee and a snack. I'm good for a while."

I grinned and thanked her, and went back to the office, where Teag was hunched over the computer. "Find something?" I asked, crossing my fingers.

Teag shrugged. "Sort of. I cross-referenced the addresses on the section of each street where Rowan's group said Alia's energy was strongest—meaning that she paused there or walked a stretch more than once. A couple of the houses showed up on lists of people willing to take in college students or foreign exchange students. When I made a couple of discreet calls, I found out they were already full—and the guests appear to be bona fide students from the university."

He gave me a guilty smile. "I'll admit that I posed as a reporter doing a story on families who welcome strangers to their Thanksgiving," he said. "They were happy to talk to me, and I got enough information that I'm sure their guests don't match what we know about Alia. They gave me the names of the students, and I hacked the college database. They're legit."

I leaned against the wall, cradling a cup of coffee. "So now what?"

"One of the houses on her route was the Wilmot House," Teag said. "Heard of it?"

I nodded. "Yeah, I just looked it up. But no one's living in it right now."

"Maybe she didn't know that," he replied. "It would have been at the top of my list."

"How about the other places Rowan identified?"

"I played the reporter card and called them, saying I'd heard they were hosting a Thanksgiving dinner for visitors," he said. "I'm still waiting to hear back from a couple places where I left messages, but the others were all private gatherings for different clubs that welcome members traveling over the holidays. They were very clear about the fact that only members were welcome. I think it would be hard for Alia to fake it."

Charleston can be wonderfully hospitable to tourists and newcomers, but there are certain social circles that are incredibly cliquish. Private societies are fanatic about their membership requirements, and secrecy is part of the appeal for some people. Party-crashers need not apply.

"So we've got nothing?"

Teag sighed. "Not yet. Like I said, I'm waiting to see if a few more people return my calls. But I'm afraid I struck out."

My phone buzzed in my pocket, telling me I had new email. I was feeling rather discouraged about the wall Teag's research had hit, and I glanced at my inbox to distract me, then let out a low whistle.

"We've got a complication." I swore under my breath as I read my emails on my phone.

"What's wrong?"

"Check your email. Did you get something from the Historical Archive's Holiday Events Committee?" We're on their email list since the store makes a nice donation every year in thanks for all the help the Archive provides with our research projects. That means we're among the first to hear whenever there's a new exhibition or special event.

Teag glanced down at his phone and thumbed through a couple of screens. "Just an invitation to—holy hell."

I figured he'd come to the same conclusion as I had, looking at the announcement. Charleston is a huge historic preservation city, and the Archive often throws a cocktail party, holiday ball, or special dinner to raise money to restore a neglected historic home or acquire an important piece of art.

"Thanksgiving dinner at the Wilmot House," Teag read, looking a little stunned. "A fundraiser to support restoration of the Josiah Wilmot House, a Charleston architectural treasure."

"You think this might catch Alia's eye?"

Teag nodded. "Yeah. I haven't been able to find out a whole lot about Brevard since he was turned, but he came from a wealthy family when he was mortal. If Sorren's right and Brevard is a psycho vamp-child, he might like the idea of having his holiday 'feast' somewhere that has a connection to his mother."

Teag looked down at the invitation. "Seating is extremely limited, so respond early. This will be a night to remember."

"You're not just whistlin' Dixie," I muttered.

"Do you think you could persuade Mrs. Morrissey to hold the party on another night?" Teag asked. Over the years, I've gotten to be good friends with Mrs. Benjamin Morrissey, the doyenne Director of the Historical Archive. She knows everyone in town, and she's been an invaluable asset as we've researched some past problems. But she doesn't know about the Alliance, although she may suspect that the store and I are a bit more than we appear to be.

"What do you suggest? Maybe call her up and tell her we need to cancel the fundraiser because there's a child vampire with a nasty disposition on the loose?" I was frustrated, and it showed in my voice.

"If we don't do something, it's going to be a bloodbath," Teag replied.

I studied the invitation. "There are only a dozen seats available at the table," I noted. "The price per plate is pretty pricey."

"Mrs. Morrissey won't have any problem filling that," Teag predicted. "She'll probably have a waiting list."

"Let's find out." I have Mrs. Morrissey's number on speed dial because she's one of our best sources when we need to research something about the city's history. I expected to need to leave a message, but to my surprise, she picked up on the third ring. I put the call on speaker so Teag could hear.

"Cassidy! Lovely to hear from you. Happy Thanksgiving!" Mrs. Morrissey is a dynamo, despite being up in years. "How can I help you?"

"I just got the email about the Wilmot House event," I replied. "And I was wondering how the ticket sales were going."

"We've had a few inquiries from the sign we posted at the house, but the announcement just went out a couple of minutes ago," she replied. "And the tickets are priced to raise money, so they're not in everyone's budget. But any event with limited seating always sells out, so I'm sure we'll fill up. We've got one paid reservation already if you can believe that!"

I could, and a chill went down my spine. "Anyone I know?"

"Doubtful—it's not one of our usual donors," Mrs. Morrissey replied. "Lovely woman, said she was here on business and just happened to see the sign. Maybe she'll become a long-time friend of the Archive."

I doubted it. "I'm sure you'll fill up quickly," I said. "I just wanted to ask because we'd be glad to tell our customers about the event, but I didn't want to mention it if you were already full." It was an outright fib, but for a good cause.

"That would be wonderful!" Mrs. Morrissey replied. "Much as I love having our regular donors at events like this, there's so much potential to bring new patrons into the fold." She chuckled. "But remember the ticket price. You may not want to mention it until you've rung up their purchase!"

I promised to stop by for a visit after the holiday and said goodbye, wishing her a happy Thanksgiving. "I think we've found Alia," Teag said. "And Brevard's going to have his fill of Charleston blue-bloods if we don't do something to stop them."

I cocked my head to one side, thinking. There was the germ of an idea in what he'd said. "What if we filled the event for her?" I said, as a plan formed in my mind. Before Teag could respond, I was texting Sorren.

"Did you see how much each of those tickets cost?" Teag replied.

"Sorren always says that immortality is good for gaining wealth," I said.

THE WILMOT HOUSE glittered with holiday welcome. It had once been a showplace, but now the old house just slightly north of Broad Street that had fallen on hard times. The building had "good bones" in terms of architectural style, although years of neglect had turned it from a showplace into a fixer-upper. Still, a little imagination made it easy to see how the old brick house could return to its old grandeur.

I paused before I started up the steps, stretching out my magic. Some places were so polluted with dark power that I could feel it through the soles of my shoes. I waited, listening to my senses.

"Well?" Teag asked.

I shook my head. "Nothing evil. Just a very sad feeling. I have the oddest feeling that the house might actually like being a tourist attraction."

Teag and I arrived early, wanting to make certain everything was in place for the evening's encounter. Sorren had purchased all the remaining tickets for Thanksgiving Day, and Mrs. Morrissey set the next night as the event for the big donors. I hadn't told her exactly what we were doing, but she was a good friend of my Uncle Evann, who left the store to me, so I think she suspects more about what we do than she lets on. We told her we were trying to catch an art thief. Mrs. Morrissey was glad to help, especially when I told her that the patron whose art we were trying to retrieve wanted it handled quietly and privately.

"Cassidy and Teag! Come on and tell me what you think of the food!" Niella Teller and her mother, Ernestine, were in the kitchen.

"From what I can smell, it should be heavenly!" I said. Teag and I wandered back to the kitchen. The room was dated but functional, like the rest of the house. Niella and Mrs. Teller stood near the big stove, their aprons spotted with food.

"You know we can't eat any of this," I said, feeling guilty at the feast that was going to go to waste. "If Sorren's right, the witch will find a way to poison the food."

"I know," Mrs. Teller said, dusting her hands on her apron. "And it's a crying shame. But if we don't put some effort into this, that witch will figure something's up. We might miss our chance."

I had to give Ernestine Teller credit—she was feisty. She's in her seventies, and one of the best sweetgrass basket makers in Charleston. Niella is her daughter and an excellent basket weaver in her own right. Both women are talented with Hoodoo and root magic. Mrs. Teller is known far and wide as a root woman, someone who can cure illnesses, repair relationships, and ward off evil. Lucky for us, she and Niella are also damn fine cooks.

"You tell Sorren that we're going to have to do this meal over right when this is done," Mrs. Teller said with a look that wasn't about to take no for an answer. "I get that you don't want caterers involved since they've got no way to defend themselves. We're happy to help. But Lord Above! Thanksgiving dinner was meant to be eaten." She shook her head. "So this Sunday, Niella and I are doing this all again at my house, and you're all to come over and eat."

I grinned. "You don't have to twist my arm," I said. "That sweet potato casserole looks marvelous, and the collard greens are making my mouth water."

Mrs. Teller beamed. "Child, that's nothing compared to how that turkey is going to look when it comes out of the oven. Niella and I do Thanksgiving right!"

I thanked them profusely, still feeling guilty about wasting the food and their preparation. But if we wanted Alia and Brevard to fall for the ruse, it had to look like the real thing. And if they did, that beautiful food would end up drugged.

When I walked into the dining room, I stopped in my tracks. Teag was setting out the china from the auction on the table. He grinned as I came in. "Don't worry—I'm not expecting you to help. But I thought it just seemed right to have the set here. What do you think?"

The dining room, like the rest of the house, had seen better days. Scuffs and dents marred the wainscoting, time and disuse dimmed the paint on the walls, and the elaborate tray ceiling had some water damage. But the table down the middle of the room was set with a beautiful tablecloth and runner, crystal candlesticks from the store, and the murdered family's china and silverware. Despite everything, it looked beautiful.

If Alia Corona was as powerful as we thought she was, she would be able to sense Sorren and Rowan from a distance. The plan was for them to barge in when the going got rough, but not until Alia made her move. That meant the "guests" had to have special abilities to protect themselves without having too much magic to tip our hand.

Fortunately, we have a lot of friends who are good at kicking super-natural ass. Father Anne is an Episcopalian priest who's also part of a secret society to battle paranormal bad guys. Chuck Pettis is a retired special ops soldier whose unit specialized in neutralizing occult dangers, and he's helped us out from time to time. Lucinda is a powerful Voudon mambo, and so is Caliel. Mrs. Teller and Niella had orders to serve the food and then fall back to a safe distance, where they could use their root magic to help us without putting themselves in danger.

"Everything's ready," Teag said, standing back to admire his handiwork.

"It looks great," I replied. "Here's hoping we don't have to destroy the house to save Charleston."

It gets dark early on Thanksgiving. Teag and I left the Wilmot House after we had made our preparations, and went home to get changed. That's the kind of dilemma I face on a daily basis. What can I wear that looks suitably dressy or professional, and still gives me maximum flexibility for a fight to the death with a dark witch and a rogue vampire?

Niella and Mrs. Teller had borrowed uniforms from friends at a local catering company, so they looked the part. They were waiting to welcome us as our "guests" arrived. Teag and I were first. Teag opted for a more casual look that would give him better freedom of movement. I had chosen a pantsuit with a lot of give in the fabric and a pair of flat shoes. All of my jewelry included gemstones known for magical protection.

Teag is a competition-level martial arts fighter. His wooden fighting staff packs a real punch, especially after he souped it up with runes and magic. He put it to one side near his chair, where it would be handy if needed. I was sure he had more weapons in his messenger bag, which he put on the floor next to his chair, and I saw the hilt of one of his Spanish daggers protruding from the bag.

I had my wooden athame up one sleeve and the old dog collar that called my protective familiar spirit on my other wrist. I'd brought a huge purse, the better in which to hide a couple of nasty weapons for hunting supernatural bad guys.

Lucinda and Caliel arrived next. We had to pretend like we didn't know them, in case the witch was watching. Lucinda had opted for an elegant blouse and pants in navy blue and blood red, the colors of Voudon Loa Erzulie Dantor. I caught a faint whiff of Reve d'Or perfume, that Loa's favorite. Lucinda was ready for the fight. Caliel wore a loose-fitting guayabera shirt over slacks that would give him room to move.

"Happy Thanksgiving," I said, doing my best to play my part.

"And to you, also," Lucinda replied, then I heard her murmur a blessing under her breath. "The Loas are watching," she added, just loud enough for Teag and me to hear.

Next came Chuck Pettis. Chuck looks like a grumpy middle-aged man, and that's exactly what he is—except that he also has some kick-ass fighting skills. I could hear him ticking when he walked in. It wasn't a bomb; Chuck has an odd superstition about clocks and never leaves home without a vest that is covered with small, working watches. He wore a baggy jacket over jeans and a rumpled shirt, and I was certain that he had a full armory of weapons under that jacket.

Father Anne was the last of our group to arrive. She was wearing an all-black shirt and slacks combination but without her clerical collar tonight. Father Anne's dark hair was cut short in a spiked pompadour. Her shirt hid the beautiful tattoos of St. Expeditus and her other patron saints that covered both arms. Seeing that might have been a giveaway for Alia.

We were already seated when the last guest walked in. I tried to study her without being obvious. Alia Corona had an average build, and her brown, short hair was unremarkable for cut or color. The outfit she wore was dowdy, and she looked around tentatively, as if unsure whether she was in the right place. It was a good disguise, and it might have worked if I hadn't accidentally met her eyes. The same malice glinted in them that I had seen in the vision. *Game on.*

"Everyone here? Let's have Thanksgiving!" Mrs. Teller said, poking her head in from the kitchen.

I rose in my chair. "Mrs. Morrissey asked me to thank all of you for coming tonight to benefit the renovation of the Wilmot House. Her hope is that we will enjoy the food and the company and know that she is thankful for us and our support this holiday season."

The others played along, commenting on what I had said and making small talk as if we had never seen each other in our lives. Mrs. Teller and Niella brought in the food, and it smelled so good that it was difficult to remember the danger. My stomach growled, although I'd eaten before we came. *Has Alia managed to taint the food yet? Does her magic make everyone hungrier than usual, too?*

As in the vision, Alia Corona said very little, even as the others attempted to engage her in conversation. If I hadn't known better, I'd have bought into her portrayal of an introverted, slightly awkward person who was content to let others do the talking. Watching her eyes, I saw her sizing each of us up. Her eyes were calculating and shrewd. She was going to be a dangerous enemy.

Conversation continued as we passed the serving dishes. Pretending to eat but not actually consuming anything was going to be tricky, but I figured that if we kept up a lively discussion and the focus of attention constantly shifted, the rest of us could hide our food in our napkins or under our plates. Alia nodded when the conversation turned to her and murmured the minimum possible to be polite, quickly deflecting the discussion.

Yet as the meal stretched on, I spotted Alia drumming her fingers. She was restless, anxious for the kill. Maybe wondering why we hadn't started feeling the effects yet. I rose from my seat. "Let me see what's keeping the dessert," I said, a phrase we had agreed would be our cue.

I took two steps toward the kitchen, and staggered, reaching out to the table to steady myself. Teag stood up to assist me, but he crumpled to the floor next to his chair.

I slumped to the ground, still in reach of my purse full of weapons. "I really don't feel good," I said in my best seasick voice.

Chuck slid out of his chair, landing on his side. Lucinda remarked in alarm and headed for the door, but staggered and fell before she reached it. Caliel went to help her but only got as far as the end of the table. Father Anne slid down in her chair, head back and eyes closed.

Through it all, Alia had said nothing, made no move to help, seeming unsurprised by our sudden distress. She hesitated for a moment to make sure we were all down, and then rose from her seat, stepping over Lucinda. She opened the door to welcome the final guest.

"Come in," she said in a voice full of energy and purpose, no longer the mousy visitor. "Thanksgiving dinner is ready."

From where I lay, I got a look at Brevard LaRive. He had the body and face of a ten-year-old boy, but the eyes of a hit man. His mouth was a cruel line as he walked past our prone bodies, taking in the scene with absolutely no emotion except one: hunger.

A loud boom rattled the windows, and then a flash of light flared as one of Chuck's whiz-bang incendiaries triggered. Alia and Brevard froze, but the rest of us were expecting it. Sorren burst in through the front door, while Rowan appeared in the kitchen entrance.

Everyone moved at once. Chuck kicked his chair hard, sending it airborne—aimed right for Alia. Sorren went after Brevard in a blur of motion. We'd already agreed to let him handle the vampire.

Rowan raised one arm, and the air between her and Alia shimmered and rippled, a blast that took Alia off her feet and threw her against the wall hard enough to crack plaster. Alia struck back with a bolt of blue energy that would have fried Rowan if she hadn't dodged out of the way. It splintered the wooden doorframe and put a crack down the length of the solid oak door.

Teag came up with his fighting staff in one hand and a net of silver mesh in the other. His Spanish fighting daggers hung from his belt. He wheeled the net once and let it fly, but Alia batted it away before it came close. I let my spoon athame drop into my hand and called to the strong memories it evoked, channeling my will to send a cone of cold, white force that sent Alia tumbling. In the same breath, I let the dog collar rattle on my left wrist, and the ghost of a large, solid and very angry Golden Retriever materialized beside me, my old dog, Bo. Bo snarled and lunged, snapping his teeth and landing on Alia, harrying her as she tried to get to her feet.

Teag swooped in, landing a solid thwack across Alia's shoulders with his staff that sent her sprawling. He reached for the net, but Alia was already rolling with the blow, and sent a torrent of fire in Teag's direction that barely missed him, singing his hair and blackening the wall where it struck.

I had pulled another weapon out of my huge purse, an old walking stick that once belonged to Sorren's maker, Alard. I leveled it at Alia as she took aim at Teag, and a split second after she loosed her fiery blast, I shot off one of my own. She didn't see me, since she was focused on Teag, and the flames blistered her shoulder, burning away her jacket and setting one side of her hair on fire.

Alia shrieked and rolled to snuff out the flames, then sent a blast of power toward me that took half the dishes off the table, throwing me against a built-in china cabinet and shattering the glass in one of the cabinet doors. Alia stalked toward me, but she forgot about Father Anne, who had taken the opportunity to shift positions while everyone was busy blowing someone up. Father Anne crouched beneath one side of the table, and as Alia moved past her, Father Anne dove forward, driving Alia to the ground and bringing a slim, bone-handled boline knife down with single-minded intensity.

That knife was blessed, and it packed a punch, but Alia seemed to realize her danger. She grappled with the priest, one hand clamped around Father Anne's wrist to hold the knife away, while her other hand wove sigils in the air that blazed like fire.

Father Anne brought her knee up sharply, grinding it into Alia's thigh. Alia yelped in pain and Father Anne wrested her knife free, stabbing down toward Alia's shoulder. Alia barked a curse, and Father Anne's skin turned beet red, blistering like she had been burned. Alia took advantage of the distraction to tear loose, avoiding the knife. But as she got to her feet, Teag's silver net dropped down over her, tangling her in its folds.

Silver works great against certain kinds of supernatural creatures like nephilim, but it had no special power against witchcraft. Still, Alia had to fight her way free of it, letting me get in a solid blast of cold power with my athame. It threw Alia across the room, where Rowan got a clear shot. This time, Rowan's magic lifted Alia off the floor, suspending her in mid-air.

"Not so tough now," Rowan muttered.

Alia snarled. She threw off the silver net and flung both arms out wide, then brought her palms together with the sound of a thunderclap, rattling the entire house. Alia dropped to the ground, landing in a crouch, while Rowan stumbled backward, momentarily stunned. Alia went after Rowan, but Teag scythed his fighting staff, taking her out at the ankles. I got in a blast from my walking stick that blistered Alia's left leg as she rolled beneath the big dining table.

Chuck had thrown off his jacket, revealing a bandolier filled with enough spy-gadget weapons to singlehandedly stock a whole covert operation. He had a huge gun in his hands and was circling where Sorren and Brevard fought, waiting for an opportunity. I couldn't spare much attention for the fight since Alia was proving to be a real handful, but Chuck was squeezing off a round now and again when he could get a clear shot at Brevard. Chuck's an ace marksman, but it's difficult to hit someone who can move in a blur. So far, I guessed Chuck hadn't managed to get in a headshot or get Brevard in the heart since the vampire was still moving. Or maybe, subconsciously, Chuck was unsettled shooting someone who looked like a little boy.

Sorren had obviously made his peace with Brevard's appearance. It wasn't slowing him down. Sorren's shirt was ripped and bloodied, and his eyebrow and lip were split. Parallel cuts, like deep fingernail scratches, scored down one arm. Brevard was equally battered, with bloody gashes showing through the tatters of his clothing. At least four bullets left their mark, but he was healing rapidly enough that anything that didn't kill him wasn't going to stop him for long.

Still, Brevard was less than a century old, while Sorren was close to six hundred. I wondered if Sorren was holding back since I'd seen him go up against much bigger monsters. Perhaps Sorren wanted the chance to question Brevard. But somehow I didn't think Brevard would cooperate.

Lucinda and Caliel were chanting, and I realized that while our attention was elsewhere, they had already sown salt in a circle around themselves and were opening their connection to the Loas, and to Erzulie Dantor, protector of families, a Petro Loa with a volatile temper.

Rowan and Alia had squared off at one side of the dining room. They stood across from each other, cut off from the rest of us by an iridescent curtain of power, locked in a battle of magic and will. From my vantage point, it didn't seem like they were doing much, just a twitch of a finger or a subtle hand motion, or the muttered words of a spell. But whatever was going on inside that bubble was consuming their full attention. They appeared to be equally matched.

Alia's disguise was gone completely, revealing the hatred in her gaze and her contempt in the twist of her mouth. Rowan's expression didn't betray her feelings; instead, it was a mask of cool concentration. Now and again, the energy field around them crackled and sparked, a hint to the deadly power they were wielding within its confines.

Brevard tore loose from Sorren's grip and staggered into Teag, throwing him out of his way. Teag careened into the iridescent curtain of power, sending up a shower of golden sparks and wisps of smoke as his clothing smoldered from the contact. The force field bubble wavered. Father Anne had regained her feet, and when the shimmering curtain faltered, she dove for Alia, knife out, sinking her blade deep into the witch's back. Just for good measure, I leveled my walking stick and blasted Alia with a stream of flames.

Alia's body contorted in the fire as she tried to pull the blessed knife from her back. She burned, but she was not consumed by the flames. I had no idea what to do next if fire and a sacred knife weren't enough. Father Anne was thrown several feet. She landed on her back, hard enough I was sure it had knocked the wind out of her. I kept the stream of fire going, but my magic wouldn't last forever. Drawing on the memories and power of an object drains me, and I'm still pretty new at this. But I was determined not to let Alia get away again. Bo's ghost leaped and charged at Alia, but he couldn't get through her defenses, even if his spectral teeth could have taken a bite out of her.

Rowan looked worse for the wear, and I could see the toll her battle with Alia had taken. But she set her jaw, adding a ripple of magic to what I was sending Alia's way. Encased in power, bathed in flame, Alia began to laugh, taunting us.

Blood streaked down Brevard's face. His eyes were wild with madness and hunger, his mouth twisted in a feral howl of anger. No one would have mistaken him for a choirboy now. A cruel glint came into Brevard's eyes and he dove toward Teag, not Sorren. Hitting the witch's curtain of power had rattled Teag, and his reactions were just a fraction of a second too slow. Brevard grabbed him by the throat, lifting him off his feet.

I nearly needed an instant replay to make out what happened next. Sorren moved in a blur, ripping Teag out of Brevard's grip. Chuck got in a clean shot, and the bullet tore off the back of Brevard's head. Teag spun as he landed, sinking one of his daggers into Brevard's heart. Brevard collapsed, his body turning to dust as it fell.

Before I could get my wits about me, I realized the feel of the room had changed. The air was heavy with the smell of cigarettes and a sweet perfume, the same scent Lucinda was wearing, the favorite of Loa Erzulie Dantor. Power swelled around us, not from Alia or from Rowan but from *elsewhere*, not of this world.

The image of a dark-skinned woman with sharp, handsome features began to materialize. A red and blue shawl was draped across her head and shoulders, and in each hand, she clutched a sharp, double-sided dagger. Lucinda and Caliel chanted louder, and the image of the Loa grew more solid. As we watched, Erzulie Dantor took one slow step and then another toward Alia. She moved unharmed through my fire and Rowan's rippling power as if it was nothing to her. We halted our attack, holding our breath, watching to see what the Loa would do.

Alia had stopped laughing, and her eyes grew wide as Erzulie Dantor stood in front of her. Then a smug smile twisted Alia's mouth, and the power protecting her flared. The Loa stretched out her arms, and then brought both daggers down in streaks of silver, slashing through Alia's protections. Alia gasped, stunned and weakened. The Loa's image winked out, and both Rowan and I willed our power toward the damaged witch.

Fire from my walking stick consumed her as the force of Rowan's magic ripped Alia's body apart. She burned like paper until there was nothing left. Just like that, it was over.

We all stood frozen in our places, staring at the two piles of ash, as if we couldn't quite believe it was over. Lucinda and Caliel's chant had changed from petition to praise, thanking the Loas for their assistance. I felt lightheaded and sank into a chair at the head of the table. Bo's ghost padded over to me. I reached over to pat him, although now that he wasn't fighting, his image was insubstantial. His tail thumped, and then he was gone.

Rowan looked dangerously pale, but she waved off my concern. Sorren was as battered and bloodied as if he had been in a bar fight, but I could see his wounds already beginning to heal as he helped Teag to his feet. Father Anne's blisters had faded, and she stood with hands upraised and face upturned, giving thanks for our deliverance. Her boline knife lay amid Alia's ashes. I had enough presence of mind to walk over and retrieve it, cleaning it on the ruined tablecloth, before handing it back to her.

Teag's lip was split, one eye was swollen, and he had a nasty gash down one arm. "Anthony's going to give me an earful about showing up like this," he said ruefully. "He worries a lot." I couldn't help but smile at him as I thought of the greeting he'd get.

"We'd better get out of here. Someone's sure to have called the cops about the shots and noise," I said, glancing worriedly toward the windows.

"Relax," Rowan said. "My coven has been supporting us from a distance. They dampened the noise and added a spell that distracts people so we wouldn't get any unwanted interference."

Chuck holstered his gun and walked over to the pile of ash that had been Brevard, sorting through it with his foot and taking back the spent shells, whistling a tune. When he realized we were all staring at him, he stopped and gave us a look.

"What? Can't a guy be in a good mood? Beats hell out spending the holiday with my sister and my boring brother-in-law."

I was taking in the wreck we had made of the dining room. There was no way Mrs. Morrissey would be able to host her post-Thanksgiving fundraiser here tomorrow night. I glanced toward Rowan. "Can you do something to put this place back together?"

She gave me a wilting look. "I'm a witch, not Mary Poppins. Call a contractor."

"It's all right, Cassidy," Sorren said, managing a chuckle even after all we had been through. "I'll make a few adjustments after the rest of you leave, and we'll blame it on faulty wiring. Another check should smooth things over and pay for repairs. Mrs. Morrissey can host the meal at the Archive—she's had larger dinners there before."

I was staring at the ruined feast on the table. "Did Alia really manage to poison the food, even with Mrs. Teller and Niella watching it closely?"

Rowan walked over to the table and ran her hands along the contours of the turkey an inch or so above it so as not to come in contact. "It's tainted," she said. "Not something I know how to do with magic, but I'm guessing Alia had made a specialty out of it."

Much of the china was broken. The remnants of the feast were cold and congealed. It looked terribly sad. I took a step, and my foot bumped against something. When I looked down, I saw the gravy boat that had started it all. Without thinking, I stooped to pick it up and realized that the resonance had changed.

"It's gone," I said, cradling the bowl in my hands. "The memories, the energy. It's not there anymore. Maybe the family that owned this is finally at peace."

"I don't know about the rest of you, but I'm starving," Father Anne said, slipping the knife back into a scabbard on her belt.

"We can't go out for dinner looking like this," Chuck said. "And besides, it's Thanksgiving. Everything's closed."

I grinned. "I had a feeling we might be hungry, so I bought one of those Thanksgiving package dinners from the gourmet market. Turkey, side dishes, rolls, and a pecan pie. Plenty for everyone. We can all go over to my place. Anthony and Maggie should be there by now, getting things ready—and setting out the first aid kit. Come as you are."

And that's exactly what we did.

PART III
REDCAP

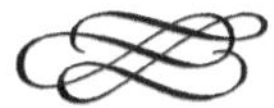

REDCAP

I ran through White Point Gardens as fast as I could. Behind me, teeth snapped, and feet crunched on gravel. The redcap was gaining on me. I turned and caught a glimpse of the creature that was hunting me, and let loose with a blast of cold white force from the athame in my right hand.

The energy bolt sizzled through the air, but the redcap was gone. They're devilishly hard to hit.

Mocking laughter came from the shadows. The redcap was enjoying his game. He was toying with me, letting me get ahead of him, saving his speed for the kill. Legend says it's impossible to outrun a redcap. I had hoped to draw him off, away from the homes that bordered on the garden, where there were fewer prying eyes and a lesser chance of collateral damage. I'd offered myself as bait to draw the redcap toward the waterfront. Now, I dodged around the statues and war memorial cannons, trying to out outwit a bloodthirsty pixie with a taste for human flesh.

Unfortunately, this wasn't the strangest way I had ever spent a Friday night.

The redcap was chattering in excitement, stoked about getting a good feast—me. I was predictably less enthusiastic about the possibility and determined to make sure he stayed hungry. The back corner of the park was coming up, where it was a darker thanks to a burned-out street lamp. Just a few more feet.

The redcap gave a feral cry and sprang at me, snapping his sharp teeth on my jeans and barely missing my skin. I wheeled and gave him a good kick in the face, knocking him a few feet away. The redcap howled in anger and jumped to his feet; eyes fixed on me as he sized up his prey.

A larger shape moved fast enough to blur, and in the next instant, Sorren tackled the redcap. Sorren hung on, using his own immortal strength to restrain the redcap, who despite being two feet tall and built like a stringy old man was as tough as a tiger.

"Now!" Sorren cried out.

Teag darted from behind a monument. I heard the redcap scream as Teag pulled the creature's head back and swung his blade, neatly severing the vicious pixie's head. The redcap's body went limp in Sorren's grip, but the mouth kept snapping even as the head fell to the ground, and its beady dark eyes glared at us balefully until the light finally left them.

Sorren dropped the headless body and stood up, wiping the worst of the pixie's blood from his shirt. Teag pulled a garbage bag from his backpack and scooped up the head and body to dispose of elsewhere.

"Third damn redcap in a week," Sorren muttered.

Just another weekend here in the Holy City.

I'm Cassidy Kincaide, and I own Trifles and Folly, an antique and curio shop in historic, haunted Charleston, South Carolina. Obviously, we're not the average second-hand shop. I'm a psychometric, meaning I can read the history, magic, and emotional resonance of objects by touch. Teag Logan is my assistant store manager. He's got Weaver magic, which lets him weave spells into cloth or weave electronic threads of data into information—making him a wicked-good hacker. Sorren is my business partner, and he's also a nearly six hundred-year-old vampire who founded Trifles and Folly back in the 1600s. We work for the Alliance, a secret coalition of mortals and immortals who keep the world safe from dangerous magical or supernatural objects. When we succeed, no one notices. When we fail, lots of people die.

The redcap wasn't the worst monster we had fought, not by a long shot. But redcaps were still dangerous, as the sudden jump in the number of missing people in Charleston attested. The murderous pixie we had battled tonight had friends out there, and they would kill again unless we did something to stop them.

Just in case someone noticed us running around, we left the park quickly and met up back at the store, gathering in the small break room. Teag handed off the bag with the dead redcap to Sorren. "You'll take care of this one, like the others?" he asked.

Sorren nodded. "I'll handle it." Sorren's blond hair was cut short, playing up his high cheekbones. He looks like he's in his mid-twenties, although he's centuries older.

"Where are all the redcaps coming from?" Teag asked as he checked my calf to make sure the pixie hadn't broken the skin. Lucky for me, I had been just fast enough to escape those razor-sharp teeth. I poured us both a glass of sweet tea, and we toasted the success of tonight's hunt.

"I don't know, but I'm never going to look at Santa's elves with their little red hats the same way again," I said, collapsing into a chair. Now that the danger was over, I felt a little weak in the knees.

It was a week until Christmas, and Charleston was beset with ugly little evil pixies. There was nothing jolly about it. "I thought redcaps were only in England and Scotland," I said, and took a sip of my tea. There are few things in life—even counting murderous elves—that can't be made a little better with a good glass of sweet tea.

Sorren raised an eyebrow. "Next you'll be telling me that vampires are only in Transylvania." Before he was turned, Sorren was the best jewel thief in Belgium.

"Plenty of people who settled in Charleston came from the British Isles," Teag replied. "As we've seen, when people relocate, they bring their gods, ghosts, and monsters with them."

Sorren frowned. "Maybe," he said. "But creatures like redcaps can also be summoned if magic is strong enough."

"You don't think the redcaps are working by themselves?"

"Unlikely, since they haven't historically made Charleston their home. They prefer abandoned castles," Sorren replied. "After all these years, I doubt they suddenly decided to relocate. Supernatural beings tend to be creatures of habit."

"What would someone get out of bringing redcaps here?" I asked, and took another gulp of the sweet, strong tea. "There doesn't appear to be any connection among the people who've gone missing." The police might still be looking for missing people, but I was certain they wouldn't be found. Redcaps ate their prey.

"The only reasons I can think of are to sow fear, or get revenge," Teag replied. "As far as the police are concerned, the disappearances are random." Teag's magic makes him one hell of a hacker, and that includes an ability to get past protections on law enforcement sites. Since the police wouldn't believe us if we tried to tell them what was really going on, we couldn't count on cooperation, so we handled problems ourselves.

"I agree," Sorren said. "And unfortunately, that casts a wide net."

"And your sources haven't heard anything?" I set my empty glass aside. Sorren is well-connected in the supernatural community in Charleston and around the world. He has contacts everywhere, and they feed each other information like a paranormal intelligence network.

He shook his head. "Nothing, at least not that I've heard. I'll make some more inquiries." He hefted the bag with the dead redcap. "I'd better get this taken care of. Keep me updated on what you find. I have a feeling we haven't seen the worst of this yet."

"Don't you love the holiday decorations?" Drea Andrews asked as we stood in line at Honeysuckle Café for a morning latte. "I think they're prettier than ever this year." Drea is a good friend of mine, and she's also the owner of Andrews Carriage Rides, a tour company that is very popular with the hordes of tourists who vacation in Charleston.

"I've been so busy; I'm ashamed to say I haven't paid a lot of attention," I admitted.

Drea grinned. "Don't feel bad—it's part of my job to notice that kind of thing. But I agree with the tourists—I think the beautification committee outdid themselves, especially on the Market area. Magnolia garlands, sweetgrass stars, sea shells, and those long-needle pine wreaths—it's all fantastic." No one outdoes Drea on enthusiasm.

"How's Valerie?" I asked. Valerie works for Drea, and she's one of the top tour guides.

Drea's light-hearted mood suddenly sobered. "You didn't hear?" When I shook my head, Drea continued. "Her cousin went missing last week. Valerie is absolutely beside herself, and she asked for a few days off to help with the search."

My heart sank. "Where was her cousin before she disappeared?"

"Here in Charleston. That's what makes the whole thing so strange," Drea replied as we inched up toward the counter to order our coffee. "It's not like we're New York or New Orleans. People don't just up and disappear here."

That might have been true before the redcaps showed up, but unless Sorren, Teag, and I put an end to the killer pixies, Charleston might end up being the missing persons capital of the U.S. "Were there any leads?" I asked.

Drea shook her head. "Beth—that's Valerie's cousin—went out for a run one night and didn't come back. Her suitcases and clothing—and her car—are still at Valerie's place. She didn't take her wallet or keys, or her credit cards and ID. Valerie swears her cousin seemed happy, no big romantic break-up, nothing like that. The police took Valerie's report, but they haven't turned up anything yet."

I felt sick to my stomach. Odds were good that Beth had been one of the redcap's victims. "I'll keep an eye out," I replied. "Are there flyers?"

Drea reached into her bag and pulled out a poster with a picture of a young woman on it. "I know Valerie would be grateful if you'd put this up in Trifles and Folly."

"Sure," I said. "Anything to help." Although I was almost certain Beth was beyond our help, at this point.

My mood was gloomy as I walked back to the store, still brooding about Beth. I had to force myself to pay attention to the decorations Drea had mentioned. Charleston does holiday décor right; after all, that's part of what tourists come to see. We err on the side of classy and elegant, which goes well with Charleston's beautiful architecture. I tried to push visions of redcaps out of my mind as I walked, noticing the beautiful wreaths on doors and gates, the garlands hung around doorways and the glimpses of lit and decorated trees in the windows of houses and stores.

What would bring a bunch of redcaps to Charleston? Why now—and why here?

I swung through the City Market, taking the long way back to the shop. The City Market is in the heart of the historic district, with three mostly open-air permanent pavilions filled with artists, bakers, jewelry makers, and gifts of all kinds. It's always a treat to walk through, better than ever with Christmas right around the corner. Just smelling the pine wreaths and the scent of cinnamon lifted my spirits.

"Cassidy! I was hoping you would come by." Mrs. Teller and her daughter, Niella, weave some of the best sweetgrass baskets in Charleston. They have a spot on one end of the main pavilion, where they can set out a display of their beautiful work for shoppers.

"I hope your baskets are selling like hotcakes for the holidays," I replied. Mrs. Teller sat in a lawn chair, fingers flying as she wove the intricate baskets. She made it look easy, but her skill came from a life-time of practice. She has magic of her own as well. Mrs. Teller and Niella are root women, Hoodoo practitioners skilled in old African magic to bless, curse, and protect. They knew all about what we really did at Trifles and Folly.

"They are, child. They are," Mrs. Teller replied. "Been some prob-lems around town I hear," she said, dropping her voice as Niella moved to where she could make sure no one interrupted or overheard.

I was certain she meant the redcaps. "What are you hearing?"

Mrs. Teller shook her head. "I've sold more gris-gris bags and jack-balls than baskets in the last few days, that's for certain." Those were protective talismans, which meant word had gotten around about the killer pixies. "People are scared. Folks are goin' missing. You know anything 'bout that?"

"Not much," I admitted. "Sorren called the things 'redcaps.' We don't know where they came from or why they're here, but they're dangerous."

"Sure are," Mrs. Teller agreed. "And there's something else you need to know. Got a new vendor in the Market, and there's something *wrong* about his merchandise, sure as I'm born."

I felt a chill go down my back. "What do you mean, wrong?" I asked.

Mrs. Teller slid me a look like I was dim. "*Wrong*," she repeated, with enough emphasis for me to know she meant in a supernatural way.

"I grabbed a flyer," Niella said. "Had a feeling you'd want to see it." She handed me a piece of paper with an advertisement for "Hearth Hobs," appealingly homely little statues.

"Put a Hearth Hob beside your fireplace to welcome Father Christmas," the flyer said. "Or set one on the windowsill to watch for flying reindeer. Perfect for your holiday decorating!"

"Just don't feed them after midnight," I muttered. Something about the adorably ugly figures gave me the willies.

"Did you see these Hearth Hobs yourselves?" I asked.

Niella shook her head. "We've been too busy to leave our spot. But a man came through early this morning passing out flyers, and I heard someone say the artist was going to sell out fast."

Great. Just great. The last thing we need are any more evil elves scurrying around Charleston. "All right," I said with a sigh. "Where did you say the booth was?"

Niella gave me directions, and I maneuvered through the holiday crowds. The City Market is always busy, but so many tourists had come to shop for the holidays that the aisles were shoulder-to-shoulder.

Even with the likelihood of a new kind of killer gremlin to deal with, I couldn't help taking in a deep breath and enjoying the Market for a moment. I could smell fresh pecan-flavored coffee, hot cinnamon buns, steaming apple cider, and warm roasted peanuts. Holiday music played from speakers overhead and the vendors' tables were heaped with beautiful things to eat, buy, and give.

I reminded myself that I had an errand, and dove back into the crowd. But when I reached the booth, everything was gone. "Do you know anything about the person who set up here today?" I asked the merchant in the next stall.

She was a plump lady selling embroidered table linens from Eastern Europe. "Sorry. Never saw the man before today. I'm not sure how he got permission to be in the booth—it's been McCartney's Art Prints for as long as I've had a stall here."

I remembered the art vendor who was normally in the space. The other merchant brought up a good point—prime stalls were prized and hard to come by. Once an artist or business owner snagged a good spot, he or she didn't let it go. I suspected that subletting your space to other people was probably against the rules. That made the whole thing even stranger.

Since my magic lets me read the strong emotions and magic of objects, I'm very attuned to the mood of physical places. Certain locations resonate so strongly with me that I can pick up on the vibes through the soles of my shoes. That's one of many reasons I don't tour battlefields. I usually enjoy the City Market because of its resonance, which is overwhelmingly positive. Most people who come here are happy.

That's why I was puzzled when I stepped into the empty stall and felt very different energy than what I picked up in the rest of the market. The energy in the booth swirled with anger, vindictiveness, and dark, wild magic. Whoever the man was with the Hearth Hob figures, he was barely in control of himself, a loose cannon ready to blow. I didn't know whether his little statues had anything to do with the redcaps or not, and I couldn't tell whether he was the danger or the hob statues were malicious themselves. But Mrs. Teller was right about the danger. I just didn't know what to do about it.

Just then, my phone buzzed. "Hey Cassidy, did you forget about going over to the Museum? Alistair just called wondering where you were."

I rolled my eyes. "Yikes. I forgot. Can you let him know I'll be over as fast as I can get there? And give him my apologies, please."

Teag chuckled. "Already did. So you'd better get going."

I was glad the day was cool by the time I speed walked over to the Museum. Alistair McKinnon is a good friend and a valuable professional contact. I knew he would forgive me for being late, but it's not something I like to make a habit of doing. I jogged up the stairs to the Lowcountry Museum, waved at the receptionist who knew me, and never broke stride until I got to Alistair's office.

"I'm sorry I'm late," I puffed as Alistair opened the door.

He shrugged. "No harm done. I just wanted to walk you through the new exhibit, since Trifles and Folly was kind enough to loan us several pieces to put on display."

Once I caught my breath, I remembered that the Museum would be debuting its *"Charleston Christmas Through the Ages"* collection this coming weekend. Our store and the Museum often helped each other out on appraisals and provenance, as well as loaning items for events like the Christmas program. I had been so deep in my thoughts about redcaps and Hearth Hobs that I couldn't remember what items Trifles and Folly had provided this year.

"I think we've got our strongest collection ever this year," Alistair said as we walked toward the closed doors of the exhibit room. He unlocked the door and flicked on the lights.

"Wow," I said, as a row of Christmas trees with decorations from various time periods lit up. Display cases were filled with all kinds of holiday memorabilia. Fragile blown glass ornaments adorned trees along with decorations of woven straw and sweetgrass, hand-painted porcelain balls, and figures made from felt. Glass cases held examples of period clothing, old fashioned toys, and programs from long-ago Christmas pageants and parades. "You've really outdone yourselves."

Now I remembered the items Trifles and Folly had loaned the museum: A big iron cowbell and a long Dutch wooden horn. "Your items are right here," Alistair said, drawing me over toward one of the cases. The Dutch and the Germans were among Charleston's early settlers, and Alistair wanted displays highlighting all of the immigrant groups who made the city their home.

Sorren had procured the horn, called a *hoornblazen*, and loaned it through Trifles and Folly. Long ago, it had been used to send messages across the Alps in the holiday season. I wondered after all the centuries and all the places he had lived what kind of holiday celebration Sorren preferred. The cow bell was featured in parades in certain parts of Germany.

"They're something different people don't think about being part of Christmas traditions," Alistair said, jolting me out of my thoughts.

I spotted a strange figure on the other side of the room, and startled. Alistair noticed my reaction. "Ah, I see you've noticed Krampus. He's part of our 'Dark Side of Christmas' display." Alistair led the way. I hung back, reaching out with my senses to determine whether or not the exhibit was likely to knock me flat with a strong vision. I tamped down on my gift and decided that I needed to take a better look.

My control is getting better; the displays don't usually throw me into a vision or overwhelm my emotions the way they used to. I felt strengthened from all the positive, happy energy that practically radiated from the rest of the holiday display. But as I moved toward the Dark Side part of the exhibit, it felt as if a shadow fell across my mood.

"This was part of Christmas?" I asked, staring at a man-sized costume of a horned creature with a face like a goat skull, and a body covered with dark, shaggy hair. One of the monster's feet was deformed, and the other was a hoof. The hands ended in long, wicked claws. The costume was well made; it looked real.

Alistair chuckled. "Say hello to Krampus," he replied. "Some very strange, very old customs have survived from the Middle Ages in the Austrian Alps and on out into Eastern Europe. Krampus is kind of like Santa Claus's evil twin. Saint Nicholas—the old school Santa—gave gifts to good children. Krampus beat bad children with sticks or carried them off in a sack."

"That's a whole lot worse than getting a lump of coal in your stocking," I said.

"Actually, the idea of a lump of coal comes from the same set of legends. I guess that was getting off easy for a bad child," Alistair answered.

"So someone actually wore a costume like this at Christmas?" That certainly didn't sound merry at all.

Alistair nodded. "They still do, in some parts of Bavaria and Austria. There's a big parade, and men dressed up like Krampus—and the Perchten, who are even uglier—walk through the streets. Some people say it scares off evil spirits, but some say they are the evil spirits." He shrugged. "The cow bell you lent us would have been used in these parades. There are other creatures like this—Buttnmandl that look like walking straw men, Glockler with big elaborate lanterns for heads, and all the way over in Bulgaria, the Kukeri, which resemble the abominable snowman."

Waiting for Santa was starting to look rather tame compared to the alternatives. "Did they actually hold those kinds of parades in Charleston?" I asked.

Alistair laughed. "I rather doubt it. I can't imagine their dour Scottish and English neighbors looking favorably on the practice. But it is a part of the heritage of the people who settled here, so we wanted to represent it."

Redcaps hail from Scotland and England. Alistair's comment jostled my memory. "What do you have in the way of elves, pixies, that sort of thing?" I asked.

Alistair gave me an odd look, but he's used to strange questions from me. "We have a few. I think they're over there." He gave a nod of his head toward another display case, and led the way.

Elves and pixies of every kind sat and crouched on the shelves in the case. Some were obviously old, others looked newly made. Statues, dolls made out of cloth, straw, crystal, wood, resin, and even origami-folded paper stared back at me through the glass. I leaned forward, careful not to touch anything, looking for a figure that looked like the Hearth Hob in the flyer.

"Looking for something in particular?" Alistair asked.

"Just fascinated," I replied, although it was only half of the truth. "Some of these look pretty new."

"The Museum collects pieces from local artists as well as items with historic value," Alistair answered. "We put out a call months ago to the Charleston art community for Christmas-themed art, and bought the ones we considered to be the best."

"You don't happen to have something called a Hearth Hob, do you?" I was pretty sure I would recognize the ugly little statue, but I figured I'd ask, just in case.

Alistair frowned, then shook his head. "Can't say that it rings a bell. Do you recommend we get one?"

"No!" My answer was sharper than I intended. I forced myself to laugh. It sounded fake, even to my ears. "I'm actually relieved. They're a new fad over at the City Market—this year's 'pet rock.' I don't know much about them, but from what I've seen, they wouldn't be up to the Museum's standards."

Alistair nodded sagely. "It's a fine line to walk between nostalgia and kitsch. I'm afraid it's often in the eye of the beholder."

I hadn't noticed the holiday-themed artwork on the exhibit walls before, but now I saw the paintings, tapestries, and photographs. Some of the work I recognized from other art shows; others were unfamiliar. "That's got to be a hard job, picking the 'best' from all the submissions," I said. "I imagine that's hard to do tactfully."

Alistair rolled his eyes. "You can say that again. Artists are passionate about their work and quite dramatic about rejection. We actually had to have one young man physically removed because he was irate."

"Fortunately, we've never had someone get quite that upset when we turned down buying their heirlooms at the store," I said, commiserating.

"It got ugly," Alistair said with a sigh. "I really don't like that kind of confrontation."

None of the pixies or elves on the shelves gave me bad vibes. "Tell me more about the exhibit," I said, knowing that would move Alistair into lecture mode and help me get my mind off the redcap problem. I spent the next fifteen minutes following him from one case or piece of artwork to another as he told me about the donors who loaned the piece or its history. It worked: I found my mood much improved by the time Alistair walked me to the door.

"Don't be a stranger," he said with a smile. "I know your… abilities… make some of our exhibits difficult," he said, careful with his words in case others were listening. "But we're always pleased to see you when you can come."

I was glowing a little with residual Christmas cheer by the time I got to my little blue Mini Cooper in the parking lot. My phone buzzed, and I looked at it, sure Teag was wondering when I was coming back to the office. To my surprise, it was Maggie, our part-time helper. She was off today, so I really hadn't expected to talk to her until tomorrow.

"Cassidy?" Maggie asked. She sounded rattled, worrying me. "I hate to bother you, but could you make time to come over—soon?"

"What's wrong?" I asked. Maggie never seems to have a care in the world. Now, I could hear fear in her voice.

"I'm not sure," Maggie said. "But I think there's a poltergeist loose in my house."

I CALLED TEAG, and let him know that Maggie was having a supernatural emergency. Then I filled him in on the Hearth Hob problem. I still didn't know what I was going up against.

"It's only half an hour until closing," Teag said. "Why don't you grab your things and go make sure Maggie's safe, and I'll be over right after I close up the store to help out. You shouldn't go up against something by yourself."

Much as I hated to delay solving Maggie's problem, Teag was right. "Okay," I said. "I'll see you there. And remind me to tell you about what I found out at the Market and Museum today."

I'm still new learning to use my touch magic for defense. At first, my visions usually knocked me flat on my ass, pulling me in and taking me over. Now, I've got a little better control, although a powerful object can still knock me for a loop. But I learned that I can draw on the magic and memories of an object, and with practice—and more than my share of life-threatening encounters with things that go bump in the night—I worked out some reliable ways to channel my magic to protect myself.

Some of those "weapons," like an old dog collar and a wooden spoon, I carried with me all the time. A few, like an old walking stick that used to belong to Sorren's maker, Alard, I only used when the chips were down. I had a variety of other protective amulets, energy-cleansing gemstones, and handy weapons stashed in a bag in my trunk. Teag had his own set of weapons that worked well with his Weaver magic, and he was a champion martial artist. What we'd been able to dish out had been enough to beat the bad guys. So far.

Maggie lived in a charming bungalow. I was surprised to see her waiting for me on the porch. "Thank goodness you're here!" she exclaimed, running to meet me. Usually, nothing flusters Maggie, but she definitely looked spooked.

"Why are you out here? It's cold!"

Maggie pulled her sweater closer around her. "I didn't want to stay in there another moment by myself. I really think I goofed this time."

I led Maggie over to the porch swing and sat down with her. "How did you goof, and why do you think there's a poltergeist in your house?"

Maggie looked embarrassed. "I was down at the Market this morning looking for Christmas gifts. There was an artist I'd never seen before selling these adorably ugly little elf-things."

"Hearth Hobs," I supplied.

Maggie nodded. "I bought one for myself and brought it home. That's when things started to get strange. I put it on the table, and when I went back, it wasn't there."

"Are you sure you didn't accidentally leave it somewhere else?" I asked. "I do that with my car keys all the time."

"So do I," Maggie admitted. "But I know I left it on the table because I put it down with my purse. When I went back, the purse was right where I left it—but the hob wasn't."

"Was anyone else with you?"

Maggie shook her head. "Nope. Just me. Oh, and Biscuit." I knew Biscuit was Maggie's big yellow cat, so named because that's exactly what she looks like when she curls up.

"Then what?"

"Well I went looking for that darn statue, and all of a sudden, Biscuit let out a god-awful caterwaul and comes streaking out of the living room like her tail was on fire," Maggie said. "Bless my heart, I never heard a sound like that in my life. The next thing I know, Biscuit is under the couch and won't come out for anything."

Cats and dogs have long been said to be more attuned to the supernatural. I'd had plenty of examples of that with my own little Maltese dog, Baxter.

"Back up," I said, remembering something important. "You bought the hob from the artist himself?"

Maggie nodded. "He was an odd sort, but then again, he's an artist," she said with a shrug. "The workmanship was nice, all hand-made and hand-painted. But he seemed jumpy," Maggie added. "Not very friendly."

"Did you get his name?"

"No. I didn't think to—"

Just then, there was a huge crash inside Maggie's house. Her face paled. "Come on," I said, grabbing her by the hand. "Let's go take care of your 'poltergeist.'"

I let my athame slip down my sleeve into my right hand, and gave a jangle to the dog collar on my left wrist. The ghost of a big, solid Golden Retriever materialized beside me, my old dog Bo. Maggie took Bo's ghost in stride and grabbed a rake from the porch. She opened the door, and a butter-colored streak tore past us as Biscuit made her escape.

Something moved past me in a blur. I wheeled, but it was gone. Another crash came from elsewhere in the house. The sound of faint, demented laughter carried down the hall. I heard the *scritch-scritch* of claws on the hardwood floor, and caught a glimpse of something gray and white. Bo lowered his ghostly head, and his hackles raised. A low warning growl rumbled, and then he sprang into action.

The crazed laughter became a yelp of panic. Bo was barking like he meant to rip that hob to shreds, and the hob seemed to believe it. I was ready when I heard Bo bounding back toward the hallway, and sent a blast of cold white energy from my athame across the doorway. I knew the magic wouldn't hurt Bo, but it packed a wallop on anything solid.

Lucky shot. I caught the hob and knocked him down the hallway like a bowling ball. Bo sprang after him, growling and snapping his teeth. The hob squealed and dashed off, heading back our way. I got in another blast from my athame, and this time, the energy picked the hob up and threw him down the hallway.

Maggie wielded her rake like a pro, slamming the hob to the floor. Her jaw was set, and her eyes flashed. Bo came leaping down the hall-way, sailed through the air and pounced on top of the rake, still growl-ing. I thought I heard an *oof* from the hob as Bo landed. In life, Bo weighed over ninety pounds. I don't know what that translates to as a ghost, but I've seen him take a bite out of more than one monster during a fight.

The hob decided to fight his way out. Maggie was using both hands to hold him down with the rake. Bo lunged toward the trapped hob, slapping at him with his big paws. I heard the sound of plastic splitting and Maggie wrestled with the rake handle to keep the hob contained.

Behind me, the door to the porch slammed open. Biscuit streaked into the hallway one step ahead of Teag. Biscuit took one look at Bo's ghost and rose a foot straight up into the air, coming down—claws out —onto the hob as he finally tore free of the rake. Bo sprang toward the hob, which was coincidentally also toward Biscuit. The cat's hackles had risen enough to make him look like a puffer fish. Biscuit howled and took off, freeing the hob from its claws just in time for the little monster to be tackled by Bo, which sent him sprawling.

I heard the swish of cloth and a fine silvery metal net settled over the hob. In the next instant, a solid wooden fighting staff came down with a *thud* on the hob's head. That stunned the hob, but didn't completely knock him out. Everyone froze.

"What the hell is going on?" Teag asked. He looked at the hob, and then at Maggie, who looked scary in her own right, hair askew, eyes wide and holding the ruined rake like a weapon. Bo wagged happily to see Teag, then sat down, gave me a doggy grin, and vanished.

"Ask that *thing*," Maggie said, giving the captured hob a poke with her rake. "I'm afraid to go see how much damage he's caused!"

"It's one of the Hearth Hob figures I told you about, from the Market," I said.

Teag looked at the wriggling hob and back to me. "You didn't tell me they were alive."

"They aren't supposed to be," I replied.

Teag pinned the hob with his staff as a precaution and leaned down for a better look. "Ugly little bastard." The hob had a head that was too big for its body, with a shock of white hair that stood straight up. His naked body was gnarled, with a pot belly and oversized hands and feet that ended in sharp claws. The mouth was filled with pointed teeth, and the hob's eyes were red as blood. It squealed in anger at being restrained, and Teag thumped it again with his staff.

"I'm guessing that it really is a hobgoblin," I said. "I've heard of them, but never thought I'd end up fighting one."

"The real question is why was someone pretending to be an artist selling statues that turn into hobgoblins?" Teag asked.

"What are you going to do with him?" Maggie asked. She's been around us long enough to have figured out our real role as supernatural vigilantes on her own, and she's cool with it; in fact, she insists on helping out behind the scenes whenever we need her.

"I need salt," Teag said with a glance toward Maggie, "and the burlap bag that's in my trunk," he added with a look toward me. We went to fetch the items, returning in a couple of minutes.

"Give me the salt." Teag held out his hand, and Maggie handed him a big canister of Morton's. Teag poured a circle of salt around the hob, which began to squeal and thrash with renewed desperation. Then

Teag dumped half the canister right on top the hob. The goblin's skin began to smoke, and it let out an ear-splitting howl.

"Open the bag!" Teag ordered, and I held the stiff burlap bag wide. Teag scooped up the hob in his metal net and dumped the whole thing into the bag.

"Won't he get out? Burlap's not very strong," I asked, looking askance at the sack.

Teag grinned. "I've spelled the cloth and then soaked it in colloidal silver and salt water for good measure. And there's an iron cage in the trunk that I made to hold a redcap if we caught one. He's not going anywhere. We'll let Sorren figure out what to do with him."

Now that the fighting was over, Maggie sagged against the wall. "That was a lot more excitement than I bargained for," she said. She took a deep breath and rallied. "How about some sweet tea? I was just about to put cookies into the oven before all hell broke loose. Why don't you stash that nasty hob in the cage and come into the kitchen?"

I knew Maggie was worried about what the hob might have damaged. "Would you like me to have a look around and see whether anything's broken?" I asked.

Maggie looked relieved that I had guessed her thoughts. "Thank you, Cassidy. I was thinking I'd have to add a shot of bourbon to my tea before I worked up the nerve to do that myself."

I had only been to Maggie's house a couple of times, but the bungalow wasn't big, so it was easy to find my way around. The hob had been busy. Several decorative plates had been thrown from their place on the wall and lay smashed in the middle of the dining room. Books were scattered across the floor of the guest bedroom, and the bookshelf was lying face down. That was probably the crash we heard. Any knick-knacks on the shelves were likely broken, but the shelves themselves and the books would probably be fine.

The hob seemed to have been bent on destruction just to cause havoc. Small items had been thrown from tabletops and shelves. The bathroom mirror was broken, and the carpet runner in the hallway had deep gouges in it that weren't caused by Biscuit's claws. I hoped

Maggie wouldn't be too upset. I found a broom and dustpan and cleaned up the broken pieces.

"Could have been worse," she said when I told her the news. "I'm okay and Biscuit's all right. Neither you nor Teag got hurt. I needed to clean out some clutter anyhow."

"Now what?" Teag asked. "Maggie wasn't the only person who bought a hob at the Market. What happens when other people's goblin statues come to life and wreck the house?"

Good question. Maggie knew to call us because of the store. Most people thought we just ran an antique store, so they wouldn't be calling for goblin extermination. "It would help if we knew who the artist was, but Maggie didn't get his name," I replied.

"Someone at the Market must have a name on the vendor booth rental," Teag said. "I bet Mrs. Teller could find out for me."

"Do you think the hobs are connected to the redcaps?" I asked.

Teag shrugged. "I hope not, but it seems like too much of a coincidence to dismiss. We'll have to assume they're connected until we find out otherwise. Maybe Sorren will know something."

Maggie put out some tuna in Biscuit's bowl. The yellow cat slunk into the kitchen with her ears flattened against her head, hyper-alert for an attack. "You know, Biscuit didn't like that statue from the moment I brought it in the house," Maggie said. "Hissed at it before I even took it out of the bag."

"BIG SURPRISE—OUR Hearth Hob vendor was a squatter," Teag announced when I arrived at the store the next day. "Turns out the merchant who has a lease on that stall was suddenly taken ill, and the hob guy showed up and took over."

"Mighty convenient, wouldn't you say?" Working with Sorren and the Alliance has taught me that there aren't many true coincidences when magic and the supernatural are concerned.

"Yeah," Teag replied, sarcasm heavy in his tone. "But the security cameras did get these shots," he added and turned his laptop around for me to see a photo of a license plate and another picture of a man's face. "I got a match on the plates. They're registered to a guy named Brian Kessler."

I didn't ask exactly how Teag had gotten the security camera pictures or managed to trace a license plate. His hacking skills—enhanced by magic—are world-class. "The name doesn't ring a bell," I replied.

"I'd never heard of him either," Teag said. "But I did a little digging. He's an artist. He's been in a few regional shows, gotten some installations at small, local galleries, done some street sales. No arrest record. But get this—his soon-to-be-ex wife has a restraining order out on him." Obviously, some of his information came from hacking into the police system.

"So he's got a bad temper," I said, and the comment triggered a memory. "You know, Alistair said that there was an artist whose work wasn't accepted for the Christmas exhibit who pitched a fit about being rejected. I wonder if it's Kessler?"

"Even if it was, I'm not sure how it connects to our redcap and hob problem," Teag replied. "That's the other thing I found out. There have been two more people reported missing, and about a dozen complaints of wild animals loose in people's homes."

"Wild animals?" I mused. "You think that's how people are explaining the hobs?"

Teag nodded. "It makes sense—if you don't believe in the supernatural. Squirrels, raccoons, feral cats—they could all make a mess, knock things over and move really fast."

"Go back to Kessler," I said. "If he's the one who gave Alistair problems, then he might have been in the Christmas exhibit before it opened. Alistair showed me the Dark Side of Christmas display—it's all about monsters from old legends who punish bad children and cause havoc."

"You think it gave Kessler ideas?" Teag asked. "That might explain the ugly hob statues—but not their ability to come alive. To do that—and summon the redcaps—Kessler would need some kind of magic."

"See what you can come up with," I said, "and I'll call Alistair and get the name of his problem artist. It's the only connection we've got, and I have the feeling that the closer we get to Christmas, the worse this is going to get unless we do something about it."

Teag stayed up front with his computer while I went back to the office to call Alistair. A few minutes later, I rejoined Teag. So far, the morning had been slow for customers, and Maggie was off, so we still had the shop to ourselves.

"Alistair confirmed it; Kessler's the guy who caused problems at the museum. And he also confirmed that Kessler had access to the exhibit before it opened, which would have included the Dark Side of Christmas display," I reported. "And one more thing—someone broke into the museum last night. The only thing missing was the Krampus costume."

"Since we're not busy, why don't I go see what I can research about this guy while you cover the front?" Teag suggested. "We might want to pay a call on his studio."

I nodded. "That works for me."

Not long after Teag went into the back, the first wave of tourists hit. Charleston draws a big vacation crowd, and clearly, some people had arrived without bringing Christmas presents with them because they were in the mood to shop. I helped them look at estate jewelry and old silver picture frames, delicate antique teacups, and pretty cut glass vases. It looked like a good day for the bottom line.

The last of the tourists was leaving when Alicia Peters walked in. "Hi, Cassidy! Do you still have that lapis lazuli jewelry I asked you to hold for me?"

"Sure thing. Let me get it out of the safe." I brought out a beautiful gemstone and silver necklace, ring, and bracelet. "I really love this set," I said, setting it on the counter. "The blue is so intense."

Alicia nodded. "Pretty, and practical too. Especially with *Rauhnachte* coming up."

"*Rauhnachte*?" That was a word I hadn't heard before.

"It goes by a lot of different names," Alicia replied. "Smoke Nights, Twelfth Night, *Glockelnacht*—all pretty much the same thing. Twelve days around the Winter Solstice where the veil between our world and the next is especially thin. It's especially good for divination, but it's also when ghosts get lively. And it's prime for demons to cross over."

Alicia has worked with Teag, Sorren, and me before on Alliance cases. She's a very talented spirit medium, so when she talks about ghosts, I listen.

"So you want the necklace for protection, or to amplify your abilities?" I asked. I'm still new at using my touch magic, so I have a lot to learn from other people with supernatural talents.

"A little of both," Alicia replied. "*Rauhnachte* is a very old custom. Maybe even from before the Middle Ages. Back in the day, in parts of Germany, people dressed up like monsters and waved cow bells around to scare away the demons."

"You mean like Krampus?"

Alicia nodded. "You've heard of him? He was just one of the monsters. There are others."

"What's so special about the Solstice?" I asked. "And isn't that tomorrow?"

She shrugged. "Yes, the Solstice is tomorrow. As for why it's special, it's the shortest day of the year—people have always sensed stronger supernatural power then. And it's also when the 'dead days' fall."

"I thought Day of the Dead was in October?"

"Completely different thing," Alicia said with a laugh. "A long time ago, they changed the calendar to be based on the sun, not the moon. There's an eleven day—twelve night—difference between the two. Some people say that those days exist 'outside of time' now and that they're prime season for things from the other side to come through."

"You didn't just pick out this jewelry because you like blue," I said.

"Nope. Shelly says we're in for a worse than usual *Rauhnachte*, and you know she's rarely wrong." Our mutual friend Shelly was a wicked-good clairvoyant.

"Do you think the *Rauhnachte* could have started early?" I asked as

I rang up Alicia's purchase. "We're sure that something—or someone —brought redcaps through, and people are going missing."

"I heard. And I don't know," She admitted. "But in the old days, people were afraid to walk around after dark because the demons would carry them away during the Smoke Nights. Maybe someone's been reading up on old myths."

Alicia paid me for the necklace and left, after we agreed to get together for lunch the next week. Half a dozen more tourists came in, and I was so busy helping them with their purchases that the next hour flew. By the time I looked up, it was almost five and nearly dark outside.

That's when the knight walked in.

"You are the demon fighters, are you not?" The man had a heavy German accent. He was a few inches over six feet tall and broad-shouldered, with black hair and a trimmed black beard. I could tell from the way he held himself that he had a military background. The long brown coat he wore seemed out of place in Charleston, but then again, so did the chain maille I saw beneath a tunic that looked like a knight's tabard.

"This is an antique shop," I replied.

He gave me a look. "This is Sorren's place. We are acquainted. I am Knight Ruprecht. I have come here because this is where the demons will be. Krampus is coming. So I am here."

SOME NIGHTS, THE best you can do is just order pizza and roll with whatever comes.

An hour later, there was an empty pizza box from Jocko's on the counter, and a war council of mortals and immortals seated around the break room table. Sorren and Teag were there, as well as Alicia. Knight Ruprecht sat stiffly at one end of the table. Father Anne sat next to him. She's a member of the secret St. Expeditus Society, a group of priests who kick demon ass, and she's good in a fight.

Chuck Pettis was next to her. I could hear him ticking from across the room. Chuck's superstitious and he wears dozens of wind-up watches sewn to the inside of his jacket. He's a retired special ops guy whose unit went after supernatural threats, so he's cool with our whole Alliance connection. The last member of the team was Rowan, a witch who had helped us out against some bad nasties not long ago.

"I think we've found where Brian Kessler may be holed up," Teag said. "I pieced together his movements based on his license plate, and everything triangulates right around the old Saint Adalgar's church."

"That burned down ten years ago," Father Anne said. "It wasn't rebuilt because the neighborhood had become mostly industrial."

Teag nodded. "The section where the old church is has a lot of vacant buildings. It's not the best part of town. Perfect place for someone to set up a studio if they didn't want to be bothered. I've hacked into a security camera on a business across the street that shows the parking lot. His car comes and goes."

"Teag asked my coven to sense the energy of the area near the old church," Rowan said. "There's a lot of electromagnetic noise in that area from overhead wires and some factories nearby. Handy for covering up magic, unless you have a reason to look and know what to look for. Someone's been meddling with some very dark energy, and what they lack in skill, they make up for in brute force."

"Do you think Kessler is working alone, or does he have a witch helping him?" I asked.

"The kind of magic we picked up on felt more like untrained, raw talent," Rowan replied. "The kind that's fueled more by rage than training."

"That sounds like Kessler," I said. "We already know he's got anger management issues."

"Saint Adalgar's is an old church," Teag put in. "It dates back to the early eighteen hundreds, but it wasn't considered architecturally important enough to restore after the fire. Here's the thing—it was built on land that was a potter's field a century earlier, the place they buried pirates."

"That would help an untrained witch with bad intentions," Rowan replied. "Those damned souls would gravitate toward the anger and malice in the magic, boosting his power. With enough raw talent, he might even be able to control them."

"Could he bind those spirits to statues?" I asked. "Like the Hearth Hobs? Because they were just statues in the marketplace, but they came alive once people got them home."

"Maybe," Rowan said. "It would be difficult. But it's possible."

"How is a guy like Kessler managing that kind of magic?" Father Anne leaned forward. "Did he show any signs of power before this?"

"Actually yes, in hindsight," Teag replied. "One of those cases where no one sees what they're not looking for. He's been fascinated with occult themes in his art for a while, but in the last six months, it's become more of an obsession. Some of the information I found suggested that it cost him gallery showings and lost him commissions —like the one for the Museum. Take a look." He turned his laptop around so the rest of us could see the screen.

The slideshow of images was a descent into madness. Monsters haunted a shadow city that looked like Charleston distorted by nightmares. Twisted faces stared back at us, barely human. I felt a chill run down my spine as I realized that the shadow creatures in some of the paintings resembled redcaps and hobs.

"Once I tracked him down, I hacked his credit card," Teag admitted. Chuck looked amused; Father Anne raised a questioning eyebrow. "He's been buying books on witchcraft—spellbooks, grimoires, and that sort of thing—from used bookshops all over the country. I'm sure some of them are total bunk—"

"You might be surprised," Rowan said. "In among the utter nonsense, it's not uncommon to find truly dangerous information. Like leaving razorblades in a toy box."

"He's got all the earmarks of a supernatural terrorist," Chuck spoke up. "Just like the kind we used to profile. I bet if you could find his wife and get her to talk to you, she'd tell you that he changed over time, got a lot worse. Started pulling in on himself, cut off everyone else. Probably always a bit paranoid, the kind that blames everyone else for his problems. Dark magic would make all that worse. People don't realize that the taint starts in the spellbooks. They're like magical poison."

"The Solstice is tomorrow," Alicia said. "And from everything you've found, it sounds like Kessler wants to bring the Smoke Nights down on Charleston full-force with real monsters. What are we going to do about it?"

"That's why I'm here." Everyone turned to look at Knight Ruprecht. "I hunt the Krampus and his horde. When *Rauhnachte* comes, I fight them." His English was stilted, and the German accent made me listen carefully. I shared a glance with Teag that said we were on the same wavelength. *This guy is either totally nuts, or there's more to him than meets the eye.*

"I knew of Knight Ruprecht back in Belgium—when I was mortal," Sorren said. "Back then, the Smoke Nights were common— and feared. We've worked together on occasion since then."

A faint smile touched the knight's stern mouth. "Many times, my friend." Ruprecht turned to the rest of us. "I swore a vow, long ago, pledging my sword against Krampus. God heard my vow and made me an immortal warrior. Once, I fought for the Church, and then for Kings. Now, I fight because it is the right thing to do."

"But Krampus keeps coming back," Teag replied.

Ruprecht nodded. "And so do I. He and his horde can't be permanently destroyed, and neither can I. I win, and push him back through the veil. He wins, and I wait to fight again. And on it goes."

"You fight Krampus and his horde by yourself?" Rowan asked skeptically.

Ruprecht looked embarrassed. "When I must," he replied. "The odds improve with help."

"Just to be clear about this, you and Sorren might be immortal, but the rest of us aren't," Chuck snapped. "So factor that into your plan. I've got better things to do than get killed by some goat-headed goon and a bunch of elves."

"Working together, we have the skills to stop Krampus and hold back more of his horde from coming through," Sorren said.

"What about the redcaps and hobs?" I asked.

"The ones that are already here, we'll deal with. Stop Krampus, and we keep more from crossing the veil," Sorren replied. The thought of more of those evil elves made my blood run cold.

"Be quick about it," Father Anne advised. "Solstice is tomorrow—and the sun sets early."

~

St. Adalgar's stone walls were mostly intact. The holes where stained glass windows had been were like a skull's empty eye sockets. A rickety chain link fence surrounded the ruin, rusted and twisted from long neglect. We had studied the floorplans Teag had found. The sanctuary and narthex were roofless, but the back part of the building was still in pretty good shape.

"When they deconsecrated the church after the fire, they forgot about the effect on the old potters' field," Father Anne murmured as we approached the grounds. "The pirates were buried in unhallowed ground. The church built on top of the graves was consecrated, and that kept the ghosts at bay. But now—"

"Now there's nothing holding the ghosts back," I supplied.

She nodded. "Bingo."

"Can you re-consecrate it and seal the ghosts back up?"

"Not quickly. Not in time to stop Krampus. After we win this, I'll bring it up to the St. Expeditus Society," she replied.

We moved through the ruined church in silence. Knight Ruprecht went first, a gleaming sword in his hands. He had left behind his drab coat and now looked the part of a real knight in his tabard and maille.

Rowan was second, with Father Anne, Teag, and me next. Chuck and Sorren brought up the rear, on guard for an attack from behind. Alicia Peters stayed outside with the rest of Rowan's coven. The witches would raise a magical perimeter to deflect mortal interest in the battle and help contain anything Kessler brought across from the other side. Alicia's job was to keep an eye on the ghosts and warn the witches if an attack came from that direction. It was the best plan we could come up with on one day's notice. I just hoped it would be enough.

The stone walls jutted up toward the night sky like ancient ruins. Their energy felt all wrong. My touch magic can pick up on old buildings if there's enough memories or magic to resonate. Normally, old churches feel peaceful to me, the collective effect of people coming together in gratitude and worship. St. Adalgar's had a dark, brooding feel as if it knew it had lost its special status and resented it. I saw no movement in the shadows, but I couldn't shake the sense that we were being watched.

We came ready for a fight. Knight Ruprecht had his sword in one hand and a deadly-looking morning star club in the other. Sorren had swords too, and his immortal strength and speed made him formidable even without weapons. Teag has his fighting staff and a set of daggers plus a messenger bag full of extra weapons. I had no idea what Rowan had with her, or if her magic was enough by itself. Father Anne has a blessed boline knife, and she was good at hand-to-hand combat. I had my athame and dog collar, and my own bag of extra surprises, along with an old walking stick. Chuck looked like he belonged in a SWAT team, with a bandolier of EMF grenades, knives and who-knew-what along with several large guns and a pair of night-vision goggles. None of us was overconfident. We knew that even with all our weapons, things could still go terribly wrong.

"Has Krampus come across from beyond yet?" I asked Ruprecht.

"Not yet. But soon. I feel the power building," the knight replied. After centuries of fighting each other, I wondered if that meant that Krampus would know Ruprecht was waiting for him. So much for the element of surprise.

Ruprecht signaled us when we came to a doorway to a part of the old church that was still largely undamaged. We readied our weapons, and Ruprecht threw open the door.

Banks of lit candles lit the stone-walled room, casting the whole space in a fiery glow. A pentacle had been drawn in the center of the floor, and inside it stood a monstrous figure that towered at least seven feet tall. Even in silhouette, I recognized Krampus.

We tensed, readying our weapons, but the figure remained motionless. Ruprecht moved forward, then stopped. "Not him," the knight said. "Just a statue."

Even from where I stood, I could feel malevolence radiating from the figure. "Not a statue," Rowan said quietly. "A focal point. It's the gateway he's used to bring the other monsters through."

"If we destroy the statue, does that shut down the gateway?" I asked, doubting it could be that simple.

Just then, the redcaps attacked.

The redcaps swarmed down the walls like spiders, clinging to the rough stone. At least a dozen of them came at us, howling in rage.

I shook the collar on my left wrist, and Bo's ghost materialized. He dove into the fray, pouncing on the malicious pixies with the same vigor he once used to chase squirrels. Claws tore into my sleeve, and I kicked a redcap away, leveling my athame and calling to the magic and memories it contained. A cone of cold white force blasted from the wooden handle, bowling over a whole row of redcaps.

I cried out in pain as sharp teeth gashed my shoulder, and struggled to shake free of a redcap that had jumped onto my back. Father Anne wheeled, bringing down her boline knife and impaling the redcap's body on its razor-sharp blade. The creature let go of me, thrashing to free itself from the knife. Father Anne brought her Doc Marten boot down on the redcap's feet and ripped upward with the knife, cleaving his body in two.

I was spattered with blood—the redcap's and my own. The bite hurt like hell. Peeved, I pulled out the old walking stick, concentrated my magic and pulled hard on the resonance of Alard, Sorren's maker. Fire streamed from the point of the walking stick, and I moved back and forth as if it were a flamethrower, incinerating three or four of the killer pixies before they could get out of the way.

I heard a metallic zing, and saw a flash of silver. Teag snapped a whip of coiled steel, and its wicked edges sliced the head right off one of the redcap's shoulders. In the next instant, Teag scythed his fighting stave, clubbing two of the redcaps out of the way.

"Fire in the hole!" Chuck yelled. We shielded our eyes, and in the next instant, a brilliant light flared as one of his EMF grenades exploded. I don't pretend to understand exactly how they work, but somehow their electro-magnetic frequency messes with ghosts. The blast stunned the redcaps, and I wondered if Father Anne was right about Kessler using the ghosts of long-dead pirates to animate the creatures.

There would be time to argue about it later. Right now, we seized the moment. Sorren and Ruprecht set about themselves with their swords, cutting down all of the redcaps near them. I burned up two more with another blast from the walking stick, while Teag took out the last three. The room smelled of blood and scorched flesh.

Rowan had poured a circle of salt around the Krampus statue, and while the rest of us fought, she kept a wary eye on the figure in the pentacle, using her magic to repel any redcaps that came close as if they had walked into a forcefield. "We're running out of time," she warned. "Krampus is getting closer to the threshold, and he's got a lot of friends with him."

I caught a glimpse of motion out of the corner of my eye, just before something caught me in the shins and knocked me to the ground. A wave of hobs flooded through the door, claws scraping on the stone floor, teeth gnashing.

They overwhelmed me before I could get to my feet. I was at the wrong angle to shoot fire without blasting one of my allies. Bo's ghost lunged at the hobs, tearing them free and throwing them across the room with a shake of his head. Claws scratched me and teeth tried to bite through my jeans and leather jacket, which wouldn't hold them off for long. I brought up my athame and willed the power to fan out flat instead of shooting forward, something I had never done before. It worked, and the hobs tumbled away, blasted loose.

Chuck backed himself into a corner, threw a metal net on the floor and pulled a long cattle prod out of his rucksack. He fired up the prod, put the tip close to the net, and sent jolts of electricity through the woven metal. Chuck didn't need to see the hobs to fry them; if they came close to the net, they got zapped.

Sorren's vampire speed made him just as fast as the hobs, but they were too short to fight with his sword, so he kicked and threw them hard enough to crack the stone walls when they hit. Teag wielded his staff like a golf club, swinging quickly enough that he was guaranteed to hit an attacker even if he couldn't see them coming. Ruprecht swung his morning star just above ground level, impaling the hobs on its sharp iron points or slamming them into the stone.

Rowan was chanting, and, I could see sweat breaking out on her face. She couldn't stop Krampus and his horde from coming through, but she was using all of her magic to make it as difficult as possible for him until we had fought clear of the hobs and redcaps.

A bolt of red fire streaked across the room, slicing through Rowan's wardings and striking her between the shoulders. She screamed with pain and collapsed. I pivoted and dove, coming up between Rowan and the surviving hobs and fanned out the athame's cold power again, trying to keep the goblins away from her.

A red streak of fire crackled toward me. Sorren moved in a blur, jerking me out of the way. The fire hit the stone where I had been seconds before. I looked up to see a tall creature covered with dark, shaggy fur framed in the far doorway. It had a goat-skull face and long, twisting horns, and one leg ended in a hoof instead of a foot. Scared as I was, I recognized the stolen Krampus costume from the museum and figured we had found Brian Kessler.

Teag's urumi whip flashed toward Kessler, ripping a hole in the costume and taking a strip of the skin beneath. Kessler yelped in pain and sent another blast of red fire toward Teag. Rowan had gotten to her knees, and she thrust out one arm, sending a shimmer through the air that looked like heat rising from asphalt on a hot day. The shimmer absorbed Kessler's fire, giving Teag the chance to dive out of the way.

"It's too late to stop me," Kessler taunted. As long as he stayed in the doorway, we could only come at him head-on. "Krampus is coming, and he won't be alone. The redcaps and hobs were just a warm-up for the real show. After tonight, this city will never be the same."

Teag sent his coiled steel whip flicking toward Kessler again, tearing another hole in his costume, then diving and rolling before

Kessler could hit him with the red fire. I had crawled into the shadows, and took aim with my walking stick, returning fire with fire, and dodging behind the statue in the center of the room.

Buzz-zap. Kessler pitched forward, twitching. Chuck had worked his way along the wall, and now he stood in a firing position, taser still in his hand. We swiveled to look at him.

"What?" Chuck challenged. "It shouldn't kill him unless he's got a weak heart. Damn sight better than letting him barbecue the rest of you."

Teag grabbed some rope from his bag, and I knew he had woven spelled strands and magic into the cord to strengthen it against a supernatural foe. He bound Kessler's wrists and gagged him, then sat him up next to the doorway.

"We've got trouble!" Rowan yelled. I turned just as the monster stepped out of the gateway that had appeared in front of the statue.

The real Krampus was terrifying. There was no mistaking him for someone in a fur suit. He stood at least eight feet tall, and his twisted horns made him even taller. His dark fur was matted with blood, and more blood darkened the mouth of his skull-face. His body was solidly muscled like a wild animal. Long claws extended from his arms, and from the single human foot. The hoof on the other leg looked sharp. He smelled like spoiled meat. A long, pointed red tongue lolled from his deaths-head grimace, and his eyes glowed hellish red.

Ruprecht charged from the left, his sword leveled at shoulder-height, meant to drive home a killing blow. Sorren attacked from the right, swords moving in a blur backed with vampire strength. Rowan raised a shimmering wall in front of Krampus, blocking his forward movement. Teag came at the creature from the back, swinging his staff with enough force to crack a skull.

Krampus lurched forward, shattering Rowan's warding. Ruprecht's sword was angled for where the monster's heart should be, but the creature turned, ducking his head and using his sharp, curled antlers to twist the blade to the side, nearly wrenching it out of Ruprecht's hands as he forced the knight to stumble.

Sorren sank one sword deep into Krampus's side, while the other sword slashed bone-deep on the monster's arm. Krampus howled in rage, shaking Ruprecht's sword free, and wheeled to face Sorren, turning so quickly his sharp horns cut deep into Sorren's shoulder.

With his right hand, Krampus grabbed Teag's staff, halting its motion and hurling Teag toward the other side of the room, where he landed with a thud and lay still. I came up firing, pouring a stream of fire from my walking stick fueled by my concern for Teag and pure, primal terror.

The fire hit Krampus in the chest, and the air stank of burning hair as his thick pelt caught fire. Krampus howled, turning to fix me with a glare from those hideous, red eyes. I stood my ground, pouring my energy into the walking stick, drawing from the magic and memories of its last owner. I wouldn't last long, but for the moment, it was keeping him at bay.

Chuck opened fire. The shots were deafening in the stone-walled room. Round after round from the huge gun in Chuck's hands pumped into Krampus, each one forcing him back half a step, tearing into his body. Blood flowed from a dozen wounds, but Krampus remained standing, and a hideous leer twisted his thin lips.

My fiery torrent sputtered out, and I staggered back, spent. The battle was far from over, but I needed to recharge before I could use my magic again. The others would have to hold him off until I got my breath.

Krampus still stood in the gateway, but I could see shadows behind him, creatures eager to cross into our world and feast on blood. We had to keep Krampus from moving fully through the threshold, or we stood no chance of winning against his demon horde.

Ruprecht came at Krampus again; his sword pitted against the creature's sinewy arms and sharp claws. Krampus blocked the blade with one arm, heedless of how deeply the edge bit into his skin or how the blood ran freely from the deep wound. He swung his other arm, and sharp claws raked along the knight's shoulder and arm in bloody furrows. None of the rest of us could get in a strike without endangering Sorren and the others. Father Anne shifted position, trying to get close enough to strike at Krampus with her blessed blade, but the flurry of swords and flash of claws and horns kept her back.

Rowan said that the statue was the focus. "Chuck! Go for the statue!" Chuck turned his gun on the hulking figure just behind Krampus, Kessler's statue of the monster. Chuck's bullets pinged off the plaster, sending shards into the air. Holes pock-marked the statue's torso, and one arm crumbled away.

Rowan had gotten to her feet, and I guessed from her chanting and the way she wove her hands through the air that she was placing invisible impediments to keep Krampus trapped on the threshold. I dodged back and forth, looking for an opening to do something useful.

Kessler had regained his senses and managed to push himself up to stand, even though his wrists were bound. The gag muted his shrieks of protest, as the assault began in earnest on the monster he had worked so hard to call into the world. He ran forward, trying to body block Ruprecht, who shouldered him aside. Bo's ghost lunged for him, and Kessler stumbled toward Krampus.

What if the statue is just the gateway—and Kessler is the focus?

Sorren plunged toward Krampus, ramming both swords deep into the creature's belly. Teag had regained his feet, and swung his staff against the monster's knees. Krampus doubled over, and Ruprecht brought his sword down in a two-handed grip aiming for its neck.

I leveled my athame, hoping I had one more good blast in me, and I loosed a cone of cold power just as Kessler careened between me and Krampus.

The white blast of energy caught Kessler in the chest, throwing him backward as if he'd been hit by a truck—right onto the points of Krampus's lowered horns.

Kessler screamed as the horns skewered him, protruding from his belly, poking right through his stolen monster costume. He wriggled like a gigged frog, but the long, twisted horns made it impossible for him to free himself.

Chuck tossed something toward the statue from behind. "Fire in the hole!" he shouted, turning and covering his ears.

Father Anne dove forward, sinking her boline knife into Krampus's back as Ruprecht's sword severed the monster's head. Kessler sank to the floor, still pinned by the horns to the creature's skull.

The statue blew into a million pieces.

For an instant, it looked as if a black hole hovered in the center of the room where the statue had been. Krampus's body and Kessler's corpse were pulled into the darkness, and in the blink of an eye, they were gone.

We all stood frozen, stunned by the explosion as much as by the sudden end to the fight. My ears were ringing, and I wondered if I would ever hear properly again.

"What the hell was that?" Teag demanded, shaking his head as if to clear water from his ears.

Chuck grinned. "A souped-up M-80, military grade. Figured it would knock that ugly statue off its pedestal, and it did a little more than I hoped." Considering that we were all going to be picking plaster bits out of our skin for days, I regarded Chuck's triumph with mixed emotions.

Rowan was making a slow circle around where the statue had been, still chanting and motioning with her hands. Finally, she stopped and looked back at us. "The gateway is closed," she said. "Whether it was destroying the statue that did it or Kessler's death, there's nothing supernatural about this room anymore."

The floor was littered with plaster chunks. Blood pooled on the stone floor, fortunately, mostly Krampus's and Kessler's. Sorren and Ruprecht had taken the worst of the damage, and I doubted any of the rest of us would still be alive, let alone standing if we were as badly injured as they appeared. I had some gashes to show from the battle, and so did Teag. Rowan looked spent enough to fall down at any moment, and a dark bruise was beginning to color her temple where she had been thrown to the ground. Father Anne was still reeling from the impact of the blast and her shirt was torn and bloody. Chuck was covered with plaster dust and spattered with blood, but as far as I could tell, none of it was his own.

"Ruprecht and I will get rid of any inconvenient evidence," Sorren said. "The rest of you need to treat those wounds before they fester.

I'm certain the claws were tainted." The fact that he and the knight looked like death warmed over went without comment.

"Come on back to my place," I offered. "I've got enough first-aid supplies to patch us all up, and a fresh bottle of bourbon if anyone wants some—for medicinal purposes." I managed a tired grin. "Consider it a holiday toast."

PART IV
BLOODLINES

BLOODLINES

"Cassidy, all I know is, we've got an angry ghost—and it's getting more pissed off every day." Kell Winston ran a hand back through his light brown hair and glanced at us as if he expected an answer, his blue eyes a stark contrast to caramel-tanned skin. "And I'm hoping you and Teag can help me figure out what to do about it."

"Okay," I replied, glancing over at Teag Logan. "Let's see what all the fuss is about."

Kell led us up to the side door of the old mansion near the Battery. I recognized Boyce House, one of Charleston's architectural gems, newly restored to its antebellum glory. Shell-pink stucco covered the walls, making the white trim stand out in bright contrast, even by moonlight. "It's okay," Kell replied to my unspoken question. "The Historical Society gave me a key and permission to be here. After all, they're the ones with the ghost problem."

I nodded. "Then lead on. Let's see if your ghost friend puts on a show tonight." I tried to sound nonchalant, but both Teag and I knew that poltergeists—if that's what this haunting really was—were nothing to be taken lightly. Restless, vengeful spirits could do real damage, even kill. I hoped that we would get a look at the problem, and then come back later without Kell to handle the situation. I trusted Kell, and he knew a little about my magic, but I wasn't ready to let him in on all our secrets just yet.

The door opened onto the side of the wide, covered porch—what Charlestonians call a "piazzo"—and afforded a view of a beautiful, manicured garden that was a showpiece even at night. Inside, electric candles glowed in the windows and lights on timers gave the empty show home a lived-in look.

"You know, I've been dying to get a peek inside since they announced the Boyce House was ready to open." I glanced around, taking in the view.

Teag lifted an eyebrow. "You might want to rephrase that." His dark hair was tucked behind his ears, making him look more like a skater boy grad student than a bad-ass demon fighter.

I gave him a sidelong glance. "Not helping."

"So here's the deal," Kell said as we stood on the porch and he dangled the key in his hand. "We can't take anything out of the house tonight because everything has to be accounted for with the Historic Trust manager. But I can show you where our gear lit up like a Christmas tree when the team went through here with me, and you can let me know if any of the objects tingle your spidey sense. And if you think you find something that's setting off the... occurrences... I'll get permission to remove it so it can be studied, okay?"

Kell's "team" was the crew of SPOOK, Southern Paranormal Observation and Outreach Klub, a group of high-tech ghost hunters trying to document supernatural activity in one of the most haunted cities in North America. We had worked together on several situations, enough that I trusted Kell's judgment and knew he wouldn't bring us on a wild goose chase.

I nodded. "Sounds like a plan to me." What Kell didn't know, and what I couldn't tell him, was that Teag and I had faced down things that were a lot scarier than a bratty socialite ghost, maybe even saved the world a time or two. And when we did our job right, no one was ever the wiser.

I'm Cassidy Kincaide, owner of Trifles and Folly, an antique and curio store in historic, haunted Charleston, South Carolina. The store has been in my family almost since Charleston's founding nearly three hundred and fifty years ago, and it comes with some big secrets. I'm a psychometric, able to read the history and magic of objects by touching them. Teag's my best friend, wingman and assistant store manager—and he's got magic of his own. We're both part of the Alliance, a coalition of mortals and immortals who defend Charleston—and the world—from supernatural threats and dangerous magical items. One other secret—my business partner Sorren is a nearly six-hundred-year-old vampire. Kell knows a little about my psychometry, but what we do is far too dangerous to tell him the rest.

Kell turned the key in the lock and tapped a code into the security keypad. He shut the door behind us and turned the deadbolt. "We went through the house with the full set of instruments. EMF reader, audio recorder, night vision camera—everything. And honestly, if I hadn't seen it for myself, I would have thought it was one of those cheesy TV shows where they fake the 'paranormal activity' to make everything happen at once." He shook his head. "This place has a lot of bad mojo."

"Show us," Teag said.

Kell took a few steps into the foyer. The wide hallway ran from front to back with two rooms opening off both sides and a rear door at the other end. A staircase with a mahogany balustrade sat in the center of the foyer, leading up to the second floor. Family portraits, embroidery samplers, and paintings hung on the walls, along with a huge gold-framed mirror. Antique furniture and decorative items original to the Boyce family lined the hallway and filled the rooms. That meant plenty of options for haunted and tainted objects.

"So we've got this," Kell said, holding up the EMF reader near the sideboard that held a glass hurricane lamp, several silver candlesticks, and the guest book. The scanner was designed to pick up on electromagnetic frequencies that often coincided with spectral activity, and when Kell held it near the sideboard, the full row of red lights lit up, and the device squealed like a cat with its tail under a rocking chair.

"Think we should sign the registry?" Teag teased. The leatherbound guest book looked like it was an antique itself, as did the beautiful onyx fountain pen that laid beside it. Several names were written in dark black ink on the lines of the book, but I was too far away to read them.

A glance in the mirror had me smoothing a stray lock of my strawberry-blonde hair and wincing at the fresh sunburn on my nose. I was about to answer Teag when I caught sight of motion out of the corner of my eye. "Did you see that?" I asked, staring into the big mirror. "I could swear I saw someone on the stairs."

"Maybe you did," Kell replied. "That's where Judah Elliott Boyce, the first owner of the house, fell to his death."

I kept my gaze glued to the mirror for a few moments, but the image never reappeared, and I finally turned away, taking in the rest of the well-appointed foyer. "Impressive," I commented, eyes widening.

Kell shot me a look. "We're just getting started."

Teag and I had not come unarmed, but I hoped we didn't need any of our "arsenal." We both had a variety of magical and technological items hidden in our pockets in case we needed to fend off the ghost, and we were wearing some heavy-duty protective amulets and charms, just in case.

In the dining room, an ornate silver tea set had the EMF scanner screaming. "If family legend is true, I might know why this object has so much resonance," Kell said, glancing back to Teag and me as he lowered the scanner. "Tradition holds that Olivia Boyce, who was the lady of the house during the Civil War, used this tea set to serve tea to Union sympathizers. Oleander tea," he added with a knowing look.

"Ouch," Teag said. Oleander was a beautiful plant but a deadly poison. "Not exactly the hostess with the mostess."

"Or just channeling her inner Borgia," I replied, studying the tea service from a distance, certain that anything that set off an EMF reader would probably throw me for a loop if I touched it.

"I figured that you'd want to study anything really suspicious back in the shop, where you could control the conditions," Kell said, and I shot him a grateful smile. He's seen me trance out when a tainted item knocks me on my ass. Most of the time, a mild resonance will show me images, or maybe a full-fledged vision. Sometimes, if the item's mojo is strong enough, I get pulled into a nightmare that won't let go. Teag and Sorren know how to deal with that using magic, but that's another area I'm not quite ready to share completely with Kell, for his own safety.

"Come on—we've barely started the tour," Kell said, pulling me out of my thoughts. Teag lagged a step behind us, staring down at the worn Oriental carpet.

"Does your scanner get anything from the rug?" Teag asked. Teag's power is Weaver Magic, which can mean weaving spells into cloth or weaving far-flung bits of information into powerful data. He stared down at the faded old carpet, and I was certain it was telling him its own story.

"Hard to tell in this house what's setting off the scanner," Kell replied, "but we did get a blip over there. Why?"

"Did anyone die violently in the house?" Teag's gaze stayed on one particular spot on the rug.

"Several people," Kell replied. "A hanging in the attic, a fatal accident on the stairs, and a shooting between jealous suitors."

"Betcha a cold beer the shooting happened right here," Teag said, eying a portion of the carpet that was more faded than the rest.

"Bet you're right," I replied, acknowledging the uneasiness I felt since stepping onto the rug. It wouldn't be the first time I picked up an item's juju through the soles of my shoes.

Kell led us into the living room. Again, the scanner lit up, and the alarm went off. "We saw the ghost in here when I brought the team," he said. "She was standing next to the mantle, so I don't know whether the scanner is picking up on residual energy from the ghost, or from something near the fireplace."

"She?" Teag asked.

Kell nodded. "Definitely a woman."

"One of the violent deaths?" I walked closer to the fireplace, studying the items on the mantle, which included a clock, a vase, and a bird sculpture, as well as a few photographs in silver frames."

"I don't think so," Kell replied. "Pretty sure we saw her," he added, pointing to one of the pictures behind me. The snapshot was black and white, but much more recent than many of the vintage photos in the home, probably dating to the 1990s from the way the people were dressed. "Esther Pettis Boyce, the last of the Boyce family," Kell supplied. "Last private owner of the house, died without heirs or descendants five years ago."

The front room grew colder as we talked, and I felt the hackles stand up on the back of my neck. "Does she have a reason to be pissed off about something?" I asked, turning slowly as the sense of being watched grew stronger. The temperature plummeted until my breath misted.

"Other than the fact that her will made it clear that the house and everything in it was supposed to be burned—and that clearly didn't happen—I can't imagine why she's angry," Kell replied with a deadpan expression.

Teag let out a low whistle. "That might rile someone up. Why would she want to torch a beautiful old home and all these antiques?"

Kell shrugged. "From what Esther said in letters and mentioned in her diary, she was certain her family was cursed, and that something here in the house was the cause."

I shivered as the sensation that someone was behind me grew stronger, though I saw no one except Teag and Kell. Leaving the room only lessened the feeling of foreboding a little bit, and I was certain that Esther—or one of the house's other ghosts—was keeping an eye on us as we moved on with our tour.

The EMF scanner went off a couple more times in the back rooms, but not nearly so strongly as in the dining room and parlor. But as we climbed the stairs, the prickle on the back of my neck grew more uncomfortable, and my gut tightened. "Definitely some bad mojo on the stairs," I murmured to Teag. Yet the nearer we got to the top of the stairs, the more the knot in my stomach grew. I had the awful feeling that we had only seen the pre-game warm-up.

Crash. We had no sooner cleared the landing when the sound of shattering glass made us all jump.

"What the hell was that?" Teag asked, drawing a small iron dagger from his belt. I shook my right arm, and my athame—the handle of an old wooden spoon imbued with strong emotional memories of my childhood—dropped down into my hand.

"The house is waking up," Kell replied, and I noticed that his hand, that wasn't holding the EMF reader, had gone into his pocket, probably for a fistful of salt. Ghosts hate iron and salt because while they're past being hurt, they can be dispelled, and both items do the trick.

Kell led us into the nearest bedroom. Below, on the first floor, doors slammed, one after the other, hard enough to make the china dishes in the cupboards rattle. The electronic box in Kell's grip squealed like microphone feedback, painful and piercing. I could barely focus my attention to look around the room, but my instincts drew me toward a small inlaid music box on a bedside table, right before the bathroom door swung shut with no one nearby.

"Told you it was a hopping place," Kell said with a nervous smile.

"You weren't just whistling Dixie," Teag muttered.

"Let's make it quick," I urged. "Whatever's going on is building up to something, and I don't think we want to be here for the grand finale."

Overhead, I heard a thump that sounded like the right heft to be a body. *Did the rope break?* I wondered about the Boyce ancestor's suicide in the attic. I had no intention of going up there to see what made that noise.

Gooseflesh rose on my arms, and my breath fogged although the old home's air conditioning was nowhere near cold enough to make that happen. The constant squeal of the EMF recorder rendered it useless to spot "hot" items, and my intuition screamed for us to get out *now*.

Another crash downstairs made me wonder if something had swept every dish and piece of silverware from the dining room table. Heavy footsteps sounded on the attic steps. "I think we need to leave," I said.

"Yeah, I think you're right," Kell replied, stuffing the EMF reader in his pocket but keeping a firm grip on a length of iron pipe he pulled from beneath his jacket.

Too late.

Esther Boyce's ghost stood in the hallway glowering with fury. She flung her hands forward, and we slammed against the walls as if we had been dolls tossed by a vengeful child. For a few seconds, I couldn't move, couldn't breathe, and my heart thudded like it would rip from my ribs. Cold stole heat from my blood, the chill of the grave, and I felt the unyielding grip of corpse-stiff fingers pinning me against the wall. A moment later, that same unbreakable grip tore me away from the wall and threw me toward the stairs so that I landed on my knees. Kell and Teag barely caught themselves to keep from landing on their faces.

Get out. I heard her voice ringing in my head, and from the shocked looks on Teag and Kell's faces, I was sure they heard her as well.

"Run!" I yelled, heading for the steps. I shook my left hand, jangling the tags of the old dog collar wrapped around my wrist, and the ghost of Bo, my late, beloved Golden Retriever, materialized next to me, barking ferociously at the spirit.

Esther glided toward us, arms outstretched, hands grasping. *Get out! Burn! Burn everything!*

Teag and Kell were right behind me as I started down the steps. Bo's ghost stood between Esther's spirit and the top of the stairs, growling and snarling. We nearly made it to the bottom. I reached the riser where I'd sensed bad mojo, and for an instant saw a clear image of Judah Boyce, eyes narrowed with malice. Then I felt a hand between my shoulder blades and grabbed too late to steady myself as I fell forward.

"Whoa!" Teag yelled, grabbing my arm and wrenching me backward, pulling hard enough that I saw his hand tighten white-knuckled on the balustrade. I thought I heard a man's sinister chuckle, but it was hard to hear anything the way my heart thumped like it would tear free from my chest.

The front hallway felt like a meat locker, cold enough that tendrils of frost encroached on the surface of the mirror, which I noticed was unbroken despite the crash we heard earlier. "Look!" I pointed as we ran for the door.

A man in Civil War-era clothing stood glowering on the stairs, invisible except in the mirror. Esther Boyce's ghost manifested right on the balcony as we opened the front door and ran for the piazza.

Get out. All of you, out! And don't come back, she shrieked, her voice echoing in my head loudly enough to make my temples ache.

～

"YOU HEARD ABOUT Parker Jackson?" Trina asked as she totaled up my order. The Honeysuckle Café buzzed with conversation as King Street merchants lined up for their coffee and muffins before stores opened and tourists filled their shops.

"Good news or bad news?" I asked, handing over cash.

"Good news. His architecture firm just got a big contract for a historic renovation in Savannah, and one of the cable channels wants to do a television show about it." Trina handed back her change and sighed. "It's about time something good happened, you know?"

I nodded. Charleston's business community was fairly small, and news traveled fast when it touched on one of their own. Lately, that news had been nothing but bad. A car crash claimed the life of a well-regarded investment banker. The CEO of a local firm lost his rapidly-growing company and his marriage when charges of embezzlement surfaced. The suicide of a society matron made the front page.

"Happy to hear it," I replied.

"Have you gotten a look inside the Boyce House?" Trina asked as they waited for the lattes to be ready. "I know you're connected to all the historic groups."

Trifles and Folly's position as Charleston's oldest antique store meant it was the first place local historians and preservationists turned for the perfect items to complete a display or furnish a period home. "Just a glimpse," I said. "Why?"

Trina shrugged. "Just wondered if you'd heard about it being haunted."

I hoped I didn't give anything away with my expression. "What have you heard?"

"The usual rumors. Family secrets. Tragedy. Usually adds up to a ghost or two, at least in the movies," Trina replied with a grin.

"Sounds like the kind of story that will sell plenty of tickets once it opens to the public," I answered, gathering my purchases. With luck, my smile didn't look as fake as it felt. "Gotta run!"

Teag already had the store ready for the morning rush by the time I walked in the door. I grinned, and handed over his drink and one of the fresh muffins, taking my share of the bounty over to a spot near the register. "Recover from last night?" I asked before I took a bite of the muffin, savoring the fresh blueberries.

"Got a few new bruises," Teag confessed. "Esther's one hell of a strong poltergeist. Makes me wonder what she's so angry about."

"Can't imagine Anthony was too happy about you getting thrown around." Anthony is Teag's long-time partner, and while he knows what we really do behind the scenes, he's understandably less than thrilled when saving the world puts Teag in harm's way.

Teag chuckled. "No, he wasn't—until I asked for a massage to work away the sore muscles," he added with a grin.

I filled him in on the news I'd heard from Trina. "Good for Parker," Teag replied. "Anthony passed along some news of his own. Jenkins Filbert had a heart attack yesterday. Guess he didn't get much time to enjoy landing that sweet deal." Filbert's company signed a multi-million dollar contract to supply equipment for a new research facility just the week before.

"Sorry to hear about Filbert," I replied, taking a sip of my latte. It felt like lately, things had been feast or famine, the wins, and losses canceling each other out. I'd sent nearly an equal number of congratu-lations emails as I had condolence cards. "Did you hear anything from Kell?"

Teag nodded. "Yeah, he called while you were getting coffee. I texted him the list of the objects we wanted to see from the house, and he said he'd bring those plus some extras he wanted us to look at. He needed to clear taking the items with the head of the Historic Trust, but he figured he'd be here by noon."

I laughed. "Since Mrs. Morrissey is a board member for the Trust, I don't think that's going to be a problem." Mrs. Morrissey was a good friend and a long-time source for information on anything about Charleston's past.

True to his word, Kell brought everything we requested, except for one piece—the large mirror. "Too big and too fragile," he replied. "Sorry. Though you're welcome to come back during daylight if you want another look at it."

He slapped a hand down on a cardboard box. "I thought you might also want to take a look at these," he added, opening the lid. Inside lay two bundles of yellowed envelopes bound with twine, a couple of journals, and a folder full of newspaper clippings and articles.

"The preservation people found these in the house when they did the renovation," Kell said. "They're supposed to go to the Historical Society, but I figured Mrs. Morrissey wouldn't mind if they had a small detour. From what I can tell, they're family letters, some old photographs, journals that belonged to Esther and other family members, and a file of things related to news about the Boyce family. There's probably some stuff in there that goes back even before Esther. Thought it might be useful."

"Definitely," I confirmed. "Kell—have other people been through the house besides your team and the renovation workers, and us?"

Kell frowned. "Not very many, but some. A few key donors, some VIPs in the architecture and preservation circles who were interested in the project, and some of the committee members who are overseeing the project. Why?"

"Just wondered if anyone else got the kind of welcome we did from Esther," I replied, wincing as I moved my left shoulder, which was sore from my near tumble down the steps.

"Oh yeah," Kell said, leaning back against one of the display cases. "That's how SPOOK got involved. I'd heard rumors about the Boyce house, and I intended to try to get permission to take the team in once it opened to the public, but they called me first."

"What happened?" Teag asked. Now that we'd had a look at the house first-hand, "haunted" didn't quite cover it. "Spook-a-palooza" was more like it.

"Apparently there've been problems since they started the renovation," Kell replied. He was eying my blueberry muffin, so I gave him half, which he accepted with a guilty grin. If I had remembered he was coming over, I would have picked one up for him as well. I knew they were his favorite.

"Little things at first, like tools going missing or damage to repairs that had just been made. They thought vandals were getting in, but they could never find evidence of anyone messing with the locks."

"Anyone get hurt?" I asked.

He nodded. "From what the construction crew told me, the 'pranks' always had an edge to them, like someone wanted to make them go away. Broken equipment, for example, or making them re-do work. When that didn't work, I guess Esther stepped up her game. One of the workers swears he got beaned by a block of wood that just flew through the air and hit him on the head. A couple of guys got shocked or burned by electrical surges. One of the carpenters almost lost his hand on an electric saw that suddenly turned on all by itself. So many people tripped or fell on the steps that they started using the servants' stairs instead. And no one wanted to go into the attic."

"And they stayed with the project?" Teag asked, raising and eyebrow. "Talk about persistent."

Kell shook his head. "It wasn't persistence—it was politics. Too much fundraising and bally-hoo had gone into this project. The Historical Society couldn't afford to just walk away from it. So they paid for repairs and replaced workers who quit, and sprang for bonuses for people who stayed on the job."

"Yikes," I replied. I took another sip of my coffee while I thought about Kell's story. "So we've got at least three ghosts from different time periods actively haunting the place. And all of them sound dangerous."

"That's why I'm counting on you to figure out what's going on and how to get rid of them," Kell said. "They'll hold off the opening for a short time, but not forever."

"It's not going to be good publicity the first time old Judah pushes a visitor down the steps," Teag noted. But I knew what Kell meant.

The Historical Society could hardly cite "ghost problems" as a reason not to open their big new project to the public. There would be no face-saving way for them to abandon the effort at this point. So we not only had to figure out what pissed off the Boyce family ghosts, but do it quickly, before anyone else got hurt.

"We're on it," I promised. "I'll let you know as soon as we have something."

Kell grinned. "You're the best!" He leaned over and gave me a quick kiss, then headed out with a wave.

"So I take it you and Kell are still an item?" Teag asked with a smile.

"Four months in and going strong," I replied, before turning to examine the items Kell brought in.

"I'll carry them back to the break room, so you don't have to touch them," Teag offered. "Then let's take turns going through the papers. Maybe we'll crack the secret."

"Works for me." I followed Teag into the break room and sat down at the table.

I glanced at the objects we had requested from the Boyce House. Nothing had struck me as the anchor for the hauntings, but then again, my senses had been overloaded by the sheer volume of pieces that glimmered with resonance. Since we couldn't examine everything, I had asked for a personal item from Esther, Judah, and other family members—something small that might have been used daily or carried with them.

Reading those items with my psychometry would have to wait until Teag could help me. Given how strong the hauntings were, I had to assume the psychic taint that clung to personal items would be equally powerful, easily enough to knock me flat on my ass. I glanced at my watch. Sorren was traveling, but he expected to be back in Charleston tonight. Maybe he would remember something about the Boyce ancestors. Having a first-hand witness to history as an immortal business partner came in handy.

In the meantime, I'd see what I could learn from the letters and journals. My hand hovered above the box with the papers, trying to decide whether it was safe to touch. I felt the residue of strong emotion, but it was distant, faded with time. The sensation was strongest over the journals, which I expected since the leather-bound books were more substantial than the faded envelopes. I reached in, grabbing one of the newer journals.

For a moment, images overwhelmed me as my psychometry kicked into gear. I smelled roses and black tea, and the scent of soap and linen. I heard the chime of a mantle clock and the rattle of a spoon inside a teacup, elements of Esther Boyle's daily life. I opened the cover and began to read.

"How's it going?"

I startled at Teag's voice, and a glance at the clock in the break room told me I'd been reading Esther's journal for hours. I chuckled and put down the book, then rubbed my eyes. "Going well enough I didn't realize how much time had passed."

Teag grinned. "The afternoon's been quiet. I thought maybe I could take some of those letters out with me and start reading, and then once we close up, I'll spot you if you want to touch the objects Kell brought."

"Sounds like a plan," I agreed. "We could order pizza—unless Anthony's waiting dinner on you?"

Teag shook his head. "Nah. He's working late—big case coming up." Anthony was a lawyer. "Kell expecting you?"

"No. I'm pretty sure he knew we'd dig into this when he brought over the box."

Teag grabbed a pack of stained and faded envelopes. "Find anything in the journal?"

"Nothing concrete, just that Esther didn't have a high opinion of some of her ancestors," I replied. "And I get the definite idea that the house was actively haunted while Esther lived there, so that might have been part of her reason for wanting to see the place get torched."

"It wouldn't be an old South Carolina wealthy family if it didn't have a mess of skeletons in the closet—and a few in the backyard, too," Teag commented. Dealing with ghosts and haunted objects meant that we dug up a lot of dirt on things people would rather leave buried.

I got up and stretched, deciding to make a pot of coffee since I guessed we'd be pulling a late night. I read through all but the last few pages of the journal by the time I heard the bell on the shop door ring and the click as Teag threw the latch, signaling five o'clock. I'd been so immersed in Esther's diary that the time flew by.

"Any juicy details?" I asked as Teag came into the break room with his handful of envelopes. He set the letters on the table and poured himself a cup of coffee, then took up a chair across from me.

"The Boyce's weren't a happy family," Teag observed. "The letters I read were between Judah and his wife before the Civil War. He's the one who made the family fortune."

"He's the grumpy ghost on the stairs. Kell brought us his pocketknife," I supplied, glancing at the box.

"Right. He had quite the rags-to-riches story. Straight out of Horatio Alger. Poor boy makes good and ends up owning the cotton mill where he originally swept the floors. And all it cost him was his decency."

"What do you mean?"

Over the course of the afternoon, Teag read all of Judah's letters, while I finished both of Esther's journals. "He was ruthless," Teag replied. "He broke contracts, double-crossed old friends, and pushed the limits of the law—and was proud of it. Nothing mattered except rising to power and wealth."

"Well," I said, "he got what he wanted. It must have taken a lot of money even back then to build that house, and leave a nest egg substantial enough to keep several generations living comfortably."

"Yes and no." Teag leaned back in his chair, staring at the letters. "Judah got rich and powerful. But everything else seemed to go wrong. His health failed, his oldest son died in a carriage accident, his business partner committed suicide, and from the tone of the last letters, his marriage was on the rocks."

"Sounds like a soap opera." I drummed my fingers on Esther's journals. "Actually, for being an heiress, Esther didn't seem too happy toward the end, either. The early entries were different. She was in love with a man back during the Second World War, a pilot. She was really over the moon for him, and her diary talked about how she would do anything for him to come home safely to her."

"Did he?" Teag leaned forward, caught up in the story.

"Yes—and no," I replied, echoing Teag's earlier answer. "He came home from the war, and they married. But then everything took a turn for the worse. Esther had several miscarriages and never was able to have a child. Her husband had what she called 'battle fatigue'—we'd say PTSD—and couldn't hold a job. He died young. Drank himself to death."

"So both Judah and Esther were unhappy, and both died in the house—which might explain the hauntings," I mused. "How about the lady in the attic? Do we know who she was or why she hanged herself?"

"We've got a name—Alice Boyce Sandoval," Teag said. "Esther's great aunt. Kell knew that much. He brought a pocketknife from Judah, a necklace from Esther, and Alice's signet ring."

"Let's get through the rest of the letters, and then we'll tackle the items," I suggested. "Maybe Sorren will be back by then."

By the time we finished with the remaining correspondence, the pizza arrived. "I didn't get much from the letters I read, except that for as much as the Boyce family prospered, they sure had a lot of personal tragedies," I said after I finished my slice.

Teag swallowed his last bite of pizza and nodded. "Same here. Although a few of the letters did mention Alice. She married the man of her dreams—quite the society wedding. And then a few years later, her Prince Charming took off with Alice' dowry and another woman and skipped town to Bermuda. She was completely disgraced."

"Which explains why she hanged herself in the attic." I poured myself a cup of coffee. I stared at the box with the personal possessions of our three ghosts and realized I had run out of excuses.

"Come on," I said. "Let's finish this."

Teag pulled out a small strip of handwoven cloth, one I knew he had made himself. "Hold onto this when you touch the objects. That way, I can see what you see."

"Not going to do much good if we both land on our asses," I replied, trying not to sound nervous.

"That's never happened the other times we've done this," Teag said. "I think the version I see is a little… watered down."

"Here goes nothing," I said and reached out for Judah's pocketknife.

The handle of the old knife slipped against my palm, slick from years of use. Judah no doubt carried the knife in his pocket every day, handled it frequently for a dozen uses, an all-purpose tool. Strong memories washed over me, and I saw Judah sitting behind his desk, slitting envelopes open with his knife, cutting the twine from packages, trimming his nails. I caught the scent of pipe smoke, leather, and bay rum.

The knife witnessed the minutia of Judah's life, absorbing his resonance over decades. I struggled to make sense of the onslaught of remembered moments, looking for clues to reveal the murderous specter who had tried to push me down the stairs.

Determination. Strength of will. Cold, hard purpose. Never-say-die stamina. Clear-eyed practicality, unfettered by sentiment. Judah embodied all those attributes, wrapped in a resolute and single-minded drive to achieve. Beneath everything, I sensed ruthless anger. Judah was an ice cold son of a bitch.

I knew that Teag felt what I felt, through the spell-woven cloth that we both held. Later, we'd compare notes on what we saw. Now, I held tight to the pocketknife, determined to glimpse something that might reveal what bound Judah to his mansion and fueled his fury.

I slowed my breath and sank deeper into a trance, willing myself to read more from the images supplied by the knife. A woman's face emerged, and I recognized her from the old photos as Judah's wife. Other scenes flickered, of business meetings and intense conversations in wood-paneled offices and dark back alleys. More than once, I glimpsed blood. Judah was willing to do whatever it took to achieve his goals, and people who got in his way got hurt.

One memory felt especially laden with importance, and I turned my attention toward its flickering images. Judah spoke with a thin man in a black suit whose back was turned to me. I could not hear their voices, but from the intensity of Judah's expression and the fire blazing in his eyes, I knew I witnessed a pivotal moment. Judah said something to his visitor, then leaned over to sign a ledger on his desk. When he looked up, his gaze held a mixture of victory and finality--and fear. The last impressions happened in a blur of movement and pain. I saw Judah start down the stairs in Boyce House, felt his anger and fear surge as something shoved him hard from behind, and saw the reflection of his fall in the large hallway mirror as his body tumbled in a tangle of limbs to lie broken and bleeding at the bottom of the steps.

"Cassidy!" Teag's voice brought me back to myself, and I came out of the vision with a start. "You okay?"

I nodded, trying to clear my head. "You saw all that?"

"Yeah. He was a real hard-nosed guy. Not exactly Mr. Personality."

I scrubbed a hand over my face. "I think the scene at the end was the most important, but I don't know why. It felt urgent and... dangerous."

"Agreed—but I've got no clue what the big deal was," Teag agreed. He pushed my iced tea toward me, and I took a gulp, calming my nerves. "Ready to look at one of the other pieces?"

I took a few deep breaths. "Sure. Let's see what Aunt Alice's ring can tell us."

Teag pulled the ring box out and opened it, then slid it over to me. A silver signet ring sat on a silk cushion. Delicate filigree decorated the sides, and the monogram "ABS" worn but readable in the center of the ring.

Anger and longing hit me like a punch to the gut. Strong passions swirled through my mind as the face of a petite, dark-haired woman came into focus. Alice's delicate features suggested fragility, but her eyes glinted with the same steel I saw in Judah's gaze. She moved with energy and purpose, and while I could not hear her words, from the reactions of those she addressed, I gathered that Alice did not mince words.

Another image came into focus, a handsome man with blond hair and startlingly blue eyes. I knew from the first glimpse of this young man that he was Alice's ill-fated lover and that the desire to acquire him consumed her. A montage of memory fragments swept through my mind, of Alice checking her reflection in the hallway mirror before dances and dinner parties, of carriage rides and stolen kisses, tracing the steps as Alice won over her beau.

I dug deeper and found myself in a dark garden. The smell of gardenias hung heavy in the air. Alice stood in the moonlight, talking to someone who stood in the shadows. A shiver ran down my spine. Alice's unseen visitor filled me with foreboding, and I recoiled instinctively. The scene changed, and I saw Alice sitting at a writing desk, and an ebony fountain pen moving smoothly over paper. She signed her name with a flourish and looked up to stare out the window with an expression filled with triumph and sorrow.

Once again, Teag called me back to myself. This time, he pressed the cup of coffee into my hand. "You with me?"

I gulped the coffee, eager for its sugar and caffeine to replenish the energy the visions drained. "I will be. You still tuned into the same channel?"

"Loud and clear. Did you get the feeling that Alice met someone in the garden—someone who didn't want to be seen?"

I nodded. "Yeah. And I wish I could have gotten a better look at what she had in front of her on the desk. I got the sense that it was very important to her."

Teag grimaced. "Too bad it wasn't a prenup. Might have saved her dowry from that loser she married." He shot me a worried glance. "You sure you're up to one more?"

"Nothing short of a good night's sleep is going to make me feel better, so we might as well get it over with," I replied, pushing my hair out of my face. "I'm still hoping Sorren will show up. He's been in Charleston almost from its founding—maybe he's heard something about the Boyce family."

Teag put Esther's necklace on the table in front of me. I gripped one end of the woven strip in my left hand, and let the fingers of my right hand touch the elegant silver and onyx pendant.

The touch sent me reeling. I saw Esther looking back at herself in the huge hallway mirror dressed in 1940s-era clothing. Her eyes looked haunted as if dark dreams and worry kept her from a sound sleep. I glimpsed a picture of a good-looking man in a pilot's uniform and a memory of a hurried wedding. Newspaper headlines chronicled heavy fighting, and I felt Esther's fear clutch my own heart so tightly I could not breathe.

Pages filled with Esther's neat handwriting gave her something to do, and I recognized the journals I'd just read where she chronicled her fears for the safety of her beloved. I could feel Esther's fierce independence and the indomitable streak of will that ran in the Boyce family. I could also sense her disquiet, as she argued with herself over a decision that kept her from sleeping and never strayed far from her thoughts.

The war brought hard times, and bad news from the front. Esther's stubborn refusal to give in kept the business afloat, but the family's fortunes diminished, adding to her worry. I saw her at the desk in a business office late at night, the room lit by a single lamp, Esther's pinched features shadowed by an accountant's eyeshade as she poured over ledgers.

And then one night, I knew Esther was not alone in the office. I saw Esther argue passionately with someone I could not see, felt the fear and worry come to a head, and then sensed Esther's resignation and despair as she filled out a sheet of paper with a flourish of that same black fountain pen and handed the unseen stranger one of the ledger books. After that, the images flashed by like a manic slideshow and I saw her aviator beau return, only to slide into despondency and alcohol. I saw Esther kneel weeping in a cemetery next to a tombstone with the carving of a lamb, and sensed heartbreak settle deep to become a dull, furious ache that grew more bitter as the years went on.

Get out! Once again, Esther's voice screamed in my mind, and I recoiled. *Get out all of you, out, and stay out of this cursed place!*

When I came back to myself, Teag was patting my cheeks with a cold, damp cloth. I sagged against the back of the chair with a shaky breath. "There goes my fearless reputation," I joked in a weak voice.

Teag gave me an encouraging smile. "I think it's pretty damn fearless going into those visions when you know they're going to kick your ass."

"What did you make of that?" I asked, thinking that I was about ready for a slug of bourbon after all we had seen.

Teag sat back when he was sure I would be all right, and pursed his lips as he thought. "Esther seemed the most level-headed of the three of them," He mused after a moment. "She didn't seem as ruthless as Judah, or as flighty as Alice. She struck me as a strong woman trying to make the best of a bad situation."

"Me too," I agreed. "In fact, I'm kind of surprised Esther's one of our ghosts," I added. "I get why Judah's spirit would hang around—he was a cold bastard, and he was murdered in the house. Alice was despondent and killed herself. But Esther died of old age. Her tragedies happened seventy years ago, and she soldiered on long afterward. So why haunt the place?"

A soft rapping at the back door jolted us both to attention. I let my athame slip into my hand, just in case, as I went to answer the knock, and relaxed when I saw Sorren in the alley behind the shop.

"Good to have you back," I greeted as Sorren stepped into the room, and Teag gave him a wave in welcome.

"Nice to be here," he replied. Sorren looks like a twenties-something grad student, dressed in a t-shirt and jeans with his blond hair cut in a trendy style. But one look in those grey eyes the color of the sea before a storm, but it's easy to see his real age. Even he can't hide the weight of centuries. "I got your text message. Fill me in."

Sorren sat down at the table while I caught him up on our tour of the Boyce House and what Teag and I learned from the objects, letters, and journals. While I talked, Teag scrolled through messages on his phone. He let out a low whistle.

"Guess it's a good thing Parker Jackson won those big contracts," Teag observed. "He'll need the money. His office building just burned to the ground."

"That's terrible," I replied. "Anyone hurt?"

"Just Jackson himself—the news report says he was taken to the hospital with serious burns."

Sorren looked up sharply. "Am I correct that Jackson recently had a huge success of some kind?"

"He landed a big business deal," I replied. "Why?"

"Have there been any surprising reversals of fortune among prominent people?" Sorren pressed, and I knew from the look on his face that he was on the trail of something. I thought about the socialite suicide and the CEO arrested for embezzlement, and the investment banker in the car crash, and Jenkin Filbert's heart attack.

"Actually, several," I replied. "Why?"

Sorren met my gaze. "Because it fits an old pattern," he replied. "And I'm afraid the Boyce family curse has expanded its scope."

"Curse?" Teag asked, leaning forward.

Sorren shrugged. "Maybe it would be more accurate to say that the Boyces had a tendency to make very poor business deals."

From what we'd learned, the Boyce family seemed to have more than its share of tragedy, but I wasn't seeing the connection. "How does that have anything to do with the other people who've had their luck turn?"

"I don't know, but I doubt it's a coincidence," Sorren replied.

Teag was already reaching for his laptop. "I'm on it." His Weaver magic also lets him weave strands of information into data, making him one hell of a hacker, so if there were connections to be made, I knew Teag would find them.

"You knew the Boyces?" I asked Sorren.

"Several generations of them. Never liked the way they did business, but their dealings only brought grief on themselves, so it was never Alliance business."

I frowned. "Why would the Alliance care? Unless they were using witchcraft—"

Sorren shook his head. "Old Judah Boyce wouldn't have had the patience for witchcraft. He liked to cut out the middleman and get down to brass tacks. That's why making a deal with a demon appealed to him."

I sat back, stunned, and let Sorren's words sink in. Now that he said it, I could see the pattern. "Judah made a deal for wealth," I said, remembering his rags-to-riches rise. "Alice made a deal for love. And Esther made her deal to bring her husband back alive from the war."

"And the Devil, as they say, is in the details," Sorren supplied as Teag searched the internet. "They weren't the only ones over the years to call on the 'old family friend.' That's one of the problems with single-mindedness—no appreciation for long-term consequences."

"So they got what they asked for and more—but the price was having other things fall apart."

Sorren nodded. "Exactly. Now you see why the Boyce family gained the notice of the Alliance. Dealing with demons is a dangerous business. But so long as they kept the consequences in the family, we decided it wasn't really our concern." He glanced toward Teag. "It seems something has changed all that."

"The house is getting ready to open to the public," I supplied. "Against Esther's wishes. Which explains the hauntings and the poltergeist activity. But how would that have anything to do with other people suddenly making deals with demons?"

"Bingo." We turned to look at Teag. "I found a connection," he said, stretching in his chair and lacing his fingers together to crack his knuckles. "Every one of the people was either a donor to the Boyce House project or involved in some major way. The woman who killed herself hosted fundraisers to raise money for the renovation. The investment banker managed the funding. Jackson's architecture firm did the plans. Some of the others served on the preservation committee."

"If you're right, then there are other people who could be in danger," I replied, thinking of Mrs. Morrissey and the Historic Society. "See if you can find out from Kell whether any of the people who've had their luck turn on them toured the house." I turned back to Sorren as Teag got up and walked a few steps away to call Kell.

"Do you think it's something in the house that's letting the demon latch onto people?"

"That's my first instinct." Sorren replied.

I thought about the visions I'd had, and what happened the night we were in the house. "That big mirror in the hallway," I said. "I saw it in all of the memories from the objects I touched. When we were in the house, it sounded like the mirror crashed and broke, but it didn't, and twice I could have sworn that I saw someone reflected in it who wasn't there."

"It's as good a place as any to start," Sorren said. "But if we're going up against a demon, we'll need some backup—and we definitely don't want your ghost hunter friend involved." He didn't have to explain. Kell was good at finding ghosts, but fighting demons should be left to the professionals.

THE NEXT NIGHT, we headed out to the Boyce House to kill a demon. Father Anne Burgett came with us. She's not your average Episcopalian priest, and her membership in the secret St. Expeditus Society means she's one of the inner circle when it comes to kicking supernatural ass. Tonight Father Anne wore a black t-shirt over a pair of black cargo pants and solid Doc Marten boots. The colorful tattoo of her patron saints covered most of her right arm, extending beneath the sleeve of her shirt. I knew the silver crucifix on her necklace could double as a weapon against a demon, and wondered whether the blessed boline knife in a sheath on her belt, so effective against vengeful spirits, would work against hellspawn.

Teag carried silver and iron knives, as well as a variety of protection charms. I had my athame and Bo's collar, plus a silver knife of my own and a lighter in my pocket, just in case, since fire served as a weapon of last resort. Sorren's immortal strength was a formidable defense, and I was certain he had other protections hidden on his body. We were armed for the fight.

Sorren picked the locks to get us into Boyce House. Back when he was mortal, he'd been the best jewel thief in Antwerp. Teag hacked the security system, and we were in.

"The mirror is right over there," I said as we gathered in the foyer.

The temperature plummeted and my breath puffed out in white

clouds. Esther's ghost materialized between us and the mirror. In the reflection, I saw Judah on the stairs.

Get out! I heard Esther clearly in my mind, and from the looks on the others' faces, I knew they heard her as well. Esther's image broke up like a bad TV signal and then reappeared right in front of Sorren, crowding his space. *Get out!*

Sorren lunged forward with an iron knife in his hand, plunging the blade into the apparition. Esther's ghost shrieked and vanished.

"Teag! Behind you!" I glanced toward the big mirror and realized Judah was no longer on the stairs and had reappeared right behind Teag, with his walking stick raised like a club. "Down!"

Teag dropped and I brought up my right hand, athame already in my grip. I sent a surge of my will into the wood, drawing on the depth of the emotions that old mixing spoon held, and a blast of cold white light streamed forward, catching Judah's spirit in the chest and blowing it apart.

"They won't be gone for long," Sorren said as Teag climbed to his feet. Neither iron nor the cold energy of my athame would destroy a ghost, but for the moment, we were alone in the foyer. I shook my left arm and heard a jangle as the old dog collar wound around my wrist slipped down. Bo's ghost materialized at my side.

"Let's get this mirror taken care of," Father Anne said. "Cover me." Teag and I moved behind Father Anne as Sorren stepped to one side, knife in hand, wary in case Esther and Judah returned. I heard a muffled thud overhead and knew that our presence had awakened Alice.

Father Anne withdrew a black marker and drew a large sigil in the middle of the mirror, one I recognized as being a warding against demons. I moved to take Sorren's place on guard as Teag and Sorren moved to lift the large piece down from the wall. It was heavy and awkward, and as they brought it down, the bottom edge of the mirror knocked the guest book and its pen to the floor. I glimpsed Judah and Esther's spirits in the mirror, and a third woman whom I guessed was Alice. And then, out of the corner of my eye, I saw a dark, blurred image there and gone. Frost was forming on the mirror, and gooseflesh rose on my skin as the ghosts' presence sent the temperature even lower.

"Incoming!" I warned. Bo's ghost growled and took a step ahead of me. Judah's ghost formed to Teag's left, while Esther appeared behind Sorren, still screaming for us to get out.

"Do it now!" Sorren commanded, and Father Anne drew a silver flask from the pocket of her cargo pants and splashed the mirror with holy water.

"I exorcise thee, every unclean spirit, in the name of God the Father Almighty..." Father Anne began the ritual. Teag pivoted and slammed into Judah with an iron dagger, and the ghost's image flickered and blinked out, only to reassemble right next to me.

I felt Judah's hands around my throat as I brought my right hand up to where his chest should have been and willed my power through my athame. The cold light blew Judah's image apart, as Bo's ghost stalked Esther, who continued to shriek at us to get out.

"We cast you out, every onslaught of the infernal adversary..." Father Anne continued, and as she spoke, she drew back a booted foot and smashed its steel-reinforced toe into the center of the mirror.

The security lighting in the house flickered wildly, and a deep, unsettling laugh rolled through the darkened rooms. Esther's ghost blinked out with a look of panic on her face, and Judah vanished a second later, his angry scowl replaced for once with real fear.

A dark form took shape just inside the parlor door. Unseen hands tossed us all into the air as if we weighed nothing. Sorren crashed against the stairs with enough force to break bone if he were mortal. Father Anne slammed up against the foyer wall, pinned. Teag flew back against the door like a rag doll. I leveled my athame and managed to send a blast of cold white force toward the new threat, but the blast parted around him, flowing by without effect, though it would have slammed a normal man into the next room. In the next instant, a twist of the newcomer's hand threw me against the sideboard hard enough to force the air from my lungs. I collapsed in a heap next to the guest book, which lay where it had fallen among the shards of the broken mirror.

"Did you really think that you could be rid of me that easily?" The man's deep voice sent a shiver through me. Bo's ghost backed up to put itself between me and what I realized must be the Boyce family demon.

"*Exorcizamos te, omnis immunde spiritus...*" Father Anne switched to Latin, but the demon only laughed.

"You're going to have to do better than that, sister. This family is bound to me by blood. I've got iron-clad contracts on their souls."

I could see the demon more clearly now. He looked cocky and slick, like a Mafia hit man right out of Scorcese central casting. Teag got to his feet and launched himself at the demon, a silver knife replacing the iron weapon. The demon barely glanced his way, then flicked his wrist and slammed Teag against the wall.

"The Boyce family died out with Esther," Sorren said in a low, gravelly voice as he slowly got to his knees. I wondered whether being a vampire made it more difficult for the demon to control Sorren. "Your claim on them is forfeit."

The demon laughed. "Don't recall anything about my contracts having an end date." His laugh faded, and his expression grew predatory. "They're mine for eternity."

I had been wrong about the mirror being the demon's anchor, and now all of us were likely to die. My head pounded from where I hit the sideboard hard enough to knock over an oil lamp and smash its hurricane globe. Drops of lamp oil splattered on the floor and splashed the guest book.

I pushed up to sit with my back against the solid piece of furniture, and frowned as I stared at the guest book, which lay in a heap beside me, its cover splayed and pages crumpled. Falling from the top of the sideboard damaged the book, and I could see where the cover started to come apart, pulling the canvas away from the inside paper lining to reveal a much older hidden binding, one that looked like cracked leather.

Memories flashed through my mind, recalling bits of the visions I'd had of Esther, Alice, and Judah. In each one, I had seen them writing in a book. At the time, I'd thought they were making notes in a ledger or a journal, but now I realized the significance of what I had witnessed, and when I saw the same onyx-black fountain pen lying next to the guest book that I had glimpsed in my visions, the missing pieces of the puzzle came together.

All of the recent victims of the Boyce curse were involved with the renovations. VIP donors, the architect—people who got a personal tour of the house, and would have signed the guest book with pride.

A guest book I was now certain was really the demonic ledger on which Judah, Esther, and Alice signed away their souls—as did Parker and the rest of the victims, without their knowledge.

Bo's ghost sprang at the demon, teeth bared. The demon fluttered his fingers, and Bo's image flickered and vanished.

A desperate plan formed in my mind. Sorren climbed back to his feet, starting toward the demon again, his face a mask of concentration as he battled the creature's will with his own immortal strength. Father Anne kept chanting the Latin exorcism, until an unseen hand clamped around her throat, cutting off her words and her breath. I saw her eyes grow wide and her face flush and I knew we were running out of time. Teag lay slumped where he had fallen, a bad gash open across his fore-head, blood running down his face.

Sorren tackled the demon, and the two of them fell to the floor, wrestling for control. I made my move, knowing it was now or never.

I snatched the blessed boline knife from Father Anne's belt and jammed it down into guest book, then grabbed the lighter from my pocket and with a flick lit the lamp oil that coated the torn leather and yellowed pages. The book burst into flame, stinking of sulfur.

Father Anne gasped as the pressure on her throat eased, and picked up the exorcism where she left off.

"Cassidy! Throw me the pen!" I looked up to see Sorren still pinning the demon, and while the hilt of his silver dagger protruded from the man's chest, the creature still bucked and twisted trying to get loose from Sorren's grip.

Instinctively, I knew to touch the pen gingerly, and I managed to send it flying in Sorren's direction without ever closing my hand around the onyx shaft. Sorren caught the pen in midair and wrapped his fingers around it. Blood began to drip from his palm, and the demon screamed.

"Not exactly what you had in mind?" Sorren growled. The demon tried to buck Sorren clear, but Sorren yanked the silver dagger free with his left hand and severed the demon's head with one slice of the razor-sharp blade.

Father Anne finished the exorcism rite, voice strong despite a tremor, and then sagged back against the sideboard. "Wow," she breathed, in what had to be the understatement of the year.

Blood trickled down Sorren's face from a jagged cut and livid bruises around his throat showed where the demon had tried to strangle him. Rips in his shirt and bloodied skin beneath testified to the ferocity of his combat with the demon. Sorren eyed the corpse warily, moving clear a moment before the body and its severed head vanished.

I stared at the remains of the guest book as it rapidly burned to ash, then a groan from Teag had me crawling over to where he lay against the wall where the demon threw him. "Did I miss something?" He managed as his eyes struggled to focus.

I gave a shaky laugh that revealed more panic than humor. "Don't worry; we'll fill you in," I promised, then leaned forward and gingerly felt along the back of Teag's head until he winced when I touched a growing goose egg beneath his hair. I relaxed when I saw his pupils were normal, and he batted my hand away gently.

"I'm all right. Just hit my head. Is it over?"

Sorren helped Father Anne to her feet, and to my relief the priest appeared to be no worse for the wear. "I don't know how we'll explain this to the Preservation Society," she said, taking in the shattered mirror and the charred remains of the guest book.

"The book was older than it looked," I said, staring at the ashes. "I realized that when it fell off the table and the new cover pulled away. There was old leather underneath the cloth."

"Tanned human skin," Sorren remarked, and I repressed a shudder. "It never was a guest book. It was the demon's ledger, and it held the contract the Boyce descendants used to make their deals." He held up the broken remnants of the onyx pen in his bloodied hand. "The pen drew blood from the user and mixed it into the ink, sealing the agreement." He smirked. "I suspect my blood didn't set well with the demon."

"So Filbert and Jamison and the others—they were actually making a deal with the demon when they signed their names to the guest book?" Teag asked, horrified as the reality of the situation hit him.

I nodded. "Yeah. So they got a windfall—and then catastrophe, just like the Boyce family."

Teag shivered, and I bet that he recalled joking about signing the guest book himself when Kell gave us our tour.

"Esther just wanted people out of the house and away from the ledger," I said. "She wasn't trying to hurt anyone; she was trying to protect us."

"You can let Kell know that Boyce House is officially un-haunted," Sorren said as we headed for the door, ready to be done with the night's work. We were limping and bloodied, bruised, and battered— but alive, an outcome not to be taken for granted. "But just to be on the safe side," Sorren added, "he might want to recommend that they skip replacing the guest book."

PART V
PREDATOR

BLACK DOG

Teag Logan glanced over his shoulder and repressed a shudder.

"Don't worry. They won't eat much since they're already dead."

Teag shot me a murderous glance. "Since when has that stopped anything from eating?"

"Point taken. But in this case, I think you're safe," I replied.

Teag looked unconvinced but returned his attention to the shrimp basket in front of him. "All I've got to say is, this is one of the strangest places I've ever had lunch."

I had to agree with him. We were a little way out from Charleston on the South Carolina coast, and we had stopped for dinner at a mom-and-pop restaurant friends had recommended. Down here, we call this kind of place a "fish camp," a no-frills, fried seafood hole-in-the-wall.

"Most of the time, these places look like a barn with picnic tables," Teag continued, eyeing the decor. "But this takes the cake."

The building itself was unimpressive. But the owners had deco-rated with hundreds of taxidermy animals salvaged from a defunct wildlife museum, many in "natural" habitats with tree trunks and fake plants. It felt as if we were eating in a forest surrounded by bear, deer, elk, moose, coyotes, wolves, and other wildlife which all seemed to be watching with their beady glass eyes. It would have been intimidating —if the owners hadn't decided to string Christmas lights between the displays year-round, just because.

"It's memorable," I laughed. "And the food's good, so don't complain."

Teag swallowed a mouthful and nodded. "True, on both counts. At least they didn't shoot all these critters."

"Pretty sure from the signs on the displays that most of these creatures were plugged and stuffed when my grandmother was still a kid," I replied, taking a sip of my sweet tea.

Teag grew serious as he stared at the taxidermied fox not far from our table. "Seriously, what do you think you'd read if you touched one of those?"

I shivered. "Not sure I want to try. I don't know whether there'd be any sense of the animal itself left after all this time, or whether I'd get more of a read on the taxidermist—or the events that have left an impression on the piece in all the years it's been on display."

I'm Cassidy Kincaide, and I run Trifles and Folly, an antique and curio store in historic, haunted Charleston, SC. Teag is my assistant store manager, best friend, and sometime bodyguard. I'm a psychometric—meaning I can read the magic or emotional resonance of an object by touching it. That's a talent that's been passed down through my family, and it goes along with being the one to inherit the store, which has been around for over three hundred years.

It's just one of my secrets. Teag's got his own kind of magic, and the store itself isn't what it seems. We do more than sell cool old stuff; we're part of the Alliance, a coalition of mortals and immortals who locate and neutralize supernatural threats and get cursed and haunted objects out of circulation. My business partner, Sorren, is a nearly 600-year-old vampire. There's no such thing for us as "just another day at the office."

Except that today wasn't about ghostbusting. We were on our way back from an estate sale where we'd picked up a load of non-haunted, particularly attractive antiques to resell, along with a few that I knew right away needed to stay out of the wrong hands.

"Earth to Cassidy!" Teag teased, noticing I'd gone quiet. He flipped a lock of lank dark hair out of his eyes and grinned. Teag looks like a grad student—and he used to be before he found his calling kicking supernatural ass. He's still got a skater boy look—tall and thin, longish hair, and a fondness for vintage t-shirts and ripped jeans. It hides the fact that he's a championship mixed martial arts fighter, which comes in handy given the kind of company we keep.

I laughed and pulled myself out of my thoughts. "Sorry. Just wondering how weird the 'spookies' and that 'sparkler' are that we picked up at the auction." My magic identified which items had a touch of "something extra," but since I hadn't wanted to go into a full-out vision right there at the auction house, I left reading the details for later. Touching tainted objects can land me flat on my ass and lead to uncomfortable questions.

"From everything we've heard, the guy who owned that stuff was a bit... eccentric," Teag replied and dipped a french fry in ketchup. "Maybe he dabbled in the Black Arts on the side."

I glared at him. "Not funny. Remember what happened the last time that was true?" I knew he did from the look on his face. We had managed to neutralize a particularly nasty curse just in time, but Teag ended up with a concussion, and I'd needed a transfusion before all was said and done. "I could do without a repeat."

"I don't think we need to worry about that," Teag said. "I didn't get any vibes about dark magic when we went through the house, and from what people say, Mr. Broward was a real back-to-nature guy who got his kicks going to nudist retreats in national parks."

I looked up. "Can you even imagine the mosquitoes?"

Teag laughed. "No—and I don't want to. And with the way you attract bug bites—"

"Let's not even go there," I said with a shudder. Pale skin and strawberry blonde hair must be an irresistible attraction to mosquitoes because I'm always the one who gets bitten more than everyone else.

"As I was saying—the old guy might have had a few kinks, but he sounded harmless."

"I hope so—although 'harmless' people don't usually have magically tainted objects lying around." I was done with my meal and leaned back in my chair, trying not to feel watched by the stuffed moose that loomed over my shoulder.

Teag shrugged. "He might have inherited the pieces or picked them up from a flea market somewhere. You know as well as I do that most people are completely tone-deaf when it comes to picking up on super-natural vibes."

"Yeah—until it all goes massively sideways," I muttered. Then people like Teag and Sorren and I ended up wading in to clean up the mess.

"Ready to head out?" Teag asked after we settled up the bill.

I jerked back to attention. My mind wandered again, and I was keeping a close eye on a taxidermied ferret that I was almost positive had just moved. "What?"

"They aren't moving, Cassidy. This restaurant has been here for thirty years. We'd have heard if the decorations were eating the customers."

"I don't trust the ferret."

"Personally, I thought the elk looked shifty, but that's probably just me," Teag replied with nearly-believable fake sincerity. "Let's go—we've got a drive back to the shop, and we've still got to unload."

I finished my sweet tea and followed him out, with one backward glare at the untrustworthy ferret. *I'm watching you.* I was only mostly kidding.

The almost-empty parking lot felt a lot more ominous at night. The fish camp drew a big dinner crowd, and a parked-full lot meant we had found a spot at the far end, near the marsh. Now, I couldn't shake the feeling that something a lot worse than a stuffed ferret watched from the shadows.

A growl sounded an instant before the large black dog leaped from the brush at the edge of the lot. "Watch out!" I yelled, throwing myself out of the way and only partially succeeding as claws ripped through my jeans and down my leg. The big dog looked like a Newfoundland, as heavy as a grown man and massive with black, shaggy fur. And right now, it had Teag pinned under it, teeth bared.

I pulled my large handbag around and dug my hand in searching for the wooden spoon. Sad that my life had come to the point where I felt I always had to have a weapon handy. A spoon may not sound too dangerous, but when it carries my grandmother's mojo and serves as an athame – it works for me. I held the wooden athame in my right hand and gave a shake to the old dog collar looped around my left wrist. The athame focused my concentration, pulling from the strong emotional resonance of my grandmother, and I sent a blast of cold white force that hit the black dog right behind its front shoulders, knocking it away from Teag.

The dog snarled and came at us again. The ghostly form of a large, angry Golden Retriever blocked its way, as the spirit of my dog Bo manifested to protect us. The black dog eyed the ghost warily, and what Bo lacked in bulk against the massive canine, he more than made up for in a seriously bad attitude.

Teag scrambled to his feet, and I saw a wicked knife in his hand as he took a fighting stance, waiting for the dog to attack. For its bulk, the black dog moved fast. Bo's ghost latched on with teeth that I knew from experience could put a dent in supernatural creatures, but the Newfoundland shook Bo off and came right at me.

I dove out of the way and still got off a shot from my athame, a glancing strike that shoved the big dog out of the way but didn't send it tumbling as I hoped. Teag let out a yell and threw himself onto the creature's back, driving his knife into its right shoulder deep enough that blood flowed across his hand and down onto the gravel.

The dog snapped its powerful jaws, barely missing Teag's arm, then threw Teag to one side and barreled into the scrub and darkness beyond the parking lot, leaving a blood trail. I helped Teag to his feet. Bo's ghost padded over and looked at me with a goofy grin, then vanished. Teag and I stared into the brush where the dog vanished.

Teag took a step to follow, and I grabbed his arm. "Are you crazy? Let it go."

I saw common sense war with the desire to finish the fight. Finally, tension drained from Teag's shoulders, and I released my grip.

"You're right. But I don't like unfinished business."

Neither did I, but the thought of heading into unfamiliar woods in the dark after a wounded and angry supernatural creature kept me from seeking revenge, at least for now. "We've got no idea what it was or why it attacked," I said, regaining the presence of mind to unlock the car and climb in. Teag opened the passenger side and joined me a moment later. "You okay?"

Teag glanced down at himself and nodded. "Yeah, just winded and I'll probably have some nice bruises tomorrow. You?"

"I've got some scratches on my leg we'll need to treat when we get back to the shop, but nothing deep."

"Do you think it was after us?" Teag mused as I turned out of the parking lot. We kept our eyes open, in case the dog followed us, but we saw nothing unusual in the tall brush along the side of the road.

"No way to know," I replied. "I'd almost rather think that we were just in the wrong place at the wrong time—even though that opens up a whole different can of worms."

"Right. Because either that thing was actually after *us*, which is one kind of problem, or it's randomly prowling, in which case it's still our problem, just in a different way," Teag summed up.

"There's lore about black dogs," I said as I drove, keeping a careful eye on the side of the road in case the creature or its friends decided to make another appearance. "Why don't you take a look at what you can find, and I'll see what I can learn from the tainted items."

"You up to this tonight?" he asked.

I shrugged. "No time like the present. If that dog really did come after us in particular, I'd sure like to know why—because it's likely to be the least of our problems."

BACK AT THE store, we unloaded the boxes from the estate sale and cleared the table in the break room. I made a pot of coffee while Teag carried in the box holding the objects that triggered my internal alarms. Teag grabbed his laptop and settled into a chair at the end of the table. It didn't take him long before he glanced up at me.

"Black dogs are trouble," he said. "How much trouble depends on which mythology you follow. They can be death omens, or demons, or even hellhounds. Sometimes they're even the watchdogs for the gods —like Cerebus is for Hades."

"That's pleasant," I remarked drily. "Any chance that for once, a dog is just a dog?"

Teag leaned back in his chair. "I guess it's possible—although how often does that work for us?"

He had a point. We were usually safer assuming the supernatural explanation for any situation and being pleasantly surprised if it turned out to be mundane.

"Speaking of which, let's get a look at your leg," Teag said, standing and grabbing our first aid kit out of the cupboard. Given what we deal with, our kit is stocked with enough supplies for a small mobile emergency room.

I swiveled in my chair and stuck out my leg. Teag pulled on latex gloves and carefully pushed up the shredded hem of my bloody jeans. "Looks worse than it is," he said, probing carefully. "Not deep, but enough to make a mess."

"Use the holy water," I prompted, and Teag nodded, already reaching for the flask we kept on hand. He poured a trickle of the water over the wound. It hissed and bubbled, and I gripped the sides of the chair and gritted my teeth to keep from crying out.

"Well, that answers one question," Teag said, his lips set in a grim line. "It's definitely not a regular dog."

Once the pain subsided, Teag knelt and spread antibiotic ointment along the gashes, which fortunately did not require stitches. Then he bandaged my leg carefully and went to wash up. "Keep an eye on that," he warned. "We don't know what we're dealing with, but you definitely don't want supernatural cooties."

Teag brought us both cups of hot coffee, and I sipped mine slowly, recovering. "You don't have to take a look at the items tonight, Cassidy," Teag said. "They'll keep until tomorrow."

I shook my head. "Whether that thing came after us specifically or not, it's still out there, and it's a hazard. And right now, the only potential leads we have are the tainted items from the sale. If they're not connected to the dog, then we've got two mysteries instead of one. But if they are—"

"We might pick up something we can use," Teag finished my sentence.

"Exactly." I drank my coffee, letting it steady my nerves. "Either way, we'll have something to tell Sorren, and maybe he can help make sense of it all."

Teag pulled the objects out of the box. Under the break room light, they hardly appeared threatening. The antique man's wristwatch no longer worked, and the crystal was broken, but its strap suggested everyday wear, which could give an item strong resonance. A St. Francis medallion hung from a fine stainless steel chain, worn and scratched from long use. The final piece was the oddest of the three, a single glass eye.

I took a few deep breaths to steady myself, and Teag unrolled a small ribbon of hand-woven material, which he set on the table between us. "You know the drill," he said, pulling his chair up to the table. "Keep hold of one end of the ribbon, and I'll see what you see." Teag's Weaver magic meant that he could weave spells into cloth, and the shared connection was something we had only recently discovered. It definitely saved on needing explanations.

"Let's get to it," I said, and reached for the watch.

I don't control my visions when I touch an object. The object shows me what it wants to show me, or more to the point, I see the emotions and memories—or in some cases, magic—most closely linked to the piece. Sometimes it's like seeing through someone else's eyes, while other times, all I get are an onslaught of images and feelings, and I've got to somehow make sense of them. Of course, I never know what I'm going to get until it hits me right between the eyes.

As soon as I picked up the watch, the feeling of being constrained made me immediately uncomfortable. I didn't get pictures, just impressions, and what I felt from the object was overwhelming. *My body felt wrong, awkward and clumsy, and I was frustrated at being restricted in a form that moved slowly, with limited sight and decreased hearing.*

The sensation of being trapped filled me with panic, but I didn't realize that I was moaning and straining for breath until Teag pulled the watch from my grip.

"Breathe Cassidy," Teag coached, in a voice warm with worry.

"What... the hell... was that?" I croaked out.

"I don't know," Teag replied. "Do we know anything about the man who owned the watch? Because the impression I got was that he felt limited by his body—as if he'd been in an accident, or maybe had a stroke or a long illness."

I nodded and took several swallows of my sweet tea trying to regain my composure. "Yeah, I wondered the same thing. Almost as if he felt locked in inside his body."

"Once we're done, I'll see what I can find on the former owner. Shouldn't be too hard to find out if he ended up injured or paralyzed."

After a few minutes, I reached for the St. Francis medal and let my hand hover just a moment. "Let's see what I get from this one," I said, as Teag picked up his end of the woven ribbon. "Whoa, this one has juice Teag. I think it's been charmed or spelled."

"Maybe you shouldn't touch it until Sorren's here..."

Joy thrummed through me as the cold metal of the medallion settled in my palm. I smelled pine trees and fresh air, heard the rush of wind. Beneath it all, I could feel the thrill of moving sure and fast, graceful as an acrobat, tireless and strong. I felt blood rushing through my veins, heart pumping with exertion, lungs burning, muscles work-ing. A sense of invincibility settled around me, and I felt giddy with the way my body moved at my command.

This time, I set the item down on my own accord and looked at Teag in confusion. "How can those two items belong to the same person?" I asked, utterly baffled.

"Maybe they're from different times in his life," Teag mused. "Any idea of what it was spelled for?"

"I guess that's possible. I can't really tell what the magic does, but it's almost comforting – like a warm blanket." I felt certain we were missing something, but for the life of me I couldn't figure out a better explanation. Teag pushed the box closer, and I grimaced as I looked down at the last object. "Why the hell did he have a glass eyeball?"

"That's something else I'm going to try to track down tomorrow," Teag replied. "While I'm poking around to see if the old man was sick or in a wheelchair, I guess I also need to find out if he had a glass eye."

The images hit me hard and fast as my hand closed around the cold glass orb. *Fear, visceral and overwhelming shook me to my core. I struggled to breathe, felt the blood pounding in my ears as my heart beat in utter terror. Loss swept over me, deep and raw. Horror—the sense that something I had seen would haunt my dreams for the rest of my life. But mostly fear, that something in the shadows knew my name and wanted me for its own, and if it caught me, death would be a kindness—*

"Cassidy! Cassidy!" Teag's voice held an edge of panic as he wrestled the glass sphere out of my white-knuckled grip and tried to break through my terror. When I finally came back to myself, my heart pounded like I had sprinted a mile, and a thin sheen of sweat covered my face and arms. Teag held me by the shoulders, trying to calm me as I shook so hard my teeth chattered.

"What the hell was that about?" I managed, once I found my voice.

"Obviously that's the 'evil eye.'" Teag replied, trying to lift my spirits.

"Or the stink eye." I stared at the glass orb from a safe distance. "Of all the impressions I thought I might get, utter terror, wasn't really what I expected." My hand was still shaking as I lifted my coffee.

Teag grabbed a folder from the regular boxes we bought at the estate sale. "Malcolm Rendell's obituary doesn't tell us much about the guy. Not married, no kids, retired electrician. Bowling league. Shot-and-a-beer kinda guy from what I can tell."

"Except for the nudist colony part," I reminded him.

"Yeah, except for that," Teag muttered, pulling out his laptop. His fingers flew over the keyboard. Teag's Weaver magic extends beyond cloth. He can pull threads of information together far beyond normal Google-fu, making him one hell of a hacker. If Malcolm Rendell was hiding something, Teag would find it.

"I don't see anything in his obit about military service," Teag mused. "So he didn't lose an eye in the war." That might have explained both the glass eye and the sense of pervasive terror. "But give me time, and I can hack into his eye doctor's records."

"Maybe we should look into that nudist colony," I suggested, the felt my cheeks color. "Let me rephrase that—"

Teag snorted. "I'll get right on it. Anthony and I were thinking about taking a weekend getaway," he added with a knowing grin. Anthony is Teag's long-time partner. He's a lawyer with a prestigious firm, the scion of a family with a home on the Battery, and definitely not likely to hike around in the buff.

"I meant perhaps a little research into the group's history and membership is in order," I laughed.

"Agreed. No recon required. Malcolm seems like an odd fit for a group like that."

I frowned as I looked at the three items and replayed the impressions I had received. "Everything I saw felt very personal, but so different from one piece to another, it's hard to believe they all belonged to the same person. In fact, the more I think about it, the more I'm almost positive the glass eye didn't originally belong to Malcolm."

Teag shrugged. "Maybe Malcolm bought the pieces somewhere, or received them as a gift, and the visions you saw belonged to prior owners."

"Maybe," I allowed, but my gut told me otherwise. "I'm wondering if we should go talk to his neighbors, see if anyone can tell us more about him."

Teag shook his head. "Way ahead of you. I made the rounds while you were bidding at the auction," he said, and I raised an eyebrow, impressed. "Figured it couldn't hurt, especially after you zeroed in on the 'spookies.' Zilch. Nada. Nothing. Old guy, kept to himself, didn't bother anyone, didn't make a fuss. No girlfriend, no pets, but he did feed stray dogs, which was the only negative thing anyone mentioned. And he liked to go for walks in the woods—fully clothed," Teag added with a grin. "Birdwatcher."

"Huh." I digested what Teag uncovered as he reached over for the watch and medallion.

"Well, that shoots down two-thirds of my theory," he said, and held up both pieces, flipped over to reveal engraving on the back. *To Malcolm Christmas 1958* read the watch, while the medal was engraved, *To Malcolm with love, Mom and Dad.*

"Okay, so no flea market," I said, finishing my coffee and staring at the pieces on the table. I leaned forward to study the pieces more closely. "Teag, look at this. It's not your standard St. Francis medallion. A symbol was stamped on the back, like a charm of some kind, and it's engraved." I held it out. "Have you ever seen that symbol?"

Teag picked up the medallion to see the markings in better light. He shook his head. "I think the same thing is engraved on the watch."

"You're right. Same mark on both pieces. But it's not something I've seen before." I paused. "The glass eye might not have originally belonged to Malcolm, but all the pieces have strong supernatural resonance," I said. "When has anything like that turned out to be a coincidence?"

Teag concentrated on his computer, and a few minutes later he looked up, shaking his head. "Security sucks on his eye doctor's computer system. It took me more time to figure out which doctor he went to than it did to hack the records. No glass eye. Some glaucoma, and cataract surgery, but two real peepers."

I glared at the glass sphere. "It looks old," I said, studying the orb from a distance. "And I don't see any way it could have been connected inside an eye socket. Do you think it could have been part of a doll? Or maybe just a really creepy decoration?"

Teag shrugged. "I'll call the lady we get to appraise old dolls, first thing in the morning. Maybe she'll know more about it."

"What about the symbol?"

"I'm on it." Teag carefully drew the marking on a piece of paper, then took a photo with his phone, uploaded it, and called up another program. "Image recognition software," he said, although I hadn't asked. "It'll look for matches across the internet and show me the best results."

A loud thump sounded near the back door to the shop. At this hour, no one had a good reason to be in the alley. Sorren was traveling and I wasn't sure when to expect him, but I had the feeling that's not who was out there. No windows on the first floor looked out into the alley, so anyone approaching from that direction would not have seen the lights on in the break room, and given the hour, might well have expected the shop to be empty. With a glance, Teag and I both got to our feet, grabbed a weapon, and moved carefully toward the door.

A man lay unconscious on the pavement, just beyond the doorway. "Looks like Lucinda's wardings still pack some juice," Teag observed. Lucinda, a friendly Voudon mambo, keeps protective magic active around the shop and our homes, something that's come in handy more times than I like to think about.

"Let's get him inside, tie him up, and find out why he was trying to jimmy the door open," I said, wondering whether this would turn out to be a matter for the police, or something more supernatural in origin.

Teag and I dragged the unconscious man into the break room and tied him to one of the chairs. Lucinda's warding had knocked him out cold. While we waited for him to wake up, I looked the man over. He appeared to be in his early thirties, shorter than Teag, and fit enough to be a body builder. Long black hair fell to his shoulders. He wore a gray field coat with unusual buttons. I frowned as I noticed blood on the man's t-shirt.

"He's injured," I said, pointing.

Teag grabbed a pair of latex gloves from our med kit and gently lifted up the man's shirt to reveal faded bruising across his back and ribs. "Those bruises are pretty impressive even though they're mostly healed," he said, raising and eyebrow. "They must have really been something when they were fresh. And something got him behind his shoulder," he noted, pointing toward a pink scar of new skin. "Huh. The wound is closed, but there's blood on his skin and on his shirt like it just happened."

"He didn't get that from Lucinda's warding," I replied. "Her protections are supposed to keep people out, maybe knock them for a loop, but not tear them up."

Teag looked at me, as if debating whether to say what he was thinking. "This is going to sound really strange... but that fresh scar of his is in the same place as where I stabbed the black dog... if the dog were a guy."

I remembered that Bo's ghost tried to take a bite out of the black dog. "Check his right side, on the waist just above the hip."

Teag pulled up the hem of the stranger's shirt to reveal a newly healed bite scar. "Right where Bo got that dog-thing yesterday."

"Is there a wallet in his pocket?"

Teag checked, and came up with a battered leather fold-over. "Derek Eiford. License is either legit or a damn good fake. Address looks like an apartment; guessing it's north of the city."

Teag and I looked at each other. "There are no such thing as shapeshifters—are there?" I asked quietly.

"A few years ago, I would have told you there were no such thing as vampires, or ghosts, or any of the things we've fought."

"Why wouldn't Sorren have mentioned if there were shifters or weres?"

"Maybe it just didn't come up," Teag replied.

I took another look at our prisoner and would-be burglar. Given his bulk and weight, if I imagined him on his hands and knees, he wouldn't be far off size-wise from the black dog that attacked us. So it wasn't impossible—if you believed that a person could turn into a dog and back again.

When I looked up, I realized Teag was watching me. "Yeah," he said, guessing my thoughts. "It would work. If that sort of thing is possible. So I'm wondering, is it good or bad that I didn't use a silver blade? Or does silver even really affect shifters?"

Teag's laptop gave a soft *ding*. "Got a match on that symbol," he said, scooting around me to look at the screen. I joined him.

Multiple images of the same marking filled the display. Some were chiseled in stone, inked on parchment, tattooed onto human skin, carved into wood or etched into metal. The objects bearing the mark ranged from new pieces of jewelry to manuscripts and obelisks that were hundreds—or thousands—of years old.

"Ancient symbol… used worldwide," Teag read aloud. My breath caught a moment before he looked up at me as we read the same phrase. "Associated with were-creatures and shape-shifters."

"Do you think Malcolm—"

Teag raised his eyebrows. "That would reconcile the two very different images you got from the watch and the medallion. The watch gave you his human side, and the medallion must have been a resonance from when he was in his animal form."

The more I thought about it, the more Teag's suggestion made sense. "Still doesn't explain the glass eye."

"Let me work on that," Teag replied and turned back to his laptop.

I pulled my phone out of my pocket and called Sorren, not surprised when it rolled to voice mail. I left him a brief message about a mugger, a burglar, the symbol, and a black dog, and asked him to call. When I finished, I realized that Teag had been busy. A net of knotted rope woven with spells and soaked in colloidal silver now blanketed our unwilling guest and the cord that bound the man's wrists had been looped with silver chain. A human wouldn't notice, but many supernatural creatures would be immobilized by the metal's presence. I noticed that Derek's skin was red where the silver touched him. Teag grabbed a silver blade and an iron knife, both good against certain kinds of non-human beings, and a few more weapons from our bag, just in case.

"What now?" Teag asked. "We just wait for Sorren? We can't keep him here indefinitely."

The man groaned and lifted his head. Confusion and fear crossed his features, then panic as he tested his bonds. Anger quickly overshadowed everything else. "Who are you? Let me go!"

"Not until you tell us why you tried to break into our store," I replied, letting my athame slide back down into my hand.

"I don't know what you're talking about," the man replied, but I could see he was a little freaked.

"You jumped us last night, at the fish camp." Teag made it a statement, not a question.

"No idea what you're talking about," the dark-haired man replied.

"How'd you get the knife wound on your shoulder?" I asked.

Derek startled. "Knife wound? Lady, you've got it all wrong. A shelf fell on me at work and poked a hole in my side."

I gave him a look that made my disbelief clear. "And the dog bite on your hip?"

Derek glared at me. "What'd you pervs do, strip me down while I was out? You some kind of sickos?"

"These what you were looking for?" Teag held out the three tainted items we reclaimed from Malcolm's sale.

Derek's eyes gave him away before he caught himself and sputtered a denial. "You're crazy," he said.

I shook my wrist, and Bo's ghost appeared by my side. Derek flinched away so hard he nearly tipped over his chair. "Keep that thing away from me!" Bo seemed to recognize him as well and gave a low, warning growl.

"So here's the problem," Teag said, hitching up to sit on the corner of the break room table. "We could turn you over to the police and report an attempted break-in. They'll haul you in and question you, might keep you a while, cause you a real hassle."

"What do you think they'll say about tying me up and keeping me prisoner?" Derek challenged.

"We just restrained you until the police could respond," Teag replied with a shrug. "In fact, I'm pretty sure that we could cut the ropes and you still couldn't move, as long as that silver net is over you." He gave a patently insincere smile. "Wonder why that is?"

"How did you know Malcolm, and why do you want the things we bought at his sale?" I asked, deciding it was time to work the other side of the good cop/bad cop deal.

Derek glared at me. "I was a friend of Malcolm's, and he intended to leave me those things. So as far as I'm concerned, you stole them."

"Got a bill of sale that says otherwise," Teag replied.

"Bite me. The auction people screwed up," Derek's anger was clear in his voice. "I'll buy the pieces back from you if I have to." That's when I realized that I had seen him at the auction. He had bid on several boxes of odds and ends, junk that looked like it came from tag sales and pawn shops. I wondered why he was so intent on getting these three items when he had bought boxes of junk legitimately.

I regarded Derek as possibilities swirled in my mind. "A broken watch. A beat-up medallion, and a creepy glass eye. Strange bunch of things to risk getting arrested over."

"Sentimental value."

"Or maybe, you know that in the right hands, they'd 'out' Malcolm—and maybe you by association."

Derek squirmed in his seat. "I'm not gay, and neither was Malcolm."

"Not gay—shifter," Teag countered. "Or do you prefer 'were?'"

Derek kept his face impassive, but I saw fear in his eyes. "You people are crazy. Watchin' too much TV. No such thing as shifters or weres."

"Then why the symbol on the back of the watch and the medallion?" I challenged. Derek tried to keep his face impassive, but his eyes gave him away. "You didn't want anyone seeing that marking, or getting their hands on a spelled medallion. You were afraid someone would figure it out."

Derek looked away. "Malcolm didn't hurt anyone. And even if there were such things as shifters and weres, being one isn't against the law. So you've got no reason to keep me here."

I heard the click of the back door as it opened and closed. Sorren moved into the room silently, standing between me and Teag, facing Derek. "We both know better," Sorren said quietly.

Derek's expression twisted in sudden rage. "Keep that goddamn biter away from me!"

MEET THE FAMILY

"You two know each other?" Teag asked, gaze flickering between Sorren and Derek.

"I know what he is," Sorren replied, and I picked up an edge of distaste. "But not this one individually."

"Rich coming from your kind," Derek snapped, whatever hard feeling he harbored rising despite the fact that he was still a prisoner. "Like your transformation doesn't count."

I rarely saw Sorren angry, unless someone close to him got hurt. Now, I saw him clench his jaw, saw a muscle tighten around his eyes that told me Derek poked at some deep trigger. "Not going to argue this," Sorren said, his voice carefully controlled. He looked to Teag and me. "Why is he here?"

Teag jerked his head toward the back door. "Tried to break in. The wardings knocked him cold. We wanted some answers."

"I want to know if he's the black dog that attacked us last night." Derek's head snapped up when I spoke, and for a moment before he regained control, I saw fear in his eyes. Sorren's attention moved to take in Teag and me in a long glance, and I suspected he let his heightened senses scan us for signs of injury.

"Answer her." Sorren's quiet voice held lethal promise.

"No matter how I answer, I'm screwed," Derek retorted. "It's just a question of whether you kill me or my own people put me down for being too stupid to live."

"No, it's a question of whether or not I use compulsion to force you to tell Cassidy everything you know about the packs in the area, bleed you out for threatening my people, and send your body back as a warning." Sorren's flat voice and unreadable expression made my breath hitch, unsure just how far he was willing to take this.

"You want a war?"

"Seems to me, we've already got a war, if I'm right about the disappearances that have been going on for the last year," Sorren replied, never turning his gaze from Derek. "A war I intend to stop."

"Damn vampires, so sure you're better than the rest of us," Derek snarled.

Sorren moved so fast he blurred, then stopped with his hand wrapped around Derek's throat. "I don't give a damn about your petty prejudices," he said in a dangerously quiet voice. "Right now, what matters is that I'm older, stronger, and a lot more powerful. My allies and I protect this city from all enemies. And since you're not among my allies—"

"All right!" Derek croaked, hatred glinting in his eyes. "Get your filthy hands off me."

"Were you the black dog?" Sorren eased his grip but did not move his hand completely.

"Yes, dammit. I wanted to get that box back."

"Because you were afraid someone with magic might figure out Malcolm was a shifter, and his friends were, too?" I asked.

Derek's head twitched in a nod constrained by Sorren's hand on his throat.

"So I'm guessing all that business about Malcolm liking to bird-watch and go to nudist retreats in the forest were just cover for pack hunts?" Teag put in.

"Yeah. And everyone bought the story—until you two showed up." He licked his lips nervously. "They promised me they'd hold that stuff for me. But someone screwed up, and it ended up in the auction. I was supposed to make sure nothing got into the wrong hands, and then you had to go and outbid me. You can't keep that stuff or me; the pack won't stand for this. Even if you kill me, they'll come after you."

"They can try." Sorren let go of Derek's neck, and the man pulled back as if the touch burned him.

I watched Derek as he and Sorren argued. Something about the situation didn't add up. There weren't a lot of psychometrics running around Charleston—I was the only one I knew of—so the risk that someone else would handle Malcolm's items and realize his secret seemed like a flimsy excuse. Malcolm was dead; it wouldn't matter if his cover was blown. Nothing about the items tied them to Derek. The mark was unusual, but it could always be passed off as decoration. Yet our prisoner had a desperate, wild-eyed sense about him like a man on a mission. That's when I remembered what Sorren said about people going missing.

"Who did you lose?" I asked.

Derek jerked, startled. For a second, before he collected himself, I saw fear in his eyes. "Don't know what you're talking about," he muttered.

I knew he was lying. "You bought those boxes of junk at the sale. We figured Malcolm bought them at pawn shops and yard sales. You're looking for something. Maybe a clue to find a missing person?"

Derek struggled with himself for a moment, then lifted his head defiantly. "My brother, Jesse. He's been gone for four months now." Pain glinted in his eyes. "I don't figure he's still alive. But I want to find out what happened—and kill the bastard who took him."

So much raw pain colored Derek's voice that I knew he wasn't lying. I glanced at Sorren, and his nearly imperceptible nod validated my impression. "Tell us what's so special about the stuff you bought—and were trying to steal—and maybe this can go easier on you," I offered.

Derek looked from me to Sorren to Teag, distrust clear in his eyes. Then he let out a long breath, and his shoulders sagged. He suddenly looked tired and worn.

"Jesse's my older brother. We've always been close. He and I were going to meet up out at Sumter Forest and have a good run." His gaze was far away, and a sad smile touched his lips. "We hadn't done that for a while, and we were both looking forward to it. But when I got there, Jesse had vanished."

"You're sure he didn't just change his plans?" Teag asked.

Derek shook his head. "No. Jesse wouldn't stand me up like that. He would have called. And his car was parked in the lot. He didn't show up for work, didn't go back to his apartment. No one's seen him since."

"No trouble with the law? Romance problems? Bad debts?" Teag asked.

Derek glared at him. "Jesse kept his nose clean. He had a good job, a girlfriend he adored. Stayed out of trouble." His jaw set. "Someone took him."

"Okay," I said. "Let's say that's what happened. Why would someone kidnap him—or the others who've gone missing?"

"That's what Malcolm was trying to figure out." Derek glowered at us. "The guy was an oddball; that's true. He was also a hoarder. Loved to cruise through yard sales, pawn shops, and flea markets on the weekend and buy whatever caught his fancy. Did some dumpster diving, too," he added with a smirk. "But that's how he found the stuff that got him killed."

"Back up," Teag said. "What stuff? Killed by who?" I noticed that Sorren stayed quiet, letting Teag and me handle the questions since Derek was actually talking to us.

"Malcolm realized that some of the things he bought belonged to shifters that went missing. Little things, not much value, but they showed up for sale when they shouldn't have. We were trying to figure out who was pawning the stuff and where it was coming from. Then Malcolm ended up dead."

"What about the glass eye?" I asked.

Derek looked honestly stumped. "Malcolm was working on some leads, and he was too spooked to tell me much. Said it was for my own good. So I don't know what it means, but if he had it, then he thought it was important."

"And you think someone killed Malcolm to make him stop looking into the disappearances?" Teag asked.

Derek nodded. "Yeah. I'm sure of it. Although we hit nothing but dead ends. So far. Just means I'll pick up where Malcolm left off. " He looked up as if he expected us to try to talk him out of it."

"Won't that mean whoever killed Malcolm will come after you?"

Derek's eyes narrowed. "Let them. I've got a score to settle —for Jesse."

"What about your pack?" Sorren's voice made Derek jump.

Derek looked away. "They'd have to admit something was wrong," he said, bitterness clear in his voice. "It's a lot easier to blame the victim."

"There've been too many disappearances for the packs to keep denying there's a problem," Sorren said. "I intend to push the issue."

Derek snorted. "Good luck with that." He tilted his head, giving Sorren an appraising glance. "Look, I'm no fan of biters. But if you're serious about this, I can help. I'll share all the information Malcolm and I put together. Whatever it takes to either get Jesse back or avenge him." The look in Derek's eyes assured me he could be a dangerous ally.

"What now?" I asked, looking to Sorren for a hint of how he wanted to play this.

Sorren's lip twitched in a grim smile. He bent down until he was on eye level with Derek. "Sleep."

For an instant, I saw Derek's will struggle against the command, before his eyes closed and his face went slack. He slumped in his bonds, chest rising and falling in even, deep breaths.

Sorren motioned for us to move into the office, leaving Derek bound and draped in silver netting in the break room. He closed the door behind us as I turned on the light. "Why didn't you tell us were-things were real?" I asked as the adrenaline from the night's work turned tension into annoyance.

"I didn't keep their existence from you," Sorren replied. "We haven't had to deal with them, and the truce with the packs is fragile enough—if you weren't aware of them, you couldn't accidentally encroach."

"Isn't that exactly what we've done since we've got a shifter tied up and glamored in the other room?" Teag asked.

"I'll admit this is awkward," Sorren answered, in what I thought might be the understatement of the year. "But technically, the fault is his. He attacked people under my protection—and shifted to do it. He attacked this shop—also well-known to be off-limits. And if you and Teag hadn't managed to subdue him, I have no doubt that he would have hurt you to get what he wanted." Sorren's jaw was set, and his eyes had a hard glint. "That is unforgivable."

"I'm not thrilled about it, but he had a good reason. I can't imagine it will make anything better if we kill him," I said. Now that we were out of the thick of the fight, the idea of just killing Derek in cold blood made me pause, although I knew we couldn't leave him tied up and wrapped in silver forever.

"His pack wouldn't like it, but they would accept it as punishment due," Sorren replied. "Fortunately, there is another alternative."

"Take him to the pound?" Teag quipped, but I could hear the nervousness in his voice.

"Hardly. Although it's a lovely mental image. I intend to return him to his pack leader, in exchange for information."

"What about his offer to work with us?" Teag asked.

Sorren nodded. "We have to return him to his pack. If he still wants to collaborate, that's fine with me, although the pack might have other ideas. I have the feeling he's going to keep looking for his brother, with or without anyone's help or blessing."

"Back up to the part where you tell us that were-things are real and they live in Charleston," I said, taking down the bottle of bourbon I keep for emergencies and pouring some for Teag and me as we settled into chairs.

"The packs in Charleston are shifters, not were-creatures," Sorren replied, leaning on the door and crossing his arms over his chest. "It's an important difference. Shifters can change shape at will. Were-creatures' change is driven by the lunar cycle."

"Okay," I said slowly. "So he can just change himself into a big black dog whenever he wants to?"

Sorren shrugged. "It's a little more complicated than that, but basically—yes. Shifting takes energy, so he can't do it a lot, and he'll need rest and food to recover. I figure that's why he tried to break in as a human, instead of tracking you to your car again as a dog. Shifters can't stay in their animal form for too long without... unpleasant side effects."

"Are there a lot of shifters in Charleston?" Teag asked. I knew he'd be doing research on the Darke Web, the ensorcelled encrypted part of the internet frequented by those familiar with the supernatural.

"A few dozen," Sorren replied. "Enough for several packs—none of which like or trust each other."

"Lovely." I'd learned the hard way that supernatural creatures were masters of holding grudges.

"And I'm guessing they don't care for vampires," Teag added.

Sorren grimaced. "Those of us who began as humans remain more human than not, despite the other significant changes. Even immortality doesn't temper love, hate, jealousy, anger—or prejudice." If he had needed to breathe, he might have let out a sigh. "You've glimpsed it a bit among the different types of magic-practitioners you've met. Everyone's convinced his or her power is the most desirable."

"Are there other vampires in Charleston?" I asked, and realized it was something I'd never questioned.

Sorren's eyes narrowed. "Not without my permission. I claimed this city as mine to protect three hundred and fifty years ago when I worked with your ancestor to found Trifles and Folly. The signs are unmistakable for those who need to know. Coming here uninvited would be rightly considered a challenge—and a threat."

"But the packs co-exist," Teag put in, steering us back to less dangerous topics.

Sorren nodded. "Shifters aren't usually solo predators. They form small groups that function like a family of choice for self-protection. It helps them stay hidden because they cover for each other. And for more than a century, the Accords have held. Mortals have forgotten most of the tales about local people turning into animals because the packs have been careful to hide themselves and police their own members." He paused. "Clearly, something has changed."

"He couldn't get through Lucinda's wards," I said. "They knocked him out."

"Lucinda's protections against hostile magic are nothing to be taken lightly," Sorren replied. "There's even more animosity between the Voudon community and shifters than there is between shifters and my kind."

I wasn't a big fan of political maneuvering, and the idea that the hidden world of supernatural creatures had its own internal drama left me vaguely disappointed, even as I had to confess that it made sense. "You said you wanted to trade Derek to his pack for information. Do you know what group he belongs to?"

"I can smell the mark of his pack on him," Sorren replied. "And it's a bit of luck in our favor. His pack leader, a man named Marshall, is a reasonable man—less blinded by bias than most."

"You think there's a common thread to the disappearances?" Teag asked. "If so, then whoever killed Malcolm is likely to come after Derek—and us."

Sorren nodded. "That's why we need to talk with Marshall before this whole situation gets completely out of hand."

Teag and I followed Sorren out of the office and back to the break room. He spoke quietly to Derek, who woke up looking pissed. He raised his head to glare at us. "You gonna kill me now or what?" The split lip slurred his words, but the intent was clear.

"We're not going to kill you," Sorren replied, standing in front of Derek. "I'll dial your phone for you, and you're going to call Marshall and arrange a trade. You for some information."

Derek snorted. "I screwed up. What makes you think Marshall wants me back?"

Sorren shrugged. "You're pack. I suspect he'd want to deal with what happened himself, rather than letting outsiders handle it." Derek winced, validating Sorren's guess.

"The pack isn't going to be keen on having a biter around," Derek warned, glancing from Teag to me as if he was still trying to figure out what we were and how he ended up knocked for a loop.

"Leave the details to me," Sorren replied. He reached down and dug Derek's phone out of the man's pocket. "Give me Marshall's number." Derek's expression wavered between baleful and uncertain, trying to hide his fear of the pack leader behind bluster. Finally, he swore and rattled off the number.

Sorren dialed, and a moment later, a man's voice answered. "Hello."

"Marshall," Sorren said.

"Who is this? Where's Derek?"

"This is Sorren. We've met."

Silence, and then: "The biter?"

"I have someone who belongs to you—and you have information I want. Let's trade."

From the string of curses that followed, I gathered Marshall was less than pleased with the suggestion. "I'd be within my rights to kill him," Sorren continued after a moment, managing to sound completely unruffled. "He attacked two of my people and tried to break into my shop. You've been in Charleston long enough to know I protect what's mine. Giving him back to you is a gesture of goodwill. All I want in return is some information—and for you to let your people know that my people and places are off limits."

Marshall launched into another stream of profanity, but even at a distance, I could hear the frustration in his voice. Sorren held the cards, and it was clear from the angry words spewing from the phone that Marshall knew it. "When and where?"

Sorren gave Marshall a time to meet and directions to a cabin on St. John Island. I knew the place. Lucinda and Rowan, our favorite Voudon mambo and local witch, had warded the cabin against everything they had a protection spell for. Sorren, Teag, and I carved the walls and doors full of sigils and runes, to go with the amulets and talismans that hung from the rafters. We'd used the place as a neutral zone to meet with other players in the supernatural community when no one dared to take "good intentions" at face value. And more than once, we'd stashed a prisoner in the cabin when the risk of using any other location outweighed the inconvenience. Now, the plan called for a little of both.

"I'm invoking the Accords," Sorren told Marshall. I couldn't hear Marshall's reply. "Safe passage in and out for both sides. I'll have two people with me; you can bring two of your own. No more."

This time, Marshall's terse agreement carried across the distance. "Derek's alive?"

"A little worse for the wear," Sorren replied. "Within my rights to do worse, for what he did."

"Agreed." I shot a glance at Derek, and he dropped his head at Marshall's words, knowing trouble was headed his way.

"No reason we can't all come away from this with what we want, if everyone keeps a cool head," Sorren continued.

"Suits me." Marshall was obviously a man of few words.

Sorren ended the call and turned back toward Teag and me. "He'll be there in an hour. Let's go—I want to make sure we get to the cabin first."

I drove, glad that I recently traded my blue Mini Cooper for a more practical RAV4. Not as sexy, but much more useful for hauling around boxes and bodies. *And when did my world go sideways enough that evaluating trunk space meant figuring out how large a person would fit inside?*

Teag rode shotgun. Sorren sat in the back with Derek, who was handcuffed and partly wrapped in the silver-infused net. The net wasn't pure silver, but the residue was enough to raise welts and make Derek fidget. I almost felt bad for him, until I remembered fighting his dog alter-ego off in the parking lot last night.

The meeting with Marshall was supposed to be peaceful, but the three of us had enough weapons to protect ourselves if something went wrong. I'd only just found out that shifters were real, but if they were half as dangerous as TV shows and movies made them out to be, we were well-served going in prepared.

The cabin sat in the center of a large clearing, just as I remembered. Sandy soil kept the grass sparse and short. Nothing nearby gave cover for an ambush. Sorren had been playing this game for nearly five hundred years. Being good at it kept him—and us—alive.

"Let's get inside." Sorren manhandled Derek while Teag and I grabbed our weapons. We escorted them into the cabin. Sorren paused for a moment, scanning the clearing, and sniffed the air. "No one's here yet. Good."

Sorren paused in the doorway before flipping on the lights, just to assure that no surprises waited in the dark. By design, the cabin left no hiding places. Just a large main room and a small bathroom with its door wide open, exposing a shower and commode. The main room held a couch, a table, a few chairs, and along one side, a galley kitchen. Emergency supplies filled the shelves, along with basic canned goods. We used the cabin for awkward meetings, but in a pinch, it could serve as a well-provisioned safe house. I knew for a fact that Sorren had a day crypt beneath the floor, and that another secret compartment held sufficient weapons—supernatural and conventional—for a lengthy stand-off. The cabin itself could withstand even hurricane-force winds, with metal storm shutters covering the windows and fireproof walls and roof. We were as safe as possible—which somehow, didn't seem like much of a guarantee.

Sorren sat Derek down in a chair in the middle of the room, and Teag looped rope around his arms to keep him seated. I went to the window and looked out through the shutters, scanning the darkness for movement. I gripped my athame in my right hand and brushed the fingers of my left hand against an agate spindle whorl—the gift of a Norse *seiõr*—to rein in my nerves. The collar on my left wrist jangled, and Bo's ghost appeared next to me, silently vigilant. Teag had his martial arts staff in one hand, his spelled dagger in a scabbard on his belt.

We were here for a meeting, not a showdown, but we all sensed just how quickly one could become the other.

"He's here." I nodded toward the approach to the cabin. Sorren moved to glance out between the slats of the shutters. A tall, muscular man stalked across the open field with two lean, athletic shapes walking in sync on either side. They moved with the grace of dancers and the ferocity of wolves. Even with them at a distance, a warning prickled in the back of my mind.

"Let him in," Sorren said.

I opened the door, and Marshall strode inside. Clean-shaven, with dark hair that held just a hint of gray at the temples, Marshall looked like he belonged in a business suit, though tonight he wore a plaid shirt over jeans and boots. He looked to be in his early forties, and I wondered if shifters aged differently the regular humans. How many of them I had passed on the street never realizing?

Marshall's backups, a man and a woman, carried themselves like ex-military. I wondered if shifters gravitated toward jobs like that, where aggression fit the requirements. The woman's dark hair fell in a braid to her shoulders, her face defiantly free of make-up. Tension radiated from her body, but she defaulted to a parade rest stance. I glanced at the knife on her belt and wondered if she needed a weapon to kill. The man appeared equally lethal, with short dirty-blond hair and features that managed to be attractive in a rough way despite a nose that had been reset a few times.

"Derek." Marshall's gaze took in Sorren, Teag, and me, evaluated our potential danger, and then fixed on the object of the trade. "We need to talk."

Derek did not raise his head, and his mumbled apologies sounded garbled as he spoke them into his chest.

"He's here and alive—a little worse for the wear but quite good, all things considered," Sorren opened the negotiations.

"I'm here." Marshall replied. "Tell me why we couldn't have just done a drop-off out on the edge of town?"

"Because we agreed to a trade—your man for information. I want to know how many of your kind have gone missing—and how long it's been going on."

Whatever Marshall expected, Sorren's question sucked the wind out of him. For an instant, his eyes were unguarded, and I saw a glint of fear, something I didn't think Marshall revealed often. His expression slipped from surprise to anger. "Biters keeping an eye on us now?"

"Keeping an eye on Charleston is my job," Sorren replied, refusing to rise to the bait. "Has been for a long time. And in all those years, I've left your kind mostly alone, unless they gave me reason to do otherwise. If you don't believe me, ask your elders."

"I know it's true. I just don't like outsiders nosing around our business." Marshall's defiant voice held an edge of something else, and I wondered if he felt he needed to put up a good front for his backup.

"How many?"

Marshall looked away and let out a long breath. "In our pack? Three this year. Three I'm sure didn't just leave on their own."

"And in the other packs?"

Marshall hesitated. "You know we don't talk much. But word gets around. Maybe eight, nine total—just since January."

"Any theories on who's behind it or what's going on?"

Marshall shook his head. "No. And it's got people scared. Malcolm's was the exception. He's the first killed outright, the others are just missing. There's no connection among the victims that anyone's heard about, no common enemies, no old grudges. Just—gone."

Marshall looked like the kind of guy who solved his own problems, and I could see that it killed him to admit weakness. On the other hand, much as he scorned "biters," I was pretty sure anyone who had been in Charleston's supernatural underground as long as Marshall would have heard about Sorren and the Alliance—and us. We'd saved the city— and the world—from some pretty bad nasties, and Sorren's longer track record couldn't have gone unnoticed. *Maybe Derek's attack had been a skewed kind of gift. Marshall never would have offered up what he knew on his own.*

"So the disappearances started in January?" Sorren and Marshall stood facing each other, just farther than arm's length apart, as if neither were certain whether to talk or throw a punch.

"It's pack business. We'll handle it."

"You've had eight months to 'handle' it," Sorren snapped. "People keep dying. And I'm guessing that even so, the packs aren't working together."

Marshall shrugged, uncomfortable. "We don't have much to say to each other. Better if we keep our distance."

"Bet the killer knows that," Sorren goaded. "Bet he's counting on it. The longer the packs avoid working together on this, the more of your people are going to die."

"We don't know they're dead!" Marshall's head swung back to fix Sorren with a glare. His set jaw and the glint in his eyes sent a clear warning.

"Nobody's come back, have they?"

Marshall's right hand closed in a fist. Behind him, his bodyguards tensed, ready to move. Derek kept his eyes averted, but I could see the way his jaw clenched, and knew he was thinking about his brother among the missing. Sorren stood motionless, though Teag and I waited on high alert. Physically, we were no match for two shifters, but our magic gave us a more than human edge, maybe enough to even the odds.

After a moment, Marshall swallowed hard and let his fist loosen. "What can you do? You're not one of us."

"You know this will spill over eventually, outside of the packs." Sorren's voice, low and cold, carried the weight of centuries of authority. "Bystanders will get hurt. When—not if, but when—that happens, not only will outsiders pay far more attention to 'pack business' than you'd like, but I won't have any choice except to finish it. With or without the help of the packs."

"You wouldn't dare."

"You know better."

Sorren and Marshall eyed each other again, a momentary stand-off. "All right," Marshall said, and ran a hand up through his hair, shaking his head as if fighting a silent battle with himself. "This isn't going to be pretty. The other packs will be harder to convince than I was. And they like biters even less."

"Someone is picking off shifters. Since none of the packs are sharing information, the attacks look random. I suspect they're anything but," Sorren said. "Separately, none of you can put the pieces together. The killer's counting on that."

"We don't know they're dead," Marshall repeated.

Pity tempered Sorren's stern expression. "You know that's likely."

Marshall blinked slowly, composing himself.

I wonder if he lost someone who was more than just a pack mate. I thought.

"So you get us to come to the table, share information. Then what? The packs take care of their own."

"Then you let the professionals deal with it." Sorren's tone, razor-sharp, cut through Marshall's denial. "Because there will be blood, and this way, the pack stays clean. We will deal with it," he added, emphasizing each of the last five words, driving his point home.

Marshall nodded quickly, and I wondered whether he was trying to convince himself, or get Sorren to shut up. "Okay. All right. I get it. Yes. At least, for my pack. That's all I can promise, but I'll do everything I can to bring the others to the table."

Sorren watched him closely, looking for a sign that Marshall might be lying, and seemed satisfied with what he saw. "How long will it take?"

Marshall snorted, shooting Sorren an incredulous look. "A lifetime? Forever?" He rolled his eyes. "Give me a few days. It's not like I've got them on speed dial."

"Make it quick. We don't know when whoever—whatever—is behind this will strike again. There've been enough deaths already—and maybe more we don't even know about."

"I'll call you, once I've talked with the other pack leaders. In the meantime, try not to piss them off. This is going to be hard enough to sell them on without anybody stepping on toes." He paused and looked at Derek as if considering his presence for the first time. Throughout the conversation, Derek had not dared to raise his head.

"I believe I've found a use for Derek," Marshall said, a cold smile touching his lips. "He can start working off his penance by being the go-between and your pack-appointed bodyguard." Derek lifted his face, his expression a mix of relief and trepidation. "Cut him loose. I'll take him tonight. When I send him to you, don't kill him before you find out why he came."

Teag glanced toward Sorren, who gave a curt nod. Teag moved behind Derek and untied the rope.

Derek moved away from Teag like a spooked animal, but he kept his eyes on me with wary hope, as if he thought I might be a skeptical ally.

"He will be safe—so long as he doesn't act against me or mine," Sorren warned. "I can't promise we might not ruffle some fur while you're setting up the meeting," Sorren returned. "Better for everyone if we keep working the leads. Maybe I'll have more to share when we get together."

"I'll be in touch." With that, Marshall signaled his bodyguards, and they strode out of the room

HEADED FOR TROUBLE

THE NEXT DAY, I HEADED TO THE CHARLESTON CITY MARKET BEFORE it opened to the public. Just as I hoped, Ernestine Teller and her daughter Niella moved busily around the south doorway to the second building, setting up their table and laying out their elaborate sweetgrass baskets. A local magazine recently ran a feature on Mrs. Teller, hailing her as a master basket maker, and I knew Niella's skill did not lag far behind her mother's. Several of their baskets decorated my home, among my prized possessions. But today, I didn't come looking for baskets.

I needed answers from the best Hoodoo woman in town.

"I told Niella you'd be comin' round today," Mrs. Teller said in greeting, giving her daughter a nod and a smug smile.

Niella rolled her eyes. "Since you come by most days on your way to or from getting coffee, that was a safe bet," she said, fond exasperation coloring her tone.

"Looks like you've had a good week," I remarked since the number of baskets set out for sale was more sparse than usual. Other sweetgrass weavers had tables in the market, but Mrs. Teller had a following to match her reputation, and many in-the-know tourists would only buy from her.

Mrs. Teller's smile broadened. "Business has been good," she allowed and touched the gris-gris bag on her belt in gratitude. "Niella and I are working on more baskets. Should have them out soon." She fixed me with a look. "That's not what you came to talk about today."

Mrs. Teller knows about my psychometry, and she's teaching Teag to deepen his Weaver magic. She's one of the few who knows the whole story about Trifles and Folly, the Alliance, and Sorren. Even so, it always takes me by surprise when she knows what I'm thinking. I forget that her abilities go far beyond hexes and divination.

"So ask me." Mrs. Teller raised an eyebrow, waiting. Niella gave an exasperated sigh.

"What do you know about shifters?" I kept my voice down since other merchants were setting up inside the building, going back and forth to fetch merchandise from their trucks. This wasn't the kind of conversation I wanted anyone to overhear.

"They exist." Mrs. Teller met my gaze. "And they're closer than you think."

I nodded. "Can they take on any form?" I'd seen enough movies for my imagination to go into overdrive picturing shifters taking on the appearance of people I knew and trusted.

Mrs. Teller shook her head. "No, or at least, none that I've ever known could. Each one is born with the gift of becoming a certain type of animal. Even the ones who can turn into the same type of animal each have unique markings. Can't turn into just anything—or anybody, if that's what you're wondering."

I relaxed, just a little. "Do you know why anyone might be out to get them?"

Mrs. Teller frowned. "I heard some people—shifters—have gone missing. I've known there are packs here in town, but they keep their distance, and I keep mine. But people talk." She shrugged. "Some of the shifters are scared. They've come to me for gris-gris bags, for protection." I'd seen first-hand what Mrs. Teller's magic could do.

"Can you keep them safe?"

A glance passed between Mrs. Teller and Niella. "Maybe," she admitted. "It depends on who's after them, and what kind of power is being used." She lifted her head as if sizing me up. "How did all this get to be your concern?"

I gave her a very short recap. "Sorren's afraid something big is behind the disappearances, but until the packs will work together, it's difficult to get enough information on what's been happening. And I have the feeling that the only thing the packs dislike more than each other is Sorren."

A faint smile touched Mrs. Teller's lips. "Old rivalries never really fade. Both sides want to believe they're the top predator, the biggest badass in the room," she added. "And you know that t-shirt about what happens when mere mortals meddle in the affairs of dragons?"

I grimaced. "Yeah. We get deep fried and dipped in ketchup."

Niella chuckled at that. "What mama's trying to tell you is that pride is as much a part of the problem as whoever's causing the disappearances. The packs don't want to let the other shifters know they've been hurt. They sure as hell don't want help from someone like Sorren. No one wants to lose face by asking for help, but if the disappearances keep happening, they're going to have to do something soon."

"If the packs start fighting each other, it's going to spill over. People will get hurt. I won't be able to stay out of it—and neither will the Alliance."

Mrs. Teller sighed. "I know. But shifters are a close-mouthed bunch, and they're used to keeping to themselves. Asking for help makes them feel weak, and they'd rather fight to the last than lose face."

"Amazing they've lasted this long, with an attitude like that," I muttered.

Mrs. Teller reached out to take my hand. "Listen to me, Cassidy," she said, a warning tone clear in her voice. "Whoever is behind the disappearances is strong enough to take on the packs. You and Teag need to be very, very careful. The shifters will turn on you if they think that stopping the killer might reveal them to the outside world. Don't trust them. Even if you find out who the killer is, they might decide to make sure that what happens among the packs stays among the packs."

I shivered but nodded. "If they're that private, why let us help at all?"

Mrs. Teller fixed me with a look. "They might be hoping you'll force the killer's hand, draw him out."

"In other words, we're bait."

AFTER I LEFT the marketplace, I called Lucinda, but the calls went to voice mail. Still mulling over Mrs. Teller's warning, I stopped by Honeysuckle Café to grab lattes for Teag and me. I was so deep in thought that I didn't see Alistair McKinnon until he hailed me.

"Cassidy! What have you been up to? Haven't seen you at the museum lately!"

Alistair was the curator for the Lowcountry Museum of Charleston and a good friend. He often helped us out authenticating antiques that came into the shop, and on more than one occasion, he had turned to us when one of the museum's acquisitions carried a hint of haunt.

"You're right—I'm overdue," I admitted. "I need to come over and see the new exhibit."

Alistair laughed. "It's a good one. What's been keeping you busy?"

Alistair knew Teag and I dealt with ghosts and tainted old objects, but nothing about the real scope of the supernatural threats we fought. Well, truth be told, he had known a lot more but Sorren glamored him so he'd forget. It was best for us and for Allistair.

"Lots of people anxious to sell off old family heirlooms, and lots of others looking to buy second-hand treasures," I replied as casually as possible. "You know. The usual."

"Don't knock it," he said as we stood in line to order our caffeine fix. "Excitement is rarely a good thing." Something about his tone made me glance back at him.

"Problems?"

He shrugged. "One of our exhibits was vandalized last weekend. We're still not sure how someone got in—or why they left pieces that were far more valuable."

"What went missing?"

"Pieces from our new Natural History of the Lowcountry exhibit," he replied. "And the thing is, we're not the only museum to have a theft recently." He shook his head. "I don't get why they wanted what they took, but I guess there's a black market for everything."

"Any chance the police can get back what was taken?" I really hated the idea of people stealing anything, but taking one-of-a-kind pieces of history from a museum seemed especially low.

Alistair sighed. "I wish I could believe that, but this kind of theft doesn't usually get recovered. Some collectors are obsessive enough that they will stop at nothing to acquire what they want—even if they can never show it to anyone because it's stolen."

I remembered reading about art thefts where famous paintings had been cut out of their frames in museum galleries and vanished without a trace. It made me angry to think that one person's greed and selfishness could deprive the world of the chance to enjoy an artifact. "I'm sorry."

Alistair nodded. "What we really can't figure out is how the thief got in. Nothing tripped the alarms or the motion sensors. It's spooky."

A chill went down my spine. "Were there any legends about the pieces that were taken—any stories that they might have had something supernatural about them?"

"Not that I'm aware of," Alistair replied. "I guess anything's possible. Are you thinking the thief might have been some kind of cultist?"

I gave my most disarming smile. "You know how some people get when an item has a reputation for being haunted or magical. Some people will believe anything."

When I got back to Trifles and Folly, I found Maggie, our part-time assistant, handling the lone shopper in the front of the shop. She waved to me, and I headed to the break room, where Teag sat hunched over his computer.

"Brought you a latte," I said, setting it on the table beside him. "Find anything?"

Teag glanced up. "Yeah. Maybe. I started tracking all the missing persons in the Charleston police reports for the last eight months. And then I expanded it and looked at who went missing over the last couple of years, just in case. Then I mapped their social networks for clues about whether or not they were shifters."

"And?"

He slid a scribbled list my way. "Bingo. Got about a dozen that I'm almost positive are not quite mortal."

"Can you tell if they're shifters?"

Teag grimaced. "No, but there are other clues. If Sorren will share more names of confirmed shifters, I could do more." He paused. "But I think I figured out one piece of the puzzle."

This time, he turned his computer around so I could see the screen. The news site carried a story about a break-in at a mansion elsewhere in the state, but what drew my eye were the photos of the home's interior. The subtitle read "Thieves poach trophies from big game hunter's home." Every room featured large taxidermy animals—bears, deer, elk, and wolves. I shuddered, trying to imagine living in a house surrounded by dead, stuffed creatures and remembered how the glassy eyes of the specimens at the fish camp had weirded me out.

The glassy eyes. I met Teag's gaze as I realized the connection.

"Oh my god," I murmured. "You think—"

Teag nodded. "Yeah. You know that glass eye from Malcolm's auction? After I saw the news clip, I took a photo and sent it over to Horace." Horace was our oddities appraiser. "Recognized it right off as being a taxidermist's piece, but very old—seventy years or so at least."

I stared back at him. "Why would Malcolm have—or want—something like that?" A chill went down my spine as I remembered Derek's conviction that the items Malcolm picked up at pawn shops and flea markets had a connection to the disappearances.

Teag shrugged. "Not sure. I'd think being around trophy animals for a shifter would be like us keeping a mummy in the house." He met my gaze, and I registered the moment we both realized the connection.

"That theft at the big game hunter's house," I croaked, still grappling with the idea. "Have there been other break-ins like that?"

Teag took back his computer and started typing. On impulse, I pulled out my phone. "Alistair? It's Cassidy. Hey, strange question, but can you tell me what was stolen?" I listened, feeling a chill go down my spine. "Thanks."

I pocketed the phone and turned to look at Teag. "Someone broke into the museum's new natural history exhibit last night—"

"Let me guess. All that's missing are some taxidermy animals."

I watched Teag's fingers fly across the keys. In a few moments, he looked up. "There've been a dozen thefts from museums, national parks, and collectors in the last six months. All of taxidermy animals. Large specimens. And the thief was choosy. Reports say whoever did the break-ins didn't take the most valuable mounts. The police don't seem to have any idea why he—or she—took some and left others."

"You're thinking what I'm thinking?" I asked, feeling a knot in the pit of my stomach. Teag nodded.

"Shifters," he said, and his voice sounded like he was going to be sick. "Bad enough for them to be hunted for sport but—"

He swallowed hard, unable to say the rest, but I knew what he meant. *Hunted for sport. Shot down for someone's idea of fun. Mounted and preserved...* I ran to the bathroom and threw up.

When I came back to the break room, Teag handed me a glass of sweet tea. My hand was shaking as I accepted it. He met my gaze, and I saw the horror I felt reflected in his eyes.

"Do you think the owners of the mounted pieces knew the 'animals' were really people?" I managed when my stomach settled and I had nearly finished my latte.

Teag frowned, then shook his head. "I doubt it. But whoever's taking them now has to know. So is it one thief or several? Are the packs in on it?"

I set aside my empty glass. "I could sympathize if someone from the packs was behind the thefts," I said slowly, thinking out loud. "It's like when the Native American tribes sue a museum to get back the bones of their ancestors or important relics. Some things should never have ended up in a collection."

"Yeah, but the tribes can at least explain why they want the pieces back without everyone thinking they're nuts," Teag replied. "What would the packs say? 'Hey, that polar bear you've got on display, it's really my uncle?'"

A dark suspicion surfaced. "What about the disappearances?" I asked, afraid of the possibilities forming in my thoughts. "Derek and Marshall seemed to think the kidnapper was someone outside the packs, not one group turning on the others." Something Alistair said at the coffee shop made my blood run cold.

I met his gaze. "Alistair said that stolen museum pieces aren't usually recovered—that obsessive collectors don't care about keeping the hot artifacts a secret because they just want to own them."

"What if the same person is behind the thefts and the disappearances?" Teag finished my thought aloud. "A collector with very specific—and unusual tastes."

I nodded. "Someone who's filling in the gaps with the exotic pieces he doesn't already have—either by stealing them or hunting them." My mouth went dry. I hadn't made peace with the idea of shifters, and the ones we'd met seemed unlikely allies. Yet if I could accept a vampire as a friend, a mentor, and an employer despite knowing that others of his kind were dangerous, then I had to believe that some shifters could live safely among regular humans, too. If Marshall and the other packs weren't killing anyone, they weren't Alliance business. And if someone was stalking and killing them, the paranoia we had seen when we met with the pack leader suddenly seemed a little more justified.

"See if you can find anything else out about the thefts or the disappearances," I said. "I'll go up front and help Maggie. It sounds like she's busy out there." Maggie was handling the front room while Teag and I brainstormed the shifter problem. Maggie knows what we do, and while she steers clear of the big fights, she's always had our backs by holding down the fort or helping to pick up the pieces afterward.

Teag dug into the research, while Maggie and I kept customers happy. The day started out slow, but a couple of busloads of tourists made for a very busy afternoon. Before I knew it, we were a few minutes away from five o'clock, and I was starving.

"I'm going to call Sorren, right after I order food," I said as I went to find out what Maggie wanted to eat. After figuring out the link between the stolen items and the missing shifters, I wasn't hungry anymore. The idea of skinning, preserving, and displaying a trophy that was a human in another form made me nauseous.

I froze mid-step as an even more awful thought occurred to me. "You don't think that their souls are trapped in those display pieces, do you?" I could scarcely force out the words.

Teag's eyes widened. "Shit. Maybe. It would depend on how the magic works for the shifters. And whether the taxidermist has magic of his own." He stared at me as the pieces clicked. "We might have a renegade necromancer on the loose."

I wandered back into the front of the shop as I called in the order. Maggie went over the day's new acquisitions as we waited for dinner. When I glanced out the front window and caught sight of someone I didn't expect to see.

"Hey Teag! Do you know why Derek's hanging around outside the shop?"

"His boss volunteered him for guard duty—remember?"

I'd forgotten that Marshall had assigned Derek to us as his "punishment" for screwing up. Given the circumstances, I couldn't imagine how effective he'd be at the job since he could hardly be faulted for resenting the duty.

Derek's parked car sat across the street from the shop. The choice of a black pick-up truck didn't surprise me; it seemed like the kind of macho ride I'd expect from the shifter. I saw Derek fidget and wondered how long he'd been sitting outside. If he'd been there all day, I hoped his truck had good air conditioning, since it was warm.

All of a sudden, Derek opened his door and stepped out of the truck. I frowned, wondering if he had decided to head to the shop for some reason. To my surprise, Derek strode off down the block, walking like a man with a purpose.

Before I could ask Teag's opinion, I heard a knock at the back door. I glanced outside, surprised to see the food delivery man. Then again, parking out front was hard to find, and no one would care if he left his car running in the alley. I opened the door, reaching for my wallet.

Derek appeared out of nowhere, springing at the delivery man with supernatural speed and strength. I yelped as I dove out of the way. Derek and stranger hit the pavement hard enough to break bone. That both were giving as good as they got made me suddenly certain that the delivery guy was a shifter, too.

I'd never seen two shifters fight each other, and up close, the battle was brutal and terrifying. Teag and I couldn't have stepped in if we wanted to, although self-preservation instincts kept us back. Sorren might have had a chance in matching their speed and strength, but the only way we could have held our own was with a gun, and there was no way to take a shot without hitting Derek.

The delivery guy twisted in Derek's grip and threw him at the back door of the shop, blocking our exit and knocking Derek senseless for a moment. Before we could react, the attacker had vanished.

"What's going on?" Teag closed the distance to the door in a few steps, a silver knife in his hand. Belatedly, I realized that the take-out pasta we ordered spilled across the alley.

"The food was drugged." Derek hauled himself to his feet. Blood trickled from a cut on his eyebrow and a split lip, and I knew the angry red bruise on his left cheek would be black and blue tomorrow. "Permission to enter?"

I just stared at him. "What?"

Derek rolled his eyes. "The wardings? The ones that knocked me flat on my ass before? You have to allow me inside."

"Permission granted," I replied. As I watched, Derek's injuries healed themselves, until only dried blood remained.

"Shifter metabolism," Derek said, watching me as I stared at the prisoner. "Makes us hard to kill."

"How did you know about the drugs?" Teag asked.

"Smelled them," Derek replied, with a look at Teag that implied he was simple. He tapped his nose. "Enhanced senses. Roofies have a particular smell."

"Why would someone want to roofie us?" I looked up sharply, glancing from Derek to Teag.

Derek raised an eyebrow. "I can think of at least four good suspects —the heads of the other packs. That's assuming you haven't pissed of anyone else recently. You and Teag would make good collateral, especially if your biter friend cares whether you live or die."

Sorren definitely cared, which meant Teag and I had hostage potential. That wasn't a revelation. Teag and I were both trained fighters, good with magic. We'd handled ourselves against some badass bad guys and come out on top. That didn't make me cocky, but it did put the threat in perspective.

"That's not going to make it any easier to have a peaceful meeting with the pack leaders," Teag pointed out.

Derek rolled his eyes. "I imagine that a 'peaceful' meeting isn't what whoever sent him had in mind."

"Do you know which pack he belonged to?"

"None. He's a lobo."

"A wolf?" I asked.

"No. 'Lobo' is what we call shifters who operate outside of the packs. Wild cards. Lone rangers. They don't trust us. The feeling is mutual."

"Why would a... lobo want to derail the pack meeting?" Teag asked.

Derek shrugged. "Most lobos used to be in a pack, and either got thrown out or left on their own. We leave them alone, they leave us alone, and most of the time, no one gets hurt. But there's a reason they're flying solo—lobos are all a little edgy. Tightly-wound. Or to put it another way, they're unstable, even by shifter standards."

"So the guy could just want trouble for trouble's sake," I supplied.

"Maybe," Derek replied. "Or he might not want to see the packs work together. After all, that would put the lobos even more on the outside."

"Did you recognize him?" Teag glanced back toward the door, though the guy was long gone.

"No—but I'll know his scent again if I ever get close to him," Derek answered.

~

TWO HOURS LATER, Teag, Derek, and I waited inside the cabin on St. John Island and tried not to look nervous. I knew why Sorren chose that spot for the pack summit meeting. Small, private, remote, and providing no cover for assassins. Each pack master came with two bodyguards, who took their places against the walls, silent and lethal. Marshall and Derek exchanged terse words, and Derek went out to stand sentry on the porch. No one would mistake Teag and me for Sorren's bodyguards, and his insistence that both of us flanked him in seats at the table made the four shifters worried and uncomfortable.

I sized up the competitors. Marshall wore a polo shirt and khakis, sticking with his business casual look that would have been at home at a corporate retreat. Nico, sitting next to Marshall, looked more like a biker, with a shaved head, leather jacket and tat sleeves peeking from beneath his cuffs. Patty, beside Nico, looked like a soccer mom in her thirties in a matching twinset—except for the feral gleam in her eyes. That just left Sarah, a thin woman in her fifties with bottle-red hair and the world-weary look of a truck stop waitress.

"We don't need your help." Nico spoke first, and while Patty and Sarah remained silent, I could see in their eyes that they agreed.

"We've tried handling this on our own, and it's not getting better." Marshall might not have exuded support in our last meeting, but his resolve was clear now. "We need to work together. Share information. Hell, we don't even know how many of our people are actually missing because we haven't talked about it."

"Then why don't *we* talk—alone?" Patty's icy tone left little doubt about her feelings.

"Because we need the help, dammit!" Marshall's voice rose. Suddenly he froze. "Unless your packs are in on it."

I expected a brawl at that. Anger rose in the other three pack leaders' faces, swift and spontaneous.

"I lost four of my people this year." Nico's voice dropped to a low growl. "Four *friends*. How dare you—"

"We lost my cousin's son and two young women—both college students with promising careers," Patty snapped, lips set so tightly they paled. "This is *not* our doing."

"Our pack lost its master of the hunt and two elders," Sarah said in a whiskey rasp. "So either there's an outsider picking us off, or the other packs are trying to whittle us down."

"You actually think that we'd send… assassins against your pack?" Nico looked stunned and seriously pissed off. "How in the hell does that make any kind of sense?" His eyes narrowed. "Unless you suspect that from us because it's what your people are doing?"

"Are you out of your mind?" Patty slapped her palm against the table. "My pack doesn't slink down alleys throwing people into the trunks of cars."

"No, they stick to white collar crime," Sarah muttered. A corner of her mouth twitched upward at the look of disgust Patty afforded her.

"Beats clerking at the liquor store," Patty replied.

I found myself profoundly disappointed to discover that even in the supernatural community, Charleston still divided into those who lived South of Broad—and everyone else.

"No reason to be ashamed of honest work—not that you'd know," Nico sniped.

"That's enough," Sorren said. He might not have used true compulsion, but his voice silenced the room. "You don't have to like each other, or trust each other. But be smart about this. Your packs aren't large enough for each one to hide a secret killer. So if you're not hunting each other—and I don't think any of you believe that's the case—then the killer wins when you don't work together."

"And you have a solution?" No one could mistake the cold sarcasm in Patty's voice.

Sorren met her gaze and raised an eyebrow. One predator sizing up another. To no one's surprise, Patty blinked first. "Not yet," Sorren replied, completely unruffled. "And without full disclosure from all of you, this situation will just drag on. So I want to know the details about everyone's who's gone missing or died under suspicious circumstances for at least the last year—longer if you think it's relevant. We need information to find a pattern."

"I've got the list of everyone reported missing to the Charleston police for the last eighteen months," Teag said, distributing copies around the table. "It would be a huge help if y'all could positively ID the ones who are shifters. I was able to make an educated guess about a third of them, but I'd like confirmation." He looked up. "Here's a tip—if you don't want to be outed, watch who you friend on Facebook."

The room grew quiet as the pack masters scanned down through the list. From their solemn expressions, I figured that the seriousness of the situation finally sank in, outweighing their differences. Marshall read off four names, his voice thick with emotion. "But they're not the only ones," he said, grief clear in his eyes.

"Two of these are mine, but one's not on the list from this year—and if we're going back that far, you can actually add two more on top of that," Sarah admitted grudgingly. "And if the rumors are true, there might be up to half a dozen lobos no one would bother to report that have vanished."

Teag and I glanced at each other. We needed to find out more about the stalker delivery guy and the rest of the lobos.

"You've got the names right for my folks," Patty said, identifying her missing members. "But now that we're talking about this, a couple of people left town suddenly last year—at least, that's what I thought happened to them. Blamed it on a new job, bad breakup—but maybe not." She gave those names to Teag, just in case, and actually had the good grace to appear slightly rattled.

"None of my people are on the list," Nico said, leaning back in his chair. "We didn't report them to the cops, because the cops couldn't help. They just would have stuck their noses where they didn't belong." A sidelong glance in Sorren's direction made his unspoken sentiment clear. Even so, he provided the names of the missing shifters, and Teag wrote them down.

Marshall looked at Sorren. "You got what you wanted. Are we done?"

"It's not just disappearances." They all turned when I spoke. "We tracked a series of break-ins and thefts that might be related. Someone's targeting hunters and stealing very specific trophies. Taxidermy trophies."

Marshall paled. Nico cursed under his breath. Patty recoiled, looking physically ill. Sarah swallowed hard, trying and failing to hide an expression of horror. "You think—" Marshall began.

"It's a possibility," I replied. I wasn't going to bring up Marshall's cache of pawn shop items just yet, deciding it would be best for everyone to leave Derek's part out of the story, at least for now. "The thefts started a little more than eighteen months ago—same as the disappearances from what you told us tonight. The thieves are choosy. They're not taking the most valuable pieces, or even the rarest specimens. It's like the thief is looking for something in particular."

"I thought that was urban legend." We all turned to look at Nico. Slowly, the others nodded. "You know, like the guy with the hook for a hand at lover's lane or seeing Bloody Mary in the mirror? Makes a good boogeyman story, but c'mon—you don't really think—"

"I've learned that in more cases than not, the boogeyman is real," Sorren replied. "The missing shifters and the stolen trophies happening at the same time are too similar to be coincidence."

"Why?" Marshall licked his lips as if his mouth had gone dry. "Why would someone want the trophies? They're... ghastly."

A mental image of a sitting room filled with stuffed human corpses flashed in my imagination, and I had to agree with Marshall. I never had liked the idea of posing dead animals to look alive. Not killing them in the first place made a lot more sense to me.

"We don't know," Sorren replied. "But we'll find out. In the meantime, if you hear anything about the thefts, we need to know about it. Warn your people. At best, we're dealing with a sociopath who knows enough about the supernatural community to target shifters, and at worst, we're up against dark magic."

"So you want me to tell my pack to watch out for witches?" Nico echoed.

"Because being a shifter is possible, but being a witch isn't?" Sarah mocked. "Come on. We all know people who dabble in the Art." She looked at Sorren. "This goes a long way past love spells and putting curses on ex-husbands."

"Do you think the stolen trophies are... were shifters?" Patty had gone green in the gills.

"Maybe," I replied.

"Oh, god." Patty pulled a hand to her stomach reflexively. I couldn't blame her. "So that would mean that whoever's taking the new people is—" She couldn't finish the thought.

"You'd better not be making this shit up," Marshall said.

"We're not." Sorren's tone remained even, though I saw a flash of impatience in his eyes.

"If you can find out who's behind this, fine with me," Nico said, cocking his head as he looked at Sorren as though trying to take his measure. "But when it comes to dealing out justice, it should be done by the pack."

"Let the professionals handle it." Sorren's voice had the edge of authority. "You all know what the Alliance is and what we do. Let us take care of it. Keep the blood off your hands."

I could see that didn't set well with the pack masters by their expressions, but to my surprise, no one argued. Hard to know whether that meant they grudgingly accepted the truth in Sorren's words, or just intended to do as they pleased, regardless. For everyone's sake, I hoped they would stay out of it, but I doubted it would be that simple.

Given the drama involved in setting up the meeting, the aftermath seemed anticlimactic. When the arguing and shouting finished, and Sorren had the last word, the pack masters and their bodyguards got up and left with barely a nod to acknowledge our existence. We heard their cars leave the drive, and that's when I remembered Derek.

Teag and Sorren put the furniture back in place as I walked out on the porch. Derek stood a few feet from the door, blending in to the shadows. "Are you okay?" After the attack at the fish camp, and at the store, Derrek hadn't been one of my favorite people. Now that I knew he had a personal stake in the situation and had saved us from the drugged food, I found it hard to dislike him.

"It wasn't quite the suicide mission it looked like, being sent out here," Derek replied, self-deprecation clear in his voice. "Each of the pack masters had a guard stationed outside. Marshall was just reminding me that I'm just the hired muscle."

"Did Marshall lose someone close to him too?" My voice was soft, but I knew the shifter's extra-sensitive hearing wouldn't miss my words.

"Gossiping about the pack doesn't usually end well." He looked away.

"It's not gossip when it provides key information we need to stop this thing," I replied. "Knowing you lost Jesse, I understand how committed you are to this. So anything you can tell me about the others—"

"Marshall lost his mate." Derek looked away. "Marshall and Kayla were inseparable, and then she just vanished. He went a little nuts."

"How long ago?"

"Three months. Not too long after Jesse disappeared."

He was silent for a moment. "Do you have a picture of Jesse?" I asked.

Derek's gave me a wary glance. "Why?"

I shrugged. "If I see a face, it makes the fight to find him more real."

Derek hesitated, then pulled a wallet from his pocket and thumbed out a worn photograph of the two of them together. Derek looked younger by a few years, but no one could mistake the resemblance between him and Jesse. Jesse stood few inches taller and with his black hair cut in a short, trendy style compared to Derek's unruly mop, but the dark eyes and angular cheekbones marked them as brothers.

"Thank you," I said quietly. He put the photo and wallet away.

"Why did you replace the buttons on your coat?" That detail had bothered me since the first night we found him in the alley.

Obviously, Derek didn't see that question coming from the look he gave me. "What?"

I pointed to the buttons on his field coat. Someone had punched two neat holes through shiny quarters and secured the coins with leather as fasteners.

Derek chuckled, and for an instant, his face lost its wary, haunted look. "Jesse did that. You know how they brought out those quarters for each state a while back? Jesse took one from each of the states we lived in for more than a couple of weeks and made them into buttons."

He smiled at the memory. "We moved around a lot when we were younger. All shifters do. So it's kind of like my personal scrapbook, sort of. Jesse always liked doing things like that." Abruptly, his smile faded.

We sat in silence for a moment. "So someone took your brother. What about the others who disappeared? Were they especially close to anyone?"

Derek let out a deep breath. "The other two from our pack—Gregory and Jackson—were good friends. Marshall is a good pack leader. As families go, ours is closer than most—and he doesn't tolerate drama."

I chuckled at that, trying to picture a shifter version of the Brady Bunch. "How about the other packs?"

"Nico lost Rick—his cousin, but they were close. Patty's daughter was one of the ones taken. Sarah's best friend—or lover, depending on who's talking," Derek replied. "I'm not sure about the rest, but their packs are pretty tight, so I'd bet that at the least, they lost friends."

"Then why not work together, if they all lost people who were that close to them?"

Derek looked away. "That would mean exposing weakness—which could be used against them later."

I could think of a million arguments, but none of them mattered. "Well, the secret is out now, I guess. They'll have to deal with it." Derek gave me a look suggesting how unlikely that was. "Now what?"

"Now I go looking for the lobo who tried to drug you." Derek raised his head and met my gaze as if he expected an argument. "Marshall and the others don't want to be bothered. They won't believe anything a lobo would do could be important. But whoever drugged your food knows something, or he wouldn't have come after you—and I want to find out what he knows."

"We'll come with you."

Derek shook his head. "You can't. It's dangerous—"

I met his gaze and set my jaw. "Marshall assigned you to us. So, we're coming."

"Lobos trust non-shifters even less than the regular packs," Derek argued.

"Then we'll hang back. Be your bodyguards for a change. Teag and I aren't your average humans. We have… skills." I didn't want to elaborate too much on our magic since I wasn't sure that the shifters were long-time allies. On the other hand, we all had a stake in the game, and I had a strong feeling that Derek was going to need backup.

Derek bit his lip as he argued with himself. He knew that we could shut him down completely with a call to Marshall. I didn't want to go that route because I thought tracking down the lobos was a good idea. Now it was a battle of wills between me and Derek.

"All right," he growled, with a look that let me know he was distinctly unhappy. I resisted the urge to smile. Before either of us could say anything, the door opened.

"What's up?" Teag walked out, glancing from me to Derek and back again.

"Just checking in to get Derek's impressions of our guests tonight," I said, with a look, I knew Teag would interpret as "not now." Sorren was in the cabin, and while he might not have overheard my conversation with Derek with the door closed, he'd surely hear anything we said now. I wasn't sure that Sorren would like the idea of going after the lobos, so I decided to beg forgiveness instead of asking permission.

"You'll have to fill me in," Teag replied, and I knew he got my unspoken message.

Sorren stepped out onto the porch a minute later, turning off the lights and locking the door. "Not too bad, considering," he said in a tone that suggested the opposite. "No one's bleeding, no hearts got ripped out—pretty much of a win."

"Sometimes, you've got to take what you can get," I said, mustering up a tired smile.

~

"HEY, DO YOU know where Derek went?" I glanced out of the big windows in the front of the store, used to seeing Derek either in his truck or lounging nearby. If he kept this up, someone might report him for loitering. But now he was nowhere in sight, and that worried me.

"Maybe he needed to use the bathroom," Teag suggested. "Or he went for coffee—and lunch. He can take care of himself, Cassidy."

I frowned. "I know that," I snapped, then regretted sounding so sharp. On the other hand, something was getting the drop on shifters. Teag and I might be in danger, but so was Derek. A few moments later, I heard a knock at the back door.

Derek stood in the alley. He didn't try to come inside. "I went down to the pizza place where you and Teag ordered the take-out that night," he said. "Found out who the guy was I tackled. Seems he quit the next day, but I gave the manager a line about how I was a bill collector, and he gave me the guy's address." Derek added. "Seems pizza boy—Caleb—pissed off his boss by quitting like that, so his manager didn't mind handing him over."

"Nice," I replied drily.

Sarcasm didn't bother Derek. "Hey, I didn't have to rough anyone up—I'd say that was successful."

"Now what?"

Derek grinned, more like baring his teeth. "We go pay a visit, and see why Caleb came after you. One way or another, he's in this up to his neck."

I debated waiting until after the store closed, but if Caleb's boss changed his mind and decided to give him a heads-up, we could miss our man. "All right. I need to make sure Maggie's okay minding the store, and Teag and I will follow you."

Maggie assured us she was fine and offered to stop by my house and make sure Baxter, my little Maltese dog, got fed on time if we were late. I thanked her profusely, and then Teag and I followed Derek in my RAV4. We wove through traffic until we were past the trendy part of town, into neighborhoods that had seen better days. Derek pulled up outside a by-the-week apartment complex. I glanced up and down the street. Even though it was daytime, I was glad Teag and I were armed.

"What now?" Teag asked.

I shrugged. "We go around back, and make sure Caleb doesn't take a runner." Without magic, Teag and I would be useless as backup, or worse—sitting ducks. Our human strength was no match for a shifter, and on our own, we weren't fast enough, either. Magic evened the odds.

Teag and I both carried silver knives. The wicked sharp blades could decapitate if necessary, but even a small cut would burn a shifter badly. Teag had his silver-infused rope net and his fighting stave. I had both my athame and an antique walking stick that once belonged to Sorren's mentor, and Bo's collar jangled on my left wrist.

We saw no one as we got out of the car and made our way carefully around to the back of the apartments. I guessed the building started out as a hotel and fell on hard times. The last hurricane had damaged the roof, ripping up shingles that had yet to be replaced. Dingy white paint needed a touch-up, and the anemic, spindly plants in front of the sign looked ready to expire. I'd never seen a better visual metaphor for desperation.

A moment later, a man came clattering around the corner. It was Caleb, though he wasn't wearing his uniform now. I leveled my athame and caught him with a white blast of pure energy, knocking him off his feet and slamming him hard into the wall. In the next instant, Bo's ghost leaped past me, pinning the shifter to the ground. Bo kept him down while Teag bound his wrists.

"Let's get him back inside." Derek grabbed the man by the arm, holding on although our prisoner put up a struggle. We followed Derek into a sad efficiency apartment with all the charm of a cheap roadside motel. It stank of grease and cigarette smoke. Derek threw the man into a chair, and Teag draped the silver-rope net across his legs, effectively preventing him from changing form.

"Let's try this again," Derek began.

I took another look at Derek. I'd seen him contrite and submissive in front of Marshall. Now, I could see him as the predator he truly was. Tension coiled his muscles. Derek circled the prisoner, all lethal energy, and barely controlled anger. He might be our ally at the moment, but Derek could be dangerous if he chose. I wouldn't forget that lesson.

"Go to hell."

"I want to know why you drugged the food." Derek clenched his fist and released it as if fighting with himself about whether to take a swing or to keep using his words. For now, words won out.

"Because I got paid." Caleb eyed Derek. "Tips sucked last week. I needed to make some extra cash."

"Who paid you?"

Caleb looked at Derek as if he were stupid. "A guy."

Derek took a swing. His fist connected with a crack, knocking Caleb's head back. A non-shifter would have gotten a concussion or worse. Caleb just glowered and worked his jaw.

"Another lobo?"

"Maybe."

Derek's fist shot out again, and this time, I heard bone snap. Blood started from Caleb's nose. "I'm not fooling around."

Caleb's eyes narrowed. "Neither am I. What do you think happens to me if I tell you what I know?"

Derek shrugged and pulled a knife from his belt. "I know what's going to happen if you don't tell me."

I kept my athame trained on Caleb and looked around the room. Beer bottles littered the counter in the efficiency kitchen, and pizza boxes filled the garbage can. Either Caleb hadn't lived here long or he traveled light. Then I spotted the shirt from Caleb's uniform and caught Teag's eye. He nodded, realizing immediately what I meant to do.

Caleb's attention focused on Derek. I eased around to the side without either of them noticing. Teag shot me a worried glance, and I shook my head. Questionable pieces like the ones from Malcolm's sale might knock me flat on my ass, but I didn't think Caleb's uniform shirt was haunted. I bet that if he'd been wearing it when the person hired him to roofie us, I might catch the resonance of that image and perhaps find a clue to whoever was behind the attack.

Before I could overthink the situation, I put my hand on the uniform. In the next breath, I saw the kitchen at Ciao!, the pizza and pasta restaurant where Caleb used to work. I saw another worker, a man with short, dark-blond hair, replace the phone and I guessed he took our order. He handed in the ticket and walked over to the back door, where Caleb leaned against the door frame, taking a smoke between deliveries. I couldn't hear what the man said, but money changed hands, and Caleb nodded. The vision wavered, and I saw Caleb with our food in white Styrofoam containers. The blond man slipped him a vial of liquid and then went back to the phone. Caleb opened the containers and sprinkled half of the mixture on each meal and closed up the boxes.

I came back to myself with a gasp. Caleb and Derek stared at me. "What did you do?" Caleb growled. Derek didn't say anything, just looked from me to the shirt and back again. I could almost hear the wheels turning in his mind.

"You need to do laundry," I snarked. "Your clothes stink."

When Caleb's attention returned to Derek, I gave Teag a brief nod. He answered with a relieved smile. We were both glad I didn't need to be peeled off the floor after a bad vision.

"What's a lobo care about these two?" Derek asked. "What did your buddy want from knocking them out?"

Caleb shrugged. "Didn't ask; don't care. He paid cash." He paused. "Whatever he wanted, he was just waiting for a chance. Seemed to recognize the names right away."

I grimaced. So much for being predictable. Ciao! was one of our favorite options because they were good, cheap, and quick—and they delivered. I decided I was swearing off take-out and delivery for a while.

Derek threw a few more punches, but I had the feeling he did it more to work off frustration than because he believed Caleb had more to say. Finally, he nodded to Teag, who removed the rope net. Bo's ghost remained in front of Caleb, and a low growl warned the man not to rise from his chair.

"Get out of Charleston." Derek glared at Caleb. "The packs know what you did. The lobo who paid you won't have your back—if he's even still in town. I hope you got enough for bus fare to somewhere far away. Stay out of my sight. If I see you again, you'll wish I hadn't." Derek turned to us. "Let's go."

"You're going to leave him tied up?" Teag asked.

"He'll get out of the ropes—eventually," Derek replied. "Even if he has to chew his way out," he added. "We'll be long gone."

Getting out suited me fine, and I only relaxed once Teag and I were back in my car. Bo's ghost gave a wag and vanished, and I slid my athame back up my sleeve as Teag tossed his staff and the rope net in the back seat.

"You got something from his shirt." Teag didn't have to make it a question.

I nodded. "Yeah. Got a look at our man with the roofies. If he's still at Ciao!, I can ID him." I got lucky with the vision. I don't completely control what the psychometry shows me, or where I drop in on the impressions resonating from an object. Usually, I pick up something relevant because situations linked to strong emotions make the biggest impression on the energy of the object. Sometimes, it's like coming into the middle of a TV show and not knowing when you'll get to the part you want to see. I might have needed to relive Caleb's last whole day at work to get to the part I wanted, but I gambled that his nervousness about drugging the food would increase the emotion associated with the memory. I love it when things work out.

"Then let's head to the restaurant and see if we can track this guy down before he skips," Teag said. He paused. "Do you think Caleb told the truth about not knowing any more than the target?"

I nodded. "Yeah. I saw it when I touched his shirt. He didn't care about anything except the payoff." Sad to think we'd been sold out for twenty bucks.

Derek followed us back into town and parked behind my car. "What's up?" he asked, looking around warily as we got out of the car.

"Cassidy thinks she knows who paid Caleb to drug us," Teag said quietly, keeping an eye on the restaurant. We had parked down the block, so no one inside would spot us easily.

Derek gave an appraising look. "You read things by feel?"

I hesitated. "Yeah. I saw Caleb's memories from his shirt."

"That's how you knew about Malcolm—you got something from the pieces in the box."

I nodded. "The items filled in some of the blanks. You supplied the rest."

For the first time, Derek looked impressed. He eyed Teag as if wondering what magic, if any, he might possess, then seemed to think better about asking.

I described the man from my vision to Derek. Once again, Teag and I circled around back, letting Derek go in the front, gambling that the suspect wouldn't want to make a scene by making a break through the restaurant's seating area. Teag and I braced for another fight, athame and staff at the ready, but after a few minutes, I saw Derek coming down the alley toward us.

"It's a bust," he said, disgust thick in his voice. "The manager wasn't happy to see me again. First Caleb quit, and now the blond guy —Jim Kramer is his name or at least the name he used."

"You get an address?"

Derek nodded. "Yeah, but I had to promise to never come back." He snorted. "Didn't like their food anyhow."

"So could you tell if any of the other workers were shifters?" I asked.

Derek hesitated, and I realized that I had asked him to out others of his kind, people who might have nothing to do with Caleb or Jim. "No," he said finally. "There's no one else there we need to worry about."

We weren't hunting shifters, just looking for individuals tied to the disappearances, so I let Derek's half-truth slide. "All right then, let's find Jim—or at least his apartment—and see what we can figure out from there."

Jim's address led us to a mobile home in a run-down trailer park on the outskirts of town. The place looked as if it had been deserted for weeks. Weeds grew up around the base of the trailer, and the blinds hung askew behind dirty, cracked windows. Whoever Jim was, domesticity wasn't his strong suit. Cigarette butts littered the gravel around the hard-worn wooden steps.

Since no car sat in the driveway, I bet that Jim had already skipped out.

Derek headed for the front, while once again, Teag and I circled around back. I heard the door slam open as Derek chose not to knock. We waited, ready to capture a fugitive, but the back door did not move.

"He's gone." Derek's voice carried through the thin trailer walls. A moment late, the back door opened to admit us.

Derek stood in the dimly lit trailer, which was even gloomier on the inside. A sagging, stained couch looked like it had been picked up off the curb from someone else's trash night, as did an equally sad recliner with a broken footrest and two scarred end tables. I glanced around and saw no personal items. It looked as if Jim had already cleared out.

I heard Derek curse under his breath, and had to agree with his sentiments. "Now what?" Derek asked, an undercurrent of anger and frustration clear in his voice.

"Now we play CSI-Shifter," I said. "Look around for something that Jim might have touched very recently, the more personal, the better. Clothing would be best, or something he carried with him.

I guessed Jim left in a hurry, because he didn't do a good job of packing. That might work to our advantage. A few minutes rummaging around turned up some possibilities. Teag found a pocket comb on top of the battered dresser. Derek spotted a t-shirt behind the bathroom door. I found a disposable lighter in a bowl in the kitchen I bet Jim used to hold his keys and wallet.

"Are you going to try and 'read' them?" Derek asked, giving me a suspicious look. "Are you some kind of witch or something?"

"Or something," I murmured. "Why don't you keep poking around, see if you can find anything—hand-written notes, receipts, even match books from bars—that might clue us in to Jim's whereabouts. Teag and I will work with these."

I could tell from the expression on his face that Derek knew we were trying—nicely—to get rid of him for a while, but he did what I asked and headed into the other room. I sat down at the kitchen table and tried not to notice how sticky it was as Teag gathered the objects and put them in front of me.

"You really want to do this?"

I shrugged. "No, but do I have a choice? Jim either had a reason of his own for hiring Caleb to drug us, or he's working for someone else. Either way, it's got to be related to the disappearances, and face it—we've got diddly-squat."

Teag pushed the comb in front of me. "Hold on," he said before he dodged out to the car and returned with a bottled sports drink. "Just in case," he said with a nervous smile. We didn't have Teag's woven cloth strip to let him share the vision, but since we weren't in a secure location, I was okay with him standing guard while I got trippy.

I took a deep breath and closed my hand around the cheap plastic comb.

A torrent of images assaulted me. Jim's face in a mirror, here in the trailer. Riding in a car—an old Ford compact with a blue hood that was missing some of its paint. Another glimpse in a mirror and more of a men's restroom than I wanted to see, likely at a dive bar. Fighting the wind down at the Battery overlooking Charleston Harbor and this time, I caught the silhouette of another man. Sitting on the step outside the trailer, staring at the glowing tip of a cigarette…

I pulled back, and the images receded. "Get anything?" Teag asked.

The sports drink tasted wonderful as I took a couple of gulps while I pulled my thoughts together. "I know what Jim's car looks like—at least unless he decides to ditch it. Saw what might be one of his hang-outs, but only the men's room." I added with a grimace. Teag chuckled. "Saw him talking to someone, but didn't get enough to recognize who the guy was."

"Okay, that's still useful," Teag said, sliding the comb away and slipping me the t-shirt. "Don't worry: I've got hand sanitizer in the car," he added as if reading my thoughts.

My lip curled at the dirty shirt, but I closed my eyes and laid my hand on top of it. Once more, images flashed in my mind and as usual, in no particular order.

I saw what I recognized at the kitchen at Ciao!, where Caleb told us Jim also worked. I got another look at a seedy bar, this time of the main area and not the bathroom. Next a gym, and after that a convenience store. The next thing I saw was a woman, eyes closed, lips parted, and it looked to me like Jim was going to get lucky. I lifted my hand, not wanting to see more.

"So?"

I leaned back in my chair, feeling the strain of multiple readings. Teag pressed the drink into my hand, and I took another sip. "Saw a bar—think it might be same place. Derek might recognize it. A gym too. Looked like one of those cheap by-the-month chains. And a girl, either a girlfriend or a hook-up. I'd recognize her if I saw her again."

"One more to go," Teag said, swapping out the shirt for the lighter. "You up for it?"

I nodded, and picked up the plastic cylinder. A blue flame lit the tip of a cigarette, and then the image broadened to be the view from a bench at White Point Gardens, down by the harbor. Seeing a flash of the same sketchy bar didn't surprise me, although a glimpse of a local coffee house on King Street wasn't what I expected. When the scene changed back to the Battery, I got another look at the harbor, but this time, I saw Jim's companion straight on.

When I lifted my hand this time, I smiled. "I think I've got him—Jim's contact."

"I'll ask you again—what the hell are you? How do you do … that?" Derek leaned against the doorframe from the bedroom. I had the feeling he'd been watching for a while.

"Like you already guessed, I can read impressions from objects by touching them," I replied. "Depending on what I touch, that can include strong emotional resonance and magic."

"Witchcraft?"

I shook my head. "Psychic gift. No spells or rituals necessary. The images aren't always easy to interpret. Sometimes I don't see enough to make sense of anything, or what I do see is jumbled up, out of order. I don't control what I get to see."

"Tell me about the bar." Derek pushed away from the doorway.

"I didn't see the outside. The inside had a tacky Western theme, wood-paneled walls, and a stuffed jackalope."

"Denver Joe's." Derek looked from me to Teag. "It's a lobo bar. Figures he'd like a place like that."

"Just lobos?" Teag asked.

Derek shrugged. "Not just shifters, if that's what you mean. It's a regular bar. Most of the people in there aren't anything special. But none of the packs hang out there, so the lobos feel comfortable. Sometimes, some of the pack rebels go to Denver Joe's for a drink when they feel like slumming."

I described the gym, and Derek nodded in recognition, even though I thought the place looked generic. "Fitness Den. It's run by a shifter, so our kind is welcome, pack and lobo. Guy who owns it is a real alpha, so there's never any trouble."

After I told him about the girl, Derek was quiet long enough that I wondered if we'd hit a wall. "I've seen her," he said quietly. "But I don't know her name." He fell silent even longer when I described the man. "He's not a local. Doesn't sound like any of the shifters around here, either pack or lobo. If he's an outsider, he might be the guy who put Jim up to trying to drug you."

I could tell something was bothering Derek, but he held back so I dived in. "I don't need to be a mind reader to know you've got a question you want to ask me. Go ahead."

"If I gave you something that belonged to Jesse, would it help you find him?" He looked down, embarrassed by the worry and fear in his voice. "I'm just afraid that the longer he's missing, the less likely it is he'll come home," Derek said quietly. "He's my brother. I've got to find him."

"You two are close, aren't you?"

Derek nodded. "Shifters move around a lot. That's how we keep from getting caught. So me and Jesse always watched out for each other. Parents don't stay with pups once the pups can care for themselves—so when I was sixteen, mom and dad went their own way. Jesse and I stuck together. And now something's happened to him and I'm letting him down."

The guilt and pain in Derek's voice reminded me that the stakes were higher than just finding whoever was behind the disappearances.

"If you gave me things that Jesse owns and uses every day, I'd get images from them, but unless one of the items was something he carried when he got taken, I won't read anything useful. I'm sorry."

Derek looked down, letting his long black hair cover his eyes. "That's okay. I had to ask."

"Unless…" I said, getting a sudden thought. Derek looked up, hope and grief in his eyes. "It's a long shot. We've been betting that the kidnapper takes the victims by surprise, grabs them off the street. It's riskier for the kidnapper to make contact before the snatch, since someone might remember seeing him with the victim, but it could make sense if the victims are being chosen for a reason."

"Like their pelts?" I heard the edge in Derek's voice and winced, because that had been my thought exactly, thinking about the museum exhibits stolen for their "exotic" coloring.

"Yes." I saw no point in lying when Derek knew better.

Derek swallowed hard and then raised his head. "All right. I'll bring you some things of Jesse's tomorrow—things he usually carried in his pockets or wore just before… before. I mean, hey, nothing ventured nothing gained, right?" He tried to sound casual, but I heard the desperate hope in his voice, and the undercurrent of pain from the suspicion that we were already too late.

"I'll do whatever I can to help," I said, finding that I'd grown to like Derek despite first impressions. "We'll find out what happened to Jesse." We both knew it was the best I could promise, since the odds weren't in our favor of a happy ending, even if Derek did cling to hope.

Teag listened closely as Derek questioned me. "Let's get back to the shop," he said finally, reminding us how long we had been in Jim's trailer. "I have a couple of ideas."

When we got back to Trifles and Folly, Derek decided to wait outside, returning to his role as bodyguard. I promised to call his cell phone if we uncovered anything else he might be able to help with. Teag fired up his laptop while I made a pot of coffee. It didn't require a premonition to know this was going to be a late night.

"People forget that public parks have surveillance cameras," Teag said as he tapped away on his keyboard. "Too many movies about spies making a drop or Mafiosi handing off payola where they can't be seen or heard." He snorted. "Might have worked thirty years ago, but between cell phones, wifi, and all the city cams, it's pretty hard to go anywhere and not get caught on video."

"So you're hacking into the park's security cams?"

"Yeah, but first I'm hacking Ciao!'s payroll system," Teag said, biting his lip as he concentrated. It didn't take long for him to find what he was looking for—Jim's employee photo.

"Got it," he murmured as he saved a copy of the picture. "Now on to the park." After another few minutes, he sat back with a satisfied smile. "I'm in."

I moved behind him so I could look over his shoulder. Teag's Weaver magic lets him pull together data streams just as expertly as threads in fabric, so his hacking skills are crazy good. Good enough that he's been in and out of all kinds of "secure" systems including government and law enforcement sites and we haven't been arrested… yet.

The pictures on Teag's screen changed rapidly as he searched for the video feed he wanted. "Here," he said finally, a note of triumph in his voice.

"How are you going to find those few moments Jim and his contact were sitting on the bench out of hundreds of hours of video? We don't even know what day my vision picked up."

Teag grinned. "That's the beauty of facial recognition software. I've set it to match Jim's photo, so anyone he's with will get pulled along with it."

"You're scary good," I said, shaking my head and moving to get a cup of freshly-brewed coffee.

Just as I turned away, my phone rang. I expected Sorren, but the caller ID caught me by surprise. "Alicia! It's been a while."

Teag raised a curious eyebrow when he heard the ringtone, then went back to what he was doing as soon as I identified the person on the other end of the phone. "I'm going to put you on speaker, if that's okay," I said. "Teag's here with me."

"I've been getting messages for you, Cassidy," Alicia said without preamble. Alicia is a gifted psychic medium, and she's helped us make contact with restless spirits on several of our cases. Nothing ever seemed to rattle her. Now, she sounded edgy.

"Messages?" I echoed. "For me? From dead people?"

"You tell me," Alicia replied. "I've had four spirits come to me in the last twenty-four hours, trying to reach you. Three men and a woman."

"What did they look like?" I asked, and jotted down notes. Alicia's connection to the departed is as close to 4G as you can get to the after-life, and her descriptions had been used by police sketch artists more than once. Now, as I looked at what I'd written, I was almost certain one of those ghosts was Jesse, Derek's missing brother.

"So what were the messages?" I asked.

"Always the same thing," Alicia said, and this time, I couldn't miss the fear in her voice. "They kept saying 'free us' over and over. That's it. Just 'free us.' Do you know what that means?"

Teag and I looked at each other, and I thought about the missing taxidermy animals from the museum. "I'm afraid I do."

HUNTING THE HUNTER

AFTER THE LAST DINNER DELIVERY DISASTER, ORDERING TAKE-OUT
didn't appeal to either Teag or me. His face-matching software took
time to run, so we locked up the store and headed out for a quick bite
to eat. Ciao! did not make the short list of choices. I saw Derek sitting
in his truck across from Trifles and Folly. He held up a burger that he
must have gotten at a drive-through on the way back and waved to let
us know he'd keep an eye on us.

My stomach felt like one big knot, so I didn't care where we ate, as
long as no one tried to drug us. Charleston is a foodie city, so the
number of choices is staggering, but we opted for two orders of baked
mac and cheese from a pub down the street and walked back just as the
sun set. Derek still sat in his truck, which he had parked in a spot that
gave him a full view of our side of the street for several blocks. He
gave a mock salute and watched us go back into the store.

"Anything?" I asked as Teag checked on his laptop.

"Making progress," he replied. "The new software is faster and
almost scary good at making matches." Teag shook his head. "Kiss
your illusions of privacy goodbye."

Part of me wondered whether Teag was running a pilfered NSA-grade facial recognition program, but the voice of common sense decided I didn't really want to know for sure. I poured another cup of coffee, then sat down at my laptop and answered emails for another hour until Teag's program delivered its results.

"Bingo!" he whispered, smiling broadly. I hurried over and peered at his screen. The video clip matched my vision from Jim's lighter exactly.

"It's kind of grainy. Can you get a fix on who the other man is?"

Teag knew his way around the software, isolating the stranger's face and improving the resolution. With a few more keystrokes, he submitted the photo to the database for a match. A *ding* announced that we had a winner.

"Benjamin Gevers," Teag muttered, reading the name and frowning as he scrolled down through the information linked to the photo. "Last known address, Philadelphia. Couple of prior arrests, but no convictions. Not minor charges; we're talking about assault, possession of stolen goods, breaking and entering." He paused. "That's interesting."

"What?"

"Either Gevers has money or he's got a patron. The law firms that defended him on those charges don't come cheap." He looked up. "Anthony talks shop, so I know the names of the powerhouse law firms. Gevers wasn't getting sprung by the local bail bondsman."

"Anything else?"

Teag fell silent as he digested the data on the screen, and reached for a notepad. "This lists Gevers known employment, previous addresses. Now that we've got a name and address, I can data mine for credit card information, utility bills, phone records, social media if he's careless enough to leave a trail." Teag gave a cold smile. "Put enough data points together, and you can find anyone. And if we follow the money, we'll know who owns Gevers."

"How long will that take?" I asked.

Teag stretched. "Should have something by morning, if I let it run all night. Anthony's out of town on business, so he won't miss me as long as I answer my phone."

"You can crash at my place," I offered. I'd hosted late-night strategy sessions plenty of times, with the roster of guests changing depending on the sort of supernatural mayhem we were fighting at the time. "Besides, it's been a while since you've seen Baxter."

"Sounds like a plan," Teag said, finishing off his coffee. He gathered his things and grabbed his backpack. "I've got everything I need including; you'll be relieved to hear, a change of clothes. Learned the hard way it comes in handy," he added with a sidelong glance. The antiques business didn't get dirty, but fighting off demons and fugly monsters ruined more clothing than I cared to remember.

"I'll go let Derek know," I said, heading for the front door. I froze as soon as I got outside. Derek's empty truck sat across the street. The shattered glass on the driver's side door and a set of parallel scratches in the paint confirmed my worst suspicions. "Teag! Someone's grabbed Derek!"

Teag reached my side in a few running steps. We both took in the scene. Blood tinged the broken glass and left streaks on the driver's seat, confirming that Derek had not left voluntarily. We circled the truck, but saw nothing to indicate where Derek could be, and I guessed his kidnapper had a car nearby.

"Damn." Teag ran a hand back through his hair as I peered into the truck once more. On the passenger seat lay a worn ball cap and a leather wallet. "Grab those," I directed, not wanting to touch them yet. "I'm going to try getting a read from the truck."

Teag didn't question why I wanted the items from the seat. He took them and then moved closer to me as if to shield me from passers-by with his body. "Can you do that?"

"I don't know. Never had a reason to try." In the course of a day, I handle hundreds of objects that give me absolutely no psychic imprint, thank god. If I got a stream of memories and emotions from everything I touched, I'd lose my mind.

While working with Sorren and the Alliance gave me plenty of chances to practice my psychometry, most of what I learned came through trial and error. Often, that meant finding out the hard way whether something I tried was a bad idea. I closed my eyes, and let my hand fall onto the driver's door of Derek's truck.

Irritation. Surprise. Anger. Fear. Pain, and then blackness. A moment later, I found myself leaning against the truck, gasping for breath as Teag's hands clasped my shoulders, holding me on my feet.

"Come back, Cassidy," he urged, trying not to make a scene in the street. His fingertips dug into my arms, and if he let go I knew my knees would buckle.

"I felt it." The words came between panting breaths as I tried to still the shaking that made my whole body tremble.

"Tell me when we get inside," Teag urged, gently turning me to slip an arm around my waist. He made it look like a casual stroll back to the shop, when he held me up the whole way. Teag locked the door behind us, pulled the shades and maneuvered me into the break room. A moment later, he returned from my office with the bottle of bourbon we keep for emergencies, and poured a couple of fingers' worth into a glass, which he slid in front of me.

"Drink. Then tell me what you saw."

I took a sip, letting the liquor burn down my throat, anchoring me to the here and now. Behind closed eyes, I tried to sort out the sensations and images I'd received. The burst of impressions knocked me for a loop, coming at me so hard and fast I struggled to make sense of them.

"He knew the person." I opened my eyes and looked at Teag. "It irritated Derek to see him… I'm sure it was a man… and then Derek got angry." I tried in vain to get a good look at the mental picture of a figure outside the driver's window, but the night was dark and a hoodie hid the man's features. "I think he drugged Derek, maybe used a tranq gun," I said slowly, piecing impressions together. "It hurt. Derek didn't expect it, and then when he realized what was happening, he was terrified."

My hand shook as I reached for another sip of bourbon. Teag managed a worried smile and removed the cap and wallet from his pockets. "What about these?"

I eyed the items, but didn't reach for them, afraid of what I might see. "Derek asked if I'd try to read something that belonged to Jesse. It wouldn't be anything Jesse had with him when he disappeared, of course, but he hoped maybe we'd get a clue from… something."

"You don't have to do this tonight, Cassidy." Teag's worried tone gave me an idea of just how much the truck's vibes had affected me.

"Derek's in trouble. Jesse's probably dead. And whoever's out there is still taking shifters." I shook my head. "Let me get a grip, and then I'll touch them."

"Why don't we go to your house, like you suggested, and do it there?" Teag coaxed. "You'll feel better with Baxter nearby. I'll fix us a snack, and you can read Jesse's items somewhere comfortable. Then we can watch a movie while the recognition software runs, and kick back a little."

I nodded, thinking that sounded like a great idea. "You can drive," I added since I intended to finish the bourbon. "And then I'll call Sorren later on, see what he's come up with."

We left my RAV4 at the shop and drove to my place in Teag's old Volvo. Baxter yapped up a storm when he heard us coming, and I immediately felt better when I scooped him into my arms and snuggled him close as he stepped into the house.

"Let me get the laptop set up, and then I'll pillage your kitchen for snacks," Teag said with a grin. "Go pick a movie."

"Let me read Jesse's things before that," I said, sitting at the kitchen table with Baxter in my lap. "Just in case I pick up on something important."

I felt steadier now than at the shop, whether that was due to catching my breath or the bourbon, I couldn't say. Teag grabbed a pitcher of sweet tea from the fridge and poured us both tall glasses, coming over to sit next to me. He slid the wallet and cap in easy reach.

"Hat first." My fingers settled on the worn fabric of the cap's bill. I saw a sudden image of a man who strongly resembled Derek only a few years older, with a scruff of dark stubble and coal black hair. More pictures flowed from my connection to the hat. Jesse and Derek in the truck, talking. An apartment I guessed to be home for both brothers.

The same bar I'd seen in the other visions. A large, shaggy Newfoundland dog with long, sable hair save for a blaze of white on its forehead. And then another image, one I'd feared—Gevers, relaxing at the bar, chatting it up with Jesse.

I came back to myself as I sucked in a deep breath and swayed in my chair. Teag put out a hand to steady me, and Baxter slipped a small, cold nose against my hand. "He knew Gevers—met him in that bar."

Before Teag could stop me, I reached for Jesse's wallet and closed my hand around the worn leather. A rush of emotions surged over me, feelings rather than sounds or images. I don't control what my gift pulls from an object, just like I can't turn down the volume or change the channel if what I read from a piece is too intense. Anger swept over me, strong enough it took my breath away. Fierce protectiveness, coupled with worry bordering on mania and beneath it, dark ripples of gut-deep fear.

I surfaced like a drowning woman coming up for air. "Jesse was afraid," I said, my voice trembling. "He wasn't used to being afraid of anything, but he was terrified." I tried to make sense of the strong impressions. "Not for himself; for Derek. Jesse worried himself sick about Derek, and not being in control made him really angry."

"Maybe Jesse knew something about the disappearances, and he was afraid something would happen to Derek," Teag speculated. "Jesse might have started putting the pieces together, but maybe Gevers nabbed him before he could warn Derek."

I nodded. "That's what I think, too." I met Teag's gaze. "We've got to help Derek. Even if it's too late for Jesse, we've got to stop the killing."

Just then, my phone vibrated in my pocket. "It's Sorren," I mouthed to Teag, and when I spoke, I hoped my voice held steady.

"Derek's missing," I said before Sorren could get out a full sentence. "And we've got new information." I listened for a minute, then nodded. "Okay. We'll be waiting for you." I looked to Teag. "Sorren's coming over—and he's bringing Archibald Donnelly with him."

"What about Derek?"

"Sorren said he'd call Marshall. Even if Derek wasn't his favorite, I hope he'd care that another of their pack went missing."

Teag glanced at the progress of the tracking program on his laptop. "Still got a few more hours to run, but it's racking up matches. If this works, we might be able to narrow down the search."

Any relaxing effects from the bourbon faded as I paced, waiting for Sorren and Donnelly. Baxter started to bark as soon as the two men came to the door, and then he went silent, looking goofy and bemused when Sorren entered.

"You need to teach me how you do that," I said.

"I can't teach you to glamor him," Sorren replied with a chuckle. "You wouldn't like the package deal." I knew what he meant. Glamoring was a vampire talent, but there were times it would really come in handy.

"Hello, Archibald."

Donnelly gave me a wink in reply and waved at Teag. "Good to see you both." Archibald Donnelly looked to be in his late sixties, though I suspected he was much older, perhaps by hundreds of years. Shaggy white eyebrows and a fondness for safari jackets always made me think of the man as a Victorian colonel, and perhaps he had been, but his power as a necromancer made him a powerful friend and a formidable enemy.

"Tell me about Derek." Sorren and Donnelly settled on the couch and as usual, Baxter curled up at Sorren's feet.

I caught them up on the information we gathered from tracking down Caleb and Jim and what I gleaned from the objects I read, then let Teag fill in what we learned from his computer hacking. Finally, I shared Alicia's call about the ghosts' warning messages.

"I'm impressed," Sorren said, leaning back. "And what you've discovered dovetails with what Archibald and I turned up."

"This all happened once before, a long time ago," Donnelly said, folding his hands across his belly. "Not long after your Civil War. Nasty business when a big game hunter found himself a new taxidermist—who happened to be a necromancer."

Teag and I exchanged glances, and I knew we both remembered Alistair's comment about the stolen museum exhibits.

"I suspect it was no accident that they got together," Donnelly went on. "The hunter—Henry Sheldon—rivaled Teddy Roosevelt for his love of the chase, and he excelled at his sport. The perfect dupe for a necromancer like Ezekiel Green."

"Dupe?" I leaned forward, equally intrigued and unsettled.

"Green's use of magic fell outside accepted ethics," Donnely said, distaste curling his lip. "He managed to keep his dealings just ambiguous enough to evade the Alliance's interest, but those of us with magic kept an eye on him, looking for an excuse. You'd probably call Green a sociopath now. We just called him a sick son of a bitch."

Donnelly shook his head. "When we finally got to the bottom of it, we caught Sheldon hunting shifters, which Green was only too happy to… preserve."

My gut twisted. "I thought shifters reverted to human form after death."

Sorren met my gaze. "They do—unless something interferes."

"So Green used magic to keep the shifters in animal form and then… preserved them?" Teag sounded like me might throw up.

"Please tell me he let them die," I murmured.

Donnelly's eyes were haunted. "I wish I could. He used the energy from their trapped souls to replenish his magic, like infernal batteries."

I swallowed hard to keep from losing my dinner. "Damn. And you think someone's copying what happened back then—"

Donnelly shook his head. "Not copying. Repeating. We caught Sheldon and punished him, but Green got away. A necromancer of his power could easily be alive a century later."

"Then where has he been all that time?" Teag asked.

Sorren shrugged. "Not in Charleston or nearby any of my other stores, that much I know for certain. I imagine he went elsewhere and laid low for a while. Why he decided to come back here, resurface now, I can't imagine—but we're going to put a stop to it, once and for all."

A ping from Teag's computer interrupted the discussion. Teag jumped up and ran to the laptop as a cat-that-ate-the-canary smile flashed across his features. "Got you, you bastard," he murmured.

Sorren, Donnelly and I came to look over his shoulder. "For the last eight months, Gevers has been getting gas at a station on the outskirts of Walterboro," he said, naming a small town in a rural area not far from Charleston. "He makes other routine purchases in the area—groceries, convenience store, and a hardware store."

"So you think Gevers's boss is in the area?" Sorren asked.

Teag's grin broadened. "I've got a theory on that, too. I checked Gevers's car registration. He's got a truck with one of those fancy emergency signal systems—and those systems use GPS. Let's hack in and get a look at Gevers's driving habits."

Teag cracked the system in less time than it took me to go out to the kitchen and set out a tray of cheese, meat, and crackers. "Interesting. He drives to and from a farm just outside Walterboro. Give me a second, and we'll find out who owns the place."

"That's impressive magic you've got, young man," Donnelly said.

"Only part of it's magic," Teag confessed as he typed. "I jacked the rest from the NSA. Your tax dollars at work," he added with a smirk.

Before long, Teag looked up, triumphant. "The farm belongs to Jackson Emory. He's a local doctor, and—get this—he's been featured in the hometown newspaper for his worldwide hunting trips. Says he's hunted on all seven continents and according to the article, he's got a huge collection of mounted trophies, some of which he lends out to museums."

"Hells bells," Donnelly murmured. "I think we've got our hunter."

"What about Ezekiel Green?" Sorren asked.

Donnelly frowned. "I imagine he wants to stay close to the trophies if he's using them to store power. He'll be nearby."

I kept staring at the screen as they talked. "What about Derek and the others?"

"We'll find them," Sorren assured.

Teag looked up at me. "What are you thinking, Cassidy?"

"Can you get a satellite image of Emory's farm? He's not likely to keep his kidnapping victims in the house. Is there a barn or an outbuilding on the property big enough to stash a few people—maybe even house Green's taxidermy workshop?"

"Let's see." In a few minutes, Teag called up photos that gave us a good idea of the lay of the land on Emory's property.

"He's got a lot of land out in the middle of nowhere," Sorren mused. "No nearby neighbors."

"And I was right—there's a building that's a good distance from the house big enough to hide a multitude of sins," I said, and moved closer for a better look. "Can you zoom in?"

Teag obliged, and I pointed to the screen. "What's that?"

Teag played with the image until we got a ground level close up. He let out a low whistle as the picture came into focus. "It's a fence."

"Not any fence," Donnelly observed. "That's heavy-duty chain link with razor wire."

"Like a game preserve—or a prison," I said, going cold with horror.

Teag looked stricken. "You think Emory is hunting them."

"Hunting them for sport, and when he gets the kill, Green preserves the trophy." Sorren's voice held a deadly chill.

"Then we hit the barn, not the house," Donnelly said. His eyes had a hard glint to them that reminded me how dangerous he could be. "Teag and Cassidy extract the survivors. Sorren and I will take out Green."

Hearing Donnelly frame up the strike in military terms made my gut clench, but I forced the fear aside. Derek and the other shifters lost family members and friends to Emory's sick hobby and Green's cruel magic. We were their only hope, and that meant getting them out alive or putting down the sons of bitches who killed them.

"What about Marshall and the packs?" Teag asked.

Sorren and Donnelly exchanged a glance. "We bring in an army, Emory will skip out and Green will know we're coming. He'll kill the prisoners, and we'll lose any advantage of surprise."

"What's the point of the summit if we don't use the resources?" I asked. I knew Sorren had valid concerns, but Marshall and the others lost people they cared about. The fight belonged to them too, maybe even more than it did to us. Then again, I'd grown to like Derek as a friend. This was personal now.

Sorren thought for a moment. "I think I know how to do this." He pulled out his phone.

"Nico. It's Sorren. We've got a bead on who's taking your people." He waited out a loud torrent of profanity. "I need backup. We need to lock down a perimeter around a hundred-and-fifty-acre farm." I heard more swearing, and sharp questions.

"No, you're not going in hot," Sorren said, and his voice dropped into a tone that demanded obedience. "There's a necromancer involved in this, and that means you leave the magic to us. We'll take out the ones responsible and get your people out. But we do it my way, or I cut you out of the action."

Nico's tone would send a sane man running. Not much frightens a nearly six-hundred-year-old vampire. Sorren waited him out. "Yes or no, Nico. We don't have time to waste. Are you in or out?"

From the cold smile that touched Sorren's lips, I gathered Nico agreed to terms. "Tomorrow night. I'll call an hour before the strike with coordinates, so your people can get into position." I couldn't hear Nico's protest, but Sorran gave an amused snort. "No, I'm not tipping my hand a day early. I trust you. I just don't trust anyone that much. Assemble your people by nine tomorrow night outside Cottageville and wait for my call."

He paused. "And Nico? Double-cross me or screw this up, and the Alliance will make sure no packs come within a hundred miles of Charleston for a century." Calls to Patty and Sarah followed the same pattern, with varying degrees of profanity as the pack leaders grappled with not being in complete control of the operation.

"What about Marshall?" I asked as Sorren eyed his phone for the last call.

"He wants in; he's in." Sorren dialed Derek's pack master and waited for an answer, setting the phone on speaker. "Derek's missing. We know where he is and who took him. Your people up for blood?"

Marshall's swift, vehement answer left no room for doubt.

"Here's how I'm playing it," Sorren explained. "The other packs will cordon off the area, hold the perimeter, so no one gets in or out. We'll be going up against an assassin and a necromancer, and at least one or more lobos the shooter uses to acquire his targets."

"I'm listening." Marshall's clipped, tight voice held lethal promise.

"I need four hand-picked members of your pack, people you'd trust with your life because I'm trusting them with Teag and Cassidy." Sorren sounded like a general. "Two will go with them, and two come with me. The rest of your pack will hold the inner perimeter. That is if you want to be on the front line."

"Hell, yes."

"I'm trusting you," Sorren warned. "Letting your pack in closer than the others. Don't share what I tell you, and don't get creative." He repeated his instructions about time, place, and sending coordinates.

"Bring them back, Sorren. And stop the bastards who took them." Anger and grief roughened Marshall's voice.

"That's the plan." Sorren ended the call, and lowered his phone, then turned back to us. "Cassidy. You and Teag go into the barn and free the prisoners. Assuming they're still alive. Marshall's people will back you up, in case Gevers isn't the only traitor to his kind."

The thought of shifter guards had crossed my mind. Even with our magic, Teag and I would have a real challenge trying to get wounded prisoners out and fight off opponents that were faster and stronger. "What about Emory and Green?"

"Don't worry about Green." Donnelly's tone sent a chill down my spine. "I'll bring Rowan with me. She'll handle the regular magic, and I'll shut down Green's necromancy." His lips curved in a dangerous smile. "This fight is long overdue." Donnelly looked like he relished the opportunity and I knew that Rowan, a powerful witch who some-times helped us on cases, would enjoy the fight.

"That leaves Emory for me—and Marshall's people," Sorren said. "I've got no doubt Marshall will come himself. I'm counting on it. Emory is about to find out what it is to be hunted."

NINE O'CLOCK the next night found us on the other side of the chain link fence that marked Emory's private hunting grounds. Teag I had spent the day pouring over as many satellite images as we could acquire. I'd realized that if you only knew where a crime would occur, mighty few places were exempt from surveillance. The trick, of course, came in knowing when and where to look.

Our recon equipped us with a good idea of the terrain. Most of the area was wooded, with some rocky outcroppings and a few rough trails. Thick forest and underbrush made for a challenging hunt. *Does Emory hunt them as people, or force them to shift?* I wondered, both options equally terrifying.

We came armed for a fight to the death. I had a long knife on a belt scabbard and a small silver dagger, as well as my athame, Bo's collar, and Alard's walking stick. A necklace of protective agate circled my throat. Teag carried a knife as well as his martial arts stave and an array of silver-tipped throwing knives. An *Agimat* charm hung next to a Hamsa on a chain around his neck, both protective symbols. Carefully knotted lengths of cord hung from Teag's belt, and I knew he used his Weaver magic to store power and spells in the knots for future use. Beneath our jackets, we both wore Kevlar vests, one of Sorren's non-negotiable requirements. I knew what shifter teeth and claws could do, so I didn't argue, even though the vest felt stiff when I moved and held enough of my body heat to make me sweat on a cool autumn night.

"Get in and get out," Sorren warned in a barely audible hiss. "If you find survivors, you'll have your hands full just making it back to the perimeter, because I don't imagine they'll be in good shape." He left it unsaid the slim likelihood of finding the prisoners alive, even Derek.

Rowan assured us that the fence had no protections beyond a mundane alarm system, which Teag quickly disabled. Marshall came with us and Vivian, a black-haired, violet-eyed shifter who looked twice as lethal as Uma Thurman. The other two shifters, Alex and Hendrix, went to back up Sorren and Donnelly.

Wire cutters got us through the fence. We stopped, and Marshall lifted his face to the wind. "This way," he said, taking off into the shadows of the forest. The shifters' supernaturally-enhanced vision let them see in near-darkness, but Teag and I required night vision goggles. Marshall and Vivian moved silently, with a preternatural grace I'd never seen duplicated by anyone fully human. Teag and I did the best we could to keep up and make as little noise as possible. The look on Vivian's face let me know how much we sucked at stealth by shifter standards.

A glimpse of something shiny below a bit of scrub vegetation caught my eye. I bent down and saw a quarter with two neat holes drilled through it. Teag signaled for the others to stop, and they looked at me questioningly.

"Derek knows I can read objects," I whispered to Teag. "He dropped this on purpose, I'm sure of it."

Do I pause and risk a vision here and now, or have Teag pick up the button and keep going after Derek? My gut told me Derek meant to leave a message, and so I grabbed the button and closed my eyes.

Images flew past like a DVD on fast-forward, almost too quickly to process. Derek's truck, parked in front of Trifles and Folly. Gevers with a gun, and a struggle that ended with a tranquilizer dart. Waking up in the dark, probably the barn on Emory's farm, naked and bound. Then a gaunt-faced, hollow-eyed man speaking an incantation and the shift, forced and painful, to become the large black dog I'd seen at the fish camp. In the final image, the dog nipped the buttons of Derek's discarded jacket and held them in his mouth.

I came back to myself with a muted gasp. "They made him shift," I murmured to the others. "He's out here."

A rifle shot split the night air.

Marshall gave the military gesture for us to follow him, and we took off toward the sound of the shooting.

I gave the dog collar around my left wrist a shake, and Bo's ghost materialized next to me. My athame slipped into my right hand, and I could draw Alard's walking stick faster than Billy the Kid at high noon if I needed to. Teag had his blades out. Vivian shifted into a svelte gray wolf. Marshall pulled out a .45 and stayed in his human form.

Another shot sounded, closer now, and a pained yelp.

Vivian ran ahead, while Marshall indicated that he planned to flank the hunter. We were close to the action; I could hear heavy footsteps, and then a made out the image of a man stalking along the edge of a natural clearing. Jackson Emory lifted his rifle.

"It's over, Derek," Emory called out to the darkness. "I know that shot clipped you. You've led me a good chase. Time to end this."

My foot scuffed against something hard in the leaves, and I saw another one of Derek's special buttons. Blood smeared across the silver quarter. Trusting Bo and Teag to have my back, I grabbed the button.

This time, the vision gave me a good look at the hunter's face, confirming the identity as Emory. I saw Derek, in dog form, run for his life from the big barn, tearing at full speed into the forest, only to discover the fence that blocked any hope of escape. Emory nearly caught him then, but Derek doubled back, keeping to the shadows. Emory might be a skilled hunter, but he was merely human. Derek had a man's brain and a shifter's heightened senses. For a while, it was enough. Then he underestimated Emory's abilities and found himself staring down the barrel of a rifle. A shot fired, and I felt Derek's pain as the bullet grazed his ear. I also felt Derek's terrified certainty, as he ran into the darkness wounded and bleeding, that Emory missed making the kill on purpose, intent on stretching out the pleasure of the hunt.

I jerked back to myself and shook my head to clear it. "Sick bastard," I muttered. "Go!" I hissed to Teag. What I'd learned from the button confirmed important details, but right now, we had to get to Derek before Emory decided he'd had enough fun.

Just then, I caught a glimpse of movement and flung my arm out across Teag's chest, stopping him before he could step into view of the man on the other side of a row of large trees. Enough moonlight filtered down for our night vision goggles to function, and I wondered whether Emory used them too.

"You can't run forever, Derek." Emory's voice carried on the night air. "Give up. I'll make it quick. You know what they say: You never hear the bullet that kills you."

Emory's taunting tone made it clear how much he enjoyed his hunt.

I thought about the information Teag found about the man online, all his trophy kills around the world, even of species considered to be endangered. He'd hunted everything—except humans. The thought turned my stomach. *Was that what Green offered him? The hunt for more challenging prey, something that thought like a man and had the animal abilities of an apex predator?* Deep inside, I was sure I knew the answer.

"That's far enough." Marshall spoke from behind Emory, holding his gun in a firing stance, aimed at the center of the hunter's back. "Drop the rifle."

"Get off my land. This private property." Emory never flinched, and his voice gave no sign that he worried about an armed man behind him. For an entitled sack of shit, he had balls.

"Last time I checked, murder was still murder on private property."

"You're the one holding a gun on me."

"And you're the asshole hunting one of my people."

Emory's laugh sounded sharp and hard. "Not hunting any *people*, son. Just some rabid dog that needs to be put down."

"Drop your rifle," Marshall repeated. "I won't ask again."

Emory raised his left hand in a gesture of surrender and bent over to place the rifle on the ground. At the last moment, he dropped and rolled, firing at the spot where Marshall had been standing seconds ago.

A large gray malamute sprang from the shadows like a wolf, teeth bared, knocking Emory to the ground. I raised my athame, but I couldn't get a clear shot to hit Emory without hurting Vivian. She had his left forearm in her teeth and they rolled on the ground. A heard a shot, muffled from beneath the big dog's body, and then Vivian fell backward, fur matted with fresh blood. Emory held a pistol in his hand, pointed right at me.

"Get out of here," he snarled. "Before I kill the lot of you. I'm friends with the sheriff. No one will question it if I plead self-defense."

Everything happened at once. I raised my athame and sent a blast of cold white force at Emory as he squeezed the trigger. His shot went wide, missing me and *thunking* into a tree behind me. Marshall's gun fired an instant later, as Teag brought his staff around in a bone-crunching swing to knock the gun from Emory's hand. Bo's ghost leaped at Emory with all the weight of a ninety pound Golden Retriever, pinning him to the ground. That's when I saw the bullet's exit wound through Emory's right shoulder.

Teag sank down on one knee next to Vivian, who had shifted back to human form. He looked up and met Marshall's gaze, then shook his head. "I'm sorry."

"I think your hunt is over," Marshall grated, keeping his weapon trained on the wounded man. "Don't give me an excuse to shoot you again." He looked up to meet my gaze. "Go find Derek."

Teag and I started out in the direction Emory had been traveling. Teag glanced down and brushed his hand against a bush. His palm came away smeared with blood. "He came this way."

I thought about calling out to Derek, but we didn't know where Green was, or whether Sorren and Donnelly had captured the necromancer. So I kept silent, looking for Derek's trail. That's when I spotted another coin-button.

This time, a single image seared into my mind. I felt Derek's pain and fear, but the picture I received showed me a rocky outcropping like a shallow cave. I raised my head to look around, and in the moonlight, spotted a ridge not far away. "He's over there," I said, pointing. "Come on. Let's get him out of here."

Teag and I scrambled through the underbrush, climbing the rocky rise. "Derek! It's Cassidy. Emory's done for. You're safe. We're going to get you out of here."

A dark shape moved in the shadows. The big black dog limped into the open, bleeding from his shoulder and left ear. "Can you shift?" Teag asked. The dog gave a very human shake of the head "no."

"Green. He's still got his power, and he's locked Derek in." I managed a tired smile. "Good job dropping the buttons. They helped." The dog ducked its head in acknowledgment.

"Cassidy—look over there." My gaze followed where Teag pointed. From the high ground where we stood, I could see beyond the woods to the yard by Emory's barn. Two figures squared off against one. If Sorren and Donnelly were at an impasse, we were in a load of trouble.

"Where the hell are the shifters?" Teag muttered.

"Maybe Green took them down." I looked beyond Sorren and Donnelly toward the house, its windows ablaze with light.

"Remember what we guessed, that Green used the trophies of the shifters to store death magic for him, like witchy batteries?"

"You think that's why Donnelly hasn't handed him his ass yet?"

I nodded. "The house and the barn. We've got to get to the trophies and burn them."

Teag turned to Derek. "Can you walk?" This time, the big dog nodded.

"Follow us. We'll take you to Marshall," Teag said.

Derek limped behind us as we made our way back. Marshall had covered Vivian's body with his jacket. Emory lay where he fell, eyes open and staring at the night sky. I guessed that he had bled out from the wound. When Marshall spotted Derek, he let out a sigh of relief. "Thank God." He glanced at me and then at Teag. "Why hasn't he shifted?"

"We think Green's magic locked him in," I said, looking in the direction where we had last seen Sorren and Donnelly. "We've got to destroy the trophies. Can you make it to the barn, check for survivors and set any trophies there on fire? Teag and I will take care of anything in the house. Until we do, Sorren and Donnely are at a stalemate."

Marshall glanced at Derek. I don't know whether they could actually communicate by thought, or whether Derek just guessed intent, but the big black dog sat down beside Vivian's body and even wounded, he made a formidable guard.

"Go." Marshall grabbed Emory's fallen rifle and helped himself to a long knife from the hunter's belt. "I'll handle it."

"Watch yourself," Teag warned. "We don't know if Emory has 'helpers' out here." Marshall gave a curt nod, then headed in one direction while Teag and I jogged in another.

Teag and I found our way back to the cut in the fence, and stuck to the shadows, moving swiftly and silently. We kept the barn between us and Sorren's fight with Green, knowing we helped best by knocking out the necromancer's power supply. Bo's ghost loped beside me as I ran, adjusting his pace to mine. It didn't take long to cross the wide, dark lawn between the barn and the house, but I felt exposed with every step, knowing we presented an easy target.

"Where do we start?"

The square, three-story white clapboard house with a wide wrap-around porch looked like something from the pages of an upscale magazine. Lights blazed from the huge picture windows that ran the length of the first floor.

"We find the trophies and light them up."

Teag's expression made clear the words he did not say aloud. *What could possibly go wrong?*

JUST BEFORE WE reached the steps to the porch, a dark form hurtled from the shadows, knocking me to the ground hard enough that the air rushed from my lungs and my head spun. Teeth snapped, so close to my neck I felt a spray of saliva. I struggled to get free, pinned by the shifter's weight and strength. Teag's staff swished through the air and cracked against the man-sized Rottweiler's skull, and Bo's ghost sank its teeth into the creature's haunch. The Rottweiler twisted, trying again to bite and this time, its teeth grazed my shoulder.

I forced my right arm to bend, painfully wedging my elbow into the ground and my palm against the shifter's chest. Drawing on the resonance of my athame and my own pain and fear, I called to my magic and let loose a cold, white blast of power that threw the shifter off me, slamming him against the steps.

Teag followed up with another blow to the creature's head, and this time, the shifter stayed down. Taking no chances, Teag tied up the shifter with silver-infused rope.

"Come on!" I whispered, leading the way toward the windows that showcased the trophy room. Teag had managed to find a floorplan from the building permits, so while we had no way to know if alterations had been made, we weren't going in blind.

The trophy room took up half of the first floor. I couldn't know which of the taxidermy creatures might be shifters without touching them, something I had no intention of getting close enough to do. Breathtaking in its scope, Emory's collection included complete, mounted figures of large mammals and apex predators from around the world. Those that would not fit easily had been carved up into parts, like the rhino and elephant heads above the mantel.

We came prepared. Teag dug into the small rucksack he had carried all night, handing off two modernized Molotov cocktails to me, keeping two for himself, and grabbing a sawed-off shotgun. A little finesse and better materials meant assurance the home-made incendiaries wouldn't blow up in our hands. We pulled off our night vision goggles, not wanting to be blinded by the flames. Teag fished a lighter from his pocket. "Ready when you are."

"Go!"

Teag racked the shotgun and blasted the windows, taking no chances our explosives might bounce off bullet-proof glass back into our faces. Apparently Emory hadn't been worried about anyone shooting him, because the windows shattered in a spray of glass. I heard the snick of the lighter, saw the blue flame and a moment later, we lit the Molotov cocktails and let them fly.

"Run!" I yelled, as we turned our backs on the house and sprinted away at top speed.

A shot rang out, and I felt a sudden, searing pain in my calf that dropped me to my knees. Blood ran down my leg. Teag grabbed my arm and yanked me to my feet. "Can't stop!" I stumbled after him, just trying not to fall as we zig-zagged through the garden, hoping to use its bushes and plantings as cover.

A second shot kicked up dirt inches from Teag, and we careened in the opposite direction. We were easy targets in the moonlight, and the small garden hedgerow wouldn't hide us for long.

Over by the barn, I saw a flare of brilliant red light, as if hellfire had surged up from the ground. Behind us, the house exploded, sending plumes of flame into the night sky, deafening me and shaking the ground. I seized the opportunity, trading out my athame for Alard's walking stick. I took aim, tapping into the history and magic of those who had used the cane before me, gathering its power and drawing on my pain and fury to send a torrent of fire at the shooter.

Flames illuminated the man's face as he dodged aside, seconds too late. Gevers's hair and jacket caught fire, and he dropped, screaming, to roll on the lawn. Before I could breathe a sigh of relief, a large dark form slammed into Teag with a feral growl, taking them both to the ground.

I saw a flash of silver, and as Teag rolled the shifter, he buried his blade in its belly. The Mastiff howled, and as it reared back, firelight revealed other bites along its shoulder and sides, making me certain it had already encountered some of Marshall's pack. Teag seized the opportunity and got his feet under the creature's rib cage, hurling it away from him with his legs. I turned toward where the shifter lay, stunned and injured in the underbrush as Teag scrambled to his feet. He grabbed a weighted net of fine silver-coated chains from his belt and hurled it, unfurling as it flew, so that it covered the downed shifter, pinning him to the ground until we could get backup.

I looked at Teag, panting with exhaustion and pain, relief flooding through me. Then I registered the horror in Teag's eyes.

"Cassidy! Behind you!"

Too late. Charred, bloody arms grabbed me from behind, pulling me against Gevers's ruined chest. Any normal human would have been unconscious from the trauma and the pain, but shifters can withstand far more punishment. Even wounded, Gevers's grip threatened to break my ribs.

"Drop your weapons."

Teag raised his hands in surrender and moved slowly to comply, giving Gevers no reason to tighten his grip. I wondered why Gevers didn't have a gun on me, and then I looked down at his clawed, blackened hands and fought not to throw up at the smell of burned skin and blood. My left leg buckled, and would have taken me to the ground if Gevers hadn't held me up, using my body as a shield.

"Keep that ghost at bay," Gevers ordered when Bo took a step toward him, head lowered and teeth bared. I shook my head, and Bo stopped, but he watched Gevers's every move. Gevers held my upper arms pinned to my sides and encircled my chest like a vise with his forearms, but I could still move my hands. My fingers fumbled at the clasp on the sheath holding my silver knife, and I hoped he wouldn't feel the twitch of my muscles.

"She's my ticket out of here. So here's how it's going to work. I take her to my car. You stay here, and I won't break her neck on my way out of the driveway." Gevers's voice held steady considering the pain, but I could hear his breath hitching and feel the trembling in his failing body. He might live long enough to get away, but barring healing miraculous even for a shifter, he wouldn't get far.

"Not today," I muttered as I palmed the knife and turned it in my hand, driving the blade back into Gevers's belly. I fell forward the moment Gevers's grip eased, and a shot rang out from the bushes to our right. Gevers stiffened and gave a croak of pain, then dropped to the ground, a bullet hole in his temple.

Teag and I froze, unsure whether we had been rescued or merely passed off to another captor.

"Stand down." Marshall stepped out of the shadows, still holding his gun ready to fire.

Shaking with pain and relief, I fell forward onto my hands and knees. Teag moved to verify that Gevers was really dead, but I had all the proof I needed when I saw that half the man's skull was blown off. The other wounded shifter groaned beneath the metal net. I was more than happy to let Marshall deal with him.

"We found bones and freshly skinned pelts in the barn, but no survivors," Marshall reported. Barely controlled rage colored his clipped words.

That meant Derek's brother Jesse and the other missing members of his pack were dead, including Marshall's mate. I closed my eyes, saddened at their loss.

"Sorren and Donnelly?" I asked, as Teag eased me to a seat and took out a flashlight to examine my leg.

"Setting fire to the trophies burned Green along with them." Sorren stepped out of the darkness, startling all of us with his silent approach. Donnelly followed a few steps later. They both looked exhausted, blood-spattered and soot-streaked, but I didn't see any serious wounds. "Green held us off as long as he could draw on the stored energy, but once the trophies burned, he was overextended, and he went up in a ball of fire."

"We need to get you home and have Sorren's doctor take a look at your leg," Teag said, removing his t-shirt and wrapping it around my leg as a bandage. "A hospital will ask too many questions. Looks like the shot went through—didn't hit bone. You're lucky. Shouldn't be too bad to stitch up."

"How about Derek?" I looked up at Marshall. He and his pack had really come through for us tonight, and the cost had been high.

"Derek's in my truck. We'll see that he's properly fixed up."

"Can he shift back?" Teag asked.

Donnelly frowned. "Now that Green is dead, the magic that bound Derek should be gone, but I can check on him before we leave, just in case."

"I'd be grateful for that. Oh, one more thing. That stuff you picked up? Think maybe we could have the medallion back? Those are handed down through families; they mean a lot to us. I'd like Derek to have it," Marshall said.

I didn't have to think about it. "Sure. We'll destroy the watch and the eye, so they don't fall into the wrong hands, but I'll have the medallion delivered to you." I was about to ask if he was okay, but one look at his eyes gave me the answer. He wasn't, and he wouldn't be for quite a while, not after the losses he and the others suffered because of Emory and Green.

I felt battered and bruised, and Teag looked equally exhausted and injured. Still, I knew it could have turned out much worse, and for Marshall and Derek, there would be no celebration, just a cold sense of completion. I'd take my wins where I found them, and be grateful for any fight my friends and I walked away from.

"Come on," I said, struggling to my feet as Teag gave me a hand up and got under one shoulder to help me to the car. "We set fires they can probably see from space. Police will be here soon. We'd better not be here when they arrive."

I was alive, and so were my friends. The bad guys were dead. For tonight, it was enough.

PART VI
FAIR GAME

EARTHQUAKES, EPIDEMICS, AND EXPOSITIONS

"Two disasters and a World's Fair? How did you come up with this exhibit?" I glanced around the room at the display cases, shaking my head. "Isn't it a strange group of things to put together?"

My host, Mrs. Benjamin Morrissey, laughed, and the mirth reached her eyes. Slim and regal in a St. John suit, she looked every bit the society maven. "We've been displaying items from Charleston's history in decade groupings all year," she replied. "This is 1880 – 1910."

"I knew about the earthquake," I said as I moved closer to the wall mural covered with a montage of photographs, etchings, and newspaper clippings. "Anyone who's toured the historic district has seen the earthquake bolts through the old houses."

"At least we didn't have to include Yellow Fever epidemics," Mrs. Morrissey replied. "The last one in Charleston happened in 1877."

I shivered, despite myself, and took a step back from the nearest glass case. My magic can read the history of an object by touching it, and I'd learned the hard way to steer clear of pieces with tragic pasts when I could.

"Where did the items come from?" I asked to distract myself. Mrs.

Morrissey knows a bit about my magic. I suspect she knows more about my business than she lets on.

"We put out the call to the old families in town for memorabilia," she replied. "Some were happy to donate; others want the pieces back at the end of the exhibit. What makes this special is these items have never been on public display before. I don't think most of them have been out of attics or closets in decades." She sounded triumphant, and she had reason for it. Under her direction, the Historical Archive had gained a new prominence in Charleston, on the forefront of preservation efforts and seeing its best fundraising outcomes in years. Unique exhibits like this one, coupled with exquisite donor receptions and deft diplomacy with the city's moneyed elite were directly responsible for the Archive's rise in status.

"Your family's been in Charleston almost since the city was founded," she said, glancing at me. "I'm surprised you didn't have anything we could borrow."

"Given the business we're in, we don't hang on to old things too long," I replied, trying to keep my tone light.

I'm Cassidy Kincaide, and I'm the latest in my family to own Trifles and Folly, an antique and curio store in historic, haunted Charleston, SC. The store has been around for 350 years, since the city was an outpost. We've kept a lot of secrets in that time. The biggest is that antiques are only part of what we do. We're really a cover for the Alliance, a group of mortals and immortals who fight supernatural threats and get haunted and cursed objects out of the wrong hands. The second secret is that my business partner Sorren has been with the shop since its founding. He's a nearly six-hundred-year-old vampire, and he helps run the Alliance. When we do our job right, no one notices. I had to wonder if the hurricane and earthquake were how people explained the damage if my ancestor and Sorren didn't quite cover their tracks.

"Tell me about the World's Fair," I said, shifting the subject. The large upstairs room which housed the exhibit felt overly air-conditioned, probably in an attempt to protect the artifacts from Charleston's killer humidity. I ran my hands up and down my bare arms, feeling goosebumps rise.

"It wasn't really a true World's Fair," Mrs. Morrissey replied, leading me over to a bank of cases. I peered inside, feeling more comfortable around souvenirs of a gala exhibition than I did near the reminders of disease and natural disaster.

"Its real name was the 'South Carolina Interstate and West Indian Exposition.' That's quite a mouthful, isn't it?"

I leaned closer, looking at the elaborately printed tickets made from such detailed engraved plates that they almost resembled currency. A few specially-minted commemorative coins rested on a velvet pillow, along with a souvenir silver spoon that had a scene of a large Victorian building in the bowl and the name of the event etched into the stem.

"It wasn't sanctioned by the World's Fair organization," Mrs. Morrissey continued. "Some of the city promotors and business men put the deal together. It was controversial at the time. The Old Guard considered it a bit unseemly to be so forthright about wanting to attract more business. You know Charleston likes to do things the old fashioned way," she added with a wink.

Charleston was built on back-room agreements and hand-shake deals between descendants of families that had known each other for generations. Old school decorum meant pretending that money didn't matter, while in reality, it was always the primary goal. "I don't recognize the buildings," I noted, leaning forward to peer at the faded postcards and broadsides.

An elaborate white-domed Victorian palace sat at one end of a majestic sunken garden. On the other end of the long reflecting pool lined with classical statues was a round gazebo. I knew I had never seen the palace, but the gazebo looked familiar.

"The exposition was held on the land that's now Hampton Park," she said. "Some of the sunken garden and the gazebo are still there. That building was the Cotton Palace," she said wistfully. "Several fine, imposing buildings were constructed. After all, the whole point was to attract the world's attention and get people to invest in businesses here in South Carolina."

"They look so magnificent, but I'm sure I'd remember them if I'd seen them."

"They weren't built to last," Mrs. Morrissey said. "In fact, they were so poorly built that the city tore them down at the end of the exposition." She sighed. "That's almost a metaphor for the entire event. It never got the funding the organizers wanted, the weather was poor and attendance fell short of projections, and despite all the grandeur, the organizers went bankrupt with little economic impact to show from the whole, grand debacle."

"But it makes for one heck of a tragic, romantic story," I said, as my gaze lingered on the old photos.

I drifted back and forth among the glass cases, looking at the memorabilia. Among the items in the earthquake display were a broken porcelain doll, journals, and letters by survivors chronicling the cataclysm, some period photographs, and a length of iron railroad rails bent by Mother Nature into an unmistakable S-curve.

Experience has taught me to stay alert for impressions I receive through my "gift," even when I'm not actually touching objects. If the resonance is strong enough, I've picked up on emotions and energy from the ground beneath my feet. Even without handling the items in the case, I sensed the residue of fear and confusion, the weariness of a city that had barely survived war only to be crushed by nature itself. I'm not a medium, but everyone in Charleston has seen a ghost or two, and my abilities seem to attract more ghosts to me than my fair share. I caught a glimpse of movement, the impression of a woman and a girl in long-ago clothing, a man with a top hat, another fellow dressed like a laborer. I glanced at Mrs. Morrissey, but she either didn't see the shades or wasn't concerned.

Curiosity pulled me over to the cases showing the devastation left behind by the hurricane of 1893, what folks around here call the "Sea Island Hurricane" because it hit the coastal islands hardest. Old photos showed houses and piers destroyed by the force of the storm. Small items retrieved as flotsam from the waters lay carefully arranged on velvet inside the case. A stamped metal button lay next to a scratched and twisted silver fork. An unblemished porcelain teacup sat next to a card noting that it had been carried away by storm waters that destroyed its owner's entire home, only to be gently deposited yards away in the fork of a tree. Near it sat an invitation to a wedding that never happened, both the would-be bride and groom among the storm's casualties.

I paused again, closing my eyes this time. Mrs. Morrissey has a pretty good idea about my psychometry, and since she was friends with my late Uncle Evann who left me the store, I suspect she knows more about our real mission than she lets on. She didn't say anything though, just stood nearby waiting as if she hadn't seen everything in the display dozens of times already.

The ghosts felt stronger near this case, or maybe just tied more closely to the objects on display. After a long time, many ghosts begin to hollow out, become less of themselves and more like a lingering memory. Except, of course, for the ones so driven with rage or unmet needs that they seem to grow stronger with the passage of time. I didn't sense a danger from the storm's ghosts. If anything they felt... uneasy. That struck me as odd. What unsettles a ghost?

I opened my eyes and startled. A dark black *something* glided along the edge of the room. Not person-shaped, like a regular ghost. Not shaped like anything in particular that I could make out. There and gone so quickly I almost doubted what I saw, but I've been doing what we do for long enough that I know not to mistrust my instincts. In its wake, the black shape left a sense of dread and a visceral curl of fear. It seemed like an odd resonance to be left by a storm, no matter how devastating. Storms might kill as many people as a battle, but unlike man-made carnage, storms bore no ill will, harbored no resentments, did nothing out of malice. In a way, that almost made it worse for the impersonality of the devastation. *That's why it's called an Act of God.*

I repressed a shiver and moved to the next case. Out of the corner of my eye, I could just glimpse the black shadow, as if it hovered just at the edge of my sight, waiting.

The "World's Fair That Wasn't" filled a large case. Unlike the other displays, this one made me smile. A commemorative silver spoon lay on a velvet cushion; its bowl pressed with a scene of an ornate Victorian building and the name of the fair engraved up the handle. Several souvenir coins gleamed in the light, along with a gaudy, painted porcelain ashtray, commemorative plates, and a sheaf of yellowed postcards.

I leaned closer as one of the cards caught my eye. "That gazebo looks familiar," I said.

Mrs. Morrissey nodded. "The bandstand is one of the few things that survived, along with one building and a bit of the sunken gardens. It's rather amazing, really, with how grand the grounds were at the time, that it's as if it were all a dream."

A few of the postcards were turned picture-down to reveal the writing on the other side. "Can't believe I'm really here. I'll tell you all about it when I get home," the faded ink read. "Love, Stephen." The precise handwriting had the swoop and flair of a confident young man.

"The fair might not have gotten the crowds the promoters wanted, but those who did attend came from far and wide," Mrs. Morrissey said with a sigh. "It's just a shame that the whole thing was a bust."

"I'd heard most World's Fairs don't really turn a profit," I remarked, drawn to the display by something I couldn't explain. "Kind of like hosting the Olympics. Lots of prestige, big expenses, big bills to pay once the party's over."

The darkness felt closer. I turned sharply, expecting to see that it slipped between the displays or puddled beneath the cases like spilled water, but saw nothing. Mrs. Morrissey gave me a look. "Something wrong, Cassidy?'

I managed a smile and shook my head. "Just a little jumpy today. I thought I saw something."

Mrs. Morrissey laughed. "Well, you probably wouldn't be wrong if you did. It's an old house, and this is Charleston. Ghosts are part of the package."

Quiet ghosts didn't bother me, but the dark shadow made me nervous. I was about to ask a question when the lights went out. Downstairs, that wouldn't have been a problem with the tall windows in the old converted house. But the exhibit room was windowless, to protect fragile fabrics and paintings on display. That made it pitch dark.

I froze, expecting the emergency lights to flicker on at any second. The temperature in the room plummeted, and I felt goosebumps rise on my arms. All of a sudden, the texture of the darkness around me changed. This new dark felt heavier, not quite solid but more than mere air. Its touch felt cold like corpse-flesh, and fear slithered up my spine as the blackness licked around me, opaque enough that I feared if it engulfed me I would not see light again.

I could hear screaming from a distance, many voices raised in anguish, pleading, begging, crying out in terror and pain. Another voice carried on the darkness, this one just a whisper, murmuring fearsome ideas of what might happen next. *Free us. Please, free us!*

Abruptly, the lights went on, blinding me. The voices fell silent, and the strange, solid darkness vanished. I realized that I had wrapped my arms around myself and was rocking back and forth, braced against the threat of that deep, fearsome voice.

"Cassidy? Are you all right?" From the tone, I gathered Mrs. Morrissey had been calling to me for a while without reply.

"Yeah," I said, hearing the stutter in my lie. "Just got a bit of a vision. Not a surprise considering the circumstances behind all this," I added with a vague sweep of my hand to indicate the cases.

"I was afraid of that," Mrs. Morrissey tutted. She took hold of my elbow and guided me back downstairs to her office, then disappeared for a moment to fetch me a cup of coffee. When I took a sip, I realized she'd laced it with whiskey.

"I've called you a cab," she said, smoothing her skirt under her as she sat down behind the desk.

"That's really not—"

"I insist." She smiled. "I'm sorry about the display—"

I sighed. "I need to learn better control. And it's getting better, just not quickly." I didn't know what the timetable was for learning not to get knocked flat on my ass by my psychic gift. Surprisingly, it wasn't the kind of thing people wrote self-help books about, and the people I'd asked who might know just said "it depends."

"What you sensed up there—was it dangerous?"

I frowned, trying to parse through the impressions I'd gained, and took another sip of the Irish coffee. The whiskey warmed me, stopped the shivers, grounded me in the here and now.

"Not actively," I said slowly. "It didn't try to hurt me. The ghosts just seemed to be spectators. But there was something else, a shadow that felt bad. I don't know what it was."

"I'll have the whole area smudged with sage, just to be careful," she promised. "And I'm sorry for giving you a scare."

I shook my head. "It's a very interesting display. I think it'll do well for the Archive. And seriously, in my business, and living in Charleston, it's not like I can get away from ghosts or haunted heirlooms. So I'll just have to deal with it."

TEAG LOGAN, MY assistant store manager, looked up when I walked into Trifles and Folly. "Everything okay?" he asked. "Mrs. Morrissey called."

I rolled my eyes, exasperated at myself. "Yes. I'm fine. I just got a glimpse of something at the new exhibit. Not sure what it was, but I know it's not friendly."

Teag came out from behind the counter. No customers in the shop at the moment meant we could speak freely. "You think it's a danger to the people who visit?"

I shook my head. I'd spent the whole cab ride trying to figure out what exactly I did get from the glimpse I'd seen. "There's something old and evil, but I don't think it was actually there in the Archive if that makes sense. Almost like what I saw was a shadow of the real evil. And I don't even know which of the events it was tied to—or if the exhibit had anything to do with it at all." Teag listened closely as I recounted what I'd seen, giving him the full account, not the heavily-edited version I'd told to Mrs. Morrissey.

"Since you never sensed it before in all the times you've been to the Archive, I'd say odds are good it has something to do with one of the featured displays," Teag said. He's got magic of his own, and we're partners in the whole eliminating supernatural threats work of the Alliance.

I stashed my purse in my office and came back from the break room with a cup of regular coffee. Mrs. Morrissey's doctored brew had gotten me over the vision, but I needed to get back to work and clear my head. "It spooked me, which is odd given what we've seen."

Teag and I had faced down demons and vengeful ghosts, vicious witches, fallen angels, and plenty of nasty paranormal threats. I'd mastered my psychometry enough to hold my own in life-or-death battles. Which made me wonder again what had rattled me at the Archive.

"You said the ghosts begged you to free them. Do you think that might have had something to do with the effect on you? Like maybe it wasn't just the shadow—it was the ghosts, too?"

"Maybe. I'd like to find out more about the hurricane, the earthquake, and the World's Fair," I said. "There's a piece missing, and I think it's important."

The door opened, ushering in our first customer of the day, and Teag and I stayed busy with a steady stream of visitors until after lunch. I didn't have a chance to check my phone until I went to the back to grab my sandwich from the fridge. That's when I realized I'd missed a call from Kell.

"Hey," I greeted him when he picked up my call. "What's up?"

"Hey yourself," he bantered, his voice warm. Kell Winston ran Southern Paranormal Observation and Outreach (SPOOK), a local ghost hunting group. SPOOK handled their research in a credible manner, and while Kell didn't know the full story about the Alliance, he knew Teag and I had some special skills when it came to supernatural stuff, and he'd been a help on several of our investigations when haunted or cursed objects showed up in the store. One thing led to another, and Kell and I started dating. We'd been together for several months, and things were going well. Very well.

"We're going out on a hunt tonight; thought you might want to come with." Kell's tone was light, but I could tell he really wanted me to say yes. Our work schedules had kept us too busy to get together for over a week, and both of us had noticed the absence.

"What's up?"

"We've been getting reports of people seeing orbs and other things out in Hampton Park," Kell replied. "Out by the old World's Fair bandstand."

My heart thumped. "Oh?" I tried to keep my voice casual, but my heart thumped. I didn't believe in coincidence, and after what happened at the Archive, this had to be related.

"Yeah. There've always been ghost sightings there and in the one remaining building left over from the Fair, but the reports have really spiked lately, and we want to find out why. I actually wondered whether it had anything to do with the two new exhibits."

"Two?"

"Yeah—the Museum has a new exhibit on World's Fair Scandals, and it's got some juicy stuff, including bits about the exhibition here back in the 1800s."

My mind raced. I'd have to get to the Museum in the next couple of days and see if the shadow showed up there, too. "Sure," I replied. "Just tell me when and where."

Kell laughed, and I relaxed a little. While I couldn't tell Kell everything about what we did—the truth was too dangerous—it was nice not having to hide everything about my abilities and feel accepted.

"How about dinner first, then some ghost hunting?"

"You sure know how to show a girl a good time," I snarked, but I liked both suggestions.

"I'll take that as a 'yes' and pick you up at your house—say around seven?" Kell replied. I smiled, knowing that he'd worked out the timing, so I had the chance to close up shop, get home and take care of Baxter, my little Maltese, and get changed. Anyone who factored Bax into his plans was okay by me.

"Hot date?" Teag asked with a grin.

"Yep. How about you? Is Anthony still working long hours?"

Teag pushed a hand back through his dark, skater-boy hair. He still looks like the grad student he was before he started working at the store and he found a whole new purpose in life—eliminating supernatural threats. "He's a lawyer. So long hours go with the territory. I knew what I was getting into when I signed on." His expression took any sting from his words. Teag and Anthony were crazy in love and had been together for a while now. Anthony was as buttoned-up Brooks Brothers as Teag was Urban Outfitters, but somehow, it worked for them.

"But he's between cases right now, for a day or so, and we're going to make the most of it," he added with a smile that was pure sin.

"Have a good evening," I said, heading out the door.

"Planning on it!" He called in response. "You, too!"

SEVEN CAME FASTER than I expected. Kell sat on the couch and played with Baxter while I finished getting ready. There's no such thing as "just" a ghost hunt. Charleston is one of the most haunted cities on the continent, and the majority of its ghosts are peaceful, thank goodness. Many are just "stone tape" images, powerful memories that get imprinted on a thing or place and reply like the loop on a recording. Those can be disturbing, but they're harmless. There's no actual spirit present; just an over-active memory stuck in time.

Lucky for us, at least seventy-five percent of the ghosts we encounter aren't dangerous. They're lost, stuck, confused, or bound to a task or mission. As long as they don't harm anyone, we don't bother them. It's the other twenty-five percent that cause problems. Poltergeists. Vengeful spirits. Dangerous hauntings. That's when Sorren and Teag and I step in. Ghosts aren't the most powerful or the most evil creatures out there, but it would be a mistake to underestimate them. I didn't plan on making that mistake.

I glanced at the mirror, double checking. My strawberry-blonde hair was tied back in a scrunchie to keep it out of my eyes if tonight turned out to be more action-packed than Kell expected. Even though it was a date of sorts, I dressed for practicality—a black long-sleeved t-shirt, dark jeans, and a jacket over Doc Martens. A silver and agate necklace filled the neckline of my shirt, a powerful protective amulet. I had my athame up my sleeve, where it could be in my hand in seconds if needed. It was an old wooden spoon that had been my grandmother's, and the strong emotional resonance it held for me activated my touch magic enough to turn it into a powerful weapon, when necessary. I hoped it wouldn't be needed tonight, but better safe than sorry.

Just in case, I had an iron knife in a sheath on my belt. Iron blades are hard to keep sharp, but with a ghost, it's the iron itself, not the razor edge that matters. An agate spindle whorl, another protective talisman that enhanced my magic, lay snug in the pocket of my jeans. My coat pockets held a canister of salt and a bag of iron filings. Ghosts hate salt and iron. It fries their signal, disrupting the energy that enables them to manifest. I also had a lighter and a bundle of sage, to dispel negative energy. Kell said the ghosts were more restless than usual. I wasn't taking any chances.

I ran through my mental checklist of weapons and protective charms. Satisfied, I headed downstairs, where Baxter yipped his welcome and Kell's appreciative once-over made me think I managed to pull off functional *and* stylish. I returned a glance of my own. Kell was tall and lean with light brown hair and a tan that highlighted his blue eyes.

"See something you like?" Kell teased.

I stretched up to kiss him. "Definitely."

We went to Jocko's Pizza for dinner, a neighborhood favorite. While we waited for our order, Kell filled me in.

"The bandstand and one dormitory are the only buildings left from the World's Fair," Kell said, calling up photos on his phone and flipping through them so I could see. I recognized the distinctive, blue-domed gazebo immediately.

"The bandstand is the original structure, but it was moved from its original location," Kell explained. He showed me photos of the current site, and where it had been before. "We're hearing reports of ghost activity and orbs in both places. No one seems to be getting hurt, but I'm curious about what's made this kick into high gear now, all of a sudden, after all these years."

"There weren't ghost sightings before?"

Kell waited until our server had situated the steaming hot pizza between us to continue. "Ever since the World's Fair ended, people have said the grounds were haunted. Maybe it's because one of the

Fair's producers killed himself in the bandstand a few months after it closed. The event never brought in the tourists or money the organizers had hoped it would, and several of the investors went bankrupt."

"Okay, that explains one ghost. But who are the others?"

Kell shrugged. "No idea, but we'd like to find out. From what I've read about the Fair, there were no big catastrophes, no tragic fires, no crazy serial killer like at the 1893 Chicago World's Fair. You know, the *Devil in the White City* guy—H.H. Holmes."

I shivered. "Yeah, I saw a documentary about him. Built a murder house, killed lots of women who rented a room from him. I remember."

"Everything I've read about the Charleston Expo says that it was a very normal exhibition—if anything, a little too boring for its own good." Kell cut a slice of pizza for me and then wrangled another slice dripping with gooey cheese onto his own plate.

"What about traffic accidents?" I mused. "Carriages, trolleys, trains —anybody get killed like that?"

"Not related to the Fair, or it didn't make the newspaper if it was," Kell replied. "That's what's got me stumped, and with the sudden surge in activity, we decided we'd check it out. I'm glad you could come along."

"None of the ghosts have tried to hurt anyone or do damage?"

"Not that we've heard. Just a lot of evening joggers and dog walkers freaking out from seeing Victorian visitors who disappear into thin air and balls of light that dive bomb them out of nowhere."

I ate a few bites, savoring Jocko's homemade signature sauce and thought for a moment. "And you think the exhibits at the Archive and Museum shook something loose? I didn't sense anything major at the Archive from the items they had on display, but I did get an ominous feeling I couldn't shake." That was the truth, even if it wasn't the whole truth. I told myself that I was protecting Kell by shielding him from knowing too much about the supernatural. He believed in ghosts and magic. He would sleep better at night not knowing about the things Teag and Sorren and I hunted and destroyed. Now that I knew, I would never sleep soundly again.

"Maybe. It just seems like too much of a coincidence," Kell allowed. "The Museum's display doesn't open until tomorrow. I just saw the announcement online. It's not even just focused on the Charleston expo—it's all the World's Fairs and their scandals."

I finished off my slice and reached for another one. "Hey, nothing sells history like dirty laundry," I replied. "Let's face it: history is the original reality TV."

Just as the check came, my phone buzzed. I glanced down to see a call from Teag. He knew I had a date with Kell, and Teag didn't call without good reason, so I figured something was up.

He started talking before I could say anything. "Cassidy. Are you at the bandstand yet?"

Kell gave me a questioning glance. I mouthed "Teag" and he nodded. "No. Just finishing dinner. Why?"

"Not sure it's a good idea to go. Or if you do, be careful." Teag sounded really worried.

"Something happen?"

"Anthony didn't get home as early as he intended, so I did a little digging online, in some databases," he said, emphasizing the last word. Teag's Weaver magic lets him weave spells into cloth, but it also means he can weave disparate bits of data into information, making him one hell of a hacker. Cracking passwords and getting around firewalls doesn't even slow him down, and he can hack into law enforcement and government computers faster than Bonnie and Clyde could crack a safe. So I guessed he'd been poking around in the local police computers, looking for strange complaints that might actually be supernatural. Not the kind of thing he'd admit to his lawyer boyfriend.

"And?"

"A guy was reported as a missing person yesterday. Name's Peter Morrill. The last time anyone saw him, he was taking a smoke out at the old bandstand."

I thanked Teag and relayed the intel, omitting the source of the information. "Might just be a coincidence," Kell said, finishing his sweet tea. "It's a public park. Lots of people stop for a smoke."

"Maybe. But just in case, let's be extra careful."

Kell leaned across and kissed me on the cheek. "No complaints from me on that."

We met up with the rest of the SPOOK crew at Hampton Park. Calista still rocked the goth librarian look, dark makeup and severe hair at odds with a blouse under her leather jacket that could only be described as "prim" if it weren't unbuttoned down to *there*. She already had her audio recording equipment mostly set up in the center of the bandstand, favoring us with a glare I knew from experience not to take personally.

"Glad you could make it." Sarcasm laced Calista's voice like arsenic. Situation normal. The only time I had ever heard her not doling out sarcastic barbs was when she was running for her life, so by comparison, this was better.

"Haven't seen anything yet." Drew wandered around the bandstand staring at an EMF scanner that so far remained stubbornly mute in his hand. He looked even skinnier than usual in his black jeans and t-shirt, with his dark hair tied up in a ponytail.

"Keep it that way until I get the cameras in position," Pete ordered. He was a short, wiry ginger built like a welterweight wrestler. A pair of modified smart glasses were pushed up on top of his head, riding in his short red hair. "Can't prove it if we can't get it on camera."

I'd seen the circular gazebo many times, but I'd never had a reason before this to walk out to it. Before I went up the steps, I paused, trying to get an idea of whether or not stepping onto the main platform would pack a psychic wallop. I could feel a resonance strong enough to travel from the ground through my shoes, but nothing that made me worried about getting knocked for a loop. Kell was watching me, and I knew he understood why I hesitated, but I flashed him a reassuring smile and headed up the steps.

The rest of the team would be busy for a while with the equipment, so I ambled over to the far side of the round platform and drew in a deep breath before placing my palms flat on the white wooden railing.

The bandstand had been disassembled, moved and put back together, muting its resonance, but the impressions were strong enough that they hardly seemed dimmed by that at all. I heard strains of music and the hum of conversation. When I opened my eyes, I saw the grand, gleaming white Victorian palaces of the Exposition grounds, and looked out on sunlight glinting from the still water of the pools in the sunken garden.

The view was breathtaking, and I wish I could show it to Kell and the others, but Teag is the only one I've ever been able to share a vision with, and it's his magic that makes it possible. I'd seen pictures of the grand expo, but their faded images didn't do it justice, not by a long shot. It was so much bigger in person, designed to impress the world with the wealth and opulence of the American South. Everything about it screamed plantation pride, bruised by the War, desperate to regain its footing. Like everything about that turn-of-the-century period in Charleston, it felt bittersweet.

I concentrated, and more of the scene came in to focus. I could see people now, not ghosts, just images trapped in the memories retained by the bandstand. A group of young women in their long bustle skirts and elaborate hats giggled as they passed a knot of equally dapper young men, who bowed deep in exaggerated courtliness, grinning widely.

I got so caught up in the vision that the seeping darkness took me by surprise, making me inhale sharply. I frowned, honing in on the emotions, trying to discern both cause and location. Behind me, toward the center of the bandstand where Calista had her equipment, I felt a pang of despair and loss, desolation and fear, and I remembered that one of the Exposition organizers had committed suicide near this place.

"Cassidy?" Kell's voice broke through the vision, and I felt his hand on my arm. "Are you okay?"

"If she's getting one of those vision things, she needs to share it with the class," Calista said in an exaggerated drawl that somehow sharpened the sarcasm.

"Just glimpses," I said, turning away from the park toward Kell and Calista. "Memories." I stared at the floor of the bandstand beneath Calista's equipment, and for a moment, I could have sworn I saw a pool of blood, though I knew the boards had been replaced long ago.

"If you're looking for the spot where the event investor killed himself, I think you're on it," I said, and Calista actually flinched, looking down as if she might have stepped in something nasty.

"Starting to get readings, people!" Drew called from out on the lawn. "It's showtime!"

Drew's meter glowed red and began to whine, signaling that it picked up fluctuations in the electromagnetic frequencies that often accompanied ghost sightings.

"Getting something on the audio," Calista said, pressing her fingers against the receiver in her ear. "We've got a hot one tonight."

"Son of a bitch, will you look at that?" Pete's whisper had us all turning toward where he stood. Pinpricks of light rose from the grass like fireflies; only this was the wrong time of year for lightning bugs. "Fairy lights" the lore called them, or "will-o-the-whisps." You could chase them but never catch them, and those who tried came to grief.

"Over there!" Kell pointed, snapping photos with his own modified camera as Pete went for video footage. I saw two young men dressed in white linen suits and boater hats strolling down one of the gravel walkways, deep in conversation, their images glitching now and then like a bad video feed, or wavering and then disappearing altogether.

"What are you picking up, Cassidy?" Kell asked me quietly. I knew he realized I saw a vision since the death grip I had on the railing would have been a dead giveaway.

"I see the scene from the postcard, only like it's real," I replied. "Nothing dangerous."

But that wasn't exactly true. The hair on the back of my neck rose, and I felt a prickle against my skin like a storm rising. I looked around at the resonance served up by my contact with the railing, but nothing seemed amiss or threatening. Yet there was something… waiting.

"Hey!" Drew yelled and staggered back once, then again. "Something's pushing me!"

"Get off me!" Pete hollered, stumbling as if someone shoved him hard from one side.

"Watch your hands, freak!" Calista slapped at empty air in outrage.

"We need to get out of here," I said to Kell, drawing my iron knife in one hand and pulling out a canister of salt in the other. Just then, I felt cold hands in the middle of my back pushing me forward. The wind had kicked up from nothing to gusts that whipped my hair into my eyes.

"Yeah, I think you're right," Kell agreed. "Everyone, pack up!"

I held on to one of the bandstand columns and looked out over the empty park, no longer seeing the long-ago vista. The temperature plummeted, and my breath misted in air far too cold for the season this far south. Just outside the glow of the streetlights, I caught a glimpse of movement. Darker shadows glided just on the edge of the light, and I wondered if it was the same thing I saw at the Archive. I figured the odds were good, but that didn't tell me what we were up against.

Calista packed her gear, swearing as unseen hands battled her. Pete and Drew continued their work, though they stood back to back against an invisible threat.

"Levels are off the charts!" Drew reported as his EMF scanner squealed, its read-out glowing bright red.

"Getting blurs and movement," Pete said changing a look up from his camera. "But what I see with my eyes isn't showing up on the display."

A gust of wind swept around the base of the bandstand, catching something shiny and swirling it into the air. I bent to pick it up without thinking and froze as my hand closed around a crumpled, empty cigarette carton.

This time, the vision hit me hard. *I saw the park through someone else's eyes. A glance down took in long legs that weren't my own over boots far too big for me. I saw hands strike a match and light a cigarette. A man's hands, with broad palms and long fingers, and an old, deep scar just below the right knuckles.*

The cigarette glowed against the twilight sky. No one else was in sight, and the man took a long drag, resting. He fidgeted as if afraid someone would see. His thoughts churned restlessly, and I could feel his unhappiness. He felt poised on the brink of making a big decision, and I sensed he didn't like any of his options.

The wind picked up, tugging at his clothes and making him shiver. He pushed away from the bandstand, almost finished with his smoke.

He shivered in the sudden cold. Too late, he recognized that he was no longer alone.

"Who's there?" He tried to sound defiant. "Quit screwing around with me. If you followed me, have the balls to admit it. I told you, I'm done with this kind of bullshit!"

No answer came. He glanced around, more nervous now. "I mean it! Go away!" I could tell that he thought he knew who lurked in the shadows, but I feared he was wrong.

He dropped the cigarette and ground it out under his shoe, squaring his shoulders and heading down the bandstand stairs, unaware of the shadow that followed him. He looked over his shoulder, aware on some level of the danger, but he searched for human faces, not an inhuman threat.

Overhead, the streetlight flickered and faltered, then went dark. I heard the man cry out in fear and pain, felt him drop the crumpled cigarette pack, then everything went black.

"Cassidy!" Kell's voice sounded from far away.

"What's going on with her?" Calista asked, the edge in her voice between fear and annoyance.

Kell didn't answer, and my attempt sounded more like a groan than actual words. I felt Kell pull me up and wrap an arm around me. "We've got to get you moving, Cassidy," he urged, barely hiding his fear.

"I saw him," I managed. "The missing guy. He was here."

Kell steered me toward our parked cars, keeping me on my feet. "We knew that, Cassidy. Before we came."

"No," I protested woozily. "I saw him—I saw what happened to him."

"That cigarette pack? You got a vision from it?"

I nodded, trying to ignore how the movement made the world blur around me. "Something chased him and took him. Not human. Not normal."

"What's she saying?" Drew asked, jogging up alongside us. "Did she touch something? See something?"

"Yeah," Kell replied. "Give her some space. I'll fill you in later."

We got back to the cars without incident. The black shadows didn't follow us outside the park, but I knew they could go farther if they wanted to. Hell, I'd seen them all the way across town. Kell got me settled in the passenger seat of his car while he went back to talk to the SPOOK team. We had all worked together enough times that I knew the others were concerned for me, even Calista despite her tough-as-nails façade.

Kell talked with them for a few minutes, calming them down and reassuring himself that they were all right. I had no idea whether their instruments registered even a fraction of what happened out there, but I knew none of us questioned that we'd been at the epicenter of paranormal activity tonight.

Kell came back moments later. "Don't let them go back out there tonight," I said, finally catching my breath after the vision.

"Don't worry. They won't. They saw enough for one night," Kell reassured me. "C'mon. Let's get you home."

I felt absurdly grateful that Kell had given me a ride that night since I didn't feel steady enough to drive yet. My thoughts spun, trying to put the pieces together. So many questions and not enough answers. Before I knew it, we were parked in front of my house.

"Thanks for coming along tonight," Kell said. "Although I'm sorry it turned out the way it did."

I managed a smile and stretched up to kiss him. "That's all right. I think we saw something important; I'm just not sure what it meant." I felt the adrenaline crash, and suddenly I couldn't keep my eyes open.

Kell chuckled. "Go to bed, Cassidy. I'll call you tomorrow."

"Some date," I muttered, too exhausted to consider doing anything else but awake enough to feel disappointed.

"Next time, I promise we'll go someplace un-haunted," Kell replied, walking me to the door.

"Where's the fun in that?"

He gave me another kiss, one that promised a much better evening on a future night, and then I went inside and closed the door behind me, sagging against it. Baxter jumped at my feet, anxious for attention. I scooped him up into my arms and collapsed onto the couch. As soon as Bax settled down, I dug out my phone although I knew it was too late to call Teag.

Need to know everything you can find out about the missing guy, I texted. *Think I saw him in a vision. Definitely our kind of thing.* I added, remembering the creepy opaque shadow and how it seemed to swallow up the frightened young man. Bax nestled under my chin in comfort. I kicked off my boots, pulled a throw down over us, and fell asleep right there, too tired to bother going upstairs. I suspected tomorrow was going to be a busy day. We had a shadow to catch.

SCANDALS AND SERIAL KILLERS

THE BIG CLOTH BANNER READ "SCANDALS OF THE WORLDS' FAIRS." It draped across the front of the Museum of the Lowcountry like a tabloid headline.

"What do you think?" Alistair McKinnon, the museum's curator, had a pained look on his face as we stood together on the sidewalk, looking up at the banner.

"It's a bit salacious," I allowed.

Alistair winced. "It's practically clickbait," he said with a sigh. "Welcome to the art of peddling history in the modern era. We've got TV to thank for it. Unveil a new archeological find and everyone yawns. Reveal some of history's dirty little secrets, and the tickets sell out in minutes."

I grinned. "Then you're lucky that history has such juicy gossip. Admit it; the banner is good marketing."

Alistair gave me a long-suffering look and nodded. "I know. And we all win when ticket sales and memberships go up. It just seems so… sordid."

I clapped him on the shoulder. "As if sorting through old bones and reading dead people's diaries and letters isn't?"

Alistair and I are old friends and professional colleagues. We call on each other's expertise regularly for appraisals and restoration advice. Alistair knows a bit about my gift, but not the whole truth. Actually, that's not completely right. He did have an encounter where he witnessed far more than was safe for him to know, and Sorren used his vampire mojo to alter a few memories.

"Why the sudden interest in Worlds' Fairs?" Alistair asked as we headed up the steps.

I thought about the incident in Hampton Park the night before and repressed a shiver. Teag texted me early, letting me know he was on the trail of the information I requested, and I told him that I wanted to stop by the museum on my way in. "I saw the display at the Archive," I answered truthfully. "It got me thinking." Quite the understatement, but true nonetheless.

Alistair laughed. "I'm actually surprised you haven't come across any of the memorabilia at the store. Sooner or later, everyone decides to clean out their old stash of great-grandpa's souvenirs."

"I don't recall anything," I replied as we went inside. "Maybe the fair was unique enough that people wanted to hang onto the items. Mrs. Morrissey didn't seem to have any trouble getting folks to loan her what they had."

"Mrs. Morrissey could charm the gold out of Fort Knox," Alistair said. "Why doesn't that surprise me at all?"

We walked into the large room reserved for rotating exhibits. Another large banner hung over the entrance. "Were the Fairs really that scandal-prone?"

"See for yourself," Alistair replied. "You know, we're also pointing up the technological advances unveiled at each of the fairs, but that wouldn't draw the crowds nearly like a hint of scandal. And any time you've got a high profile, big money event, there's going to be something that goes wrong or someone who misbehaves."

Near the front of the room, a series of bold, graphic paintings caught my attention. "Are those Andy Warhol paintings?"

Alistair grinned. "Not originals, no. But that's a copy of his *13 Wanted Men* artwork for the 1964 World's Fair. It caused such a scandal that the Fair organizers had it covered over in silver paint before the Fair even opened. Warhol recreated it elsewhere, but it never actually appeared at the Fair itself."

I moved closer, intrigued. The enlarged black and white photographs were clearly mug shots, taken from the front and side. "What was so scandalous? These look like they came from the police blotter."

"They did," Alistair replied. "And it's an odd tale. Some people say that the Fair feared legal trouble from the accused men. Others said it was political, or glorifying violence. There are even some whispers that the way the photos are arranged, so that the men seem to be looking at each other, put the censors on alert that it was some kind of gay message."

I almost laughed, then remembered what things were liked back in 1964, and realized that was no laughing matter. "Really?"

Alistair shrugged. "It's possible. Warhol liked to push the limits, and he made no attempt to hide his own orientation, despite the times."

I squinted at the black and white mug shots, trying to imagine a censor reading forbidden love into such stark images. "Makes you wonder why some things were so much on the censor's minds," I remarked.

"That's always the case," Alistair replied. "Of course, to play up the scandal, we've got profiles on all of the thirteen men—they weren't angels. They deserved their place on the Most Wanted list." I trailed down the row of photos, clippings and personal effects linked to each of the hardened criminals featured in Warhol's ill-fated display. While the initial set of art prints didn't elicit a reaction from my gift, I kept my distance from the small cases containing the wanted men's belongings and didn't pause too long in front of the headlines describing their crimes.

Even without getting close, I sensed a darkness that hung over the dead men's possessions. Anger, alienation, vengeance, and a demand to be seen, to be acknowledged radiated from the mundane items like watches, wallets, rings, and tie tacks. I backed away, eager to move beyond the reach of the unsettling resonance.

He led me to the next section, and I startled to look up at a huge metal man. It had the retro-futuristic look that made me think *Flash Gordon* and picture pulp magazines from the 1930s. Smooth, golden metal skin covered the robot. He had a broad, boxy chest, cylindrical legs and arms, and a face that had blocky, almost sculptural features.

"Meet Elektro," Alistair said. "He was the star of the 1939 World's Fair. This is the real Elektro—on loan from Mansfield, Ohio. He even had a metal dog." Alistair laid a hand on the huge robot's bulky arm. "Elektro could walk, say several hundred words, and smoke a cigarette."

I raised an eyebrow. "I guess he doesn't have to worry about his lungs."

"He's quite remarkable," Alistair said, patting the robot fondly. "Believe it or not—there was no person inside, pulling strings. Elektro was the real deal—run by electricity and vacuum tubes."

I looked up at the smooth, emotionless face. "He reminds me of a golem." I'd read tales of large hollow men made of clay and animated by magic, and I knew enough about the supernatural to believe they were true.

"You aren't the first to say that," Alistair said. "But to my knowledge, no one's seen him move without permission. In fact, he spent about fifty years in a box in an abandoned museum before the new owner reopened the place and dug him out of the crate."

The impassive metal features made me vaguely uncomfortable. "What's the scandal?"

"On a mild scale, I've heard that some of Elektro's recorded phrases sound a bit sexist by today's standards. Not really a surprise," Alistair said. "But the real scandal was a lot darker, and it didn't have anything to do with Elektro. There was a bomb at the UK pavilion. After all, war had started in Europe, and New York was getting around four hundred bomb threats a week. A few bad explosions, too. In this case, the police removed the bomb and took it somewhere else to defuse it, but it detonated and killed the policemen who tried to disable it."

"Sounds like something ripped from today's headlines," I remarked. I wandered past the wall of pictures and information about

Elektro toward the somber collection of newspaper articles and photos showing the bomb's damage.

"The more things change, the more they stay the same," Alistair agreed.

Around the next corner, I confronted two life-size, wax figures of men in nineteenth-century garb, one of whom held a gun pointed at the other. "Is that supposed to be President McKinley?" My history geeki-ness came in handy sometimes.

"Very good," Alistair said as if I were a star pupil. "But even the people who vaguely remember that William McKinley was shot don't know it happened at the 1901 Pan American Exposition in Buffalo, New York, in the Temple of Music."

"At a World's Fair? Wow."

Alistair nodded. "It gets even more interesting. The president's secretary was afraid of an assassination attempt—the setting was too public—and tried twice to cancel, but McKinley insisted. An unem-ployed anarchist shot him as he went through the receiving line, and McKinley died a few days later. The killer got the electric chair."

I tried to decide which seemed more unsettling, the seven-foot robot or the hyper-realistic wax figures depicting an assassination in progress. Behind the figures loomed another display wall of photos and headlines, as well as a Victorian man's coat in a glass case, with a card noting that it was the one worn by McKinley when he was shot.

My eye followed the banners to the one proclaiming the Charleston exposition. "What do you have from the exposition here?"

Alistair chuckled. "Nothing that rivals Elektro or McKinley's assassi-nation, thank heavens. But two of the investors ended up going bankrupt, and the press coverage in the day was lurid. Of course, when the press begins digging, there's no telling what they'll find, and they hit pay dirt. One of the men was having an affair, and the other had fathered a child out of wedlock with his business partner's wife. And one of the show's promoters turned out to be nearly insolvent due to gambling debts."

He raised an eyebrow. "When the tabloids got hold of it, you can imagine. One of the bankrupt investors shot himself. The man with the illegitimate child did not kill himself, but he was ruined, and the woman involved overdosed on Laudanum shortly thereafter, though it was said to be accidental." His voice gave me his opinion.

"And the one with the gambling debts?"

"Drowned in a boating accident," Alistair replied, "or so the family claimed. Although the water was calm that day and he was an experienced yachtsman."

"Uh huh," I replied skeptically. "Did the families object to the museum's dredging all this up?"

Alistair brightened. "No. We haven't said anything that isn't a matter of public record, and as for the questionable pieces, we just present the facts and let readers draw their own conclusions. The family of the man who shot himself died out in the next generation—no male heir to carry on the name. The others either moved away or faded into obscurity."

I remembered the ghosts from Hampton Park the night before, and the way the Archive display gave me the heebie-jeebies. "Anything else salacious happen at the Expo?"

Alistair gave a wave of his hand. "Oh, the usual. Crime went up—muggings, vandalism, public drunkenness—people skipped town, made questionable business deals, even a bar fight that might have spawned an honest-to-goodness duel. But nothing like what happened in Chicago."

I lingered for a moment as Alistair moved off toward the next display, trying to see if I picked up any of the resonance I felt at the Archive or in the park. I didn't see the shadow. But I did pick up an uneasiness that made me jumpy. Peering into the case of memorabilia, I saw a souvenir watch, a few more coins and engraved silver spoons and two admission tickets along with a train pass that had never been punched.

"Alistair? What's the story about the items here?" I asked, unsure why it was important and at the same time, certain that this meant something.

He retraced his steps to stand beside me. "There's no particular story behind anything except the train ticket. That belonged to Harris Jubal Tomlinson."

I glanced up. "The cotton Tomlinsons?"

Alistair nodded. Tomlinsons were still prominent in Charleston, though not perhaps at the level they had been a hundred years ago when their cotton plantation provided a quarter of the state's output. "Yes. He was the natural choice to be the host at the Expo's Cotton Pavilion, squiring the out-of-towners around, showing off the place. By all accounts, a very sharp young fellow, educated at William and Mary, a savvy businessman, and a natty dresser," he added with a chuckle. "That's his photo on the wall."

I moved away from Alistair to gaze at the image. Harris Tomlinson looked to be in his early thirties. He exuded confidence and privilege, yet something about his stance suggested he wasn't completely comfortable. Harris was a good looking man, blond, tall, and fit, wearing an expensive suit that showed off broad shoulders and a trim waist. "What about the train ticket?"

"Tomlinson was due in Atlanta for an important business meeting the day after the Expo closed. The meeting was critical to his family's interests, and the other parties were some of the movers and shakers of their day. Tomlinson never showed up."

"So the train ticket—"

"Never used," Alistair replied. "The family loaned it to us. There was a hullaballoo in the papers, as you might imagine. All kinds of conjecture, reasons why he might have skipped town-or left the country. But nothing stuck. No evidence of foul play. No fraudulent business dealings, no suggestion that he was being blackmailed—nothing."

I frowned. "A man like that doesn't just walk away without a good reason."

Alistair shrugged. "No body was found, and no one ever claimed to see him again." He met my gaze. "Then again, a man of Tomlinson's means might be able to engineer his own disappearance better than most."

I knew from hearing Sorren talk about some of the vanishing acts he had to pull in his long, undead existence that having means certainly helped make it easier to assume a new identity. But when I turned my attention back to Tomlinson's photo, I didn't get the sense that this was a man ready to turn his back on everything he knew. He looked like the world was his oyster.

"Do you know anything else about Tomlinson?" I asked. Something about the long-ago disappearance caught my attention, and I learned long ago to pay attention to hunches.

"I don't, but Rand might." Alistair glanced up as a young man in his early twenties crossed the back of the exhibit room. "Rand? Can you come here please?"

Rand brushed a lock of blond hair out of his eyes. "Mr. McKinnon?"

"This is Cassidy Kincaide, from Trifles and Folly—the antique store on King Street. She's got some questions about the Tomlinson exhibit."

"Sure. I mean, nice to meet you."

I smiled, trying to put Rand at ease. "I was intrigued by the Tomlinson story. It seems so… unusual. Did you have any other materials that didn't get used in the display?"

Rand thought for a moment, then nodded. "The family gave us a whole box of personal items. I think they were grateful he was being remembered. It's down in storage, but if it's okay with Mr. McKinnon, I can get it for you, and you can sign it out."

"Cassidy's a donor, a patron, and a friend, Rand. She has my permission to borrow whatever she needs."

I smiled my thanks. Rand nodded. "All right then. I can have it ready for you tomorrow morning if that's okay."

"That would be fine," I assured him. "Thank you," I added, directing my comment to Rand and Alistair. Rand ducked his head in acknowledgment, then went back to what he had been doing as Alistair continued his tour.

"Interesting," I commented, and let Alistair lead me to the Chicago display. Exhibit walls papered with big newsprint told a grisly tale. "Murder House." "World's Fair death toll rises." "Fiend's Victims Still Uncounted."

"Dr. H.H. Holmes, aka the Devil in the White City," Alistair said. "Born Herman Webster Mudgett. Built a rooming house that was actually a fancy killing box. Secret rooms, trapdoors to dispose of bodies, special equipment to gas or incinerate his victims. He was executed for twenty-seven murders, but experts think he might have killed as many as two hundred."

I felt a sick twist in my stomach. In a glass case, a faceless mannequin wore a man's spectacles, top hat, and dark black suit. "Someone actually kept his clothing?"

"That's the suit he wore to his trial. It's on loan from the Serial Killer Museum in Los Angeles."

"Serial Killer Museum?"

"It's L.A. There's a market for everything, I guess."

I stayed at least four feet away from Holmes/Mudgett's suit, and even so, I fought the urge to squirm. Such a sense of darkness emanated from the clothing that I was amazed anyone could stand to be in the same room for long. Malice exuded from the clothing, strong enough that I almost expected to see a green churning fog like movie special effects. The resonance was strong enough that I had trouble breathing. The clothing didn't trigger visions of the victims; it revealed the man who did the killing. Smug. Convinced of his superiority. Completely unrepentant.

I've been in the presence of some really evil sons of bitches—vengeful ghosts, blood-crazed monsters, even a demon or two. Mudgett's resonance ranked with the worst of them.

"I need to get back to the shop," I said abruptly and knew I wasn't fooling Alistair.

"Of course," he said, guiding me away from the exhibit with a barely-there hand on my elbow like he was afraid I might collapse. Unfortunately, before I had a more solid grip on my Gift, I had given him good reason for his fears. Now, I didn't feel so much like passing out as I did like I needed to retch, then take a shower with lye soap to remove the taint.

Thankfully, the oppressive blight of Mudgett's resonance faded as we put distance between ourselves and the display. Even so, now that I knew what it felt like, I was surprised it hadn't hit me when I first walked into the room. It didn't completely leave my awareness, and while nothing made me think the taint was sentient, it felt like a stain inside me, where I couldn't wash clean. I knew that if I ever went to L.A., the Serial Killer Museum would not be on my list of things to do.

"You never did say to what I owed the pleasure of your visit." Alistair gave me a canny look as we reached the main lobby. He's got a mind like a steel trap, and not just gets by him.

"Mrs. Morrissey showed me around the Archive's exhibit," I replied. "The two complement each other well."

"It's not an accident. We probably talk by phone every other day," Alistair laughed. "We do our best not to duplicate, or steal each other's thunder. Her focus is very local, while we try to connect Charleston to the grand scheme of things." His eyes narrowed. "And you've dodged my questions, Cassidy."

I fidgeted, knowing he had caught me. "Mrs. Morrissey likes to get my take on new displays before they open to the public." I grimaced. "There have been a couple of notable incidents where things got a bit too lively." I wasn't going to bring up Nephilim or old vengeful judges. Nope, not going there.

"A wise strategy," Alistair agreed. "I might have to do the same. What did you make of it, Cassidy? Are we posing a danger to the public?"

"I don't think so," I replied. "If anyone else with a little psychic mojo wanders in, they might get more than they bargained for, but I don't think anyone else will notice." I managed a wan smile. "I'm not worried about anyone getting possessed or going 'Redrum' on you."

"That's a relief." Alistair's laugh made me think he wasn't completely joking.

When I got to back to Trifles and Folly, a few busloads of tourists kept us too busy to talk. I mulled over what I had seen at both the Archive and the museum and tried to make sense of the heightened ghost activity at Hampton Park. Something didn't add up, and I doubted the ghosts were confused, which meant we were missing a piece of the puzzle, an important piece.

"I know you'll be very happy with your teacups," I assured a customer, carefully wrapping the fragile porcelain set of four gold-rimmed cups decorated with violets.

"They're just like the ones my grandmother had," she assured me, looking thrilled at the purchase. The day-to-day conversations with customers in the shop are so far away from the saving-the-world stuff we really do that sometimes; it's a little surreal sometimes. I watched the lady nestle the package in the crook of her arm and head out, sublimely unaware that ghosts, demons or supernatural big bad uglies went bump in the night. And if Teag, Sorren, and I continued to do our job well, she and all the other people would never be any the wiser.

"I looked up a few things between customers," Teag murmured as he slipped behind me to take down a blue vase from the shelf. "I'll fill you in later. Still on for dinner?"

"Wouldn't miss it," I assured him.

We didn't slow down until I turned the key in the lock at the end of the day. I slumped against the door, exhausted, but happy. "Wow. I think that had to be our best day in at least a month."

Teag grinned. "We're going to have to restock the shelves. Those bus tours don't fool around. They come ready to shop."

Sorren compensates Teag and me well for running the store, with extra for "hazard pay" as he calls our Alliance work. I know that Trifles and Folly is primarily a cover for smacking down supernatural bad guys, but the store has been in my family for over three hundred years, and it's a point of pride for me to run it well and turn a profit, or at least make ends meet. Today's sales went a long way toward making that happen.

"So what did you find?" I asked as I started moving the jewelry trays from the glass cases to the safe.

"I looked into the people who've gone missing in Charleston lately."

"Do I want to know how?"

"Probably not."

"Okay," I replied. "Find anything noteworthy?"

Teag brought over trays from the other side of the room. "More people than you might think get reported missing, even for a city the size of Charleston. Of course, some of those are more misplaced than missing—sleeping off a bender, staying with a friend without telling anyone, going on an impromptu road trip. And some are pretty obviously runaways, so no supernatural element there. But when I accounted for all of that, I still came up with two people missing since the Archive and the Museum started to put their displays up. Peter Morrill and Jon Werther."

He pulled up some pictures on his phone. "That's Morrill," Teag said, pointing at a young blond man. "And that's Werther." The chubby dark-haired man didn't look familiar, but I knew where I had seen Morrill before.

"He's the one I saw in the vision at the bandstand," I said. I pushed a lock of hair out of my eyes and closed the safe, then set the lock and leaned back against the heavy steel door. "Anything in common?"

"It took me long enough to get that far since I only had a few minutes at a time thanks to the tourists," he replied. "I'll look for connections tomorrow."

I filled him in on what I had seen at the Archive and Museum, as well as the reactions I'd had to the displays. "I can't shake the feeling that pulling all the items together for the exhibits has stirred something up," I told him. "Hampton Park had enough orbs that it looked like a firefly swarm."

"And you didn't find anything out that uncovered a big, sordid scandal to account for it?" Teag asked.

I shook my head. "Not yet. And given the focus of Alistair's exhibit, I think he'd have been all over it if there had been anything noteworthy. Just a couple of suicides and some sordid business dealings."

"Not enough to make so many ghosts edgy enough to haunt the park," Teag mused. "Have you talked to Sorren?"

"He should be back soon. Maybe he'll remember something that didn't make it into the newspapers."

"I have a couple of leads that might or might not turn out to be something," Teag said. "And I'll look into the guy you mentioned from the exhibit. I'll let you know what I find out when you and Kell come over."

He walked me out to where my RAV4 was parked. I missed my zippy little Mini Cooper, but I needed more cargo room for hauling boxes and the occasional body. "See you tonight," I said with a wave.

~

"WHATEVER YOU'RE COOKING smells delicious," Kell groaned as Teag welcomed us into the house he and Anthony shared. Teag clapped Kell on the shoulder, gave me a quick hug, and took the bottle of wine I held out.

"Anthony's in charge of the pasta. I'm doing the appetizers and salad, so I'd better get back to the kitchen," Teag said with a grin, and I realized he was wearing an apron that read "kiss the cook."

We followed him toward the source of the smells that made my stomach growl. "Hi Cassidy! Hi Kell!"

We returned the greeting and settled in at the kitchen bar. Teag poured wine and handed us each glasses. He came up behind Anthony, who was stirring a pot of sauce on the stove and laid one hand on his hip, reaching around with his right hand to place the goblet of wine on the counter. "Looks good enough to eat," he murmured, just loud enough for us to hear, a wicked grin on his face.

Anthony cheeks reddened, just a bit, as Teag intended. "Don't distract the cook," he replied, though he didn't seem to mind.

"Get a room, you two," Kell teased. Anthony stopped stirring the sauce long enough to flip Kell off.

Kell laughed. "Some things never change." He turned to me. "Anthony lived down the hall from me freshman year at college. I expected a pre-law student to use a lot of big words, but he tended more to gestures."

"Got the point across just fine," Anthony replied without looking up. "You somehow always had movie marathons with lots of loud explosions when I had tests to study for."

"You were pre-law," Kell replied. "You always had a test to study for. Your study team kept taking over the common room and plastering the whiteboard with morgue photos and Latin."

Anthony gave an exaggerated huff. "Introduction to Forensics, and Latin 101. Had a professor that would throw in the occasional dirty poem in ancient Latin to keep us interested. For some reason, that's what I remember best."

"Not surprised," Teag laughed, intentionally bumping Anthony's shoulder as he reached for the salad tongs. Anthony stood just a little shorter than Teag, with short blond hair and blue eyes. Even relaxed and at home, he had a GQ vibe, with a button-down shirt open at the throat, untucked over dark jeans that might have been ironed. Teag wore a concert t-shirt over ripped jeans, his brown hair long enough to tuck behind an ear on one side. Anthony was legacy Charleston blue-blood. Teag was a former struggling grad student. They couldn't have been more different, or more perfect together.

"Munchies are served," Teag announced, bringing in a tray with olives, cheese, crackers, and some flaky triangles I recognized as spanakopita. "Don't be too impressed. The Greek stuff came frozen." He snagged one as he set down the plate and fed it to Anthony, who was in the process of folding the pasta into the finished sauce.

"Where'd you get the recipe?" I asked. "It smells wonderful."

"Cooking show," Anthony confessed. "They're a guilty pleasure. After I get home from the office, it's nice to watch something where the biggest decision is olive oil or canola." Anthony was a rising star in his family's law firm, with a solid South of Broad clientele. With his good looks and his career, Anthony was quite a catch, but what I liked best was that he was crazy in love with Teag enough to stick around even after he found out the whole bloody truth about what we really do.

A few minutes later, we sat down to a feast. "Everything looks as good as it smells," Kell said, taking an exaggerated breath.

"Here's hoping that it tastes as good, too," Anthony said, but he smiled as if he was fairly certain we'd be pleased. One bite proved that suspicion to be true.

"This is fantastic," I said, savoring the taste and following a perfect bite with a sip of wine. Kell nodded his approval, his mouth too full to speak.

We chatted about local news and friends in common, focused on polishing off the fabulous meal. "Did you hear about the preservation work, down by The Citadel?" Anthony asked. "Our firm's been asked to handle the details. Half a block of old Victorian homes that have largely been neglected, getting re-done to their former glory." He grinned, and I remembered that Anthony served on several preservation and architecture boards in the city. He and Teag shared a passion for history, among other things.

"I've seen a little about that in the news," I replied. "Sounds like a win for everyone. The neighborhood gets an upgrade, some fine old houses get rescued, and The Citadel gets some classy new office space."

Anthony nodded. "Some of the properties are in rough shape, so it won't be easy, but I think in the long run, everyone will be happy. I'm heading over there later this week, so I'll be able to tell you first-hand just what a mess we'll have to clean up once I've seen the properties."

Finally, when dessert was over, and Teag poured more wine, we sat back, full and lazy. "Leave the dishes," Anthony said to Teag, pausing only long enough to put leftovers in the fridge. "Let's go into the living room."

Kell and I sat on one couch, and Anthony settled next to Teag on the couch facing us, one arm slung companionably over Teag's shoulders, mirroring Kell and me. "So about those scandals..." Teag said with a raised eyebrow.

"Am I going to have to recuse myself if I listen?" Anthony asked, only half-kidding.

"You're about a hundred years too late," Teag replied. "Cassidy went to see the exhibits at the Archive and the museum about the World's Fair, and that made me see if I could find some untold stories."

Teag spun the cover story for Kell's benefit. Anthony looked skeptical as if he suspected there might be more to the issue, but if he intended to call Teag on it, he'd do it later. Kell grinned. "Scandal? Do tell!"

Teag sipped his wine and leaned back into Anthony's shoulder. "So the first bit of gossip I dug up was about Josiah Harcourt. He was quite the star of the Charleston fair, in the technology building. Had a model of a wondrous machine that he said would revolutionize textile manufacturing. People lined up for hours to see the model, which didn't actually do anything except move a bit where it was connected to a steam engine. That was enough for investors, who practically got in a fist fight over who could give Harcourt the most money."

Teag warmed to the tale, enjoying his audience, flush with wine and dinner. "Harcourt moved into a big warehouse near the river, and rumors circulated that his competitors were trying to steal plans to his wonderful machine, so no one was allowed in while the equipment was constructed."

He leaned forward. "Here's where it gets murky. Construction dragged on, lots of delays, and the investors started to get edgy. Then one night, the warehouse burns to the ground, destroying the machine and—so the record says—killing Harcourt."

"I'm guessing there's more to the story?" I asked, leaning against Kell.

Teag grinned. "Yep. Seems that no one could make heads or tails out of the slag in the warehouse debris, and no body was ever recovered. Harcourt's investors lost their money and couldn't sue the estate because all the funds mysteriously vanished from his accounts."

"So the whole thing was a scam?" Kell finished off his wine and set his glass aside.

Teag nodded. "It gets better. Five years later, one of the investors happened to be traveling in Europe. He swears he saw Harcourt in Paris, alive and well. If so, Harcourt skipped town before he could be caught. No one ever heard from him, and the money was never recovered."

"I wonder how that lovely tidbit escaped notice," I mused.

"Perhaps because the Harcourt family is a donor to both the Archive and the museum," Anthony replied, his tone as dry as the wine. "Descendants of Josiah's brother, I believe. Since some of the investors who got burned were likely to have been some of the Charleston upper crust, that's a second reason not to go picking old scabs. Old grudges aren't easily forgotten."

I made a mental note to ask Teag if any of the investors took a dive off the roof of a building or met a similarly untimely end, qualifying them for the spook-a-palooza down at the park, but I'd wait until Kell and Anthony weren't around to pursue that. "Good story. You had something else?"

Teag nodded, and I knew he loved spinning his tales. "More of a tidbit than a full-blown story. Apparently, a New Orleans madam who went by the name 'Revienne la Nuit' laid claim to a large, fancy house a couple of blocks from the exposition grounds. There's speculation that she might have received some funding from silent partners who were backers of the Expo. VIP visitors to the commerce pavilions got their visits underwritten in exchange for promises to bring new business to town. Gossip had it one of the visiting dignitaries died during a visit due to a bad heart."

Kell choked on his wine. Teag grinned wide. "I know, right? Good stuff! There were whispers that the cops were paid to look the other way, and that the city fathers got special treatment if they didn't object."

"I refuse to confirm or deny anything," Anthony said when we glanced at him for confirmation.

"Well I don't." We all turned to look at Kell. "The current owners actually called in SPOOK because they were having ghost problems. There's a B&B in that house now. Seems the spirit of a young lady appeared to several of the guests and tried to climb into bed with them. One gentleman actually checked out in the middle of the night, claiming he had been molested by a very forward ghost!"

No one could top Kell's story, so the conversation moved to other topics, and all too soon, the time came to head home. Kell and I thanked Teag and Anthony for the lovely dinner, promised to repay the evening in kind soon, and headed out. I glanced back to wave, smiling at the sight of the two of them framed in the doorway, Teag's arm around Anthony's waist, and Anthony's arm around Teag's shoulders.

"They're so darn cute together," I murmured as Kell and I walked to his car. Kell snugged his arm around my waist and pulled me into a kiss.

"Not as cute as you are," he murmured, and I laughed.

Kell fell silent as we drove away. "You don't know how glad I am that Anthony found Teag," he said after a few minutes. "Remember, I knew Anthony in college. He was going through a... rough patch then."

"Oh?" I counted Anthony among my closest friends, but his college days hadn't come up much aside from his friendship with Kell and some fondly remembered sporting events.

"I don't think I'm saying anything I shouldn't," Kell said. "Anthony came out to his family about the time he left for college. His parents and most of his family was cool with it, or at least they didn't give him grief. But his grandfather... that was another story. He was very fire and brimstone, and he was the senior partner in the firm."

"Ouch."

Kell nodded. "Yeah. Anthony already knew he wanted to be a lawyer, but the old man gave him a hard time about his 'lifestyle.'" Kell's disdain came through clearly in his voice. "Anthony cared about his grandfather, but some things aren't negotiable, you know?"

"I'm guessing they worked it out."

Kell winced. "Actually, the old man died of a heart attack Anthony's second year in law school. He was planning to go to Columbia, practice up in the state capital. Then that happened, and his father took over as senior partner, and let Anthony know he was welcome as soon as he passed the bar."

"I'm sorry it had to happen the way it did, but glad that it ended up okay."

"Some of Anthony's boyfriends weren't my favorites," Kell said with a grimace that told me he was understating his opinion. "I didn't think they were good for him, or that they deserved him. He's a really great guy. And then Teag came along, and they just seem so right together. He makes Anthony so happy." Kell smiled, and reached over to give my hand a squeeze. "I like to see nice people find nice people and make it work."

I squeezed his hand back. "I like that, too. And for the record, Teag's pretty over the moon about Anthony, too."

When we pulled up to the curb near my house, a familiar car sat nearby. Kell and I exchanged a glance, since I knew he recognized the gray Subaru, same as I did. "Were you expecting Ryan?" he asked.

I shook my head. "No clue." I checked my phone. No messages, no texts, nada.

I opened up the door that leads to the front porch from the street. It's a Charleston single house, with the porch—what Charlestonians call a "piazza"—facing an inner, walled courtyard, with the side of the house facing the street. Thanks to Lucinda, our friendly Voudon mambo, the door and wall is warded, so only friends may enter. I was surprised to find Ryan Alexander sitting on the porch, holding a cardboard box against his chest.

"I'm sorry to surprise you like this," Ryan said, glancing from me to Kell, aware that he had just ruined our date. "But I didn't know what else to do." He looked a little freaked out. Kell and I exchanged a glance.

"What's wrong?" I asked.

Ryan looked up at me with wide eyes, far too pale. "Hypothetically speaking, if I discovered evidence of a felony while I was committing a misdemeanor, would I still be in trouble?"

GHOSTS AND MISDEMEANORS

Kell and I ushered Ryan into the house. Baxter yipped and bounced until Kell picked him up as I steered Ryan to the kitchen and put on water for tea. Kell took the box from Ryan and put it on the table, handing him Baxter instead.

"Pet Bax. Therapy dog. Do you good," Kell said. Ryan rolled his eyes, but he took Baxter and absently stroked his fur.

"Sorry to interrupt," Ryan apologized belatedly.

"We'll survive," Kell replied, with a wink in my direction.

"Go back to the part about the felony and the misdemeanor," I said, getting three cups ready and measuring out the tea.

Ryan took a deep breath, and Baxter seemed to sense his nervousness, because he nosed Ryan, as if to prompt him to go on. "So lately, the team and I have been going places that are slated for either teardown or renovation, so we can see and document what's there before it's gone." Kell and I nodded.

Ryan is part of a group of urban explorers, adventurous—and sometimes reckless—rogue archeologists who spelunk through the ruins of modern civilization—abandoned buildings, drains, subway tunnels, bridges, maintenance conduits, and the like. Needless to say, these largely unsanctioned activities usually involve trespassing, if not a little breaking and entering, though ethical Urb-Exers like Ryan's group take a hard line against looting and vandalism. They approach the wastelands of urban decay much like wilderness hikers, taking nothing but pictures and leaving nothing but footprints. So I was surprised at the box that Ryan had brought with him.

"Okay. Go on," Kell nudged when Ryan felt silent. Given their interests, Kell and Ryan often coordinated forays, with Kell putting Ryan's group onto cool old ruins and Ryan calling in Kell and SPOOK when they found a place with signs of paranormal activity. Both of them tended to come to Teag and me for our input on history and antiques, and on more than one occasion for my gift.

"There's a block that's going to be renovated, so we wanted to get in and document the properties before we can't anymore," Ryan said, gratefully accepted a cup of steaming tea as I pushed it toward him. Kell and I took our mugs and settled in at the table, waiting for Ryan to tell his story.

"On an empty lot between old houses, there's a well. It's been bricked up for a long time, and probably went dry even before that. But the walls were in good shape, so Corey wanted to go down and see what was down there."

I'd met Corey. He seemed likely to climb anything just because it existed, so the thought of him rappelling into an old well didn't surprise me, although it wasn't my idea of a good time.

"About halfway down, he found an old leather wallet caught on an outcropping. He picked it up, thinking it had gotten lost somehow, meaning to return it if we could. But then the farther down he got, there were more—"

Kell and I looked at each other, then back to Ryan. "More wallets?" Kell asked, frowning.

Ryan nodded and took a gulp of his tea. "Yeah. First just a couple, and then more. Corey thought that was pretty weird, and since the well's going to get destroyed when the lot gets renovated, he figured there was no harm in bringing them up with him. We thought maybe there'd been a pickpocket, you know, taking the cash and ditching the ID. People might still want the wallets back."

"How were you going to explain finding them, without getting arrested either for theft or trespassing?" I asked, curious.

Ryan gave me a sour look. "Stick it in their mailbox, put it through the mail slot, leave it on the porch—"

"Okay, we get it," Kell said. "So what went wrong?"

"Corey picked up all the wallets he saw that hadn't fallen apart," Ryan said, looking too pale and his eyes too wide. Something had weirded him out. "He thought there might have been more at the bottom, but with the rain and debris, everything down there had rotted. Even so, he came back up with almost fifty."

I looked at him in surprise. "Fifty? That's some pickpocket."

Ryan met my gaze. "It's not just the number, Cassidy. When we opened them looking for ID, they're all much older than we expected. None of them is newer than 1902."

"Fifty wallets—more, probably—from the same time period?" Kell echoed. Ryan nodded.

A cold knot of dread tightened in my stomach. "Where was the well located?" I asked, hoping my suspicions were wrong.

"A couple of blocks away from Hampton Park," Ryan replied.

Kell looked at me. "You're thinking something."

I nodded, feeling sick. "The Expo was held in 1902."

"So maybe there were pickpockets," Kell said. "Makes sense—lots of out of towners, big crowds. It's the kind of place thieves love."

I nodded, but my gut suggested a much worse truth. "Let's go through them," I suggested. "We'll make a list of who they belonged to."

Ryan looked at me as if I were nuts, and I had the feeling that he shared my suspicions. "Cassidy, even if those men were in their twenties when the wallets were taken, they're long dead by now. That's over a hundred years ago."

Kell watched me closely, coming to his own conclusions. "You think foul play? I mean, fouler than just theft?"

"I hope I'm wrong, but that's exactly what I'm thinking."

Ryan looked from me to Kell and back again. "Wouldn't someone have noticed if fifty-plus men just disappeared? You'd think with the research the Archive and museum have done for their exhibits, someone would have picked up on that."

I remembered what Teag said at dinner, and shook my head. "Not necessarily. If they were from out of town, here for the Expo, who would notice? Their families would make inquiries—maybe if they knew they had come here, but what would the police have to go on?"

"And even if the police did get questions, it might have been hushed up," Kell speculated. "After all, the whole point of the Expo was to bring new business to Charleston and show off to the world. Wouldn't do much for the city's reputation if people disappeared off the streets."

We spent the next hour going through the old wallets, a sobering process. From the faded, damaged photos and identification, it appeared the wallets' owners had all been young men in their twenties and thirties, and from the lack of pictures of wives and families, single. I wasn't ready to touch them and risk getting knocked on my ass, so Kell and Ryan handled the wallets, and I dutifully copied down names and addresses. The longer we worked, the more certain I became that these men and the others whose wallets had decayed at the bottom of the well met an early and tragic end.

"All from out of town," Kell confirmed as we compared notes.

"No one would miss them right away," Ryan said. "It's not like people phoned home every weekend back then, and they weren't updating on Facebook. They probably didn't live at home, and it could be weeks before someone noticed they hadn't gotten a letter lately."

"Families might not have even known they were going to visit the Expo," I mused. "They could have come in on the train from Columbia or Atlanta or further, maybe from colleges, or for work. Schools or employers would have noticed if they didn't come back, but they might not have gone out of their way to go looking for them."

"Wallets are one thing, but if someone killed them, where did the bodies go?" Kell asked.

"Holmes," I said, remembering the display at the museum.

"Sherlock?" Ryan asked, confused. "Yes, I imagine he'd figure this out—"

I shook my head. "No. H. H. Holmes. From the Chicago World's Fair. The serial killer."

Kell frowned. "Couldn't be. I read that book someone wrote about him. He got caught and executed before the turn of the century. He was dead by 1902."

"Copycat?" Ryan wondered aloud.

"Maybe," I murmured. I needed to put Teag to work tracking the dead men and pick Sorren's brain to see what he remembered from having been in Charleston at the time. But I couldn't really say that aloud. "Maybe it really is as simple as a pickpocket ring. If so, there should be something in the police archives, or somewhere. Even if the authorities kept it quiet, there should be a log of the reports."

"You really believe that?" Ryan asked.

"No. But I hope I'm wrong."

"THE CHARLESTON EXPOSITION? I haven't thought about that in a long time. A very long time." Sorren, my vampire business partner, stared into the distance, thinking. Teag and I sat at the break room table in the back of the shop, a take-out pizza box pushed out of the way, and waited for Sorren to sift through his memories.

Sorren is nearly six hundred years old. I wondered what it was like to have that many memories, whether the mind sent old recollections to the mental equivalent of salt mine storage, or whether it was like a really big database that took a while to index. For all his vast experience, Sorren looks like he's in his mid- to late twenties with blond hair in a trendy cut and gray eyes the color of the sea before a storm. Before he was turned, he was the best jewel thief in Antwerp, maybe all of Belgium. Now, he's one of the leaders of the Alliance, and he spends his time checking in with his many shops like Trifles and Folly and human partners all over the world.

"We did have a few problems with the Expo, as I recall," Sorren said after a few minutes. "All those businessmen anxious—maybe desperate—do some deals attracted a few demons who were more than happy to make dreams come true in exchange for a soul or two. Had to put a stop to that. Found a couple of psi-vamps hanging around, feeding off the energy of the crowd. Not unusual when you have a big gathering like that. Took care of those pretty quickly," he chuckled. "The succubus who infiltrated the exotic dancers was a bit more of a challenge."

"Exotic dancers?" Teag asked. "Back then?"

Sorren gave him an amused look. "Ever hear of Salome, in the Bible? You think sex is a modern discovery? Of course, at the Expo, they called them 'hoochie coochie' dancers, but while the music changes, the song remains the same."

I'm never sure whether it's unsettling or comforting to realize that for all the world changes, people don't. If I spent too much time thinking about it, I'm pretty sure I'd be depressed, so I don't know how Sorren manages.

"So there *was* supernatural activity at the Expo," I pressed.

"Any time you get a large gathering of people, there will be super-natural opportunists," Sorren replied with a shrug, as though it was the most obvious thing in the world. "Even more so if ambition and greed are involved. But I wouldn't have called it a 'hotbed' of activity or said that the creatures were even particularly powerful. Mostly low-level spirits or monsters, looking for easy prey."

I told Sorren about the spike in ghostly activity at Hampton Park, and the shadow entity I'd seen at the Archive, as well as the resonances I'd picked up from the items in both displays.

"Oh, I remember the Chicago World's Fair quite well," Sorren replied. It seemed odd to hear that from someone who looked younger than thirty, though in an unguarded moment, I could see centuries, not decades in his gray eyes. "Holmes—his name was actually Mudgett—and his 'murder house.' The press had a field day. You can imagine. Crime of the century and all that."

His expression turned grim. "The Alliance investigated, of course. Such an atrocity, we wanted to believe there were demons, monsters involved." He shook his head. "Just a twisted, sick man. Evil doesn't need demons when it's got men to do its work.

Reminded me of another time, right here in Charleston. Lavinia Fisher."

Teag and I nodded. We knew the story about the notorious innkeeper and her husband who killed and robbed their guests, all but two. Sorren, and one other man who led to Fisher's downfall. The case was a sensation, even in the 1700s, and Lavinia's hanging is one of Charleston's most famous stories, along with her ghost, said to still haunt the Old Jail.

"The man who 'survived' to turn her in had help," Sorren said, as a cold smile touched his lips. "There would have been too many questions if I came forward. We needed a mortal. I made sure he stayed that way."

"No demon there either," Teag said quietly.

Sorren shook his head. "No. Evil comes as much from the heart as it does from the Pit."

I'm not sure that if I existed as long as Sorren has that I would retain any hope in humanity. Yet he does, and that hope is what keeps him fighting supernatural threats when he could just as easily retreat to a safe fortress and watch the world go by.

"Was there a serial killer loose at the Expo?" I asked, and filled him in on the wallets Ryan's team found.

Sorren frowned. "If there was, it wasn't supernatural in nature. We were monitoring closely, just in case something dark decided to feed. I don't recall anything in the papers. Something like that should have been in the news."

"Unless no one connected the dots," Teag said and held up a sheaf of papers. "I just got started on the list of names Cassidy, Kell, and Ryan compiled from the wallets. It's a slog through old newspaper archives, and not everything's been digitized. But from what I've found so far, the men who lost those wallets were reported missing—and later, presumed dead—within a few weeks to a month or so after the Expo."

"Did they have anything in common?" Sorren asked.

"They were young and single, and all of them but one from out of town. Some were college students, but others were doctors, teachers, businessmen, as well as a butcher, tailor, and farrier, from the ones I've looked into. Strangers, travelers, away from home and family —vulnerable."

"What about the one? You said—all but one from out of town," I asked.

Teag smiled. "James Hibbard. His family was from Aiken, but he had a married sister here in Charleston, and he was a student at The Citadel. The sister is long dead of course, died in 1960, but her granddaughter is a retired school teacher, still here in the city. It's a long shot, but I found an address, and it's the closest thing we've got to a personal connection to any of the wallet men."

"Let's go see her tomorrow," I urged. "I'll get Maggie to cover the store." I looked to Sorren. "I can't shake the feeling that we've got to figure this out before something bad happens. That energy I felt in the Archive, it might not have made the men go missing, but it didn't intend anything good."

Sorren nodded. "That's what I meant by 'supernatural opportunists.' There are creatures out there that feed on pain and fear, and that latch on to people with evil intent and intensify it for their own benefit. The exhibits brought all the memorabilia together and into the public eye, giving the resonance energy. It would have been like a dinner call to a creature like that."

"Do you think there's a connection to the people who've gone missing recently?" I asked, glancing at Teag.

He shrugged. "Until we know more about what happened back then, it's hard to say. People go missing every day without supernatural causes. But yeah, maybe. If we can find out what we're dealing with, maybe there's a way to stop it, or at least bottle it back up for a hundred years."

"I'll make some inquiries through the Alliance," Sorren said. "Very few entities are entirely unique. Someone else has likely either dealt with it or found a record of it."

I tried to ignore the warning tightness in my gut and plastered on the bravest smile I could muster. "And tomorrow, we'll go see Hibbard's grandniece. Sooner or later, we'll find the missing piece."

~

THE NEXT DAY, Teag and made coffee in the break room before the shop opened. I called Alistair while we waited for Maggie. "I just wondered if Rand was able to pull that box we discussed out of storage," I said. Harris Tomlinson was one more man who had gone missing, and I thought we might find a clue in his possessions.

"Not to my knowledge," Alistair said. He sounded much grumpier than usual.

"Something wrong?"

"Rand hasn't shown up for work today. It's not like him, and he's not answering his phone."

A cold shiver slithered down my spine. "Has anyone seen him?"

"He lives at home with his parents—he's going to college part-time to finish his degree—and his mother said he didn't come home last night. She's worried, says he's good about letting her know if he's going out with friends."

"Any idea where he went last?"

Now that I knew what to listen for, I could hear the concern beneath Alistair's gruff tone. "Not really. We're doing a 'then and now' wall for the exhibit with photos of a scene back in the day overlaid with the same view on Plexiglass. He went down to the area that had been the fairground to get some photos. No one's seen him since."

"If you hear from him—"

"Looks like I was wrong," Alistair interrupted. "The box is at the front desk. You just need to sign off on the inventory."

"I'll come by for it," I promised. And if you hear from Rand, please let me know. I have a couple of questions."

I ended the call and turned back to Teag, whose expression grew grim as I summarized Alistair's comments. "So we've got another missing person," Teag said.

"I'm afraid so."

Teag was silent for a few moments, fingers flying over his keyboard. "Two."

"Two what?"

"Rand makes the second new missing person since I the last time I checked," Teag said. "Mike Irwin was reported missing two days ago, but it looks like he might have really been gone longer than that."

"Does he fit the pattern?"

"You mean, was he young and single? Yes. And… oh—"

"What?"

Teag looked up. "He was an intern at the Archive."

We stared at each other for a moment. "Rand worked for the museum," I said. "Did you look for any connection with the others?"

Teag made a face. "No, but I will." He sounded pissed, but I knew not to take it personally, that he was mad at himself for overlooking a connection, though how we might have protected Rand had we known, I had no idea.

Just then, the bell over the door chimed as Maggie let herself in with her key. "We're back here," I called.

Maggie swept into the room like a patchouli-scented hurricane. She's got a head for business and a vibe from Woodstock, and she's decided that kicking supernatural ass is much more fun than yoga and book club. Hard to believe that she used to be a retired teacher, and now she's happily playing backup to our screwy little band of misfits trying to save the world without anyone noticing.

"All right. I'm here. Go do what you need to do," Maggie said, pulling off her sweater and going for the coffeepot all in one smooth movement.

I hugged her. "What makes you think we need to do something?"

Maggie fixed me with a "not born yesterday" look. "Because I'm sure there's something afoot. So go. The store will be fine. I've got plenty of coffee. Scoot."

I had already called Catherine Landry, Hibbard's grandniece, so she knew to expect us. We found her in an apartment building not far from downtown. She looked to be in her seventies, with gray hair pulled back into a ponytail, spry and curious.

"No one's talked about great uncle James since my mama died," Landry said. "Why now?"

"The museum and the Archive both have exhibits about the 1902

World's Fair here in Charleston," I said, skirting the truth. "We were doing some research related to the displays and found out several young men went missing, including your great uncle. You're the only family member we were able to contact."

"I know it happened long before you were born," Teag took up the story, "but we thought maybe you might have heard stories from your mother or grandmother, about James Hibbard."

Catherine Landry leaned back in her chair and folded her hands in front of her, lips touching her fingertips as she thought. "It's been a very long time," she said finally. "Grandma seemed... conflicted... about talking about him. Like the stories made her sad, but at the same time, she wanted—needed—to make sure someone remembered."

Teag and I said nothing, waiting out her pause. "James was grandma's older brother, and she worshipped him. She was so proud when he went to college here in Charleston, even though she hated him being away. She worried about him," Catherine said, frowning as if filtering childhood memories through an adult lens. "He was a kind man, but he didn't always fit in easily."

"Did she know he was coming to the World's Fair?" I asked.

Catherine nodded. "He was going to graduate soon, and he'd heard that there would be a lot of businessmen at the Fair, maybe looking for people to hire. He thought he might get a good job, make enough money to send some home to the family, even help grandma go to school." She chuckled. "Grandma was a smart girl, and James told her she should get an education, that he'd help her."

"Did James send any word about being at the Fair?" Teag nudged.

"He sent a couple of postcards," Catherine replied. "I lent them to the Museum. The last thing grandma ever heard from him, he sent her one of those souvenir coins, with a note that he had met some nice people and thought he had a job arranged, that he'd be home to visit soon and tell her all about it."

She sighed. "That was the last anyone ever heard from him. A telegraph came from his new job, informing him that he was being let go for not showing up. Grandma's parents came to Charleston, went to the police, but no one knew anything. They hoped, for a long time, that maybe James had been hurt, hit his head, lost his memory—that sort of thing. That he might show up and be able to explain everything. Hoping for a miracle," she said quietly. "But they didn't get one. And after years went by, they accepted that he must be dead. Only I think grandma held out hope, all the way to the end, that he was out there, somewhere. Or that at least she would find out what happened."

Catherine picked up a framed picture and handed it to Teag. "That's the last picture she had of James. It was taken about a year before he left for school."

I didn't try to touch the frame since I figured the photo held a lot of emotional resonance, but I leaned forward to get a better look. James was a good looking young man in his teens with a wide grin, and Catherine's grandmother was a young girl of about ten who shared a strong resemblance to James. They stood arm in arm, and their body language made it clear they were close to each other.

"Did your grandmother have any theories about what happened to James?" I asked in a gentle tone.

Catherine stared at the picture as if imagining the young girl her grandmother had once been. "She said that Aiken was too small for James, not enough opportunity, small-minded people," Catherine recalled. "Said that he blossomed in the 'big city' where he met more people full of ideas, like him. I don't think she ever got over his death. I hope that they're together again, wherever they are."

I blinked back tears at her tone and managed a smile. "Thank you. I appreciate you sharing your story—with us, and with the museum."

"My mom spent years trying to find out what happened to her Uncle James," Catherine added, looking up sharply. "Although she never met him, she knew what an impact his death had on her mother. She hired a private investigator and found nothing. She even went to a psychic." Catherine wrapped her arms around herself and repressed a shiver. Teag and I exchanged a glance.

"Did the psychic tell her anything?" Teag ventured.

Catherine nodded, but I took her a minute to speak. "Mama never told Grandma about the psychic. Didn't tell me until much later." She looked up, a defiant gleam in her eyes. "You've got to understand what it took for my mama to go have a séance done. All the church people said that kind of thing was sin. But she went anyway. And then she wished she hadn't."

"This would have been long enough past when he disappeared that one way or the other, James had to be dead?" I confirmed.

Catherine nodded. "Grandma never acknowledged it, but mama and I knew. After a while, the calendar outweighed any optimism we might have had left." I knew what she meant. James would have been born around 1880, and we were well past the centenarian milestone.

"What did the psychic tell your mother?" Teag kept his voice soothing.

Catherine looked away. "She said James never left Charleston. That his spirit was trapped here." She swallowed hard. "He was murdered. And that he wouldn't rest until his murderer was caught." Catherine turned back and met my gaze. "It's too late to catch and punish James's killer. But do the next best thing. Figure out who did it, so that we can tell the whole story."

SECRETS AND LIES

"ALL OF THEM." TEAG'S VOICE HELD A FLAT, ANGRY TONE I HAD rarely heard before.

"You're sure?" I held on to the last, small glimmer of hope, but it died as Teag gave a curt nod.

"I'm certain. The men who owned those wallets came to the Charleston Exposition and were never heard from again." Teag sat back in his chair and drummed his fingers against the break room table.

"And the police?"

Teag stood up and began to pace, fairly vibrating with nervous energy. "Anthony got a friend of his down at the department to see what he could find in the old records. We're going back over a hundred years here, but he found a log book. All of the wallet men were reported missing or had relatives ask the police to track them either during the Expo or within six months after it ended."

"And did the police find anything?" I had to ask, but I could guess the answer from the look on Teag's face.

"No. Anthony's contact didn't straight-out say it, but it didn't look like the police took the reports too seriously. I guess they figured 'boys will be boys,'" he added in a tight voice. "Just a note with each one

"""

saying that no evidence was found of foul play, missing presumed voluntary departure."

"Fifty 'voluntary departures' that didn't bother to inform their families?" I asked incredulously.

Teag nodded. "Yeah. It looks bad. The guy at the police department seemed to think so too, because he asked Anthony if the information was going to be made public."

"Not that it would do a lot of good now," I said with a snort. "You think it was a cover-up?"

Teag shrugged. I could see how much this bothered him. All of the young men were about our age. They had families who loved them, friends, classmates, lives ahead of them. Fifty people—maybe more—gone. No trace. And apparently, the police were more worried about how that might look to business investors than they were about stopping a killer.

"No idea who was doing it?" My throat was tight, my mouth dry. The enormity of the crime, and the apparent lack of interest staggered me.

"I don't think the cops ever considered looking for a pattern," Teag said. "Either they didn't want to be bothered, or they didn't have the manpower, or someone paid them to look the other way."

"When was the first disappearance reported?" I asked, and the words felt thick on my tongue.

"January, 1902. Two months after the exhibition opened."

I looked up at Teag, stunned. "So if the cops had done something—anything—about the first missing man, maybe the others wouldn't have been taken?"

Teag nodded. "And there were more, Cassidy. Anthony's contact looked at the ledger through January of 1902, six months after the Expo closed. One hundred and fifty inquiries about men whose last known destination was the Charleston Fair." I heard anger, grief, and frustration in Teag's voice, and all three emotions bunched in my gut like a chunk of ice.

"We need to look through James Hibbard's box," I said finally.

"Harris Tomlinson's things too, from the museum. And I need to see if I can read the wallets."

"We can go through the Hibbard box and the Tomlinson items. As for the wallets—let's wait until we know more. God, Cassidy! If you read fifty wallets owned by men who were offed by a serial killer, you'll be traumatized for life! And for what? They're dead, and the killer is dead."

"Dead—but not gone," I replied. I dreaded reading the wallets. My gift is visceral, and uncompromising. It can show me the resonance of a situation like watching a movie, or throw me into the mind of the object's owner so that I see, hear and feel what that person felt. But I remembered the malevolent presence from the Archive, and the darkness I sensed at Hampton Park. "It's back, Teag. Whatever—whoever —it was, they're back. And I'm really afraid that it might have something to do with Rand and the other new missing men."

Teag nodded soberly. "I know, Cassidy. But using your gift costs you. Reading fifty wallets might only tell us that the men are dead— and we can assume that, being murdered, they died badly—it's just going to wear you down for nothing."

I raised my head defiantly. "The murderer can't have been careful all the time. Not if he killed at least one hundred and fifty people. Probably more." What about tourists who hadn't thought to give a detailed itinerary to anyone? Or someone who came in on the train for the weekend, not thinking the jaunt warranted notifying family and friends? If we could look at the missing persons' reports for the entire East Coast from December 1901 until the June of 1902, how many more men vanished, without a clue to their fate?

"We know that whatever did this is human," Teag said. "Or Sorren and the Alliance would have shut it down. So that black entity must be a really twisted ghost."

I shook my head. "What if something possessed the killer? Maybe not a demon. Sorren and the Alliance would have picked up on that. But there are so many other kinds of energies out there, so many malevolent spirits. What I felt at the Archive and in the park, it seemed too dark to be fully human."

"You think Sorren wouldn't have noticed?"

"I think Sorren can't be everywhere at once, and if this was mostly-human, maybe it slipped under the radar."

Teag was quiet for a moment, considering what I'd said. "Maybe," he allowed. "But what do we do about it? We can't go to the police and say that we think the men who have gone missing are being grabbed by a century-old serial killer?"

I didn't have an answer to that, so I glanced toward the cardboard box. "Let's look at James Hibbard's collection."

Teag fetched the stained wooden container and set it on the table not quite evenly between us. He went to the office and grabbed a couple of thin woven strips of fabric from a jar on the desk. He wove those strips, and they are filled with his magic. When I use my psychometry and hold one of the woven strips at the same time, Teag can see what my visions reveal to me. That not only saves time on recaps, but it's also more likely that Teag might notice something I don't.

"Where do you want to start?"

I took a deep breath. "What are my choices?"

Teag rummaged through the box. "There's another postcard from the Expo, so it was obviously written before Hibbard got into trouble. We know where his wallet is," he added with a wry look. "Otherwise, odds and ends, the kinds of bits and pieces you leave in a drawer at home when you go off to school."

"Anything that might give me an idea of him—before?"

Teag sorted through the items. "How about a nice fountain pen?"

"Let's give it a try."

Teag picked up the pen and handed me the fabric strip, then settled in to a chair next to me before passing over the pen. The sleek shape and retro styling made a functional item into usable art. Just the kind of thing for a young man on the edge of seeking his fortune.

An image of a young man came to mind, and I recognized him from the wallet's contents as Hibbard. I picked up a hint of nervousness, and an image of Hibbard concentrating hard as he wrote something on a tablet. *Taking a test? Filling out a job application?* I couldn't see the paper, but the resonance of Hibbard's desire to do a good job carried through. The images shifted, and I saw Hibbard shaking hands with a man in a business suit who looked pleased and friendly. Although I couldn't glimpse Hibbard's face, I sensed that the meeting succeeded. After another moment and a few images of Hibbard in classrooms, presumably taking notes, I shook myself awake and set the pen down.

"Nothing particularly useful there," Teag said with a sigh.

I shrugged. "Not a bad warm-up. Better than diving into the gruesome guts of something right away." I'd done that enough times. "Besides, it's helpful to have a sense of Hibbard before whatever happened, kind of a level set."

Teag passed me a yellowed postcard. Unlike the one claimed by the exhibit, this card had been damaged by time and water. Those scars didn't affect its resonance, and I caught my breath the minute my fingers touched the fragile paper.

Excitement. Loneliness. Anticipation. Longing. Hibbard's emotions washed over me, strong enough that I struggled to remember that he had been dead for over a hundred years. Sometimes visions feel like I'm inside the person's head, and other times I watch from the outside, still me. Now, I was an invisible observer, standing in the midst of the hustle and bustle of the Charleston Expo. The grand, gleaming white palaces of commerce built to impress foreign and domestic business magnates loomed tall, even more impressive than in their pictures. So much promise, so many dreams packed into the exposition grounds that the air fairly hummed with the electricity of it.

I recognized Hibbard right away, dressed in his Sunday best suit. He tried for natty with a pocket watch on a chain, but his wide-eyed expression made it clear he was a country boy set loose in the big city. Despite knowing how the story ended, I smiled at the unabashed youthful enthusiasm. Hibbard looked to be only a year or two younger than I was, with his whole life ahead of him. A life that had been stolen—

Hibbard crossed the grounds with two friends his age. They laughed and talked, and I heard them joking and making plans.

Hibbard stopped at one point and bid his friends goodbye, then continued on alone, walking a block or so beyond where the Exposition grounds ended, past the sunken garden. The bandstand from Hampton Park still stood in its original location, where it would remain until after the grand Expo closed its doors and workers dismantled its plywood palaces.

I watched Hibbard walk past homes, trying to commit what I saw to memory, hoping something might still look familiar. Charleston valued its history, but it's a living city and a lot had changed in a century. He stopped in front of a gray clapboard house memorable for the ornate wooden 'gingerbread' trim that decorated its cornices and for the colorful accents that made it the kind of house people called a "painted lady." Hibbard took something from his pocket and dropped it in a mailbox. My vision went dark.

This time, Teag pushed a glass of sweet tea into my hand, giving me a minute to take several deep gulps before I was ready to talk.

"Nothing bad," I told him, and drank more of the tea, relishing the mix of strong and sweet. "He looked so happy and normal, taking in the sights with his friends. And let me tell you—the Expo is a lot fancier in person. The photos don't do it justice." I paused, trying to sort through the images I'd read from the postcard.

"He seemed excited, and a little nervous. Not like he thought he was in danger; more like being in a strange place on your own. And he was either homesick or missing someone special."

Teag looked at the postcard, which had been addressed to Hibbard's sister. "Train ride uneventful. Charleston beautiful as ever. Wish you and S could see the grand fair. Tell you all about it. Love, James." He shook his head. "Nothing out of the ordinary. I wonder who 'S' was?"

"Friend? Girlfriend? We could ask his grandniece, but I doubt she'd know."

"She said her grandmother said James never really fit in. Are you picking up anything like that?"

I thought back over what I had seen and sensed. "He seemed to be comfortable with the friends or traveling companion I saw at the Expo. Maybe he hid his insecurities well?"

Something about the comment made me feel like I'd missed a clue, but nothing that I'd seen in the vision suggested an answer. "All right. I've dodged a bullet twice now. Let's get to the wallet."

Teag refilled my glass and set it aside, knowing that if this vision proved more traumatic I would need it. I swallowed hard, knowing Teag could see my fear, and reached for the worn leather billfold.

As soon as I touched the wallet, everything changed. *My head pounded, and my sight blurred. Drugged. I'd been drugged. I was certain; a single glass of beer at dinner shouldn't have nearly knocked me out. But who? And why?*

My brain felt sluggish. I tried to stand up, and fell back on my bed like a marionette with cut strings. I saw the teacup and plate on the bedside table, and I knew.

"Enjoy your nightcap, Mr. Hibbard?" The voice from the doorway made me try to shift backward, away. Brannigan, my landlord.

"Why?" The words sounded slurred, even to my own ears.

The man silhouetted in the doorway shrugged. "Easier for me to handle you. Quieter. Don't worry. It won't be long."

"Why?" I repeated, and struggled again to rise, only to collapse beside the bed.

"The fairgrounds makes for such a good hunt," Brannigan replied. He shifted, and I could see him in the gaslight, tall and spare, with wiry brown hair and blue eyes that regarded me with the cool gaze of a predator. "Because you're far from home, and no one will notice. Because no one will care about the likes of you."

I felt the chill of his words into my bones, knew the truth of it. My family dared only push so far to find me, for fear the police might uncover secrets best not spoken aloud. Secrets that had to go to the grave.

"What?" One word at a time seemed the best my body could do with the drugs coursing through my system. The man moved into my room, bent down and lifted me as if I weighed nothing, and moved to

the small closet. He pressed against something I did not see, and the back panel swung inward, into darkness.

"I'm afraid you'll have to trust me on this," he said, and hiccupped an obscene giggle at the thought—me, trusting him as he hauled me somewhere I knew in my bones would be a very bad place.

"Ten steps in," he said as if dragging a body was an everyday occurrence. My heart clenched at the fear that perhaps it was. So many men came and went from the boarding house. I hadn't paid attention. No one had. Where did they go? Elsewhere. We assumed they went on about their lives, left the Expo behind. Now, I feared that some— perhaps many—did not.

"Five steps down." I fell more than walked down the stairs, supported by my captor. "Not much farther."

He stopped and I heard a door creak as he opened it. "Don't worry. I'll come back to take care of you very soon," Brannigan said. A hand patted me down, searching my pockets, and found my wallet, which he removed. The vision went dark.

I came back to myself with a shudder and a gasp. "He took them," I managed as Teag reached for my wrist to steady me and put the sweet tea in my grasp. "He took them. Killed them." My head pounded and my heart thudded like it would jump out of my chest.

Teag waited for me to drink the tea and slow my breathing, leaving his hand on my wrist to anchor me. "Who did it, Cassidy?" he asked when I had recovered enough to be able to speak.

"Brannigan. The landlord. Oh god, Teag. Just like in Chicago."

Teag frowned. "Did you get a full name?"

I shook my head, and realized that the glass trembled in my grip. "No. But I can describe him, and I could probably recognize him in a picture."

Teag moved Hibbard's wallet back to the cardboard box with the other billfolds, and when he came back, he handed me a package of peanut butter crackers. "Here. Eat. I'll do some digging."

We had done this kind of thing enough to have a routine. The pitcher of sweet tea—strong a hurricane, sweet enough to make your fillings buzz—the crackers, and in my office, for really bad visions, a bottle of bourbon, were the mainstays, along with enough coffee to keep a hospital awake. I told Teag what I saw from the wallet's resonance, describing the house and Brannigan in as much detail as I could manage.

"So he walked a few blocks from the Expo grounds to mail his postcard, into a residential area," Teag mused. His fingers flew on his keyboard, and I knew he had shortcuts to all the old maps of the city. "Did you get any landmarks from inside the Expo? That might help me figure out which side of the park he was on."

I gave Teag all the information that I had seen, though some of it made little sense to me. Unfortunately, what I could provide did little to narrow the search. "How about that 'painted lady' Victorian house by the mailbox? Maybe there's a photo of it. Maybe it's still around."

"Working on it," Teag muttered. I know better than to be hurt by how short he gets when he's on a digital trail. He gets single-minded, laser-focused, and I know he's harnessing his own hacker magic, which takes a concentration all its own.

Half an hour later, Teag sat back, irritated at himself. "Nothing. Bupkis. Nada. The house is a bust."

"Okay, let's come back to that," I said, setting aside my empty glass and the cracker wrapper. I felt mostly human again. My headache had receded and my heartbeat had returned to normal. "How about this Brannigan character?"

"Give me some time. Maybe we'll find a deed that ties Brannigan to the house." Teag's optimism seemed strained. We were rarely that lucky. He gave me a look. "You ready to see if the box from the museum tells you anything?"

I wasn't, but we had a job to do. "Let's see what Harris Tomlinson left behind."

Business records filled most of the box Rand left for me, along with yellowed clippings and program flyers about the Expo. Only a few were personal items: a single cuff link, and a broken watch fob.

Bracing myself, I reached for the cuff link, and Teag stretched the woven strip between us. Images hit me in a jumble. *Exhilaration and nervousness, confidence and a sense of accomplishment. Anticipation and longing, the sense of being separated from someone beloved, and looking forward to a reunion. Shame and fear—of discovery, punishment, consequences. Determination and loyalty, worry and evasiveness.*

I blinked, clearing my mind. "I think Harris Tomlinson was having an affair."

Teag passed me more iced tea, and raised an eyebrow. "He wasn't married, so what makes you think that?"

"He felt excited about the business aspect of the Expo, but being here took him away from someone he cared about," I said, sorting through the resonance. For whatever reason, Tomlinson's memories felt vague, as if even long after his disappearance and death he would not relinquish his secrets. "But he looked forward to going to Atlanta. I think that's where the person he loved was, or they were going to meet up there. But he was afraid of being caught, that something bad would happen. That's why I think his beloved must have been cheating on a spouse, or at least breaking a betrothal."

"Or maybe it was a Romeo and Juliet thing," Teag suggested. "Maybe Tomlinson fell in love with someone from the wrong side of the tracks." Unfortunately, we would probably never know.

The watch fob fit in the palm of my hand, a simple silver circle engraved with Tomlinson's initials. It looked well-worn, as if its owner toyed with it as a nervous habit, and I could see where the link that connected it to the watch chain had pulled loose, allowing it to be lost. *Nervousness, to the point of feeling sick. Fear of discovery, of scandal, being ruined. Anger at being forced to do something hated. A bribe? No, a payoff. Blackmail.*

I came back to myself, gasping. "Someone was trying to blackmail him. He was terrified. Whatever the blackmailer had on him, it was enough to make him consider suicide. But the love he felt was real. That came through, too."

Teag put the items back in the box and moved it away from me. "Since the Tomlinsons are still players here in Charleston, I doubt we'll get anyone to 'fess up even if they do know the truth. Let me see what I can find about Brannigan."

While he ran through databases, I texted Sorren. "We don't know what Sorren has found out. Maybe he'll remember something important."

"Or maybe Brannigan wasn't on his radar because until now, there was nothing supernatural involved, just good old fashioned blood-thirsty psycho," Teag muttered.

"I could look at more wallets," I offered. "Maybe if we put enough of the victim's memories together, we'd have more to go on."

"Cassidy—" Teag's growl told me he worried that I would push myself too hard.

"The longer this takes, the more men go missing—and we don't know what happens to the men who are vanishing now," I argued. "If we can get to the bottom of this, maybe it all ties together—the men who disappeared back then, the ones now, the ghosts, the entity. We won't know until I see what I get from those wallets."

Teag glared at me, reluctant to agree but I knew he saw the logic in my argument. "All right," he said, setting a search program to run while he came to steady me. "But we're not going to try for all fifty tonight."

"No argument from me on that," I said, and meant every word.

I managed to get through ten wallets before a headache nearly had me on my knees. Teag got me a couple of ibuprofen, and sat with me, rubbing the tension from my shoulders, until the pain subsided.

"All that, and we don't know much more than when we started," I said, feeling defeated.

"Not exactly," Teag said. "You got a much better look at both Brannigan and the house, even glimpses of the street."

"They haven't been enough for us to narrow it down," I argued.

"Yet," Teag emphasized. "You don't know which detail might click at the right time."

I gestured at the wallets on the table. "I just feel so helpless. What good is my magic if I can't get answers?"

"This Brannigan guy was good at being evil," Teag said, coming around to sit next to me. "If he wasn't, they would have caught him back then. Cassidy, he got away with almost two hundred murders. For all we know, he had magic of his own and used it to fog his victim's memories. Hell, maybe he anticipated having someone with magic come after him."

"Sorren said the Alliance was watching," I countered. "Don't you think they would have noticed a homicidal witch?"

Teag grimaced. "Okay, then we're back to a Hannibal-level psychopath. It's possible. Sorren's often said people don't need the supernatural to be evil. Think of all the serial killers who've gotten away with their murders for decades because they're smart sons of bitches and good at covering their tracks. If the police and the FBI and whole teams of detectives take years to put the clues together, don't beat yourself up for not getting the right answer on the first try."

Before I could answer, both our phones went off. We gave each other a look of exasperation, then went to different corners of the room to answer.

"It's all right, Anthony. I'll be waiting when you get back—"

"Hi, Kell. Okay, thanks for telling me. For the record, I still think this is a bad idea—"

A few minutes later, Teag and I regrouped at the break room table. Maggie had closed up the shop and gone home, reminding us to call her if we needed someone to back us up. She doesn't try to help out with the fights, but Maggie is an unstoppable force when it comes to having dinner ready along with enough hospital supplies to staff a MASH unit.

"Anthony has to take care of some business before he comes home," Teag reported. "He's going to be late."

"Kell's still determined to go check out the well," I answered. "And he wants us to join them."

"Let's do it," Teag replied. "There's no time like the present for bad decisions."

KELL HAD INVITED Teag and me to go along with the SPOOK crew to check out the old well, and my answer had been that we would catch up with them. The more we learned about the missing men, the more certain I became that any resonance left behind would be powerful and dangerous. Kell and his team were good at paranormal investigation, but they weren't trained fighters, so battling either humans or supernatural entities was out of their league. I didn't want them getting hurt, and since they couldn't be allies on the battlefield, the less they knew about our "extra" abilities, the better.

"It would have been simpler to talk Kell out of coming, and have a go at this ourselves," Teag grumbled as we parked a few block away and headed toward the empty lot with the well.

"Have you ever tried to talk Kell out of something when he's fired up?" I countered. "He's like a kid on the Fourth of July. Once Ryan told us about the wallets, having SPOOK come out and take a look was a foregone conclusion. Bonus points since the property is going to be redeveloped soon."

Kell's team would have all their ghost hunting gear in hand to document activity. Teag and I came prepared with a different kind of gear. Both of us wore several protective charms, as well cloth into which Teag had woven defensive magic. I had my athame and an antique walking stick. Both items carried a strong emotional resonance for me, and served as conduits for me to focus my touch magic into a formidable protective force. Teag had an assortment of blessed, silver and iron knives as well as a staff. He's a competition-level martial arts practitioner so he can handle himself against foes human and otherwise. We both carried plenty of salt, holy water, and small iron pellets the size of BBs, items that tended to dispel or at least annoy most supernatural creatures.

With luck, nothing would happen, and we could all go home safe and sound.

We were never that lucky.

Teag and I kept to the shadows, moving up on the empty lot along the sides of the buildings, wanting to observe before we made our presence known. The nearest streetlight hung dark and useless overhead, and the next closest gave an anemic glow at less than full power. This area had remained largely residential, although new developments that mixed condos and retail seemed to be moving in on all sides.

"Did you find anything out about the well?" I asked as Teag and I watched from a nearby alley. Since we both have magic, it's debatable whether having us along on a ghost hunt helps or puts Kell's team in danger. Some entities are frightened by magic, while others are drawn like moths. I wanted to see what showed up on its own for the SPOOK investigators before we went barging in.

"Nothing interesting," Teag replied quietly. "We're at the outside edge of the old Expo grounds, so this section was never built up with Fair buildings. It's always been residential. A number of the homes that were here in 1901 are still here. Some of them became boarding houses while the Expo was open, homeowners making an extra buck off all the tourists. Pretty enterprising bunch. Since all those out-of-towners were walking right past their doors, the people who owned the houses found a way to earn some extra cash selling fried chicken and pound cake, taking in laundry, even boarding horses in their carriage houses."

"Sounds like the whole city got in on the excitement. How about the house the well belonged to? Anything special?"

Teag shook his head. "Not that I could find. The owner had no criminal record, didn't get in any trouble, no reports about problems to the police. He took in lodgers, but there's nothing in the police files implicating him in any of the disappearances."

"So how did the wallets end up down his well?"

Teag shrugged. "No idea. I'm still poking around, trying to see if I can find out more about everyone who owned the buildings around the Expo. It's slow going."

"Look!" I jabbed Teag with my elbow and pointed. Pinpricks of green light winked on and off on the lot near the well. At another time of the year, I might have wondered if they were fireflies, but we were too late in the season, and the color was wrong. I could hear Kell's crew remarking as they moved to capture video, audio, and EMF.

"The lights are centering around the well," Teag noted.

"There's more of them every second, and they're... agitated." If the dancing lights were spirits manifesting, then anything that made them anxious couldn't be good. I let my athame slip down my sleeve into my right hand, and patted the walking stick where it hung from my belt alongside my left leg.

"The entity is here," I said, sensing the same apprehension I felt at the Archive. "I can't see it yet, but it's here."

"The wind is picking up," Teag said, glancing skyward. "And it's supposed to be calm tonight."

"Gotten colder, too," I replied, as the air grew unseasonably nippy.

"There!" I grabbed Teag by the arm and turned him toward the broken streetlamp. The shadows that pooled beneath it looked too dark, too solid.

"I really don't like the look of that," Teag said, eying the distance between the opaque shadows and Kell's group.

The resonance I picked up from the shadow thing grew stronger, and through the muddy impressions, I could piece together a sense of purpose, maybe sentience. Enough to know it had Kell's group in its sight, and the ghost hunters were about to become the prey.

"We've got to get them out of there," Teag murmured, whether he read my expression or picked up something on his own from the entity.

Before I could agree, a cold blast of wind came out of nowhere and swept across the empty lot with enough force to make Calista grab for her audio equipment, cursing a blue streak. Drew bent against the wind, EMF reader clutched in one hand, while the other shielded his eyes from the dust and small debris carried in the wind. Pete hung onto his camera, wrapping his body around it protectively, as he struggled to keep from being bowled over by the gusting wind. Kell grabbed at the edge of the old well, then lost his footing and staggered backward as the old masonry came loose in his hand and gave way.

For a second, I thought the wild wind meant to tumble Kell down the shaft, but he managed to fall away from the well instead of taking a header over the edge. *That was too close.*

Bounded on three sides by other buildings, the empty lot trapped the wind, which circled with dangerous strength, carrying leaves, dirt, and paper with it.

"Get them out of here!" I yelled to Teag. "I'll see if I can slow down the shadows."

I knew from the look on Teag's face that he didn't like splitting up, but I had the distance weapons, so we both knew how it had to go down. Teag muttered something under his breath and then sprinted off toward Kell and the others as I drew the walking stick and tightened my grip on the athame. *Showtime.*

The entity seemed to register Teag's arrival, because the wind gusted again, harder and colder, and although I was still on the edge of the vortex, the airborne dirt stung where it hit my skin and my eyes burned from the dust. Hoping its attention stayed on Teag and the others, I sidled up closer, sticking to the regular shadows that stretched out from the neighboring houses. My athame and the walking stick could channel powerful magic, but I needed to be within range, which was strongest within about a dozen feet. And that was the weak point in my plan.

Behind me, I could hear Teag shouting above the wind, trying to get Kell's people to safety. I raised my right hand and leveled the athame, pulling on the strong emotions and memories my touch magic drew from the wand.

Cold, raw force blasted out from the tip of the athame, a bright white jet of power. It hit the shadow entity square on, blasting through it into the wall behind, sending up a shower of brick fragments and carving a depression into the solid wall. The creature shredded around it like mist, undamaged.

I backpedaled a few steps as I watched the entity regroup. The wind grew stronger, whipping my hair and burning my face. It tore at my clothing and made it difficult to breathe. The cycling air carried more debris aloft, battering me with pebbles and sticks, dry leaves and empty paper coffee cups. I'd survived enough Charleston hurricanes to know bigger things could go airborne too, big enough to cause real damage. This needed to end before someone got hurt.

"Cassidy!" Kell's shout barely carried above the roar of the vortex. I forced myself forward. It took two hands to raise the walking stick, fighting the press of the wind.

Bang. The sound of a shotgun firing at close range made me flinch, and as my heart hammered, it took me a second to realize the shot aimed past me, at the entity. For a few seconds, the wind lessened.

I called up the memories held in the walking stick, of Alard, Sorren's master, and the power he commanded. The resonance leapt to my touch, and in the seconds before the shadow creature regrouped, I sent a streak of fire arcing from the cane's tip, blasting against the darkness.

A scream echoed from the walls of the surrounding buildings, and then the tattered shadow caught the last of the swirling wind and rose into the night sky before vanishing. I fell to my knees, ears still ringing from the too-close shotgun blast.

"Cassidy!" Kell sank down in front of me, anxiously looking me over for injuries. I realized a moment later that he had a shotgun in one hand.

"We need to get out of here. Someone will call in the gunfire."

Kell helped me to my feet. "Rock salt. The shells were filled with rock salt."

I gave him a confused look. "Why?"

He shrugged. "You told me spirits don't like salt. Salt cleanses, right? Figured I'd give it a try. It always works for those guys on TV."

I let myself lean on him, enjoying the warmth of his arm around my shoulder. "You made it blink."

"And you somehow incinerated it with an old cane, after you pointed a stick at it and blasted it," he murmured as we crossed the rubbish-strewn lot. "When you're ready to tell me about it, I'm ready to listen."

I smiled, despite how worn I felt from the fight. My battle with the entity had taken only minutes, but drawing on my magic takes a lot of out of me. While this wasn't the longest or the hardest I'd fought, it had still drained me.

Teag looked us both up and down when we got back to the group. Calista sat behind the wheel of Kell's car, which was running and ready to go. "Get out of here," Teag said, clapping a hand on Kell's shoulder. "I'll get Cassidy out in the other direction. We really don't want to explain this to the cops."

Calista had the car moving before Kell even got his door shut, while Teag and I had already sprinted a block in the other direction toward where we left my car. Sirens wailed in the distance, and we picked up our pace, rounding the corner a few moments before the patrol cars closed the distance from the other direction. I threw open the car door and flicked the locks, then we were gone, heading through the darkened alleys without lights for a few blocks until we were certain we left both ghosts and cops well behind us.

I would drop Teag off at his car back at the shop. "What did you make of tonight?" I asked.

Teag flopped back against the seat and closed his eyes. "Whatever the hell that shadow-thing is, it's definitely supernatural—you heard all of SPOOK's equipment going wild. And it's strong enough to cause a whirlwind like a freaking hurricane." He opened his eyes and met my gaze. "It could have killed us."

"My athame didn't do anything to it. But salt made it flicker, and fire sent it packing."

"Fire made it leave, but it wasn't destroyed. It'll be back—and now it knows you hurt it. It could hunt you."

I considered that for a moment and shook my head. "I don't think so. It's run into me before. And it wasn't aiming at me—it sent the wind against the group investigating the well. It's tied to those wallets and whatever else is down there. Somehow, it's connected to what happened all those years ago."

"And now? Do you think there's a connection to the new missing men?"

I thought for a moment. "Yes, but I don't think we've got all the pieces. I'm not sure that what's happening now is something a black ghost can just mojo on its own."

"You think it's got help of some kind?"

I shrugged. "I think we don't know enough, and we don't know what we don't know." The convoluted sentence summed up my frustration.

"You okay?" Teag asked.

"Yeah. But if Kell hadn't gone cowboy on us, I'm not sure I would be. Force and fire weren't enough to dispel it. The salt wasn't either, but at least it disrupted the… thing."

"I know we usually try to avoid guns for the noise, but maybe Kell's on to something," Teag said. Most of the time, knives or relics are enough to do the job, although when we've fought creatures that took on human form, silver bullets did the trick. "It wouldn't hurt to add a shotgun or two, just in case."

"What's next? Water balloons filled with holy water?" I realized it was only partly a joke.

"Do you think it would work? Father Anne would bless them. Although she might never let us live it down," Teag added with a grin.

"Thanks for getting Calista and the others out of there."

"All in a day's work. Although I was glad when Kell went after you. Everyone needs backup."

"Amen to that," I muttered. I managed a smile. "Don't you have dinner to cook? Anthony's going to blame me if it's late."

Tired as he was, Teag's face lit up. "Nah. Everything's already done, I just need to warm it in the oven. No harm, no foul."

"So get out of here. You've got dinner with your honey," I urged.

Teag's grin turned wicked. "Bet you could have dinner with your honey, too, if you gave Kell a call."

I batted his shoulder in mock indignation. "Maybe another night. Kell's got a freaked-out team to settle, and I need to go feed Baxter before he thinks the world has come to an end." I paused, mustering my nerve. "And tomorrow, we'll tackle the rest of the wallets and see what happens."

Teag nodded. "Then you better get a good night's rest and bring a latte with you in the morning, because we'll be in for stormy weather."

I waited until he had his Volvo running before I eased my RAV4 around the corner and headed home.

I didn't expect my phone to ring so late. Baxter and I had just curled up on the couch to watch TV. Dinner had been eaten and leftovers put away, and all that remained was some quiet downtime before bedtime. I'd decided to take Teag's advice and get some sleep because handling those objects at the store tomorrow would be an emotional rollercoaster.

"Alicia Peters" shone on the caller-ID. Now I really was curious, since I figured it might be Sorren or Kell, or even Teag. Not our friend the psychic medium.

"Alicia? Is everything all right?" Alicia and I were colleagues more than friends, making me pretty sure she hadn't called to chat.

"Cassidy, there are so many."

Goosebumps rose at her tone. "So many what, Alicia?" I asked carefully, afraid I knew the answer.

"All the dead men. So many. So young. They want you to find them."

Alicia doesn't usually sound like something out of a late-night horror movie. Every other time we've spoken, she's sounded perfectly normal, and while I knew she had a strong gift, I'd never seen it overwhelm her before. "What's going on, Alicia? What are you hearing?"

"There are more than you know," she said as if I hadn't spoken. I don't have Alicia's gift with spirits, but if it works at all the way my touch magic does, then the pictures can be maddeningly incomplete, fuzzy, or all mixed up. Real psychic gifts don't work the way they do on TV. Ghosts don't speak in complete sentences, or always have correct information. Spirits can be misled by anger or jealousy, or go dark and crazy with guilt and grief. Visions can be spotty, providing just enough bits and pieces to tell you danger is coming without any help on where or when.

"More ghosts? So more murders than what we've found so far?" My mouth went dry. If Kell's count was correct, there had been far too many deaths already.

"Happening again," Alicia said, her voice raspy and not at all her usual tone. "Now. He's back. The ghosts want... justice."

"Help me," I begged. "I want to find out the truth about what happened to them. And I think the disappearances are connected to what happened before. But I need more—"

"Blue to green. Green." Alicia's words made no sense to me, but I wrote down everything she said, because the ghosts knew, even if they couldn't easily share the answers with the living.

"What else, Alicia? What can the ghosts tell me?"

"Urn. Shining urn."

"Okay. Do they remember anything else?"

"So many voices. So many all at once." Alicia sounded like she was in pain. I knew what having a single vision could cost me. I couldn't imagine having hundreds of dead people screaming in my mind at the same time. "The walls are hollow."

That at least squared with my vision. I waited, but Alicia remained silent. "Alicia?"

I heard her take a shaky breath. "They're gone," she said finally. "Did it help?"

"I don't know," I replied. "Nothing about this is simple."

"If they come back, or if I remember something, I'll call you," Alicia promised. She sounded totally wrecked.

"Are you okay?"

"I will be," she said, rallying a bit. "Goes with the gift, you know?"

I did and promised to check in on her tomorrow, and ended the call.

Baxter and I settled in on the couch to watch a movie and eat popcorn, and somewhere along the line, I fell asleep. A knock at the door and Baxter's yipping roused me, and a glance at the clock said it was almost three in the morning. The knock came again, harder this time I frowned, and grabbed my athame from where it lay near my purse, just in case. Only a handful of people can get through the wardings around the house to come up on the porch unescorted, so most visitors ring the bell from the sidewalk door, outside the piazza. I wasn't expecting anyone, certainly not at this time of night.

Teag stood on my doorstep, pale and haggard. "What's going on? What happened?" I asked, thinking he might have been in a car accident. Red-rimmed eyes met mine.

"It's Anthony. He never came home, hasn't answered his phone. I found his car, but he's gone and no one's heard from him. Cassidy, I think he's been taken."

HAUNTED MEMORIES

I PUT ON A POT OF COFFEE, BECAUSE I KNEW NEITHER OF US WERE
going to get any sleep. Teag looked like hell. He'd obviously been
awake all night, and I could see his barely-controlled panic every time
I met his gaze.

"Here. Hold Baxter. Certified therapy dog, and all that. Make him
earn his biscuits," I said, jokingly gruff, and handed off the little
furball. Teag took Bax gratefully, settling in on the couch like he was
in shock. A few minutes later, I came out with two cups of coffee and
handed one to Teag.

"Okay. If you're up to it, tell me what happened. Then we'll call
Sorren and get out the laptops and crack this wide open," I said with
more confidence than I felt. Anthony wasn't the first man to go missing, but he was the only one I knew, and that made it worse.

"Anthony had to stop by the new project—the real estate deal he
talked about at dinner, remember?" When I nodded, he continued. "He
was running late because one of the investors wanted to tour the property. Anthony agreed to show him around. But that was at seven
o'clock, they were done by nine. Even if he had stopped by the office
on the way home—he didn't—he would have been home by ten." Teag
swallowed hard. "He knew I had dinner in the oven. He always calls."

"One thing at a time," I coaxed, watching Teag's hands tremble as he held his coffee. "How do you know Anthony didn't go to the office?"

Teag blushed a little. "I hacked their security cameras. No Anthony. And he hadn't logged onto his computer there since five."

Teag has hacked the NSA and the FBI, so how hard could it be to get into a small law firm? "Do you know anything else about the big project he was working on?"

"I didn't—until I got into his computer." For the first time, Teag looked guilty about breaking into something. "I know it's a violation of privacy. Screw the law. I wouldn't have just done it if I didn't think he was in danger. I wouldn't—"

I put my hand on Teag's shoulder. "I know. It's okay. What did you find?"

Teag took a deep, steadying breath. "The real estate project is down by The Citadel. Taking old houses and tearing them down, building 'mixed use' retail/condo units instead." That squared with what Anthony had told us, but something niggled in the back of my mind.

"The Citadel?" I echoed. Teag met my gaze.

"I never put two and two together, Cassidy. This is all my fault. I should have realized, I could have protected him—"

"I don't—"

"When the Expo was over, the city made part of the land into Hampton Park. They sold the rest off—to The Citadel. So the murder house wouldn't have been near the well. It could have been a few blocks over, along the part of the Expo property that now belongs to The Citadel."

"Oh, god," I murmured. "So you think… that the houses in his project… one of them was the Brannigan house?"

Teag looked like he might be sick. "When I adjusted my search, I found a house on that street registered to a 'Victor Brennan.' Brennan —Brannigan—might be the same guy. And it's not far from the well. Easy for someone to walk by and toss something in on their way to or from the Expo. He owned some other properties, too."

"Who owns the place now?" I asked.

"Technically, the developer who is working on the project. The house has been vacant for a while. From what I could find, the title's been enough of a mess that no one's lived there for at least ten years. Rentals before that, but the records aren't worth much." He pulled up a photo of the old house on his screen and I gasped.

"Blue to green," I murmured, pointing to a section of the front where on layer of blue paint had peeled off, revealing an older green color underneath." A stained glass window above the front door caught my attention.

"Can you enlarge the photo?"

Teag did as I asked. "Shining urn," I said, as I made out the image in the Victorian window. A classical urn, which would shine if the lights were on behind it." I looked at Teag. "Alicia called me. She had a spook-a-palooza going on, and those were the two solid things she said, but it didn't make any sense until I saw the picture."

"So this is definitely the house."

I nodded. "You're sure Anthony was taken?" Of course Teag was sure. At three in the morning, there were few places Anthony could be, and taking off without telling Teag didn't fit.

"When he didn't come home by midnight, I called his parents. They hadn't seen him. I knew he didn't stop by the office and lose track of time. Ryan and Kell hadn't seen him, and neither had our other friends. So I hacked the GPS on his phone." Teag dropped his head. "Jeez, I sound like a stalker." He looked up defiantly. "But it was gone, Cassidy. Not turned off, just *gone*."

I took Teag's empty coffee cup and curled my fingers around his hand, steadying him. "All right. That's bad. But—"

"While I was waiting, I researched," Teag went on as if I hadn't spoken. "I looked at the Facebook pages and other social media sites for the men who've vanished lately. They did have something in common. And I can't believe I didn't realize it. They were all gay."

An awful possibility hit my stomach like ice. "You don't think—"

Teag nodded. "Remember what Hibbard's niece said, about him 'not fitting in?' How we figured none of the wallet men were married because there were no photos of pretty girls in their billfolds?" I fought down bile, and nodded. "And Tomlinson, how you thought he might be blackmailed about an affair?

"I dug up what I could online about the wallet men. Of course back then, being gay was illegal. They didn't dare come out, be open. They could have been thrown in jail, disinherited. But there are usually hints, ways people said things back then that implied a wink and a nod."

"The equivalent of liking ice dancing and Streisand?"

That got the barest of wan smiles. "Yeah. And it was all there, for most of them at least. I can't believe I missed it."

Another piece of the puzzle came together in my head with a *thunk.* "At the Chicago World's Fair, Holmes—Mudgett—preyed on young single women because they were vulnerable."

Teag nodded. "Brennan, or Brannigan or whatever the hell his name is, he saw easy pickings. Gay men wouldn't go to the police. They might not be able to count on their families. And if their families did make inquiries, if they suspected at all about being gay, they wouldn't press too hard. Wouldn't dare have the police look too closely."

"Son of a bitch," I muttered under my breath.

"Yeah. And one more thing—all of the men who've gone missing lately had some tie to the Expo. Alistair's assistant, working on the exhibit. One of the other missing men interned for the Archive. Another worked for a company involved in the renovation. And Anthony—" his voice choked off.

A knock came at the door. Baxter jumped down off Teag's lap and ran barking to the door, then abruptly sat down and shut up, tilting his head with a goofy look. "Sorren," I said over my shoulder to Teag as I went to open the door.

"How do you know?"

I jerked my head toward Baxter, who hadn't moved. "Vampire mojo."

Sorren barely spared Baxter and me a hello, looking immediately for Teag. He didn't hide the worry in his expression. "I got your message. This definitely forces our hand."

"Ya think?" I muttered. "Except we don't even *have* a hand right now."

"Maybe more than you give us credit for," Sorren said. "I verified my memory of the Expo with the Alliance. No one knew about the murders or sensed the kind of entity you've described. So whatever killed those men was human at the time."

"But a human from 1901 isn't snatching men now," Teag replied.

"No, but that entity might be influencing someone, returning to old habits," Sorren said. "I went to see Archibald Donnelly. He's certain there's no necromancy involved." Donnelly was head of the Briggs Society, a member of the Alliance, and a powerful necromancer. "But he did say that a particularly twisted soul can work some dark magic to make its ghost into something almost demonic. An entity like that can possess a willing victim."

"So what's happening now could be the same guy from back then, with a new… host?" Teag asked.

"And when I saw the shadow? Did it go walkabout and leave its body behind?" I tried not to sound sarcastic, but I'd been up all night, and this was a lot to take in.

"An inelegant comparison, but accurate enough," Sorren replied. He paused and lifted his head, his extra-sensitive vampire hearing picking up a sound we didn't. "They're here."

"Who?" I asked.

"Father Anne and Chuck Pettis," Sorren replied. "I told them what was happening, and what we knew so far. We're going to need backup. Donnelly said he had to check with some resources, and he'll be here too."

"It's oh-dark-thirty," Teag protested.

Sorren raised an eyebrow. "So? Chuck's ex-military. Father Anne still keeps grad student hours. And Donnelly is… Donnelly."

"The Briggs Society exists outside of time, right?" The odd time-traveling building, a private club for adventurers throughout the ages who had vanished on the hunt, still made my head spin when I thought about it too hard. "Could he go back to the Expo? Find out what happened, even if he can't change history?"

Sorren nodded. "And that's exactly what he meant to do, assuming his building will oblige. I don't pretend to understand how the magic works, but I get the feeling that Donnelly is more of an empowered caretaker than actually in charge. And I think the building has a mind of its own."

At another time, I'd be intrigued. Now, I just wanted to help Teag find Anthony before it was too late, and stop the entity from hurting anyone else.

I opened the door and stood aside to let the newcomers enter. Father Anne led the way. She's taller than I am by a few inches, with short-cut, spiked black hair. A complex tattoo wound down one arm beneath the black shirt with the priest collar, marking her as a member of the St. Expeditus Society, a secret group of hunter-priests. She's fast with an exorcism as well as a gun, and her knife skills are scary awesome. Dressed all in black down to her Doc Martens, she looked almost as dangerous as she really was. "Hey, Cassidy. Hi, Teag."

Chuck trudged in a few steps behind her. He's in his middle years, short and stocky, and everything about him says "former soldier." He also has a superstition about watches and wind-up clocks, fearing that if all of his timepieces wind down, he'll die. Chuck wears a vest lined entirely with working watch faces. He ticks if you get close to him. Hell if I'm ever going to try to get through airport security with the man. But he's good in a fight, and since he was special ops against supernatural threats in his military days, he gets his hands on very cool, useful weapons and we don't ask how.

They listened as I filled them in on Alicia's desperate phone call and what had happened with the ghost hunt at the well. Teag recapped everything else.

"You're right about the Brennan-Brannigan connection," Sorren said. "I remembered a men's boarding house—several of them—near the Expo grounds. And when Donnelly and I talked, he reminded me that Holmes had helpers with his murder house in Chicago. One of them was a man named Victor Brennan. He was just a janitor and claimed he hadn't known what was going on. The police let him go; he never faced charges. But I always wondered how Holmes managed to do everything himself. I don't think he did. I think Brennan was more involved than he let on, and I think it's mighty suspicious that he turned up here, just in time for another Expo and a slew of missing people."

"The closest match we can come to is a Chindi, which is a Native American vengeful spirit that takes all the bad traits of a person and magnifies them," Father Anne said. "Ghosts don't worry about ethnicity, they just do what they do, but it's a helpful description. Chindi kill with 'ghost sickness,' which is kind of like supernaturally-induced Spanish flu."

Teag paled. "How do we get rid of it? And if the men it's taken are… infected," He paused and swallowed, then went on, "how do we cure them?"

Father Anne laid a hand on Teag's shoulder. "Fortunately, that's the easy part. Once we get rid of the Chindi, the ghost sickness goes away." I heard what she didn't say. *If Brennan's ghost works like a regular Chindi.*

"Or, as I like to say, let's blow the fucker up and let the chips fall where they may," Chuck said.

"Brennan-Brannigan came from Charleston originally, moved around a bit through the Midwest, and came back," Sorren said. "He was a distant cousin to Lavinia Fisher."

Great. The crazy innkeeper psycho killer. This just kept getting better and better.

Teag looked up. "So he decided to recreate his family history here? It would make sense—and Brannigan would be ripe for ghost possession."

"That's what we think," Sorren confirmed. "And if Archibald was able to convince the Briggs' building to do us a favor, we might know for sure that Brennan-Brannigan is our guy. We'll see what else he comes up with. It's amazing what you notice once you know what you're looking for."

As if on cue, the doorbell rang. Sorren, Donnelly, Father Anne, and Chuck were on the short list of people who could get through the warding. Baxter sat quietly in Sorren's lap while I went to open the door.

Archibald Donnelly stood framed in the entrance. He was a tall, broad-shouldered man with a British accent and the look of someone who had been a colonel somewhere during the height of the Empire. A shock of white hair looked windblown over unruly eyebrows, and his pale cheeks had a flush to them that might have been windburn or good scotch.

"Bloody Hell. I had forgotten how much I hated the Edwardians." He tramped inside and only then seemed to notice the others. "Don't mind me. Been arguing with the damn building all day. Never bet against the house, my ass." Charleston's most powerful necromancer, wrapped in the guise of an eccentric English uncle.

"Come on in Archie, we're just starting to strategize," Sorren invited. Donnelly huffed into the room, made a beeline for my liquor cabinet and poured himself a stiff bourbon, then settled into a wing chair.

"I found the murder house," Donnelly said after we had all turned to stare at him expectantly. "Took pictures. Pretty sure it's still standing."

He handed his phone around to share the photos, and for a moment, the idea of a necromancer shooting photos on a smartphone made me want to laugh uncontrollably.

"That's the house," Teag said, pointing at the building in the center. "The 'painted lady' from your vision, in front of the mailbox where Hibbard mailed his postcard is on the left, and the middle house is the one that turned up in my web search."

Donnelly cleared his throat. "And while I was taking in the sights, I learned a little about that wallet well. Seems the house that stood on that lot was a competitor to Brennan. Everyone knew there was bad blood between them."

Maybe people knew about the animosity, but no one at the time suspected just how much blood was involved. "So Brennan dumped the wallets down his competitor's well so that if anyone did come looking for the missing men, they'd not only get the wrong guy but take out his rival."

"Sure as Bob's your uncle," Donnelly said, pointing a finger at Teag. "Got it in one."

I looked up at Sorren. "So what's the plan? This Brennan-Brannigan guy and his Chindi have Anthony—and maybe the other missing men, too. How do we get them out?"

Father Anne smiled. "Easy. I read the exorcism, Archie uses his dead-guy magic to grab the Chindi, and y'all storm the haunted house and rescue the captives. Then Chuck does what he does best."

Chuck grinned. "I make things go boom."

"Works for me, I said, and looked over to Teag. He squared his shoulders, and a look of quiet, deadly confidence glinted in his eyes.

"Let's go get Anthony back and burn this son of a bitch."

JUST BEFORE DAYLIGHT, Sorren retreated to the basement to rest. Father Anne and Chuck dozed in the armchairs in the living room. I made Teag lie down on the couch, and I curled up with Baxter on the loveseat. Donnelly mumbled something and left, promising to be back at dusk. We had been up all night, and going into a hunt dead tired was as reckless as going in unprepared. Much as we all wanted to charge in with guns blazing, and as fearful as we were for Anthony and the other missing men, we had to wait for nightfall.

Sorren couldn't go until after dark, and we needed his supernatural strength and speed. I had the feeling that Brennan's ghost and the Chindi weren't going to go down easily. We also couldn't go barging into a house in daylight for a firefight with a ghost and not find ourselves facing down a SWAT team when we came out. So no matter how we chafed at the delay, we had no choice except to wait until late evening to make our move.

THE OLD HOUSE loomed over us, inky against the night sky, blotting out the stars. Chuck's EMF reader pegged the meter, though he set the audio on silent. No surprise, but it did confirm we were in the right place.

Teag had found the floorplan from the construction documents online, though if Brennan had learned anything from H.H. Holmes, I was betting he'd made some modifications. Still, knowing the basic layout was better than nothing and gave us a plan of attack.

Sorren went through the front door, while Donnelly led the way through the back, with the rest of us behind him. That sent our two most bad-ass fighters in first, the ones with a supernatural unfair advantage. Chuck came in last, watching our backs, armed to the teeth. He wore the same night goggles as the rest of us, everyone except Sorren and Donnelly, who didn't need them. Now, in the creepy quiet of the abandoned house, I found myself feeling twitchy, ready for a fight.

"You sure we can't just toss an EMF grenade on each floor and be done with it?" I muttered.

Chuck glared at me. "We could. But that just pushes the ghost and the Chindi into one of the damn secret rooms you know Brennan must have built, and that's not going to do anyone any good. Or it gets pushed in with the prisoners, and decides to finish them before we finish it."

So much for doing things the easy way.

We moved carefully, weapons at the ready. Teag and I had everything that we'd brought to the fight at the well, plus a few more weapons we didn't want to use in front of Kell's group. Chuck had given both of us retrofitted German H&K signal pistols and shotgun shells full of rock salt and iron pellets. I had a silver knife inscribed with protective sigils, and Teag carried a silver-coated metal whip that curled up like a coiled spring. Knowing we were going up against amped-up ghosts, we both had iron knives, and Teag added an iron cap to one end of his staff.

Father Anne could recite exorcisms and rituals from memory, and coupled with her faith, that was formidable enough. But we had fought together enough times that I knew she had a blessed boline knife that could do a number on corporeal and non-corporeal creatures alike, and I was betting she had a shiv or two somewhere on her person.

We moved slowly from the back of the house toward the central hallway, where we met up with Sorren. He gave a curt shake of his head, indicating he'd found nothing in the front rooms.

"Basement?" I mouthed. Teag and I moved to scout the kitchen, while Father Anne looked beneath the front stairway as Chuck and Donnelly kept watch. Cellars were rare in Charleston given how close we were to sea level, and I hadn't expected much from the elevation of the house, but it never pays to assume. We returned to the foyer, shaking our heads.

The Brennan house had three floors and probably an attic. Teag and I had poured over the sketchy floorplan, marking where it would be structurally easiest to build in hidden rooms or passageways, and we had shared our notes with the group. "Alicia told her the ghosts said 'the walls are hollow,'" I reminded them. "So he didn't just line up his captives in the parlor."

"Check the walls," Teag said. His eyes held a dangerous glint. Tension and the need to fight fairly thrummed through his body. He looked cold and resolute, and God help anything that came between him and finding Anthony.

We split off, tapping walls and checking room dimensions, but we couldn't find any modifications on the first floor. Brennan might have been a psychopath, but he was a clever bastard who managed to evade detection in his lifetime.

"Ghosts?" Father Anne asked, directing her question to Donnelly.

"Plenty of psychic residue, but for a place where so many people died violently, no ghosts," Donnelly said quietly. "I think we can blame the Chindi. It's either scared them away or devoured them. And it's definitely here, watching."

I carefully avoided touching anything as much as I could, and still my gift had me on edge. When the resonance is strong enough, I can feel it through the souls of my shoes, or in the air like static electricity. The house made me feel sick on a gut level, the psychic equivalent of mild food poisoning. I could sense layer upon layer of pain, fear, hate, and beneath it, a vengeful glee that lived for the game, for the thrill of the hunt.

"Where is it?" Father Anne murmured.

"Moving," Donnelly replied. "Through the ductwork maybe, or the spaces between the lathe and the studs. Stalking."

At that moment, every door downstairs slammed shut. The light fixtures, long cut off from electrical power, flickered wildly with an unnatural foxfire glow. The temperature plummeted, and a cold draft grew quickly to a gust that ripped at the stained, damaged wallpaper and sent dust swirling into the air.

"There!" I saw the inky stain seeping down from the stairway like cascading crude oil. Chuck and I moved in the same instant. The *bang* of his signal pistol came an instant before a *pop* and a wet *squelch*. As suddenly as it came, the wind vanished as the lights gave a final flicker and went dark.

"What the hell was that?" Chuck demanded.

"Water balloon filled with holy water," I said. "I brought a few, although a Super Soaker might work better."

He laughed and clapped a hand on my shoulder. "Not bad. But not as spectacular as the time we got the chaplain to bless the fire hydrant before we opened it up on some *dimme-kur* that tried to attack an outpost."

Father Anne raised an eyebrow, and I couldn't tell whether she was impressed or offended.

"It's gone. Let's keep moving." Teag's voice sounded so tight and curt I almost didn't recognize it.

"Father Anne and I will take the third floor and attic," Sorren said. "The rest of you can tear the second floor apart." We had already decided that the most likely place for Brenner's bolt holes.

Sorren again led the way with Father Anne behind him, Teag and me in the middle, then Donnelly and Chuck bringing up the rear. Adrenaline made me twitchy as if I'd had too many shots of espresso. Teag's set jaw, mouth in a hard line, body tensed let me know he was aching to take his fear and worry out on the nearest suitable target. I couldn't blame him, knowing Anthony's life hung in the balance.

When we reached the second floor, Sorren and Father Anne split off, and we faced a long hallway of closed doors. I knew from what we had found online about Brannigan's Rooming House for Men that the second floor had been subdivided into nine "premium" private rooms and that the third floor and likely the attic held additional beds in an open dormitory layout. We had no choice but to search each room.

"In my vision, I saw Brannigan take one of the men through a closet," I reminded the others. "Let's start with that."

Teag paused. "Why nine rooms? Why not ten?" He suddenly walked toward the end of the hallway, pacing off the distance. "I think there's something at the end of the hall," he said when he returned. There aren't any windows on that side of the house, and the distance from front to back seems too short."

"All right. Let's start with that." I had my athame in my right hand and an iron knife in the other. Alard's walking stick hung from my belt, but I didn't plan to burn the house down, at least not until we had found Anthony and the other prisoners. Ghosts didn't like iron, and the sharp blade would serve against other threats as well. Teag held his staff in his left hand and the silver metal whip coiled in the other.

Overhead, we heard a sudden series of thumps, then Father Anne's voice shouting in Latin, and Sorren's curses.

"It's trying to distract us," Donnelly said, looking around. "Get moving. I'll hold it off."

"I'd like another shot at it myself," Chuck said, his signal pistol in one hand and an EMF grenade in the other.

Teag and I sprinted to the other end of the hallway, carefully watching each of the closed doors as we went. We tried the last room on the right. It had a shallow closet against the rear wall, but neither of us could find a catch to open a hidden door.

"Stand back," Teag warned, and drew back with his staff, then smashed the iron-clad tip through the back of the closet. A fine rain of plaster, insulation, and lathe crumbled to the floor, but behind that was a solid barrier.

"That's not the outside wall," Teag said through gritted teeth. "So there's a secret room, but no door from here."

"Let's try the other side." I led the way, athame and knife both at the ready. Not for the first time, I mentally thanked Chuck for the night vision goggles, because it meant we didn't have to juggle flashlights as well as weapons.

Overhead, we heard more thumps and swearing. Out in the hallway, I heard Donnelly shouting, and Chuck's muttered curses.

I stopped as soon as we entered the tiny bedroom. "This is it," I whispered. The room from the vision." Teag didn't bother asking if I were sure. He had seen the vision too. I pointed to the small closet in the back corner.

I led the way. Teag was right behind me, watching my back as I reached up like I had seen Brannigan do, running my fingers across the wood trim until I heard a catch snap open at my touch. "There!" I said, a note of triumph in my voice.

The door swung open. But instead of a dark passage, Peter Morrill stood waiting with a twisted smile and lunged forward with a knife aimed to kill.

"Down!" Teag snapped, but I was already dodging. Teag's staff whirled over my head and the iron cap connected hard with Morrill's right wrist, leaving no doubt by the crunch that bones snapped. In the next breath, I willed cold force from my athame, throwing Morrill backward into the blackness and keeping him pinned against the passageway wall.

"Where are they?" Teag demanded, hooking his metal whip onto his belt and drawing out the signal gun from his waistband. "Where are the prisoners?"

Morrill's wrist hung at an odd angle, obviously broken. He should have been in agony. But the look in his eyes was pure crazy, not entirely human. "He took me to be his hands and feet," Morrill bragged. I felt sick realizing what he meant. Brenner-Brannigan's spirit needed a solid body to gather prisoners for the Chindi. And whether or not Morrill had originally been a willing host or the possession had driven him mad, he now clearly sided with the monsters.

Donnelly crowded up behind us as the blast from my athame waned. I couldn't keep Morrill pinned forever.

"Depart!" Donnelly commanded. Father Anne handles the demons, but there's more than one kind of unclean spirit, and Victor Brennan's ghost was as foul as they come. I'd never seen someone cast out a possessing ghost before, and I startled when green, glowing liquid began to ooze, then drip, from Morrill's eyes, ears, nose, and mouth. His body convulsed, eyes rolling back, limbs shaking. The phosphorescent liquid ran in thin rivulets that left foxfire tracks across his skin and clothing. Morrill's chest heaved and his breath staggered. Brenner was not letting go easily.

"I'll keep him pinned," Donnelly said, sparing a glance to Teag and me. "See to the prisoners. Sorren and Father Anne won't be able to keep the Chindi bottled up much longer."

Teag and I stepped into a long narrow room, just a little wider than the small bedrooms on the hall. It appeared to run the length of the house, and it stank of sweat and human waste, death and rotting flesh.

Several heaps that might be bodies slumped against the far wall. "Anthony!" Teag called quietly, and my heart ached when no response came.

We moved forward carefully, alert for traps, waiting for the Chindi to make an appearance. I knelt next to the first form, and put a hand out, then withdrew with a gasp and jerked back so hard that I nearly fell on my ass. Two piles of clothing had been men, dead long enough that their eyes and mouths crawled with maggots and the bloated features appeared mottled even in the glow of my night vision goggles. I tried to remember the names of the other men to go missing. We'd accounted for Peter Morrill. I feared Jon Werther and Mike Irwin were the rotting corpses.

Teag choked back a cry and moved forward. The next form groaned but did not wake to Teag's frantic shake. Rope bound the man's wrists and ankles securely, and a dirty cloth stuffed in his mouth served as a gag.

"That's Rand, Alistair's assistant," I said, recognizing him from our one meeting. Teag was already moving toward the fourth figure.

"Anthony?" Teag's voice held a note of fear. He hunched in front of the fourth prisoner who sat with his back to the wall, head resting on his bent knees. Teag tipped his head up and let out a long breath. "Anthony." Anthony stared at Teag bleary-eyed, and I wondered whether magic or drugs caused the lethargy.

Before Teag had a chance to reach for Anthony, a wave of darkness swept down from overhead, opaque enough to hide the injured prisoners from our view. The energy the creature gave off felt foul, like being splattered with sewage inside and out. Nightmare visions clawed at the edges of my mind. Behind the Chindi, cut off from our sight, Anthony gave a panicked groan. Teag went flying in one direction, colliding with the opposite wall with a grunt, and an invisible force hurled me back the way I came, to land on my back at Donnelly's feet.

I had no way to get off a shot from the signal pistol without risking a hit to Anthony or Rand. The battle at the well showed how useless my athame was against the Chindi, and the walking stick's fire would incinerate all of us in these close quarters. I heard Teag cursing as he got to his feet while I scrambled upright. One hand went for my iron knife, while the other grabbed a squishy orb from my pocket.

Teag and I launched ourselves at the Chindi. I slashed down with my knife, and the blade sank into something neither solid nor mist, dragging down through air suddenly too thick and clammy. Teag lunged with his staff, iron end first, careful to angle upwards so as not to hit Anthony or Rand. I stabbed once more with my knife and lobbed a holy water balloon at the floor with all my might.

Water splashed up as high as my shoulders as the thin latex burst. The Chindi swirled and writhed, but did not completely dissipate. Teag hurled a handful of loose salt from one pocket, and the creature folded in on itself only to unfurl once more, crackling with energy now that it identified us as a foe.

"Fire in the hole!" Chuck shouted from behind me.

I dropped to the floor and covered my eyes a second before a flash of bright light illuminated the narrow room, doubly blinding with my night vision goggles. The oppressive presence of the Chindi vanished.

"That won't keep him gone for long." Sorren pulled me to my feet and then reached to help Teag. "Let's get the prisoners out of here, and then we'll take care of the Chindi and the ghost."

I hadn't heard Sorren join us, and now that I looked at him, I saw the toll the fight in the attic had taken. Blood oozed from a gash on his cheek, and Sorren carried himself in a way that suggested deep bruises, maybe broken bones. Deep cuts scored his back and shoulder. I suspected whatever abuse he had taken from the Chindi would have been enough to kill a mortal, if it did that much damage to a vampire. And while Sorren healed with supernatural speed, the pain of injuries didn't change, nor would the healing come fast enough to help if we were attacked again.

Teag knelt next to Anthony. He reached out gently to cup Anthony's cheek and raise his head. "I've got you," he murmured. "It's going to be okay. You're going to be safe." He used his silver knife to cut through Anthony's bonds as I did the same for Rand. Anthony at least seemed groggy but conscious. Rand lay still, breathing but completely unconscious.

"I'll carry him," Sorren said with a jerk of his head toward Rand. Donnelly and Father Anne already had Morrill tied up and gagged, though his wild eyes held the promise of terrible retribution. A glance at Father Anne affirmed that she had been in the thick of the fight upstairs. One eye darkened with a bruise, and I wondered how she would explain that to her parishioners. A deep cut on her left shoulder bled steadily through her shirt, and she held herself as if her ribs ached. The Chindi had put up a hell of a struggle.

"I've got your back," Chuck said. "But move your asses. We don't have all day."

Anthony staggered and would have fallen without Teag's arm around his waist. Teag's staff hung across his back in a specially-made holster, but I saw that he kept his iron knife in his right hand, supporting Anthony's weight with his left arm. Sorren lifted Rand as if he were a child, and Morrill succeeded in struggling only for a moment before Donnelly muttered something under his breath that made the man go limp in his arms.

Sorren still led the way, with Father Anne beside him, long knives in both hands. Donnelly went next, then Teag burdened with Anthony's unsteady weight. Chuck and I brought up the rear. I glanced at the rotting corpses, sorry we couldn't do better for them.

By the time we reached the stairs, the Chindi's anger manifested behind us as a growing whirlwind, starting slow but building rapidly. Once again, the temperature plummeted, and even unconscious, Morrill writhed in Donnelly's grip.

"Move!" Chuck urged. "We'll hold it at the steps. Get them to the cars!"

Father Anne fell back to stand with Chuck and me, shoulder to shoulder. But before Sorren and the others reached the exit, the Chindi swept down over us like an arctic wind, slamming all the hallway doors so hard the glass rattled in the windows.

"Close your eyes!" Chuck yelled, lobbing another EMF grenade. I squeezed my eyes shut against the glare, only to feel myself picked up off my feet and hurled against one of the walls with enough force that my elbow went through the crumbling plaster. The grenade might have sent the Chindi away the first time, but it was on to our tricks now, and angrier than before.

I climbed to my feet and saw a sickly green orb hovering against the solid black of the Chindi. It dove first at Morrill, then at Sorren, but when it dipped toward Rand's pliant body, Donnelly barked out words of power in a language I did not understand.

The orb stopped in mid-air, then took off at full power straight toward me. Father Anne stepped in between before I could move, holding up an iron crucifix from a chain around her neck as I grabbed a handful of salt from my pocket and threw it right at the orb.

"We've got to contain the Chindi," Donnelly said. "Without its energy, the ghost is too weak to be a threat." I could figure out the rest. Contain the Chindi. Power-down the ghost. Burn the house.

We had counted on dispelling the Chindi, not boxing it up. I glanced around and spotted the door to a small closet. I lurched toward it, jerked the door open, and began firing with my signal gun, loading rounds of rock salt and iron pellets and shooting until every surface was peppered.

Chuck got the drift without me saying a word. "Teag, plow the road with that whip of yours. We've got a plan."

I saw silver streaks against the darkness, and felt the Chindi's energy lurch as it winced away from the strikes, clearing their way to get out. Donnelly chanted, low and steady, forcing the Chindi back from the door, toward us. Father Anne took up a position at the foot of the stairs, and I heard her start into the Rite of Exorcism, and I chanted along with her, doing my best not to mangle the Latin.

"Exorcizo te, immundissime spiritus, omnis incursio adversarii…"

Once Teag and the others made it to the door, he tossed the coiled metal whip to Chuck. With Father Anne blocking the stairs, me and my salt, holy water, and buckshot blocking one end of the hall and Chuck lashing the Chindi from the other, the darkness condensed, folding in on itself, sliding toward the closet.

"Careful," Chuck urged. "If we dispel it, the damn thing will just go somewhere else and we'll have to do this again."

With a few more snaps of the silver whip and warning slashes from my iron knife, we backed the Chindi into the newly spirit-proofed closet. It surged back toward us as I tried to force the door shut. I saw a blur of motion and then Sorren was beside me, using his strength against the entity.

"Cassidy! Shoot into it now!"

I sent a shot of salt and iron into the closet, right at the center of the writhing mass. It screeched in anger and pain, and Sorren slammed the door shut. Donnelly was right behind him, raising both hands to seal the closet with a muttered spell and a sudden, faint glow.

"Teag's in the car with the prisoners. We've got to finish this," Sorren said. We moved to the back door, and just before I crossed the threshold, I lifted the walking stick lose from its holster and leveled it at the stairs. Part of me felt bad that the missing men's remains would never be recovered, but the alternative, allowing the Chindi and the bloody history of the house to fester and raise more unholy energy, was far worse.

I took a deep breath, centered my magic, pulled hard from the resonance of the power within the old walking stick, and sent a jet of fire from the silver tip. I didn't stop until the flames burned like a bonfire, until the walls and floor crackled with fire, until Sorren's hand fell gently on my shoulder, telling me that it was time to go. Even so, I sent one more pulse blasting down the hallway, aiming for the Chindi's prison.

"That's for Anthony," I muttered, unashamed for feeling triumphant as a preternatural scream filled the air.

I ran for the car. With all the shots we'd fired and now the flames, police cars had to be on their way, and we needed to be hell and gone. I slid into the shotgun seat of Teag's Volvo next to Sorren who was at the wheel so Teag could cradle Anthony in the back seat.

"How is he?" I asked as Sorren pulled away, moving with as much speed as we dared.

"Donnelly didn't sense any serious injuries," Teag said, barely masking a hitch in his voice now that the heroics were over and the adrenaline let-down settled in. "But he's been drugged, tied up and held prisoner in the dark next to a rotting corpse."

"In case you're wondering, Donnelly said Rand was dehydrated and hungry, and both he and Anthony appeared to have been beaten and cut. Since no one even found the bodies from Brenner-Brannigan's house of horrors, we can't compare the pattern, but it's consistent with serial killers who like to play with their victims before killing them." The cold, flat tone in Sorren's voice let me know that he would be perfectly fine with ending Morrill if Donnelly determined the man willingly allowed Brenner's ghost to possess and use him.

"Do they need a hospital?"

Sorren shook his head. "I've already called my private physician. He'll take care of Anthony at your house—if that's suitable to you— and then swing by the Briggs Society to see to Rand."

"Did Donnelly get the building to agree to that?" I asked. "You could end up God knows where in time."

Sorren chuckled. "I think Donnell and the building have an… agreement of sorts. We'll get Rand patched up, I'll take care of any troublesome memories, and we'll drop him off somewhere safe where he can be miraculously reunited with his family."

"And Morrill?" I hesitated to ask, torn between wanting vengeance and not sure I desired to know.

"It depends," Sorren answered. "I'm leaving the determination to Donnelly. If he wasn't a willing accomplice, we'll do for him what we're doing for Rand." He left unsaid what would occur if Morrill had knowingly sold the others out. The Alliance's job protecting the world had plenty of gray areas, but proven cold-blooded killers didn't get a reprieve.

"Once we get Anthony seen by the doctor and know how he is, I'll call his family," Teag said. He hadn't stopped carding his fingers though Anthony's hair since I got in the car. The two of them barely fit in the backseat together, but Teag had his back up against the door, Anthony pulled up against his chest, legs mostly stretched out on the seat and Teag's arm across him. Anthony looked pale and haggard, and the bloody slashes on his chest and arms attested to his ordeal, but he his breathing was regular.

We made it. Rescued the prisoners, zapped the ghost, torched the monster, saved the city. I'd have new bruises and pulled muscles to show for it, but compared to how it could have gone down, we got off easy.

Just another day in paradise.

PART VII
UNRAVELED

RESTLESS SPIRITS

"Are you sure you didn't mean to invite a priest? I can't bless restless spirits, and I suck at exorcisms," I said as Teag Logan and I followed Kell Winston and his paranormal investigators through back alleys in a part of Charleston, South Carolina that doesn't make it into the tourist guidebooks, for good reason.

"Maybe later," Kell said, and the tension in his voice told me he wasn't joking. "We've been checking back on this haunting and a couple of others for a while now. There've been reports of a minor haunting here for years, but it was always things like cold spots, orbs, and people feeling like they were being watched. Over the last few weeks though, it's juiced up."

"How?" Teag asked. He flicked a lock of lank dark hair out of his eyes and looked around the dimly lit alleyway warily. Teag stood a little taller than Kell and the others in his group, and I saw Teag go up on the balls of his feet, trying to see ahead, impatient to know what we got ourselves into.

"Much higher EMF readings, for one thing," Calista said, from near the front of the group. Instead of the big computer setup she had for exploring reportedly haunted houses, tonight she just had a tablet and an earbud. "All kinds of readings going off the charts."

Peter, who had two different kinds of EMF readers going, nodded as both units pinged and whined. "Yeah. Definitely stronger than last week. Don't need to look the numbers up to know that. Meters are at the top of the yellow zone, nearly red. Not something you see every day."

Drew, their cameraman, let out a whistle. "Will you look at that?" We followed the direction of his nod and saw a glowing blue orb form out of nowhere. The temperature in the alley dropped rapidly, until I found myself shivering—something that didn't often happen on a Charleston summer night.

"Down ten degrees within a minute," Calista reported.

"Go slow," Kell warned. His group, the Southern Paranormal Observation and Outreach Klub (otherwise known as SPOOK), earned its reputation for being the most credible group of its kind by doing good work and thorough documentation. "If it's getting stronger, we don't want to find out the hard way that it's angry."

Kell turned to me. "Picking up anything, Cassidy?"

I shook my head. "Nothing clear," I replied. "You do remember that I'm not a medium?"

Kell grinned. "I know. I'm not sure there's enough of a personality manifesting for a medium to be able to get much, but for the haunting to amp up like this, I'm thinking something has to be anchoring the spirit to this place. And if there's an object involved, you're the first person I call."

I'm Cassidy Kincaide, owner of Trifles and Folly, an antique and curio shop in historic, haunted Charleston, SC that has its share of secrets. My touch magic is one of those secrets, but not the only one. The shop has existed for nearly 350 years as a front for the Alliance, a coalition of mortals and immortals that get dangerous magical items out of the wrong hands and keep Charleston—and the world—safe from supernatural threats. When we succeed, no one remembers. When we fail, the damage gets blamed on a natural disaster. Teag Logan is my assistant store manager, best friend, and sometimes bodyguard. He's got a secret of his own—he's powerful with Weaver magic, the ability to weave spells into cloth and unlikely data into information, making him one hell of a hacker.

I didn't think Teag's magic would do much for us tonight, in a very haunted alleyway, but mine might shed some light on the situation.

"Give me a sec," I said to Kell, as the rest of his team fanned out to gather data. Drew kept his camera on the orb, which had not tried to flee or come closer, a good sign. It hovered near one side of the old alleyway as if it were waiting for something. Teag and Kell protectively stepped closer to me as I shut my eyes to focus on what my magic could pick up.

My gift is strongest when I'm actually in contact with an object that carries a deep emotional or magical resonance. Sometimes, if the energy is strong enough, it sinks into walls, floors, even the cobblestones beneath our feet, and I can feel it despite my shoes.

"It's hazy," I said. "Impressions more than actual images, but without an object, it's rarely as clear." I hesitated, sifting through the feelings that what I picked up raised in my gut, trying to put them into words. "Female. Young, but not a child. Terrified. Pain. Loss." I shook my head to clear it and opened my eyes.

"Sorry, that's not much," I said. "Whoever she was, a woman must have been murdered here, and without a particular object, I'm guessing she's anchored to the place where she died."

Kell gave me a supportive smile. With his brown hair and blue eyes, Kell had a way about him that put people at ease. Lucky for me, we'd gone from good friends to a couple, so I got to see that smile of his a lot. "Anything else?" he pressed.

"Urgency," I said, frowning as the word formed because it came straight from my intuition, an interpretation of what I had picked up. "I think that's why she's manifesting. She's trying to tell us something. Maybe warn us."

"Can you tell how long ago she died?" Kell asked. "Are we talking Colonial era or something more recent?" Charleston, SC is one of the most haunted cities in the US, and it's been settled by Europeans since 1670. Plenty of people have died here under tragic circumstances, and many never leave.

"Years, maybe a decade or so, or a little longer," I said, going on feeling instead of fact. "Remember, I'm picking up on her energy, not making a spirit connection. Another reason I think she's new at this. She doesn't seem to know how to make herself seen."

I opened my mouth to say more, but a sudden clatter and Calista's potent curse stopped me cold. Pebbles rose from the ground, wobbling in mid-air. They hovered, as if waiting for us to notice, and then began to pelt us like hail.

"Hey!" Calista yelled. "Don't damage the equipment!" She curled protectively around her tablet and fell back. Drew did the same thing a moment later as a small rock smacked into the side of the camera, but Peter remained where he was, oblivious in his audio readings until Kell grabbed him by the collar and hauled him back a few steps, out of range.

"You notice anything?" I asked Teag, feeling shaken and wary.

"Nothing beyond what the rest of you have seen and heard," he replied. "Remember—I sense things from cloth. Maybe if we had a bit of what she'd been wearing, I'd get a reading. But this trip, I'm just the muscle," he added with an ironic smile. Teag's thin but whipcord strong, and he's won martial arts championships, proof that looks can be deceiving.

I glanced at Kell as his folks put their gear back in his SUV. We'd only hit the first of three stops tonight. "Do you have any idea who the ghost is or how she died—other than violently?" I asked, staring past him into the alley that now stood empty once more. The orb was gone, and the temperature edged back up to its usual sultry heat.

Kell shook his head. "No, but now that you've narrowed down the timeframe a bit, we might be able to figure it out. Big difference looking at ten to twenty years versus over three hundred!"

The SPOOK group got into the SUV and headed to the next location. Teag and I piled into my RAV4, which held our gear bag in the back full of additional weapons good against supernatural threats. I knew Kell had a shotgun with shells filled with rock salt in his car, but I hoped we didn't need to use it. Not only would that mean a very dangerous ghost, but I didn't want to have to explain shooting at something most people don't even believe exists.

As I drove, Teag watched out the window, but the streets at this hour were deserted. Even the tourists had gone to bed. "So, was there anything else you sensed that you might not have wanted to mention in front of SPOOK?" he asked. Kell knows a little about what I can do—and I'm sure he suspects more—but we haven't told him everything just yet, for his own safety.

I kept my eyes on the road, following Kell. "Not really. I didn't get a look at her; the spirit isn't strong enough to manifest that much. At least, not yet," I added, an ominous thought. "I don't think she was trying to hurt us. As odd as it sounds, I think she was trying to warn us, to send us away from danger."

"You think it's a trapped spirit or just a stone tape?"

Ghosts come in several different forms. Some are tied to objects, while others to locations or even to the date when something important —often, their death—occurred. Many of those ghosts, fortunately the most common kind of spirits, are what ghost hunters call "stone tape" manifestations, as if they've imprinted somehow on something real and solid and they replay a loop of activity, like an old cassette tape (hence the name) but there's no personality or sentience. Some ghost hunters call them "repeaters." Other ghosts, often the more dangerous kind, are more like trapped spirits who either chose not to move on after death because they wanted to finish something or protect someone, or because they got lost and didn't know what to do. Over time, these ghosts often get frustrated and vengeful as they become more powerful, and they're the ones that can be a real problem.

"I'm not sure," I replied. "If she's gaining power and abilities, then probably not a repeater. I got the feeling that throwing stones was new, so definitely not a loop of the same actions they've seen before."

"So maybe like the Gray Man?" Teag asked. Everyone around here knows the story of the Gray Man of Pawley's Island, who appears as a warning when a bad storm is about to hit the Charleston area. That ghostly protector's actions and locations change, suggesting a personality and sentience.

"A little," I said. "Just newer at the game, perhaps? After all, the Gray Man's been around since the early 1880s."

"Can ghosts learn how to be better at being ghosts?"

I shrugged. "Maybe it's like everything else. Some people are born knowing what to do, and others have to figure it out by trial and error. I don't think anyone's out there giving ghost lessons!"

Kell stopped in another run down area along the edge of the city. Despite all the colorful brochures and magazine articles that focus on the Historic Area, Charleston—like every city—has its less desirable sections, places where people moved away or businesses closed and the neighborhood hasn't gotten a second wind yet.

We'd circled part of the way around the downtown, and where the first ghost haunted an alley behind a strip mall that had seen better days, this street had office buildings from the 1970s that could use upkeep and some remodeling.

"Back here," Kell said, as his crew got their gear and set up their cameras and tablets. He looked at Teag and me. "Same kind of thing as before. Been watching this place for a while, but the activity's picked up lately. Just wanted to see if you pick up anything we didn't."

This time, I was nervous as we moved into an alley that appeared to get little recent use. I saw real estate signs out in front of the building and guessed that the outdated office complex sat vacant, and had for some time. That made it doubly odd for the ghost to pick up steam if there was no one around to witness the haunting.

Teag must have been thinking along the same lines. "If a ghost haunts a forest and no one sees it, did it really manifest?" he joked. We had bandied that idea around with Kell many times over pizza and drinks, without ever coming to a conclusion.

"I don't know about that," Kell chimed in, "but this ghost seems to know we're here."

A cold wind picked up in what had been heavy, humid air seconds before. The gust that swept down the deserted alley made me shiver, and I could see the steam rise from my breath.

Calista began reading off her numbers, as Drew's night-image camera tried to capture a glimpse of the ghostly presence. Peter mumbled to himself, but the EMF readers he held told their own story, squealing high and shrill.

No orb formed this time, but as I stared into the darkness, I thought I saw a ripple, a barely-there shimmer of light that shouldn't have been present.

"Did you see that?" I whispered.

"Yeah," Teag and Kell replied, almost in unison. "Something's there. That's new," Kell added.

The wind swept by us again, cold enough that a darkened plate glass window facing the alley fogged up with the sudden temperature change.

"Look," I gasped, pointing as something began to take shape in the condensation. As if drawn by an invisible finger, we watched as one dot was joined by a second, then an upturned curve to make a smiley.

"Did you see that?" Calista breathed.

"Did you get that on camera?" Kell asked Drew.

The wind died, the air warmed, and the image vanished. We stood in the middle of the street, staring at each other.

"What the hell was that about?" Teag asked. "Did the ghost just tell us to have a nice day?"

Kell looked to me. "I know you didn't have much time, but did you get an impression, Cassidy?"

My heart pounded, excited and a little scared by the power that had just made itself known. "No face again, but female, I think. Afraid. Pain." I looked up. "Whoever killed her wasn't quick about it," I said, and then stumbled to the side as emotions caught up with me and I bent over and threw up.

Kell and Teag followed, and Teag laid a hand on my shoulder to steady me. "Are you okay?"

I nodded, feeling embarrassed at the reaction. Kell pulled a bottle of water from his pack and handed it to me, giving me an encouraging smile. "Not surprised a resonance like that would upset you," he said. If Calista and the others noticed, they were now pretending to be completely engrossed in the readouts of their equipment.

"You still feel up to making the last stop?" Teag asked, with a look that meant he was worried.

I swallowed and nodded. "Yeah. I think we need to. Something's going on, and I don't know if it's all related, but what are the odds?" I knew from the look on their faces that we were all thinking the same thing: "coincidences" usually aren't accidental at all.

Our last stop that evening was a long-shuttered middle school. We drove back in toward town, but not as far as the main district to get to the school. The hulking building looked like it was built in the 1940s, solid brick and steel. I vaguely recognized it and realized that I had driven past it many times without paying much attention.

Butler Middle School sat, dark and brooding, a little ways back from the road. A chain-link fence cordoned off the area close to the building, cutting off its wide front steps from curiosity seekers and winding around its long footprint. The center of the school stood a story taller than the wings on either side, and I wondered what had led to its shutdown.

"Butler Middle School closed in 1990," Kell said as we parked behind the building and got our stuff. This time, Kell took out his shotgun, and waited as Teag and I retrieved salt, holy water, and some weapons, including our own shotgun in case this supernatural problem proved more dangerous than the two ghosts.

"From what I've found out, the school board wanted a new school with better wiring and amenities, and it would have been too expensive to retrofit," Kell said. "Then this building took storm damage, and that was the last straw. They built a new building that was closer to the residential areas, and shut down Butler."

"Why let it sit for over twenty years?" Teag asked.

Kell shrugged. "Old buildings can have lead paint or asbestos, especially ones built back in the Forties and Fifties. That's safe until you knock the place down, and then dangerous and expensive to contain and clean up. Or maybe the school district doesn't know what to do with the land and hasn't had to make a decision. Whatever the reason, Butler's sat vacant for a long while, but there've always been stories about ghosts, even before it closed."

I didn't usually consider an old school building to be creepy—not compared to abandoned hospitals or mental institutions or jails—but something about Butler Middle School gave me the heebie-jeebies.

"What kind of ghosts?" Teag asked as we hefted our gear and headed for a place in the back of the fence where thrill-seekers had long ago bent the metal to allow entrance.

"There's supposed to be a black cat that crosses the parking lot and disappears," Kell said, leading us across cracked asphalt toward the rear of the building. "People hear dogs barking, but there's never a dog in sight. A girl on a bicycle rides by and then disappears, but people swear they heard the bell on her handlebars ring. And some people say they've seen a boy with a baseball cap and catchers' mitt sitting on the back steps, in the middle of the night, inside the fence, but he vanishes when they call out to him."

"Like he's waiting for a ride that never showed up," Calista said, and despite her usual too-cool-for-words persona, even she looked a little creeped out.

"Looks like the kind of place Ryan's group would love," I said. Ryan Alexander is a mutual friend of Teag, Kell, and me, and he runs a team of Urban Explorers who love to skulk through abandoned buildings, old drainage pipes, mothballed factories, and similar places. They go for the thrill of discovery, and to document decaying history, but Ryan and his team have often run into supernatural phenomena they couldn't explain. That's when Ryan turns it over to Kell and if it's more than a simple haunting, Teag and I end up getting involved.

"Big surprise—he's the one who put us onto this," Kell said. We walked toward the loading dock, and a crumbling brick enclosure I guessed might have been where the dumpsters were once kept. The doors that once hid the trash bins from view hung open and askew on broken hinges.

"Ryan likes to revisit places they've photographed every five years if the buildings are still around, to show how decay sets in," Kell went on. I was a fan of Ryan's photography. His pictures were starkly beautiful reminders that everything dies and a humbling comment on how we too often expect the world around us to remain unchanged. "He says they picked up a little ghost activity the first time, but when they came back a few weeks ago, the energy had gotten a lot worse."

"Anywhere in particular?" Teag asked.

"Two areas," Kell replied. "Here in the parking lot, and in the mechanical room. They had a bit of a close call getting out the last time, so I didn't plan to go in if we can avoid it, but I thought we might pick something up out here that would shed a little light, especially with what's happened at the other sites."

Teag regarded the shadowy old building for a moment. "And it's not all the haunted sites that are getting new mojo, just some of them?"

"Yeah, and we don't know why those particular sites, since we haven't figured out anything in common."

"There's got to be something," I said. "Let's see if it wants to put on a show tonight."

Kell's team set up their equipment, and Drew panned his camera across the dark, quiet parking lot. Teag kept his bag on his shoulder, but he had the shotgun in his hand. I dropped my athame into my palm, the handle of an old wooden spoon that belonged to my grandmother. It has a lot of resonance for me to ground my magic. I'd learned to always keep it with me, just in case. In my left hand, I held a canister of salt.

"Is that a real cat? Or a ghost cat?" Drew asked, and we turned to catch the back half of black cat disappear behind the dumpster enclosure. A few seconds later, from the far side of the parking lot, the cheery sound of a bicycle bell rang out, all kinds of wrong at one o'clock in the morning.

"It feels like a storm's rising," I said, barely needing to reach out my magic to sense the danger. "Something in that building is very dark, sorrow and pain, and it doesn't like us being here." The impressions were so strong I couldn't believe Ryan, and his explorers could have even entered the building, despite them not having any magic or clairvoyance of their own. My skin crawled, and all my gut instincts told me to run.

"Look," Drew said, pointing. The broken wooden doors to the garbage enclosure began to swing back and forth on squeaking hinges, slowly, and then with enough force to send them banging into the cement block walls. A dog barked, a whine that rose high and frightened, then changed into a warning. Once more, the temperature plummeted, and I caught a glimpse of a ghostly figure on the back steps frantically waving us off.

"Y'all, we need to be gone from here. Now," I said. I expected resistance, but Kell and the others seemed to be getting the same vibes I was, which were not good at all.

"Keep recording, and we'll see if we can make anything of it later," Kell told his team. He brought up his shotgun, as did Teag, guarding our flanks as we moved back toward the break in the fence where we entered.

The sharp sound of breaking glass made us freeze. No one else was nearby, but long cracks webbed across a pane in a window whose plywood covering had fallen away.

The *cha-ching* of the bicycle bell sounded again, closer, and a cat yowled. The figure I'd glimpsed by the steps had vanished, but I had an impression of a billowing black cloud, welling up from the center of the old school, like a storm tide ready to rush for the shore.

"Run!" I shouted, and that snapped the others into action. I urged Calista, Drew, and Peter to make for the fence, and hung back to guard the rear with Teag and Kell, readying my athame for a fight. "Put a ring of salt around your car, then get in and don't get out, no matter what you see," I called to the Drew and the others, and hoped they had time to follow my instructions. The presence had already begun to surge toward us, and I knew we wouldn't make it back to the car before it hit.

"Stay in the circle!" I yelled, pouring out the salt into a circle around the three of us large enough to give us a bit of maneuvering room. I closed the line and hopped inside, just as the darkness reached us.

Teag and Kell fired their shotguns into the pitch black, freezing cold cloud that enveloped us. I sent a cold white cone of energy blazing from my athame into the midst of the tide. The darkness parted around the rock salt blasts and my streak of light, but it did not dissipate completely. Yet the salt line around our feet held, obliging the gloom to part around us.

Outside the fragile line of protection afforded by the salt, I glimpsed nightmare images and felt fury bordering on madness. The wind grew cold enough to raise frost on the asphalt outside the salt, buffeting the invisible boundary that protected us. We fired again, two blasts and the column of pure magical force punching through the shadows, and we heard a shriek of rage and frustration. Across the lot, the wooden doors rattled so hard I felt certain one would rip off its hinges and come flying toward us.

As quickly as it came, the darkness vanished, leaving us in the wan light of a partly-burned out street lamp. My hand shook as I lowered my athame, but I could feel the temperature of the night air rising. Teag and Kell kept their shotguns up as we scanned the lot. The doors on the enclosure looked worse for the wear but still remained intact. Nothing moved, and the only sounds were the hum of cars on distant, more heavily traveled roads. We were alone.

"Think we can make a run for it?" Teag asked, and I noted that his voice wasn't entirely steady. Kell had paled, but his grip on the gun remained sure.

I tried to read what my senses were telling me. "I think it wore itself out, for now," I said. "It doesn't have the juice to do that again until it recharges. But just to be on the safe side, let's hurry."

I smudged the salt and scattered the circle, then we ran to the break in the fence and squeezed through.

"What was that?" Kell breathed as we ran. He motioned for Teag and me to go through, keeping the shotgun leveled at the darkened school until we were safely on the other side. Teag returned the favor, covering him until Kell stood next to us.

"No idea, but something really, really bad," I said. From what I could see, the force of the strange storm tide had not reached past the fence. An unbroken salt line circled Kell's SUV, and I could see the frightened faces of his team pressed up against the tinted glass. My RAV appeared undamaged. "Let's figure it out somewhere else after we get some sleep. Call me tomorrow," I said, and Kell nodded, gave me a quick kiss, then jogged to the SUV and got in. I relaxed, just a smidge, when I heard the engine roar to life.

Before I got into the RAV, I looked back over my shoulder. Maybe it was my imagination, but the old building loomed even more menacingly as if it felt smug in having run us off. I got in, locked the door, and peeled out, glad to leave Butler Middle School in my rear view mirror.

UNFINISHED BUSINESS

Cassidy?" Teag teased as we headed into the Lowcountry Museum of
Charleston on a sunny summer day. Despite the heat and humidity, I
couldn't suppress a shiver.

"There had better not be," I warned, knowing he was joking and
not entirely amused. "If I pass out or throw up, you'll be the one
making apologies and hauling me out of here."

I didn't expect trouble, but it always seemed to find me. When your
gift is the ability to read the history and magic of objects by touching
them, it doesn't take much imagination to realize that a lot of things in
museums could set that off in all kinds of not-fun ways. Fortunately,
the resonance for many objects had either faded or was never strong in
the first place. But other pieces, the ones that have a connection to a
tragic, horrific, or emotionally powerful event, can put me into a tail-
spin. My control over my gift has gotten better with practice, but I've
been surprised enough to always be on my guard in a place like this.

A few days had passed since our eventful night of ghost hunting.
I'd talked to Kell several times, and both he and Teag were doing their
best to find information that might shed light on what happened to the
two ghostly women, and why the old school had turned into a house of

horrors. They didn't find quick answers, so in the meantime, I figured Teag and I could spare an hour to support our local museum.

Fortunately, the new exhibit, "Textiles: Weaving the History of Charleston," seemed like a safe bet.

Teag's Weaver magic and his interest in all things woven convinced me to brave an outing to the museum, a decision I'd already begun to rethink now that it was too late to turn back.

"Hey, look at this!" Teag said with such enthusiasm I could have mistaken him for a kid in a candy store, instead of a guy in his mid-twenties who abandoned his Ph.D. thesis to help save the world from haunted heirlooms. He grabbed my elbow and guided me over to a realistic-looking tableau of a Native American woman sitting cross-legged in front of her loom.

"I can't get over what beautiful pieces people could make with just a simple loom," he gushed, eyes alight. "Have you ever tried to use one of these?" he asked me, gesturing toward the frame loom in the recre-ated vignette.

"No, but I always thought it could be relaxing," I admitted. "Sort of like the way people who knit find the repetition soothing."

Teag nodded excitedly. "It is. That's one of the great things about weaving. And look, the basic design doesn't change all that much for a long time, until the foot-treadle looms," he added, leading the way to the next display.

"And don't forget the spinning wheels," I said, glancing at the mannequin sitting at an antique wheel, while a child's figure used a spindle whorl to twist fiber into yarn. Unconsciously, my fingers went to the smooth agate stone of a much older whorl I carried in my pocket, one that carried with it the magical protection of an old Norse demi-goddess.

"People have always linked spinning and weaving with magic," Teag said, peering intently at the old loom in the next display. I wasn't an expert on weaving, but I could tell that as time moved on, the looms became more complex and added more features.

"There's certainly an art to planning how to switch back and forth with the different colors," I said with admiration. Teag had been practicing with a variety of weaving techniques for the love of the craft itself and studying with a local master of sweetgrass basket making, Mrs. Teller, for a couple of years now.

"That's part of the fun," Teag replied with a grin. "And most artists end up creating signature patterns and designs that become uniquely theirs. I'm still working on that," he admitted. "But then again, it's not like I'm planning to make pieces for galleries or sale. It's just a hobby."

I shook my head. "You've got a Gift," I said, and I knew he would hear the word with a capital "g" as I intended, meaning both magic and talent. "Just because you don't plan to sell what you make doesn't mean your pieces are any less important."

He shrugged, and the red flush of his neck told me I'd actually embarrassed him a little. "Maybe," he admitted. "Come on; there's more to see."

The next few displays showed the impact of the Industrial Revolution, with big mechanical looms and factory automation. The massive, metal looms made me sad, thinking of how much artistry got lost in the rush for faster production. Once we passed the final displays with the "looms of the future" and their computerized, robotic, enhancements, we emerged into a bright white gallery showcasing some of the finest textile artists of the Lowcountry and the Southeast, past and present.

I felt a tug at my intuition, a warning that something nearby had at least a touch of magic. That didn't surprise me since many artists have more magic than they realize guiding their innate talent. The gallery showcased shawls and rugs, delicately woven fabrics, and sturdy blankets, along with all kinds of decorative items and some textile creations that were just meant to be pretty to look at, true art pieces.

Some of the items roused no flicker of awareness from my gift at all, and I was careful to keep my hands away from any of the pieces, just in case. Others filled me with a sense of calm and satisfaction as if I could feel the weaver's happiness at a job well done.

We moved around a couple of large-scale art pieces that took up the center of the gallery and angled around to see more of the rugs and smaller pieces. I had been idly scanning the crowd and thinking about stopping for a cookie in the museum cafe when Teag stopped so suddenly in front of me that I ran into him.

"Hey, signal next time!" I said, stepping back. Then I realized that he hadn't moved, and his shoulders and back were stiff with apprehension. "Teag?" I asked quietly, moving up beside him. "What's wrong?"

I maneuvered him out of the center of the aisle and over to one side, but his gaze remained fixed on a hand-woven rug in a display in front of us as if it might attack. "Cassidy, don't get too close, but tell me if you pick up anything from those pieces over there," he said, gesturing as if the rug and its nearby display items might hear him.

I took a couple of steps closer, and recoiled, surprised at the intensity of the emotions I felt at a distance of a few feet. No way in hell did I want to get any closer, let alone touch anything. I closed my eyes and tried to put words to the influx of sensation. *Darkness. Fear, Despair. Anguish.* I shook my head, trying to clear my thoughts, and my heart thudded in my chest. On an instinctive level, my body had picked up on a threat, and my "fight or flight" impulses were working well since my breathing had become shallow and the hair on the back of my neck and on my arms stood up in warning.

I put some distance between myself and the bothersome display and took another minute to get myself under control. "I don't know what's wrong, but whoever wove those must have been terribly unhappy."

"We've got to find Alistair," Teag said, with an edge of desperation in his voice.

I reached out to grab his arm, and searched his face, trying to figure out what lay behind his sudden insistence. I could have sworn he looked panicked. "Teag, what's wrong?"

"I've got a bad feeling about the pieces by that artist," Teag said. "We need to find out if there are others that aren't on display." He noticed my concern and swallowed hard. "Please, Cassidy. Just trust me on this."

I nodded, knowing that something had seriously freaked him out, and hoping he would tell me more later. "All right. Let's go."

Teag and I were very familiar with the museum from attending many events over the years. Alistair knew a little about my gift, enough to call me in as a consultant for an antique appraisal, or whenever a new acquisition created problems of a supernatural sort. We wound through the crowd and slipped into the corridor toward Alistair's office. A light shone under the door, and Alistair answered Teag's knock with a look of surprise.

"Hello. Didn't know you'd be here. What's up?" Alistair McKinnon had the buttoned-down decorum donors loved in a museum director, and the degrees and pedigree to go with it. I admired his work with the museum and knew that his very proper demeanor hid a wicked wit and dry sense of humor.

"Are there any other pieces by Edna Willers that aren't on display?" Teag asked, sounding breathless enough Alistair's brows furrowed with concern trying to figure out the problem.

"I don't think so. Why? Is something wrong?"

Teag seemed at a loss for words, a true rarity, and another indicator that whatever bothered him meant trouble. I gave him a worried glance and jumped in. "I picked up some very strong negative emotions from her pieces in the gallery, and it was enough of a shock that we're worried that there might be other pieces that give off an even stronger vibe," I said, filling the gap. Now, I was really concerned.

He knew something he wasn't ready to talk about, and it scared him shitless.

"Do you think they're dangerous?" Alistair asked, looking from me to Teag. Anyone who's worked long in museums has had experience with ghosts and curses and knew to take them seriously, even if it's nothing they'll admit in public. We've helped Alistair out with some hauntings and other spooky situations, so he trusts us to be discreet, and knows that if something gives us the heebie-jeebies, it's worth worrying about.

"Maybe," I said, and Teag gave a curt nod.

"I'm not sure where the items for that exhibit are stored, but I'll have one of my staff look into it, and if there are other pieces, I'll let you know," he promised. "In the meantime, should we remove the works of hers on display?"

I looked to Teag since he knew more about the possible threat than I did. He deliberated for a moment, then shook his head. "I wouldn't want to take them home with me, but I don't think they're going to hurt anyone. People who are sensitive to those kinds of things will probably give that display a wide berth." He frowned. "None of your staff had anything bad or weird happen when they were mounting the pieces, did they?"

"No, and I think I'd have heard," Alistair replied. "Museum people have their superstitions, you know," he added with a smile. "Then again, I don't think anyone handled them for long. It got pretty chaotic in there before the opening, since some of the items came in at the last minute, so we had everyone who could lend a hand hanging and tagging. Not exactly the kind of environment for anyone to have time to notice feeling unsettled."

"Thanks for checking," Teag said, sounding a little sheepish. "It's probably nothing, but I thought it was worth checking into."

"No problem at all," Alistair reassured us. "I'll let you know as soon as my staff can get a chance to look."

We thanked him and found our way back to the main lobby. Teag still looked flustered, so I decided to forego the museum coffee shop and try to get Teag's mind off whatever had spooked him. "I could use some caffeine and sugar," I suggested. "Let's stop by Honeysuckle Café on the way back to the shop and pick up lattes and cookies."

Teag looked relieved and readily agreed. When we arrived, the place was packed. Honeysuckle Café is a favorite of the King Street crowd, both merchants and shoppers, and tourists in the know have also gotten wind of it. Rick, the barista, slings joe with the hangdog charisma of a modern-day Bogart, and Trina, the owner, always seems to know everything that's going on in town.

"Hi, Cassidy! Hi, Teag!" Trina greeted us when we worked our way through the line to pay for our order.

"Busier than usual," I said, noticing that not a single table sat empty. "What's going on?"

Trina shrugged as she rang us up. "Nice weather brings people out," she replied. "But most of the buzz is about the murder."

"Murder?" I echoed. Charleston's a fair-sized city, and bad things can happen in cities, but murders rarely become big gossip unless there's something unusual or the crime involves someone famous.

"They found a woman dead down in White Point Garden," Trina said, noting the park down along the Battery by the harbor. "And according to the rumors, it looks like there might be a serial killer on the loose."

We couldn't find seats inside, so Teag and I found a bench in the shade a little ways from the café. That suited me fine since I hoped to get him to spill the beans about what had him so jittery.

"You ready to talk about what happened at the museum?" I asked, giving him a hopeful smile and laying an encouraging hand on his arm.

Teag shifted uncomfortably and shrugged. "Not much to tell," he said, looking down at the cup in his hand. "The pieces by that weaver, Edna Willers, felt *wrong*. She was an art teacher of mine, back in college. That's why I was so surprised to see her work. I'm sure she had magic, Weaver magic, but those pieces in the museum carried so much despair, I don't know how you could even breathe around the display. It made me think of some stories I'd heard, about weavers who used their magic to do really bad things, which is why I wanted to find out if there were more pieces that might be even worse, down in the storage area."

"What kind of really bad things?" I asked.

Teag had such a tight grip on his cup I thought he might squeeze it until it exploded. "Weaver magic has a very checkered history," he said quietly. "It's never gotten the respect it deserves, in part because for a lot of centuries, it was put down as 'women's magic,'" he said. "Same old misogyny and homophobia," he sighed. "In fact, back in the Viking days, a male witch could be put to death for being a *seiðr*, a Weaver."

I stayed silent, letting Teag tell the story at his own pace.

"Some of the negative feelings had to do with a fear of being manipulated," Teag said, easing his grip on his cup. He took a sip of the latte and tried to relax. "There are stories about Weavers using spells in the cloth to control people—love spells, business deals, major decisions. Of course, the magic was used to make the person who received the woven item act against his own interests. You can see why people would be afraid."

"Sort of sounds like the Salem witch trials to me," I replied. "Someone gets a run of bad luck and blames it on some poor woman who doesn't have the power to fight back."

Teag shrugged. "I imagine there was some of that, as well. A lot of people would rather claim to have been bewitched than admit they made a bad call." He drank some more coffee. "I got really bad vibes from the pieces at the museum. And you know how it goes sometimes with art that's tainted by bad magic or haunted somehow. The original owners guard it, and then when they die, the heirs sell it off or put it on display somewhere, and then things go wrong."

"Maybe when we go back to the store, you could look up the artist and see if there's anything in the bio that clues you in on why the mojo was so freaky," I suggested. "We ought to go—Maggie's coffee and cookie are going to get cold." Maggie was our godsend assistant who knew the truth about what Trifles and Folly did and hadn't run away screaming. She had nerves of steel and a heart of gold.

Teag nodded, and I had the sense he still hadn't told me everything that bothered him about the display, but he'd probably said all he intended to for now. I gave him a hug when we stood up. "C'mon. Put it out of your mind for a little while. If there's a problem, we'll handle it. It's too nice a day to let it get you down."

Teag managed a smile, but as we walked back to the store, neither of us really felt any better.

When we got back to Trifles and Folly, Maggie accepted the coffee and cookie with enough reverence you'd have thought it was the Holy Grail. "You're the best!" she squeaked. "I'm glad you're back. We've been slammed, and everyone wants to talk about the murder."

I blew out a long breath. "Yikes. Thanks for holding down the fort." I glanced to Teag. "Why don't you look up that weaver from the museum? Maggie and I can handle the front." He nodded gratefully and went into the break room.

Maggie gave me a look. *Is he okay?* she mouthed.

I nodded. "He'll be fine," I murmured, though I didn't feel entirely sure. Teag was one of the steadiest people I knew. We'd been through a lot of freaky and downright terrifying stuff together, and I'd never seen him this rattled. It scared me because I worried about his safety, and I figured that anything bad enough to knock him off his game must really be bad. So I took a deep breath and tried to calm myself.

Which meant turning the conversation to discuss a serial murderer. "What do you know about the Smiley Killer?" Maggie asked me.

"Not much," I replied. "I've heard the name. It was a long time ago. Why? Are people saying he's back?"

Mid-afternoon is often slow in the shop, so we didn't have any customers. Maggie perched on her stood behind the counter, and nibbled her cookie. "This would have been back in the late nineties, before you were paying attention to such things," she added. I'm in my mid-twenties and had to admit she was right, although it made me feel wet behind the ears.

"Let me tell you; it was quite a big deal in Charleston. We weren't nearly so cosmopolitan then as we are now," she added without a touch of irony. Maggie gathered her tie-dye broomstick skirt around her as she rutched in her seat to get comfortable. Maggie is an amazing combination of Grateful Dead and general accounting, and all heart, with the spine of a true steel magnolia.

"Some people were a little excited that we had our very own serial killer as if that meant we had made the big time, like New York or Chicago," she said with a moue of distaste. "Of course, they were being stupid. Five women died, bodies left all over the historic district, all killed the same way. Two punctures on the throat and a curved slice, sort of like a really sick smiley face, hence the name," she said, rolling her eyes. "The media had to give him some kind of catchy name, and 'Smiley Killer' caught on."

"What happened?" I asked, feeling a knot of suspicion deep in my gut as I recalled the dots and curve the ghost had drawn on the fogged window.

"The killings just stopped," Maggie replied with a shrug. "Everyone was all keyed up, waiting for something else to happen, but eventually as time went on and no one else got killed, I guess we all figured that either the killer died, or moved on. Although if he—serial killers are almost always men, you know—did move, I never heard of more deaths with that 'signature' happening somewhere else."

I wrapped my arms around myself and shivered. Even the hot latte didn't take the chill away. "And no one ever found out who it was?"

Maggie shook her head. "Not that I heard. I guess it's not that uncommon, killers stopping for years after going on a spree. I read a few 'true crime' books when everything happened, but it was too damn depressing. So the Smiley Killer remains one of Charleston's modern mysteries, and now it seems like maybe he's come home."

"Or someone else wants us to think he has," I replied. I tried to drink the rest of my coffee, but it made my stomach churn.

"On the cop shows on TV, that's what they call a 'copycat' murder. I don't know what's worse," Maggie mused. "Having the real killer back, or having someone who wants to celebrate his greatest hits."

The bell jingled as a customer walked in. I stood up to greet her. "Welcome to Trifles and Folly."

The woman looked a little unsure. "I'm not sure I'm in the right place. Do you handle heirloom jewelry?" She wore a nice twinset sweater combination with dress slacks and looked like she might have stopped in on a break from work. The woman looked to be in her mid-forties, with short, neatly cut hair and manicured nails. But from the way she fidgeted, I could tell something made her nervous.

I gestured toward a display case to her right. "Yep. We have a really nice selection, both fine jewelry, and costume pieces. Are you interested in buying or selling?"

She tightened her grip on her purse. "Selling. Do I need to make an appointment?"

I smiled. "Nope. Come over here, and I'll be glad to do an appraisal." She followed me to an open spot atop the glass display case and reached into her purse.

"I'm Jenny Mitchell," she introduced herself. "I'm helping my aunt downsize, and she went through her things," the woman said. "I'm not sure whether they're what you handle—"

"Let's take a look, and we'll see," I said brightly. She reached into her purse and took out a wrap-up jewelry holder, which she unrolled. I knew at a glance that most of the items were nice costume jewelry, but not expensive enough for us to resell, although she might find a buyer at a yard sale. One piece, a pretty crystal brooch, caught my eye.

"That's very interesting," I said, pointing.

Jenny removed the pin and put it on the counter. "I don't know much about it, except that it was a gift. A boyfriend maybe, or a suitor my aunt never wanted to pursue," she added.

I gave her a conspiratorial grin. "Unrequited love? A nice story to go with it. It looks like it's in good shape." And like an idiot, I reached out a picked up the pin.

The world spun. I cried out, but the vision already gripped me. *Terror. I couldn't breathe for the thudding of my heart as I struggled, but the hands that gripped my arms and pinned me were too strong. I fought, kicking and twisting, and my captor swore before a brutal fist against my temple sent me reeling. I kicked off my shoes and tried to run, but he caught me, tackling me to the pavement, where I hit like a body blow and had the wind rush from my lungs.*

"Stupid bitch. You could make this easy on yourself."

The voice made my blood run cold. I bit down on his forearm, earning more swearing and another cuff to the side of my head that made my ears ring. My heel connected with his gut and once again I made a break for it, only to be grabbed around the knees and slammed hard against the cobblestones.

"So pretty," my assailant said in a sing-song voice that sent a shudder through me. His hands came up against my throat, pressing with murderous intent, and I bucked beneath his weight, clawing at his arms with my fingers, scratching at his skin with my nails. He kept eye contact as he choked me, smile broadening as I gasped and my mouth moved, trying to pull in precious air.

"Don't fight it," he urged, beaming down at me like a psychopathic angel. "It'll be over soon."

Black spots danced in front of my eyes. I tried to fight, but my body failed to obey my command. Blood thundered in my ears. He tightened his grip again, and my lungs burned as my body spasmed, autonomic reflexes taking over trying desperately to draw air into my lungs. Pain lanced through me, and my thinking slowed and vision blurred. My body lurched one more time, a valiant, doomed effort, and the hands tightened once again.

Something snapped, the air cut off, and everything went black

<h1 style="text-align:center">OLD GHOSTS</h1>

I woke up on the floor, with a pillow under my head and Maggie peering down anxiously. "Cassidy, are you back?"

I groaned in response and then tried and failed to sit up. Maggie put a hand on my shoulder and gently pressed me back. "Easy there," she cautioned. "You went down hard."

"The pin—"

"Teag bought it, and put it in the safe until Sorren can take a look at it," she reassured me. "We told the seller you had low blood sugar."

I closed my eyes and enjoyed having a nice, solid floor under me. The images from the vision loomed far too real in my memory, made worse because I knew what I glimpsed had actually happened. "Teag—"

"Teag's out handling the front. He already texted Sorren. And he got as much information as he could from the seller about her aunt, so you can follow up when you feel better. Now rest, and I'll fetch you some sweet tea."

Maggie patted me on the arm and went to the fridge to pour a glass of that ice cold elixir known as southern sweet tea, equal parts water, tea, and sugar. Folks in these parts widely held that it was good for what ailed you, no matter what that might be, and they were mostly right. Maggie helped me sit up, and steadied the glass while I drank. Then she gave me a hand up and stayed close as I moved from the floor of the break room where Teag must have carried me, into the office to plop down on the small couch.

Closing my eyes just made the vision real once more, but I couldn't keep them open forever. "Someone murdered the original owner of that pin," I said to Maggie, who drew in a sharp breath. A lot of haunted and cursed items come through Trifles and Folly, and we make sure they don't hurt anyone ever again. Some of the pieces pack a real psychic wallop. Usually, there's a reason an owner chooses to get rid of a problem item, and it often has to do with a vague feeling of wrongness or uneasiness they get around the heirloom. For those without strong or developed psychic gifts, that edginess is intuition sending up an emergency warning flare.

"And you saw it happen."

"Yeah. From the victim's point of view. It wasn't an accident, and it wasn't a crime of passion. The killer hunted her, and killed for sport."

Maggie crossed herself, although I knew she wasn't Catholic, a warding against evil. "Did you see anything that would help you identify the victim—of the killer?"

I started to shake my head and stopped as a headache reminded me that was a bad idea. "I was seeing the victim's perspective, so no idea what she looked like. And the killer's face was blurry like maybe he had a stocking over his features or something. But I heard his voice. Definitely a man."

"Time period?" Maggie knew from experience with my visions that details faded with time, so as uncomfortable as it made me to recall disturbing images, we stood our best chance of preserving important information by pressing me to talk while the memories were fresh.

"The cars looked older. Maybe 1990s?" I replied. "Around that time. Not recent."

Maggie went to refill my glass. "Rest a bit," she urged. "You went down hard, and you're likely to have a bit of a goose egg on your head.

Take it easy. I imagine Teag and Sorren will want to go over everything anyhow."

I dozed on the couch and roused when I heard Teag come back into the office. "Closed up for the night," he said and looked me over with concern. "You doing better?"

"Yeah," I said, remembering at the last minute not to nod. "Hell of a vision."

"Maggie told me a little bit," he said, leaning against the wall. "When you're up to it, I want to go over the details, and we'll see what I can find online, although linking what you saw to an old murder probably won't be easy."

"It happened in Charleston," I said, and had to stop to figure out how I could be sure. "I recognized the place. Anson Street, out behind the horse stables for the carriage rides."

Teag smiled. "That's good. I can use that. I'll ask Drea if she remembers anyone saying something about a murder over there. That's her territory." My friend Andrea, "Drea" ran Andrews Carriage Tours, a business which had been in her family for decades. If she didn't remember, odds were her parents might.

"That poor woman," I murmured. "She was so terrified, and then... it wasn't an easy death."

Teag nodded. "Your gift sucks sometimes, Cassidy," he replied. I couldn't disagree. As often as my touch magic helped us stop some kind of supernatural menace, it took a toll.

"I'm just not sure what we can do about a murder from ten or twenty years ago. The police won't take my word for evidence. And the killer seemed human—not supernatural. We're not cops. The killer has probably already been caught, and I hope he rots in jail."

He sipped his tea. "I know what it's like to have a piece of a puzzle and not be able to connect the dots. For a long time, I've had a dream that recurs. Just a scene, with two men in business suits looking at me so intently, and they say 'what did you see?.'" Teag shivered. "Something about it always upsets me. I can't tell you how many times Anthony's had to wake me up because I'm having the nightmare."

Anthony Benton, Teag's long-time partner, came from an old Charleston family and was a lawyer with the family firm.

"And you don't know what it's about?"

Teag shook his head. "I think it's a memory, but I've had it for so long, I can't be sure. If it really did happen, then I've either forgotten everything else about the situation or pushed it way back in my mind where it can't bother me."

"If you discover something about the killer and it turns out to be a cold case, do you think Anthony could get access to the files—just in case there is something supernatural about it?" I asked.

"Maybe," Teag replied. "I hate to put him on the spot, so I'll see if I can hack into the database first. But if the case is old enough, the files might not be digitized. Let me see what I can find, and we'll keep Anthony as our Plan B."

Anthony knew about our real mission with Trifles and Folly and about our work with the Alliance. He found out the hard way after one of our battles against a crazy dark witch and a bunch of nephilim nearly killed Teag, and Anthony had to make a choice between ignorance about things that go bump in the night, and the man he loved. He chose Teag.

Still, Anthony's role as a lawyer often created potential dilemmas. Teag, Sorren, and I sometimes had to bend some laws—especially about trespassing and breaking and entering—that it was better if Anthony didn't know about. Plausible deniability and all that. I felt sure that Anthony suspected far more than he ever tried to confirm, his own version of "don't ask, don't tell."

"Could you pick up any information from the pin or anything the seller said?" I asked.

Teag shook his head. "You spooked her pretty good going down like that."

"Low blood sugar," I mumbled, feeling my cheeks heat in embarrassment.

Teag laughed. "Oh, is that what we're calling it now?"

"Shut up," I retorted, but without any sting in my words. "Did Jenny say anything else about the piece?"

"No, she just wanted to finish the sale and leave. I did get her contact information, so when you're feeling better, we can make up a reason and call her or go visit, and you can see if there's more to the story, or if the old aunt can recall who gave her the pin."

"Sounds good. You didn't notice anything unusual about the pin itself?"

Again he shook his head. "It's costume jewelry, department store quality. Classic design, but I think pins like that made a comeback in the 1990s for women's suits, so that might go with what you saw in the vision. But there's nothing special about the pin itself—probably one of thousands just like it, mass produced."

I set the empty glass aside. Between the rest and the tea, my headache had dimmed, and I felt much better. "It's still light outside—going to be a while before Sorren can come out. Are we still on for the four of us to go to dinner?" Kell and I often double-dated with Teag and Anthony.

"If you feel up to it."

"It would be nice to think about something else for a while," I admitted. "Since I'll have to go over everything again once Sorren gets here." Sorren has adapted to many things about modern life, from fashions to using a cell phone and email, but being a vampire—even one who is nearly 600 years old—means he can't come out in daylight. It's an inconvenience we've all just learned to work around.

An hour later, the four of us were ensconced in a booth at Jocko's Pizzeria, our favorite pizza place. We were regulars, so the servers tended to just bring out our usual unless we made an effort to order something new. Tonight, everyone seemed content to stick with comfort food.

"You'd have thought it was the full moon this week," Kell said, as he filled his plate with slices of pizza. "It's been quiet lately, and then —bam! Spook-a-palooza. Still can't figure out why."

"Is there an anniversary of anything?" Teag mused, digging into his pasta. "Pirate battle? Slave uprising? Street riot from the Colonial days?"

Kell shrugged. "Not that we've found, but we're still looking.

We're getting activity from locations all over town that aren't usually active. Cold spots. Orbs. Interference with cell phones and computers and TVs. Strange lights. So far, no human figures or voices, but the activity seems to be growing stronger, so that might happen." He paused to take a bite and wiped the sauce from his lips. "No one's gotten hurt, thank heaven. But it's scared some night watchmen and drunk tourists out of their gizzards."

I glanced at Anthony, who seemed intent on stealing as many bites of Teag's pasta as he was on eating his own. "How about you?" I asked. "Anything interesting you can share with the class?"

Anthony sighed. "Nothing I'm personally working on that's remotely interesting," he replied. "And before you ask, I don't have any good scoop about the murder everyone's talking about, and I couldn't tell you even if I did."

"After all this time, do you think the Smiley Killer could actually have come back to Charleston?" I asked.

Kell shrugged. "I've heard about that happening—killers who stop killing for years and then start up again. But it happened so long ago. Hell, in that much time, he might even be dead. Probably a copycat."

"I can tell you that the cops are really edgy," Anthony confided. "So if you've got any 'after-hours extra-curricular activities' planned, realize that the police are twitchy," he warned. He knew that Kell's group often teamed up with our mutual friend Ryan Alexander's urban explorer group and that Teag and I sometimes went poking around places that weren't exactly public property. I appreciated the warning. Bad enough to get thrown around by vengeful ghosts; I had no desire to get arrested or shot.

"It probably doesn't help that the media made the connection between the new killing and the old killer's signature style," Kell observed, with a nod of his head toward the TV monitor by the bar running the local news.

Anthony swore and took a drink of his wine. "That definitely doesn't help. I'm all for freedom of information, but sometimes an investigation goes better if all the details aren't public. At least until the killer gets caught. Can't tell you how many times a whole investigation gets compromised because important details got leaked too soon."

That reminded me of the disturbing insight I'd had earlier in the day. "Two dots and a curved line," I said, looking from Kell to Teag. As comprehension dawned, I could see it in their faces. "I think those two hauntings have something to do with the Smiley Killer."

"Shit," Kell said. "I was afraid of that. I'll look into it. That might narrow things down." I knew that Teag would be on it as soon as he got back to his computer.

Conversation steered away from troubling topics, and soon we were laughing and joking. A bottle of wine helped to lighten the mood. Once the sun set, Teag and I exchanged a look. "We've got to head back to the shop," I said with a sigh, leaning against Kell's shoulder and giving his hand a squeeze. "We have an appointment with a seller." That wasn't exactly the truth, but although Anthony knew about Sorren, Kell didn't, and for his own safety, I meant to keep it that way until I had to do otherwise.

"This late?" Kell asked, concerned. I couldn't blame him. A crazy killer was on the loose.

"Teag and I are going back together, and we'll be in the thick of the tourist crowd the whole way," I reassured him. Charleston stayed just as busy after dark as it did in the daytime, with carriage rides, ghost tours, and foodie-favorite restaurants and bars.

"Text me when you get home," he said, giving me a gentle kiss.

"I will. And you and the team be careful, too," I cautioned. "No telling where this guy is hiding out, so watch your back if you go poking around old dark places."

Kell chuckled. "Always. I promise."

Out on the sidewalk, Kell gave me a goodnight, lingering kiss of promise, and I took my time to enjoy it. Out of the corner of my eye, I saw Teag and Anthony in a clinch as well, and I heard murmured cautions. Anthony and Kell both knew Teag and I could take care of ourselves, but it was sweet for them to worry.

Teag and I headed back to the store, both of us hyper-vigilant. We were rarely unarmed, although not in the conventional "concealed-carry" sense unless the supernatural threat was solid enough to take a bullet. I wore agate, silver, and onyx jewelry that provided a level of protection, and Teag had his own amulets to ward off dark energies. Since you can't shoot a ghost, I made sure I had bags of salt and iron shavings in my pockets, which could disrupt all but the strongest spirits, at least for a while. We both had silver and iron daggers, and I always kept my athame up my sleeve or in my purse. Teag's martial arts training wasn't much good against ghosts, but the salt-soaked small rope net he kept tucked in his backpack could definitely scramble their signal.

I couldn't shake the feeling of being watched as we walked back, although no one we passed appeared to pay us any attention. Evening didn't tend to cool things off much in a Charleston summer, but now and again, I felt a whisper of an icy breeze when we weren't close to any open doorways. I wished for one of Kell's EMF readers that picked up on the energy pulses of ghosts.

"You feel that?" Teag murmured.

"Yeah. Not sure where it's coming from." Charleston is one of the most haunted cities in the country, and the ghost tours claim restless spirits haunt nearly every street and old building, but while we have more than our share of real spooks, most remain in a fixed position. Whatever caused the cold spots seemed to be moving with us, following us. That idea didn't make me happy at all.

Just before we reached Trifles and Folly, I felt a presence strongly enough that the hair on the back of my neck prickled. I wheeled, but saw no one anywhere close to us on the block. From the look on Teag's face, I could tell he sensed something, too.

Without needing to ask, we opted to go in through the front door, instead of around to the alley behind the store through the delivery entrance. When we crossed the threshold, the protection of layers of old magical wardings closed over us, and I felt as if a weight had been lifted from my shoulders. The oppressive presence that I had felt outside was gone.

The security light gave enough illumination for us to make our way to the break room. "Sorren?" I called quietly. He can see just fine in the dark, so I didn't expect him to have the lights on.

"I'm here."

We lacked his supernatural senses, so Teag closed the door between the break room and the front of the store and turned on the light. Sorren sat at the table, dressed in a t-shirt and jeans. His new haircut made him look a little European hipster to me, but whenever I mentioned that he just rolled his eyes and pointed out that in 600 years, he had seen far too many styles come and go to feel complimented or insulted by my observation. I knew he paid attention mainly for camouflage, to fit in with the mortals around him. Still, it made me chuckle when I tried to imagine him dressed like those people in the old Flemish paintings, back from when Sorren had been one of the best jewel thieves in Antwerp.

"I got your message," Sorren said. "What do you want to do about the pin?"

"As much as I'd like to drown it in the ocean, it might end up being evidence, if we could come up with an explanation the police would believe," I said. "Someone murdered the woman who originally owned it. But the seller said it had been given to her aunt as a present. So either the aunt lied about how she got it—"

"Or she had some kind of really freaky boyfriend," Teag finished.

"Either explanation is possible," Sorren answered. "What else do you have?"

I started to mention Teag's reaction to the woven rug at the museum but stopped. I still didn't know what prompted his concern and intended to get the details out of him sooner or later, but it was his story to tell.

Sorren listened while I recounted my vision, and Teag added what he learned from the seller. "I've tried hacking into the police files, to see what I could find out about this 'Smiley Killer,'" Teag said. "It's long enough ago that I don't think everything's been scanned, but there was enough to get us started." He poured me a glass of sweet tea and one for himself—Sorren rarely consumed food or drink, except for the blood he needed to survive, which he assured me long ago came from "willing and sustainable sources."

"According to the files, the Smiley Killer murdered five women over the course of several months back in 1997. He was never caught, but the murders ended abruptly that Fall and the police figured he either died or moved elsewhere, although there are notes that his 'signature' was never seen on serial kills elsewhere."

"Interesting," Sorren mused.

"The 'smiley' part came because of the punctures and the shape of the cut on the throat," Teag said. "I double checked—despite the punctures, none of the bodies were drained."

"So it's not a vampire," Sorren supplied.

Teag shrugged. "Had to check. Just in case. Anyhow, the police tried to keep the method of killing quiet, but there was a journalist who wouldn't leave the case alone, and he leaked the information to the press. The lead detective was really pissed. But one detail didn't get leaked. The killer stole jewelry from each victim. Police kept an eye on pawn shops and flea markets, in case the pieces turned up, but they never did."

"You think the pin we bought was one of those 'trophies?'" I asked. I'd read about serial killers keeping mementos of their kills, everything from driver's licenses to body parts, so by comparison; jewelry wasn't as bad as it could have been. Still, the ghoulishness of wanting to relive the thrill of the murder turned my stomach.

"I think it's entirely possible," Teag said. "Other serial killers confessed to enjoying giving their trophies as gifts, getting off on the idea of knowing the truth when the recipient had no clue."

"That's so sick," I muttered.

Sorren shrugged. "Indeed. But unfortunately, more common across the course of history than most people like to think about. More proof, perhaps, that what makes a monster is what you do, not what you are."

Most people would automatically put a vampire in the "monster" category. Yet Sorren had been helping save the world for most of his existence. From what I'd seen, regular people gave supernatural creatures stiff competition when it came to mayhem and bloodshed.

"Let's go see the seller tomorrow, and find out whether her aunt will talk to us. If the guy who gave her the pin actually was the Smiley Killer, it might be a break in the case," I said.

"Which we'll have a hell of a time getting the police to accept," Teag grumbled.

"Yeah, but if the killer is back—or there's a copycat—it might be important," I said.

"I did find out a little bit about the recent murder," Teag added. "All of the Smiley Killer's victims were found in public places as if he were taunting police—and he probably was. The woman who was just murdered was found in a locked room, and the security cameras in her building didn't show any visitors. But there was a ring next to the body —and it was one of the pieces stolen by the original killer."

"Shit," I swore. "That doesn't sound good."

"I vaguely remember the murders," Sorren said, frowning as he tried to recall. I couldn't imagine having to sift through centuries of memories. "I didn't pay much attention at the time, once I determined it wasn't a supernatural killer. We're usually so busy dealing with our own kinds of problems; mortal crimes just don't stick in my mind. But these 'Smiley' murders were gruesome, and I had originally also worried about the punctures. When the killing stopped, I guess I just assumed he had been caught."

"Did the police look for a connection between the woman who was murdered and the Smiley Killer?" I asked.

Teag shook his head. "But she *was* the sister of the textile artist whose pieces gave us the jitters at the museum. Ann Delarue."

I was just about to ask him to tell Sorren about it when Teag's phone buzzed. He pulled it out of his pocket, glanced at the screen, and blanched, then swore under his breath.

"Problem?" Sorren asked, concerned.

Teag looked up. "That was Anthony. He said to turn on the news. There's been another murder."

I had a small TV in the office, and we gathered there while I turned it on and flipped to the local news channel. The unflappable anchor person sat behind the desk, droning on.

"—just in. Police have confirmed reports that a woman was found dead under suspicious circumstances earlier this evening. The dead woman's identity has been confirmed as Sophie Johnston. Police are not releasing any details at this time, other than to confirm that the victim was murdered. If anyone has information that might aid law enforcement, please call the number on the screen. All tips will remain confidential."

I flicked off the TV, and we looked at each other. "Want to bet it's another 'smiley' murder, and they're playing it cool to avoid panic?" I asked.

I nodded. "The question is, what's the connection to the killer?"

Sorren frowned. "Did the police ever find a connection between the original victims? Did they know each other? Or did he have a 'type?'"

"As far as the police ever knew, the original murders appeared to be random. They were all women, and all fairly young, but the builds and hair color all varied," Teag said.

A horrible thought occurred to me. "Do you think he picked them for their jewelry?"

Teag raised an eyebrow. "It's possible, I guess. There was one serial killer who stole his victim's shoes, but I never heard that he targeted them for their Louboutins."

"Let me ask around to some of my sources," Sorren said. "If this is a mortal copycat, then there may be little we can do since ghosts can't testify. But just in case, I'll talk to Alicia Peters, and see if she's picked up any unusual 'chatter.'" Alicia was a gifted medium who helped us when a situation required her specialized skills.

"I'm going to see if I can find any photos or descriptions of the stolen jewelry," Teag said. "There must be something in the files if the cops knew the jewelry had been taken. Let me poke around, and maybe I can turn up something useful."

We all agreed to reconnect the next evening. Teag and Sorren walked me to my RAV, and I was nearly home before I realized I had forgotten to press Teag about his reaction to the woven exhibit pieces.

I felt frustrated and useless and vowed to go back to the museum on my own for another look at those rugs. I didn't know if there was a connection to the pin and the long-ago serial killer, but if there was a chance I could help, I knew I wouldn't be comfortable until I had run every possibility to the ground.

That night, I double-checked all my locks and wardings, and just to be safe, laid down a salt-soaked length of rope across the doors and windows to my room. Then I grabbed my little Maltese dog, Baxter, and hugged him tight. Even so, it took a long time to drift off to sleep, and my dreams were dark.

~

ALISTAIR CALLED ME before I finished breakfast. "Cassidy. We found another piece by the artist Teag seemed so concerned about, Edna Willers. It's damaged, so it never made it out of storage. Do you two want to come have a look at it? I'm sorry to call you, but I don't have his number in my phone."

"I'll stop by on the way to the shop," I said, although the store and the museum were in opposite directions. "Let me finish feeding Baxter and drinking my coffee, and I'll be right over."

Alistair chuckled. "I'll have more coffee for you when you get here. See you soon."

I took Baxter out and let him run around in my little walled garden, and then made sure I picked him up and loved on him for a few minutes since I'd been out late the night before. He licked my nose and wriggled closer, and I fed him treats, before setting down more food and water for the day and finishing my own coffee. Bax gave me a reproachful look as I went out the door.

"I don't think I'll be late tonight," I promised, but I could tell he wasn't convinced.

I told myself I'd take him to the dog park this weekend, feeling like a guilty parent as I got into the SUV and headed toward the museum.

True to his word, Alistair had a fresh pot of coffee waiting when I made it to his office, and I accepted a cup gratefully. "Before we go down to storage, would you mind taking me past the rugs we saw in the exhibit room?" I asked. "I picked up some strong vibes from them, and I want to see if I read any more off them than I did before."

"Do you think it's something dangerous?" Alistair might not know the full truth about what we do, but he's been part of enough strange circumstances to understand that the supernatural is real and it can be dangerous.

"I don't know," I replied. "That's why I want another look—and why I need to see the piece in storage. If I think there's any danger to people viewing the exhibit, I will definitely let you know."

This time, I focused in on my gift as we walked through the other woven pieces on display. My magic kicks in the most strongly when I actually touch something, but being close can trigger impressions if the energy is strong enough. I moved past the rugs, textile sculptures, and other beautiful items, picking up either no vibes at all, or calming, peaceful sensations.

That changed like the last time as I came around the corner, and confronted the woven pieces that had rattled Teag. I kept my distance so the impressions wouldn't overwhelm me, and sorted through what I picked up. Sorrow, fear, and despair were strongest. I screwed up my courage and moved closer. Sometimes, I get images; other times, it's just feelings. Whoever made these beautiful rugs had been terrified of something, and felt guilty, too—although that emotion ran second to the fear. I sensed that the weaver had used her craft as catharsis, a way to ease her conscience. I wondered what might have weighed so heavily on her mind, but part of me was afraid to find out.

When I got closer, I let my palm hover just above the fabric. Up close, I could feel a faint tingle of magic, and that made me remember how viscerally Teag had reacted. Edna Willers had Weaver magic, but it had a different feel from what I'd sensed of Teag's power. Edna's magic felt strong and mature, carefully controlled, intentional. Protective. That's when I realized that she'd created a bulwark in her weaving, a cocoon of defensive energy. *What was she so afraid of, to make her art into a fortress?* I wondered.

"Cassidy?"

I could tell from the tone in Alistair's voice that he had been calling my name without a response. I looked up, blushing a bit at being caught up in my thoughts. "Sorry. I'm just getting a lot of feelings from these pieces, and I wish I knew more about the artist."

"She was local," he replied. "Very talented, but never sought the spotlight. Her executor sent us the pieces for the exhibit."

"So she passed away?" I frowned, feeling like there was a piece missing, something important.

"Edna died of a heart attack a month ago. It's so sad—her sister was just murdered two days ago."

My head jerked up. "Sophie Johnston?"

"No. Ann Delarue."

Of course the last names might be different if one or both of the sisters married. "The copycat killing?"

Alistair nodded. "I guess that's what they're calling it. Terrible thing. Neither of them had any living family, so the bank's taken over the estate."

"Let's go see that other piece," I suggested, and as we walked away, a sense of relief swelled through me as I left behind the sadness of the woven pieces behind.

"It's really a shame," Alistair said as we went downstairs to the museum's storage area. "I'm not sure what happened to the one rug, but it's been torn, and that made quite a bit of it unravel. It's not her best work, thank heavens, but there's a somber beauty to it. Like a storm on the horizon. Makes me think of thunderclouds, looming. You'll see what I mean."

I followed Alistair through a maze of aisles between tall wooden shelves chock full of tagged and labeled bits of history. Some shelves held boxes, while others had taxidermied animals and birds, clay pots, woven baskets, and other pieces not currently on display. I held my arms close to my body and tightened control over my gift. Far too many things in a museum held strong resonance, and I didn't want to get sidelined.

"Here we go," he said, stopping to pull out a marked cardboard storage box. He set it down in the middle of the aisle and opened it up.

I crouched beside it and caught my breath. Even from a foot away, I felt a psychic stench that made my gorge rise.

A ruined woven rug lay in the box, and I guessed it had originally been about the size of the other pieces, perhaps three feet by five feet. The colors were black, gray, and a muted green the color of stagnant water. Its pattern looked jagged, a harsh and brutal clash of color and geometric figures. Now that I could compare it to Edna's work upstairs, this piece resonated with anger, vengeance, and hate so strongly my throat closed and I struggled to breathe. Just being close to it made my skin crawl, and I fought an instinctive reaction to scramble away.

Alistair laid a hand on my shoulder. "Are you okay?"

I nodded, though my stomach clenched and my mouth felt dry. No way in hell did I intend to touch the weaving, and I didn't think it was a good idea for Alistair to come in contact with it either. Forcing myself to peer more closely, I could see where something had caught on the rug and torn across rows of weaving, releasing the threads from the warp and woof to let them dangle like viscera.

The rug felt like a corpse, I realized with a shock. Something about it made me think of an empty vessel, a body that had held a soul which had departed. What remained was an empty, discarded shell, cast aside as the spirit within went free.

My heart froze with the possibilities. *Did Edna trap some kind of demon in the rug, and it's been set loose?* Something truly evil had touched this woven piece, and the psychic residue clung to what remained like toxic sludge.

"This... thing... is dangerous," I managed, getting to my feet and backing away. "Is there a safe you can put it in until we can figure out what to do about it? Preferably a nice, thick lead safe?"

Alistair gave me a questioning look, but he didn't call me crazy. "I thought it was just my imagination, but the rug gives me the creeps," he admitted. "And since we put it down here, none of my staff will come into the storage area alone."

"Good instincts," I replied. "Let me do some research, and I'll get back to you as quickly as I can. Just... don't let anyone near that."

Alistair agreed, and I knew he would keep his word. I felt skittish until I was out of the museum. As soon as no one was around, I called Teag.

"Can a Weaver trap a demon in a rug?"

Teag's silence gave me the answer I feared. "Come to the shop, and I'll tell you a story."

ANCHORS

When I got to Trifles and Folly, Teag and Maggie were taking care of customers. I put my questions aside, and went to help, sending tourists on their way with their new-found treasures until the rush of visitors slowed to a trickle. I ordered in pizza, and Maggie shooed us into the back room, promising to let us know if she got swamped.

"Okay, spill." I sat down at the table and leveled a look at Teag that made him squirm.

He turned a chair around and straddled it, resting his arms across the back. "Before I knew anything about magic or being a Weaver, I took a textiles class in college. I'd always been intrigued by looms and fabrics, and I thought it would be fun. It was, and—big surprise—I had a knack for it," he added with a wan smile.

"Looking back on it, I'm certain the teacher had magic," he said. "And maybe she knew that I did, too. She never mentioned anything woo-woo, but she definitely encouraged me to stick with textiles, even suggested I get a small loom to work on at home. We stayed in touch, and she retired a couple of years later. When I was working on my doctorate, she had a stroke, and I went to visit her once she was well enough to have visitors."

His expression grew pensive. "She knew she was dying. So she

"

told me something she had never told anyone else. She wanted to get it off her chest, I guess. She said that she had done a bad thing for good reasons, trapping the soul of a monster in the weaving of a rug."

"Did she say what kind of monster?"

Teag shook his head. "She said that someone begged her for help with a monster they couldn't control and couldn't kill. She wove the thing's soul into a rug and left it there. I guess she figured it would be forever. I didn't ask questions because I didn't really believe her at the time. Thought maybe the stroke messed with her mind. I told her it was the right thing to do because, hell, I wasn't going to guilt-trip a sick old lady. She lingered on for a couple of years in poor health, and I heard she died about a month ago. Heart attack."

"Your teacher was Edna Weller."

Teag nodded. "When I started working to develop my Weaver magic with Mrs. Teller, I thought about asking her whether what Mrs. Weller told me would be possible. Then one night, Mrs. Teller needed to borrow from my strength to trap an imp in a special kind of basket. That's when I knew the other story must have been true."

"Well, whatever your teacher wove into that rug is gone now," I said. "Something strong... and nasty had been trapped there, but all that's left is a husk and some real bad resonance." I took a deep breath. "So... we need to find out what kind of monster it was and how to trap it again or kill it, before more people die."

"Do you think Alicia's sensed anything?" Teag asked.

"Crap. Sorren hasn't called back on that. I forgot about her. Let me call." I dialed, and Alicia picked up on the second ring.

"Whatever it is, the answer is no," she said, sounding a little prickly before I had even opened my mouth.

"Um, just checking in to see if you've gotten any strange messages from beyond," I replied.

"Hell, yes. Which is why I've left town—and so has every other real clairvoyant and spirit medium I know," Alicia said. What I'd originally thought was anger in her tone I realized now was fear. "I don't know what's going on, and I don't want to know, but there's something evil and powerful loose in Charleston, and it's the kind of thing no one with my kind of talent should be within a hundred miles of."

"Can you tell what it is? A demon, maybe?"

"Not a demon. They don't need a medium; they can possess anyone who's vulnerable. If I had to guess, I'd say this was an amped up ghost chock full of anger and ready for revenge. And since a strong ghost can possess an unwilling medium—well, that's why I got the hell out of Dodge, so to speak."

"Any suggestions on getting rid of it?"

Alicia was quiet for so long I wasn't sure she intended to answer. "A ghost like that is anchored to something. That's how it hangs on to its power. Destroy the anchor, and the ghost loses energy. It probably won't cross over on its own, but you'll be able to wrangle it a lot easier if it isn't juiced up."

"Thanks," I said. "Want me to call you when it's over?"

"You won't have to," Alicia replied. "Whatever's out there is strong enough, even the ghosts are scared of it. When they calm down, I'll know it's safe to come home."

I ended the call and could see from Teag's expression that I wasn't hiding how bad it was. Hell, he might even have heard most of it. "Teag, give me a second, and I'll tell you what she said, but I've got to make a quick call first." I slipped into the office and fretted until Kell picked up. "Hey," I said. "I need you to trust me on this. Can you and your team promise not to go out hunting for a little while? It's dangerous."

Kell snorted. "Yeah, we figured that out when the ghosts blew out our equipment last night. Readings off the charts. And the really strange thing was, they weren't trying to hurt us. I could have sworn they were trying to warn us away."

I swallowed hard. "I think you're right."

"Cassidy, we mapped out where the ghost readings went ballistic. They match the locations where the Smiley Killer's victims were found. What the hell is going on?"

"I don't know, but I think there's a really strong... hell, I don't know what… 'spirit' maybe, that's escaped from where it had been bound. Now it's loose, and it's angry."

"Like that World's Fair ghost?" Kell had helped us out with another dangerous haunting a little while ago, so this wasn't his first rodeo.

"Yeah," I replied. "And you remember how much fun that was, right?" It hadn't been, not at all.

"You need a bodyguard?" he asked. "I've still got a shotgun loaded up with rock salt."

"Keep it handy," I said. "Just promise me you won't go looking for trouble."

He paused. "Do I get to make you promise, too?"

"I won't take any unnecessary risks," I said.

"Not the same thing. Dammit, Cassidy! I worry about you—and about Teag, too."

"We'll be okay," I replied, though I couldn't guarantee that.

"If I can stand down from investigating, and I'm the ghost hunter, why can't you? How is this your business?"

This wasn't a conversation I wanted to have right now, and certainly not over the phone. "I've got to go," I said. "But I promise I'll do everything I can to stay safe. You just do the same and Kell, please… trust me."

Kell swore under his breath and sighed. "I will. I do. But I don't like it. Are you part of some secret government agency that hunts monsters or something?"

"No," I said honestly. "I'm not part of a secret government agency." The Alliance transcends borders, and it's been doing its job longer than most of the governments have been in existence.

"Just… be careful. I care."

"So do I," I murmured. "And I will be. If I find out more, I'll let you know. See you soon." I ended the call and closed my eyes. I liked Kell a lot, and I didn't want him to get hurt. But until I knew our relationship might be permanent, I couldn't bring him in on the secret. Anthony had been willing to accept the truth rather than let Teag go. I didn't know if Kell and I had reached that point yet, or if we would, and until then, I didn't want to try my luck.

Teag glanced up when I came back to the break room. "Let me guess—Kell doesn't like you investigating."

"Got it in one," I sighed. "I don't imagine Anthony's thrilled, either?"

Teag shook his head. "No. Although I think he's more worried that we'll spook a trigger-happy cop than get killed by a ghostly psychopath." He ran a hand back through his hair. "Anything else from Kell?"

I relayed the news about the ghostly activity, and Teag grimaced. "How much of the conversation did you catch with Alicia?" He actually had picked up on most of it, but I filled in the missing pieces.

"So the question is: are the ghosts trying to warn us that the killer is back, or chomping at the bit to get some revenge?" Teag said.

"I don't know. Both, maybe."

"Let's go see the aunt of the seller who brought in that ring," Teag suggested. "It's still early, and Sorren won't rise for a while, so we've got time. Maybe we'll figure out how her aunt knew a killer."

Teag had the address from the sale, and before long we pulled up in front of a neat house in North Charleston. We walked to the door and knocked, but the woman who answered looked much different than she had when she came into Trifles and Folly just days before. Jenny's red-rimmed eyes and the tiredness in her face suggested recent tragedy.

"I'm so sorry to bother you," I said gently. "But it's really important. Could we please possibly speak with your aunt about the ring you sold us?"

Jenny stared at us. "I wish you could. God, I wish I could. But she's dead. Aunt Sophie was murdered last night, locked in her bedroom. How in the hell did a serial killer do that?"

Aunt Sophie. Sophie Johnston. The last name didn't match because both women had changed theirs for marriage. A tangle of emotions made it hard to find my voice. "I'm so sorry," I finally managed. "We had no idea."

"She never liked that pin," Jenny said. "Swore it brought bad luck, but I think she was also afraid to get rid of it, you know? And maybe she was right. Sold if off and look what happened."

"I'm sure it's just an awful coincidence," Teag consoled. Maybe he was right. Then again, perhaps the Smiley Killer's ghost took it personally that she had gotten rid of the trophy. "Did she ever tell you the name of the man who gave her the pin? It's important—for insurance reasons," he added, managing to look entirely sincere.

Jenny shook her head. "I asked her about it, but she just clammed up and said it was a bad bit of business and the less said, the better. I got the feeling he might have stalked her, you know? Like she wasn't actually dating him, but that he wouldn't take 'no' for an answer?"

I nodded sympathetically, thinking that Jenny's aunt might have avoided becoming one of the killer's victims the first time around, but he had still managed to wrap up his loose ends from beyond the grave. "We're so sorry to intrude," I said. "And I know this is a bad time. But if you find out something as you're going through your aunt's effects, please let us know. It's important." I handed her one of my cards, and she took it, then closed the door as we made our way back to my SUV.

"Well, that was awful and awkward," Teag said with a sigh as we got back into the car. "But it confirms your vision. I've got an idea. Let's go back to the store, and I'll see what I can pull up from either the police or old news accounts about the victims and the missing items. We might be able to narrow down what we're looking for."

We still had several hours until sunset, and Maggie had already promised to close up and feed Baxter, so we picked up some Chinese take-out and got back to the store after Maggie was gone. I didn't want to freak Teag out, but I had the feeling we were being watched, although I knew no one had followed us, and no one suspicious lingered around the shop when we returned. I've learned the hard way to trust my intuition, but this time, I couldn't spot a tail, or figure who would want to shadow us.

Teag and I fired up our laptops on the break room table, with him sifting through hacked police files while I searched old files in online newspapers.

By the time we finished our food, Teag had a list ready. He slid it across the table. "That's what the cops have in the file about victims and missing jewelry, with as much of a description as they bothered to write down."

I scanned the list. "Kelly Atkins, garnet cocktail ring. Valerie Stevens, gold and pearl brooch. Roberta Warde, crystal and silver pendant necklace. Polly Wright, gold pin in the shape of a 'P.' Lisa Wentworth, gold signet ring." I read the bit of description provided, which wasn't much.

"We know the gold and pearl pin was given to Jenny's aunt," I said. "Do you know which ring was found with the body of the first victim?" I asked. "And what was found with Sophie Johnston's body?"

A few minutes later, Teag had my answer. "The garnet ring was found with Ann Delarue's body," he replied. "But with Sophie, it was her own ring removed from her hand and placed next to the body."

"So what do you think? Maybe he gave Ann a trophy as well, and she was wearing it, so his spirit took it off the body, but that might be as far as he could make off with it, if he's limited as a ghost," I mused.

"But Sophie had sold the brooch and didn't wear it, so he followed his pattern with what she had with her."

I nodded. "So it's not so much he's 'leaving' the jewelry as he's still removing it, just not very far now, because he can't."

"That's one really sick ghost," Teag said with a shudder.

I worked in silence for a while, and then looked, up, grinning in victory. "I managed to find pictures of all the victims online, both their obituary photo and in some cases, pictures from receptions and business events. Let's see if any of them were wearing their special jewelry in the photos."

Teag brought his chair around, and we went through the photos together, making them as large as possible to see details. I felt a stab of sorrow as I eyed the faces in the pictures, seeing them young and happy and knowing what lay ahead of them.

"Look," he said, crowding close to my shoulder. He pointed to the screen, and I zoomed in even more. "A gold pin shaped like a 'P,'" he said, and sure enough, Pamela's picture showed her wearing a scarf with a large monogram pin securing it to her shoulder. When I switched to Roberta's photos, she wore the silver and crystal necklace in nearly every one we found of her.

"Must have been a favorite," I mused. None of Lisa's photos showed her hands, so we struck out with an image of the signet ring, but I figured it would be the easiest of the pieces to identify.

"So what did he do with the other trophies?" I wondered, leaning back in my chair. "Are there other people out there who've been wearing his sick prizes for decades—and is he going to try to kill them next?"

"What if he's not after the trophies?" Teag questioned. "What if he's back for revenge against the people who didn't let him get his way?"

I chewed my lip as I thought about that. "So Sophie died because she rebuffed his advances. But what about Ann? And Edna died of a heart attack—but could it have been caused by seeing a ghost she thought she had bound in a rug for all eternity?"

Teag went back to work and let out a low whistle. "So we knew Ann was Edna's sister, right? But according to her obituary, she was preceded in death by a husband, Vincent, and one son, Steven, who was declared dead in 2005."

"Declared dead?" I echoed. "As in, missing for seven years and then pronounced 'legally dead' as opposed to finding-a-body-dead?"

Teag nodded, and I searched for the name Steven Delarue. "Hey, here it is. A notice in the paper back in 1997 about him going missing, asking for anyone with information to contact the police. And then another notice, from 2005, declaring him dead. There's an obituary, but it's really short." I stared at the photograph that went with the obit, a smiling young man in his early twenties, although something about the look in his eyes made me cringe.

"So Steven went missing the same year as the Smiley Killer attacks," Teag mused. "Is there a date for when he disappeared?"

I shook my head. "More likely to be in the police files."

Teag did a little more hacking and came up looking queasy. "The last Smiley Killer attack happened in August of 1997. Steven was reported missing at the end of September. So he vanished after the killings stopped. Shit, Cassidy... I know this is far-fetched, but you don't think he could be the one Edna..."

I fidgeted with a pen as I thought. "Let's think it through. *Reported* missing," I repeated. "Which means if he was the Smiley Killer, and if someone got rid of him, they could have done it any time after the last murder and waited a bit to report him missing to blur the connection." I sighed. "I'm thinking your idea isn't so crazy. Edna helping her sister, Ann by trapping him somehow in that rug is looking more and more likely," I said.

"Last time, all the Smiley Killer's victims were women under thirty," Teag said, tapping his finger on the table as he thought. "But if Ann was his mother, she was much older, and if he stalked Sophie, she was probably around his age back then, so she had to be around fifty now."

"Another break in the pattern," I replied. "Which looks more like taking revenge than going on a new spree."

Just then, a text from Kell drew my attention. "Shit," I muttered. "Check the news. There's another murder."

Teag streamed the local news channel, just in time to catch the end of the coverage. "Authorities have identified the victim as Vernon Walker, age sixty-five. Police have not released details, but they say they are treating the death as a homicide." The picture of the man on the screen behind the news anchor showed a man with a fringe of gray hair around a bald pate. He had a stubborn set to his jaw and intelligent eyes, but a hard glint made me think he wasn't the trusting sort.

I met Teag's gaze. "He's never killed men before," I said. "Breaking pattern again. Why?"

Teag went back to his computer. "Oh, hell," he murmured. I came around to peer at the screen. "He was the lead detective on the Smiley Killer case," he said. The search results showed a series of commendations and accolades, plus charity involvement after his retirement. Teag's cursor hovered over an old headshot that showed Walker in his forties, probably around the time of the killings.

He looked up at me, and I saw that he had paled. "I've seen him before, Cassidy. That dream I told you about? The one I've had since I was a kid? This is one of the two men who keep asking me what I saw."

I swore under my breath. "How is that possible? Wouldn't you remember it if you had witnessed a serial killer at work?"

Teag stood and began to pace, running his hands through his hair. "I would have been seven years old," he said. "How much do you remember from when you were seven?"

"I think I'd remember a murder."

Teag's expressions and gestures made me think he was carrying on a lively conversation with himself. "Maybe. If you knew that's what it was. But what if you didn't really see much? What if you didn't know what was going on? Suppose they wanted to know if I'd seen someone in an alley, or leaving a building. It wouldn't mean anything to me, wouldn't be the same as having seen a dead body or actually seen someone die. It would be scary because strangers kept asking questions I couldn't answer."

"Who was the other man?"

Teag looked up at me, eyes wide and a little panicky. "I don't know. A cop, maybe? Another detective? That was twenty years ago. He could have moved away, died from natural causes."

"If he's still in Charleston, he's a prime target," I said. "And maybe you are, too."

Teag dropped into a chair as the realization sank in. "There's nothing to say I told the detective anything useful," he said, and I could tell he was breathing fast. "Just because I got scared over being questioned doesn't mean I actually knew anything."

He dove for his computer, and I guessed he was hacking back into the police records. We sat together in silence as his fingers flew over the keyboard, and then he sat back with a sound like he'd been punched in the gut.

"What?"

"Detective Walker interviewed T.L., a boy who was waiting for a school bus near the alley where Roberta Warde's body was found, close to the estimated time of the murder. He saw nothing," Teag read from the report.

"But does the Smiley Killer know you didn't set the cops on him?"

Teag rested his head in his hands, elbows on the table. "I don't know. The detective didn't even catch Steven."

"Maybe Walker was closer to finding the killer than he thought," I said. "Maybe Steven was afraid of getting caught, but Ann and Edna trapped him in the rug before Walker caught up to him."

"What do I tell Anthony?" He asked, not raising his head. Teag's voice was wrecked. "I've got to tell him. He'll want to tell the cops, but they won't believe us. Hell, they'll think it's suspicious that we know so much, probably think we're in on it."

"Let's take things a step at a time," I said. "Sorren should be here soon. We'll try to destroy Sophie's brooch, and see if that damages the ghost. And if we have to, Sorren can probably steal the rings they found with Ann and Sophie from the evidence room."

"There are three other missing pieces of jewelry, Cassidy," Teag argued, his voice rising. "We don't even know where they are. If he gave them away, they could be anywhere."

I shook my head. "I doubt he gave one to the detective," I said. "But it would be interesting to see if they found one of Walker's own pieces near the body."

"I'll check later. It's probably not written up yet."

"I think the other pieces are somewhere here in Charleston," I said. "Call it intuition. I wish we could get Alicia to question Ann's and Sophie's ghosts."

"You heard what she said. Asking a medium to poke around a case where the serial killer is a ghost is just asking for trouble," Teag countered.

"I know. And I agree. It just feels like we're missing something."

"We've got to stop him, Cassidy," Teag said. "Right now, he's killing the people who tried to trap him, but if he succeeds, what's to stop him from going on another binge? And the police won't be able to do anything because he's a ghost." His gaze was intent. "We're the only ones who can."

∼

Sorren showed up right after sunset and listened with a grave expression as we recounted what we had discovered. "I think we need to destroy the mementos," he said when we finished our story. "If the trophies all still exist, then he's probably using them as anchors, and each one we destroy weakens his hold."

"Like a Horcrux?" I asked. Teag snorted. I didn't expect Sorren to get the reference, but he did.

"A little, only in Steven's case, an unintentional anchor. I doubt he planned on ending up disembodied," Sorren replied with a wan smile. "The fact that he took the pieces as trophies implies a strong emotional connection. Let's deal with the one we have, and I'll see if Rowan and I can't get the other piece away from the police." Rowan is a witch who's helped us out on more than one occasion. She and Sorren together probably wouldn't have much of a problem stealing the ring back, or at least, not compared to the odds for Teag and me.

"How do we do it?" Teag asked, lifting his head and straightening his spine. I knew he was frightened, but he wasn't going to let that stop him.

"I've heard volcanos work well on cursed rings," I replied.

Teag rolled his eyes. "We don't have a volcano handy. But I've got a friend with a pottery kiln. They get pretty hot. And at least the pin is just costume jewelry. It should melt pretty easily."

"And how do we explain that we need to borrow his kiln to melt a pin? Not suspicious at all," I replied. "What about a bonfire?"

"Not exactly stealthy," Teag countered. "What about a welding torch?"

Sorren nodded. "That could work."

"My dad has one in his garage," Teag said. "He showed me how to use it back when I took a shop class one summer to help him work on the cars he likes to tinker with. And even better—he and my mom are on vacation, so no awkward explanations."

Which is how we ended up in my car heading toward Goose Creek just outside of Charleston. I drove, and Teag rode shotgun, armed with an actual shotgun which was just beneath his seat, with shells filled with rock salt, a tactic Kell picked up from something he'd seen on TV.

If it worked, I didn't care who thought of it. Sorren was in the back-seat. We stashed the brooch in the back in its own lead box, to mask its resonance from my magic.

Just in case, we brought canisters of salt and a couple of iron crow-bars, since both salt and iron play merry hell with ghosts. I had several protective charms, my athame and the old dog collar that summons my ghostly protector, my late Golden Retriever, Bo. Teag had holy water and a silver-soaked rope net in his bag. Sorren carried an old iron dagger, but his biggest weapons were his speed, strength, and vampire resistance to ghostly mojo. With any luck, we'd pull the plug on Steven the serial killer's rampage before he knew what was happening.

Teag's parents lived out in the country, down a long lane off the secondary highway. I pulled into the driveway, backing in, so the hatch faced the detached garage that served as his father's workshop. A secu-rity light overhead glowed brightly.

"No neighbors close by," Teag said. "So we don't have to worry about anyone seeing us, although it wouldn't be the first time I've come by to borrow a few tools. I have a key."

That meant we didn't have to worry about turning on lights, although Sorren did lock the door behind us, just in case. Teag went to get the propane torch and returned with a welder's apron and mask plus fire-proof gloves. He also brought an old cast iron frying pan.

"Dad uses the pan for small welding jobs. We'll take it with us when we're done—in case crazy ghost cooties linger—and I'll buy him a new one," Teag said.

"Get what you need," Sorren said. We'll set the wardings." Teag set up the welder while Sorren and I put down a circle of salt and iron filings to keep ghosts at bay. We made the circle large enough to give Teag space to work and still have room for Sorren and me inside the warding.

Outside, the wind picked up. I felt the hair on the back of my neck prickle. Teag pulled on the protective apron and welder's mask, holding the welder's wand in one gloved hand as he readied to turn on the power with the other.

"Don't look at the arc while I'm working," Teag warned. "It can damage your eyes. That's why I've got the mask."

Sorren and I turned our backs, watching the shed for any sign that Steven had somehow guessed our whereabouts. I had a bad feeling, and as the shutters began to bang against the outside of the garage—on a night that had been still—my sense of foreboding grew stronger. From the way Sorren held himself, ready for a fight, I knew he picked up on the same uneasiness.

The welder hissed, and I felt the heat on my back, although Teag hunched several feet away. "Here we go," he warned us, and I knew without looking he lowered the flame to the brooch.

A sudden gale-force wind rocked the garage, ripping shutters free from their moorings and howling around the small building. An inhuman force pounded on the door until I was sure the wood would splinter or the lock would break. The howl of the wind rose to a banshee screech, and I heard shingles rip free from the roof.

"Almost done," Teag said through gritted teeth.

Three large trees stood close enough to the garage that the unnatural wind lashed the building with their branches. I wondered whether any other houses in the area were also being assaulted with the ghostly temper tantrum, or whether Steven reserved his strength for us alone.

"There it goes!" Teag called out in triumph, though we could barely hear him over the wind. The hiss of the welder stopped, and I turned to congratulate him just as a deafening boom sounded overhead and the roof came down on us.

For a moment, my head rang as if a thunderclap sounded right next to my ear. I staggered, in pain and disoriented, and then Sorren pulled me down and jerked Teag forward, throwing himself over both of us as the ceiling collapsed.

"We're easy prey here," Sorren said when the last of the roof had fallen around us. "We need to get to your car. I don't think the ghost can keep up this level of energy for long."

"Got a plan?"

"Teag takes the shotgun with the salt rounds. Cassidy—call your dog and use your athame. I'll go after the ghost with iron." Sorren paused. "Are you injured?"

"Had the wind knocked out of me and I can't hear much, but otherwise okay," I assured him.

"Same here," Teag agreed.

I lifted my head and saw that the door still stood open and beyond it, I could see my RAV4 looking mostly untouched. Already, Steven's attacks waned as he depleted his energy. The wind no longer howled as loudly, and the bits of roof still overhead appeared likely to remain so.

Sorren shifted his weight off of us, allowing Teag and me to get our feet under us. "I'll meet you at the car. Get in the passenger side; I'll drive. Go!" He hissed, and sprinted to the largely intact rear of the garage, grabbing a crowbar from the workbench and pulling the iron knife from his belt. I shook the dog collar that wrapped around my left wrist, and a large, spectral dog appeared beside me. Teag put the cast iron skillet under his arm as he loaded the shells, and together we broke from cover and ran.

The ghost of a young man popped up between us and the car, blocking our way. His eyes blazed with rage and madness, and his mouth opened in a feral howl. Even so, I recognized Steven Delarue from his obituary photo. We were the Smiley Killer's next target.

Teag couldn't get in a shot without blowing out the windows on the RAV, but Bo's ghost leaped for Steven, ninety pounds of pissed-off poltergeist, teeth snapping. Steven vanished, but Bo remained on guard, hackles raised.

"Cassidy! Behind you!" Teag shouted. Before I could turn, I felt a whoosh of air and heard metal clang.

"Get in the damn car!" Sorren yelled.

We ran, as the wind picked up again, hurling chunks of gravel from the driveway. Teag got off a shot in the direction the wind was coming from, and immediately the air stilled. I jerked open the rear door of the RAV. "Get in," I yelled. "Cover yourself with the net."

Before I could slam the door, Steve was practically in my face, ghostly hands outstretched. I fit his victim preference, and he had me pinned between him and the car.

I threw a handful of salt with my left hand, and brought my athame up in my right, blasting him with cold power. Bo snarled and lunged, sinking spectral teeth into Steven's leg.

The ghost flashed and disappeared, and I scrambled to the passenger door, heart pounding so hard I could barely breathe. I threw myself into the car just as Sorren slammed in from the other side. We were moving almost immediately, as Steven lunged at the car, ripping long gouges in the hood as if he had clawed the metal with his fingertips.

"Teag, stay down and under the net," Sorren ordered. "Cassidy— any time you want to take some shots to clear the road, be my guest."

I rolled down the window, angled the shotgun and pulled the trigger, sending the blast out in front of us. A hail of rock salt hit the hood, but Steve's ghost vanished.

"He's losing strength." Each time he came back, the vengeful spirit appeared less solid.

"Destroying the brooch hurt him," Sorren said, his inhuman reflexes serving well as Steven appeared right in front of us. Sorren dodged, and the ghost blocked us again, but each appearance grew fainter. I wasn't sure Steven had enough juice to actually hurt us, but I didn't want to find out for sure.

I racked the shells again, and this blast took Steven through the chest. The ghost flickered and disappeared, and this time, he did not come back. "How long do you think that'll keep him down?" I asked, my heart thudding like I'd been on a rollercoaster.

"No idea," Sorren replied grimly. "But we're coming up on the main road, so you'd better hide the gun."

Good thinking. I tucked the shotgun under the front seat and rolled up my window, then patted the dog collar, sending a silent "good dog" to Bo's ghost, wherever he went between appearances. I hoped his afterlife included plenty of puppy biscuits.

"You okay back there?" I called to Teag, never taking my eyes off the road around us and the shadows along the sides.

"I'm in one piece," Teag replied. "Think I'm gonna have bruises from where some of the roof came down, but nothing's broken."

I glanced at Sorren, knowing he had taken the brunt of the fallout. He had dust and splinters in his hair and a gash over one temple that practically healed as I watched. Otherwise, he looked unharmed, although I felt certain that without his protection, Teag and I both would have been seriously injured. I also sent up a prayer of thanks that he adapted with the times as he drove us to safety.

"Thanks," I said.

He shrugged. "You're welcome. Healing quickly has its benefits."

"What now?" Teag asked, still staying down and under the salted rope net.

"If it's all right with both of you, I'd like to take you back to Cassidy's house. It's more thoroughly warded than yours, something I intend to rectify shortly," Sorren replied. Anthony had only recently come into full knowledge of what we really do, and so fully protecting the house would have raised difficult questions. Now, he'd be grateful for the added security, but that would have to wait until the current crisis was over.

"Is it okay if Anthony comes to your place, too?" Teag asked, just as I opened my mouth to make the offer. "I'd feel better knowing he's safe."

"I suspect Kell is going to show up as well," I said, and the thought warmed me. Kell might not have magic, but he stood his ground in front of forces that had sent others away screaming. "Maggie's probably already there. I don't imagine she left after she fed Baxter, and if we're lucky, she's got food waiting for us."

I thought about suggesting we pick up Anthony on the way but then changed my mind. He's a lawyer, and I didn't want to compromise him if anyone caught us with weapons and a bag of questionable relics and supplies.

We must have worn Steven out because he didn't appear again, although Sorren and I stayed on alert until we pulled in beside my house. It's on-street parking, but I had a friend put a distraction spell on the spot by my door, so other people don't notice it's open. It helps when we come back bloody to not have to circle the block for parking.

We hustled Teag inside, and as soon as we crossed the wardings, I felt my shoulders relax. Baxter heard us coming and barked up a storm, a six-pound ball of attitude. Sorren gave him a look, and Bax quieted immediately. Glamoring a dog to make him stop barking doesn't seem fair, but it works.

Maggie met us at the door. "Are you all right?" She asked, taking in the three of us in her question.

"Yeah. For now," I replied.

Teag's phone rang, and he reached for it. "Anthony," he mouthed. His partner didn't wait for a hello. Even though the phone wasn't on speaker, Anthony was loud enough for me to hear.

"Teag! Where are you? And why are there police here asking about the Smiley Killer? What's going on? They want to take you into protective custody."

Teag paled. "Oh, God. Has there been another death?"

"Teag, you're freaking me out," Anthony warned. "And yes, they found another body. One of the cops from the original investigation."

Teag choked. "The blond," he stammered and met my eyes. I knew what he meant. His dream-memory had two men asking questions. Now, both were dead.

"Teag?"

Teag swallowed hard and pulled himself together. "Tell the cops I'm safe for now and decline protective custody. Then get a bag together for both of us. Sorren will be by as soon as he can get over there, in Cassidy's car."

"Where—"

"Don't ask, and you can't tell," Teag warned, but I felt sure Anthony could figure it out. We've used my place as a safe house before.

"And if they won't take no for an answer?"

"You're a lawyer. I'm a witness, not a suspect. If they're not going to arrest me, they have to let me walk. Besides, you can tell them honestly, you don't know where I am."

After a moment of silence, Anthony spoke again. "All right. But I want to know what the hell is going on."

"I'll tell you everything. I promise. Just… get here. I need to know you're safe," Teag begged, and I could see the strain of the last few days in his face. He ended the call and sagged against the arm of my couch. Sorren was already out the door, heading for the car.

"Come in the kitchen," Maggie said. "I've got coffee on, and I figured you wouldn't mind if I made pizza rolls and cookies. I had a feeling it might be a late night."

I hugged her. "You're the best."

She grinned. "Damned straight." In one move, she scooped up Baxter and deposited him in Teag's arms. "Here. Hold him. He's a therapy dog. Then come sit down before you fall down. I want to hear all about it, but I figure I can wait until Anthony and Kell get here, so you don't have to go through it twice."

My head snapped up. "Kell's coming?"

She nodded. "Yep. Called right before you got here, said he's on his way with 'supplies' and information."

"Then pass me a cookie, and let's wait for the reinforcements to arrive," I said, as Baxter snuggled into Teag's arms and Maggie poured coffee for all of us.

MEMORY REMAINS

K ELL ARRIVED FIRST, WITH A DUFFLE BAG SLUNG OVER HIS SHOULDER
that I felt sure included his ghost hunting equipment as well as salt, an
iron blade or two, and a shotgun with rock salt rounds.

"The new deaths have something to do with the Smiley Killer," he
said after he hugged me tight and kissed me hard enough to let me
know he'd been worried about me.

"Afraid so," I said, taking his hand and drawing him into the
kitchen where Teag and Maggie—and Baxter—still waited.

"The victims' ghosts are really active," Kell said, and I frowned as
I realized he sported a freshly blacked eye. He noticed my gaze and
looked chagrined. "Yeah, I got clocked by a flying trash can lid. She
was trying to get my attention."

"Didn't know her own strength?" I asked, glad he hadn't been seriously injured.

"They often don't," he replied, meaning ghosts. "You know, the
team and I went looking for the ghosts of the Smiley Killer's victims a
couple of years ago, and didn't find anything. We thought maybe
they'd moved on. After all, not everyone who dies violently sticks
around as a haunting."

"Which is a good thing or Charleston would be shoulder to shoulder with spooks, as if we aren't already," I muttered.

"Isn't that the truth," he said. "But then when the new killer's first victim was found, we started hearing about hauntings—strong manifestations—showing up where nothing had registered before. I'd forgotten about the last time, but the spots looked familiar, and that's when I realized what was going on—plus the 'artwork' the ghosts drew."

"Other than making a ruckus and throwing trash can lids, did the ghosts try to send a message?" I sipped my coffee and wolfed down a cookie, needing a sugar and caffeine boost.

"You saw the smiley one ghost drew on the glass. Then the ghost of Kelly Atkins wrote 'him' in the condensation on a window near where her body was found," Kell said. "And after Lisa Wentworth's ghost threw pebbles at us, we found two eyes and a smile drawn in the dirt."

"Yikes," Maggie said, scooting her chair a little closer.

"I thought that meant that the killer had come back—alive. And then a friend who works at the morgue told me the new vics were found inside locked rooms." He grimaced. "Of course, the cops wouldn't have let me get anywhere near the crime scenes, but even from out on the sidewalk, the meter pegged," he added.

I knew what he meant. His EMF reader picked up the energy frequencies ghosts gave off, and strong readings meant a spook with mojo.

"How did you figure that meant Teag and I were involved?"

Kell gave me an "oh, please" look and rolled his eyes. "Whenever this kind of shit hits the fan, there's usually a connection."

Just then, I heard Sorren and Anthony come in the front door. With the wardings on the house, strangers can't get through the sidewalk door to the porch without me with them. The list of who can enter on their own is very short. As Anthony headed for Teag, Sorren pulled me aside.

"I'm going to go get those other items," he said, giving me a meaningful look. "I'll be back as quickly as I can. I'll take care of the skillet and residue while I'm out."

I knew he meant to "liberate" the piece of trophy jewelry from the police department, as well as anything that had been found with the other bodies. "You might also want to get the remains of the rug he was trapped in from the museum. It's in the safe. Watch your step," I cautioned.

Sorren tilted his head and gave me a rakish smile. "Remember who you're talking to, and what I used to be," he replied and slipped out the doorway. Maybe the opportunity was catnip for a former jewel thief. He actually looked excited.

"Teag." Anthony pulled Teag into his arms and held him close. Teag winced, and Anthony let go, immediately worried. "You're hurt."

"Just bruised. Could have been a lot worse," he said, although I could see from the look on Anthony's face that didn't do much to dispel his concerns.

Anthony stretched up to kiss him on the cheek and took his hand to pull him into the kitchen. Kell slid back to make room at the table and slipped an arm around my shoulders when I came to sit next to him.

"Fill me in," Anthony said. "Start from the beginning."

Kell and Anthony listened as Teag and I took turns explaining what was going on. I omitted anything legally incriminating for Anthony's sake, or that gave away too much about the Alliance or Sorren since Kell still wasn't in on that secret.

Anthony ran a hand down over his face. "Shit. So you've already destroyed evidence—for a good cause, but try explaining that to a judge. And you've actually identified the Smiley Killer, which even the FBI didn't manage to do. Plus you know what made him disappear. I don't know if weaving someone into a rug counts as kidnapping, but it's got to be illegal. And you know the identity of the 'new' killer, but the cops would never believe you. Oh, and then there's the part where you're actually in more danger than the cops already think you are, but you've declined protective custody!" His voice rose throughout his recap, and he looked overwhelmed and a little panicked.

"Yes, to all that," Teag said, reaching to grasp both of Anthony's hands in his own. "But Anthony, think about it. We can actually stop him—this time for good. Weaving him into a rug bound him, but didn't destroy him. We can finish him, send him on to hell, and he won't hurt anyone ever again."

"He knows who you are. The fucking Smiley Killer knows who you are," Anthony replied, his voice unsteady with worry. "How do you fight a serial killer ghost?"

Teag's smile was brave and gentle. "It's what we do," he said quietly. "We'll fix this. I promise."

"If I thought there was anything the cops could do—that they'd even believe—I'd insist you turn yourself in," Anthony chided. "But this is out of their ballpark. Hell, it's certainly beyond anything I learned in law school."

"Trust us, we're the professionals," Teag said with a wan smile. Anthony's grip tightened on his hands.

"I do. You know that. But I also want you safe. All of you," Anthony said, looking me first, and then to Kell and Maggie. If he registered that Sorren was gone, he didn't question it or perhaps decided it was better not to know.

"Cassidy, when this all settles down, I think you and I need to have a talk... but for now, we'll just leave it. There's something else you need to know," Kell said, giving my shoulder a squeeze and then leaning forward. He clasped one of my hands in his as he rested his elbows on his knees. "That school we went to the night we checked those hauntings—the abandoned one? I think it's got something to do with this."

I felt a knot in my stomach. There was too much that was happening and that had just been discussed for Kell to brush off why Teag and I were so involved. But like he said, that was a problem for later. I consoled myself with the thought if it went bad, Soren could glamor him. Sadly, that just made me feel worse.

Kell let go of my hand and pulled a piece of paper from his messenger bag, spreading it out on the kitchen table. It showed a map of part of the downtown, with five red dots, and one larger dot in the middle.

"These," he said, pointing to the small dots, "are where the Smiley Killer's original victims were found. "Now look at this." He pulled out a pen and connected the dots into a circle, drawing lines into the larger dot at the center like the hub and spokes of a wheel. "I don't know what it means, but it's too much of a coincidence to overlook," he said. "Butler Middle School is the dot in the center. Something about that old school got juiced up, just like the ghosts of the victims. There's got to be a connection."

Teag grabbed his backpack and pulled out his laptop, setting it up quickly on the table. He started typing, and I noticed that Anthony stayed where he was, rubbing Teag's shoulders and making no effort to see the screen. *Plausible deniability,* I guessed.

When Teag looked up, his face held a haunted expression. "In the mid-Eighties, two kids who attended that middle school went missing and were later found dead. Murdered. Police wondered if the deaths had anything to do with the dead cats and dogs they found every few months behind the school's dumpsters."

I felt sick. "Steven Delarue was twenty-five when he disappeared, in 1997. He'd have been in middle school in the mid-eighties."

"Want to bet Steven lived near there when he was in school and started his career a little earlier than the cops gave him credit for?" Teag asked. We both knew serial killers often abused other children or animals early in life, before working up to the main event. Family sometimes covered up for them, hoping for a cure, or the crimes were never linked to the actual perpetrator.

"You need to send that son of a bitch straight to hell," Maggie said, blunt even for her, but none of us disagreed.

"You think his victims are haunting the school?" Anthony asked.

Teag and I exchanged a glance. "I think it's a pretty good bet that's where Steven stashed the missing trophy items he stole from his known victims—and probably things he took from the others as well," I said.

"What good does it do us knowing this?" Anthony asked.

Teag met his gaze. "We have to destroy what's anchoring the spirit here, what he remained so connected to that he could return from being bound in the rug. It's got to be missing trophy items. Destroy the trophies, and we break his link."

"That's illegal—and all kinds of crazy," Anthony protested.

Teag shrugged. "The cops can't use evidence against a ghost. It's not like he can stand trial. But we can stop the murders. On the whole, not a bad trade for some costume jewelry, don't you think?"

"We need to get back in there and find the trophies," Kell replied.

"Not we," I corrected.

Kell stood his ground. "You need my help, Cassidy. Teag's got to stay inside the wardings, here with Anthony and Maggie. I'm not letting you go on your own. I may not be in your league but I 'know' ghosts and don't freak easily."

Teag moved to argue, but Anthony put a firm hand on his shoulder and stared him down, the look on his face resolute. "The ghost has already tried to kill you. Even the police know you're in danger. You can't go marching into its lair," Anthony said. "Your magic can't directly help, and if it links you to the weaver who trapped him, it'll go even worse. If this thing is as smart as you all seem to believe, it'll use you against each other, and that puts Cassidy and Sorren—"

"And me," Kell said defiantly.

"—and Kell in danger," Anthony said. He met Teag's eyes and lifted a hand to touch his cheek. "Please, babe. Let them handle this one. Maybe you can be the surveillance guy giving them intel over a headset, like in the movies. Sit this out. For me. Please."

I could see the struggle in Teag's face, and I knew he didn't want to leave the fighting to the rest of us. "He's right," I said. "And you know it."

"But—"

"I'll get on my knees and beg if it makes a difference," Anthony said.

I couldn't help but smile at Teag's reaction and knew at least one problem was solved.

"I just bought motion cameras like the snowboarders wear for my SPOOK team," Kell interrupted. "We adjusted them for low light. I've got my laptop with me—the video feed is already set up, and so is the audio for the earpieces we wear. Cassidy and I will go in wired, and that way, you guys can see and hear everything and guide us."

I raised an eyebrow, asking a silent question. Teag chuffed out a long sigh and nodded. "Okay. I get it. But I don't have to like it."

Anthony leaned over and kissed him. Then he turned to look at Kell and me. "Come back safely. That's not negotiable."

"What he said," Maggie added, crossing her arms over her chest and fixing me with a glare.

"We'll be careful. And we'll be back before you know it," I said, although from the look Teag gave me, I felt sure he also knew I was lying.

Kell set up his ghost hunting computer and readied the cameras and microphones. Teag only needed a quick primer to figure out the system, and he donned his own headset, ready for the night's work.

"Anything else you can tell us about the murders in the Eighties to help us identify the trophies if we find them?" I asked.

Anthony moved off to get more coffee and lingered with his back to the table while Teag dug around on the police server. "Kevin Robart, age eleven. They found his bike near the school, and his body two days later by the dumpsters. Looks like he was missing a baseball cap he always wore. His dad gave it to him before he died in a car wreck. Kid wouldn't have lost it or left it behind."

"Damn," I swore under my breath. Details would help us put an end to the killer, but they made the victims far too real.

"Connie Strand, age ten. Disappeared on her way home from school. She was missing a charm bracelet with an angel on it. Never took it off—present from her grandma."

"Anything else?" I asked, my voice thick.

"Give me a sec; I'm looking at the murders from 1987 to 1996," Teag replied. "Crap. Charleston isn't New York City, but there are still enough reports, this is going to take some time. But I bet there will be at least a few unsolved killings that might not fit the wound profile but are missing items with sentimental value."

"The school closed in 1990 when a new building opened to replace it. I guess the old school got too expensive to repair," Kell said. "If we knew where Steven went to high school, you might find a link to more victims."

"Whatever we find, we'll salt and burn," I said. "That will release Steven's anchor, and should make it possible for any trapped ghosts to find peace, too."

Anthony's jaw tightened. I knew he was thinking about the possibility of closure for the families who had gone so long without knowing who killed their loved ones. But even Anthony had to recognize the impossibility of convincing the police of the truth. At best, they'd disregard the information. At worst, we'd find ourselves locked up as accomplices.

"Maybe when this is all over, an anonymous tip could point the finger in Steven Delarue's direction, and suggest police take a fresh look at the earlier murders," I said. If anyone would know how to make that happen without being traceable, it would be Teag and Sorren.

Anthony gave a curt nod. "All right. That'll do."

Sorren returned without fanfare at some point during the discussion. He gave me a look, and I knew he had gotten hold of the missing trophy items and the damaged rug. By now, it was after eleven o'clock, plenty late to skulk around an abandoned school without attracting undue attention.

"Let's go," I said, standing. Kell stood with me, and I expected a protest from Sorren, but he turned instead to Teag, Anthony, and Maggie.

"Whatever you see on your cameras or hear on your audio, whatever happens, do not leave this house," Sorren warned. I wondered if he would go so far as to use some of his vampire mojo on Anthony and Maggie to make sure they did as he said. Teag was probably immune, and I knew for sure that not only did my family's long acquaintance make me able to meet his gaze without being glamored, but I had Sorren's word that he would never abuse my trust like that.

Baxter, it seemed, fell outside that understanding.

SORREN, KELL, AND I didn't talk as we headed for the old school. I drove this time, and Kell rode shotgun. Sorren sat in the back, watching for any sign that either police or vengeful ghosts pursued us. As urgent as our mission was, I kept to the speed limit, having no desire to explain the small occult arsenal in the gear bags in the back or the strange damage to my SUV.

I'd brought my athame and walking stick, along with plenty of protection charms and Bo's dog collar. The bag held more than enough salt and lighter fluid, plus holy water and iron filings. A couple of iron knives would help keep ghosts at bay, and the crowbars not only were good against spirits but helpful if we had to do a little demolition to find the missing trophy items. We also brought a portable propane torch that Sorren picked up when he was out, to melt or burn whatever trophies we might find. Sorren had slipped the signet ring and other mementos he stole from the evidence room into a lead box along with what remained of the damaged rug. Kell carried the bag, keeping a flashlight in one hand and his shotgun in the other.

Kell and I dutifully put on our hats with the action cams and hooked up the earpiece microphones. "Do you copy?" Kell asked, and I felt like I'd been dropped into *Mission: Impossible.*

"Yeah, I copy," Teag replied. We'd all watched enough movies to know not to use names. "Good luck. Give him hell. He deserves it."

"Will do," I said. "You have the floor plans?"

"Roger," Teag answered, getting into the spirit. "Hate to go all Freddy Krueger, but I'm thinking the basement is the best bet."

"Seems logical. We'll head there first." I paused. "If this goes badly, you know how to reach Archibald, right?" Archibald Donnelly headed up the Briggs Society, one of our Alliance allies. Donnelly was a powerful necromancer, and while I hoped we didn't need his help, I knew he'd settle the matter permanently.

"Got it. Not planning to need it," Teag said, and he knew he projected more confidence than he felt. "Go get 'em."

We went radio silent then until Sorren picked the lock on the back door. Kell glanced at me with a raised eyebrow, and I shrugged. Tomorrow, I'd have to explain and answer some tough questions, but right now, we had a job to do.

The old building looked just like I remembered my own middle school, with painted cement block walls, doors with window panels opening into classrooms, and ugly beige floor tiles. No one had bothered to rip down the posters on the walls before the lights went out for the last time. The drama department announced an upcoming play that opened nearly thirty years ago, the football team urged school spirit, and a fundraiser offered cheap donuts to help support the band. Once lively posters hung askew, faded and mildewed.

Kell supplied us with night vision goggles, courtesy of SPOOK, and he pulled his EMF reader from his pocket. "Nothing nearby," he muttered, keeping his voice down although we were alone.

I stretched out my magic. When resonance is strong enough, I've picked up vibes through the soles of my shoes. Now, I felt a vague restlessness, but nothing nearby or imminently dangerous. Still, the back of my neck prickled, and all of my intuition told me to leave and never come back.

"You came in by the rear student entrance," Teag said in my ear. "Stay on the first floor, and look for the gymnasium. The doors to the half-basement and mechanical rooms are near there." Charleston has a high water table, so true basements are few and far between. More common was a half-basement that was only partially underground, and then rose several feet above ground as well, which also provided some protection against flooding for the main floor.

I thought about the young teens who had gone to school here, the ones who would have known Steven and his victims. They'd be in their forties now, with families and careers of their own, most likely. Except for the ones whose future had been stolen from them, snatched away before they even had a chance to grow up. The thought made me angry, hardening my resolve to see this through.

We found the door on the lower level to the boiler room. No one had bothered to lock it. I'd have chalked that up to the need for whoever owned the place to check on the mechanical room now and again, only it didn't look like anyone had been in here since the last car left the parking lot when the school shut down. That made me wonder. Had the building just been mothballed, or did the owners try to sell it, only to fail for reasons far more supernatural than structural. I bet on the latter.

"Lights don't work," Kell muttered, trying the switch. The windows at ground level had been boarded up, so no daylight came in from them. Sorren went down the steps first, since he could see in the dark, and he's tougher to kill. I insisted on going next, which left Kell to watch our backs.

The boiler room smelled dank and musty, and as our flashlights illuminated the cement block room, we could see a thick layer of undisturbed dust, confirmation that nobody had come down here for a long time. Kell and I both had powerful wide-beam flashlights, and we did a first sweep, Sorren still on point, but the half-basement remained silent. Almost too still.

"Any ideas where the items might be?" I murmured into my mic.

"You know the drill," Teag replied. "Look for places he could open and close that wouldn't draw attention. Behind a loose brick, on top of a beam, under something he could move."

The temperature felt colder as we ventured deeper into the basement. I jangled the dog collar on my wrist, and Bo's ghost materialized next to me, with the same happy doggy smile I loved when he was alive. I gripped my athame in my right hand and my heavy industrial flashlight in the other.

"See anything?" I asked Kell and Sorren.

"Lots of things; none of which I want to touch," Kell replied. We'd worn gloves, for that very reason. I'd heard Kell and Ryan trade too many stories about spider bites, rusty nails, or other hazards of abandoned buildings, and I had no desire to get lockjaw or worse.

"Want to check your meter? I'll cover you," I offered. Kell slipped his shotgun over his shoulder and pulled out the EMF reader, as I kept watch. Sorren moved along the perimeter, examining a stack of concrete blocks. One wall had a dark spread of black slime I didn't want to go near, and two of the walls were largely hidden from view behind huge boilers, thick pipes, and the massive furnace. Tools lay scattered as if the shutdown crew knew no one would be checking up on them.

"I'm picking up some activity, getting stronger the farther in we go," Kell observed as the small box in his hands whined.

"Any particular direction?" I asked. Just then, I felt a cat slide against my leg, and I jumped. When I looked down, the floor around me was empty.

"Cassidy?" Kell asked.

"Nothing. Thought I felt something."

Sorren moved around the equipment, putting himself in the most vulnerable position where visibility was limited. We followed, trying to keep him in view to cover him as well since we knew Steven's ghost had enough strength to kill.

"There!" I said, pointing, just as Kell's meter blasted and I heard a warning in my ear from Teag. I saw the faint outline of a young girl dressed in a cartoon t-shirt and leggings materialize to the left of the boilers, barely holding the shape long enough for me to see her.

"Did you—"

"Yeah, that's Connie," Teag said in a choked voice. "I recognize her from the 'missing' posters I found online."

Again something slapped against my right calf, like being hit with a wagging tail. I looked down. Bo stood on my left, nowhere near where I had felt the light smack, but he turned his head curiously as if he had seen something I did not.

"Got something to share with the class?" Kell asked as the meter blipped.

"The animals the police found… I thought I felt a cat rub against me, and just now, a dog tail that wasn't Bo's hit my leg."

Kell muttered curses. "Steven's got it coming," he added.

"There's a block that looks out of place," I said, pointing to where one of the concrete rectangles jutted out from the wall. I set my flashlight aside, slid my athame up my sleeve, and Kell covered me with the shotgun and his light, as my gloved hands coaxed and wiggled at the errant block. "Nothing," I said a few minutes later. "It's mortared in. Just bad masonry."

"There's another one!" Kell's gasp and the blip of the EMF monitor got me up on my feet in a heartbeat, athame drawn and Bo ready to spring. A slightly older boy's ghost regarded us somberly, standing farther back among the tangle of pipes. I didn't need Teag to tell me that was likely to be Kevin, the other missing child that we knew about.

The two ghosts seemed to be leading us into the maze of equipment and conduits, exactly where I had hoped to avoid because the narrow space in between limited our movement and felt like we were being herded down a cattle chute. I tried not to dwell on the fact that in a slaughterhouse, the butcher waited for the cows at the bottom of the chute.

"There's a box here," Sorren said, and I saw his pale hand reach up onto one of the exposed ceiling beams. He doesn't have to worry about spiders or tetanus. Sorren pulled down a dark metal box, and we heard hinges squeal as he pried it open.

"Never mind," he called out. "Just instructions and special keys." He put the box back where he found it, although the lid looked a bit mangled.

I knew from the simultaneous gasps I heard from Kell and Teag that this time, all three of us saw the tabby cat that sauntered over to a grate in the wall and sat down, waiting for us to catch up. Kell's meter beeped, then rose to a high-pitched whine. The cat's image blinked out.

"Let's see what's behind that grate," I muttered. Sorren moved forward and ripped the metal away from the wall. He reached in as I cringed, imagining rats and roaches, and pulled out a dirty cloth bag with a drawstring. I felt my heart in my throat as Sorren loosened the string and dumped out the contents.

Even though I knew what we would find, seeing it made the horrors much more real. A metal brooch in the shape of a "P." A woman's gold signet ring. The crystal necklace. I caught my breath at the other items. Kevin's baseball cap. Connie's charm bracelet. Two other inexpensive necklaces, from victims no one ever linked to the Smiley Killer since they were part of Steven's "practice" runs. And five or six pet collars.

Sorren rose to his feet, wary and tense, looking like the predator he was. "I think he wanted to show us his treasures," Sorren said quietly.

"He wanted to show off. Isn't that right?" He asked the empty boiler room.

Never trust anything that goes too smoothly.

Kell's monitor set off an ear-splitting shriek, and Teag yelled a warning that nearly deafened me. The temperature plummeted and my breath fogged as goosebumps formed on my arms.

Steven Delarue's ghost looked almost solid when Sorren charged toward him. Steven grabbed for Sorren just as Sorren moved in a blur, slicing down with an iron dagger. The ghost vanished, only to materialize once more behind me.

"Cassidy!" Teag warned. I swiveled, sending out a blast of cold force with my athame. The magic seemed to scramble Steven's concentration, making him hesitate just long enough for Bo to launch himself into the air, snapping his teeth closed on Steven's forearm. Again, Steven vanished, and Bo dropped to all fours, hackles raised, growling into the darkness.

Kell had already fallen to his knees beside the trophies, digging out the propane torch and laying down a circle of salt around himself and the sorry pile of stolen keepsakes. Sorren added the garnet ring, Sophie's ring, a man's watch and a man's class ring—from the two dead cops—and the damaged rug to the pile. Bo, Sorren, and I closed ranks, protecting Kell as Steven flickered into existence again, lunging at me this time. I got in another blast with the athame, just as Kell's shotgun sent a salt round past me and right into Steven's chest.

"Maybe that'll hold him for a minute or two," Kell muttered as he set the gun aside and handed me the salt. My hand shook as I made an arc in front of me. Bo's ghost stepped forward, beyond the line, and Sorren finished the rest of the second circle as Kell readied the torch. I sure as hell hoped the old boiler room didn't have a gas leak, or else we'd be ending ourselves as well as the ghost, and sending the building sky high.

The torch hissed, and its blue flame roared to life as Kell pushed welding glasses over his eyes and lowered the fire toward the trophy pieces and the mangled rug. A hideous shriek filled the basement, deafeningly loud, and Steven took shape once more, right in front of me.

The photo in his obituary showed a slightly awkward young man with an unsettling glint in his eyes. The ghost revealed the Smiley Killer, the Steven his victims had seen as they drew their last breaths, the one who made himself feel powerful by causing pain. He raged against the protective barrier of the salt circle, shrieking and wailing his fury, as Bo harried him, nipping at his heels.

"Hurry!" I yelled.

Kell lifted his head as the torch flared. "This stuff isn't a quick burn," he replied. "Just keep him occupied."

"Cassidy, Kell, watch out!" I heard the creak of pipes, and the rending of metal as Teag's warning echoed in my ear. Dust and grit fell as Steven wrested a section of conduit free from its moorings and hurled it toward me.

Sorren moved faster than my eyes could track, sweeping the metal and wires aside and absorbing the force of the blow. But his foot scuffed the protective salt line, and Steven seized the opportunity, grabbing for Sorren while he was off balance and throwing him to one side.

He tackled me, ice cold hands closing around my throat, eyes alight with madness. I thrust my athame deep into his ghostly chest and pulled hard on my power, blowing him apart. Surely the repeated hits of cold force had to have sapped the spirit's strength, I thought. Then again, he'd had twenty years bound into a rug to rest up.

Steven was back before I had fully regained my feet, as Sorren disentangled himself from the mess of torn pipes and ruined machinery he had taken down with him in the force of his fall. Bo chomped down on one of Steven's legs as I slashed and missed with the iron dagger. The power I sent through my athame didn't seem to hold Steven back for long, but it was wearing me down quickly.

Out of the corner of my eye, I saw the flare of the torch and the flames rising as the killer's trophies burned and melted. Steven's ghost came at me again, hands grasping and teeth bared.

The yowl of an angry cat filled the air as two ghostly felines hurtled down onto Steven from the beams overhead. I heard angry barking, and then Bo was not alone in his defense, as three other dogs bit deep into ghostly arms and legs. Kevin and Connie jumped onto

Steven's back, clawing at him with their hands, pummeling with their feet. Steven's ghost staggered backward as Sorren closed in, holding a length of iron rebar he had found somewhere in the debris, and I readied my athame for another blast.

Borne down under the weight of his victims, Steven thrashed but could not free himself as the other ghosts got their long-overdue revenge. Claws and nails shredded his clothing and gouged into his arms, legs, and torso, digging in deeper as the Smiley Killer tried to shake them loose or tear them free.

The flames behind me flared high, and the air smelled of hot metal and burned nylon, with a tang of propane.

"Go to hell, you son of a bitch," Kell snarled, as the last of the trophies shrank down to a blackened pile of slag and ash.

Steven's ghost screamed, a wail of true terror and utter desolation. Flames licked at his body, eating away at him as his outline grew fainter and fainter, and then he vanished.

I kept my athame up, expecting a trick. Sorren had the rebar ready to swing as he moved closer where Kell still knelt over the last flickering flames. Steven did not reappear, though, despite the fire, the basement remained as cold as a walk-in freezer.

The ghostly children stood side by side, staring at me with sad eyes. Spectral dogs and cats wound around their legs, and Bo returned to sit at my feet.

"Go in peace," I murmured, raising a hand in blessing. Kevin gave me a tired smile, acknowledging a long-overdue victory, and took Connie's hand. Abruptly, the ghosts disappeared, and with them the frigid cold.

"What do you want to do about the ashes?" Kell said as he turned off the torch and sat back on his haunches. Tears tracked down his cheeks, and I knew seeing the stolen belongings of the victims had really rattled him.

"I'll scrape them back into the lead box, and see that they and the frying pan are disposed of properly," Sorren said, as we scattered the evidence of the salt circles. The last thing we needed was someone finally coming down here and starting rumors of a satanic cult.

Kell got to his feet and dusted himself off, reclaiming his shotgun and putting the torch away as Sorren found a flat piece of metal to shovel away the ashes. I slipped up beside Kell and put my arm around his waist, silently supportive, and he rested his cheek on the top of my head, wordlessly accepting the comfort.

"What's going on?" Teag sounded worried, and I realized that my camera-hat had gone askew, giving him a great view of the ceiling.

"We're fine," I reported, righting my cap. "Mission accomplished. Might want to have the place blessed, but that's for another day." Father Anne, our unorthodox Episcopalian priest and frequent ally, would be happy to say a benediction for the murdered children, perhaps back near the area where the bodies had been found. If any of the other of the Smiley Killer's ghosts still lingered, I knew Father Anne would help us send them on to rest.

"So it's over?" Teag asked. "He won't be back?"

I shook my head. "Looked pretty permanent front this end. And the other ghosts flickered out, too. I don't think they'd let go if he was still a threat." I paused. "Anything happen on your side?"

I knew we'd get the full scoop when we got back to my house, but I couldn't resist asking.

"Some freaky wind gusts and a power outage—I think you-know-who was throwing a tantrum," Teag replied. "And then all of a sudden, the lights came on, and the wind died down—guess he realized he had bigger fish to fry."

"Last laugh's on him," I said tiredly. "We weren't the ones who went up in smoke."

"Come home," Teag urged. "We've got hot cookies and a fresh bottle of bourbon to wash them down with. You deserve it."

"I'll second that," Kell said, and despite the slight shake in his voice, he managed to smile and pulled me a little closer.

I looked around the wreckage of the old boiler room, realizing this was another triumph no one else but we few would ever know about. Sorren might make that anonymous call to the cops, but without evidence, I doubted they'd believe him. At least he might be able to give the families some closure. I imagine the police would just assume that the Smiley Killer had disappeared again, and leave the case open, should future victims surface.

That's okay. We knew the truth. We'd managed to put down a serial killer with extreme prejudice, free the victim's ghosts, and do it all without anyone getting too badly injured. That earned us a celebration.

Cookies and bourbon? Hell, yes.

PART VIII
BONUS

STEER A PALE COURSE

"Bring in those nets. Let's head for home." I put my back into hauling in the nets on my side of the boat. They were full of fish, but not as full as yesterday. Over the horizon, the sun was just coming up.

"Easy for you to say, Dante. You've got the skinny nets on your side." Coltt grunted as he and Nesh leaned into bringing their net into the boat. Lucky for me they're taller, with long arms. I probably would have gone over the side trying to haul in a net as full as theirs.

We should have been out to sea with the other men, and any other year since I'd been ten years old, we would have been. The rest of the men from the village had gone a day out on the water, where the big catches are this time of year. They wouldn't be back for another couple of days, salting the fish as they caught them to keep the catch from rotting. But this year, mother wasn't feeling well, and she normally heads up harvest, her and Nady, Coltt and Nesh's mother. But Nady died over the winter, and mother said that she needed our help this harvest. So at night, Coltt and Nesh and I went out on our boat just far enough to catch what we could but close in enough to be back just after sunrise.

"Look, this one's sweet on you, Nesh!" Coltt held up a big fish whose mouth was opening and closing. "Just like Letta!" He threw the fish at Nesh, who caught it and leaned back after him, holding the fish's flopping tail to smack his brother across the face.

"And that's just what Letta would do if she heard you call her a fish," Nesh laughed, dropping the fish into the huge basket. Coltt and Nesh were cut from the same cloth. The Skinner brothers took after their mother. Tall and thin, with long, strong arms and a shock of straw-blond hair, they were freckled with the sun and still pink in the face from the summer just past.

Me, I was as dark as they were light. Their hair was a mop of yellow curls that looked like a bird's nest after a windstorm. My hair fell lank into my eyes, even more limp than usual from the salt wind. I'd cut it short at the beginning of the summer, and it wasn't quite long enough yet to catch back in a queue. Nesh and Coltt were skinny, but even at eighteen, I already had my father's build: sturdy and strong, though I was slim-built. I wasn't as tall as the Skinners either, and they'd had more than enough fun at my expense over the years tossing a ball or my lunch or my hat over my head just out of reach. Still, they were the closest thing I had to brothers, what with three sisters back home. And if I had to be left behind when the other men went out to sea, having them with me made it bearable.

"Let's head back," I said, turning the sails for home. "The sooner we get the harvest in, the quicker we can get back out here and salvage some dignity with a decent catch before the rest of the boats come back."

Coltt and Nesh kept up their joking until the boat rocked so badly we nearly lost some fish over the side. As usual, I handled the rudder while the Skinner boys kept the sails. The wind was with us, and the morning breeze was clean. Despite the prospect of harvesting vegetables for the rest of the day, my spirits were high. Everyone in our village has at least a touch of sea magic. Mine was more than a touch, by a good bit. I could listen to the wind like it was telling me a story. The stars, too. Even as a child, I never got lost. Father said I could navigate on a starless sea, and he was right. Coltt and Nesh could barely find their way home from the well at the end of the village, but they could smell where the fish were hiding.

Good thing, too, because fish kept our little village alive and earned most of the coin to be had. Mother and the women raised some vegetables and a few scrawny hens, goats, and rabbits. We did some trade with the boats and merchants who passed by our inlet. Like every village, Netters Cove had a weaver, a potter, and a blacksmith, a dyer and a hedge witch who gave cures and birthed babies and said the High Words over the bodies when some poor blokes drowned. It was enough to trade for us what we couldn't build or grow, but not so much that the pirates who sailed the waters just beyond the shoals had any reason to bother us.

"Look there." Coltt pointed as we sailed into the inlet. A strange boat was anchored just beyond the shoals, and two rowboats I didn't recognize were pulled up on shore.

"Not the usual season for traders," I mused. But a little extra coin sure wouldn't hurt.

Just then I saw a figure burst from the trees at the side of the beach. It was my little sister, Jana, and she was jumping up and down and waving her arms. We were still pretty far out, and I smiled at her enthusiasm. She always missed me when I spent the night at sea.

It wasn't until we were too close in to turn around easily that I realized something.

Jana wasn't greeting us. She was warning us away.

"Something's wrong." I had barely gotten the words out of my mouth before another figure ran from the trees, toward Jana. It was a man I didn't recognize, and he grabbed her by the arms, dragging her backward. To make his point, he held up a cutlass and then held it to her throat.

"Dante—" Coltt's voice was low, like a growl.

"I see."

"What do you think—"

"I think we'll find out more than we want to know once we land the boat."

We brought the boat ashore, but there seemed to be no one else around except Jana and the man with the cutlass. He watched us as we dragged the boat up, making sure he turned to face us as we moved, keeping Jana and the cutlass in between us. He was dirty and unshaven, and even at a distance, he stank. His clothes were torn and stained, looking like mismatched pieces he'd stolen off a clothesline somewhere.

Jana's eyes were wide with fear. Knowing Jana, she was likely to either bite the man or kick him in the shins, and that was likely to make things worse.

"Let her go." I was surprised how steady my voice was, but I was more angry than scared. "I'll be your hostage. Let her go."

The man with the cutlass just laughed. "We're going to the big building. You three go first."

I could feel how angry Coltt and Nesh were without needing to look at them. My worst fears were confirmed when we reached the lodge, a building large enough for our whole village of about fifty people to gather. We used it for holidays or smoking meat or important meetings. Now, all of the women, children, and the men too old to go out on the boats were sitting in silence on the floor. I saw my mother sitting with my other two sisters in the front row. She looked up at me, scared and sick—and defiant. Letta, Nesh's girlfriend, sat with his younger brother on her lap, holding him close to her and patting his head. They both looked close to panic. Six men who looked as worse for the wear as the man who held Jana were in the building. They had muskets. We were out of luck.

I had a fishing knife in a scabbard on my right leg, underneath my trousers. Coltt and Nesh probably did, too. I had a small, curved knife on my belt, good for gutting fish and not much else. In my pockets, I had some dirty twine and a few small iron balls we used to help weight the nets. Nothing that would counter six muskets and a guy who looked like he knew how to use that cutlass.

I knew Coltt and Nesh were waiting for me to make the first move. It's been that way since we were kids. My heart was pounding, but I took a step forward, careful to keep my hands away from my sides. "What do you want from us?"

The tallest of the men stepped forward. He stood a head above even the Skinner boys, but his neck craned forward. Dressed in black, missing several of his teeth, with a ripped and dirty cloth wrapped around greasy blond hair, he reminded me of a buzzard. He smiled, showing his rotted teeth. "We've been waiting for ya," he said, and his smile wasn't pleasant. "They said you'd be home after dawn."

"What are ya waitin' for, Jammer?" A short, wiry man waved his musket toward the captives, and the women shrank back, wrapping their bodies around their children. "Just shoot the lot of them exceptin' the boys."

Jammer took on a crafty look, and I noticed that one of his dark eyes turned out to the right, where an old scar ran along the brow. "I don't think that's necessary—yet." Jammer stared at me. "Of course, it depends on what the boys say to my business deal."

"If you need goats and rabbits, take them," I said, knowing that giving up our livestock would mean a hungry winter. "We've got no coin."

Jammer's eyes narrowed. "I don't want your poxy goats. I want someone to go into the barrows and bring out something for me. Someone with magic."

"No one goes into the barrows."

Jammer leered and waved his musket toward the hostages. "Then I guess it's time to start killing until we find someone with the guts to try." He pulled back the hammer with his thumb.

"I'll go." My voice sounded too deep, since I was trying not to let it waver. To keep from squeaking, my throat tightened, making it sound like the words came all the way from my toes. I figured that I couldn't hide that I was shaking, but I hoped I looked less scared than Coltt and Nesh, although to give them credit, they were still at my back.

Jammer smiled his unpleasant smile. "That's a good boy. There's a very special necklace buried down there. I want you to bring it to me."

"And then you'll leave? Without harming anyone?"

Jammer seemed to find my bargaining amusing. "Sure, boy. I'll leave. And I won't kill anyone if you do as I say."

I didn't trust him. But I'd bought us time, and maybe the men would come back and save us. Maybe there'd be a way to warn them. If all the pirates wanted was a necklace, then why would the dead care?

They weren't using it. But Jammer wasn't asking me to go to the cliffs where we'd buried our dead for generations. He was asking us to go into the barrows. We didn't know who or what made the barrows. Maybe they were graves, maybe something else. The entrances had been walled up long ago, but the stories remained. Men had gone in, looking for treasure. No one came out.

We left the barrows alone most of the time, except in the Dead Moon, when we brought offerings and left them by the walled-up entrance. The hedge witch took a goat and sacrificed it, letting the blood run down into the barrow. He left the carcass there and said the Old Words, something he called a binding spell. Next morning, the carcass was gone. I swallowed hard. If whatever lived in the barrows liked goat blood, maybe it would like Coltt, Nesh, and me even better.

"Tell me about this necklace."

THEY DIDN'T SEND someone with us to the barrows. They didn't have to. We knew what would happen if we didn't come back with the necklace. The look in my mother's eyes bound me more to see it through than my word to Jammer. I didn't doubt Jammer would kill them if we failed or ran off.

"We could light a big fire and warn the men." Coltt had obviously been giving some thought to our options.

"One of us could run for the next village," Nesh offered.

I shook my head. "If we light a fire, Jammer will see it. We'd have to get the whole way to the other side of the cliffs to hide it, and if we do that, the men won't know it's for them. And it's a day's walk to the next village. Jammer said to be back by dawn. Even if one of us got there, he couldn't get back in time with a mob." I'd thought of the same things on the hike to the barrows. From the looks on their faces, Coltt and Nesh had reasoned through it, too. We had no choice but to go on.

For autumn, it was a hot day. We were all sweating by the time we reached the barrows. I stopped and took a deep breath. The barrows were about a candlemark's hard hike directly inland from the village. There were three of them, and they might have been mistaken for hills if the rest of the land weren't so flat. I'd heard about the barrows since I was a kid. The old women warned children that the barrow wights ate children who wandered away from the village. At first, I thought it was just a tale to keep the children from running off. Then I noticed that even the hunters made a wide circle around the barrows. I'd gone out once with my father to look for deer, and I'd asked why we couldn't just climb the "hills" for a better view. He'd gone gray in the face and told me they were an evil place and to stay clear.

Now we were going into them.

Jammer let us take equipment to unseal the barrows. Coltt and I had picks, and Nesh carried two shovels. The pirates seemed pretty confident we couldn't use them for weapons. Hell, they hadn't even cared about taking our knives. After all, they had muskets. I had the awful feeling that whatever was in those barrows wouldn't be scared of either knives or muskets. Nesh also had a bag of reeds and a flint and steel for torches. Jammer had thrown us some dried meat and cheese with a laugh that told me our meals were numbered.

"Can you feel it?"

"Feel what?" Coltt asked. Then he closed his eyes for a moment, and so did Nesh. I could see the change in their expression. My magic felt jangly, like warning bells in my mind. It was the same feeling I got when there was a bad storm coming at sea, long before we saw the waves. That jangle had saved us many a time out on the ocean, warning us to head home before the squall hit. Only now, we couldn't head home. We were heading straight into the storm.

Then I heard it. It was faint, like a voice calling from a distance. I pictured the necklace Jammer had drawn with a stick in the dirt floor of the lodge. The more clearly I pictured it, the louder the voice called to me, directing me to its barrow. I didn't like the voice, but I'd heard it before. I'd heard it in my dreams, bad dreams where a voice tried to call me out into the night, or onto the dark water. It was the kind of voice you knew in your bones only wanted you for your meat. I shuddered.

"Let's do this."

Coltt and I set to with the picks, while Nesh cleared away the rock from the entranceway. We took turns with the shovel. It was hard work, and it wasn't until the sun was overhead that we broke through. Whoever had blocked that entrance wanted it to stay blocked. I wondered again what was down there, but I really didn't want to know. I was afraid I'd find out anyhow.

Cold air rushed toward us when Coltt's pick broke through. It should have felt good in the autumn heat, but it smelled like dead things. I saw fear in their eyes as I lit my torch, and I was pretty sure they saw the same in mine. We picked up our picks and shovels and headed in. Maybe we'd need them to dig out another blocked area. Or maybe it just felt good to have something heavy to swing at whatever lived in the darkness. I went first.

"How do we know where the damned necklace is?" Coltt whispered. Everyone down here was supposed to be dead, but I knew why he was whispering. It felt like we were being watched.

"It's calling. Can you hear it?" I could make out their faces by torchlight enough to see that they didn't hear the voice. Damn. I didn't like that it was only calling to me, not one little bit.

I ignored the voice in my head that was screaming common sense and followed the other voice, the hungry one. Inside the barrows, there were tunnels leading in every direction. There were carvings on the walls, too, and just at the edge of the torchlight, I saw statues and slabs that might have been coffins. I didn't look too hard. I was afraid something might be looking back. Whatever else was down here, it could stay. All we wanted was the necklace, and from the way it called me, I'd have said it wanted us to take it.

"No rats. No spiders." Nesh whispered, and I wasn't sure it was to himself or to the rest of us. But I knew what he meant. We'd gone caving in the cliffs by the sea all our lives. Part of the fun was discovering gross stuff, like bat poop and creepy crawlies. But not here. Things might exist here, but nothing lived. I was now sure of that. We saw nothing.

I don't know how long we walked. Without the sun, time meant nothing. The voice guided us, showing me which of the turns to take, which tunnel to follow. It kept getting louder, and I followed it, even though inside, I wanted to run. Running seemed like a sane idea. Nesh carefully marked each turn by chipping an arrow into the wall. Just in case the necklace lured us in and didn't want us to get out. It occurred to me that maybe the necklace and Jammer had different agendas. Why Jammer wanted the necklace, I didn't know. Why the necklace wanted to be found, I wasn't sure, but the suspicions I had weren't good. I was glad Nesh marked the trail.

"There it is."

"Are you sure?" Coltt didn't move closer, but he leaned forward, peering through the shadows. The necklace lay beside a small box next to what was probably once a body. It was wrapped in a shroud, but both the bones and the cloth were brittle with age. The necklace wasn't around the corpse's neck. It was clasped in its bony hand. I got a glimpse of gold and white, but I didn't have time to look closely.

"I'm sure." My sanity fought every step I took toward the necklace. My will made me keep moving. The necklace was screaming at me, screaming to pick it up. Something in me was very sure there was a good reason the necklace had been sealed in here. I didn't think it was a good idea to remove it. Then, when I got closer, the screaming was so loud I couldn't think at all. I just wanted to shut the damned voice up, and I tore it out of the skeleton's hand. I didn't care if every barrow wight in the place came after us, I just wanted that voice to shut the hell up.

I held the necklace in my hand, and there was silence. Beautiful silence. On instinct, I grabbed the box that was next to the necklace. Damn, it was heavy, like it was made from lead. Something told me to take it, too, that voice of common sense I'd ignored since we headed into the cave. The necklace didn't like it, but this time, I ignored the necklace. I took the box.

Suddenly, images flooded into my mind, pictures that were so crisp and clear it was as if someone had opened a window in front of me, although we were deep in the cave. Sunlight. Ocean. A path through the forest. The urge to run back along the tunnels for the open air was so strong I was shaking with the effort to fight it. "We've got to go," I said, the strain clear in my voice. "Now."

Whether they guessed that the necklace was pushing me or whether they just wanted out, I don't know, but Colt and Nesh found the energy to walk back a lot faster than we walked in. I didn't trust the necklace. I checked at every turn, but each time, I saw Nesh's marks. I couldn't get out fast enough. Holding the necklace seemed to open up a whole new level of senses for me, something I'd never felt before in the magic. I could feel things moving in the distance, things that were cold and long dead. Some were angry, and for some, the hatred was so intense I cringed. Some were hungry. There were a lot of them, and I didn't want to meet them. I couldn't tell whether they liked me taking the necklace or not. I didn't want to find out. Without saying a word, we ran.

Jammer met us on the path to the village. He'd been waiting for us, even though we were back before dawn. "Did you get it?"

"Yes."

"Show me."

I tightened my hand around the necklace in my pocket. "We had a deal. I give you the necklace and you leave. You promised you wouldn't kill anyone."

"Give me the necklace. I won't kill anyone."

I knew Colt and Nesh were watching me. Two more men came out of the trees to stand beside Jammer as if we might jump him and run for it. I pulled the necklace out of my pocket and opened my hand. The moonlight caught it, and it glowed. For the first time, I got a good look at it with my eyes, but I'd seen it clearly in my mind. It had a wide band of gold made from hinged squares. In the center was a huge, white oval stone that seemed to pulse and swirl. It looked alive.

Jammer laughed and took it from me. He took the box, too. I thought the necklace might stick to my hand or refuse to let me give it away, but Jammer took it like it wasn't some kind of cursed thing.

Maybe it liked him. "Good job," he said, with a smile I didn't like at all.

We walked back toward the village in silence. Jammer was in front of us, with Coltt, Nesh, and me in the middle and the two men following behind. The moon was full and high that night. But even before I saw, I knew. It was too quiet. The magic was gone from the village. Magic only leaves for one reason. It leaves when you die.

Bodies littered the beach. We hadn't heard the musket fire because we'd been deep in the barrows. Or maybe, the necklace didn't want us to hear. Mother lay dead next to my sisters, face down in the bloody sand, a chunk out of her skull visible where the musket had blown away her ear. Letta lay next to her, face up, only they'd shot her in the face and from the nose down there wasn't anything left.

"You bastards!" Nesh launched himself at Jammer.

An explosion rocked the night. The fire from the pirate's musket flashed right by my shoulder. The ball caught Nesh in the back, tore a hole through his ribs big enough to shove an arm through. He staggered forward and collapsed in the sand. The two men behind us grabbed Coltt and me by the arms before we could move.

"You gave your word you wouldn't kill anyone!"

Jammer gave me that smile again. "I said *I* wouldn't kill anyone. *I* didn't. My men did." He clucked his tongue. "If you're going to bargain with pirates, you need to be more specific."

I didn't have to look at Coltt to know what he was thinking. We both lurched forward, ready to rip Jammer apart, ready for a musket ball to tear through us the way it did through Nesh.

My head seemed to explode as the man behind me brought the butt of his gun down on my skull. I could feel the blood rushing through my ears as the moonlight turned to darkness.

"Take them," I heard Jammer say from a far distance. "They'll be useful." Then, I didn't hear anything else at all.

"DANTE?"

I heard Coltt's voice but it was faint. Must be imagining it.

"Dante?"

Louder now, close to my ear. My head was pounding, and I was afraid to open my eyes. I groaned. My hands pushed down against wood. Wood? As my senses returned, I felt rocking. I knew that feeling. We were on a boat. We were Jammer's prisoners.

"Where are we?" I tried to sit, and Coltt grabbed my arm, pulling me up. It was a dumb question. I knew. We were on Jammer's ship.

"They must have bashed you harder than they got me," he whispered. "I thought they'd killed you. I woke up in the dinghy. We're out to sea by now."

I could feel the magic. It was always stronger near water. I listened for the wind although I couldn't see the stars. "We're headed south. Towards Chasston."

"Figures."

Chasston was down the coast from Netter's Cove. The whole coastline was a haven for smugglers and pirates, the bane of the king's navy. Chasston was the main port, and no matter how many of the king's ships were in port or how many soldiers were in town, it didn't seem to bother the smugglers. Father said the smugglers and pirates paid the soldiers better than the king, so they looked the other way. Might be. Of course, Jammer might not stop at Chasston. He had hot cargo. He might meet his buyer somewhere else, someplace a little quieter.

"Dante, why did they bring us? Why didn't they just kill us, like —" He didn't say it. He didn't have to. Like Nesh. Like everyone else.

"Because of the magic." It hurt to talk. It hurt to think. "We were too good at finding the necklace. There must be more things like that, and Jammer figures we can retrieve them for him. He'll keep us as long as there's a use for us." And then… we'd join the rest.

Coltt helped me bind up the gash on the back of my head. He had a bruise on his temple, but otherwise, he seemed in pretty good shape.

"I can't hear it."

"Hear what?"

"The necklace."

Coltt gave me a funny, sideways glance, but I figured he knew what I meant. Actually, what I said wasn't exactly true. If I listened hard, I could hear something, muffled and far away. And then I knew. Jammer must have put the necklace in the lead box. And the necklace didn't like it.

I looked around as soon as I could move without wanting to pass out or throw up. My head seemed to pound in time with the swell of the waves. But I knew how the magic worked. The longer I was at sea, the stronger the magic got. Not that it would do us much good. We weren't likely to get lost. We were locked in an iron cage.

I started to get up and thought better of it. "Don't bother," Coltt said. "I had time before you came around. The lock is solid. No other welds or joints. Bars are tight. Tried to pick the lock with my knife but I couldn't."

"They left our knives?"

Coltt nodded. "Guess they were too busy to pat us down. Or they don't care. Maybe they figured we weren't likely to kill each other." Or ourselves, I added silently. I wasn't letting myself think too hard about what I'd seen in the village. There'd be time enough for that.

"They say anything else?"

"Jammer said they were due for 'the meeting' by midnight tonight. Whoever hired them didn't give them much time. Wonder who it is and what they want."

I wondered if anyone had asked the necklace what it wanted, but I didn't say anything. That sounded crazy even to me.

I could see the angle of the sun change from the light through the portals. We sailed all day. No one fed us. Maybe Jammer didn't mean to keep us for too long, after all.

The sun went lower and I slept.

In my dreams, the sea turned wild and the sky turned dark. Lightning struck on the horizon, and I could smell the way it charged the air. My dreams changed from the stormy sea to the massacre at Netters Cove. I saw the bodies of the people I'd grown up with, my mother, my sisters… all of them gone. In my dream, I fell to my knees on the shore and wept as grief and anger washed over me, as strong as the pounding waves.

What do you want?

I looked up from the bloody sands. "I want revenge."

What do you want?

"I want Jammer dead. I want them all dead. I want to kill the men who did this."

What do you want?

My voice tore from a throat raw from weeping. "I want to avenge them. I want blood."

Then blood you shall have.

Coltt's hoarse scream woke me. Our iron cage was sliding across the hold as the ship tossed like a cork. I didn't have time to brace myself before the cage slammed into a wall of crates and I hit the bars on the other side hard enough to make my teeth rattle. The cage thrummed as the shock vibrated through the iron. It felt as if all of my insides were shaking.

The cage door swung open.

Coltt and I exchanged glances, and went for the knives in our leg sheathes. We stumbled from the cage as the ship pitched hard to port, scrambling to stay out of the way of the cargo, which had begun to shift. Just then, we heard footsteps on the stairs from the deck. We hid behind the most stable thing we could find, the forward guns.

"Son of a bitch!" The first man to the bottom saw the empty cage. He was ugly even by raider standards, with a poxy face and one hollow eye socket he didn't bother to cover with a patch.

The second man's curse was more creative, but anatomically implausible. "They didn't go far." By comparison, he was the better looking of the two, although whatever fight had flattened his nose had also left a deep crease up his forehead.

"They'd better go nowhere, or Jammer will skin both of us."

We held our breaths as the two men began to search the hold. Around us, the wooden ship creaked and moaned, rushing forward as it rose with the waves and then dropping, freefall. I eyed the hold filled with barrels, crates, and logs warily.

"I think I see something!" One-eye headed straight for us. I gripped my knife, resolved to go down fighting.

The ship pitched starboard hard enough that I thought it might rip apart. Coltt and I barely kept a grip on the heavy gun that strained against its chains. One-eye and Flatnose weren't as lucky. They went tumbling. A crack like gunfire echoed in the hold. I winced, expecting musket fire. The ropes on the timber broke, and the logs surged forward, propelled by the violence of the sea. Barrels and wooden crates tore loose from the ropes that secured them, crashing into the center of the hold. Flatnose and One-eye screamed as the logs rolled over them, and their blood ran like wine from a press across the filthy hold floor. When the screaming stopped, the hold was silent, quiet in a moment's lull.

Coltt's face was ashen. I pried his hand from the gun and motioned toward the stairs as the ship began to rock once more. Carefully, we crept to the top of the stairs, holding on as the ship began to pitch once more.

Waves twice the height of a man pounded the ship's deck. Coltt and I barely kept our footing as the ship seemed to dive nose first down a steep wave. Behind us, we could hear the bloody cargo scrape across the hold as it shifted. A massive wave caught the ship from starboard, and a man screamed. Coltt grabbed my arm and pointed skyward, toward the top of the mast where the lookout had been thrown from his perch, falling to land on the deck with a sickening thud, only to be washed overboard as more waves followed the first, sweeping two of his fellow pirates with him.

Two dead down below. Three washed overboard. I'd only counted seven of them.

What do you want? I could hear the necklace, louder now. *Take what you want. Take your due.*

Rage clouded my vision. All I could see were the bodies of my family, my neighbors, left on the beach to rot. I could smell their blood above the musket smoke, could taste blood in my mouth.

Blood for blood.

I knew Coltt couldn't hear the necklace, but I saw a fury in his eyes I'd never seen before. I could guess his thoughts, or maybe the necklace told me. *They killed Nesh. Killed Letta. Killed them all. Kill them all.*

"Jammer's mine." I barely recognized my voice. It sounded more like a growl. Coltt nodded. After all, it had been Jammer's lieutenant who murdered Nesh. It was time to prove two fishermen could hunt.

I couldn't see Jammer, but I could hear him cursing even above the roar of the wind. I was betting he was at the wheel. The lieutenant had dragged himself forward to drop the sails and blunt the power of the wind.

We had a moment's reprieve between waves. Coltt and I sprang from our hiding place. Coltt was on the lieutenant before he ever saw him coming. Coltt tackled the man from behind with a cry, and I saw a streak of silver as he drew his blade across the man's throat as neatly as he'd learned to do hunting wild boar. He dropped the man's hair and spun the lieutenant around, sinking his knife hilt-deep into the man's chest for good measure, then grabbed for the rigging and watched the next wave wash the dying man into the sea.

I knew Jammer didn't dare leave the wheel, although his curses made it clear he'd seen Coltt. I'd been unconscious when they'd brought me aboard, but I recognized the type of ship, knew where to find the wheel. The storm kept pounding us, soaking me to the bone. Twice, I almost lost my grip as the ship tossed and pitched.

Take what belongs to you. Take what you want.

The necklace was screaming in my mind, or maybe I was screaming. I lurched up the last two steps to face Jammer. He stood with one hand on the wheel and one on his musket. As I cleared the last step, he pulled the trigger; musket leveled at my heart.

Nothing happened. Wet powder's a bitch.

Before he could draw his cutlass, I was on him, even as I spotted Coltt climbing his way up to help. But Jammer was mine, all mine. I think he meant to run, but just then, the ship dropped beneath us as we ran down a wave, and Jammer fell against the wheel. His right arm snapped as the wheel spun against it, out of control. He was pinned, with no way to draw his cutlass, like a jaundiced fish.

I've been killing fish all my life.

My knife rammed into his chest just below the ribs, and I let the momentum and the ship's movement force the blade all the way down. Guts spilled in a steaming mass to the deck, just like a fish. Jammer's mouth opened and closed soundlessly, and his whole body started to quiver until he gave one final flop against the knife and hung dead from the wheel.

I tore him loose to steer, and I didn't look back. I think Coltt threw him overboard, or maybe the next wave took him. The ship wasn't built for two men to sail, but Coltt and I had been on the sea since we could walk. It took all my strength to hold the wheel against the storm, but I knew that the worst was past. Whether my magic had called the storm or whether it had just fed its intensity, now that Jammer and the lieutenant were dead, all the fight seemed to go out of the wind, and out of me. I was shaking so badly I think my knees would have buckled if I hadn't been holding the wheel, and for someone who never was seasick a day in his life, I wanted to retch.

Little by little, the storm lost its fury, and the sky turned from pewter gray to twilight blue. As the clouds parted, I could see the stars. I knew where we were.

Coltt trimmed the sails and climbed back up to where I stood at the wheel.

"We can't go home." He said it flat, without emotion. But I saw his eyes. "The men'll be back. We've got no proof of our story, only bodies."

"We've got the ship." But I knew what Coltt meant. If we went back, the murders would dog us the rest of our lives, and the men would look at us with questions in their eyes forever.

"Now what?"

I shrugged. "We head for Chasston. It's thick with pirates, smugglers, and thieves."

"What if Jammer's friends come after us?"

A bitter smile crossed my face. "Doubt he had many. We know how to fish, so we won't starve. We know how to sail. We'll go to Chasston, find someone who needs a fast ship."

"And be pirates, like Jammer?"

My nerves were shot. I wheeled on Coltt. "We can smuggle whiskey and broadleaf. Father said the king's entire navy hasn't been able to plug up all the coves and inlets, no matter how many ships they send. We know the coastline. Way I figure it, cheatin' the king out of his taxes doesn't hurt anyone, and whisky and broadleaf give a good bit of satisfaction to our fellow man. Makes it almost charitable."

"We stole a ship and killed the crew to do it. That'll earn us a noose."

"If they catch us."

I put in for the night in a hidden inlet up the coast from Chasston. Exhausted, hungry, and soaked to the skin, I crawled down onto the lower deck and went looking for Jammer's quarters. Coltt had slept some while I steered us; he took night watch.

Everything in Jammer's cabin had been tossed around by the storm. Doors were open, drawers were spilled out, and most things lay in a heap on the floor. Near the heavy wooden captain's desk, I found it. The necklace lay near the empty lead box.

I can make you rich.

Dead tired, I knew I had one more task before I could sleep. I used my magic to shield my thoughts as I approached the necklace, keeping my face blank. Its voice was sultry, like the whores we'd find in Chasston, full of promises, lies, and clap. I sprang at it, shoving it into the box and slamming the lid closed even as I heard it shriek at me like a cheated tinker. I found a length of rope and wrapped it around the box, sealing the lid closed, and then I tied it to the sturdy leg of the desk, to keep it from "accidentally" opening. The storm had washed Jammer's blood from my hands, but I knew what I'd done and how I'd done it.

Coltt was right. We'd done murder. Stolen a ship. Jammer's "friends" might want us dead, and his enemies might want the ship. The king's men wouldn't care. They'd hang the lot of us. But not tonight. Every bone in my body ached as I crawled into a dead man's bed and for once, I slept without dreaming.

～

THE NEXT MORNING, the sky was bright and clear. I woke just after dawn, and went looking for Coltt. Found him dangling from a rope off the bow of the ship, and for a moment, I thought he'd saved the king the trouble and hanged himself. Then Coltt hoisted himself over the rail, and I saw the make-shift rigging he'd made.

"Can't paint the whole boat, but I struck Jammer's flag and scraped off the name on the hull," Coltt said in a matter-of-fact tone. I knew that meant he'd struggled with our outlaw status all night and come to terms with it. He wasn't much for talking about things like that. "Went down in the hold and found some black paint. Should do until we get to Chasston, or wherever."

I peered over the edge. "*Vengeance*" had been painted over a scraped-bare spot on the hull. Probably not original, but Coltt had summed it up.

I turned to find him seated on the deck, looking at me, or maybe past me at the sky.

"What now?"

I dropped to the deck beside him. I didn't look at him; I looked at the clouds. Looking at Coltt would make me think of Mother and Jana and Nesh and I wasn't ready to mourn them, not yet. So I looked at the clouds instead. "Father had an uncle in Chasston. Took me down to meet him once, a long while ago. Cagy old man. Father said he ran a curio shop. Said that meant he bought and sold old and unusual things, no questions asked. According to father, Uncle Evann had a foot on both sides of the line when it came to the law, honest enough to not make trouble with the king's men, dodgy enough to not care about where his treasures came from."

"You think he'd help us?"

I shrugged. "If he doesn't, we find a tavern to set up shop and look for someone who needs cargo run cheap. It's worth a try." I was quiet for a moment. "I'm going to take the necklace," I said quietly as if I was afraid it would hear me, lead box or not. "I don't want the damn thing around, and I don't want blood money for selling it. I just want rid of it."

"Can't blame you." Coltt might not have heard the necklace talking to him, but he was good about taking me at my word. I was glad because I had enough trouble shutting out the memory of how the necklace had fed my bloodlust. I'd killed Jammer without remorse, and I didn't like knowing that I could do such a thing, even if he deserved it. If I got rid of the necklace, maybe I'd never feel that way again. Ever.

By night, we'd hiked into Chasston. We'd looted the dead pirates' quarters for some coin, enough to buy dinner and some ale. We were unshaven and smelling of salt water, but the whores in the narrow Chasston streets came on to us anyhow. I gripped the box under my arm a little tighter and kept on going, weaving my way through the crowded alleys and ginnels, to a small shop a few streets back from the docks.

"Trifles and Folly" was the name of the shop. A bell rang as we pushed the door open. Inside, it smelled of old wood and whiskey, and a musty smell that reminded me of the barrows. Things of every description were piled on shelves, spilling onto tables and into stacks on the worn wooden floor. Sextants and spyglasses and armillaries, enough to navigate a navy, filled one corner. Carved ivory tusks and wooden masks with staring eyes and sharp, bone teeth glared down from high shelves. Boxes inlaid with gold and jade were stacked next to larger boxes of teak and mahogany in every size and shape. There was magic here; I could feel it. I looked around the shadowy interior and knew that, like my necklace, many of the "trifles and follies" in this store were not what they seemed.

"Looking for something?" The voice startled me. The words were neutral, but there was an undercurrent of something sharp as steel beneath them. I turned to find a bent old man with white hair and a long, high-necked frock coat staring at me with cold blue eyes that seemed to see straight through me.

"Uncle Evann?" My voice came out like a croak. So much for being a big, tough pirate.

The old man frowned and stepped closer. He reached out and grabbed my chin, turning my head to see my profile. His grip was tight, and his yellowed nails dug into my flesh. And then, when I thought he might draw blood, he released me. And laughed.

"You'd be Dante, wouldn't you? Eric's son."

I swallowed hard and nodded. "Yes, sir. And this is my friend, Coltt."

Evann looked from me to Coltt and back again. "You're a long way from home."

I stretched out my magic, looking for a clue as to whether or not I could trust Evann. I could sense the necklace, shrieking its fury at being restrained, muted in its box. It wasn't the only voice I heard coming from objects that shouldn't have a voice at all. The voices were muffled, like a conversation in another room, just beyond my ability to make out what they were saying. But there was magic here, and I was pretty sure Evann could hear those voices, too. We were already in this up to our necks. I decided to trust him.

"There's been a problem." I glanced at Coltt. "Is there somewhere we could talk? Somewhere a little more private?"

Evann looked at me in silence for a moment as if trying to make his own decision about whether to trust me or not. Finally, he gave a jerk of his head toward the rear of the store. "Come on. Just about to close up when you came in."

He locked the door and motioned for us to follow him. Behind the shop was a one-room apartment that held a bed, small stove, and a table. Evann took a kettle from the back of the stove and stoked the fire, saying nothing until he'd poured us all hot tea. We sat around the table, and Coltt and I stared into our cups until I got the nerve up to spill out our story. I told him everything, even about how I could hear the necklace, even about how it called to me the night of the storm. I'd set the box on the table between us, bound with rope and wrapped in rags. The necklace was silent, and if I could read its mood at all, it was nervous.

Evann listened without a word as I told the whole, painful story. He said nothing as my cheeks flamed when I told about killing Jammer and the lieutenant, even though my heart was hammering in my chest. I half expected Evann to jump from his chair and call for the soldiers, but Evann didn't move at all. Finally, I was out of words. Coltt hadn't said anything. I stared into my cup as if I could read the future from the bits of leaf scattered in the bottom.

"You brought the necklace." It wasn't a question. I nodded toward the rag-wrapped lump and moved to open it, but Evann grabbed my wrist.

"Leave it be." He took a long draught of his tea and set down the cup. "I'm glad you thought to come here. There's someone I want you to meet."

I saw the same alarm in Coltt's eyes that flooded through my system. Damn, Evann was going to give us up to the soldiers.

A slight smile softened Evann's features. "No, I'm not going to call the guards. I have a… business associate… who will want to hear your story. You can trust him. Leave nothing out. Tell him just what you've told me. If there's more to say about the barrow, he'll want to know that, too. I wager he'll know what to do about that necklace." He rose and took down a loaf of bread, some hard cheese, and a length of dried sausage and put them on the table. This time, he filled our mugs with mulled cider and rum. "Eat."

"Won't we interrupt your… associate's… dinner?" I asked, losing no time grabbing a hunk of bread.

Evann's smile was unreadable. "I hope not."

Coltt and I ate in record time, thanking Evann for our first real meal in two days through stuffed mouths. When we were done, we followed Evann out the back of his flat into the alley. It stank of urine and horse dung. Clotheslines heavy with damp shirts and sodden pants hung from side to side from the tenements above. Evann wound through the narrow, slippery ginnels, up the hill from the port. Gradually, tenements gave way to wide cobblestone streets and villas. I glanced nervously at Coltt.

"We're not dressed to be seen anywhere decent."

Evann chuckled. "Sorren won't mind."

We stopped at an iron gate set into a high stone wall. Evann said a word to the man who waited in the shadows on the other side, and we were admitted. Coltt and I exchanged wary glances, but we said nothing. We walked back a long carriage road through tall trees hung with moss. I was sweating hard enough that my shirt stuck to my back by the time we reached the large, stately home. Whoever Sorren was, he had money. I glanced at the wrought iron railings, the tall columns and the large windows hung with heavy draperies. It was an old home, and my magic told me the ghosts of former inhabitants liked it well enough to stick around.

A servant opened the door and smiled at Evann. "Good to see you again, Mr. Evann. Mr. Sorren is always happy to see you."

With a nod of thanks, we moved into the large entrance hall. Candles illuminated the foyer, but of the rooms that opened off of the entranceway, all but one were dark. Evann motioned for us to follow him down a long hall hung with portraits and artwork from distant ports. I wondered whether Sorren was a sea captain or someone with connections to royal trade. As we neared the end of the hallway, my magic made me edgy. I recognized the feeling immediately. It was the same edginess I felt down in the barrow, when I knew that long-dead things lurked in the shadows. I passed a darkened room and repressed a shiver.

Evann knocked at a door at the end of the hallway. A muffled voice gave permission to enter, and Evann opened the door, leading the way. Sorren was seated in a wing chair next to the large fireplace. He stood to greet us and embraced Evann warmly. I sized him up. He was a tall, young man with blond hair and blue-gray eyes. His frock coat was understated, but obviously expensive, in cut and cloth. Even by candlelight, he had an ashen pallor. I glanced around the room. Leatherbound books lined shelf upon shelf floor to ceiling. A desk with a globe and an armillary stood on one side. Heavy damask draperies were pulled across all the windows. Beside where Sorren sat, an open book and a goblet of red wine sat on a side table.

"I've got two lads here with a story I think you'll want to hear," Evann said by way of introduction as Sorren gestured for us to sit. His eyes seemed to follow me, and I could have sworn they saw down to my bones. My magic made me jumpy, a jangled feeling that usually warned of an impending storm. "They've brought you a gift."

At Evann's nod, I held out the cloth-wrapped box. Sorren reached toward it, then drew back. A look of concern mingled with heightened interest flashed in those gray eyes. "He brought you this?" he asked sharply, with a glance toward Evann, who nodded. Sorren looked back at me, and his gaze seemed to capture my full attention. "He has magic," Sorren said finally, breaking the gaze. "Strong magic."

"Let him tell you his story."

At Evann's prompt, I told our story one more time, the last time, I hoped. Once again, Coltt remained silent, and I could tell Sorren made him extremely uncomfortable. Maybe it was Sorren's wealth, maybe it was hearing the story again, which felt like salt in a bleeding wound. But I was betting that Coltt's own magic felt as jangly as mine.

Sorren watched me with eyes the color of a coming storm. His intensity spooked me, but I kept on until the bloody end of the tale. When I was finished, Sorren leaned forward.

"You both went into the barrow," he said. We nodded. "You used your magic to find the necklace, and it talked to you."

"Actually, it talked to Dante. I didn't hear it," Coltt said quietly.

I was surprised that none of this alarmed Sorren or seemed strange to him. Finally, he sat back and picked up his goblet, swirling the red liquid as he thought.

"So tell me, Dante, what will you and your friend do now?" Sorren asked quietly.

I took a deep breath. "Not rightly sure yet, sir. We can't go home. I guess from the king's perspective, we're outlaws. We have Jammer's boat. We thought we might run some whisky and broadleaf, other cargo. And fish. It's all we know."

Sorren took a sip of the red liquid. "Did Evann tell you why your necklace would interest me?"

"No, sir."

Sorren looked toward the fireplace, although no fire burned there. "What you sensed in the barrow was real. What's sealed in there is more than just ancestors or the ancient dead. Long ago, powerful mages fought a great battle. One side conjured… things… that should never have walked abroad. They were defeated, and what they conjured was entombed in the barrows. All that survives of those times are legends, stories that have been watered down to tell how the mounds were used for rituals." He shook his head. "Rituals. Every generation, mages must reinforce the wardings to keep what's buried inside. The magic is old and complicated. Some of the mages use anchor items—artifacts—to store power, or the spirits of familiars, in order to work their spells. So did the mages who created the… things.

"The wardings are growing weaker. It's time for them to be renewed. And there are some who would raise the barrow wights for their own purposes. And so… collectors from both sides seek the artifacts that have been stolen, lost, or misplaced. Some of these collectors hire men like Jammer. Others use men like Evann to watch what unwitting travelers bring back with them and funnel those special purchases to buyers like me."

"Which side are you on?" My voice sounded sharp because my heart was in my throat.

"I want to keep what's buried in its place." He smiled then, and I saw the tips of fangs.

Sorren is a vampire. Shit. What's down in the barrows scares him. Damn, damn, damn.

"I'd like to make you and your friend a business proposition," Sorren said. "I'm prepared to outfit a ship for you and hire a crew. But finding two mages I can trust… that's the hard part." He leaned forward. "Your village isn't the only one men like Jammer have visited. It always ends the same way. I want to find those artifacts before the other side finds them. Things like your necklace. I think you have an idea of just how dangerous they are."

I nodded, my head spinning. "You're looking for pirates."

Sorren laughed again, a deep, rich sound. Again, I glimpsed his fangs. "I prefer the term *privateer.* Help me locate the anchor items. Along the way, you'll have plenty of opportunity to rid the world of men like Jammer. I know it won't bring your family back, but it could keep many, many more people from dying."

"Why do you care? You're already dead." My fear made me bold, or maybe stupid.

Sorren smiled broadly, genuinely amused. His long eye teeth were now completely visible, and I felt Coltt shudder. "Let's just say that in this, undead and mortals share a common cause. What do you say, Dante?"

I glanced at Coltt. He shrugged. We'd been together long enough: I knew to take that as a yes. "We're in."

"Good." Sorren turned to Uncle Evann. "Daniel will see you to your rooms. It's best you stay here tonight. If the boys came in with Jammer's boat, some of his friends may be looking for his cargo."

No one asked what we thought about staying the night in a vampire's mansion. But given the choice of a rather civil vampire or more of Jammer's friends, it looked like a good idea. Upstairs, we were shown to comfortable rooms, one for each of us. I drew the heavy drapes apart and opened the window to walk out on the balcony. From here, I could see the moon on the ocean. Its light cast a pale course for beyond the horizon. A ship. A crew. In two short days, I'd gone from fisherman to smuggler.

Aw, hell. Screw that.

I'm a pirate!

THE LOW ROAD

"IT'S SO NICE TO SEE A YOUNG MAN LIKE YOURSELF TAKIN' AN interest in the pipes." The elderly woman smiled at me, and reached over to pat me on the knee like a favored grandchild. The gesture felt odd, largely because I was wearing a kilt.

"Well now, what can I say?" I murmured with a warm smile, and Mrs. Balfour sat back and picked up the knitting that she had temporarily set down in her lap. "When I heard, through friends, that you were planning to sell some of your late husband's things—God rest his soul—I knew what a piper he was and how he loved the old pipes, and I had to stop in."

"Oh, it's always nice to have company, no matter what the reason." The knitting needle in Mrs. Balfour's hands flew, with a sprightliness I wouldn't have imagined from the gnarled fingers. "But you're right; Edwin loved his bagpipes. He liked to listen to them, and he liked to play them, and he also liked to buy them." She leaned forward conspiratorially. "You wouldn't want to take the whole lot of them off my hands, would you? I loved my husband, but I never really cared for the sound of the pipes. Fifty years I heard his music, and I never did like the sound of it."

"I know your husband's collection was quite extensive, but there's one set of pipes, in particular, I'm interested in," I said, trying not to sound too eager. But when my patron sends me to obtain a particular set of bagpipes, I can't help it. "I'm looking for an old set, probably not even in good condition any more, but they have sentimental value, you see? He might have called them the Dow pipes."

Mrs. Balfour looked at the ceiling, thinking. "Dow pipes? Now let me think. Ah, yes. I think I know the set. Would you know them to see them? Come, I'll show you."

And at that invitation, I rose to follow Mrs. Balfour down a long, dim hallway. I shivered. Let me say that a kilt is not my normal attire, nor was I being won over as a convert in this drafty house. It was October in Philadelphia, and it was damn cold to my way of reckoning. Before I had a three-centuries-old vampire as a patron and mentor, I'd been a fisherman off the North Carolina coast. Now, I was a pirate in a kilt, doing my best to sweet talk an old lady out of a set of magical, and dangerous, bagpipes. Not exactly the future I would have foreseen for myself just a few years ago, but then again, water magic, not foresight, is my gift.

Mrs. Balfour narrated our whole journey down the long, narrow hallway. She pointed to the paintings on the walls, to small objects on tables and in nooks, even at the oriental rugs on the floor. Captain Balfour had been a very successful merchant, and the large old home overlooking the cold Atlantic was crammed full of the trinkets and collections he had gathered in forty years at sea.

At the end of the hallway, Mrs. Balfour pulled a jangle of keys from one of the pockets of her apron and turned the balky iron lock that secured a scarred oaken door. The door swung open into a dusty storage room lit dimly by one grimy window. The room was packed nearly floor to ceiling with all manner of goods: statues with many arms, a full suit of armor, baskets, trunks, and tall wooden wardrobe boxes of every size. Mingled with the smell of dust and mildew was the faint odor of spices from places I would probably never see in my lifetime, and the unmistakable scent of old leather.

Mrs. Balfour knelt in front of a huge trunk and fingered her keys like a rosary until she found the right one. Funny how that one trunk seemed to sit by itself, while in every corner of the room, treasures were heaped one atop another. Even silenced, the Dow pipes seemed to demand caution and respect. Mrs. Balfour might not understand why her late husband saw fit to lock up this particular set of pipes, but I knew.

The Dow bagpipes were ghost pipes.

Sorren, my undead mentor and patron, had drilled me on the identification and careful handling of the pipes. They were one of two prizes my partner Coltt and I intended to bring home this trip. With luck, neither would require thieving on the high seas, a dangerous proposition as the Atlantic waters grew wild this time of year. No, I'd hoped that flattering an old lady and a little burglary might net us both trophies and let us sail home in peace.

I really should have known better.

As Mrs. Balfour worked the balky lock on the trunk, I remembered Sorren's instructions for this run.

"Know anything about bagpipes, Dante?" Sorren had asked me as we sat in the back room of my uncle's curio shop.

My grandfather tried to teach me to play them. He said I did well, but my mother said it sounded like I was trying to squeeze a cat out of a big plaid bag through those tiny little pipes."

Sorren chuckled, and I could see the tips of his long eye teeth. When he was mortal, Sorren had been one of the best jewel thieves in Europe. While three hundred years hadn't blunted his agility one bit, Sorren now preferred to stay behind the scenes whenever possible. That's why he took Coltt and me under his wing, taught us how to blend into any level of society or social situation, made us master thieves as well as damn fine pirates.

"Well, don't play these. The Dow pipes are half of the reason you're going to Philadelphia. In the hands of a piper who's of Scottish blood and has some magic, these pipes call forth the spirits."

"Ghost pipes?"

Sorren had nodded. "They were made by a man named Ian Dow, a piper of renown two hundred years ago. When his only sons drowned off the Scottish coast, Dow went mad with grief. Legend has it he built a special set of pipes and made a deal with the Darkness so that the pipes would bring the spirits of his sons home to him again."

"I take it that his bargain was successful?"

Sorren's lips twitched upward in a predatory smile. "More than Dow intended. Dow went to a cliff overlooking the sea and began to play. But he forgot that his sons weren't the only ones to lose their lives to the dark water down below. His sons came home, all right, along with hundreds—maybe thousands—of drowned souls who heard the song of the pipes and followed it. They found him on the cliff, the pipes still in his hands, dead. Heart stopped."

"And the pipes?"

"One of my associates acquired them through family connections, knowing how dangerous they could be in the hands of a dark wizard. They've passed from caretaker to caretaker until they reached Captain Balfour, who was supposed to bring them back from Scotland and deliver them to me. Unfortunately, he died of a fever before he could do that, which is why I need you and Coltt to retrieve them before someone else does."

Sorren was the silent partner behind the curio shop in Charleston run by my Uncle Evann. Three years ago, when Coltt and I had been the only survivors of a pirate raid on our small fishing village, we'd taken our stolen ship and fled to Charleston, hoping Uncle Evann could give us sanctuary. We'd killed the pirates who had murdered our families, and had a haunted necklace to show for it, one that I knew for a fact was evil. I thought Uncle Evann would know what to do with it.

As it turned out, Uncle Evann's shop, Trifles and Folly, was more than it appeared. Sorren was one of a small, secret group of mortals and immortals pledged to keeping dangerous magical objects out of the hands of those who might misuse them. Sorren and Evann kept an ear open whenever objects with unusual pasts came up at auction or were part of an estate being distributed. One way or another, Sorren made it his business to take those objects out of circulation. Evann handled the legal acquisitions. Coltt and I now took care of the rest.

"And the other item?"

Sorren looked thoughtful. "I know who has it, but I'm not totally certain exactly what the item is that we're looking for. But I do know this—it's even more dangerous than the Dow pipes."

"If you don't know what I'm looking for, how are Coltt and I supposed to 'acquire' it for you?"

Sorren frowned. "I've had my eye on a man named Galoshin Lawry for a while now. He comes from a family of minor magical talent and few scruples. On his own, Lawry is a bit player. But lately, there's been talk of him trying to acquire 'soul cash' and that put him in my sights."

"Soul cash? Lawry's selling souls? To whom?"

"I don't know, and that worries me. By himself, Lawry doesn't have the magical power to raise the dead or tamper with spirits, so my hunch is that he's gotten his hands on a dark object, something that has power over souls."

"Like the Dow pipes."

Sorren shrugged. "There are more dark objects that tinker with souls than you want to know about. The Dow pipes are benign compared to most of them. Lawry is heading to Philadelphia on a ship from Scotland. I want you to be there when he arrives. He's connected to some wealthy people, so there'll be parties in his honor. I've arranged to get you into some of them, so you can try to get an idea of just how his 'soul cash' works. Meanwhile, Coltt can search his rooms. Between the two of you, I expect that you'll make short work of it." He paused. "Oh, there is one more thing. Both Captain Dow's widow and Galoshin Lawry take extreme pride in their Scottish heritage. So of course, you'll wear a kilt when you're in their presence."

Which is why my knees were freezing.

The lid to the old trunk creaked open, and Mrs. Down removed a protective sheet of muslin that had yellowed with age. Beneath it lay a finely crafted set of the most beautiful pipes I had ever seen. The bag was a black and red plaid, and the drone cords and their tassels were crimson. The chanters were a dark wood, and the slides were bone or ivory. Even at a distance, I could feel its magic, but Mrs. Balfour seemed completely oblivious to its power.

"It is a beauty, isn't it? Never could understand why my husband would never play them." She looked up at me. "Do you play? I'd love to hear these, just once."

No, Mrs. Balfour certainly couldn't feel the magic resonating from the pipes, or she'd have never asked me to play them. Pipes, I'd learned from my Scottish grandfather, are almost a living thing in the hands of a master piper. He fills them with his warm breath and holds them in his arms close to the warmth of his body, intimately, like his beloved. Those damned pipes held a residue of Ian Dow's spirit in them; even several paces away, I could sense his despair and overwhelming grief. No bloody way would I breathe life into to those pipes.

I hoped my weak smile looked appropriately contrite. "I'm sorry, but much to my grandfather's chagrin, I've no talent for the pipes myself. But I was a Dow on my mother's side, so there's a bit of sentimental value, if you know what I mean."

Mrs. Balfour sighed. "Ah well, I had to ask." Her eyes took on a harder glint. "Did you bring money to pay for them?"

I took a bag of gold coins from the fur sporran that hung from a chain around my waist and held the coins out to her. I waited as she counted them.

She smiled when she looked up at me. "As promised," she said with a nod. "They're yours now. Take them with you. And I hope your dreams are more peaceful than mine have been."

I looked at her and frowned. "I beg your pardon?"

"I've heard pipes playing in my dreams twice now. Once, the night my husband died, and then again last night. Woke up with the cold shivers, like someone was walking on my grave."

Ask not for whom the pipes play... they play for thee.

"I'm sure I'll sleep well, and so will you," I assured her with a confidence I did not feel. I had a bad feeling about what it might mean to hear the Dow pipes in one's dreams, and a suspicion it was a harbinger of death. From the look in her eyes, Mrs. Balfour thought the same.

"Well, off with you. I've enjoyed visiting with you, but there's work to do and potatoes to peel," Mrs. Balfour said, closing the trunk and dusting off her hands. She saw me to the door and gave a last, mistrustful glance at the bundle in my arms.

"You'll see that the pipes are kept safe, won't you? My husband seemed to think they were quite valuable."

That, I could assure her in good conscience. "They'll be very safe. I promise you."

Coltt was waiting for me in a closed carriage down the lane from the Balfour home. "Did you get them?"

I nodded. "How about you?"

"Lawry is the toast of the town," Coltt replied. "I spent the day helping out with deliveries to two of the houses where he's going to be a guest at parties in his honor. Got inside, had a look around, and loosened up a back window to make going back in later all the easier," he said with a grin.

I had magic and enough of a flair for schooling that Sorren made a gentleman of me when circumstances required. I was passable at several accents and could blend in amid high or low society. As Sorren put it, I "cleaned up well."

Coltt, on the other hand, wasn't quite as versatile, but while he lacked magic, he had a natural agility I could never match, which made him the perfect choice for climbing into windows and scaling walls. Where I was Sorren's protégé when it came to smuggling and magic, Coltt was his apprentice thief.

"I want to get these pipes stowed aboard the *Vengeance* before we do anything else," I said. "I'll lock them up in my cabin. I won't feel right about storing them anywhere else."

I paused. "Any news to report?"

"I got a glimpse of Lawry."

"Not enough for him to recognize you, I hope."

"Doubt it. I was with the servants, and everyone knows servants are invisible."

"And?"

Coltt's eyes darkened. "I don't like him. I don't have a magical bone in my body, but Lawry gives me the creeps. Can't imagine how he got the society folks eating out of his hand."

I shrugged. "Don't underestimate magic. Sorren told me that some wizards can work an attraction spell that's very specific. Maybe his spell is focused on money or pedigree or connections."

"The question is, what is Lawry after? And where does the 'soul cash' come in?"

I didn't have an answer, so I asked another question. "Did you find out where he's staying?"

Coltt nodded. "Lawry is staying with the different families that are hosting his parties. Normally, I'd say that was going to make it easy to break into his rooms, but he's got magic, so it's probably not going to be simple to get in and get out without being noticed."

"I thought you and Sorren worked something out on that."

"We did. But what it means is that I'll have to rely on some of Sorren's tools to do my spying rather than going in personally. More chance to overlook something, if you ask me." He paused. "Oh, I did overhear some talk as I was helping unload. Seems like our Mr. Lawry is soliciting contributions for an expedition he's heading up in a week. The families hosting him already have contributed to his cause, and he's hoping that their guests will be equally generous."

I rubbed my chin as I thought. From what Sorren had told me about Lawry, he didn't seem the scientific type. "What kind of expedition and what exactly is his expedition hoping to find?"

"Not sure. Maybe you'll find out at the party tonight. Whatever it is, Sorren must be pretty certain that it's connected to that 'soul cash' Lawry's interested in."

I shrugged. "I'll see what I can do. Did you overhear anything else of value?"

Coltt thought for a moment. "Not sure whether or not this has anything to do with Lawry, but I heard the servants talking, and there've been a number of servants and day laborers who've turned up dead rather mysteriously."

"Oh?"

Coltt nodded. "Not the sort of folks whose deaths get a lot of attention. Scullery maids, dock workers, some vagrants. Oddest thing about it is, none of the dead had a mark on them."

"They had to die of something."

"That's just it though. It's quite the buzz below-stairs, and in the tavern where I took in some stew and ale for lunch. They weren't stabbed or strangled, and there's no sign of poison. Most were too young to have had a bad heart. The police are dismissing it as water from a bad well, but talk at the pub says they weren't all from the same area, so they would have gotten their water from more than one pump. And besides, if it were the water, more would be sick."

"Anything that ties the deaths to Lawry?"

Coltt met my eyes. "Only the fact that they began the night Lawry arrived in Philadelphia."

"WOULD YOU CARE for another brandy?"

"Thank you." I watched my host pour a measure of the dark liquor into my glass, and then returned my attention to the evening's gathering. Tonight, a group of about twenty of Philadelphia's captains of industry and pillars of society mingled at the home of Mr. Everston Willard Cummings, III. Cummings had made his fortune in the shipbuilding industry. I looked around the room. There was Robert Towars, whose glass furnace had risen right before the outbreak of war with England. Chatting with him was John Hewson Sr., famed for the calico and linen prints his company produced. There were others, wealthy men who had built fortunes copying English and French designs in porcelain, textiles, silver, and fine furniture when the war cut off trade between the former colonies and the Continent. They were shrewd men, known for their eye for a good deal, and Lawry had their full attention.

"If you'll pardon my saying so, Mr. Lawry, I wonder about the soundness of your expedition." All eyes turned to Everston Cummings, the man whose deep, authoritative voice rang out over the small room. "You're asking for quite a tidy sum of money to fund your research in Bermuda, but I'd like to know why there and not somewhere closer?"

Lawry smiled, and I wondered if he had somehow planted the

question with Cummings because from the smug expression on Lawry's face, it was exactly the issue he'd been longing to raise.

"An excellent question, Mr. Cummings. You're correct that there are many stretches along the coast of this new United States of America that have been the sites of numerous shipwrecks. Indeed, there are no shortage of such sites all over the world, and my new invention has the potential to make us very rich from all of them," he said with a knowing wink that brought greedy chuckles from the assembly.

"But Bermuda has the enviable position on old, established trade routes to make the waters around it home to a most unique graveyard of ships. Merchant ships, galleons, ships laden with the treasures the Spaniards gathered in the darkest jungles of South America. Bermuda itself is divided on its loyalty to the crown. In fact, I'm sure I'm not alone in believing that, by proximity alone, it should belong to these United States rather than to a faraway monarch."

Lawry leaned into his crowd, and I saw that he fingered a mirrored cube that hung from a silver strand around his neck. The surface shimmered strangely in the light, as if it reflected and distorted the faces of the men clustered closely around Lawry. "The delicate instrumentation in this small cube, coupled with its larger mate that rests safely under lock and key in my room, enables me to calibrate changes in the wind and barometer as well as the temperature and currents of the sea, to find wrecks that have long evaded treasure hunters. Working with men like yourselves—in fact, with some of you in this room—I have hired a uniquely skilled group of divers from the Orient who are used to deep dives and outfitted them in special suits to protect them from cold and pressure. We have everything we need to take the lost gold of the Spaniards and the sunken treasures of the East India Company for ourselves: everything except the money necessary for a journey of the duration that would be most profitable."

Lawry leaned back. As a fisherman, I recognized the movement. He had them hooked, now he just needed to reel in the catch. "I have enough to mount a small-scale expedition right now, but of course, once that happens and the results become known, there will be a clamor for investors to get in on the opportunity. I'd like to make this as profitable as possible for the people who had faith in my vision by limiting the number of investors."

I watched as the fat fish practically jumped out of the water and into his creel. The merchant princes of Philadelphia withdrew bank notes and vowed to have promissory notes delivered the next day. Only a few hung back with me at the fringe of the feeding frenzy. With the pretense of going to refill my brandy, I slipped from the room before I would be notable by my lack of sponsorship. I'd gotten what I wanted, although I didn't have any idea of what it meant. I could only hope that Coltt's night had been more illuminating.

I found Coltt waiting for me at our rooming house. "Were you able to get a look into Lawry's room?"

Coltt nodded. "Not in person, since he had the doors and windows spelled shut. But the magic telescope Sorren gave me worked perfectly. With it, I could see in the dark, and I got a good look around. I was also in a good position when Lawry came in a few hours before the big party."

"Came in from where?"

"Don't know. But he pulled a necklace of some sort out from under his shirt. It had a small box on a chain, and the box was glowing. He placed the small box on top of a larger box and then the big box picked up the glow. Damnedest thing was, I could have sworn something was flowing out of the small box into the big one, and for a moment, the light inside the big box seemed to swirl and move. Then they both faded and Lawry put the necklace back on and started to get changed for the party."

"I saw him wearing that necklace at the reception. But it wasn't glowing. I couldn't really tell what the small box was made of, but it had some kind of magic; that, I'm sure of."

"What do you reckon he's up to?"

I shrugged. "Well, what he told the men at the reception was that he'd developed a very delicate scientific instrument to help locate shipwrecks, and he was sailing for Bermuda with a crew of specialized divers to make a fortune bringing up sunken treasure. He also hinted that he'd like to see Bermuda break away from the crown, which played well to the audience."

"But where does the 'soul cash' come in?"

I shook my head. "Don't know, but he took in enough hard cash to provision a nice expedition."

"Do you think it's possible that he's gone straight?"

"Doubt it. Sorren was sure Lawry was up to something, and Sorren's sources aren't wrong often. No, I think Lawry may be telling a half-truth at best. I'm sure he'd like to get his hands on some of Bermuda's lost treasure. But I doubt his investors will ever see any return on their money—or that Lawry will show his face in Philadelphia again."

I dressed for bed and yawned. "Tomorrow, I need to hire replacements for the crew that shipped out so that we're ready to sail on a moment's notice. I don't believe the timetable Lawry's given us. I think it's more likely that he'll skip town unexpectedly, and I want to be on his tail when it happens."

I spent the bulk of the next morning in the waterfront pubs looking for replacements for the crew members who decided to leave us in Philadelphia. I kept the crew of the *Vengeance* deliberately light at twenty-five men because most of our runs weren't the usual for smugglers and I wanted to keep portside talk to a minimum. I'd expected to replace eight men and was none too happy to find myself hiring ten when two of my crew went missing.

Since nearly all of our runs were at Sorren's behest, the *Vengeance* worked a little differently than most pirate ships. We often carried cargoes of tobacco or whiskey to cover expenses. When we raided a ship, we had a specific prize in mind, one of Sorren's missing magical objects. Sorren didn't mind if we helped ourselves to anything else of value that was easily carried off, but the crew had to be disciplined enough to understand that we weren't in the business of pillaging every ship we encountered. Sorren made sure that the crew was paid well and paid promptly, which kept the grumbling about not seeing enough "action" to a minimum.

In short, I needed a crew that could sail a Bermuda sloop and who didn't mind thievery, men who could hold their own in a fight but weren't bloodthirsty lunatics. It wasn't always an easy combination to find. I had no problem finding candidates who fit the first three requirements, but it could be difficult weeding out the lunatics.

It was the middle of the afternoon by the time I finished hiring crew. We'd given the *Vengeance* a fresh coat of paint and a new name for this trip since our ship was becoming a little too well known. As far as Philadelphia was concerned, I was captain of the *Venture*. That suited me just fine. While a reputation as a dangerous pirate was a benefit in some circles, in the company I was keeping in the city, it was more likely to result in a trip to the gallows, something I preferred to avoid. Sorren even managed to provide letters of marque for the *Venture*, making us a more genteel sort of pirate, a privateer.

When I returned to the rooming house, I found that Coltt had packed all my things and was in the process of having them put aboard a wagon. "What the devil's going on?"

"Lawry's gone. He was supposed to move from the Cummings's house to the Hewsons, but that's not where his carriage went. He left an hour ago, and I followed him straight to the port. He's booked passage on a merchant ship there, the *Sea Lass*. Our ship is faster and better armed, but they're likely to have more crew. They looked like they'd be sailing pretty shortly, so I packed your things and hoped you'd had success hiring a crew or we'll lose Lawry once he heads out."

We had to scramble, but we were under sail shortly after Lawry left port, putting us far enough behind him to hopefully evade his notice, but close enough that we could follow. I used my water magic to slow his progress, while keeping the sea friendly to the *Vengeance*. Yet every time I used my magic, something alien touched my power. Whatever Lawry had in those two boxes was strong magic, and it was dark. I didn't like its touch even at a distance. The feel of its magic gave me the shivers, and every time, the same image came to my mind. I had once passed the Half Moon Battery in Charleston late at night, and through the barred windows, I could hear the piteous wailing of those imprisoned within, criminals, debtors, and the deeply unlucky who served their sentences. It was a chilling sound, made the more so since few if any who heard it were likely to be moved to compassion for the rogues inside.

Despite our quest, my mood lifted as we left the gray North Atlantic for warmer waters. We easily kept the merchant ship in our sights, with a plan to attack that night, before we reached Bermudian waters. Yet even the warmer temperature and bright sunlight couldn't drive away my sense of misgiving. And the nearer we came to Bermuda, the more my magic tingled in the back of my mind. There was something strange about these waters. Growing up along the coast, I'd heard stories of ships lost to pirates and to the treacherous reefs. There were dozens, maybe hundreds of ships that had gone down over the last few hundred years in the shipping lanes between Bermuda and the mainland. Some blamed it on reefs while others cursed fickle winds and dangerous currents. But as we sailed onward, I recognized another reason these waters had become a graveyard of ships. Magic.

I could feel the wild magic on my skin, making the hairs on my arms rise. It waxed and waned like the wind, swirled in eddies no one else could see, and slipped along the surface of the sea in places, racing the current. It was a tinderbox, waiting for a spark.

"Do you think he knows we're here?" Coltt asked.

"More to the point—if he did know, would he care?" I wasn't sure what the limits were for the magic of those confounded boxes, or what type of magic it was. The sooner they were off Lawry's ship and onto ours, the happier I'd be.

While the *Vengeance* couldn't outgun a warship, our guns were more than adequate for frightening a merchant ship into submission. Adjusting our sails, we quickly pulled up alongside the *Sea Lass*, and readied our guns for a shot across their bow. But as my men went to load the cannons, the *Sea Lass* slowed and came around, and as it did so, wooden panels in the sides opened up, baring the muzzles of twenty cannons. That was five more cannons than the *Vengeance* carried, which wasn't good. We looked up to see Lawry smirking at us from the deck, which now brimmed with heavily armed pirates, not the passive merchants we expected.

Shots fired, close at hand. I looked up to see that eight of the ten new sailors I had hired in Philadelphia stood armed, their flintlocks pointed at the rest of the crew. Grappling hooks flew through the air, pulling the *Vengeance* closer to the "merchant" ship as rope ladders were flung over the larger ship's sides and dozens of invaders scurried down the ropes to land on the *Vengeance's* deck.

"My sources were quick to tell me of your interest in my ship," Lawry taunted. "It didn't take much to buy the loyalty of your newest crewmen. You seemed quite fascinated with my expedition at the reception," he said, fixing his gaze on me. "You're just in time to see the real show."

Lawry's pirates and the turncoat sailors prodded the rest of us to climb the rope ladders that hung from the sides of Lawry's *Sea Lass*. We were badly outnumbered and while we would have given them a fight for their money had we the chance to draw our guns, as it was, we were outmatched.

"Where are your divers?" I challenged Lawry. "Is this really all about retrieving treasure from old shipwrecks?"

Lawry did not answer. He sent the majority of his sailors and the traitors from my crew back to their posts with a jerk of his head. Several armed guards herded most of my loyal crewmembers into the hold, while Lawry and three of his guards motioned for me, Coltt, and two of my crew into his cabin.

There on the desk in his cabin sat the mirrored cube Coltt had spotted in Lawry's room back in Charleston. And as Lawry entered the cabin and locked the door behind him, I saw the small cube on its chain around his neck. Lawry wore a triumphant smile, and the armed guards made him bold.

"Treasure is only part of it," he said. "Have you never heard the strange tales about these waters? Even the Spaniards whisper about the number of ships that have gone missing and the odd things they've seen if they were lucky to pass this way and leave alive. Some blame the currents, and some say it's the winds, but I know the truth of it," Lawry said with a conspiratorial grin. "It's the magic."

I remembered how my own powers had sensed the oddness of the magic in this place, how my nerves jangled and my skin crawled. "Magic?" I said, wondering whether Lawry could sense my power. I clamped down my shielding, just in case.

Lawry lifted the small cube on its chain and caressed it with his fingers. "I intend to own these waters. I'll turn the wild magic to do my bidding, and when I am the master of this sea, I'll have the power to take Bermuda for my own. We'll control this shipping lane, and all who want to pass will pay tribute or be destroyed. We'll have gold aplenty from the wrecks, and time enough to loot them when our men aren't waylaying ships."

"How do you plan to do that? There's a British fort on Bermuda. Magic or not, why would they just give up without a fight?"

Lawry's smile broadened. "Let me show you." He jerked his head, and two of his guards pushed one of my crewmen forward. Lawry removed the cube necklace from around his neck and held it out toward the frightened hostage. The mirrored surface of the cube began to shimmer and glow. It flared, and for an instant, I thought I saw a reflection of the crewman's terrified face reflected and distorted in its surface before the man fell down dead without a word.

Coltt and I surged forward to take Lawry, but the guards held us back. He turned his cube on the second crewman, who met the same fate as the first. This time, I was certain that I saw a reflection of his face on the small cube.

"What is that thing?"

Lawry fingered the cube fondly. "A tool. What matters more are the souls in my cache that amplify my magic, giving me the power to bend this region's wild magic to my will." He walked over to the large cube and held the small cube out toward it. Both cubes pulsed with a bright glow, and I felt a surge of old, strange magic as a flicker of light moved from the small cube to the large one. Worse than that, in my mind, I heard both of my crewmen scream, and I knew in every fiber of my body that it was their souls held prisoner within that awful cube.

Coltt and I exchanged glances as the realization struck us. Not soul cash. Soul cache. A hoarding place for stolen souls, kept prisoner for eternity, robbed of their final rest. A source of power that Lawry could draw upon at will to strengthen his power. In time, he would become invincible. Perhaps he already was.

Lawry seemed to tire of impressing us. He turned to the guards. "Go aboard their ship and disable their guns. Take their firearms, and leave the two of them tied up. Set a fuse in their munitions stores, and rig their sails to carry them into the shipping lanes." He looked back to Coltt and me. "I do so love a good fireworks show."

"And my crew?"

Lawry gave an exaggerated show of false remorse. "Unfortunately, they will not be joining you. They're much more valuable to me as fuel, so to speak. But the captain and first mate of the *Vengeance*, now that's a prize that lets me send a warning to the region."

Lawry clucked his tongue. "Oh yes, I learned the true name of your ship despite its hasty repainting and new name. You've made quite a reputation in a short time, and it will serve me well to let your ship explode where others will see it, where the wreck will bear witness that someone was able to best you." He nodded to his guards. "Get them out of here."

Coltt and I struggled, but Lawry's guards had us outgunned and outnumbered. I could see anger and defeat in Coltt's eyes. Lawry left us, and within a few minutes, as the guards bound us and began to make their way back to the *Vengeance*, I heard the silent screams of my crew in my mind as Lawry fed their souls into his soul cache.

How could Sorren have missed such a thing? Then again, unless he had ever seen the words actually written, there was no way for him to know that "cash" was "cache." But I had bigger worries. I had no idea how to keep Coltt and myself from being blown sky high, let alone stop Lawry from making himself master of some of the most valuable shipping lanes in the Atlantic and Caribbean.

Lawry's guards made short work of their assignment. They tied us hand and foot, and dropped us like luggage in my cabin aboard the *Vengeance*, taking care to lock us in and leave with the key. Before they left us, they clipped us both soundly on the head with the grip of their cutlasses. Coltt was knocked cold; I ended up with a hell of a headache, but I managed not to lose consciousness, though my vision blurred and I swore I could feel every beat of my heart like a drum in my head.

I could hear Lawry's men making their way into the cargo hold of the ship, looting our guns and setting the fuse in our munitions store. Once they cut our ship free, they'd probably leave a man aboard long enough to light the fuse, and the unfortunate man would have to jump ship and swim back as the *Vengeance* caught wind in its sails to carry it away.

We didn't have much time, but I wasn't about to lie back and wait for the ship to explode beneath me. I could still hear the echoes of my dying crew's screams, and the more I thought about it, the angrier I got. I rolled closer to my hammock and kicked with my bound feet until I sent a pair of boots flying from under the bed. I managed to get my bound hands inside the right boot, and with my fingers, nudged at the blade concealed in the toe until its tip peeked into view.

Bracing the boot and its knife as best I could, I sawed away at my bonds, having no idea how long it would take Lawry's men to complete their task. They had used good hemp rope, and it seemed to take forever to free my hands and feet. Coltt was still unconscious. I paused to check for a pulse and was relieved to find that he was breathing, but he would be no help to me. I tried the door and threw myself against it, but it was made of sturdy oak and held fast. I resolved to hide a spare key within my cabin should I—and the *Vengeance* —survive.

I heard the clatter of the grappling hooks as they were withdrawn, heard the creaking of the ropes and mast as the sails were hoisted. Lawry's men were ready to light the fuse and abandon us to the current. We were running out of time.

Desperately, I cast about the cabin for a weapon. Lawry's men had been efficient in tossing the contents of my drawers and chest onto the floor in search of firearms or swords, all of which were missing. I kicked at a bundle of clothing and found it strangely solid. Curious, I bent down and moved the shirt and cloak aside. Beneath them were the Dow pipes.

I had told the captain's widow that I could not play, but that was a lie. I had been afraid of the claim the pipes might place upon my soul if my magic woke them. I stared at the pipes, knowing that whether I was blown to bits or used the magic of the pipes, my soul appeared consigned to Perdition. I glanced back at Coltt's still form, and closed my eyes, hearing the desperate, anguished screams of my murdered crew. Rage filled me. I picked up the pipes and walked to the porthole as I felt the *Vengeance's* sails fill with wind and carry us away.

The sight of Lawry's ship receding was not what filled me with dread. A strange mist had risen from the water, and as far as the eye could see from side to side, the horizon glowed an eerie green color. I stole a glance at the compass on my desk. The needle had gone crazy, bouncing from side to side erratically, giving me no indication of our course, but confirming my suspicion. Lawry had begun to draw upon the soul cache to work his magic.

I took a deep breath, and called my magic to me. First, I reached out in my own power to the water, using it to slow our progress, keeping us in sight of Lawry's ship. I sent a surge of power toward Lawry's vessel, giving it a sudden patch of rough sea to keep them occupied. Then I lifted the pipes and began to play.

I only knew one song for the pipes, *Loch Lomond*. It seemed fitting to play a song written by a man about to be hanged, a man who expected to return to his beloved homeland by the "low road"— his spirit walking through the valley of the shadow of death. I saw no way to defeat the burning fuse amid our powder kegs, but I had every intention of taking Lawry and his infernal cubes with me. And as I played, my anger called up my magic, and my magic through the pipes called to the spirits.

With the screams of my crew still fresh in my mind, I swept the magic of the pipes toward Lawry and his cube. My anger fairly vibrated through the music, and I felt the pipes find the imprisoned spirits within the cube. There were many, many more than I had imagined. Not just my poor crew; oh no, there were hundreds of souls stored in Lawry's soul cache. I remembered the feckless vagrants and servants back in Charleston that had been found dead without a mark on them, and I knew where their souls had gone. I put everything I had into playing those damned pipes, trusting its magic would do as its doomed owner had originally intended and free the spirits to go home.

All around me, I could feel the magic rising. Outside the porthole, a green glow now stretched from the sea into the heavens, but Heaven had nothing to do with this cursed phosphorescence. Above me, I could hear the winds howl, and the sea beneath us had begun to pitch with the frenzy of a storm. On and on I played, and I heard the howls of the imprisoned spirits grow to a maddening pitch, echoing the anger that moved my fingers over the chanters with more speed and skill than I had ever mustered on my own.

But the magic of the pipes was not selective, and too late I remembered what had doomed their maker. The seas of the Scottish coast were not the only ones filled with the wrecks of ships and the skeletons of the lost. These waters off the Bermuda coast held an untold number of ill-fated ships and their drowned crews and passengers. Some had gone to their watery graves by accident of fate, while many more had been sent there by treachery and murder. All had been cheated out of their full lifespan, and as they rose, I knew that they had one thing in common. They were very angry.

The spirits whipped around the *Vengeance* like hurricane winds, tattering its sails and stirring the sea to white-capped fury. The winds blasted open the portholes and the door of the hold and set upon me with such power that I feared I might not keep my feet. They tore at my hammock and sent my papers flying, buffeting me. I heard the winds howl through the hatch and heard the spirits toss the contents of the hold as if the heavy casks were empty. With a crack, the lock on the door to my cabin split in two and the door swung open.

I had loosed the ghosts from the soul cache and summoned the spirits from the sea, but I had no idea of how to set them free. Yet as they whipped around me, plunging the cabin into an icy chill, I sensed... curiosity. Oh, there was malice aplenty, but not directed toward Coltt and me.

Lawry was a different story.

I felt the spirits of the soul cache and the sea dead gather their forces, even as, across the waves of power and water, I felt Lawry summon his power. All along, I had played verse after verse of *Loch Lomond*, over and over, until my fingers ached and my lungs felt as if they were on fire. I played with crazed speed, off-key, a refrain of the damned. Lawry sent his power along the channels of magic in a blast he hoped would scatter the spirits. It was magic worked by a living mage, magic that took the high road. The spirits were ready for him, and they massed their power, aided by the Dow pipes, and the magic of a mage surrounded by the dead. The low road, the pathway of the dead, was faster.

Through the magic, I could feel when the cube prison exploded, knew it sent mirrored shards at lethal velocity all around as the tormented wraiths that had been held captive burst forth. Empowered by the magic, they did not rise as mere vapor; no, these revenants possessed the will and wherewithal to set themselves upon their captor and his guards. I heard their screams across the water even as my bond through the magic showed me the attack, and I watched the enraged spirits strip skin from bone and suck the breath from their bloodied, terror-struck keeper.

I felt the shock of the magical impact in my body. It jarred every bone, sending an immediate, blinding headache from the base of my skull to the crown of my head. I felt the spirits rip away Lawry's magical protections, strip them from him like shears through silk, felt them leech the heat from his body and the breath from his lungs and finally the twisted magic from his fingers.

Their vengeance flowed through my veins, rose and fell with my breath as the pipes played their cursed tune. My rage had fueled theirs, and their hunger for justice had enraged me even further. They, and we, were avenged. I felt the spirits pull back, and then dissipate. They had what they came for.

As suddenly as it came, the storm ended. The *Vengeance* rocked on quiet waters. It was then I realized two things. The first was that Coltt was staring at me in wide-eyed horror, very much alive. The second was that we had not exploded.

My arms were shaking as I carefully laid aside the Dow pipes. The marks of the chanter's holes were imprinted—no, burned—into my fingertips, and my lungs ached. I freed Coltt, and together we ran to the hold. We found the partially burned fuse, but it was cold, extinguished by the mighty gust of wind the spirits had sent around and through the ship. We returned to the deck, and I looked skyward. The *Vengeance's* sails hung in tatters, and one of its masts had snapped.

"Look there!" Coltt pointed. Lawry's ship was listing badly to port. Its sails were in even worse shape than ours, and two of its masts had fallen, bringing the rigging with them. Bodies lay scattered across the deck and bobbed in the water. Later, we would go aboard, but our visit only confirmed what through my magic, I already knew. Lawry and his crew were dead, and his soul cache was shattered and useless.

"If we manage to get back to port, I don't know how we're going to explain this to Sorren," I said. We had reclaimed the Dow pipes and destroyed the soul cache, and Lawry along with it. I wasn't sure whether that made our mission half successful or a half failure.

Coltt still looked ashen from the shock of it all. "I opened my eyes to hear you playing those damned pipes, and I saw spirits weaving all around you. How did you do it?"

I thought about the rage and grief I had felt over my murdered crew, the anger that surged through me to be held captive on my own ship, threatened with my own munitions. It had been sheer, blinding rage, not courage, that had driven me. I was glad to be alive, but I wasn't particularly proud of myself.

"Easy," I said with a wan smile. "I just had to put the 'irate' back in 'pirate.'"

AMONG THE SHOALS FOREVER

Sorren, my patron and mentor, leaned back in his chair.

"We're in one of the most haunted cities in the New World," Uncle Evann replied. "What's a few more 'haints' when we've got so many?" He shrugged. "I never reckoned ghosts were really any of our business."

Sorren gave Uncle Evann a look that managed to convey both exasperation and affection. "They become our business when they're bound here by dark magic," Sorren said. He swirled the red liquid in his goblet, liquid I knew for certain was blood. The glow from the fireplace added color to Sorren's pale complexion, but could never warm his skin. He might have let out a long sigh if he still needed to breathe. Instead, he looked from Uncle Evann to me.

"And it becomes Dante's business when pirates are involved," he said with a hint of a smile that just slightly exposed the tips of his elongated eye teeth.

He had me at "pirates." "Yeah," I said with a glance at Coltt, my partner in crime. "Whatever it is, count us in."

Sorren was the silent partner behind the curio shop in Charleston run by my Uncle Evann. Four years ago, when Coltt and I had been the only survivors of a pirate raid on our small fishing village, we'd taken our stolen ship and fled to Charleston, hoping Uncle Evann could give us sanctuary. We'd killed the pirates who had murdered our families and had a haunted necklace to show for it, one that I knew for a fact was evil. I thought Uncle Evann would know what to do with it.

As it turned out, Uncle Evann's shop, Trifles and Folly, was more than it appeared. Sorren was one of a small, secret group of mortals and immortals pledged to keeping dangerous magical objects out of the hands of those who might misuse them. Sorren and Evann kept an ear open whenever objects with unusual pasts came up at auction, or were part of an estate being distributed. One way or another, Sorren made it his business to take those objects out of circulation. Evann handled the legal acquisitions. Coltt and I now took care of the rest.

Sorren stretched out his long legs and watched the fire burn as he spoke. "Felicity Reynolds Barre disappeared on a voyage from Bermuda to Boston almost a year ago."

I frowned. "Sloan Barre's daughter?" Sloan Hampton Barre was the scion of an old Boston family with numerous business ties in every port city of the seaboard, including Charleston.

Sorren nodded. "The same. It appears her ship was overtaken by pirates. There were no survivors found, nor bodies recovered. That would suggest that the passengers were either killed and thrown overboard—"

"Or taken to sell in the brothels and sugar cane plantations of the Indies," I finished, distaste clear in my tone.

"Precisely," Sorren replied. "Normally, I'd say there was nothing we could do except offer a prayer for the young woman's soul. But it appears that Miss Barre was exceptional beyond just her family connections. She was given an antique cameo brooch by a young man named Islwyn Lawry, a brooch that her family believed had occult power. Lawry, it seems, convinced her that it had the power to protect the wearer, and Miss Barre never took it off."

My expression darkened. "Was Islwyn Lawry any relation to Galoshin Lawry, the gent with the fondness for black magic we went after a while back?"

Sorren chuckled. "Islwyn is Galoshin's son, but he had a big row with his father several years ago, and by all accounts, didn't approve of his father's schemes or the way he used his power. Islwyn gave the cameo to Felicity when she set sail to return to Charleston, as a token of his love. It appears they had made plans to marry when she returned to Bermuda."

"But she never did," I murmured. "So the cameo wasn't as powerful as Islwyn hoped."

Sorren frowned. "Or perhaps it didn't work in quite the way he expected. Barre made a special trip to Charleston, and he came to Evann several nights ago, referred by a trusted mutual friend. Need I say that Trifles and Folly is not among his usually frequented establishments? The good man believes he is being haunted by his daughter's ghost. She comes to him in his dreams, wearing the cameo around her neck, begging for something, but she doesn't speak."

"Grief makes people see strange things, even in a city as haunted as Charleston," I replied.

"If Barre were the only one to see the girl's apparition, I might agree," Sorren replied. "But there have been reports up and down the Battery of the same ghost, a young woman in a blue gown with upswept hair and a fine cameo at her throat."

I crossed my arms. "I'm not sure what Barre expects us to do about it. If the cameo were cursed, it's probably at the bottom of the ocean by now. Unless it's shown up in Uncle Evann's shop."

Uncle Evann shook his head. "I've had no cameos brought in for quite some time," he replied. No matter how vast the store's inventory, Uncle Evann knew every piece. The storefront was crowded with antiques and curios from around the world, while in the back rooms, Evann and Sorren dealt with the dark magic items that found their way —legally or not—into Evann's possession. Some of those dark items were destroyed, while Sorren passed others along to his network of secret operatives for safekeeping. Although the parlor was warm from the fire, I shivered. I'd handled several of those dark items myself, and I knew their power. One damned necklace had already tried to kill me; I had to admit I was skeptical of searching for another.

"If she's showing up as a ghost, that makes it pretty clear what happened to her," Coltt said. "But the cameo is probably off the coast of Bermuda. What can we do?"

Sorren took another sip of blood. "I believe the cameo is here, in Charleston. And I believe both the appearance of Felicity's ghost and the unusual ghostly activity are linked." He leaned forward and met my gaze. "I have a strong feeling that we've got a necromancer here in the city, and I fear what we've seen is just the beginning."

The only thing I like less than pirates are necromancers. Then again, maybe I should qualify that statement, since in the eyes of the navy, Coltt and I are technically pirates. I prefer to think of us as paranormal privateers, chartered by Sorren and his murky band of relic-snatchers, helping the good guys by plundering the bad guys. I avoid the navy because I don't think they'd understand the distinction.

"So who's our necromancer?" I asked.

Sorren shook his head. "Don't know yet. But I'm certain whoever it is has focused his power in the Battery. That seems to be the nexus of the disturbances."

I let out a low whistle. "That's one wealthy necromancer." The Battery included some of the finest houses in Charleston, so named because it fronted along the harbor just behind the city's port defenses. The rainbow-hued homes, reminiscent of mansions in the Caribbean islands, had long been the preserve of the wealthiest and most prominent citizens in the city. Sorren knew how to navigate in that company, but it didn't come naturally to country boys like Coltt and me.

"As luck would have it," Sorren said, with a hint of a smile indicating that luck had little to do with it, "there's going to be a grand ball at the home of a dear friend of your Uncle Evann's. Everyone from the Battery will be there, as well as the folks who live south of Broad Street. And so will you," he said, looking straight at me.

"Are you coming, too?" I asked, not sure whether Sorren could hear the uncertainty in my voice. Pirates I could handle. Old-money aristocrats I found much more frightening, on a whole different level.

Sorren chuckled. "I'm a bit too well known in certain circles," he said. "There will be more than one esteemed reverend of the church in attendance who might find my presence… unsettling."

"They'll balk at a vampire and not a bloody necromancer?" Coltt broke in. "How's that?"

Sorren gave an eloquent shrug. "Necromancers have a pulse. I don't. Unlike the undead, necromancers and their sort have survived for centuries hiding in plain sight, usually among the most privileged and pious."

"I guess I'd better dust off the company manners," I said resignedly. Give me a good sword fight any day over a social event. Both are battles, but one is at least honest about it.

"I've trained you better than that," Sorren chided. And it was true. Under his tutelage, I had mingled among the wealthiest and most powerful men in the former colonies, with them none the wiser to the charade. And usually, while I mingled, Coltt was busy thieving in the darkened rooms upstairs.

"The ball will keep the Battery's residents occupied, and it's very likely they'll give their servants the night off, so it should be easy for Coltt to slip into the houses and look for clues to the whereabouts of our necromancer," Sorren added.

"And what kind of clue is that?' Coltt demanded. "Perhaps a sign that says, 'ring bell for the necromancer' or some such?"

"You're the best thief in the New World," Sorren replied smoothly and added "trained by the best thief in the Old World," with a hint of pride, tugging at his collar to indicate himself. "I have full confidence in your abilities to find our man."

"Just make sure this necromancer likes fancy dress balls," Coltt said darkly. "I don't have your strength or Dante's magic. I'm not the man for a fight."

I personally knew that, when his back was against the wall, Coltt could be utterly ruthless in a battle, but I also knew that the memories of those few awful times weighed more heavily on Coltt than they did on me. Maybe it meant Coltt was a nicer person than I am. Or maybe I'd just lost so many of the people I cared about that I no longer worried about God keeping score.

"The ball is tomorrow night," Sorren replied. "I've had an associate get me the plans to as many of the great homes as he could; Coltt will no doubt find them useful. Evann's probably already gotten his hands on the guest list and been to his sources for news. And as for you," he said, with a glance in my direction, "A haircut and a shave might be in order. I've taken the liberty of having a new outfit delivered to your rooms. I believe you'll look quite acceptable."

I sighed. Sorren had taught me long ago that the best spies looked good enough to fit in and unremarkable enough to not be remembered. I feared it was my lot in life.

THE NEXT NIGHT, Evann and I headed out. We were dressed like aristocrats, with a carriage and driver (thanks to Sorren) that rivaled the best in the city. Coltt had caught a rental coach as far as Meeting Street, where he would walk the rest of the way to attract the least notice. Evann and I intended to have our driver let us out by the main door, but someone's coach horse had bolted, and the street in front of the mansion was a tangle of people, policemen, and panicked horses, so we had our man let us out on Church Street just a block or so from the Battery, with instructions to pick us up in the same place afterward.

The ball was just beginning to get lively when we arrived. "Welcome, gentlemen," said the servant who met us at the door to take our cloaks. "You've arrived just in time." He dropped his voice conspiratorially. "The musicians have warmed up and the crowd is lively, but the sideboard is still full if you hurry," he said with a wink.

He turned away just as I saw a button fall from my cloak. I bent to retrieve it, and saw a small, intricate design at the outside corner of the stone step. It was a symbol of some sort, drawn in a yellow, chalky powder, very small, as if not to attract notice. My button fell next to it, so I couldn't avoid seeing it, although otherwise, I would never have looked down. I stood, and for an instant, saw a look of stark fear cross the servant's face until his mask of genial welcome slammed back into place. *Odd*, I thought, vowing to ask Sorren about it later.

"Evann! How good of you to come!" I looked up to see Eudora Hallingsworth, the doyenne of the Battery, holding out her arms to greet Evann with a prim kiss on each cheek. Mrs. Hallingsworth was descended from the families whose names matched the streets and plantations of Charleston, as close as we got in these post-colonial days to local royalty.

"Honored to be your guest," Evann said, making a low bow and kissing her hand with a rakish raise of his eyebrows.

Eudora Hallingsworth chuckled. "Really, Evann! Such a show you make," she protested, clearly thrilled at the attention. "And who is this with you?"

Evann turned to me with a flourish. "My nephew, Dante Morris, of the Virginia Morrises."

Mrs. Hallingsworth smiled indulgently at me. "Pleased to make your acquaintance. Your family has an illustrious reputation."

I smiled along with the ruse. "You're too kind, m'lady," I replied. Yes, my family name was Morris, and yes, I was from Virginia, but otherwise, Evann had led the dear lady woefully astray. My father was a fisherman in a poor coastal village, not a planter aristocrat. But if privateering hadn't already damned my soul, I doubted another lie or two would tip the balance.

"You simply must try the roast duck," Mrs. Hallingsworth said, leading us into the ballroom where musicians had already struck up a lively reel. "One of the servants will get you a cup of punch, and you can't overlook Cook's benne seed wafers." Her attention turned to me with the eye of a mother.

"And you, Dante, shouldn't waste another minute when the band is playing. Come with me. I'll introduce you to the prettiest young ladies in South Carolina!"

Evann and I were swept into the high spirits of the ball. It seemed to me that for a curio shop owner, Evann seemed to know everyone who was anyone in Charleston's notoriously cliquish upper society, and they treated him with the fondness usually reserved for an elderly, quirky relative. After Mrs. Hallingsworth had made my introduction, I was accepted as an approved and eligible bachelor and managed to dance with the daughters of some of the most powerful men in the city. I was certain those same men would be horrified to know that their coddled darlings were waltzing with a pirate.

All the while, I kept my senses keen to magic. While more than one of the blue-blooded young ladies made me tingle, it had nothing to do with the supernatural. To my surprise, I picked up its traces on several of Charleston's movers and shakers. Not water magic, but other forms of power. Land magic, not surprising given Charleston's planter heritage. Charisma beyond the norm, good for swaying others to see things your way. Attraction magic, which led to the gathering of friends, power, and money.

I chanced a look at the black-frocked Anglican priest who was engaged in a lively discussion in the corner. What might the good Father have to say if he knew just how many of his parishioners had more than a hint of magic to them?

Waltzing was a good excuse to circle the room without being obvious. I could keep my eyes on my attractive partner, while my magic swept over the bystanders as we circled past. Most of the people didn't register at all with me, meaning that they were what they appeared to be and no more. But twice, as my partners and I passed the back corner of the room, my powers gave me an uncomfortable jolt, a wave of alarm.

"Thank you for this dance," I said, favoring Sarah, my latest dancing partner, with a deep bow.

"The pleasure was all mine," she drawled. She was so good at innocent flirtation that I knew it was a skill honed of long practice.

I murmured an excuse about needing more punch and found a reason to go the long way back to the sideboard. I passed within a few feet of the place where my magic had jolted me, slowing as much as I dared to get a look at its source.

The elderly gentleman had his back to me at first, but he turned as I walked past, and I wondered if he sensed something, too. He had a shock of untamed white hair over bushy eyebrows and a furrowed face. His hazel eyes had a wary glint, and his lips were pressed tightly together, jaw set. In his prime, he might have been a tall man, but age had hunched him. I shook my head to clear it. No, it wasn't age that made his shoulders slump. In my mind's eye, my magic eye, I saw him clutching a chest against him, hunched over it to protect it with his body, to hide it from view. His eyes met mine, and I got a very nasty frisson down my spine. I was pretty sure I'd found our necromancer, and at the moment, I'd bet that he was wondering whether my magic posed him any threat.

"Dante! There you are!" Ms. Hallingsworth's greeting was music to my ears. Our hostess took my elbow and steered me away from the old man whose gaze, I was sure, followed me as I headed in the opposite direction. "I'd like you to meet my niece."

"I'm embarrassed to ask," I said, doing my best to look chagrined, "but I couldn't place the older gentleman in the other corner. Should I know him?"

Mrs. Hallingsworth chuckled. "I should say not—unless you're a pirate! That's Judge Heinrich Von Dersch. He served as the king's highest magistrate in Bermuda before he moved to South Carolina on the eve of the war, and he's been an absolute bulwark against piracy on the high seas. He'll tell you that he's hanged over three hundred pirates himself, and I believe him." She cast a backward glance. "He's a stern fellow, but then, who wouldn't be in his position?"

My hostesses' words were gracious, but I could feel a tinge of fear. My good Mrs. Hallingsworth had a generous dollop of magic in the form of charisma, though she probably didn't know it and would be horrified to find out that her "charm" was indeed charmed. I was willing to bet that the tingle of fear she felt came from the feel of Judge Von Dersch's magic: dark, grasping, and vengeful.

I spent much of the next hour engaged in light conversation with Mrs. Hallingsworth's lively niece, Isabella. To my delight, Isabella was well-read, educated in the classics, and had traveled extensively abroad. She also shared her aunt's charisma, which was difficult to resist, even when I knew it to be magic. Alas, I also knew any prospects there were doomed from the start, though I was reluctant to say goodnight when Uncle Evann came to collect me for the drive home.

A different servant brought us our cloaks. As we left, I made a point to look down at the step where I had seen the chalked symbol. It had been rubbed out.

"I want to look at something," I said to Evann as soon as the door closed behind us. I led him around the house, bending low so as not to be seen out of the windows, an eye on the foundation stones of the great house.

"Look there," I said in a whisper, drawing Evann's attention to another of the intricate, graceful marks. Gingerly, I touched it. Magic quivered beneath my fingertips, of a sort I couldn't readily identify. I slipped my fingertips together, puzzled. The marks seemed to have been made in a mixture of cornmeal and ash. Strange.

"There's another one, over here," Evann said quietly. It was a different symbol, but of the same sort, and we found them at intervals all around the foundation stones, and a few more at the entrance to the servant's kitchen.

When we were safely back on the street, I turned to Evann. "What did you make of all that?" I asked, interested to hear his thoughts before I shared my own.

"You're the one with the magic," Evann replied. "I was just there to get you in the door."

I chuckled. "Forced to eat fine food and drink fine wine and be flirted with by some of the richest widows in the city."

Evann sighed. "I do what I must for the cause." He sobered. "As for those marks, I know I've seen something like that before, but not often. I'll see what I can find when I get back to the store." He gave me a sideways glance. "How about you? Did you pick up anything, or were you too addled by the beautiful ladies?"

"Considering that their fathers would line up to challenge me to a duel if they had any idea who had danced with their daughters, I'd say my attraction was tempered with a cold splash of common sense," I said. "But they were pretty, weren't they?'

"Focus, Dante."

It was my turn to sigh. "As you wish. Yes, I picked up on something besides the symbols. There was an old man in the corner. Miserable looking person, not exactly the life of the party. I saw a couple of the men talking briefly to him, but most people gave him a wide berth, and the servants did their best to stay out of his way entirely."

"Judge Von Dersch," Evann replied. "And what did your magic say?"

"He's hiding something," I answered, carefully sifting through my impressions. "I think he's able to put a glamor on his magic, to make it seem different than it is. I sensed… falseness." I paused again, thinking. "There was a feeling of doom around him, and the oddest thing was, I could swear it waxed and waned over the course of the evening. I barely noticed him when we arrived, but a few hours later, his magic seemed to fill the room so that I could scarcely think. It gradually got better, but I wondered how many of the other guests with a hint of magic felt the same thing."

"Between eighth and ninth bells, I noticed that the good Judge was standing completely alone," Evann said. "I was watching him, too, but for a different reason. Sorren didn't want me to mention it before we came, didn't want to prejudice your read on the evening, but he thinks the Judge is our necromancer."

I shuddered. "I think you're right." I glanced up at the darkened windows of the other homes along the Battery. "What do you think Coltt's found?"

Evann gave a crafty smile. "I don't know what he's discovered, but I do know the Judge's house was at the top of his list to explore."

We hustled along with our capes drawn close against the autumn wind. As we passed the entrance to one of the many small, narrow alleyways, my magic tingled. I've got water magic, and I'm strongest when I'm at sea, but close to the bay I could feel the pull of its power, and I knew from prior experience that spirits could feel it, too. Evann hadn't been kidding about Charleston being one of the most haunted cities in the former colonies. New Orleans might rival us, maybe. Both are gracious cities built on rivers of blood and a world of human suffering. The rich folks choose not to remember, but the spirits never forget.

A shot rang out at close quarters. Evann grabbed me and shoved me against the wall, and we waited, but there were no running footsteps, no shouts for the police. Exchanging a worried glance, Evann and I straightened our clothes and ventured away from the shelter of the wall, daring to peer down the narrow alley.

"Have you seen him?" The voice startled me. I looked more closely and saw a young man standing in the shadows. My eyes narrowed, and I looked with my magic instead of merely sight. The man's outline glowed faintly with a light blue nimbus. Now that I took a closer look, I could see that he bore a fatal chest wound, unfortunately not uncommon in the alleyways of Charleston. Dozens of headstrong young men met their untimely deaths at the hands of an aggrieved rival and a fast bullet in the side streets of the Holy City. But only one had bothered to hail us.

"Who are you looking for?" I asked, expecting the shade to be searching for his killer.

"The death mage."

That brought Evann and me up short. "What do you mean?" I said carefully, although I certainly had a good idea.

"Can't you feel him? You've got a touch of magic to you. There's a hocus who binds souls to the tide. The spirits run from him, those who can. But the girl can't get away."

Evann and I exchanged glances. "What girl?" I asked.

"Are ye deaf?" the spirit asked, shaking his head. "Can't you hear her wailing? She's a pretty lass in a blue dress with a fancy brooch, and she sobs something fierce."

"Where have you seen her?"

"Up and down the Battery. Mostly at high tide in the night."

High tide. Odd for that to come up again so soon. Not a coincidence, I was sure of it.

"I've been looking for that girl," I said cautiously. "Her name is Felicity Barre. Her family is very worried about her. Do you know anything else that might help me set her free?"

The ghost seemed to take my measure. "Maybe. I know someone who knows a lot about spirits and hocus. She's the one who told me I'm doomed to die in the same damned duel night after night until I put things right. She might could help you."

"Much obliged," I murmured. The ghost turned, and Evann and I followed him down the narrow alley. We wound through the back streets of Charleston, a world apart from the glittering ball we had just left. These were dark, dank streets even the harbor's burly longshoremen feared to tread. They were the province of Charleston's slaves, and they were not generally a welcome place for people like Evann and me, or for our guide, had he still been mortal.

I could feel eyes watching us as we passed the abysmal slave quarters. It was after ten p.m. curfew, and few bondsmen would risk the beating that could come if they were found in the streets after the bells rang. I could feel the suspicion that greeted us, and the fear. There was magic, too, strange and powerful, from somewhere far away, utterly outside of my own experience.

"By the way, I'm Ellison," the ghost said over his shoulder. "Ellison Hawking-Muir, the third." He paused. "My friends used to call me Hawk."

"Nice to meet you, Hawk," I said. "How did you come to be in a duel?"

"I was called out because I danced with the wrong girl at a party, and she told her brother I had somehow insulted her," Hawk replied. "I hadn't meant to. I tried to apologize. But her brother wouldn't have it, and demanded a duel for her honor. Stupid game. Turns out, he was a member of that secret dueling society. Probably trumped up a reason to call me out. He'd already shot four men dead before me. I didn't stand a chance."

"I'm sorry," I told Hawk. I'd heard about Charleston duels, a pastime of the rich, spoiled young men with more money than sense. It didn't surprise me that dueling would be just another form of one-upmanship, only a game that left the loser dead instead of just humiliated. "What happened to your murderer?"

Hawk gave a sharp, bitter laugh. "Happened? Nothing happened. Not for a while." The ghost dropped his voice, although I was pretty sure I was the only one who could hear him. "Until he came back to the alley for another duel. I could see he'd picked another easy mark, like I'd been. Poor fellow must have borrowed the gun; he could barely tell the butt from the barrel."

"And?" I asked, sure there was more to the story.

Hawk glanced at me over his shoulder, his lips pressed in a tight, pained smile. "Just as the guy who had challenged me sighted to aim, I tackled him. Went right through him. It made him shiver, and it threw off his aim. He missed, and the poor fellow he'd challenged was so frightened he managed to squeeze off a shot and got lucky. Took my murderer through the shoulder, and he bled to death before his buddies could do anything about it. The other guy ran off as fast as he could." Hawk didn't look as smug as I'd expected him to. Instead, he just looked sad. "But I'm still here."

Finally, Hawk stopped in front of an old slave cabin. I hesitated, unsure of what to do. Walking up and knocking didn't seem like a good idea. Before I could ask Hawk what came next, the door opened, and an old woman dressed in white stood in the doorway.

"That's Mama Nadege," Hawk whispered. "Tell her I brought you."

"Mama Nadege?" I managed, finding my throat had gone dry. "I'm supposed to tell you that Hawk brought me here. It's about the weeping ghost."

Mama Nadege looked me up and down, and then she did the same to Evann. When she spoke, I could see that her gaze was fixed just off to my right, where Hawk's ghost stood. "Well, of course, Hawk brought you. He's right with you, plain as day." Her voice was thick as gumbo, heavy with the consonants of the islands and somewhere else I couldn't place.

"Come in then, the neighbors won't bother you none, not now that they know you're here to see me," she added, with a glance towards the darkened buildings behind us.

We followed Mama Nadege into her house. The air was heavy with the smell of incense and candle smoke. Mama Nadege was a big woman, swathed in a white, loose gown. Her hair was tied up in a kerchief, and I couldn't tell her age from her face. Her eyes were what drew me. Black eyes, dark as her skin, like deep pools for drowning.

Her magic flowed around me, almost smothering in its intensity, but my power sensed no threat. She was curious and intrigued. And I had the unsettling feeling that she had been expecting us.

Her small cabin was hung with brightly colored block-printed cloths and filled with candles, clay figures, stuffed, crude dolls, and carved wooden images. Lanyards of shells, beads, and dried plants festooned everything.

"You're a mambo," Evann said.

Mama Nadege smiled. "Mambo asogwe," she replied.

Evann turned to me. "She's a high priestess of voodoo."

I'd heard that term before, but I hadn't associated it with Charleston. "I thought voodoo only happened in New Orleans," I replied.

Mama Nadege laughed, a deep chuckle that resonated. "Oh, there be voodoo in Charleston, all right. My mama was born in Haiti, where we know how to talk to spirits. She was brought to New Orleans and sold there, but her mistress married a man from Charleston and brought my mama with her. She raised me in the power. She wasn't the only one be brought here from New Orleans, either. Oh no, child, the voodoo is all around you. You're just too pale to notice," she said, and laughed heartily at her own joke.

She sobered and looked at me again, and I felt tendrils of her magic gliding over my skin. I fought the urge to shiver. "You've got some power," she murmured, her consonants smooth as a spicy roux. "Considerable power. Why'd it bring you to me, child?"

Evann gave me the barest hint of a nod, letting me know it was safe to tell the truth, or at least most of it. "I'm trying to stop a necromancer. He's got a dark magic object, and my master sent me to take it back from him, put it somewhere it can't hurt anyone."

She eyed me carefully. "You're nobody's slave," she said, walking slowly around me. "You might not own those fancy clothes, but you're a freeman, sure enough." She began to shake her head. "Uh, uh, uh," she murmured. "Only one kind of man be your master. You serve a nightwalker, am I right?"

"Nightwalker" seemed close enough to vampire to accept without quibbling. "Yes."

"Mister Sorren?"

I tried to hide my astonishment. "Yes."

Mama Nadege relaxed, and smiled broadly. "Well, why didn't you say so?" She gestured toward two chairs near the fireplace. "Sit down. Tell Mama what you know, and what you need to know."

I told her about the missing girl, and how she might be the weeping woman Hawk told us about. Mama Nadege listened as I recounted the ball and the encounter with Judge Von Dersch and rocked back and forth in her chair without saying anything. "There's one more thing," I added. "I saw markings by the doorway. I don't think I was supposed to see them. The man who took my coat looked afraid when I noticed it, like it might cause trouble." I paused. "Afterwards, Evann and I walked around the house, and a whole series of markings were made on the foundation stones. They were made of cornmeal and ash."

Mama Nadege nodded knowingly. "Oh, trouble it would cause, that's for sure." She bent down and drew on the hard dirt floor of her cabin with a stick, tracing an elaborate symbol very like the one by the door of the Hallingsworth house. "Did it look like this?"

I nodded. "That's one of the marks. There were others."

Mama Nadege sat back up. "Those are *veves*. Powerful magic. They can open the gateway to the spirits, bring one of the Loa, the Invisibles, across to guide us. Someone took a risk to try to protect that house."

"If the… *veves*… are there for protection, how did Judge Von Dersch get in, if he really is a necromancer?" I asked.

Mama Nadege shook her head. "Someone risked a whippin' or worse, if he got caught, but it's for nothin'. Takes a mambo to chalk *veves* with power. Those were just pretty marks. Sure wouldn't stop a necromancer none." She gave me an arch look. "I notice it didn't stop you from walking right in, either."

I hadn't thought of that. "No, ma'am," I replied. "It didn't." I paused. "Have you heard the weeping girl? Seen the spirits?"

Mama Nadege began to rock again and closed her eyes. "Oh, yes. I've seen her. I've seen all of them. Like a cloud of witnesses they are, all around us. And I'll tell you something; all of them was wronged.

Oh, most of them were pirates and thieves, like the Judge say. Most of 'em deserved hangin', they did indeed. But they didn't deserve what happened after. And that girl, she didn't deserve nothin' like that."

"Like what?" Evann asked, leaning forward.

"Most white folks 'round these parts like Judge Von Dersch because he's a hangin' judge. Had a reputation in Bermuda for hangin' more pirates than any judge alive. And he ain't stopped hangin' them since he came to Charleston. No siree. But he don't just hang them. He makes sure the bodies get thrown in the oyster shoals. That's a place of the damned, those shoals. Tide comes in and out through them, never fully dry and never fully wet. Those souls, they ain't never gonna get no rest in a buryin' place like that. They are doomed to suffer for eternity. Ain't no one, not even pirates, deserve that, and there ain't no judge but the Almighty right to pass that kind of sentence. But Von Dersch does."

"Why?" I asked, intrigued and horrified. "Why would he care what happens to them after they're dead?"

Mama Nadege shook her head. "You're as green as you are white, son. This magic is new to you, ain't it?"

I tried not to bristle. "I've had magic all my life," I replied. "But no real schooling in it, until I met Sorren. I've got a lot to learn."

My answer seemed to satisfy Mama. "That you do, son. Well, here's your lesson for tonight. A necromancer draws power from enslaving spirits. Not just killing, slaving. I imagine you can guess how I feel about somethin' like that."

I swallowed hard. For all her power, Mama Nadege herself was owned as property by one of Charleston's wealthy families. It didn't take much imagination to guess that she'd take a dim view of any slaver, before or after death. "I imagine I can," I said quietly. Another thought came to me, and I dared to look up at Mama Nadege.

"If you know Von Dersch was a slaver, why didn't you do something yourself?"

Mama Nadege began to laugh, but it wasn't a pleasant sound. "Oh, I did do something, child. I marked *veves*—powerful *veves*—around the places my people live. Those cabins out there, they're the safest place in Charleston. He has no power, not in my alley. But how you reckon an old slave woman gonna come up against a judge, 'specially when all the masters favor him? Uh-uh. All I'd get is dead, and then who's gonna protect my people?" She leaned forward. "But I can help you, if you're of a mind to do it. That I can. And I've got some powerful friends myself."

I exchanged a glance with Evann. This might be the best chance we were going to get. "All right, I said. "What do I need to do?"

"You need to get into that Judge's house, and find his object of power. By himself, his magic is weak. I know this. It's not his magic makes him so strong, it's some dark object he has; bad thing, very bad. You get in there, you gonna find that he keeps something from all of the souls he's bound, a reminder. I bet he's got somethin' belonged to the poor girl, too. How she got mixed up with him, I don't know, but she got stuck, like the others. You go in there, you make it right, hear me? You be like Moses and let those poor slaved souls go free."

I drew a deep breath. It wasn't as if I hadn't figured it would come to this, but hearing Mama Nadege say it made it entirely too real. "Sorren had someone scouting the houses," I said finally. "He might have learned something we can use. I'd like to talk with him—and with Sorren—before we do anything."

Mama chuckled. "You think I was gonna send you out tonight? Uh-uh. These things take time. I have to call the power. I have to talk to my Loa, my guides. I know who I'm gonna call to help us, just the spirits who will want to see this man get what he deserve. You come back to the alley tomorrow night; mind it be an hour before low tide. Very important—because those souls, they be bound on the shoals. When the tide is high, his power is high. Tide go out, he's weaker. That's the time to strike.

"You get Hawk to bring you back here. My people know Hawk. They'll leave you alone if you're with him. You leave it to me. I'll get you into that house—and out, too, maybe."

I didn't like the way that sounded, but it was probably the best I was going to get. Hawk saw us out to the end of the alley. "Thanks," I said, not sure what to say to the ghost.

Hawk shrugged. "If you can help that girl, I'll do what I can for you. I'm stuck here because I was stupid. I deserve what I got. But her—I don't think she did anything wrong."

I nodded. "I'll see what I can do," I said, feeling less sure of just what could be. Evann and I walked to where we were supposed to meet the carriage. To our surprise, it was still waiting for us.

"Get in." The voice from inside the carriage was Sorren's. I tried to hide my surprise as Evann and I climbed inside. Coltt was there, too. It made for a crowded ride.

"I had time to get into most of the houses on my list before your little party wound down," Coltt said. "But there was one house I couldn't enter. Wasn't the locks—I can pick them. It was dark magic, and I couldn't break it."

"Let me guess," I said with a look toward Evann. "Judge Von Dersch's house."

Sorren gave a cold smile. "I thought you might come to that conclusion."

"We found something else out," said Coltt. "About Felicity."

I looked up with interest. "And?"

"Sorren did some research on the old court cases Judge Von Dersch handled. There was a case about six months after Felicity went missing where an entire pirate crew was seized and brought to trial. They were found guilty and hanged, but here's the interesting part. The records say there was a woman aboard. She was dressed like a trollop and too drunk to give testimony, so they hanged her along with the pirates as the ship's whore."

A cold shiver went down my back. "If she'd been their prisoner for months… been dishonored… she might not have been in her right mind by the time they found her," I said quietly.

"Or the pirates might have kept her liquored up to make sure she couldn't tell anyone who she was," Coltt put in solemnly. "But it would explain what happened to her."

"And why her ghost hasn't been able to rest," I finished.

I looked at Sorren. "You know anything about a mambo named Mama Nedege?"

"Mambo asogwe," he replied. "In magic, distinctions matter." Sorren paused. "So she found you?"

"I would have said we found her, but yes, we've met."

Sorren chuckled. "More like, she led you to her. Mama's very powerful. But she can't go up against the judge on her own for the same reason I couldn't confront him at the ball tonight. The risks of exposing what we are outweigh the possibility of being able to win. That's why we need someone like you."

I grimaced. "So I've been told." Sorren and Coltt listened closely as Evann and I recounted our evening. I ended with Mama's offer to help get me past the wardings that had stopped Coltt. Sorren nodded sagely.

"If anyone can do it, she can," he replied. "Let's get you home. You've got a long day tomorrow."

I MET HAWK at the end of his alley just before two p.m., when the tide would be lowest. In the daylight, it was more difficult to see him, but when Hawk stepped into the shadows, he was nearly as clear as he had been last night. Hawk's fatal dueling wound was as raw as the first time I'd seen him, but if it still gave him pain, he did not show it. Instead, he seemed as excited as a ghost can be about the day's work.

"Where's your other friend?" Hawk asked, looking for Evann.

"Coltt and Evann have the house staked out. They saw the judge leave this morning for court. He shouldn't be home until around 4 p.m."

I followed Hawk back to Mama Nadege's cabin. The other slave homes were empty, their occupants presumably about their daily business. Mama sat on the steps of her cabin, weaving a seagrass basket and singing. Around her were seagrass baskets of all sizes and shapes, beautiful objects with intricate patterns, woven with the touch of a master.

"You like my baskets, huh?" Mama greeted me. "Now that I'm old, this is what the master has me do all day. When I've made the ones

Master needs for the household, I can make as many as I can to sell for myself down in the Slave's Market."

"They're beautiful," I replied, looking at the array of designs.

Mama Nadege laughed, a deep belly laugh. "Oh, you just looking at the surface, child. Stretch out your magic, and see what it tell you."

I did just that, and my eyes grew wide. The baskets weren't just beautiful; they were tinged with power. Magic to bring luck, to win love, to keep relationships harmonious, to prevent food from spoiling. "Household" magic my mother would have called it, often not respected as much as the great magics to affect weather or turn the tide of battle. Yet as my mother always reminded me, such small magics were the warp and woof of our lives, and without them, we would be much poorer. "Do your buyers know?"

Mama let her head fall back and gave another deep laugh. "What, you think I'm crazy, child? No one knows why, they just think my baskets are lucky as well as strong. Make them feel good when they own one, make their food last longer, make their house happier. Then they come back and buy more, and get more lucky." She gave a crafty grin. "And the more of these baskets Master has, the more he likes me. The nicer he be to my people." She chuckled.

When this is over, if I live through it, maybe I'll be back for one of those baskets, I thought. Something for protection, or to make the ladies notice me.

Mama held out a woven basket that looked like a cylinder with a matching lid. "I made this for you, child," she said, and her dark eyes grew serious. "To take into that house where you're goin'. When you find that thing your master wants, you put it in there, and my magic will keep it still. Mind you don't open the lid once it's in there and check on it. You keep that lid shut tight, and what you find will go to sleep."

"Thank you," I said. I'd been wondering how I was going to get whatever-it-was out of the house, and I sincerely hoped it would fit in Mama's basket.

She stood and waved for me to follow her into her cabin. "Mind where you step," she cautioned, and I looked down to see two intricate *veves* etched in the dirt near the center of her small house. To the side lay a skin drum and several guttered candles. Three candles: black, purple, and silver, still burned.

"We worked the magic last night," Mama said, and I could see that she looked very tired. "I called to the Loas, the spirits. I asked them for guidance. Ghede came to me. Powerful Loa. Loa of death and resurrection, huh. The right spirit for this job, no? Ghede is also the patron of vampires. I think he knows just what we doin', don't you think? Ghede Nibo came to me. He helps the spirits cross over, and he especially cares for spirits below the water."

She set her hands on her hips, pleased with herself. "Huh. I think we got the right Loa, that's for sure. We fed him and gave him rum and let him smoke his cigars, and when he be all happy and satisfied, I ask him for your protection, to get those poor souls out of that house. Ghede Nibo, he say yes. That be powerful magic on your side, child."

"Here, you take this, too." She held out a charm woven of seagrass that hung on a leather strap. The seagrass had been darkened to a red brick color, and as I held it in my hand, some of the powder that stained it colored my palm. "This *veve*, it's for Ghede Nibo. Help you take his magic with you."

"Thank you for the charm," I said, fastening it around my neck. "But Coltt said the house was warded against entry. How will I get in?"

Mama gave a toothy smile. "I'm getting to that, child. We raised two Loa last night. Ghede Nibo be one of them. Papa Legba is the other. Papa, he holds the doorway between us and the Loa. Papa Legba, he will take you to the house and open a passage for you through the magic. What happens inside is up to you. When you find the object that gives the Judge his power, you put it in my basket, seal it tight. If you can free the spirits, Ghede Nibo say he will help them cross over. The Loa will wait outside. Once you're inside the house, child, you be on your own."

I shivered, but nodded. "Let's go. I want to be in place at low tide when the Judge's power is weakest."

"I have business down by the Slave's Market, and then I'll go to the oyster beds. I'll call to Yemanja, mother of the sea, to set those souls free. Slaving them in her waters is an affront to her. Find what that judge holds over those souls and break the bond, and Yemanja will set them free." She nodded to a pile of bloody feathers in the corner that had once been a chicken. "I've done sacrifice to Lady Yemanja. She'll hear me."

Mama met my gaze. "When you're done, come back to the alley. Papa Legba will show you the way. I will keep the candles burning for you, give you my blessing." She reached into the folds of her voluminous white dress and brought out a small bag. It was made of leather and bulged with whatever was inside, tied off with purple and black string.

"You take this. It's a gris-gris bag. Very powerful. Put it in your shirt, over your heart. Keep it with you. It will give you power."

I made a slight bow, though my heart was thudding at the idea of what I was about to do. "Thank you, Mama Nadege."

She held her hands out over me in a gesture of blessing. "Come back safely, child. And set those spirits free."

Hawk walked back with me to the end of the alley, though in the sunlight, he was difficult to see. At the end of the alley, an old man waited with a dog. He was a very dark man, and a half-smoked cigar hung from one corner of his mouth. A wide-brimmed straw hat kept me from seeing his eyes. He leaned on a crutch on his left side. The dog sat quietly beside him, watching me. I'd probably passed old black men who looked just like him a hundred times in the streets of Charleston, but I knew for certain I hadn't passed him. Even at a distance, I could feel the waves of power that rippled from him. I didn't know what he was, but I was certain of one thing; he wasn't human.

The old man waved for me to follow him, and set off at a faster pace than I would have thought possible toward Judge Von Dersch's house.

I could feel the wardings around the house before we reached it. Cold, evil power. No wonder people crossed to the other side of the street when they passed. Even without magic, the house had a bad feel to it. And I was going in alone.

Evann was staked out down the street, with a big hat that hid his features. He leaned against a wall, reading a newspaper, but I knew he was keeping watch to make sure the Judge didn't return. Evann gave me a nod that might have been just friendly, but it was his all-clear signal. Coltt wasn't in sight, but I knew he was watching the back of the house, and if he'd seen something, he'd be out front along the sea wall, smoking a pipe.

I followed Papa Legba and his dog into the narrow alley between the houses. The wardings pressed on my magic horribly, screaming in my head for me to leave. I could see the warding like a dark film around the house. Papa Legba raised a hand, and there was silence in my mind. A doorway opened in the dark warding, and I stepped through. Mama Nadege said Papa Legba would help me get out again, and I certainly hoped he understood that part of the plan. I had my *veve* charm and Mama's basket, and although I didn't doubt her magic, in my belt was a loaded pistol. Taking a deep breath and clutching the seagrass basket, I stepped over the warding.

I'd been afraid that I would need Coltt's skill at picking locks, but it turned out that the Judge put a lot of confidence in his wardings. The locks on his house were easy enough for me to get open, with a little jiggling from Coltt's picks and a nudge from my magic. I glanced up at the sky. The day had grown cloudy, and now it looked as if a storm were brewing. I opened the side door and stepped inside.

The interior of the house was gloomy. Blinds were drawn closed over many windows, and a thick layer of dust lay everywhere. Cobwebs cascaded in the corners, filled with the dead husks of the spiders that dared intrude on the Judge's sanctuary. Gray sheets covered the furniture, slipcovered as if the owner had gone off for an extended trip. Yet we knew that the judge still resided here. Maybe "lived" wasn't the word. Nothing seemed to live within these walls.

The odor of mildew and the stale air made me cough. Beneath it was a strong smell of camphor. I had entered through the piazza and now made my way into the parlor. Faded curtains shrouded the windows, letting through only dim rays of light. On the slipcovered furniture, boxes, scrolls, books of all kinds and sizes and metal tins were piled haphazardly several feet above the cushions. More boxes, crates, barrels, and tins were stacked in every corner of the room, leaving only a few narrow paths. Here and there, I saw discarded pieces of clothing and old rags. I had the mental image of a dragon's lair, and a large black dragon coiled atop a mound of bleached bones and moldering treasure. Judging by the dust, none of the Judge's collections had been touched in years.

On shelves all around the parlor, I saw small glass boxes. Most of them were filmy with dust; none looked as if they had been opened or moved in a long time. There were dozens of them on the bookshelves, atop the side tables, on the mantle above the fireplace. I vowed to take a closer look on my way out.

I touched the *veve* on the strap at my throat for luck and moved further into the house. It was dark enough that I lit a small candle lantern that sat on a side table. With the draperies pulled tight, I wasn't worried that I'd been seen by neighbors. The candle's glow was comforting, and I moved deeper into the gloom.

The next room was a library. Shelves ranged all the way to the ceiling, several feet above my head. There were hundreds of leather-bound books; not surprising for a scholar and a judge. But on every shelf were three or four of the glass boxes, and here and there small urns. I struggled to remember where I had seen urns like that before, and then I remembered. One or two such urns had come into Uncle Evann's shop. Cremation urns. I shuddered. Somewhere in the house, I could hear the deep, regular ticking of a large clock, and it seemed to echo my pounding heart.

I reached out with my magic. My touch was cautious, checking for magical traps. I was astounded to see the room lit as if with captured stars as every one of the glass boxes began to glow.

I looked closer at the boxes on the shelf nearest me and had to blow on it to clear away enough dust to see inside. A button from a man's coat lay in the box and a few strands of hair. I backed up a step as my magic touched the box. A wave of anger hit me like a punch in the jaw. I had a glimpse of a man in worn and stained clothing wearing a tattered coat with buttons like the one in the glass box. He looked like a brigand, and I was glad I hadn't met him in a dark alley. Quickly, I turned my attention to the next box. Inside was a meerschaum pipe, stained with tobacco from long use, a sailor's comfort. With it, also, were a few strands of hair.

I gaped at the shelves, understanding what I had found. By holding onto a possession of each condemned man and a few strands of hair, Judge Von Dersch had been able to tap into the power of the souls bound to eternal torment in the oyster shoals. There were boxes everywhere I looked, and I was certain that if I counted them, I would find three hundred glass cases, one for every damned soul on whom Judge Von Dersch had passed sentence.

I let my magic gently skim across the shelves. The clock's ticking grew louder as I moved around the library, and then I saw it, a large, graceful Morbier clock in an ornate cabinet. The cabinet of the clock was gently curved, wider for the clock face, slim at the top of the body, then swelling to where the pendulum hung, and wider still at the feet. The cabinet was a dark Oriental lacquer, and it was covered with carvings and symbols I did not recognize.

I looked closer and realized how the clock resembled the rough outlines of a human form. Even the terms for its parts, face, body, foot, made it sound human. I looked closer, then recoiled as my magic brushed against it. The clock resonated with power, a dark magic that hissed and sang at the very edge of my consciousness. I stared at it. The clock was as tall as I was, far too large to fit in Mama Nadege's basket.

Then I saw the pendulum. A bronze disk the size of a dinner plate swung back and forth, suspended by a long metal shaft. On the shaft were three gems: a shattered moonstone, a white opal, and garnet, all unlucky. I dared another flicker of magic and realized that the clock was not the locus of power; the stones in the pendulum were. Those I could fit in my basket.

From somewhere nearby, I heard a woman weeping. I looked up and saw that one of the hundreds of boxes seemed to be glowing more brightly than the others. I climbed atop a desk for a better look and caught my breath.

Inside was a black cameo brooch with a raised white image of the three Fates. Beside it was a lock of blonde hair. My magic touched the box, and unlike the anger and rage that had responded from the other boxes, this box spoke only of mourning and loss. In my mind's eye, I saw an image of a young woman dressed in a fashionable gown. I felt the energy of the box surge toward me, and images overwhelmed me. A storm at sea, leaving a ship derelict in the water. Discovery by a ship of "rescuers" who turned out to be pirates, ruffians who killed the crew, looted the ship's hold and carried off their treasures, including the young woman.

I tried to turn my head or close my eyes as I felt the ghost's memories force upon me, memories of being cruelly used and badly beaten, plied with strong liquor to assure that she offered no resistance. Then another rescue gone wrong, this time when the pirates were captured by the navy. Dressed in a strumpet's abandoned finery, groggy from the rum and the beatings, she had been incoherent, unable to convince the sailors that she was a victim and not one of the brigand crew. The vision ended abruptly, with the snap of a gallows trap door.

I reeled back, covering my face with my hands, tears streaming down my face. There was no doubt that I had found Felicity Barre.

I heard the whispered curses and distant threats of the spirits trapped in the boxes around me as the clock's tick-tock rhythm seemed to grow louder with each heartbeat. The pirates' souls shouted and mocked, swearing in the vilest terms as if I had somehow enabled their torment. Then I heard a woman's voice as clearly as if she had bent low to whisper in my ear.

"Stop the clock and shatter the cases, and he loses his power."

Which to do first? Did the clock bind the souls, or did the trapped spirits power the clock's magic?

I set down the lantern and looked around the room for something to use to shatter the boxes. My gaze rested on a pole that stuck out from amidst the clutter. I grabbed it and pulled, setting of a small avalanche of papers and scrolls. I jumped back, careful to move the lantern so it wouldn't tip. The pole came free in my hand, a whaler's harpoon. I took a deep breath and drew my pistol, holding the harpoon in my left hand.

I fired into the face of the clock, striking it squarely in the center pin that bound the hands to the mechanism inside. A bloodcurdling shriek filled the air, the sound of something that had never been remotely human. With my left hand, I brought the harpoon down hard on the nearest shelf, smashing the glass boxes. Again and again, my harpoon raised and lowered, sweeping the boxes to the floor, or shattering them where they sat. I took particular pride when the heavy shaft of the harpoon flung Felicity's box to the floor, and it shattered, sending the cameo brooch to land near my feet.

Spirits swirled around me, angry and shrieking as the trapped pirates gained a measure of freedom. Without the clock's ticking, the room was otherwise still, but only for a heartbeat.

A blast of freezing air swept through the library, sending papers flying and clouding the room with dust. The same overpowering presence I had felt at the ball when I passed Judge Von Dersch now filled the room, and its power reached for me, enraged. The Judge might not have returned in the flesh, but some segment of his power knew that his sanctuary had been violated, and like a large, black shadow, it stretched toward me, menacing and deadly.

I cast about with my magic for a weapon since my pistol would do no good against this foe. I grabbed Felicity's cameo and threw myself toward the clock, wresting the pendulum from where it hung in the shattered clock case. The shadow's icy fingers brushed my skin, but I eluded its grip and stumbled, prizing the gems free from their attachment to the pendulum. Mama Nadege's basket was just out of reach, and the shadow was circling to come at me again from an angle that would not require crossing paths with the spirit catcher.

The shadow lurched toward me as I lunged for the basket. My foot kicked the piles that were precariously balanced on one of the old chairs, sending them sliding in a rush toward the floor, and knocking over the candle in the lantern.

The dry old papers caught fire quickly, and I knew that the crowded, cluttered rooms were a tinderbox. The shadow moved swiftly and caught my ankle as I tried to scramble clear. Its touch was icy, far colder than even a vampire's undead grip. I struggled to remove the lid from the sea grass basket without dropping either the gems or Felicity's cameo. The harpoon had fallen beside me, and my pistol was lost somewhere amid the mess.

I kicked at the shadow, but the black tendrils held me tightly. Just a few feet away, more scattered papers caught fire, and the room was beginning to fill with smoke. I grabbed at the leg of a large, overstuffed sofa to keep the shadow from dragging me backwards, but with one hand holding on, I couldn't manipulate the basket.

Outside, I heard rain lash the roof. The cameo beside me flared with brilliant light, and Felicity's ghost materialized, interposing itself between me and the deadly shadow. The air in the stuffy, smoky room began to move, gently at first, and then with the intensity of a captured windstorm. Before I had a chance to gather my thoughts, I saw a cloud of faces in the swirling air, and from the wild wind, the figures of the hanged pirates began to stream toward the shadow of the Judge's power. I reached out with my water magic and grabbed the nearest available source of power, the rain that beat down outside the mansion. I threw a burst of power against the shadow and felt its grip loosen, just as the cloud of spirits descended on the judge, shrieking and wailing. The shadow let go of my ankle, and I rolled free, twisting off the lid of the seagrass basket and thrusting the three gems inside, then slamming the lid down again.

I climbed to my feet, coughing and wheezing. I grabbed Felicity's cameo in one hand and the harpoon in the other, shoving the basket under my arm. Perhaps it was already too late. Smoke filled the room, making it impossible for me to see which way led out.

The house trembled as if shaken to its foundation. I could hear the thud of books falling from the shelves and the crash of glass as in the other rooms; the glass spirit boxes smashed to the floor. My eyes were streaming tears from the smoke, and it was growing difficult to breathe. Fire had spread to the old velvet draperies and the overstuffed furniture. Without a way out, I was sure to join the spirits I had just freed.

A dog barked frantically. Ahead of me, just visible in the smoke, I saw the shape of a large black dog. It barked again, then turned and trotted a few feet, turning again as if to make sure I had seen it. I staggered towards the dog, who jumped up and walked a few feet further, pausing to wait until I came close enough to see it before moving further.

The house rocked again, and I could hear the creak of old beams and the crash of plaster. Whatever I'd destroyed seemed to have been holding the whole damned house together, and the floor began to buckle and lurch beneath my feet. The insistent barking of the black dog kept me focused; drawing me through the smoke even as my lungs burned and skin began to blister from the heat.

Stumbling and coughing, I followed the barely-visible dog, and when I could not see him, I followed the sound of his barking. Finally, I reached the door I had entered and managed to fall more than step over the transom, still holding tight to the basket and the cameo. I let the harpoon fall, unable to see well enough to strike at an enemy.

Rain pelted me, and I felt the sting of hail. Magic convulsed around me, and I was trapped between the crumbling house behind me and the dark wards. The black dog stood next to me, still barking. For a moment, we were in the eye of the storm, and then there was silence. I felt as if I were suspended in mid-air, and then I came crashing down into the grass, landing on one shoulder so as not to lose the precious items clutched in my white-knuckled hands.

"You've done good, son." I looked up into the wizened face of the old black man who had led me here, into the depthless eyes of Papa Legaba. The black dog stood beside him, and I could have sworn it was smiling. Coltt and Evann rushed toward me, abandoning their disguises. It seemed as if everyone in Charleston had gathered, and perhaps they had. Houses on the Battery don't collapse in a puff of smoke every day. On the edge of the crowd I caught a glimpse of a figure dressed in white, and I knew that Mama Nadege had done her part, calling on the sea Loa to free whatever part of the trapped spirits' essence was bound to the oyster shoals. In the crowd, just for a heartbeat, I thought I saw a pretty young woman in a blue dress, her hair caught back in an elegant twist. She smiled at me, and then turned, and vanished.

"Let's get you out of here before there are too many questions." It was Evann's voice, and he and Coltt helped me to my feet. I looked around, but Papa Legaba and the black dog were gone. Still dazed from the fight, I let them lead me through the back alleyways until we were far enough away to call for a carriage without attracting attention. Evann made me strip off my sooty jacket, and Coltt took the seagrass basket, holding it tight with both hands. I slipped Felicity's cameo into my pocket, and the carriage whisked us back to Trifles and Folly.

Late that night, when I had gathered my wits, I returned to the alley where I'd met Hawk. He was waiting with a sad smile. "Did you find her?" he asked.

I nodded. "You deserve part of the credit. You brought me to Mama Nadege."

Hawk shrugged. "Did you free the ghosts?"

"I think so. They attacked whatever energy the judge sent to stop me, and then the whole building collapsed. Sorren told me that the Judge dropped dead of a heart attack at the bench in his courtroom at the time the house fell. The pieces in the basket, and Felicity's brooch will go into safekeeping, somewhere no one else can use them."

Hawk looked at me sadly. "I guess that's it then."

"You did me a good turn. You helped me free a woman's soul, and helped me stop a powerful necromancer. Didn't Mama tell you that you had to make things right before you could leave the alley? Maybe that counts." I removed the *veve* that I'd worn around my neck and placed it in the crossroads at the end of the alley. I blinked, and there stood Papa Legaba and his dog. Papa nodded to me, and then he turned his attention to Hawk.

"Come along, son. Best you be moving on."

Hawk glanced at me with a look of astonishment and gratitude, and then hurried after Papa Legaba and the black dog. When I blinked again, the alley was empty except for me. The *veve* was gone, too. I patted the gris-gris bag that still nestled over my heart, and began to walk home. In the distance, I heard the far-away joyful bark of a large dog, and I smiled.

AFTERWORD

Charleston, South Carolina is a real place. Some of the landmarks and a few of the historical figures in this collection do exist, and some (but not all) of the historical events were real. But the characters and their shops are all a work of fiction. So for example, if you go to Charleston (and I hope you do, because it's a lovely place to visit), you can see the real Charleston City Market and walk down King Street, but you won't find any of the businesses or restaurants I've mentioned by name. Any resemblance to real people or actual businesses is completely coincidental.

Many people in Charleston will tell you that the ghosts, however, are real. My ghosts are fictional, but that's because Charleston has enough of its own already. But don't take my word for it. See for yourself.

I hope you enjoyed the adventures with Cassidy, Teag, and Sorren. If you want more, check out Trifles and Folly, Volume 1, as well as the full-length novels, *Deadly Curiosities, Vendetta,* and *Tangled Web* available in paperback and e-book.

ABOUT THE AUTHOR

GAIL Z. MARTIN is the author of *Scourge: A Darkhurst Novel*, from Solaris Books. Gail is also the author of *Vendetta: A Deadly Curiosities Novel* and *Trifles and Folly 1: A Deadly Curiosities Collection*, the latest in her urban fantasy series set in Charleston, SC; *Shadow and Flame* is the fourth book in the Ascendant Kingdoms Saga; *The Shadowed Path* (The first Jonmarc Vahanian Adventures collection), as well as *Iron and Blood* a Steampunk series, and *Spells, Salt, & Steel*, both co-authored with Larry N. Martin.

She is also author of *Ice Forged, Reign of Ash,* and *War of Shadows* in The Ascendant Kingdoms Saga, The Chronicles of The Necromancer series (*The Summoner, The Blood King, Dark Haven, Dark Lady's Chosen*); The Fallen Kings Cycle (*The Sworn, The Dread*) and the urban fantasy novel *Deadly Curiosities* and *Tangled Web*. Gail writes three ebook series: *The Jonmarc Vahanian Adventures, The Deadly Curiosities Adventures* and *The Blaine McFadden Adventures. The Storm and Fury Adventures,* steampunk stories set in the Iron & Blood world, are co-authored with Larry N. Martin.

Gail's work has appeared in over 35 US/UK anthologies. Newest anthologies include: *The Big Bad 2, Athena's Daughters, Heroes, Space, Contact Light, With Great Power, The Weird Wild West, The Side of Good/The Side of Evil, Alien Artifacts, Cinched: Imagination Unbound, Realms of Imagination, Clockwork Universe: Steampunk vs. Aliens, Gaslight and Grimm, Baker Street Irregulars, Journeys, Hath no Fury,* and *A Haven Harbor Halloween.*

Find out more at:

www.GailZMartin.com
Facebook.com/WinterKingdoms
Twitter: @GailZMartin
DisquietingVisions.com (blog)
Goodreads https://www.goodreads.com/GailZMartin
Free excerpts on Wattpad http://wattpad.com/GailZMartin
Sign up for the newsletter at
https://www.instafreebie.com/free/JQorl,
and get a free short story.

ALSO BY GAIL Z. MARTIN

Deadly Curiosities

Deadly Curiosities

Vendetta

Tangled Web *(2018)*

Trifles and Folly: Deadly Curiosities Collection

Trifles and Folly 2: Deadly Curiosities Collection

Ascendant Kingdoms

Ice Forged

Reign of Ash

War of Shadows

Shadow and Flame

Chronicles of the Necromancer

The Summoner

The Blood King

Dark Haven

Dark Lady's Chosen

The Shadowed Path: A Jonmarc Vahanian Collection

The Dark Road: A Jonmarc Vahanian Collection *(2018)*

The Fallen Kings Cycle

The Sworn

The Dread

Darkhurst:

Scourge

Vengeance *(2018)*

Jake Desmet Adventures

(Co-authored with Larry N. Martin)

Iron and Blood

Spark of Destiny *(2018)*

Mark Wojcik Monster Hunter

(Co-authored with Larry N. Martin)

Spells, Salt, & Steel

Open Season

Most full-length works are also available on Audible.